Elmore Leonard

THREE COMPLETE NOVELS

LaBRAVA
CAT CHASER
SPLIT IMAGES

Elmore Leonard

THREE COMPLETE NOVELS

WINGS BOOKS
New York • Avenel, New Jersey

This edition contains the complete and unabridged texts of the original editions. They have been completely reset for this volume.

This omnibus was originally published in separate volumes under the titles:

This 1992 edition is published by Wings Books, distributed by Outlet Book Company, a Random House Company, 40 Engelhard Avenue, Avenel, New Jersey, 07001, by arrangement with William Morrow and Company, Inc.

Printed and bound in the United States of America

Library of Congress Cataloging-in-Publication Data
Leonard, Elmore, 1925–
[Novels. Selections]
Three complete novels / Elmore Leonard.
p. cm.
Contents: LaBrava—Cat Chaser—Split images.
ISBN 0-517-06492-8
1. Crime—Fiction. I. Title.
PS3562.E55A6 1992 91-44090
813'.54—dc20 CIP

8 7 6 5 4 3 2 1

CONTENTS

LaBRAVA

This one's for Swanie,
bless his heart.

1

"He's been taking pictures three years, look at the work," Maurice said. "Here, this guy. Look at the pose, the expression. Who's he remind you of?"

"He looks like a hustler," the woman said.

"He *is* a hustler, the guy's a pimp. But that's not what I'm talking about. Here, this one. Exotic dancer backstage. Remind you of anyone?"

"The girl?"

"Come on, Evelyn, the shot. The feeling he gets. The girl trying to look lovely, showing you her treasures, and they're not bad. But look at the dressing room, all the glitzy crap, the tinfoil cheapness."

"You want me to say Diane Arbus?"

"I want you to say Diane Arbus, that would be nice. I want you to say Duane Michaels, Danny Lyon. I want you to say Winogrand, Lee Friedlander. You want to go back a few years? I'd like very much for you to say Walker Evans, too."

"Your old pal."

"Long, long time ago. Even before your time."

"Watch it," Evelyn said, and let her gaze wander over the eight-by-ten black and white prints spread out on the worktable, shining in fluorescent light.

"He's not bad," Evelyn said.

Maurice sighed. He had her interest.

"He's got the eye, Evelyn. He's got an instinct for it, and he's not afraid to walk up and get the shot. I'll tell you something else. He's got more natural ability than I had in sixty years taking pictures. He's been shooting maybe four."

Evelyn said, "Let's see, what does that make you, Maury? You still seventy-nine?"

"Probably another couple years," Maurice said. "Till I get tired of it." Maurice Zola: he was five-five, weighed about one-fifteen and spoke with a soft urban-south accent that had wise-guy overtones, decades of streetcorner styles blended and delivered, right or wrong, with casual authority. Thirty-five years ago this redheaded woman had worked for him when he had photo concessions in some of the big Miami Beach hotels and nightclubs. Evelyn Emerson—he'd tell her he loved the sound of her name, it was lyrical, and he'd sing it taking her to bed; though never to the same tune. Now she had her own business, the Evelyn Emerson Gallery in Coconut Grove and outweighed him by fifty pounds.

Evelyn said, "I sure don't need any art deco, impressionistic angles. The kids like it, but they don't buy."

"What art deco?" Maurice looked over the worktable, picked out a print. "He shoots people. Here, the old Jewish broads sitting on the porch—sure, you're gonna get some of the hotel. The hotel's part of the feeling. These people, time has passed them by. Here, Lummus Park. They look like a flock of birds, uh? The nose shields, like beaks."

"Old New York Jews and Cubans," Evelyn said.

"That's the neighborhood, kid. He's documenting South Beach like it is today. He's getting the drama of it, the pathos. This guy, look, with the tattoos . . ."

"He's awful looking."

"Wants to make himself attractive, adorn his body. But you look at him closely, the guy's feeling something, he's a person. Gets up in the morning, has his Cheerios like everybody else."

She said, "Well, he's not in the same league with any number of people I could name."

"He's not pretentious like a lot of 'em either," Maurice said. "You don't see any bullshit here. He shoots barefaced fact. He's got the feel and he makes *you* feel it."

"What's his name?"

"It's Joseph LaBrava."

Evelyn said, "LaBrava. Why does that sound familiar?"

She was looking at Maurice's tan scalp as he lowered his head, peered at her over his glasses, then pushed them up on his nose: a gesture, like tipping his hat.

"Because you're aware, you know what's going on. Why do you think I came here instead of one of those galleries up on Kane Concourse?"

"Because you still love me. Come on—"

"Some people have to work their ass off for years to get recognition," Maurice said. "Others, they get discovered overnight. September the second, 1935, I happen to be on Islamorada working on the Key West extension, Florida East Coast line, right?"

Evelyn knew every detail, how the '35 hurricane tore into the keys and Maurice got pictures of the worst railroad disaster in Florida history. Two hundred and eighty-six men working on the road killed or missing . . . and two months later he was shooting pictures for the Farm Security Administration, documenting the face of America during the Depression.

She said, "Maury, who's Joseph LaBrava?"

He was back somewhere in his mind and had to close his eyes and open them, adjusting his prop, his heavyframe glasses.

"It was LaBrava took the shot of the guy being thrown off the overpass."

Evelyn said, "Oh, my God."

"Joe had come off the 79th Street Causeway going out to Hialeah. He's approaching I-95 he sees the three guys up there by the railing."

"That was pure luck," Evelyn said.

"Wait. Nothing was going on yet. Three guys, they look like they're just standing there. But he senses something and pulls off the road."

"He was still lucky," Evelyn said, "I mean to have a camera with him."

"He always has a camera. He was going out to Hialeah to shoot. He looks up, sees the three guys and gets out his telephoto lens. Listen, he got off two shots before they even picked the guy up. Then he got 'em, they're holding the guy up in the air and he got the one the guy falling, arms and legs out like he's flying, the one that was in *Newsweek* and all the papers."

"He must've done all right."

"Cleared about twelve grand so far, the one shot," Maurice said, "the one you put in your window, first gallery to have a Joseph LaBrava show."

"I don't know," Evelyn said, "my trade leans more toward exotic funk. Surrealism's big now. Winged snakes, colored smoke . . ."

"You oughta hand out purgatives with that shit, Evelyn. This guy's for real, and he's gonna make it. I guarantee you."

"Is he presentable?"

"Nice-looking guy, late thirties. Dark hair, medium height, on the thin side. No style, but yeah, he's presentable."

Evelyn said, "I see 'em come in with no socks on, I know they've got a portfolio full of social commentary."

"He's not a hippy. No, I didn't mean to infer that." Maurice paused, serious, about to confide. "You know the guys that guard the President? The Secret Service guys? That's what he used to be, one of those."

"Really?" Evelyn seemed to like it. "Well, they're always neat looking, wear suits and ties."

"Yeah, he used to have style," Maurice said. "But now, he quit getting his hair cut at the barbershop, dresses very casual. But you watch him, Joe walks down the street he knows everything that's going on. He picks faces out of the crowd, faces that interest him. It's a habit, he can't quit doing it. Before he was in the Secret Service, you know what he was? He was an investigator for the Internal Revenue."

"Jesus," Evelyn said, "he sounds like a lovely person."

"No, he's okay. He'll tell you he was in the wrong business," Maurice said. "Now he spots an undesirable, a suspicious-looking character, all he wants to do is take the guy's picture."

"He sounds like a character himself," Evelyn said.

"I suppose you could say that," Maurice said. "One of those quiet guys, you never know what he's gonna do next . . . But he's good, isn't he?"

"He isn't bad," Evelyn said.

2

"I'm going to tell you a secret I never told anybody around here," Maurice said, his glasses, his clean tan scalp shining beneath the streetlight. "I don't just manage the hotel I own it. I bought it, paid cash for it in 1951. Right after Kefauver."

Joe LaBrava said, "I thought a woman in Boca owned it. Isn't that what you tell everybody?"

"Actually the lady in Boca owns a piece of it. "Fifty-eight she was looking for an investment." Maurice Zola paused. " 'Fifty-eight or it might've been '59. I remember they were making a movie down here at the time. Frank Sinatra."

They had come out of the hotel, the porch lined with empty metal chairs, walked through the lines of slowmoving traffic to the beach side of the street where Maurice's car was parked. LaBrava was patient with the old man, but waiting, holding the car door open, he hoped this wasn't going to be a long story. They could be walking along the street, the old man always stopped when he wanted to tell something important. He'd stop in the doorway of Wolfie's on Collins Avenue and people behind them would have to wait and hear about bustout joints where you could get rolled in the old days, or how you could tell a bookie when everybody on the beach was wearing resort outfits. "You know how?" The people behind them would be waiting and somebody would say, "How?" Maurice would say, "Everybody wore their sport shirts open usually except bookies. A bookie always had the top button buttoned. It was like a trademark." He would repeat it a few more times waiting for a table. "Yeah, they always had that top button buttoned, the bookies.

"Edward G. Robinson was in the picture they were making. Very dapper guy." Maurice pinched the knot of his tie, brought his hand down in a smoothing gesture over his pale blue, tropical sports jacket. "You'd see 'em at the Cardozo, the whole crew, all these Hollywood people, and at the dog track used to be down by the pier, right on First Street. No, it was between Biscayne and Harley."

"I know . . . You gonna get in the car?"

"See, I tell the old ladies I only manage the place so they don't bug me. They got nothing to do, sit out front but complain. Use to be the colored guys, now it's the Cubans, the Haitians, making noise on the street, grabbing their purses. *Graubers,* they call 'em, *momzers, loomps*. 'Run the *loomps* off, Morris. Keep them away from here, and the *nabkas.*' That's the hookers. I'm starting to sound like 'em, these *almoonas* with the dyed hair. I call 'em my bluebirds, they love it."

"Let me ask you," LaBrava said, leaving himself open but curious about something. "The woman we're going to see, she's your partner?"

"The lady we're gonna rescue, who I think's got a problem," Maurice said, looking up at the hotel, one hand on the car that was an old-model Mercedes with vertical twin headlights, the car once cream-colored but now without lustre. "That's why I mention it. She starts talking about the hotel you'll know what she's talking about. I owned the one next door, too, but I sold it in '68. Somebody should've tied me to a toilet, wait for the real estate boom."

"What, the Andrea? You owned that, too?"

"It used to be the Esther, I changed the name of both of 'em. Come here." Maurice took LaBrava by the arm, away from the car. "The streetlight, you can't see it good. All right, see the two names up there? Read 'em so they go together. What's it say?"

There were lighted windows along the block of three- and four-story hotels, pale stucco in faded pastels, streamlined moderne facing the Atlantic from a time past: each hotel expressing its own tropical deco image in speed lines, wraparound corners, accents in glass brick, bas relief palm trees and mermaids.

"It says the Andrea," LaBrava said, "and the Della Robbia."

"No, it don't say *the* Andrea and *the* Della Robbia." Maurice held onto LaBrava's arm, pointing now. "Read it."

"It's too dark."

"I can see it you can see it. Look. You read it straight across it says Andrea Della Robbia. He was a famous Italian sculptor back, I don't know, the fourteen, fifteen hundreds. They name these places the Esther, the Dorothy—what kind of name is that for a hotel on South Miami Beach? I mean back then. Now it don't matter. South Bronx south, it's getting almost as bad."

"Della Robbia," LaBrava said. "It's a nice name. We going?"

"You say it, Della *Ro*bbia," Maurice said, rolling the name with a soft, Mediterranean flourish, tasting it on his tongue, the sound giving him pleasure. "Then the son of a bitch I sold it to—how do you like this guy? He paints the Andrea all white, changes the style of the lettering and ruins the composition. See, both hotels before were a nice pale yellow, dark green letters, dark green the decoration parts, the names read together like they were suppose to."

LaBrava said, "You think anybody ever looks up there?"

"Forget I told you," Maurice said. They walked back to the car and he stopped again before getting in. "Wait. I want to take a camera with us."

"It's in the trunk."

"Which one?"

"The Leica CL."

"And a flash?"

"In the case."

Maurice paused. "You gonna wear that shirt, uh?"

LaBrava's white shirt bore a pattern of bananas, pineapples and oranges. "It's brand new, first time I've had it on."

"Got all dressed up. Who you suppose to be, Murf the Surf?"

There was a discussion when LaBrava went around the block from Ocean Drive to Collins and headed south to Fifth Street to get on the MacArthur Causeway. Maurice said, we're going north, what do you want to go south for? Why didn't you go up to Forty-first Street, take the Julia Tuttle? LaBrava said, because there's traffic up there on the beach, it's still the season. Maurice said, eleven o'clock at night? You talk about traffic, it's nothing what it used to be like. You could've gone up, taken the Seventy-ninth Street Causeway. LaBrava said, you want to drive or you want me to?"

They didn't get too far on I-95 before they came to all four lanes backed up, approaching the 112 interchange, brake lights popping on and off as far ahead as they could see. Crawling along in low gear, stopping, starting, the Mercedes stalled twice.

LaBrava said, "All the money you got, why don't you buy a new car?"

Maurice said, "You know what you're talking about? This car's a classic, collector's model."

"Then you oughta get a tune."

Maurice said, "What do you mean, all the money I got?"

"You told me you were a millionaire one time."

"Used to be," Maurice said. "I spent most of my dough on booze, broads and boats and the rest I wasted."

Neither of them spoke again until they were beyond Fort Lauderdale. They could sit without talking and LaBrava would be reasonably comfortable; he never felt the need to invent conversation. He was curious when he asked Maurice:

"What do you want the camera for?"

"Maybe I want to take a picture."

"The woman?"

"Maybe. I don't know yet. I have to see how she is."

"She a good friend of yours?"

Maurice said, "I'm going out this time of night to help somebody I don't know? She's a very close friend."

"How come if she lives in Boca they took her to Delray Beach?"

"That's where the place is they take them. It's run by the county. Palm Beach."

"Is it like a hospital?"

"What're you asking me for? I never been there."

"Well, what'd the girl say on the phone?"

"Something about she was brought in on the Meyers Act."

"It means she was drunk."

"That's what I'm afraid of."

"They pick you up in this state on a Meyers Act," LaBrava said, "it means you're weaving around with one eye closed, smashed. They pick you up on a Baker Act it means you're acting weird in public and're probably psycho. I remember that from when I was here before."

He had spent a year and a half in the Miami field office of the

United States Secret Service, one of five different duty assignments in nine years.

He had told Maurice about it one Saturday morning driving down to Islamorada, LaBrava wanting to try bonefishing and Maurice wanting to show him where he was standing when the tidal wave hit in '35. LaBrava would remember the trip as the only time Maurice ever asked him questions, ever expressed an interest in his past life. In parts of it, anyway.

He didn't get to tell much of the IRS part, the three years he'd worked as an investigator when he was young and eager. "Young and dumb," Maurice said. Maurice didn't want to hear anything about the fucking IRS.

Or much about LaBrava's marriage, either—during the same three years—to the girl he'd met in accounting class, Wayne State University, who didn't like to drink, smoke or stay out late, or go to the show. Though she seemed to like all those things before. Strange? Her name was Lorraine. Maurice said, what's strange about it? They never turn out like you think they're going to. Skip that part. There wasn't anything anybody could tell him about married life he didn't know. Get to the Secret Service part.

Well, there was the training at Beltsville, Maryland. He learned how to shoot a Smith & Wesson .357 Magnum, the M-16, the Uzi submachine gun, different other ones. He learned how to disarm and theoretically beat the shit out of would-be assassins with a few chops and kicks. He learned how to keep his head up and his eyes open, how to sweep a crowd looking for funny moves, hands holding packages, umbrellas on clear days, that kind of thing.

He spent fifteen months in Detroit, his hometown, chasing down counterfeiters, going undercover to get next to wholesalers. That part was okay, making buys as a passer. But then he'd have to testify against the poor bastard in federal court, take the stand and watch the guy's face drop—Christ, seeing his new buddy putting the stuff on him. So once he was hot in Detroit, a familiar face in the trade, they had to send him out to cool off.

He was assigned to the Protective Research Section in Washington where, LaBrava said, he read nasty letters all day. Letters addressed to "Peanut Head Carter, the Mushmouth Motherfucker from Georgia." Or that ever-popular salutation, "To the Nigger-loving President of the Jewnited States." Letters told what should be done to the President of the USA, "the Utmost Supreme Ass-holes" who believed his lies. There was a suggestion, LaBrava said, the President ought to be "pierced with the prophet's sword of righteousness for being a goddamn hypocrite." Fiery, but not as practical as the one that suggested, "They ought to tie you to one of those MX missiles you dig so much and lose your war-lovin ass."

Maurice said, "People enjoy writing letters, don't they? You answer them?"

LaBrava said usually there wasn't a return address; but they'd trace the writers down through postmarks, broken typewriter keys, different clues, and have a look at them. They'd be interviewed and their names added to a file of some forty thousand presidential pen pals, a lot of cuckoos; a few, about a hundred or so, they'd have to watch.

LaBrava told how he'd guarded important people, Teddy Kennedy during the Senator's 1980 presidential campaign, trained to be steely-eyed, learned to lean away from those waving arms, stretched his steely eyes open till they ached listening to those tiresome, oh my, those boring goddamn speeches.

Maurice said, "You should a heard William Jennings Bryan, the Peerless Prince of Platform English, Christ, lecture on the wonders of Florida—sure, brought in by the real estate people."

LaBrava said he'd almost quit after guarding Teddy. But he hung on and was reassigned to go after counterfeiters again, now out of the Miami field office, now getting into his work and enjoying it. A new angle. He picked up a Nikon, attached a 200-mm lens, and began using it in surveillance work. Loved it. Snapping undercover agents making deals with wholesalers, passers unloading their funny money. Off duty he continued snapping away: shooting up and down Southwest Eighth Street, the heart of Little Havana; or riding with a couple of Metro cops to document basic Dade County violence. He felt himself attracted to street life. It was a strange feeling, he was at home, knew the people; saw more outcast faces and attitudes than he would ever be able to record, people who showed him their essence behind all kinds of poses—did Maurice understand this?—and trapped them in his camera for all time.

He got hot again through court appearances and was given a cooling-off assignment—are you ready for this?—in Independence, Missouri.

After counterfeiters?

No, to guard Mrs. Truman.

A member of the twelve-man protective detail. To sit in the surveillance house watching monitors or sit eight hours a day in the Truman house itself on North Delaware. Sit sometimes in the living room looking around at presidential memorabilia, a picture of Margaret and her two kids, the grandfather's clock that had been wired and you didn't have to wind—which would have been something to do—listening to faint voices in other rooms. Or sit in the side parlor with Harry's piano, watching movies on TV, waiting for the one interruption of the day. The arrival of the mailman.

"Don't get me wrong, Mrs. Truman was a kind, considerate woman. I liked her a lot."

The duty chief had said, "Look, there guys would give an arm and a leg for this assignment. If you can't take pride in it, just say so."

He glanced at Maurice sitting there prim, very serious this evening. Little Maurice Zola, born here before there were roads other than a few dirt tracks and the Florida East Coast Railway. Natty little guy staring at this illuminated interstate highway—giant lit-up green signs every few miles telling where you were—and not too impressed. He had seen swamps become cities, a bridge extended to a strip of mangrove in the Atlantic Ocean and Miami Beach was born. Changes were no longer events in his life. They had happened or they didn't.

One of the green signs, mounted high, told them Daytona Beach was 215 miles.

"Who cares?" Maurice said. "I used to live in Daytona Beach. First time I got married, October 10, 1929—wonderful time to get married, Jesus—was in Miami. The second time was October 24, 1943, in Daytona Beach. October's a bad month for me. I paid alimony, I mean plenty, but I outlived 'em both. Miserable women. In '32, when I worked for the septic tank outfit and wrestled alligators on the weekends? It was because I had the experience being married to my first wife."

"What about the lady we're going to see?"

"What about her?"

"You ever serious with her?"

"You're asking, you want to know did I go to bed with her? She wasn't that kind of girl. She wasn't a broad you did that with."

"I mean did you ever think of marrying her?"

"She was too young for me. I don't mean she was too young you wanted to hop in the sack with a broad her age, I mean to get married and live with. I had all kinds of broads at that time. In fact, go back a few years before that, just before Kefauver, when I had the photo concessions and the horse book operation. I'll tell you a secret. You want to know who one of the broads I was getting into her pants was at the time. Evelyn, at the gallery. She was in love with me."

"I don't think you've introduced me to any who weren't."

"What can I say?" Maurice said.

"How old's the woman we're going to see?"

"Jeanie? She's not too old. Lemme think, it was '58 I gave her a piece of the hotel. Or it might've been '59, they were making that movie on the beach. Frank Sinatra, Edward G. Robinson . . . Jeanie was gonna be in the picture, was why she came down. But she didn't get the part."

"Wait a minute—" LaBrava said.

"They wanted her, but then they decided she looked too young. She was in her twenties then and she was gonna play this society woman."

"Jeanie—"

"Yeah, very good-looking girl, lot of class. She married a guy—not long after that she married a guy she met down here. Lawyer, very wealthy, use to represent some of the big hotels. They had a house on Pine Tree Drive, I mean a mansion, faced the Eden Roc across Indian Creek. You know where I mean? Right in there, by Arthur Godfrey Road. Then Jerry, Jerry Breen was the guy's name, had some trouble with the IRS, had to sell the place.

I don't know if it was tax fraud or what. He didn't go to jail, anything like that, but it cost him, I'll tell you. He died about oh, ten years ago. Yeah, Jeanie was a movie actress. They got married she retired, gave it up."

"What was her name before?"

"Just lately I got a feeling something funny's going on. She call me last week, start talking about she's got some kind of problem, then changes the subject. I don't know if she means with the booze or what."

"You say she was a movie actress."

"She was a star. You see her on TV once in a while, they show the old movies."

"Her name Jeanie or Jean?"

"Jean. Jean—the hell was her name? You believe it? I'm used to thinking of her as Jeanie Breen." Maurice pointed. "Atlantic Boulevard. See it? Mile and a half. You better get over." Maurice rolled his window down.

"Jean Simmons?"

"Naw, not Jean Simmons." Maurice was half-turned now, watching for cars coming up in the inside lane. "I'll tell you when."

"Gene Tierney?" *Laura*. He'd watched it on television in Bess Truman's living room. "How's she spell her name?"

"Jean. How do you spell Jean? J-e-a-n."

Jean Harlow was dead. LaBrava looked at the rearview mirror, watched headlights lagging behind, in no hurry. "Jeanne Crain?"

"Naw, not Jeanne Crain. Get ready," Maurice said. "Not after this car but the one after it, I think you can make it."

3

They parked in the rear and walked around to the front of the one-story building on Northeast Fourth Street, Delray Beach. From the outside the place reminded LaBrava of a dental clinic: stucco and darkwood trim, low-cost construction; a surface that appeared to be solid but would not stop a bullet. A laminated door that would not stop much of anything. LaBrava, former guardian of presidents and people in high places, automatically studying, making an appraisal. Oh, man, but tired of it. In an orange glow of light they read the three-by-five card taped to the door.

CRISIS CENTER
South County Mental Health
EMERGENCY SCREENING SERVICE

They had to ring the bell and wait, Maurice sighing with impatience, until a girl about twenty-one with long blond hair opened the door and Maurice said, "I come to get Mrs. Breen."

"You're Mr. Zola, right? Hi, I'm Pam."

She locked the door again and they followed her—broad hips compacted within tight jeans—through an empty waiting room and hallway, LaBrava looking around and judging this place, at the low end of institutional decor. He had never seen so many stains and burns. Like people came in here to throw up or set the place on fire with cigarettes. There were cracks and broken holes in the dull-yellow drywall, fist marks. He could see people trying to punch their way out. They came to a doorway, the room inside was dark.

"She's in here. Asleep."

Maurice stuck his head in. "She's on the floor."

"There's a mattress," Pam said. "She's fine, didn't give us a bit of trouble. The cops that brought her in described her condition as staggering, speech slurred, I guess she didn't know where she was."

Maurice said, "Was there a problem, a disturbance of any kind?"

"Well, not really. I mean there's no charge against her. She was walking down the street with a drink in her hand."

Maurice frowned. "A drink? Outside?"

"They said she came out of a bar, on Palmetto. They saw her on the sidewalk with the drink and when they pulled over she threw it at them. Not the glass, the drink. I guess she was, you know, so bombed they thought they better bring her here." Pam looked at the doorway. "Why don't you go in with her? Let her wake up to a familiar face."

"Why don't I get her out of here," Maurice said. He went in the room.

LaBrava followed Pam. They came to a room filled with fluorescent light that was about fifteen-by-twenty: a metal desk standing between two mattresses on the floor, a line of metal chairs along the inside wall and a back door with double locks. The stains and burn marks seemed magnified in here. LaBrava saw skinny legs with dried sores, a light-skinned black girl asleep on the mattress in front of the desk. He saw a drunk, dirty from living in doorways, that familiar street drunk, soft mouth nearly toothless, cocking his head like a chicken. The drunk sat in the row of folding chairs. Next to him an elderly man sat rigid, his shirt collar buttoned, hands flat on bony thighs. He said to LaBrava, "You ever see an eagle?"

Pam, sliding behind the metal desk that was covered with forms and scrawled notes, said, "Walter—"

LaBrava said, "Yeah, I've seen an eagle."

The rigid man said, "Did it have hair?"

"The one I saw had feathers."

The rigid man said, "Oh." He looked at Pam now. "You ever see an eagle?"

Pam said, "Excuse me, Walter, but I have to finish with Earl first. Okay? Be nice." She glanced down at a clipboard. "Earl, if I call this person Eileen, will she come and get you?"

"She don't keep up her house," the drunk said. "You go in the kitchen . . . I tell her, Jesus Christ, get some wash powder. I can't live in a place like that."

Pam looked up at LaBrava in the doorway. "Sit down. Make yourself at home."

He took the end seat, two metal chairs away from the drunk hunched over his crossed legs, the drunk staring, trying to focus, saying, "Do I know you?"

"I don't know," LaBrava said, "we might've met one time. How you doing?"

"See, I don't want to go to court drunk. I don't want to go in there, maybe get sick."

Pam said, "Earl, I told you, there no charges against you." She said, "You ever drink anything like aftershave?"

"No, not ever. Just some home brew, some wine. Eileen, if I'm staying over there, she fixes these toddies are nice. Bourbon and ice cubes, you sprinkle some sugar on top. 'Bout a teaspoonful's all . . ."

A scream came from a room close by, a wail of obscenities that rose and died off, and LaBrava looked at Pam, expecting her to get up.

"It's okay. One of our consumers," Pam said. "She's catharting, sort of working it out on her own. But there's someone with her, don't worry."

"Consumer," LaBrava said.

The girl had a nice smile, very natural; she seemed too young and vulnerable to be working here. Psych major no more than a year out of college. "That's what we call the people we screen. They're not, you know, patients technically till they're admitted somewhere. This's just a temporary stop more or less."

The drunk said, "Then I'm leaving." He got up, stumbling against the rigid man, pushed off and tilted toward the girl lying on the mattress before finding his balance. He reached the back door and began working at the locks.

Pam said, "Come on, Earl, sit down and be good. You have to stay here till you've sobered up and you're a little more appropriate."

Earl turned from the door, falling against it. "More '*pro*priate? Shit, I'm 'propriate."

"You are not," Pam said, a young schoolteacher at her desk. "Please sit down so we can finish."

The drunk fell against the chairs, almost into the rigid man whose hands remained flat on his thighs. The girl with sores on her legs moaned and rolled from her side to her back, eyes lightly closed, lids fluttering in the overhead light.

LaBrava was looking at her and Pam said, "She's Haitian. She got stoned and walked out on the Interstate. A car had to swerve out of the way and hit another car and one of the drivers, I don't know which one, had to have twenty stitches in his head."

The drunk said, "Shit, I was at Louisville Veterans, they put sixty-four stitches in my leg. Boy jammed a bottle, broke it off, jammed the end of it in my leg. See? Right there. Sixty-four stitches. Doc said he stopped counting."

"It's a beauty," LaBrava said. "Cut you good, didn't he?" He saw the drunk look up.

LaBrava turned. Maurice was standing over him.

"Get the camera."

LaBrava kept his voice down. "You sure you want to? Maybe they won't like it."

Maurice said to the girl, "Sweetheart, would you do something for my friend here? Unlock the door? He's got to get a camera outta the car."

Pam let him out the back telling him to knock and she'd open it again.

What Maurice wanted to do—LaBrava was sure now—was take a picture of his friend smashed, blearyeyed, then show it to her tomorrow. "See what a beauty you are when you're drunk?" Shame her into sobriety. But if the woman had a problem with booze it would be a waste of time. He wouldn't mind, though, getting a shot of Earl. Earl showing his scar. Shoot it from down on the floor. The guy's leg crossed, pants pulled up, shin in the foreground, shiny crescent scar. Earl pointing with a dirty fingernail. Grinning near toothless, too drunk not to look proud and happy.

Bending over in the trunk LaBrava felt inside the camera case, brought out the Leica CL and attached a wide-angle lens.

Headlights flashed on him, past him. By the time he looked around the car had come to a stop parallel to the building, its dark-colored rear deck standing at the edge of the floodlit area that extended out from the back door. LaBrava felt in the case again for the flash attachment. He straightened, slamming the trunk closed.

A young guy was out of the car. Big, well-built guy in a silver athletic jacket, blue trim. Banging on the door now with the thick edge of his fist, other hand wedged in the tight pocket of his jeans. LaBrava came up next to him. The guy grinned, fist still raised, toothpick in the corner of his mouth.

"How you doing this evening?" Slurring his words.

He was thick all over, heavily muscled, going at least six-three, two-thirty. Blond hair with a greenish tint in the floodlight: the hair uncombed, clots of it lying straight back on his head without a part, like he'd been swimming earlier and had raked it back with his fingers. The guy wasn't young up close. Mid-thirties. But he was the kind of guy—LaBrava knew by sight, smell and instinct—who hung around bars and armwrestled. Homegrown jock—pumped his muscles and tested his strength when he wasn't picking his teeth.

LaBrava said, "Not too bad. How're you doing?"

"Well, I don't idle too good, but I'm still running." With a back-country drawl greasing his words. "You gonna take some pitchers?"

"I'm thinking about it."

"What of, this pisshole? Man, I wouldn't keep goats in this place."

"I imagine they don't have much of a budget, run by the county," LaBrava said. Hearing himself, he sounded like a wimp. He had the feeling he would never agree with this guy. Still, there was no sense in antagonizing him.

"Palm Beach County, shit, they got more money'n any county in the state of Florida. But you look at this pisshole kind of shack they put people in—I mean nice people—you'd never know it, would you? You don't see none of that Palm Beach crowd brought in here. They can be pissing on the squad car, cop'll go, 'Get in, sir. Lemme drive you home, sir.' Shit . . . Hey, you want a take my pitcher? Go ahead, I'll let you."

"Thanks anyway," LaBrava said.

"What paper you with?"

LaBrava paused. He said, "Oh," a pleasant, surprised tone. It was not recognition of himself, LaBrava the street shooter, but it was recognition of a sort. "What makes you think I'm a news photographer?"

The guy said, "I guess 'cause all you assholes look alike." He turned away as they heard the locks, the door opening.

LaBrava saw Pam's expression change, startled, the girl tiny next to the silver jacket. She said, "Hey, what're you doing—" The guy was taking her by the arm as he entered.

"I come on official business, puss. How you doing? You're new here, huh? I ain't seen you before."

LaBrava edged past them with the camera, walked toward the hall and heard the locks snapping again behind him, heard the guy's bullshit charm hard at work. "Here, shake hands. I'm Richard Nobles, puss, with the police hereabouts?" He heard Pam say, "Wait a minute. What police hereabouts?" He heard the rigid man say, "You ever see an eagle?" And heard Richard Nobles say, "You kidding me, papa? I've cooked and *ate* a eagle . . ."

Maurice was waiting in the hall by the doorway.

"Go in get a shot of her. Wait, what've you got, the Leica? Okay, go on."

"She awake?"

"I'm getting her outta here. Shoot straight down on her. What do you have it set at?"

"I don't know yet." LaBrava walked into the room. He saw bare legs in the shaft of light from the hall, sandals with medium heels. Slim legs, one of them drawn up. She was lying on her side, wearing a light-colored dress, her shoulders bare, an arm extended, partly covering her face. Maurice stooped down to move her arm, gently. LaBrava went out to the hall to make his adjustments. When he came back in and stood over the woman on the mattress, framing her in the viewfinder, dark hair against pale skin, Maurice said, "What'd you set it at?"

"Sixtieth at eight."

"I don't know . . ."

LaBrava didn't wait. The flash went off as he triggered the camera tight to his right eye, cocked it with his thumb, shot the second time, cocked and shot again.

"Set it lower and get another one."

"That's enough," LaBrava said.

"I want to be sure we got something."

"We got it," LaBrava said. "Take her out the front and I'll bring the car around."

There was another girl in the office now who seemed only a few years older than Pam but more grown up, in charge. Coming into the room again LaBrava heard her tell Nobles she was the supervisor and wanted to see some identification or there would be nothing to discuss. Right away LaBrava liked her confidence. He liked her slim build in jeans standing with long legs apart, arms folded, brown hair waved to her shoulders. A good-looking girl who knew what she was doing.

Nobles dug a wallet out of his back pocket, turning sideways and brushing his silver jacket open so they would see the checkered walnut grip of a revolver stuck in the waist of his jeans. Saying, "Boca police brought this lady here happens to be a friend of mine. See, I checked with them and they said it would be okay to release her to my custody. They said fine, go ahead." He flipped open the wallet to show a gold shield on one side, an I.D. card bearing his photograph on the other. "See what it says there? Palm Beach County."

The slim girl took a half step, extending her hand and he flipped the wallet closed. She said, "Palm Beach County what? If the Boca Police said it was okay, they'd have called to let us know. That's how it works."

Nobles shook his head, weary. "Look, I'm doing you a favor. Lemme have the lady and we'll say nighty-night, let you all go on back play with your nuts."

"No one leaves without authorization," the slim girl said, standing right up to him.

"I'm *giving* you authorization. Jesus Christ, I just now showed it to you."

LaBrava said, "Excuse me. Would somebody like to open the front door?"

Nobles gave him a look, cold with no expression, and the slim girl said, "Show me identification or get out. That's the way it is. Okay?"

LaBrava watched Nobles sigh, shake his head—not so drunk that he couldn't put on an act—and flip open the wallet again. "What's that say? Right there? Palm Beach County authorization." Giving her a flash of official wording and flipped the wallet closed.

He's not a cop.

LaBrava would bet on it. He heard the girl say, "That's not PBSO or any badge I've ever seen before."

Nobles shook his head again. "Some reason you got your ass up in the air. Did I say I was with the Palm Beach sheriff's office? You don't listen good, do you? See, long as I got credentials as to who I am and Boca PD says it's fine with them, then tell me what your problem is, puss, cause I sure as hell don't see it."

Sounding drunk, but with a swagger that was part the guy's brute nature and would not be contained for long; his size, his eighteen-inch neck giving him permission to do as he pleased. LaBrava had known a few Richard Nobles.

The guy was no cop.

He might've been at one time; he had a service revolver and the official off-duty look of a small-town cop taken with himself, but he wasn't one now.

The slim girl had already assumed as much. She was looking at Pam, telling her, "Get Delray Police, 276-4141."

Nobles said, "Hey, come on," watching Pam dial. "Look, this lady you got happens to be a friend of mine. Officer at Boca name of Glenn Hicks says they brought her in here. See, I was even with her earlier tonight, having some drinks." He watched the slim girl step to the side of the desk and take the phone from Pam. "Ask her. Go on . . ."

The slim girl said into the phone, "This is South County on Fourth Street. There's a gentleman here who's been asked to leave and refuses. I'd like you to send somebody to escort him the fuck out of here, right now . . . Thank you very much." She looked at Pam again. "Unlock the back door."

Pam edged around the desk, all eyes as she looked at Nobles standing in front of her, in the way. She said, "There *is* a Boca officer named Glenn Hicks. He's been here before."

The slim girl said, "I don't care who he knows or if he's with the FBI. This guy's got no business being here."

LaBrava was falling in love with her. He watched her look directly at Nobles again.

"You've got about two minutes to get out of here or you're gonna be in deep shit."

Nobles said, "All I need, puss." He reached for her. The slim girl pulled her arm away without giving ground, glaring at him.

LaBrava said, "Let's take it easy, okay?" Trying to sound reasonable, an observer, but knowing he was getting into it.

Nobles, close to where the drunk and the rigid man sat watching, turned to LaBrava, raised a fist with a finger pointing out of it. A clot of blond hair hung down in his eyes. He said, "I'll put you through the wall you fuck with me, you little son of a bitch."

An ugly drunk. Look at the eyes. Ugly—used to people backing down, buying him another drink to shut him up. Look at the shoulders stretching satin, the arms on him—Jesus—hands that looked like they could pound fence posts. LaBrava, with the camera hanging from his neck, did not see anything close by to hit him with.

The slim girl picked up the phone again. Nobles reached for it as she started to dial, yanked the phone out of her hands and gave her a shove. The slim girl yelled out. Nobles raised the phone over his head, as a threat or to club her with it, LaBrava wasn't sure.

He stepped in, said, "Hey—" as he raised the camera with the flash attached, put it in Nobles' face and fired about a hundred thousand candles in the guy's eyes, blinding him, straightening him for the moment LaBrava needed to hit him in the ribs with a shoulder, drive him into clattering metal chairs, close to the drunk and the rigid man. LaBrava got Nobles down on his spine, head hard against the wall to straddle his legs. Worked free the bluesteel revolver stuck in his jeans, a familiar feel, a .357 Smith. Held him by the hair with one hand and slipped the blunt end of the barrel into his open mouth. Nobles gagged, trying to twist free.

LaBrava said, "Suck it. It'll calm you down."

* * *

They got him into a room. Nobles rubbing the back of his neck, looking around before they pulled the door closed, saying, "Hey, who the hell you suppose to be?"

LaBrava said, "The asshole photographer," and locked the door.

They locked the gun in the desk. He told the slim girl he hoped the guy didn't try to bust the place up before the cops came; he 'd stay if she wanted him to. She said it had been busted up before, look at it. God. She said thanks, really, but he'd better get out of here or he might be hanging around all night, the cops playing games with him. They might be the guy's buddies. She said she wouldn't be surprised if they let the guy out and all laughed their ass off. Cops really thought they were funny. Some of them anyway. Talking, nervous now that it was over. She was some girl. Supervisor here, but forced to work all hours, the slim girl's name was Jill Wilkinson.

He asked her what she thought Nobles did. She said he was probably a rent-a-cop, he acted like one.

That's what he was, too. LaBrava checked the dark blue Plymouth sedan parked out in back before going to the Mercedes. There was a gold star on the door and the inscription *STAR SECURITY SERVICE, PALM BEACH COUNTY, FLORIDA*.

He drove around front to see Pam and Maurice coming out with the woman, Jeanie Breen, the woman with her head lowered but as tall as Maurice and as pale as her dress, letting him help her with his arm around her waist. They got in back, Maurice saying to him, "What were you doing, shooting the drunks?"

Maurice told him they were going to stop in Boca, pick up some of Mrs. Breen's things. Mrs. Breen was coming back to South Beach with them, stay at the hotel a while.

After that Maurice's tone was soft, soothing, and LaBrava would look at the mirror to be sure it was Maurice back there. The little bald-headed guy, his glasses catching reflections, the woman a pale figure curled up in his arms. Maurice calling her sweetheart, telling her a change would be good . . . talk to your old pal . . . whatever's bothering you. Get a new outlook. LaBrava heard the woman say, "Oh, shit, Maury. What's happening to me?'' Worn out. Still, there was an edge to her tone. Life in there. Anger trying to break through the self-pity.

What was her problem—living in a luxury condominium on the ocean—if her hair wasn't falling out or she didn't have an incurable disease?

Maybe living in the luxury condominium on the ocean. By herself.

It did not occur to LaBrava until later—cruising at seventy, the dark car interior silent—that the woman in the back seat could be the same one Nobles had tried to take out of there. A woman he'd been drinking with earlier in the evening.

4

LaBrava did his portrait work in an alcove off the Della Robbia lobby that Maurice said had originally been a bar: the area hidden now by a wall of cane screening nailed to a frame and clay baskets of hanging fern.

This morning he was working with the Leica, wideangle lens and strobes, shooting the young Cuban couple, Paco Boza and Lana Mendoza, against a sheet of old, stiff canvas that gave him a nothing background. Paco sat in his wheelchair wearing a straw hat cocked on the side of his head, one side of the brim up, the other down, cane-cutter chic. Lana stood behind the wheelchair. She wore a cotton undershirt that was like a tank top and would stretch it down to show some nipple in the thin material. Pretty soon, LaBrava believed, she would pull the undershirt up and give him bare breasts with a look of expectation. The two of them were fooling around, having fun, stoned at 11 A.M.

LaBrava said, "Don't you want to look at each other?"

"At him?" the girl said. "I look at him and wish I never left Hialeah."

"Why don't you go home then?" Paco said, looking straight up over his head.

The girl looked down at him. "Yeah, you wouldn't have nobody to push you. He sit in this thing all day."

LaBrava released the shutter and went down to his knees, eye level. "Come on, this's supposed to be young love. You're crazy about each other."

"Like *The Blue Lagoon,* man," Paco said, looking bland, cool, not reacting when the girl punched him on the back of the neck.

"He's crazy all right," she said.

"That *Blue Lagoon,* man, you see that? Why did it take them so long, you know, to get it on? Man, they don't do nothing for most of the movie."

The girl punched him again. "They kids. How do they know how to do it, nobody tell them."

"I knew," Paco, the lover, said, grinning. "It's something a man is born with, knowing how to do it."

''You the creature from the blue lagoon,'' the girl said, ''tha's who you are.'' Stretching now, bored.

LaBrava got it, the girl's upraised arms, the yawn hinting at seduction.

But he was losing it, hoping for luck. He had begun with a good feeling and it would be in the first two head-on shots if he got it. Now he was moving around too much. He felt like a fashion photographer snicking away as the model throws her hair and sucks in her cheeks, getting split moments of the model pretending to be someone who wanted to go to bed with the photographer or with the lights or with whatever she saw out there. He didn't want Boza and Mendoza to fall into a pose unless he could feel it was natural, something they wanted to do. But they were showing off for him now.

LaBrava said, ''I think that'll do it.''

Paco said, ''Man, we just getting loosey goosey.''

The girl said, ''Hey, I got an idea. How about . . . one like this?''

In the Della Robbia lobby, close to the oval front window, the old ladies would nod and comment to each other in Yiddish, then look at the young, frizzy-haired girl again to listen to her advice.

''It saddens me,'' the girl said, and she did sound sad, ''when I see what neglect can do to skin. I'm sure you all know there's a natural aging process that robs skin of its vitality, its lustre.'' If they didn't know it, who did? ''But we don't have to hurry the process through neglect. Not when, with a little care, we can have lovely skin and look years and years younger.''

The girl was twenty-three. The youngest of the ladies sitting in the rattan semi-circle of lobby chairs had lived for at least a half century before the girl was born. But what did they know about skin care? Rub a peeled potato on your face, for sunburn.

She told them that extracts of rare plants and herbs were used in Spring Song formulations to fortify and replenish amniotic fluids that nourish the skin. The old ladies, nodding, touched mottled cheeks, traced furrows. They raised their faces in the oval-window light as the girl told them that women have a beauty potential at every age. She told them it gave her pleasure to be able to provide the necessities that would help them achieve that potential. It was, in fact, this kind of satisfaction, making women of all ages happy, proud of their skin, that being a Spring Song girl was all about.

She gave the ladies a pert smile, realigned the plastic bottles and jars on the marble table to keep moving, busy, as she said, "I thought for this first visit I'd just get you familiar with the Spring Song philosophy. Then next time I'll give a facial, show you how it works."

A voice among the women said, "You don't tell us how much it is, all this philosophy mish-mosh."

"We'll get into all that. Actually," the girl said, "I came to see the manager. What's his name again?"

"Mr. Zola," a woman said. "A nice man. Has a cute way."

There were comments in Yiddish, one of the ladies referring to Maurice as a *k'nocker,* Mr. Big Shot. Then another sound, in the lobby, tennis shoes squeaking on the terrazzo floor. The girl turned to look over her shoulder.

"Is that Mr. Zola?"

"No, that's Mr. LaBrava, the *loksh.* He's like a noodle, that one."

"He's a cutie, too," a woman said. There were more comments in Yiddish, voices rising with opinions.

"Listen, let me give you an exercise to start with," the girl said. "Okay? Put the tips of your fingers here. That's right, in the hollow of your cheeks . . ."

LaBrava checked his mail slot on the wall behind the registration desk. Nothing. Good. He turned to see the girl coming across the lobby. Weird hair: it looked tribal the way it was almost flat on top, parted in the middle and frizzed way out on the sides. Pretty girl though, behind big round tinted glasses . . .

She said, "Hi. You don't work here, do you?"

Violet eyes. Some freckles. Smart-looking Jewish girl.

"You want Maurice," LaBrava said. "He should be down pretty soon. He's visiting a sick friend."

"You know if there's a vacancy?"

"I think somebody just moved out."

"You mean somebody died," the girl said. "I want a room, but I don't plan to stay that long."

"You want a one-bedroom or a studio? The studio's only three and a quarter.'' LaBrava looked over at the women, their mouths open saying ''ohhhhh,'' as they stroked their cheeks in a circular motion.

''Studio, that's a hotel room with a hot plate,'' the girl said. ''I've been there. In fact I just left there. I'm at the Elysian Fields and I need more space.''

''What're they doing? The ladies.''

''Working the masseter. That's the muscle you masticate with.''

''You think it'll do 'em any good?''

''Who knows?'' the girl said. ''They're nice ladies. I figure those that weren't raped by Cossacks were mugged by Puerto Ricans. It won't do them any harm.''

''You're the Spring Song girl,'' LaBrava said. ''I've seen you on the street, with your little kit. How you doing?''

''I'm up to my ass in cosmetic bottles, nine kinds of cream by the case. Also, I've got tubes of paint, sketch pads, canvases all over my room, I've got shitty light and I need more space.''

''I was at the Elysian Fields for a week last summer,'' LaBrava said. ''This place's much better. Cleaner.''

''Are you saying there no roaches?''

''Not as many. You see a loner once in a while. Think of it as a palmetto bug, it doesn't bother you as much. You paint, uh?''

''Some oil, acrylics mostly. I'm getting ready to do Ocean Drive, figure out my views before they tear it all down.''

''Who's tearing it down?''

''Progress. The zoners are out to get us, man, cover the planet like one big enclosed shopping mall. We're getting malled and condoed, if you didn't know it. Gray and tan, earth tones. The people that designed these hotels, they had imagination, knew about color. Go outside, all you see is color and crazy lines zooming all over the place. God, hotels that remind you of ships . . .''

''I'm glad you explained that,'' LaBrava said. ''I've always liked this neighborhood and I never was sure why.'' She gave him a sideways look, suspicious. Really weird hairdo but he liked it. ''I mean it. I feel at home here and I don't know why.''

''Because it's cheap,'' the girl said. ''Listen, you don't have to know why. You feel good here, that's reason enough. People always have to have reasons instead of just feeling.'' She said, ''You're the photographer, aren't you?''

Recognition. LaBrava leaned on the cool marble-top counter: artist relaxed, an unguarded moment. ''Yeah, I guess so.''

''Aren't you sure?''

''I'm just starting to get used to the idea.''

''I saw your show over at the Emerson Gallery, it's dynamite. But all the color here—why aren't you into color?''

''I don't know how to use it. I feel safer with black and white.''

''You selling anything?''

''A few more street shots than portraits.''

''Well, what do they know. Right? Fuck 'em. You have to do what you do.''

''You have to get mad?''

''If it helps. Why not? It's good to be hungry, too. You do better work.''

She had a healthy build, tan arms, traces of dark hair. She would go about one-twenty, LaBrava judged; not the least bit drawn, no haunted, hungry-artist look about her. Gold chain. Rings. The white blouse was simple and could be expensive. But you never knew. He said, ''You want some lunch? We can go across the street, the Cardozo. They got a nice conch salad, good bread.''

''I know, I've seen you over there. No, first I have to see about new digs. I'm not going back to that fucking cell I've been living in. You have to go in sideways.''

LaBrava looked up at the sound of the elevator cables engaging, the electric motor whining. He said, ''You may be in luck,'' staring across the lobby at the elevator door, a gold sunburst relief. The door opened and he said, ''You are. That's the manager.''

Maurice said, even before reaching the desk, ''Where the prints? They didn't come out, did they? What'd I tell you last night? I said stop it down.''

''I've got an idea,'' LaBrava said. ''Why don't you take care of this young lady—she's looking for a respectable place, no roaches, no noise—and I'll go see about the negatives I got hanging in the dryer.''

"How they look?"

"Just tell me if you want 'em printed soft or crisp."

"I want 'em *now* is what I want. While she's still hung-over, ashamed, kicking herself."

LaBrava said to the girl, "Did I tell you he was a sweet old guy?"

"You didn't have to," the girl said, smiling at Maurice. "Mr. Zola, it's a pleasure. I'm Franny Kaufman."

A pair of dull amber safelights recessed in the ceiling gave the darkroom form, indicated shapes, but nothing more. LaBrava hit the negative with a squirt of Dust Chaser, slipped it into the enlarger and paused. He added a yellow filter, feeling sympathy for the woman upstairs in 304, Maurice's guest suite. The exposure was timed for twelve seconds.

He moved to the long section of the L-shaped stainless steel sink, dropped the exposed eight-by-ten sheet into the first of three trays.

An image began to appear, lights and darks, the curve of a woman's shoulder, arm touching the lower part of her face. He had not seen her clearly through the viewfinder; only a glimpse in that part of a moment as the flash exploded. He didn't know what she looked like and was intrigued now, the way he had been curious about her in the car last night.

LaBrava lifted the print from the solution, dipped it into the second tray, the stop bath, drew it through and placed it face up in the third tray, in the clear liquid of the fix solution. He leaned his arms on the narrow edge of the sink, low and uncomfortable, hunched over to study the face, the eyes staring at him through water and amber darkness.

Someone he had seen before.

But he wasn't sure. It might be the look, an expression he recognized. He couldn't see her features clearly.

He lifted the print from the tray, staring as water ran from it, dripped from it, became single drops in the silence, and he was aware of a curious feeling: wanting to turn on the light and see the woman's face, but hesitant, cautious, on the verge of discovery and wanting the suspense of these moments to last a while longer. Then thought of a way.

He set the eight-by-ten aside and printed the second and third exposures of the woman's arm and face against the mattress, this time without the softening effect of the yellow filter, and ran them through the baths. When there were three images, three pairs of eyes set in pale white staring at him from the counter top, he walked to the door, turned on the light and walked back . . .

He stopped and could do nothing but stare at the familiar gaze, knowing why darkness, before, had given him a feeling of recognition.

Because he had seen her only in the dark. Had watched her, how many times, in the black and white dark of movie theaters, up on the screen.

Jean Shaw.

Dark hair parted in the middle, the awareness in her eyes even half awake. Why hadn't he thought of her in the car yesterday? He had seen her for a moment in his mind, without a name, and by then they were looking for Northeast Fourth Street.

She had changed. Well, yeah, in twenty-five years people changed, everybody changed. She hadn't changed that much though. The hair maybe, the way it was styled. But she was pale in black and white as she had been on the screen and the eyes—he would never forget her eyes.

Jean Shaw. Upstairs, right now.

The movie star he had fallen in love with the first time he had ever fallen in love in his life, when he was twelve years old.

5

Cundo Rey said to Nobles, "Let me ask you something, okay? You ever see a snake eat a bat? Here is a wing sticking out of the snake's mouth, the wing, it's still moving, this little movement like is trying to fly. The snake, he don't care. You know why? Because the other end of the bat is down in the snake turning to juice, man. Sure, the snake, he don't even have to move, just lay there and keep swallowing as long as it takes. He don't even have to chew," Cundo Rey said, watching Richard Nobles eating his Big Mac and poking fries in his mouth a few at a time, dipped in ketchup. "Mmmmmmm, nice juicy bat."

They were in the McDonald's on Federal Highway, Delray Beach, the place crowded with local people having lunch. Nobles had on his two-tone-blue Star Security uniform, but not the hat. Here he was from a family whose men spent their lives outdoors and wore their hats in the house and he hated 'em. No, he liked to leave his golden hair free and run his fingers through it from time to time. Give it a casual look.

He said, mouth full of hamburger, "I ate a snake. I've ate a few different kinds. You flour 'em, deep-fry 'em in some Crisco so the meat crackles, they're pretty good. But I never ate a bat. Time you skin it what would you have?"

There—if the Cuban was trying to make him sick he was wasting his time. If the Cuban had something else in mind and was leading up to it, Nobles did not see it yet.

Ah, but then the Cuban said, drinking his coffee, not eating anything, "You understand what I'm saying to you?"

So, he would be making his point now. Fucking Cuban hotshot with his wavy hair and little gold ring in his ear. Cundo Rey was the first nigger Richard Nobles had ever seen with long wavy hair. It was parted on the right side and slanted down across his forehead over his left eye. The hair and his gold chains and silk shirts gave Cundo Rey his hot-shit Caribbean look. The way they had met last summer, ten months ago:

Nobles was making night rounds in the company Plymouth

with the official Star Security stars on the doors—cruising past shopping malls and supermarkets, shining the spot into dark areas of parking lots, dying to see some suspicious dark-skinned character in his beam so he could go beat on him—came to the Chevy dealership out Glade Road and got out of the car. It was one of the places he had to go inside, turn off the alarm with a shunt key they gave him, and look around. This night when he came out there was this dinge standing by the Plymouth. The dinge goes, "What about you leave the door open, sir, so I can get my car keys?" Telling Nobles he was supposed to pick up his car in time for the free five thousand mile checkup before the place closed but didn't make it. See, all he needed was to get his keys—telling it to Nobles in this Cuban nigger accent like Nobles was a fool. Nobles had slapped his cowhide sap against the palm of his hand a few times, but then had to grin. Which must have given the dinge confidence, for then he goes, "And if you don't believe that, sir, how you like to put five hundred dollars in your pocket and drive yourself the fuck out of here?"

Nobles admired all kinds of nerve and this Cuban was polite and had fun in his eyes.

What Cundo Rey would do usually he'd wire a brand new car out on the lot and put on stolen plates, then drive it down to South Miami or Homestead, nighttime garages he knew, and sell the car for parts. Once or twice a month make a minimum twenty-five hundred a car. Also, couple nights a week dance go-go. Get sweaty, man, lose yourself, have some fun and make a few hundred bucks.

This had confused Nobles at first. Wait a minute. Dance *go-go?*

Yeah, Cundo Rey danced go-go as a pro in a little leopard jockstrap, let the ladies reach up on their bar stools and stuff money in there, let them have a feel, spin around and shake a finger, naughty-naughty, if they tried to grab his business. Sure, dance go-go, bump and grind to salsa riffs, sometimes steel drum, have a time, work clubs Ladies' Night from West Palm down to South Beach where he appeared at a gay bar once in a while, Cheeky's; though he would have to work up his nerve for that scene, stuff his nose good with coke, because it was the freak show at the end of the world, that place.

Was he a queer? At first, usually when they were sitting in

the Plymouth looking over a car dealership, Nobles had half-expected Cundo to reach over and try to cop his joint; but he had not tried it yet and he did talk about ass like he got his share of it; so Nobles decided Cundo was straight. Just weird.

But why would a man, even a Cuban, act like a queer if he wasn't one? "What do you do it for?" he asked Cundo Rey, and Cundo Rey said, "I steal cars in darkness, I dance in lights." Nobles had seen him dance only one time. It was a place out by Miami International and Nobles had felt his own body moving as the ladies reached for Cundo Rey's crotch and Cundo Rey squirmed and writhed above them to that booger music, mouth full of white teeth sucking and smacking. Jesus. That one time was enough. Nobles believed it would take more nerve to get up there and act crazy than it would to break and enter.

They had a deal going now. Nobles would go in a dealership and get a key, Cundo Rey would start a car with it and Nobles would hang the key back up on the board—later scratch his head with everybody else, squint and kick gravel at how new cars were disappearing off the lots. He was making an extra grand a month for a few minutes' work on dark nights.

"The snake I saw, is only this long," Cundo Rey said, moving his hands apart in the air and looking from one to the other. "What is that? Less than two meters. The snake lay in the sand and swallowed for three hour, still you see the tip of the bat's wing sticking out of is mouth. Taking his time . . . the snake isn't going nowhere."

Nobles said, "Yeah?"

"What does the snake have? Patience. What's the hurry? Now with the lady, you know you going to score good there, uh? Sure, so be cool, let it happen."

Nobles said, "I'm gonna get a present, like on my birthday? I want to know what it is. I pick the box up and shake it. I was a little kid I used to do that. You give me a hard time, partner, I'll pick you up and shake *you*."

Cundo Rey sipped his coffee—very poor coffee, like water—watching Nobles wiping his big thick hands on a golden arch napkin, sucking at his teeth. The Monster from the Big Scrub, with a neck so red it could stop traffic. Cundo Rey had come ashore in Dade County only a few years ago, boat-lifted out of Cambinado del Este prison and had worked hard to learn English—asking the girls why they didn't correct him and the girls saying, because he talked cute. Richard Nobles had come down out of some deep woods only a few hours by car to the north. And yet there was no doubt in Cundo Rey's mind that he was the American, a man of the city, and Nobles the alien, with mud between his toes. Nobles, with his size, his golden hair, his desire to break and injure, his air of muscular confidence, was fascinating to watch. A swamp creature on the loose.

Cundo Rey said, "You threaten me?" Yes, he liked to watch Nobles and he liked to annoy him, too, sometimes. Without getting too close. "I don't have to do this thing with you."

"I'm kidding," Nobles said. "You're my little helper, aren't you?"

Let him believe it. "If this is a good idea," Cundo Rey said, "I don't see why you can't wait for her to come home."

"Man, I got to get going *now,* take off this goddamn uniform and get into something sporty. I mean *all* the time, not just off-duty. That drunk asshole I work for, he's gonna go broke any minute the shape he keeps things. Hires a bunch of scudders barely out of high school, they got as much brains as a box of rocks, I'm out there humping like a four-horse weed chopper, keeping the son of a bitch in booze."

Cundo Rey was staring at him, squinting, fooling with his gold earring. "I don't know what you talking about."

"I'm saying I want to get out of there, *now,* is what I'm saying. Clean out your ears. Take that girlish goddamn thing off while you're doing it. I'm embarrassed to be seen with you."

"Yes, but you don't have the plan yet," Cundo Rey said, not the least self-conscious, fishing now, pulling the line in slowly. "You got this woman has a big place, very expensive, you been with her, what, a few times . . ."

"I was with her last night."

"Okay, she's got a big place, a car . . ."

"Cadillac Eldorado."

"Some jewelry maybe . . ."

"You spook, we ain't gonna rob her."

"No? What we going to do?"

"We gonna hang her up and flat skin her."

Cundo Rey began fooling with his earring again. "Hang her up and skin her. Flat?"

"Only first, right now, we got to find out where she went."

"You don't want to wait for her to come home."

"When's that? She in a hospital, a rest home or what?"

Nobles paused, squeezed his eyes to slits and grinned, show the Cuban he had his number along with great admiration. "Be easy to find out. Man as nervy as you are. Be fun, too. What else you got to do?"

Three young girls with trays came by. Cundo Rey, fooling with curly ends of his raven hair now, working in his mind but always aware, looked up idly as they passed the booth. Nobles didn't say a word to them, didn't reach out or make a grab. He was serious today, all business.

He had started out, with his first hamburger, talking about a guy he wanted to stomp, a guy he didn't know but wore a shirt with bananas and different fruit on it. Some guy who had . . . "sandbagged" him? He wanted to know where the guy lived. But first he wanted to find the woman who had been a film actress.

"You don't have a feeling for this woman?" the Cuban asked.

Nobles said, "I want a feel I pick one about twenty years younger. This here is old meat. Good looking, you understand, but aged." Nobles hunched over the table. "Come on. Ain't any of us getting any younger."

"I'll tell you what it is," the Cuban said, "why I hesitate. I don't like to get drunk."

"You have about five rum and Cokes, get you a little glassy-eyed's all. So it looks real. I Meyers-Act you in there and you find the record book first chance, see where they took her. Glenn says it's like a blue notebook. Be on one of the desks but not in that back office, the office to the west side of the building, in there. Bear right as you go in the front door. Blue notebook, it's got the record of where everybody's sent, whether they went to detox or the shelter or if they left with somebody, the name and address of the party."

Cundo Rey said, "Glenn knows where the book is, why don't he do it? Go in and ask where she went."

"No, Glenn ain't the person I thought he was. See, they was to ask him why he wants to know, Glenn, he'd start to sweat like he's got little bugs up his ass, become twitchy, afraid they'd call Boca Police and check him out. No, Glenn ain't casual enough for this type of deal."

"Yes, but you bring him into this . . ."

"No. No, I haven't. I come out of the bar last night looking around—was Glenn told me where they took her, that's all. See, Glenn's from Umatilla originally, me and him go way back. But this here's not any kind of deal for old Glenn." Nobles winked and grinned. "I got you, partner, what do I need anybody else for?"

"I still don't like to get drunk," Cundo Rey said.

"Hey, no, just get feeling good's all."

"I got another idea," Cundo Rey said. "You finished?"

They left the McDonald's and got in Nobles' official dark blue star-decorated Plymouth.

"One time I was picked up," Cundo Rey said, "it was up in Volusia County, strange place, man. I don't know what I was doing there, making a special delivery, 'Vette to some guy ran whiskey, I think. Everyone there talk like you."

Nobles grinned at him. "Sure, that's close to my neck of the woods. Fact I know several boys ran booze." He saw Cundo's shirt unbuttoned, Cundo leaning forward to take it off. "The hell you doing?"

"I was in the jail there, they say plead guilty, man, go to Apalachee for a year, I think was the place they tole me."

Christ, raising his skinny butt to slip his pants off now. Nobles would look from Cundo to the Federal Highway and back again, moving along north in light traffic. "Apalachee Correctional," Nobles said, deciding to be cool. "I think it's for juveniles, but I guess a squirt like you could get sent there."

"So I tore my clothes off," Cundo Rey said.

"You did?"

He had his clothes off *now,* pants and silk shirt, sitting there in skimpy red jockeys as he unfastened his gold chains.

"I told them there were all these little invisible creatures crawling all over me and I screamed and scratched myself enough to bleed."

"Invisible creatures," Nobles said, grinning. "Shit."

"So they sent me up to this place, Chatahoochee, instead. You know where it is?"

"You bet I do. Nuthouse right up there by the Georgia line."

"Yes, so one night I walked out, stepped across that line to freedom. I'm going to leave my shoes on."

"I would." Nobles turned onto Northeast Fourth, let the car coast as it approached the stucco mental health facility up on the left. There were cars at a gas station farther on, but none on the street.

"I'm going to trust you with my jewelry. So don't sell it."

"No, I'll take good care of it. Listen, I ain't walking in with you bareass."

"It's okay, they let me in. A blue notebook, uh?"

Nobles braked gently to a full stop and pointed. "Be in the office that end of the building there."

"Okay, I'll call you later," Cundo Rey said, opening the door.

Nobles said, "Wait a sec. There's a broad works in there, I think she's the supervisor. Brown wavy hair, these real long legs, nice high butt. See if you can find out where she lives or if she just works nights or what."

"Man, you don't want much, do you?" Cundo Rey got out, slipped off his red briefs and dropped them in through the window. "Hide these . . . where? So I can find them."

"I'll put 'em in a paper sack, in the bushes back there where they park. Then you come on over the public beach, nobody'll think you're strange."

"Okay. I see you."

Jesus. Nobles couldn't believe it. He watched Cundo walk around past the front of the car—bareass as the day he was born back of some sugarmill, except for his tan socks and white shoes—watched him cross the street and walk up to the mental health place, cheeks of his ass pale moons, lighter than his dusky skin and it surprised Nobles. Look at the son of a bitch, like he was out for a stroll. As Cundo turned half around and waved Nobles mashed the gas pedal and got out of there.

6

He found Maurice in 304, the guest suite facing the ocean, the room filled with sunlight and old slipcovered furniture. Maurice took the prints without comment, began studying them as he moved toward the closed door to the bedroom. LaBrava came in, followed him part way. He was anxious, but remembered to keep his voice low.

"Why didn't you tell me who she is?"

"I did tell you."

"That's Jean Shaw."

"I know it's Jean Shaw. I told you that last night."

"She's supposed to be an old friend—you couldn't even think of her name."

"I like this one, the expression. She doesn't know where the hell she is." Maurice looked up from the prints, eyes wide behind his glasses. "What're you talking about, I couldn't think of her name? Twenty years she's been Jeanie Breen. I told you she left the picture business to marry Jerry Breen, her husband. I remember distinctly telling you that."

"How is she?"

"Not suffering as much as I hoped."

"You bring her some breakfast?"

"What do you think this is, a hotel?" Maurice turned to the bedroom, paused and glanced back with his hand on the door. "Wait here." He went in and all LaBrava saw was the salmon-colored spread hanging off the end of the bed. The door closed again.

Wait. He moved to one of the front windows, stood with his hands resting on the air-conditioning unit. He thought he knew everything there was to know about time. Time as it related to waiting. Waiting on surveillance. Waiting in Mrs. Truman's living room. But time was doing strange things to him now. Trying to confuse him.

What he saw from the window was timeless, a Florida post card. The strip of park across the street. The palm trees in place, the sea grape. The low wall you could sit on made of coral rock and gray cement. And the beach. What a beach. A desert full of people resting, it was so wide. People out there with blankets and umbrellas. People in the green part of the ocean, before it turned deep blue. People so small they could be from any time. Turn the view around. Sit on the coral wall and look this way at the hotels on Ocean Drive and see back into the thirties. He could look at the hotels, or he could look at Maurice's photographs all over his apartment, be reminded of pictures in old issues of *Life* his dad had saved, and feel what it was like to have lived in that time, the decade before he was born, when times were bad but the trend, the look, was to be "modern."

Now another time frame was presenting pictures, from real life and from memory. A 1950s movie star with dark hair parted in the middle, pale pure skin, black pupils, eyes that stared with cool expressions, knowing something, never smiling except with dark secrets. The pictures brought back feelings from his early teens, when he believed the good guy in the movie was out of his mind to choose the other girl, the sappy one who cried and dried her eyes with her apron, when he could have had Jean Shaw.

There were no sounds from the other room. No warning.

The door opened before he was ready. Maurice came out and a moment later there she was in a navy blue robe, dark hair, the same dark hair parted in the middle though not as long as she used to wear it and he wasn't prepared. He hadn't thought of anything to say that would work as a simple act of recognition, acknowledgment.

Maurice was no help. Maurice said, "I'll be right back," and walked out, leaving him alone in the same room with Jean Shaw.

She moved past the floral slipcovered sofa to the other front window, not paying any attention to him. Like he wasn't there. He saw her profile again, the same one, the same slender nose, remembering its delicate outline, the soft, misty profile as she stood at the window in San Francisco staring at the Bay. Foghorn moaning in the background. *Deadfall.* The guy goes off the bridge in the opening scene and everybody thinks it's suicide except the guy's buddy, Robert Mitchum. Robert Mitchum finds out somebody else was on the bridge that night, at the exact same time. A girl . . .

He saw the movie—it had to have been twenty-five years ago, because he was in the ninth grade at Holy Redeemer, he was playing American Legion ball and he went to see the movie downtown after a game, a bunch of them went. She did look older. Not much though. She was still thin and her features, with that clean delicate look, always a little bored, they were the same. He remembered the way she would toss her hair, a gesture, and stare at the guy very calmly, lips slightly parted. Robert Mitchum was no dummy, he grabbed her every chance he had in *Deadfall,* before he ended up with the dead guy's wife. That was the only trouble with her movies. She was only grabbed once or twice before the good guy went back to Arleen Whalen or Joan Leslie. She would have to be at least fifty. Twelve years older than he was. Or maybe a little more.

He didn't want to sound dumb. Like the president of a fan club. *Miss Shaw, I think I saw every picture you were ever in.*

She said, without looking at him, "You don't happen to have a cigarette, do you?"

It was her voice. Soft but husky, with that relaxed, off-hand tone. A little like Patricia Neal's voice. Jean Shaw reminded him a little of Patricia Neal, except Jean Shaw was more the mystery-woman type. In movies you saw Jean Shaw at night, hardly ever outside during the day. Jean Shaw could not have played that part in *Hud* Patricia Neal played. Still, they were somewhat alike.

"I can get you a pack," LaBrava said. He remembered the way she held a cigarette and the way she would stab it into an ashtray, one stab, and leave it.

"Maury said he'll bring some. We'll see."

"I understand you're old friends."

"We were. It remains to be seen if we still are. I don't know what I'm suppose to do here, besides stare at the ocean." She came away from the window to the sofa, finally looking at him as she said, "I can do that at home. I think it's the same ocean I've been looking at for the past . . . I don't know, round it off, say a hundred years."

Dramatic. But not too. With that soft husky sound, her trademark.

He said, "You were always staring at the ocean in *Deadfall.* I thought maybe it was like your conscience bothering you. Wondering where the guy was out there, in the water.''

Jean Shaw was seated now, with the *Miami Herald* on her lap. She brought a pair of round, wire-framed glasses out of the robe and slipped them on. ''That was *Nightshade.*''

''You sound just like her, the part you played.''

''Why wouldn't I?''

''I think in *Deadfall* you lured the guy out on the bridge. You were having an affair, then you tried to blackmail him . . . In *Nightshade* you poisoned your husband.''

She hesitated, looking up at him, and said very slowly, ''You know, I think you're right. Who was the guy in the bridge picture?''

''Robert Mitchum.''

''Yes, you're right. Mitchum was in *Deadfall*. Let me think. Gig Young was in *Nightshade.*''

''He was the insurance investigator,'' LaBrava said. ''But I think he grew flowers, too, as a hobby.''

''Everybody in the picture grew flowers. The dialogue, at times it sounded like we were reading seed catalogues.'' She began looking at the front page of the *Herald*. Within a few moments her eyes raised to him again.

''You remember those pictures?''

''I bet I've seen every picture you were in.'' There. It didn't sound too bad. She was still looking at him.

She said, ''Really?'' and slipped her glasses off to study him, maybe wondering if he was putting her on. ''On television? The late show?''

''No, in movie theaters, the first time.'' He didn't want to get into ages, how old he had been, and said, ''Then I saw some of them again later. I'm pretty sure about *Deadfall* and *Nightshade* because I saw 'em both in Independence, Missouri, just last year.''

''What were you doing in Independence, Missouri?'' With that quiet, easy delivery.

''It's a long story—I'll tell you sometime if you want. What I could never figure out was why you never ended up with the guy in the movie, the star.''

She said, "I was the spider woman, why do you think? My role was to come between the lead and the professional virgin. But in the end he goes back to little June Allyson and I say, 'Swell.' If I'm not dead."

"In *Deadfall,*" LaBrava said, "I remember I kept thinking if I was Robert Mitchum I still would've gone for you instead of the guy's wife, the widow."

"But I was in on the murder. I lured what's his name out on the bridge. Was it Tom Drake?"

"It might've been. The thing is, your part was always a downer. At least once in a while you should've ended up with the star."

"You can't have it both ways. I played Woman as Destroyer, and that gave me the lines. And I'd rather have the lines any day than end up with the star."

"Yeah, I can understand that."

"Someone said that the character I played never felt for a moment that love could overcome greed. The only time, I think, I was ever in a kitchen was in *Nightshade,* to make the cookies. You remember the kitchen, the mess? That was the tip-off I'm putting belladonna in the cookie batter. Good wives and virgins keep their kitchens neat."

"It was a nice touch," LaBrava said. "I remember he takes the cookies and a glass of milk out to the greenhouse and practically wipes out all of his plants in the death scene, grabbing something to hold onto. Gig Young was good in that. Another one, *Obituary,* I remember the opening scene was in a cemetery."

She looked up as he said it and stared at him for a moment. "When did you see *Obituary?*"

"Long time ago. I remember the opening and I remember, I think Henry Silva was in it, he was your boyfriend."

She was still watching him. She seemed mildly amazed.

"You were married to a distinguished-looking gray-haired guy. I can sorta picture him, but I don't remember his name."

"Go on."

"And I remember—I don't know if it was that picture or another one—you shot the bad guy. He looks at the blood on his hand, looks down at his shirt. He still can't believe it. But I don't remember what it was about. I can't think who the detective was either, I mean in *Obituary*. It wasn't Robert Mitchum, was it?"

She shook her head, thoughtful. "I'm not sure myself who was in it."

"He seems like a nice guy. Robert Mitchum."

She said, "I haven't seen him in years. I think the last time was at Harry Cohn's funeral." She paused and said, "Now there was a rotten son of a bitch, Harry Cohn, but I loved him. He ran Columbia. God, did he run it." She looked up at LaBrava. "I haven't been interviewed in years, either."

"Is that what this is like?"

"It reminds me. Sitting in a hotel room in a bathrobe, doing the tour. Harry would advise you how to act. 'Be polite, don't say *shit*, keep your fucking knees together and don't accept any drink offers from reporters—all they want is to get in your pants.' Where in the hell is Maurice?"

LaBrava glanced toward the door. "He said he'd be right back."

There was a silence. He had been in the presence of political celebrities and world figures. He had stood alone, from a few seconds to a few minutes, with Jimmy Carter, Nancy Reagan, George Bush's wife Barbara, Rosalynn Carter and Amy, not Sadat but Menachem Begin at Camp David, Teddy Kennedy a number of times, nameless Congressmen, Tip O'Neill was one, Fidel Castro in New York, Bob Hope . . . but he had never felt as aware of himself as he did now, in front of Jean Shaw in her blue bathrobe.

"I was trying to think," LaBrava said, "what your last movie was."

She looked up from the paper. "Let's see, I made *Let It Ride* at Columbia. Went to RKO for one called *Moon Dance*. A disaster . . ."

"The insane asylum."

"I quit right after that. I tested for a picture that was shot right around here, a lot of it at the Cardozo Hotel. I thought sure I was going to get the part. Rich widow professional virgin, my first good girl. But they gave it to Eleanor Parker. It didn't turn out to be that much of a part."

"Frank Sinatra and Edward G. Robinson," LaBrava said, impressing the movie star.

She said, "That's right, *A Hole in the Head*. Frank Capra, his first picture in I think seven years. I really wanted to work with him. I even came here on my own to find out what rich Miami Beach widows were like."

"I think you would've been too young."

"That's why Frank gave it to Eleanor Parker. Before that, half the scripts I read had Jane Greer's prints all over them." She said then, "No, the last one wasn't *Moon Dance*. I went back to Columbia—oh my God, yeah—to do *Treasure of the Aztecs*."

"*Treasure of the Aztecs*," LaBrava said, nodding. He had never heard of it.

"Farley Granger was Montezuma's bastard son. In the last reel I'm about to be offered up to the gods on top of a pyramid, have my heart torn out, but I'm rescued by Cortez's younger brother. Remember?"

"The star," LaBrava said. "I can't think who it was."

"Audie Murphy. I took the first flight I could get out of Durango and haven't made a picture since."

"I imagine a lot of people liked it though."

"You didn't see it, did you?"

"I guess that's one I missed. How many pictures did you make?"

"Sixteen. From '55 to '63."

He could think of four titles. Maybe five. "I might've missed a couple of the early ones too," LaBrava said, "but I saw all the rest. I have to tell you, whether it means anything to you or not, you were *good*."

Jean Shaw raised her eyes to his, giving him that cool, familiar look. "Which one was your favorite?"

7

At 8:10 P.M. Jill Wilkinson told Pam and Rob, the crisis center night staff, she was getting out before anything else happened. Three consecutive shifts without sleep was about it for hanging in and being a loyal South County employee. She said if she didn't go home to bed within the next hour, they'd be admitting her to Bethesda Memorial for intensive rehabilitation due to social-service burnout. South County would have to scrounge around for another wide-eyed, dedicated supervisor willing to work a seventy-hour week. Good luck. They didn't stay wide-eyed long. During the past twenty-four hours:

First there was the big blond creep with the Mickey Mouse badge and the very real gun. (The Delray cops were good guys; they did think it was sort of funny, but only after informing Mr. Richard Nobles that if he ever came in here and bothered Jill again they would fucking break his jaw on both sides of his you-all mouth and that was a promise.) Then Earl, smoking, had set fire to a mattress during the night—after they were absolutely sure he had no cigarettes or matches on him. Walter continued to drive them nuts asking if they'd ever seen an eagle, until he was finally shipped off to Crisis Stabilization. A girl who had shaved her hair back to the top of her head, shaved off her eyebrows too, locked herself in the john most of the morning while two alcoholics threw up in wastepaper baskets. A consumer waiting to be interviewed got into the case of john paper stored in the counseling office (there was no room for it anywhere else) and streamed several rolls of it around the office. And then there was the smiling Cuban who gave his name as Geraldo Rivera and walked into the center naked except for sporty perforated shoes and tan silk socks. He was sort of cute.

At first he said he had no English. Jill picked up the phone to request a bilingual Delray Police officer and he said wait, some English was coming back to him. He said perhaps he was suffering from amnesia. He remembered dressing to go to the jai alai, but must have forgotten to put his clothes on. He said this is the fronton where they play, isn't it? Jill told him they played just about everything in here except jai alai. She left him for a minute and he wandered through the offices, God, with his limp dong hanging free. The new girl, Mary Elizabeth, said wow, she had never seen one like that before, so dark compared to the rest of him. The drunks opened watery eyes to watch without comment. What else was new? Walter, who had not yet been shipped off when Geraldo arrived, asked him if he had ever seen an eagle. The Cuban said yes, in fact his mother was an eagle. He said he had been stolen by an eagle when he was a small baby, taken to its nest and fed the regurgitated meat of rabbits. They wrapped the Cuban in a sheet, which he seemed to like, rewrapping himself different ways until he settled on leaving one arm free, toga-fashion. He seemed to quiet down.

Then their twenty-year-old potential suicide, manic depressive, climbed up on a file cabinet and punched through the screen to shatter the glass of the ceiling-high window in the main office. They brought him down bloody, blood smearing the wall, an arm gashed from wrist to elbow. Sometime while the paramedics were taking him out to the van, the naked Cuban disappeared.

They called Delray Police to report a missing consumer who might or might not be running around their catchment area wrapped in a South County bed sheet and might or might not answer to the name Geraldo. They would take him back whoever he claimed to be.

There was no positive response from the police.

About five o'clock, when first Jill fantasized going home at a normal hour, seeing herself barefoot, alone, sipping chilled Piesporter, she discovered her wallet and ring of something like a dozen keys missing from her bag. The only person she could think of responsible was the naked Cuban.

Mary Elizabeth left about 6:45. She came back in with Jill's ring of keys and wallet, the wallet empty. Found them, she said, right out in the middle of the parking lot. She had kicked the keys, in fact, walking to her car.

Something was strange. Jill had looked outside earlier, front and rear. If the keys and wallet weren't there a few hours ago, how could they be there now?

Well, if the guy was chronically undifferentiated enough to walk naked into South County thinking it was a jai alai fronton . . . yes? . . . play with a bed sheet, rip off her wallet and keys . . . who knows, he could have sneaked back during a lucid period, basically a nice guy, thoughtful, knowing she would need her keys, her driver's license . . .

It was a guess that she could accept.

Until she was driving home to Boynton Beach—FM top-forty music turned low, the dark, the muted sound relaxing—and began to wonder if there might not be more to it.

What if that whole number, the guy walking in naked, had been an act? To get her keys, find out where she lived . . . imagining the naked, possibly-undifferentiated Cuban now as a thoughtful burglar. Did that make sense?

None.

Still it was in her mind, the possibility, as she mounted the circular cement stairway to the second floor, moved along the balcony walk past orange buglights at the rear doors of the apartments and came to 214.

Would it be cleaned out?

Jill held her breath opening the door. She had paid almost seven hundred for the stereo and speakers, God, over three hundred for the color television set. Her two-hundred-dollar bike was on the front balcony . . .

The apartment was dark. A faint orange glow in the kitchen window showed the sink and counter. She moved past the kitchen, along the short hallway to the living room. Saw dim outside light framing the glass door to her private balcony. Saw her bike out there. Felt the television set sticking out of the bookcase. She let her breath out in a sigh, feeling exhaustion, relief. Thought, Thank you, Jesus. Not as a prayer but a leftover littlegirl response. And sucked her breath in again, hard, and said out loud, "Jesus!" Still not as a prayer. Said, "What do you want!" with her throat constricted. Seeing part of an outline against the glass door. Only part of the figure in the chair, but knowing it was a man sitting there waiting for her.

She turned to run out. Got to the hallway.

And a light came on behind her.

A lamp turned on in her own living room. The goddamn deceiving light that made her stop and turn, feeling in that moment everything would be all right because, look, the light was on and the unknown figure in darkness would turn out to be someone she knew who would say gee, hey, I'm sorry and offer an incredible explanation . . .

She knew him all right. Even in the two shades of blue uniform. The blond hair . . . Coming toward her, bigger in this room than he had looked last night, not hurrying. Still, it was too late to run.

Nobles said, "Bet you're wore out. I swear they must work you like a nigger mule at that place, the hours you put in. See, I figured you wouldn't want me sitting out in the car, so I come on in. I been waiting, haven't had no supper . . ." He stretched, yawning. "I was about to go in there, get in the bed. How'd that a been? You come home, here I'm under the covers sleeping like a baby."

That thin coat of syrup in his tone.

Jill concentrated. All the words, the dirty words, the sounds in her mind, screaming obscenities, she kept hold of them as he spoke, as he grinned at her; she knew words would be wasted. She concentrated instead, making an effort to breathe slowly, to allow the constriction in her body to drain, and said nothing. She would wait. As she had waited nearly a half hour for the police while a psychopath dumped over file cabinets, tore up her office . . . She knew how to wait.

Nobles said, "Yeah, you're wore out, aren't you? Come on sit down over here"—taking her to the sofa, easing her down—"I'll get you a cold drink. I notice you have a bottle of something there in the icebox. Look like piss in a green bottle, but if it's your pleasure . . ." Standing over her now, towering. "How's that sound?"

She stared at his hips, at dark blue, double-knit material worn to a shine, a belt of bullets, a holstered revolver. She said nothing.

Nobles said, "Cat got your tongue? . . . Hey, you mad at me? Listen, I'm the one should be angry here, way I got treated last night. I'd had a few, but I wasn't acting nasty or nothing, was I?

Just fooling around, giving you a flash of my I.D. I was about to show it to you and this boy I never seen before whomps me a good'n, blindsides me while I ain't looking. All I see's this flash of light, wham bam. I still don't know what it was he hit me with. Must a been like a two-b'-four."

Nobles waited. There was a silence. He hooked his thumbs in his gunbelt, looked about the room idly, taking his time, and came back to Jill.

"Who was that boy, anyway? Friend of yours?"

She said nothing.

"I know he said he was with one of the newspapers. I was wondering which one he worked for."

She said nothing.

"Hey, I'm asking you a question."

Jill eased back against the cushion. She looked up at Nobles. Saw his expression, the lines along both sides of his nose drawn tight. His face seemed to shine.

Sociopathic, if not over the edge.

She said, "You know more about him than I do."

"What's his name?"

Low impulse control.

"I don't know. He didn't tell me."

"Well, what was he doing there?"

Anger threshold you could poke with an elbow.

"I really don't know. I think he came with someone."

"With who?"

"We have people in and out all day. I don't remember their names. I don't meet half of them."

"You see what that scudder hit me with?"

It caught her by surprise. She said, "He didn't hit you with anything, he put you down and sat on you," and wanted to bite her tongue.

Seeing his expression again, the sheen of anger. She saw him draw his revolver and saw his knuckles and the round hole of the barrel come toward her face, close, almost touching her.

He said, "Open your mouth."

"Why do you want to do that?"

He said, "Open your goddamn mouth!"

Hunched over her to grab a handful of hair as she tried to turn her face, yanked her up tight against the cushion. With the pain she gasped, wanting to cry out, and he slipped the tip of the revolver into her open mouth.

His expression changed, the grin coming back. He said, "Hey, puss, you give me an idea."

8

They had dinner at Picciolo's on South Collins, Maurice telling them what it used to be like before the lower end of Miami Beach went to hell; LaBrava watching Jean Shaw raise her fork, sip her wine, coming to believe she was more attractive now than she had been in black and white, on the screen.

Picciolo's, Maurice said, height of the season you couldn't get near the place, the cars lined up outside. Now you could shoot a cannon off in here, maybe hit a waiter. Notice they still wore black tie. LaBrava studying her profile as she looked off across empty tables, head held high, purity of line against the dark color of the booth done up as a gondola, head turning in time back to Maurice next to her; he would shoot her in profile, either side flawless in restaurant light, this lady who had played spider women, enticed second leads to their death and never got the star. Maurice saying Picciolo's and Joe's Stone Crab were the only places left on the south end, the neighborhood taken over by junkies, muggers, cutthroats, queers, you name it. Cubans off the boat-lift, Haitians who had swum ashore when their boats broke to pieces, old-time New York Jews once the backbone, eyeing each other with nothing remotely in common, not even the English language. The vampires came out at night and the old people triple-locked their doors and waited for morning. Ass-end of Miami Beach down here.

Remember the pier? Look at it. Used to be nice. They sell drugs out there now, any kind of pills you want, take you up or down. (The old man of the street speaking.) Bar around the corner there, guys dress up like girls. Lovely place. "I'm telling you," Maurice said, telling them, giving his friend Jean Shaw a slow tour of the old neighborhood on the thirteen-block drive from the restaurant to the Della Robbia Hotel. The three of them in the front seat of the Mercedes. LaBrava inhaling without sound but deeply, his thigh touching hers, filling himself with her scent.

"You remember the kind of people use to come down for the season? Now we got three hundred bums, count 'em, three hundred, show up every winter. Look. Over there on the bench, look, the bag lady. That's Marilyn. Says she used to be a movie star, a singer and a gourmet cook. Look at her. She's got a shopping cart she pushes down Lincoln Road Mall, it's fulla plastic bags, bottles, old copies of *The Wall Street Journal.* Marilyn. Maybe you knew her back when."

"Go slower," Jean Shaw said. "Where does she live?"

"You're looking at it, on the bench. They live in alleys, the bums, they live in empty buildings. The respectable people, they work in a garment loft forty-five years, come down here, put their life savings in a co-op and have to triple-lock their doors. Afraid even to look out the window.

"They were suppose to start redeveloping the whole area ten years ago, put in canals, make it look like Venice. Nobody's allowed to fix up their property, they got to wait for the big scheme. Only the big scheme went bust, never happened. The boat-lifters and dopers come in, half the neighborhood's already down the toilet.

"I know a guy lives in a place called the Beachview on Collins. Listen to this, Collins Avenue, he pays four hundred seventy-five bucks-a-year rent. You know why? He's got a seven-by-ten room, no bath, newspapers on the floor, no air, no stove even. Joe, is that right? Joe took some pictures of the guy in his room he'll show you. Looks like a gypsy wagon, all the crap piled up in there. Four-seventy-five a year on Collins Avenue, you think it hasn't changed?

"Show her the La Playa."

Why would she want to see a run-down fleabag hotel?

"We already passed it."

"Show her," Maurice said.

There, corner of Collins and First. Two blocks from the Miami Beach Police station, they had over two hundred assaults, shootings, knifings, rapes, ripoffs and what have you in that one hotel alone last year. You believe it? Look. What're we on? Washington Avenue. They got video cameras mounted up on cement poles, close-circuit TV, so the cops can watch the muggings, the dope transactions, and not have to leave the station. Look. Right before our eyes, two young girls beating the shit outta each other on the street. Nice? I'm telling you . . .

But *why* was he telling her? His good friend the once-famous movie star. To frighten her? So she'd stay in the hotel and never go out alone?

No, LaBrava decided. It was to impress her. The old man was showing off. Letting her know, yeah, it was a rough place, but he knew his way around. Ballsy little eighty-year-old guy. What it came down to, Maurice loved South Beach.

Jean Shaw said she would join them in a few minutes, she wanted to change. LaBrava watched her walk down the hall to the guest suite.

She had long thin legs, still a good figure. He had liked blonds with coppery tans but was coming to prefer dark hair parted in the middle, pale skin.

He took off his sport coat following Maurice into his apartment, the gallery, a photographic record of what Maurice had witnessed in his life covering most of three walls. The rest of the room was crowded with hotel–lobby furniture, a sectional sofa, Maurice's La-Z-Boy recliner. Maurice went to his bar, a credenza by the formal dining-room table, and got ready to pour their nightcaps. Tighteners. LaBrava hung his coat on the back of a dining-room chair and, as he always did, began looking at photographs.

The way it went most times, Maurice would pretend not to notice. LaBrava would study a row of framed black-and-white prints. And finally Maurice would say:

"Terpentine camp, wood smoke and backyard cauldrons, men working that sticky mess for a dollar a day . . . and dance with their women at a jook place called the Starlight Patio, way in the piney woods . . . Sniff, you can smell the coal-oil lamps, look at the eyes shining, dirt rings on the neck of that lovely woman . . ."

LaBrava would move a step, concentrating, not looking around, and Maurice would say:

"Georgia road gang, 1938. They wore stripes till '42. That's the captain there. Gene Talmadge, used to be governor, said, 'You want a man knows how to treat convicts, get you somebody who has et the cake.' Somebody once a convict himself. Eugene believed in whipping and the use of the sweatbox."

LaBrava would move on, gaze holding, and Maurice would say:

"That's Al Tomani, known as the next-to-tallest man in the world. His wife was born without legs and together they were billed as the World's Strangest Couple. About 1936."

And LaBrava would move on to be told about men digging mole drains in canefields, migrants cutting palmetto, boy sitting under a tung tree, Miccosuki Indians drinking corn beer, called *safki* . . .

But not this evening.

Maurice came out of the kitchen with an ice tray, glanced over to say, "Arrival of the Orange Blossom Special, January 1927 . . ." and got a surprise. LaBrava stood with his back to the Florida East Coast Railway shots.

He said to Maurice, "I don't think she has a problem at all. She had two drinks before dinner, couple of Scotches, she didn't finish the second one. I think all she had was one glass of wine . . ."

Maurice slid the ice cubes into a bowl. "What're you talking about?"

"You said in the car yesterday, going to get her, she had a problem."

"I told you she called me up . . ."

"You said she sounded strange."

"I said she sounded funny. She tells me she's got a problem, I ask her what it is, she changes the subject. So I don't know if it's booze or what."

"You seemed to think it was."

"Well, it still could be. You throw a drink at a cop car, that's not exactly having it under control. But today she's fine."

"You ask her why she did it?"

"She says she was in a bad mood, should a stayed home. The cop gets out of the car, says something smart . . . she throws the drink."

"Yeah, but what was she doing out on the sidewalk with a drink in the first place?"

"Getting some air—who knows. She was a movie star, Joe. They're all a little nuts."

* * *

She sat with them in Maurice's living room wearing slacks and a white cotton sweater now, sandals; she sipped her Scotch with a squirt of soda and struck LaBrava as a person who was courteous and a good listener. But then what choice did she have once Maurice got started?

He was showing off tonight:

". . . Neoga, Española, Bunnell, Dupont, Korona, Favorita, Harwood, National Gardens, Windle, Ormond, Flomich, Holly Hill, Daytona Beach, Blake, Port Orange, Harbor Point, Spruce Creek, New Smyrna, Hucomer, Ariel, Oak Hill, Shiloh, Scottsmoor, Wiley, Jay Jay, Titusville, Indian River City, Delespine, Frontenac, Hardee's, Sharpes, City Point, Spratt's, Dixon's, Ives, Cocoa, Rockledge, Williams, Garvey's, Paxton's, Bonaventure, Pineda . . ."

On his way to naming every stop on the Florida East Coast line from Jacksonville to Key Largo, reciting the names without a pause, as he had learned them back in the early thirties.

This evening Maurice had to get off at Vero Beach to go to the bathroom and LaBrava and Jean Shaw looked at each other.

"The first time I met him," Jean Shaw said, "we were having dinner with a group. I think it was a place called Gatti's."

"It's right over here. Not far."

"He did his train stops. Exactly the same way, the same pace."

LaBrava said, "But how do we know he's not leaving some out?"

She said, "Would it make any difference?"

There was a silence. LaBrava looked toward the bathroom, then at Jean Shaw again. "I'd like to ask you something I've been wondering."

"Go ahead. About the movies?"

"No, it's about a guy named Richard Nobles. Do you know him?"

She sure did. It was in and out of her eyes.

When she said nothing, but continued to stare at him, he felt like a sneak. "Big guy with blond hair. About six-two."

"He's six-three and a half," Jean Shaw said. "He's a security cop and he thinks every woman he meets falls in love with him."

LaBrava felt relief, and a little closer to her.

She was frowning slightly. "How do you know him?"

"He came to that clinic in Delray last night, while we were there."

"Really?" She showed only mild surprise.

"He was pretty drunk." LaBrava offered it as a cue, wanting her to begin talking about Nobles, but it didn't prompt much.

All she said was, "I can believe it."

LaBrava tried again. "He said he was with you earlier. I mean he said he'd been with the person he came to pick up. He didn't mention anyone by name."

She was nodding, resigned. "The reason I left the bar was to get away from him." Her eyes returned to LaBrava. "I suppose you heard what I did."

"Got a little upset with a policeman."

"It was that flashing light. I didn't need help, I wanted to be alone. But they wouldn't leave, or turn off those goddamn blue lights."

"It can be irritating," LaBrava said. "Yeah, I wondered about this fella Nobles . . . He said you were friends."

"He did, huh. I'm surprised he didn't say we were more than that."

"Military Park, Melbourne, Hopkins, Shares, Palm Bay, Malabar," Maurice said, coming out of the bathroom, "Valkaria, Grant, Micco, Roseland, Sebastian . . . Comfort stop. Who's ready for another drink? . . . Nobody?"

Jean Shaw said, "Maury, why didn't you tell me about the guy last night, looking for me? Richard Nobles."

"What guy?"

"He didn't see him," LaBrava said. "Maurice was with you the whole time."

"Did he get rough? Threaten to punch anybody?"

"Well, the girl in charge called the police . . . He calmed down. No, I just wondered if you were the one he came to get. I had a feeling."

"What guy?"

"Maury, sit down, rest your engine," Jean Shaw said. "We're talking about someone I met a few months ago, a security cop in Boca."

Maurice said, "You're going with a security cop now?" He eased into the La-Z-Boy, his body stiff; he seemed swallowed by the chair's contour, laid his head on his shoulder to look at Jean past his pointy shoes. "What happened to the bartender and the guy works at Hialeah?"

"I'm not *going* with anyone. I met him, I was nice to him . . . I mean I didn't tell him to get lost. But that might've been a mistake." She glanced at LaBrava.

Maurice said, "Wait a minute. How do you know this guy?"

"He works for the security service the building hired. I happened to meet him one night. I was out taking a walk. He was making his rounds." Choosing her words with care. "We started talking . . ."

Maurice said, "Yeah?" Sounding suspicious.

"You have to understand, first of all," Jean Shaw said, "he has a way about him. Very friendly, comes on with a certain country-boy charm. If you know the type I mean."

"Looks up at the condos with his mouth open," Maurice said, "scratching his ass."

"He looks you right in the eye, and he grins," Jean Shaw said. "He grins quite a lot. And he stands right on top of you when you're talking. He comes on like he's trying to be friendly, a nice guy, you know? But there's something intimidating about him. He's a little scary."

Maurice said, "I never saw the guy in my life I can tell you what his game is, Christ."

LaBrava listened.

"All the rich broads that live down here, lonely, don't know what to do with themselves . . ."

"Thanks a lot," Jean said.

"Not you. But even you, you gotta be careful."

"The ladies in the building think he's cute."

"Yeah? *You* think he's cute?"

"In a way, I suppose. He's attractive . . . He's awfully big though."

LaBrava did not think Nobles was cute in any way, by any supposition or measurement. He believed Nobles was dangerous, that you could look at him funny and set him off. But he said nothing. He listened.

"They come in all shapes and sizes looking for a score," Maurice said. "Find 'em in all the classier lounges."

Jean Shaw said, "Maury, I think I can spot a snake faster than you can. Don't worry about it."

"Then what're we talking about?"

"I haven't said this guy's out for anything in particular." She paused. "Other than what they're usually out for."

LaBrava saw her eyes come to him and hold for a moment as she sipped her drink. A familiar look from long ago, the calm dark eyes. A screen gesture . . . Or was it real?

"So what's his game?" Maurice said.

"He's a little too . . . familiar. That's all."

"He call you? Want to go out?"

"I did meet him a couple of times. Just for a drink."

"Jesus Christ," Maurice said.

"I didn't encourage him, I was being friendly. I'm not a snob."

"I'll tell you something," Maurice said. "At times you're not very smart either. Guys you get mixed up with."

She said, "Let's keep it simple, all right? I've never had trouble dealing with men, because I don't play games with them. I'm not a tease."

LaBrava listened. He didn't like the sound of "dealing with men." For a moment, thinking of her with other men, he was uncomfortable.

"But you happen to let this guy get too close," Maurice said. "That why you called me last week? You tell me you have a problem, then you don't want to talk about it." He glanced at LaBrava for confirmation.

She said, "Oh," and nodded with that look of resignation. She said, "Well, I was beginning to get a little scared. So I called you. But then as we were talking I thought, no, you're going to think I sound dumb. You're going to say all the things you've been saying, I'm a big girl and should know better. So I kept quiet . . . It's not your problem anyway."

LaBrava could close his eyes and listen and see her on the screen. The easy delivery, the slight huskiness in her voice, serious but calm, almost off-hand about it.

Maurice said, "So what happened you got scared?"

"He was in my apartment that afternoon, the day I called you." She seemed to be picturing it. "It was the way he made himself right at home. Like he was taking over."

Maurice said, "Wait a minute. He was in your apartment. You let him in?"

LaBrava listened.

"Months ago, like the first or second time we talked, I promised I'd show him one of my pictures."

Maurice said, "One of your movies."

"See, the way it started, he didn't believe I was an actress. We were talking about it and, in a weak moment, I promised I'd run one of my pictures for him. I have video cassettes of a couple. I think the only two available."

Maurice looked at LaBrava. "You catch that 'in a weak moment'?"

LaBrava was wondering which movies she had.

"I didn't invite him," she said, "he just came. I opened the door, there he was."

"Forced his way in."

"He talked me into it."

"Musta taken at least ten fifteen seconds," Maurice said, "talk a movie actress into showing one of her hits. So what would you say it was outweighed common sense? You miss being a celebrity? What?"

"He's standing there at the door, hat in hand. Grinning."

"Hat in hand—so you sit him down, just the two of you. The place is dark—"

"It was the middle of the afternoon."

"You show the movie, there you are, the star, bigger than life on the silver screen."

"On a television set, Maury."

"He sees you putting the make on Robert Mitchum, Robert Taylor, whoever, with that sexy come-hither look . . . Okay, the picture ends, lights're still low, the guy tries to climb all over you and you wonder why."

"That's not what I'm talking about," Jean Shaw said. "I can handle that end of it."

LaBrava listened.

"I'm talking about his attitude. The way he walks around the apartment, looks at my things. He's possessive and he's intimidating, without saying a word. He wants something and I don't know what it is."

"He wants *you,*" Maurice said. "Guy like that, doesn't have any dough. What's he make? He wants you to keep him, buy him presents."

"I don't think so," she said. "He would've given me a few hints by now. Like he can't afford new clothes on his salary, wouldn't mind having a new car." Her eyes moved to LaBrava. "His sister's a cripple and needs an operation."

High Sierra, LaBrava thought.

"What he's doing, he's sneaking up," Maurice said.

Humphrey Bogart and Ida Lupino, LaBrava thought. He couldn't think of the name of the girl with the clubfoot.

"Doesn't want to move too fast and blow it," Maurice said. "Only he's too dumb to realize you can see it coming a mile away."

"See *what* coming?"

Maurice said, "Jeanie," taking his time, "is this guy in love with you? Is that a possibility?"

"He's in love with himself."

"Okay. Then he's looking for a free ride. Dinner at the club, some new outfits, little spending money . . . That's how those guys operate. They been around Miami Beach since the day they built the bridge."

"Maybe," she said. "But I think he's got something else in mind."

LaBrava said, "I do too."

Jean Shaw looked over. Maurice looked over.

"I don't think he has a particular lifestyle in mind," LaBrava said. "Dinner at the club . . . I think what he wants, if he's after anything at all, is a whole lot of money."

"Then there's nothing to worry about," Jean Shaw said, "because I don't have any."

On a stool in the darkroom LaBrava sat hunched over contacts of the stoned Cuban couple, Boza and Mendoza, who had posed for him this morning, moving a magnifier down the strips of miniature prints, deciding Lana had had the right idea ("How about one like this?"), the shot of her exposing herself was the best one. Not because of her bared chest, but because of her eagerness to show breasts that were lifeless and seemed too old for her, and because

Paco, sitting below her in the wheelchair, didn't know what was going on. LaBrava felt sorry for the girl; he saw ambition but little about her that was appealing and believed she would be hard to live with.

He could look at this girl, Lana Mendoza, barely a name to him, and know her, while his mind was still upstairs with Jean Shaw, wondering.

Trying to see her clearly.

He caught glimpses of her in black and white from the past and now in soft color, the same person, pale features, the lady in lamplight, dark eyes coming to rest on him. Her eyes could do things to him without half trying. He believed she was beautiful. He believed she was vulnerable. He believed she looked at him in a different way than she looked at Maurice.

He had walked her down the hall to 304. In the doorway she said, "I'm glad I came here." She kissed him on the cheek. She said, "Thank you," and was still looking at him as she closed the door.

Was that familiar? Seeing her eyes and then the door closing, filling the screen. He wasn't sure.

Why did she thank him?

He didn't do anything, offer advice. He listened.

He listened to her tell Maurice she was serious. She didn't have any money. Really. Not money as you thought of having *money*. She wasn't living on Social Security. But, she said, she didn't have that much to begin with. Jerry hadn't exactly left her set for life. Not after the IRS got through with him. Three audits in a row. LaBrava listened. All of his tax shelters disallowed. They had to sell the house on Pine Tree. Then his stock portfolio went to hell, he took a bath there. LaBrava listened. Between the government and the market Jerry was almost into bankruptcy when he died. That's what killed him, Jean Shaw said. Maurice didn't say much. He listened, watching her almost sadly, and seemed to nod in sympathy. He did ask her how she was fixed. She said well, she had the income from her piece of the hotel, she had a few stocks, she could sublease the apartment and move to a cheaper place. She said, with that dry delivery, she could always make appearances at condominium openings. "Screen Star Jean Shaw in

Person.'' A developer had suggested it one time. Or, she said, if things got really bad she could team up with Marilyn, the bag lady, work up a routine. Maurice, serious, said come on, don't talk like that. He told her not to worry about her financial situation, not as long as he was around. There was no mention again of Richard Nobles.

Now, in the darkroom, Joe LaBrava wondered which of her movies she had showed Nobles. He wondered why she had said, ''The way he walks around the apartment, looks at my things.'' Like Nobles had visited her more than that one time, to see the movie.

He wondered about her eyes, too, if she used them in a studied, theatrical way. Twice, while Maurice was speaking, he had felt her eyes and turned to see her watching him. He saw her eyes as she sipped her drink . . . as she closed her door.

I'm glad I came here.

And heard a girl's voice say, ''Boy, you put in long hours, don't you?''

Franny Kaufman stood in the doorway. He smiled, glad to see her. He liked her, with the strange feeling they were old friends. ''The Spring Song girl. You moved in?''

''Sorta. A friend of mine has a van helped me with the heavy stuff, the boxes. I still have some junk to get tomorrow.''

''What room're you in?''

''Two-oh-four. It's not bad, I get morning light. I haven't seen any bugs yet.'' She wore jeans and a gas–station shirt that said *Roy* above the pocket, intricate silver rings on her fingers. She turned, looking around ''I didn't know you had all this.''

''It's the old man's, really.''

''I was just nosing around, seeing what's here.'' She came over to the counter. ''Can I look?''

''Here, use the loupe,'' he moved aside, off the stool.

Franny took off her round glasses, bent over to study the contacts through the Agfa magnifier, inching it over the pictures, stopping, moving on. He looked at her strange hair that he liked, frizzed out on both sides—it seemed part of her energy—and looked at the slender nape of her neck, the stray hairs against white skin.

She said, "I've seen him around, but I haven't seen her. Which ones're you gonna print? No, wait. I bet I know the one you like the best. The one, the girl showing her tits. Am I right?"

"I think so," LaBrava said. "I'm gonna play with it, print it different ways, see what I get."

"It's sad, isn't it?" Franny said. "Except I get the feeling she's a ballbuster. I feel sorry for her, you know? But only up to a point. Was the pose your idea?"

"No, hers."

"What's her name?"

"Lana."

"Oh, that's perfect."

"Yeah, Lana gets the credit."

"But it didn't turn out the way she thought it would. You got something better. You do good work, Joe."

"Thank you."

"You do any nudes?"

"I have. A lady one time had me shoot her sitting on a TV set naked."

"Coming on to you?"

"No, she wanted her picture taken."

"Far out."

"It wasn't bad. She started with a fur coat on. Then she says, 'Hey, I got an idea.' Lets the coat fall open, she's got nothing on under it. They always say that, 'Hey, I got an idea,' like they just thought of it."

"I got an idea," Franny said. "Shoot me nude, okay? I want to do a self-portrait in pastels, send it to this guy in New York. I'm thinking life-size, reclined, very sensual. What do you charge for a sitting? Or a lying."

"You can buy lunch sometime."

"Really? But you have to promise not to send it to *Playboy*. This is for art, like Stieglitz shooting Georgia O'Keeffe in the nude. You ever see those?"

"They were married then."

She said, "They were?" surprised. She said, "You know what you're doing, don't you?"

"Sometimes."

"Are you tired? I mean right now."

"Not especially."

"Let's go outside, look at the ocean. That's the only reason to live here, you know it? The ocean and these weird hotels, both of them together in the same place. I love it."

They walked through the empty lobby.

"Yeah, I think reclined. Unless you've got some ideas."

"It's your painting."

"I'm gonna render myself about twelve pounds lighter and straighten my hair. See if I can turn the guy on."

They crossed the street past locked parked cars.

"I like your hair the way it is."

"Really? You're not just being nice?"

"No, I mean it."

And crossed the grass to the low wall made of cement and coral where she raised her face to the breeze coming out of darkness, off the ocean. "I feel good," Franny said. "I'm glad I came here."

"Somebody else told me that, just a little while ago." He sat down on the wall, facing the Della Robbia, looked up at the windows. Faint light showed in 304. "I'll tell you who it was. Jean Shaw."

Franny turned from the ocean, her face still raised. "Who's Jean Shaw?"

"You never heard of Jean Shaw?"

"Joe, would I lie to you?"

"She was a movie star. She was in pictures with Robert Mitchum."

"Well, obviously I've heard of Robert Mitchum. I love him."

"And some others. She was my favorite actress."

"Wow, and she's a friend of yours, uh?"

"I met her today."

"Is she the one, dark hair, middle-aged, she came out of the hotel this evening with you and Mr. Zola? We were in the van, we'd just pulled up."

"We went out to dinner." He thought about what he was going to say next and then said it, before he changed his mind. "How old you think she is?"

Franny said, "Well, let's see. She looks pretty good for her age. I'd say she's fifty-two."

"You think she looks that old?"

"You asked me how old I think she is, not how old I think she looks. She's had a tuck and probably some work done around the eyes. She *looks* about forty-five. Or younger. Her bone structure helps, nice cheekbones. And her complexion's great, you can tell she stays out of the sun, and I'll bet she buys protein fiber replenishers by the case. But her actual age, I'd have to say fifty-two."

"You think so?"

"Joe, you're talking to the Spring Song girl."

"Okay, how old am I?"

"You're thirty-eight."

He said, "You're right."

"But you don't look a day over thirty-seven."

Cundo Rey was driving his black Pontiac Trans Am that he had bought, paid for, black with black windows that Nobles said you couldn't see for shit out of at night, lights looked real weak, yellowish and you couldn't read signs at all. Cundo Rey let him bitch. He loved his Trans Am, he loved going slow in it like they were doing now even better than letting it out, because you could hear the engine rumble and pop, all that power cooking under the hood. Cundo was wearing blue silk with a white silk neckerchief, one of his cruising outfits. Nobles was still wearing his uniform, blue on blue, both the shirt epaulets hanging, the buttons torn off. Nobles said somebody had tried to give him a hard time. Cundo said, "It look like they did, too."

They were creeping along south on Ocean Drive, the strip of Lummus Park and the beach on their left, the old hotels close on their right, the other side of the bumper-to-bumper parked cars. "Netherland," Cundo Rey said, hunched over the steering wheel, looking up at signs. "Cavalier . . . There, the Cardozo. See? On that thing sticks out."

"The awning," Nobles said. "Okay, slow down."

"I'm going slow as this baby can go." He pushed in the clutch and gave it some gas to hear that rumble, get a few pops out the ass end.

A man and a girl with strange electric hair, crossing the street in the headlight beams, looked this way.

"There it is, on the corner. Della Robbia. I don't see a number but that's it,'' Nobles said, ''where her friend took her.'' And then said, ''Jesus Christ—'' turning in his bucket seat, both hands moving over the door. ''Where's the goddamn window thing?''

Cundo Rey glanced at him. ''What's your trouble now?''

''Open the goddamn window.''

''Man, I got the air on.''

''Open the fucking window, will you! Turn around.''

''Hey, what's the matter with you?'' Cundo scowling.

Guy acting like he was going crazy, like he was trapped, clawing at the door.

''That's the *guy*, the fucker 'at hit me.''

''Where? That guy with the girl?''

''Turn the fuck around, *now*.''

They had to go down to Twelfth. Cundo backed into the street and came out to move north on Ocean Drive.

''Put your window down.''

''I can see okay. Be cool. Why you want to get excited for?''

''I don't see 'em.'' Nobles hunched up close to the windshield.

''There,'' Cundo Rey said. ''On the porch.''

Nobles turned to look past Cundo, and kept turning.

''Guy is opening the door with a key,'' Cundo Rey said. ''So he must live there too, uh? Is that the guy?''

''That's the guy,'' Nobles said, calm now, looking out the back as they crept past the Cardozo. ''That's him.'' He didn't straighten around until they came to Fifteenth, where Ocean Drive ended and they had to go left over to Collins.

''I didn't see him too good in the dark,'' Cundo Rey said. ''You sure is the guy?''

Nobles was sitting back now, looking straight ahead. He said, ''Yeah, that's him. That's the guy.''

''You want me to go back?''

''No, I don't want you to go back just yet.''

Looking at him Cundo Rey said, ''You sound different.''

9

There was sunlight in the window. LaBrava picked up the phone next to his bed and the girl's voice said, "I woke you up, didn't I? I'm sorry." He recognized the voice now. She said, "I don't know what time it is and the goddamn nurse won't come when I call . . ."

He drove past the hospital thinking it was a resort motel or it might be a car dealership with all the glass and had to U-turn and come back for another pass before he saw the sign, *Bethesda Memorial.*

Jill Wilkinson was alone in a semi-private room. She looked different, smaller and younger, out of character as victim. She had been diagnosed as having a slight concussion and was under twenty-four-hour observation, chewing on crushed ice when La-Brava came in.

"This is all I've had to eat since yesterday afternoon. You believe it? They won't give me anything else till I'm all better."

"You look pretty good."

"Thanks. I've always wanted to look pretty good."

He leaned over the bed, close to her, looking into her face clean of makeup. Her eyes were brown looking at his, waiting. "You look great. How's that?"

"Better."

"You fish for compliments?"

"I don't have to, usually."

"Your head hurt?"

"It's a little fuzzy. I feel dragged out. Used up."

"That what he did, he used you?"

"He tried to. He had ideas. God, did he have ideas."

"What stopped him?"

"*I* did. I said, 'You put that thing in my mouth I'll bite it off, I swear to God.' "

"Oh."

"He had to think about that. I told him I might be dead, but he'd be squatting to take a leak for the rest of his life."

"Oh."

"He put his gun in my mouth—and you know where he got that. And then *that* gave him the other idea."

"He hit you?"

Two people talking who knew about violence.

"He pushed me around. I tore his epaulets and he got mad. I tried to run in the bathroom and lock the door, but he came in right behind me, banged the door in, and I fell over the side of the tub and cracked my head against the tile."

"He had his uniform on."

"Yeah . . ."

"Were you knocked out?"

"I was sort a dazed, you know, limp, but I wasn't out all the way. He put me on the bed and sat down next to me—listen to this—and held my hand. He said he was sorry, he was just goofing around."

"Did he look scared?"

"I don't know, I wasn't all there." She shook the ice in the paper cup, raised it to her mouth and paused. "Wait a minute. Yeah, he tried to take my blouse off, he said he'd put me to bed, and I grabbed one of his fingers and bent it back."

"Then what?"

"Nothing, really."

"He touch you?"

"Did he give me a feel? Well, sorta. He gave it a try."

"You tell the police that part?"

She hesitated and he thought she was trying to remember.

"I didn't tell them anything."

"You didn't call the cops?"

"I called South County, my office. I got Mr. Zola's name and number and I called, but there was no answer. Last night."

"How'd you get my number?"

"I had your name. I took a chance you lived in South Beach, near Mr. Zola, so I called Information, this morning."

"You haven't told the cops anything."

"No."

He waited a few moments. "Why not?"

Now Jill waited. "He really didn't *do* anything. I mean you have to consider the kind of creepy stuff I run into every day, at work. A guy making a pass isn't all that much."

"How'd he get in your apartment?"

"I don't know."

"You don't think he broke in."

"No."

"What he did comes under attempted sexual battery. In this state it can get you life."

She said, "How do you know that?"

"But you say he really didn't do anything. What would he have to do?"

"You want to know the truth?"

"I'd love to."

"I'm going to Key West for ten days. It's my big chance to get out of that place and nothing's gonna stop me."

"What do you think he wanted?"

"I sign a complaint, I know damn well what'll happen. Get cross-examined at the hearing—didn't I invite him over? Offer him a drink? I end up looking like a part-time hooker and Mr. America walks. Bull *shit*. I've got enough problems." She coaxed ice into her mouth from the paper cup, paused and looked up at him. "What did you ask me?"

"What do you think he wanted?"

"You mean outside of my body? That's why I called—he wants *you*. 'Who *was* that boy, anyway?' " Giving it the hint of an accent. " 'What newspaper he with?' About as subtle as that crappy uniform he had on. He's a classic sociopath, and that's giving him the benefit of the doubt. I know his development was arrested. He probably should be too."

"But you're going to Key West."

"I've *got* to go to Key West. Or I'll be back in here next week playing with dolls. I don't think that asshole should be on the street, but I have to put my mental health first. Does that make sense?"

LaBrava nodded, taking his time, in sympathy.

She said, "He thinks you hit him with something."

"I should've," nodding again, seeing Mr. America in his

silver satin jacket. The shoulders, the hands. "But there wasn't anything heavy enough."

"I told him you didn't hit him, you put him down and sat on him."

"Oh."

"That's when he got mad. I should've known better."

"Well, I don't think it would take much . . . Let me ask you, did he mention Mrs. Breen? The lady we picked up."

"No, I don't think so . . . No, he didn't."

LaBrava was at ease with her because he could accept how she felt and talk to her on an eye-to-eye level of understanding without buttering words to slip past emotions. She was into real life. Tired, that's all. He wouldn't mind going to Key West for a few days, stay at the Pier House. But then he thought of Jean Shaw and saw Richard Nobles again.

"How did he get in your apartment?"

"If I tell you I think somebody gave him the key, then we're gonna get into a long story about a naked Cuban who thinks he's Geraldo Rivera."

"Well," LaBrava said, "even Geraldo Rivera thinks he's Geraldo Rivera. But I could be wrong."

"Do my eyes look okay?"

"They're beautiful eyes."

"I see giant red things all over your shirt."

"I think they're hibiscus," LaBrava said. "What naked Cuban?"

Joe Stella said to Joe LaBrava, in the Star Security office on Lantana Road, across from the A.G. Holley state hospital, "You believe you can walk in here and start asking me questions? You believe I'm some wore-out cop's gonna roll over for you? I put in seventeen years with the Chicago Police, eight citations, and I've been here, right here, seventeen more. So why don't you get the fuck outta my office."

"We got two things in common," LaBrava said. "I'm from Chicago too."

Joe Stella said, "We aren't over in some foreign country on our vacation. Gee, you're from Chicago, uh? How about that, it's a small fucking world, isn't it? I run into people from around Chicago every day and most of 'em I just as soon not. You could be, all I know, from the license division, Secretary of State, come in here you don't have nothing better to do, see what you can shake loose."

"I'm not from the state, not Florida," LaBrava said. "I'm asking about one guy, that's all."

"See that?" Joe Stella said, the spring in the swivel chair groaning as he leaned back, motioned over his shoulder at the paneled wall.

LaBrava thought he was pointing to the underexposed, 5:00 P.M. color photo of a bluish Joe Stella standing next to a blue-black marlin hanging by its tail. The marlin looked about ten feet long, nearly twice the length of the man, but the man was about 100 pounds heavier.

"That's my license to run a security business," Joe Stella said, "renewed last month."

LaBrava's gaze moving to the framed document hanging next to the fish shot.

"I've posted bond, my insurance is paid up, I know goddamn well I am not in violation of any your fucking regulations 'cause I just got off probation. I spend a whole week running around, get the stuff together, make the appearance before the license division . . . I gotta show cause on my own time why they're full a shit and ought never've put me on probation. I have to show 'em it wasn't my fault the insurance lapsed *one* week, that's *all,* and long as I'm there show 'em in black and white all my guys are licensed, every one of 'em. Fine, they stamp a paper, I'm pardoned of all my sins I never committed. I'm back in business. I'm *clean.* So why don't you get the fuck out and leave me alone, okay? Otherwise I'm gonna have to get up and kick you the fuck out and I'm tired this morning, I had a hard night."

LaBrava got ready during Joe Stella's speech. When the man finished, sitting immovable, a block of stone, LaBrava said, "The other thing we have in common, besides both of us being from the Windy City, we'd like to keep the Director of Internal Revenue happy. Wouldn't you say that's true?"

Joe Stella said, "Oh, shit," and did sound tired.

"You're familiar with form SS-8, aren't you?"

"I don't know, there so many forms"—getting tireder by the moment—"What's SS-8?"

LaBrava felt himself taking on an almost-forgotten role—Revenue officer, Collection Division—coming back to him like hopping on a bike. The bland expression, the tone of condescending authority: I'm being nice, but watch it.

"You file payroll deductions, withholding, F.I.C.A.?"

"Yeah, a course I do."

"You never hire guards as independent contractors? Even on a part-time basis?"

"Well, that depends what you mean . . ."

"You're not aware that an SS-8 has ever been filed by a former employee or independent contractor? It's never been called to your attention to submit a reply?"

"Wait a minute—Jesus, you know all the forms you gotta keep track of? My bookkeeper comes in once a week, payday, she's suppose to know all that. Man, I'm telling you—try and run a business today, a bonded service. First, where'm I gonna get anybody's any good'd work for four bucks an hour to begin with? . . . Hey, you feel like a drink?"

"No thanks."

"You know who I get?"

"The cowboys."

"I get the cowboys, I get the dropouts, I get these guys dying to pack, walk around the shopping mall in their uniform, this big fucking .38 on their hip. Only, state regulation, they're suppose to pin their license—like a driver's license in a plastic cover—on their shirt. But they do that they look like what they are, right? Mickey Mouse store cops. So they don't wear 'em and the guy from the state license division sees 'em and I get fined a hunnert bucks each and put on probation ninety days. I also, to stay in business, I gotta post bond, five grand, and I gotta have three-hundred-grand liability insurance, a hunnert grand property damage. The insurance lapses a week cause the fucking insurance guy's out at Hialeah every day and it's my fault, I'm suspended till I show cause why I oughta not get fucked over by the state of Florida where I'm helping with the employment situation. I'm not talking about the federal government you understand. You guys, IRS, you got a job to do—keep that money coming in to run the government, send guns to all the different places they need guns, defend our ass against . . . you know what I'm talking about. Fucking Castro's only a hunnert miles away. Nicaragua, how far's that? It isn't too far, I know."

"Richard Nobles," LaBrava said, "he ever been arrested before?"

Joe Stella paused. "Before what? Jesus Christ, is that who we're talking about? Richie Nobles? Jesus, you can have him."

"You know where I can find him?"

"I think he quit. I haven't seen him in three days. Left the car, no keys, the dumb son of a bitch. All those big good-looking assholes, I think they get hair instead of brains. What's the matter, Richie hasn't paid his taxes? I believe it."

"What I'm curious about—guy applies for a job, you ask him if he's ever been arrested, don't you?"

"I did I'd be in violation of your federal law, invasion of privacy. I can't ask if the guy was ever a mental patient either. I can ask him, have you ever been convicted of a felony, or have you ever committed one and didn't get caught? But I can't ask him if he's ever been arrested."

"You did issue him a handgun."

"They buy their own."

"So he's got a license."

"You apply, you want to be an armed guard, you gotta get clearance through the FBI and the State Department of Law Enforcement. The guy—it takes months—he gets his license or he gets a certified letter in the mail saying he's turned down. But they don't notify me, ever."

"Have you seen his license?"

"Yeah, he showed it to me."

"Then he must be clean, uh? They checked him out."

Joe Stella said, "You ready for a drink now?"

LaBrava nodded. "Sounds good."

He watched Joe Stella push up from his desk. The man moved with an effort to get a bottle of Wild Turkey and glasses from a file cabinet, ice and a can of Fresca from a refrigerator LaBrava had thought was a safe. Pouring double bourbons with a splash of Fresca Joe Stella said, "First one today. What time is it? Almost ten-thirty, that's not bad. Long as you had breakfast." He handed a drink to LaBrava and sat down with the bottle close to him on the desk.

LaBrava took a good sip.

"Nice drink, huh?"

"Not bad."

"Refreshing with a little bite to it." Joe Stella took down half his drink. Poured another ounce or so of bourbon into it, and added a little more. He said, "Ahhh, man . . ."

"I bet he's been arrested," LaBrava said, "but never convicted, uh?"

Joe Stella said, "Richie's from upstate. Some of the boys here call him Big Scrub when he's in a good mood, call him Big Dick he'll grin at you. Otherwise nobody talks to him. You understand the type I mean?"

"I know him," LaBrava said.

"He was arrested up there, you're right, for destruction of government property. The son of a bitch shot an eagle."

"I understand he ate it," LaBrava said.

"I wouldn't be surprised. Richie'll eat anything. He'll drink *almost* anything. He came to work here he gave me a half gallon of shine with peaches in it, whole big peaches . . . That's a good drink, isn't it?"

"Nice."

"He shot the eagle he was living up around Ocala, the Big Scrub country. Richie was a canoe guide, he'd take birdwatchers and schoolteachers back in the swamp, show 'em nature and come out somewhere up on the St. Johns River. He wasn't doing that he'd run supplies for a couple of moonshiners, few hundred pounds a sugar a trip. These two brothers he knew had a still in there. So when he got busted for the eagle he traded off, gave the feds the two brothers and they got two to five in Chillicothe. I asked him, didn't it bother him any to turn in his friends? He says, 'No, it weren't no hill to climb.' " Joe Stella drank and topped it off again, the color of his drink turning clear amber in the window sunlight. "No, it weren't no hill to climb. He's around here more'n ten minutes I start to sound like a fucking cracker.'' Joe Stella took another drink and sat back. ''You ever hear of Steinhatchee?''

''Sounds familiar.''

''Way up on the Gulf side, where the Steinhatchee River comes out. Sleepy little place, the people there, they cut timber for Georgia-Pacific or fish mullet outta the river, use these skiffs they call bird-dog boats, make ten thousand a year, top. Till they saw their first bale of marijuana and found out they could make ten thousand a *night*—buy it offa shrimp boats'd come in there and wholesale it. These hardshell Baptists, all of a sudden they're getting rich in the dope business. They never smoked it, you understand, they just ran it. Well, Richie Nobles had a relative living over there and found out about it. So what do you think Richie does?''

''If he got rich,'' LaBrava said, ''I know he didn't declare it.''

''No, Richie believes marijuana is for sissies. But it bothers him these people that don't know shit're making all that money. So he tells the DEA and they send him in, see if he can join the business.''

''Professional snitch,'' LaBrava said.

''Kind you people love, huh?'' Joe Stella said. ''Once he was in tight there, part of the deal, the feds wired him. Richie comes back with enough to bust all his new friends. Testified against 'em in Jacksonville federal court, change of venue to protect his ass, and put enough on his own relative, some cracker name Buster something, to send him up to Ohio for thirty-five years. Second flop's the long one, the first time the guy only drew three.''

''What's Richard get out of it?''

''Enemies. He knows anything he knows how to piss people off.'' Joe Stella hesitated, about to drink. He stared over the rim of his glass. ''None of that's familiar?''

''Why would it be?''

''You don't know an old guy name Miney, huh? Miney''—looking over his desk, picking up a scrap of notepaper—''Combs. Father of Buster Combs, the one was sent up.''

''Don't know 'em,'' LaBrava said.

"See, you're not the first one come looking for Richie. He's a popular boy."

"I can see why."

"This old guy was in here, talk just like Richie. He's the one told me about Steinhatchee. I asked Richie—it was only like a week ago—if it was true. He says, 'Yeah, I done more'n one favor for my Uncle Sam.' "

LaBrava said, "So he left the Big Scrub, came down here to work . . ."

"Came down to Dade with a federal recommendation, wanting to join the police. Miami and Dade-Metro he says wouldn't even talk to him. He was a gypsy cop for a while, worked for Opa-locka, Sweetwater, Hialeah Gardens, got fired for taking bribes, one thing or another, and came to work for me."

"Where's he live?"

"Same thing the old guy asked. I don't know. I never was able to reach him on a number he gave me. A woman'd answer and say, 'No, he ain't here and I hope I never see the son of a bitch again.' Words to that effect, they'd say it different ways and hang up."

"Any of the women sound . . . older or educated, like they were well off?"

"I don't know how *well* off, I know they were *pissed* off."

"Why'd you keep him on?"

"I thought I explained it, Christ, try and get help aren't all misfits or retirees, old geezers . . . You want another drink? I think I'll have one."

"No, I'm fine."

Joe Stella pushed up to get himself another ice cube and the can of Fresca, stumbled against the desk as he came back and sat down again. "I think you laid a smoke screen on me. You aren't with the IRS, are you? . . . Gimme that Windy City shit, I bet you never even been to Chicago."

"I passed through it once," LaBrava said, "on my way to Independence, Missouri. It looked like a pretty nice town."

"Passed through it . . . You know, I was thinking," Joe Stella said, pouring. "Guy like you—I could fire three of my dumbbells, pay you twelve bucks an hour and give you just the cream, supervisory type work. What would you say to that?"

10

Again he experienced the strange sense of time. Having lunch on the front porch of the Cardozo Hotel with a movie star out of his memory. She wore dark glasses, round black ones, and a wide-brimmed Panama straight across her eyes. He watched her

He watched her take dainty bites of marinated conch, raising the fork in her left hand upside down, her moves unhurried. He watched her break off a piece of French bread, hold it close to her face, elbow resting on the table, wrist bent, staring out of shade at the ocean in sunlight, then slowly bring the piece of bread to her mouth, not looking at it, and he would see her lips part to receive the bread and then close and he would see the movie star's masseter begin to work, still unhurried. He wasn't sure where the masseter was located, Franny hadn't told him that. Franny said the movie star used some kind of secret cream, placenta tissue extract, and very likely said *Q* and *X* with exaggerated emphasis in front of mirrors and wore sunglasses till sundown so she wouldn't get squint wrinkles. His gaze would shift briefly from Jean Shaw and he would see:

Franny sitting on the wall in the strip of oceanfront park across the street, taking Polaroid shots of the hotels. Franny in cutoffs cut so high they must be choking her.

Della Robbia women in lawn chairs talking about Medicare and Social Security.

Maurice coming along Ocean Drive with a grocery sack, skinny legs, faded yellow shorts that reached almost to his knees.

Cars with tourists passing slowly, sightseeing.

A young Cuban guy talking to Franny now. The guy fooling with his ear, Franny laughing. The guy posing, hand on his hip, seductive, strange, as Franny aimed her Polaroid at him.

And his eyes, behind his own sunglasses, would slide back to the movie star's face, pale but in full color. The skin was smooth, without a trace of what might appear to be a tuck, a lift. He believed it didn't matter even if she'd had one. He believed he was in love with her face.

She would turn her head to him and seem to smile, used to being looked at. He wanted to see her eyes but would have to wait.

She said, "You know, that's a lovely shirt." Then surprised him, lowered her sunglasses to the slender tip of her nose, letting him see in daylight a line beneath each of her eyes, slightly puffed, a look that he liked, a slight imperfection. She replaced her glasses as she said, "I don't believe I've ever called a man's shirt lovely before, but it is. I love hibiscus." She said, "I almost married a man who wore only dark brown shirts and always with a dark brown necktie. Odd? . . . Maybe not. He made three thousand dollars a week as a screen writer, he kept an apartment at the Chateau Marmont and died of malnutrition." She said, "I want to see more of your work, I think it's stunning. Will you show me?"

He said, "I want to photograph you."

"I've been photographed."

"Maybe you have . . ."

Maurice said, "Well well *well,*" on the street side of the stone-slab porch railing, stepping up on the base to look at their table. "What're you having, conch? You ever see it they take it out of the shell? You wouldn't eat it. Gimme a bite." He lowered the grocery sack to the railing and leaned over it, face raised waiting as Jean Shaw speared a piece of conch and offered it.

"Another? You can have the rest, I'm finished."

"I don't want to wreck my appetite. We're eating in tonight, fried steak and onions, railroad-style. Gimme a sip—whatever it is."

She offered her glass. "Plain old Scotch."

"How many you had?"

She looked at LaBrava. "How many, six, seven?"

Maurice said, "It's three o'clock in the afternoon!"

"We've had two, Maury. Don't have a heart attack." In that quiet, unhurried tone. He left them and she said, "Do you like his shorts? They have to be at least twenty years old. He may be the most eccentric guy I know. And I've known a few, I'll tell you."

"Well, he's different," LaBrava said.

He saw Franny, alone now, farther down the beach . . . Paco Boza coming along the sidewalk in his wheelchair, a ghetto blaster in his lap; it looked like an accordion.

"Joe, when you're as well off as Maury and you choose to live in a place like the Della Robbia, that's eccentric."

"He said he used to have money, but I don't know that he has that much now."

She said, "Oh," and paused.

He said, "That was my understanding. Had it and spent it." He could hear Paco's blaster now, turned up all the way. "In fact the other night, he was telling me when he sold the hotel next door, the Andrea, he could've kicked himself for not waiting, get a better price."

She said, "Does he confide in you?"

"I wouldn't say he con*fides*."

"But you're close. I know he likes you, a lot."

"Yeah, we get along. We argue all the time, but that's part of the routine."

"He's an actor, Joe. He plays the crabby but loveable retired bookie, hangs out at Wolfie's, Picciolo's, all those places from the old days."

"That's his age—he lives in the past."

"He's a fox, Joe. Don't ever sell him short."

He wanted to say, Wait a minute, what're we talking about exactly? But now Paco Boza was rolling toward them, his ghetto box playing soul against his body, Paco letting it run up through his shoulders and down his arms to turn the silver wheels of the wheelchair wired to the beat, no hurry or worry in the world.

"Hey, the picture man. When do I get my pictures, man?"

LaBrava told him maybe in a few days. Maybe sooner. Come back when you're not busy.

Paco Boza left them, taking his sound down the street, soul with a kick that got into LaBrava sitting there in his sunglasses drinking Scotch with a movie star on the porch of the Cardozo Hotel.

She said, "The poor guy. He's so young." He told her there was nothing wrong with Paco. He had stolen the chair from Eastern Airlines, had his girlfriend push him out of Miami International in it because he didn't like to walk and because he thought it was cool, a way for people to identify him. She said, "What does he do?" and he told her about two-hundred-dollars worth of cocaine a day. She said, "You're part of this, you feel it." She said, "I love to watch you. You don't miss anything, do you?" He did not move or speak now. Close to him she said, "You think you're hidden, but I can see you in there, Mr. LaBrava. Show me your pictures."

"At Evelyn's gallery they sip wine and look at my photographs . . ."

Looking at them now spread over the formica table, Jean Shaw picking up each print and studying it closely—in his rooms on the second floor of the Della Robbia. 201. He paid for the rooms, he had been living here eight months, but there was nothing of him in the rooms. They were rooms in a hotel. He had not got around to mounting or hanging any of his prints, or was sure there were any he cared to look at every day. There were other prints in envelope sleeves in the bookcase and among magazines on the coffee table. He told her *Aperture* magazine had contacted him about doing a book. Call it *South Beach*. Get all the old people, the art deco look. He was working on it. He wanted to do it. He wouldn't mind having a coffee-table book on his coffee table. It seemed strange though—ask thirty or forty dollars for a book full of pictures of people who'd never see it, never be able to afford it.

"At the gallery they sip wine and look at my pictures. They say things like, 'I see his approach to art as retaliation, a frontal attack against the assumptions of a technological society.'

"They say, 'His work is a compendium of humanity's defeat at the hands of venture capital.'

"They say, 'It's obvious he sees his work as an exorcism, his forty days in the desert.' Or, another one, 'They're self-portraits. He sees himself as dispossessed, unassimilated.'

"The review in the paper said, 'The aesthetic subtext of his work is the systematic exposure of artistic pretension.' I thought I was just taking pictures."

Jean Shaw said, "Simplicity. It is what it is." Then paused. "And what it isn't, too. Is that what you're saying?"

He didn't want her to try so hard. "I heard one guy at the gallery—it was his wife or somebody who said I was dispossessed, unassimilated, and the guy said, 'I think he takes pictures to make a buck, and anything else is fringe.' I would've kissed the guy, but it might've ruined his perspective."

Jean Shaw said, studying a print, "They try to pose, and not knowing how they reveal themselves."

He liked that. That wasn't bad.

"Your style is the absence of style. Would you say?"

He said, "No tricky angles," because he didn't know if he had a style or not. "I'm not good at tricky angles."

"Some of them look like actors. I mean like they're made up, costumed."

"I know what you mean."

"When you're shooting them, what do you see?"

"What do I see? I see what I'm shooting. I wonder if I have enough light. Or too much."

"Come on. Tell me."

"I see 'images whose meanings exceed the local circumstances that provide their occasion.' "

"Who said that?"

"Walker Evans. Or somebody who said he did."

"What do you think about when you look at your own work?"

"I wonder why I can't shoot like Stieglitz."

"How long have you been doing it?"

"Or why I'll never be able to. I wonder why my people don't look at me the way August Sander's people looked at him. I wonder if I should have moved in closer, taken one step to the right or left."

There was a silence.

"What else do you see?"

"But it isn't what I see, is it? It's what I wonder when I look at the picture. I wonder if I'll ever have enough confidence."

She said, "Yes? What else?"

"I wonder, most of all I wonder what the people are doing now. Or if they're still like that, the way I shot them."

He heard her say, in the quiet afternoon apartment, "What do you see when you look at me?"

And almost answered, turning from the table of black and white prints. Almost. But as soon as he was facing her, close to her, he knew better than to speak, break the silence and have to start over. No, they were now where they wanted to be, if he could feel or sense anything at all. So he touched the face he had watched on the screen, bringing up one hand and then the other just before he brought his mouth to hers and felt her hands slide over his ribs.

They went into the bedroom and undressed without a word to make love in dimmed silence, to make love as soon as they were in bed and she brought him between her legs, Joe LaBrava believing this was unbelievable. Look at him. He was making love to Jean Shaw, he was honest-to-God making love to Jean Shaw in real life. He didn't want to be watching, he wanted to be overwhelmed by it, by Jean Shaw, making *love* to her, but he didn't want to just do it either, he wanted the overwhelming feeling of it to take hold and carry them away. But her eyes were closed and maybe she was just doing it, doing it with him, moving with him, but she could be doing it without him because he didn't know where she was with her eyes closed so tight. He wanted to see her eyes and he wanted her to see *him* . . . so close to her face, her hair, her skin and not a blemish, not a trace of a tiny scar . . . He had to stop thinking if he was going to be overwhelmed. He had to *let* himself be overwhelmed . . .

It wasn't something he would tell anyone. He would never do that. Though it seemed like the kind of thing you might tell a stranger on a train without naming names. On a *train?* Come on. He was making an oldtime movie out of it looking for a way to tell it. Or maybe write it in a diary. Though he could never imagine, under any circumstances, even in solitary confinement, writing or talking to himself.

No, he would never be able to tell anyone there was more to making love to a movie star than just . . . making love. Or, maybe he should qualify it. Say, making love to a movie star the first time . . . there was more to it than just making love. The idea of it, the anticipation, the realization, was more overwhelming than the doing of it. Although he could not say that would be true of all movie stars.

What he had almost said to her when she said, "What do you see when you look at me?" was:

"The first woman I ever fell in love with, when I was twelve years old."

But the mood, something, had saved him from maybe getting pushed out the window. He was able to move through the next steps letting heavy breathing bring them along, into the bedroom to the act itself. But you see, with all the anticipation, thinking back twenty-five years to the first time you saw her and were knocked out by her, finally when you're there and it's happening, it's almost impossible to quit thinking about how great it's going to be, how unbelievable, and do it without watching yourself doing it.

The movie star smoked a cigarette after. In bed. She actually smoked a cigarette. He went in the kitchen, fixed a couple of light Scotches and brought them back. The movie star acted a little like a kitten. She seemed much younger with her clothes off, not at all self-conscious. She gave him those secret looks, sly smiles that were familiar. (But did she have secrets? Now?) She asked him how he would photograph her. He said he'd like to think about it.

What he thought about though, what he was most aware of, was a feeling. It was not unlike the way he felt and wondered about things when he was looking at his photographs.

He felt—lying in bed with Jean Shaw, after—relief. There, that was done.

And wondered if he had learned anything about illusions, since that time when he was twelve years old and first fell in love.

There were other feelings he had that he would save and look at later. All things considered, he felt pretty good. The movie star was a regular person. Underneath it all, she was. Except that she was never a regular person for very long.

She said, "You're good for me, Joe. Do you know that?"

Familiar. But he didn't know the next line, what he was supposed to say, and the words that came to mind were dumb. So he smiled a tired smile and patted her thigh, twice, and left his hand there.

She said, "I have a feeling you're the best thing that could happen to me, Joe."

Another one, so familiar. He sipped his Scotch. He looked at the ceiling and a scene from *Deadfall,* early in the picture, began to play in his mind. Jean Shaw saying to Robert Mitchum, "I have a feeling you're the best thing that could happen to me . . . Steve."

And Robert Mitchum, giving her that sleepy look, said . . .

11

There was the Had a Piece Lately Bar. There was the Play House, the Turf Pub. There was Cheeky's. "Don't go in there without me," Cundo Rey said. "They liable to tear you to pieces, fight over you."

"Queers," Nobles said. "I love queers. Jesus."

There was Pier Park. Go in there at night and get anything you want, light up your head.

Nobles said, "Those guys have dough, huh, that sell it."

Cundo Rey said, "Yes, is true." Low behind the wheel of the Trans Am, holding the beast in as they cruised, he said, "But they got guns."

Nobles said, "Shit, who hasn't."

They cruised Collins Avenue and Washington, staying south of the Lincoln Road Mall, Nobles peering through smoked glass at the activity along the streets, all the little eating places and stores and bitty hotels, every one of the hotels with those metal chairs out front. Nobles said, "You ever see so many foreigners in your life?" After a few more blocks of sightseeing he said, "I think I'm having an idea."

Cundo Rey was learning not to say anything important unless he was sure Nobles was listening. Nobles didn't listen to very much. Sometimes Cundo wanted to tie him to a chair and press a knife against him and say, "Listen to me!" Shout it in the man's ear.

He said, "I thought you had an idea already."

"I got all kinds of 'em."

He was listening. Talk about him, he listened.

"The woman is still there," Cundo Rey said. "I saw her again. The guy is there, I think. I didn't see him good to know what he look like, but he's there. Why wouldn't he be, if he live there?"

"I'm waiting on the spirit to move me. It ain't the same as heisting cars, Jose. You gotta be in tune." Nose pressed to the side window. "You know what it's like down here, you read the signs? It's like being in a foreign country."

"You want to hear my idea?" Cundo Rey said.

"I want to get something to eat, partner. My tummy says it's time."

"Listen to my idea."

"Well, go ahead."

"Shoot the guy," Cundo Rey said. "You want to shoot him, shoot him. You want to shoot him in the back, get it over with, it's okay. You want to use a knife, you want to push him off a roof—any way you like, okay."

"That's some idea, chico."

"No, that's not the idea. That's to get him out of the way, so you can think of the woman."

"Watch the road. I don't want us having a accident."

"Okay, you want the woman? You know how to get her?"

"I'm certainly anxious to hear."

"You save her life."

"I save her life. Like out swimming?"

"Listen to me, all right? You listening?"

"Go ahead."

"She gets a call on the telephone or she gets a letter that say, *Pay me some money or I'm going to kill you.* A hundred thousand, two hundred thousand—how much has she got? You have to figure that out, how much you want to ask for. Okay, then you find the guy that sent her the letter and kill him. You her hero and she loves you. She say, take me, take my money, anything you want, baby, I'm yours."

"I find the guy sent her the letter . . ."

"Exactly."

"What guy?"

"Any guy. What difference does it make? Go in the La Playa Hotel, down the end of this street, is full of guys you can use. Set the guy up—don't you know anything? Make it look like he's the guy, see. Tell him to come to her room in the hotel—somebody want to buy some poppers from him. He goes up there, you shoot him. The woman say, 'Oh, my hero, you save my life.' She give you anything you want."

"That's how you do it, huh?"

"Listen, maybe even you use the guy you want to shoot

anyway. Is it possible? If he's on drugs maybe?"

"Little shit, he's gonna need something for pain, anyhow."

"But the best part—"

"That's if I don't put him all the way outta his misery."

"You listening to me?"

"I thought you was through."

"The best part," Cundo Rey said, "see, the woman is so ascared she *pays* the money. She leaves it some place the letter tells her. You comprehend? See, *then* you shoot the guy. The guy is dead and the police, nobody, they look in the guy's place, but *nobody can find the money*. You like it?"

Nobles said, "You been reading the funnypaper, haven't you? I love to hear boogers like you talking about setting people up and shooting 'em—Lord have mercy, like you done it all and taken the midnight train more'n once, huh? Cundo, you little squirt, let's go get us something to eat."

A place called Casa Blanca looked fine to Cundo. Nobles said he didn't feel like eating Mex. Cundo tried to tell him it was a Cuban place, there was a big difference. Nobles said dago chow was dago chow. He picked Eli's Star Deli on Collins near Fourteenth, saying he had never ate any Jew food before, he'd like to give her a try.

So they went in. Nobles had a Henny Youngman on rye, said hey, boy, sucking his teeth, and ordered a Debbie Reynolds on pumpernickel. He told Cundo, watching him pick at his cole slaw, he ate like a goddamn owl. He picked—why didn't he *eat?*

Cundo Rey tried Nobles with, "See, they all in the yard, all around the embassy of Peru, all these thousands of people waiting to leave Havana when it first started, when Fidel decided okay. But they don't have no food. So you know what they ate? They ate a papaya tree, man. The whole tree. Then they ate a dog. You know what else they ate? They ate cats, man. They killed and ate the cats."

Nobles said, "Yeah?" admiring the thickness of his Debbie Reynolds, tucking in the fat ends of corned beef hanging out.

There was no way to make him sick, to make him even stop to make a face. Look at him, sucking his teeth, waving at the man in the apron behind the meat counter, telling him he wanted a dish of potato salad.

Cundo Rey said, "Would you pay thirty dollars for a chicken? A cooked one?"

"Fried or roast chicken?"

"If you were starving?"

"Would I get biscuits and gravy?"

"At Mariel it was like a parking lot of boats waiting to leave, a thousand of them, it was so crowded with all kinds of boats. We sitting there for days and days, everybody running out of food and water. Now this boat is like a cantina comes to you. Is painted blue. The man on it offer you a cooked chicken for thirty dollars. Black beans, ten dollars a pound. Bottle of rum, eighty dollars."

"Where's this at?"

"I just *tole* you. Mariel. You never hear of Mariel?" Almost gritting his teeth, Christ, trying to talk to this guy. "The name don't mean nothing to you?"

"Yeah, I heard of it. You're talking about your boatlift back—when was that, three four years ago, brought all you boogers up here. Yeah, shit, I'd had me a boat I'd a gone down there made some dough."

"You know what it cost to leave Havana? What they charge people? Thousand dollars. More than that—some of them, they think you have the money, they charge you ten thousand dollars."

"It's what I'm saying. Get a old beat-up shrimper cheap, pack about five hundred of you squirts aboard—shit, you could retire, never work again long as you live."

"If you don't get fined, put in jail by the Coast Guard when you come back from there," Cundo Rey said. "Listen, they put twenty of us on a cruiser, a charter-boat, a nice one about ten meters with the name Bar*bara* Rose on the back. From Key West."

"That's *Bar*b'ra Rose, you spook."

"The captain, this tough guy, say he only suppose to pick up five people, that's all he was paid for. See, he got their names, given to him by their people in Miami. They came down to Key West to hire the boat. Thousands of people were doing that, to get their relatives. But see, the G-two man from Fidel say to the captain, you think so, but you going to take four for one, twenty people. See, so the rest of us on the boat, with this family that was paid for, we all from Cambinado. Brought to Mariel in a truck."

"What's Camba-nato?"

"Jesus Christ, it's the prison, Cambinado del Este. I told you I was in there—I picked up a suitcase in a hotel I find out belong to a Russian. I sell his big Russian shoes for ninety dollars—is how bad it is in Cuba, man—and a shirt, you know, that kind with the reptile on it. Where did the Russian get it? I don't know, but I sell it for fifty dollars. They give me life in prison."

"You poor little bugger, I thought they put you away for being queer."

"They put plenty of them in Cambinado, yes, and plenty of them come here, too."

"Let's go find some," Nobles said, "and kick the shit out of 'em." He licked mustard from his fingers. "Yeah, I wish I had me a boat that time."

"Not if you talk to the captain of the Bar*bar*a Rose," Cundo said. "He look at twenty people crowded in his boat, no food, a hundred and ten miles of ocean and if he reaches here he's going to make five thousand dollars."

"I don't know if I'd get seasick or not. I doubt it, but I don't know. Biggest boat—you might not believe this—I ever been in's a canoe."

"You hear what I'm telling you? The captain, this tough guy, don't like it. So all he does is complain."

"No, I been in a bird-dog boat, too, up on the Steinhatchee. But it wasn't no bigger'n a canoe."

"Listen, the captain of the boat is complaining, he's saying, 'Oh, I could go to jail. I could be fined. I could lose my business, this sixty-thousand-dollar boat because of you people. Why did I come here? Look at the ocean, the choppiness all the way.' Man, all he did was complain."

"Yeah, but he took you to Key West, didn't he? And he made out pretty good."

"First we had to lock him up in the below part, while we waiting for the approval to leave."

"You did?"

"Then, it's time to go, he say it's a mutiny, he wants to leave the boat. No, first call the Coast Guard on the radio, then leave the boat. But then, finally, we leave."

"He saw the light."

"He saw the knife we got holding against his back. We leave Mariel, but still he complain, never shut up. He complain so much," Cundo Rey said, "we come to think, this is enough. So we throw him in the ocean and take his boat up to a place, it isn't too far from Homestead, and run it in the ground, in the sand. We have to walk, oh, about a hundred meters in the water to get to shore, but is okay, we make it."

Nobles said, "Well, you little squirt, you surprise the hell outta me."

Cundo was staring back at him, giving Nobles his nothing-to-it sleepy look.

"Why you think I was in Cambinado del Este?"

"You said you stole a suitcase, belonged to a Russian."

Cundo had Nobles' attention now, Nobles hooked, hanging on, wanting to know more.

"I took it out of his room, yes."

"And the Russian got a good look at you, huh?"

"Yes, of course. Why else would I have to kill him?"

The little Cuban dude kept staring right at him, playing with his earring in his girlish way, nose stuck up in the air like he was the prize.

It took Nobles a few moments to adjust—wait a sec here, what's this shit he's pulling?—and think to say, "Well, you shoot one of those fellas up here you don't even need a per-mit. Now you want me to tell you *my* idea? How me and you can make some quick bucks while we're waiting on the big one?"

12

He was smiling before Franny reached the porch with her sack of groceries and saw him, holding the door open.

She said, "What do you do, just hang out?"

"I'm locking up."

"This early?"

It was twenty past seven. He closed the glass door and set the lock, Franny inside now looking around the empty lobby, the last of daylight dull on the terrazzo floor that was like the floor, to LaBrava, of a government building. He turned on the cut glass chandelier and Franny looked up at it, not impressed.

"The place needs more than that, Joe."

"Color? Some paintings?"

She waited as he turned on lamps and came back. "It needs bodies, warm ones. I'm not knocking the old broads . . ."

"Bless their hearts," LaBrava said.

"Listen," Franny said, "I'm gonna be an old broad myself someday, if I make it. But we could use a little more life around here. So far we've got you and me and the movie star and things haven't improved that much. Joe, there's a carton behind the desk with my name on it UPS dropped off. Would you mind grabbing it for me? I've got my hands full." She waited and said, "Let's see," when he brought it out and said, "Oh, shit, I was afraid of that. Another case of Bio-Energetic Breast Cream. Apply with a gentle, circular massaging motion to add bounce and resiliency." Into the elevator and up. "Do you know how much bounce and resiliency it's gonna add to the dugs around here? Contains collagen and extract of roses, but not nearly enough, I'm afraid, for South Beach bazooms. They've served their purpose, we hope. Right?" And down the hall to 204. "Maybe I can sell a couple bottles to your movie star . . . You're not talking, uh? I saw you having lunch, it looked like you were giving each other bites. When you were in there close, Joe, did you notice any little hairline scars?"

He said, "That's not nice," and was surprised he didn't feel protective or take offense. He was with Franny and they were old pals.

"But you looked, didn't you? Come on in. Don't lie to me, Joe." She went to the kitchen and he looked around the room, surprised at its lived-in appearance after only two days. It was all the color that gave the effect. The colors in the unframed canvases on the walls—bold abstract designs in shimmering gold, blues and tans—and the pillows in striking colors and shapes, on the floor and piled on the daybed she used as a sofa. Wicker chairs held stacks of books and magazines. Her voice remained with him as he looked around. "I'm jealous, if you want to know the truth." The venetian blinds were pulled up, out of the way, the evening blue in the windows faded, pale next to the paintings. "You asked me to lunch, sorta, and I see you over there with your movie star." There were cartons stenciled *SPRING SONG,* a portable television. She came out of the kitchen with white wine in stem glasses.

"Sit down and look at my Polaroids."

"You take pictures you don't fool around."

"I got about forty today. This bunch is sorta in order, starting at First Street and working up. But I don't like it around there; so I came up to Fifteenth, decided to work down, get the good stuff first." She sat next to him among pillows on the floor, their wine on a glass cocktail table. "I want consecutive views. Maybe do the whole street on a canvas about thirty feet wide. The face of South Beach."

He looked up at her paintings. "Like those?"

"That was my Jerusalem spacy period. I wanted to get the spirit, you know, the energy of the sabras, but what stands out? The Mosque of Omar, the part that's gold. Now I'm into echo-deco, pink and green, flamingoes and palm trees, curvy corners, speed lines. I'm gonna pop my colors, get it looking so good you'll want to eat it. Hey, how about staying for dinner?"

"Maurice asked me."

"And that star of the silver screen—here she is, Jean Shaw! . . . She gonna be there? I'll get you yet, Joe."

"Will you sell me one of your new paintings?"

"I'll trade you one for that shot of Lana showing her depressing tits. That poor girl, I keep thinking about her."

LaBrava held up a Polaroid. "She lives right around the corner from here, the Chicken Shack." He began looking at storefronts and bars along the south end of Ocean Drive. The Turf Pub. The Play House, an old-time bar with photos of Jack Dempsey and Joe Louis on the walls. There were bikers outside this afternoon, in the Polaroid shots. He saw people he knew. A drunk named Wimpy. A pretty-boy Puerto Rican dealer named Guilli. He looked at figures standing, moving in suspended motion. Another one, in shadow, who seemed familiar and he studied the shot for several moments. Another figure, in the sunlit foreground, stood facing the camera with an arm raised.

"Is he waving at you?"

"Let's see. Yeah, I ran into him a couple of times."

"This the guy you were talking to, you were sitting on the wall?"

"You noticed me. I thought you'd be too busy with your movie star."

"Is it the same guy?"

"Yeah, very friendly. A little swishy maybe. He gets into a goof"—she snapped her fingers—"like that. It's hard to tell when he's serious."

"What's he do?"

"He sells real estate. What do you mean what does he *do?* He's looking for some kind of hustle, like all the rest of 'em. They deal or they break and enter."

He was looking at a hotel now on the north end of the street. "Here we are, the Elysian Fields."

He passed it to Franny and she said, "Ten million cockroaches down in the basement holding it up, straining their little backs."

He looked at several more hotels, then went back through the shots he'd already seen till he found the one he wanted, a view of the south end.

"There's a guy going in the Play House—you can only see part of him, he's right behind your friend."

"The guy in the doorway?"

"The other one. He's got on, it looks like a white silk shirt."

Franny said, "Oh, the lifeguard. Yeah, I remember him. I don't know if he's a lifeguard, but he sure is a hunk."

"Was he with your friend, the goof?"

"Gee, I don't know. Let me see those again." She went through the prints saying, "I think he's in one other one . . . Yeah, here. See the guy I was talking to? He's got his back turned, but I know it's him. Standing with the biker. That's the hunk right behind him."

"I didn't notice him in this one."

"No, the biker catches your eye. The beer gut."

"His shirt doesn't look white here. It looks silver."

"You're right. I remember now, it *is* silver. But it's not a shirt, it's a jacket, like the kind jocks wear. Yeah, I remember him now—real blond hair, the guy's a standout, Joe, you oughta shoot him."

"Not a bad idea," LaBrava said. "Where's the one you took of your friend? You were sitting on the wall."

"You don't miss a thing, do you?" Franny found it, handed it to him. "This one."

LaBrava studied the pose, the Cuban-looking guy fooling with his ear. "What's he doing?"

"I don't know—he uses his hands a lot. Let's see . . . Oh, yeah. He's playing with his earring. That's why I thought he might be gay, but you can't tell."

"What's his name?"

"I don't think he told me. He talked all the time, but really didn't say anything. Asked me where I live, if it's a nice place, would I like to have a drink with him—no, thank you—all that."

"Did he tell you, by any chance, he's Geraldo Rivera?"

Franny paused, about to raise her glass from the table. "Are you putting me on, Joe?"

"I just wondered. He looks familiar."

"You think he looks like Geraldo Rivera? He doesn't look anything like him. Joe, tell me what your game is? Are you a narc?"

Dinner at Maurice's, the picture gallery; fried sirloin and onions in candlelight with a '69 Margaux. Jean Shaw said, "If this is railroad-style it must be the Orient Express." Maurice said it was the pan, the cast-iron frying pan that was at least 100 years old he'd swiped out of a Florida East Coast caboose.

After dinner, sitting in the living room with cognac, Maurice said, "It's a fact, they go in threes. You want the latest ones? Arthur Godfrey, Meyer Lansky and Shepperd Strudwick, the actor. Jeanie, you remember him? Seventy-five when he died."

"Yeah, I read that," Jean said. "Died in New York. We did one picture together."

LaBrava knew the name, he could picture the actor and caught a glimpse of his snow-white hair, a scene in a cemetery. "Shepperd Strudwick, he was your husband in *Obituary*. Remember? We were trying to think who it was."

She looked surprised, or was trying to recall the picture. She said, "You're right, he was my husband."

"Shepperd Strudwick," LaBrava said. "You wanted to dump him. You got together with Henry Silva . . . Didn't you hire him to kill your husband?"

"Something like that."

"I know Henry Silva was the bad guy," LaBrava said. "I remember him because he was in a Western just about the same time and I saw it again in Independence. *The Tall T,* with Richard Boone and, what's his name, Randolph Scott. But I can't remember the good guy in *Obituary.*"

"Arthur Godfrey's on the front page of every paper in the country," Maurice said. "Meyer Lansky gets two columns in the *New York Times,* he could a *bought* Godfrey. Arthur Godfrey gets a street named after him. What's Meyer Lansky get? A guy, I remember with the FBI, he said Meyer Lansky could a been chairman of the board of General Motors if he'd gone into legitimate business." Getting out of his La-Z-Boy, going over to a wall of photographs, Maurice said, "I'll tell you something. I bet Meyer Lansky had a hell of a lot more fun in his life than Alfred P. Sloan or any of those GM guys."

LaBrava said to Jean, "I don't think the plan was to kill Shepperd Strudwick. It was something else. I remember he kept getting newspaper clippings that announced his death. To scare him . . ."

"Maier Suchowljansky, born in Russia," Maurice said, "that

was Meyer Lansky's real name." He traced his finger over a photograph of the Miami Beach skyline.

LaBrava said, "I can't remember who played the good guy."

Jean said, "Maybe there weren't any good guys."

"Right here," Maurice said, "this is where he lived for years, the Imperial House. His wife's probably still there. That's Thelma, his second wife. She used to be a manicurist, some hotel in New York. Met Lansky, they fell in love . . ."

"Victor Mature," LaBrava said.

But Jean was watching Maurice. "Did you know Lansky?"

"Did I know him?" Maurice said, moving to another photograph. "MacFadden-Deauville . . . Lansky used to come in there. They *all* used to come in there. You know what I paid for a cabana, by the swimming pool, so I could run a horse book right there, for the guests? Woman'd send her kid over to place a bet. Forty-five grand for the season, three months. And that doesn't count what I had to pay S & G for the wire service, Christ."

"But you made money," Jean Shaw said.

"I did okay. Till Kefauver, the son of a bitch . . . You know who this is? The bathing beauty. Sonja Henie. We used to call her Sonja Heinie. Here's another spot, the dog track, you used to see Meyer Lansky once in a while. This spot here, the Play House . . ."

LaBrava looked over.

". . . used to be big with the dog-trackers. Also the fight fans. Fighter from I think Philly, Ice Cream Joe Savino, he used to sell Nutty Buddies in the park, he bought the place about twenty years ago. I don't know what it's like now. It's all changed down there."

"But you'd never move," Jean Shaw said, "would you?"

"Why should I move? I own the joint—most of it—I got the best beach in Florida . . ."

"Maury, if I'm actually harder pressed than I've let on—"

"Harder pressed how?"

"If I get to the point I'm absolutely broke, would you consider buying me out?"

"I told you, don't worry about money."

LaBrava listened. Watched Maurice come back to his chair.

"Maury, you know me." She was sitting up in the sofa now and seemed anxious. "I don't want to become dependent on anyone. I've always had my own money."

"This whole area right in here, from Sixth Street up," Maurice said, "we're in the National Register of Historic Places. That impresses buyers, Jeanie. We hold the developers off, the value can only shoot up."

"But if I *need* funds—"

"If we see values start to go down, that's different."

LaBrava listened. It didn't sound like Maurice, the old guy who loved the neighborhood and would never leave.

"Five years ago the Cardozo sold for seven hundred thousand," Maurice said. "Way they've fixed it up I bet they could sell it, double their investment. Almost double, anyway."

She was sitting back again, resigned. "What do you think the Della Robbia's worth?"

"Four and a half, five hundred, around in there. But listen," Maurice said to her, "I don't want you to ever worry about dough. You hear me?"

LaBrava listened. He heard Maurice talking like a man who had money, a lot of it.

They reached her door. She said, "How about a nightcap? Or whatever might appeal to you."

Was that from a movie?

Maybe it was the way she said it, the subtle business with the eyes. How did you tell what was real and what was from pictures?

She could surprise him, though—sitting close on the slip-covered sofa with their drinks, something to hold till they had to put them down—she could look vulnerable and come at him quietly with, "Tell me I'm pretty good for an old broad. I'll love you forever."

And his answer to that—like a knee jerk, reflecting his yes-ma'am upbringing—"Come on. What're you, about three or four years older than I am?"

She said, looking him right in the eye, "Joe, I'm forty-six years old and there's not a damn thing I can do about it."

Shoving numbers into his mind that would have made her a

teen-aged bride in *Obituary* in the black dress, coming onto Henry Silva, leading him on, the two of them conspiring to sting her husband.

He pushed the numbers out of his mind by thinking: She isn't any age. She's Jean Shaw. And by looking at her face, at the little puff circles under her brown eyes that he loved to look at. If she wanted to play, what was wrong with that? Play. Maybe he could've been in the movies too if he hadn't gone to Beltsville, Maryland, learned how to shoot guns and taken an oath to protect the lives of Presidents and important people. Bob Hope, little Sammy Davis, Jr., Fidel Castro . . .

He said, "Jean."

Within the moment her eyes became misty, smiling but a little sad. "That's the first time you've said my name. Will you say it again?"

"Jean?"

"Yes, Joe."

"You're gonna have to be very careful."

"I am?"

"I have a feeling you might be in danger."

She said, "You're serious, aren't you?"

Yes, he was serious. He was trying to be. But now even his own words were beginning to sound like lines from a movie.

He said, "Jean. Let's go to bed."

That sounded real.

She said, "I'm hard to get, Joe. All you have to do is ask me."

That didn't sound real.

13

I have a feeling you might be in danger. All the next day he would hear himself saying it.

The tone was all right, not overdone, and he believed it was true, she *was* in danger. But it didn't sound right. Because people who were into danger on an everyday basis didn't talk like that, they didn't use the word.

He remembered the guy who wholesaled funny twenties standing up in federal court hand at his throat—the judge banging his gavel—and saying, "Joe, Jesus Christ, all my life I been in shit up to here, but never, *never* would I a thought you'd be the one'd push me under."

The Miami street cop assigned to paperwork, typing memos, said, "I gotta get back out there, put it on the line with the fuckups, or I'm gonna be sniffing whiteout for my jags." A week later the Miami street cop, still doing paperwork, said, "Whatever happened to splitting heads, kicking the shit outta assholes? For the fun of it. Is the game still going on or what?"

The Dade-Metro squad-car cop, drinking Pepsi out of a paper cup, said, "The guy had the piece, he was pressing it against me—*into* me, right here, under the rib. He pulls the trigger, click. He pulls the trigger, click. He pulls the fucking trigger and I come around like this, with the elbow, hard as I can. The piece goes off—no click this time—the fucking piece goes off and smokes the guy standing at the bar next to me with his hands up. We get him for attempted, we get him for second degree, both." The Dade-Metro squad-car cop said, "Did you know you rub a plastic-coated paper cup like this on the inside of the windshield it sounds just like a cricket? Listen."

Buck Torres said, "Who is this guy? Do we know him from somewhere before?"

"That's what I want to know," LaBrava said, "if he has a before. Put him on the computer and we'll find out. But I can't believe he hasn't."

Buck Torres had been a uniformed Dade-Metro cop the time LaBrava was assigned to the Miami field office, United States Secret Service, taking pictures at work and play. Torres had showed him life on the street. They had finished off a few hundred beers together, too. Sgt. Hector Torres had transferred and was now supervisor of Crimes Against Persons, Miami Beach Police. He always wore a coat and tie—his men did too—because he would never speak to the relatives of a deceased person in shirt sleeves.

They left the Detective Bureau—the one-story, windowless, stucco annex on the corner of First and Meridian—walked across Meridian to MBPD headquarters—the official-looking brick building with the flag—punched "Richard Nobles" into the National Crime Information Center computer and drew a blank.

"So, he's a good boy," Torres said.

"No, he isn't," LaBrava said, "he's a sneaky kind of asshole who likes to come down on people." Hearing himself falling back into police patter.

"Yeah, but he hasn't done nothing."

"I think they pulled his sheet, gave him a clean bill. He was a federal snitch. You gotta have a diseased mind or your balls in somebody's hand to do that kind of work. Check the DEA in Jacksonville when you aren't doing anything."

Torres said, "Should I care about this guy or what? What do you want me to do?"

"Nothing. I'm gonna do it."

"Let me see—then you want me to say nice things about you, you get picked up for impersonating a police officer."

"Or pick the guy up, maybe. You still have 'Strolling without a destination' on the statutes? In case he sees me and becomes irritated. See, what I'm doing, I'm trying to stay ahead of the guy, be ready for it when it comes."

"Be ready for what?"

"I don't know, but all my training and experience tells me something's gonna happen."

"Your experience—you guarded Mrs. Truman."

"That's right, and nothing happened to her, did it?"

"You're serious?"

"I'm serious."

"Then you better tell me more about the sneaky asshole," Torres said.

Paco Boza said a wheelchair was better than a bike. You could do wheelies, all this shit, also build up your arms, give you nice shoulders, the girls go for that. Also, sometimes, it was safer to be sitting in a wheelchair than to be standing up with some people. They respect you sitting in a wheelchair, yes, and some people were even afraid, like they didn't want to look at you. He loved his Eastern Airlines wheelchair.

Though it didn't seem to be doing much for his arms and shoulders. His arms became skinny cords as he collapsed the chair and strained to carry it up two steps from the sidewalk to the hotel porch. He said he wanted to leave it where it would be safe. He was going to Hialeah for a day or two.

"I do you a favor," Paco said, "you do me one. Okay?" Grinning now, being sly.

LaBrava caught on right away and grinned back at him. "You saw him, didn't you?"

"Man, you can't miss him. He's twice as big as anyone I ever see before. Has that hair . . ."

"Let's go inside," LaBrava said. He took the wheelchair and Paco followed him across the lobby to the main desk. LaBrava went around behind it, put the wheelchair down, telling Paco it would be safe here, and brought out a manila envelope sleeve from a shelf underneath.

"Hey, my pictures."

"I know why you fell in love with Lana."

"That broad, I been looking all over for *her* too." He brought three eleven-by-fourteen prints out of the envelope, laid them on the marble countertop and began to grin. "Look at her, showing herself."

"Where'd you see the guy?"

"I saw him on Collins Avenue, I saw him on Washington Avenue. You can't miss him."

"He likes to be seen," LaBrava said. "He's the Silver Kid."

"No shit, is he? . . . I like this one of me. It's cute, uh? You like it?"

"One of my favorites. You talk to anyone at the Play House?"

"Yeah. Maybe he was in there, they don't know him. But that isn't the place. The place you want to go—a guy I talk to, he say check the Paramount Hotel on Collins."

"Who was that?"

"The guy? Name is Guilli, a Puerto Rican guy. He's ascared all the time, but he's okay, you can believe him."

"I know who you mean. So you went over there?"

"Yeah, but I didn't see him."

"Where's the Paramount?"

"Is up around Twentieth. I saw him on Washington, I saw him on Collins Avenue. Two days now. Three days—man, where does the time go?"

"You doing all right?"

"Sure, I make it. You kidding? Lana is going to like this one, showing herself. I hear she went over to Hialeah, see her mother. But I don't know where her mother lives no more, I got to look for her. Man, they give you a lot of trouble."

"Dames are always pulling a switch on you," LaBrava said.

Paco said, "What?"

"Something a guy in a movie said."

"He did?"

"Listen—how about when you saw the guy, what was he doing?"

"Nothing. Walking by the street. Go in a store, come out. Go in another store, come out."

"You're not talking about drugstores."

"No, regular stores, man. Grocery store—or he go in a hotel, he come out."

"Has he bought any stuff off anybody?"

"Nobody told me he did. Guilli thinks he's a cop. But you know Guilli. Guilli thinks the other guy is a cop too, guy drives the black Pontiac Trans Am. Shit, Guilli thinks everybody he don't know is a cop."

"What other guy? Cubano?"

"Yeah—how do you know that?"

"I might've seen him. He's got a black Trans Am, uh?"

"Yeah, he stay at the La Playa Hotel. You know it? Down the

end of Collins Avenue. There's a guy live there—you know a guy name David Vega?"

"I don't think so."

"David Vega told Guilli he *knows* the guy, from the boat-lift. He told him, he's not a cop, man, he's a *Marielito*. He say the guy was with some convicts they put on a boat, from a prison. He say he remember him because the guy wore a safety pin in his ear."

"That mean something?"

"Like a punk. You know, be in fashion. Now David Vega say he's got a gold one, a real one he wears."

"What's his name?"

"He don't know his name, he jus' remember him."

"Staying at the La Playa."

"Listen, the first night he come there a guy live there was ripped off. The guy come back from the pier from doing some business, he got hit on the head and somebody robbed him, took four hundred dollars."

"That happens all the time there, doesn't it?"

"Yes, of course, with guys like this guy. Tha's what I mean."

"Why does Guilli put the Cubano with the big blond guy?"

"He saw them talking, that's all, it don't mean nothing. But maybe. Who knows?"

"I'll see you in a couple days, uh?"

"Yeah, I have to go to Hialeah. Talk to Guilli or David Vega if you want to know something. Also, you want to, you can drive my wheelchair. I think you like it."

There weren't too many places had swimming pools around here. A pink and green place called the Sharon Apartment-Motel on Meridian and Twelfth, across from Flamingo Park, had a little bitty one out front, but nobody was in it. Nice-looking pool, too, real clean, sparkling with chlorine. There hadn't been anybody in it the other time either. This was Nobles' second visit to the Sharon Apartment-Motel office, the important one.

He said to Mr. Fisk, little cigar-smoking Jew that owned the place, "Well sir, you think over my deal?"

Mr. Fisk had skinny arms and round shoulders but a big

stomach and was darker than many niggers Nobles had seen in his life. Mr. Fisk said, "Go out and turn left and keep walking. What do you come to, it don't even take you ten minutes and I'm talking about on foot?"

Nobles said, "Let's see. Go out and turn left—"

"The Miami Beach Police station," Mr. Fisk said. "Look, right here I got it written down. I even got it in my head written. Six-seven-three, seven-nine-oh-oh. I picked up the phone they're here before I can say goodby even."

"Yeah, but see, by then it's already done." Nobles took out his wallet and held it open for Mr. Fisk. "What's 'at say there, under where it says Star Security?"

Mr. Fisk leaned against the counter separating them, concentrating on the open wallet. " 'Private protection means crime prevention.' Is that suppose to be clever? I got a son in the advertising game could write you a better slogan than that one, free."

"See, prevention," Nobles said, "that's what you have to think about here. See, you call the cops after something's done to you, right? Well, you call us before it happens and it don't."

Mr. Fisk said, "Wait a minute, please. Tell me what you're not gonna let happen the cops one minute away from here down the street would?"

"Well, shit, they could mess your place up all different kinds a ways."

"Who is they?"

"Well, shit, you got enough dagos living around here. You got your dagos, your dope junkies, your queers, this place's full a all kinds. But, see, five hundred dollars in advance, you don't have to worry about 'em none. It gives you protection all year, guaranteed."

"Guaranteed," Mr. Fisk said. "I always like a guarantee. But tell me what in particular could happen to my place if I don't buy your protection?"

"Well," Nobles said, "let's see . . ."

Surveillance, the way LaBrava remembered it from his Miami field-office days, was sitting across the street from a high-rise on

Brickell Avenue or some place like the Mutiny or the Bamboo Lounge on South Dixie. Sitting in a car that was as close as you could come to a plain brown wrapper with wheels, so unnoticeable around those places it was hard to miss. The afternoon the wholesaler came out of the Bamboo, walked across the street to the car and said, "Joe, the lady and I're going out to Calder, catch the last couple races, then we're going up to Palm Beach, have a nice dinner at Chuck & Harold's with some friends . . ." it was time to move on, to Independence, as it turned out . . .

But not anywhere near the kind of independence he was into now—protecting his movie star—standing in some bushes on the east side of Flamingo Park, catching Richard Nobles with a long lens coming out of a motel named Sharon:

Richard Nobles walking over to the swimming pool. *Snick.* Nobles turning to say something to the little guy standing in front of the office. *Snick.* The little guy with his hands on his hips, feisty pose, extending his arm now to point at Nobles walking away. LaBrava saying, eye pressed to the Leica, "I see him."*Snick.*

The guy turned to his office, then turned back again and yelled something at Nobles. Nobles stopped. He looked as though he might go back, and the little guy ran inside the office.

LaBrava got in Maurice's car, crept along behind Nobles over Twelfth Street to Collins and parked again, got out with his camera and followed Nobles up Collins. Silver jacket and golden hair—you didn't have to worry about keeping him in sight. There he was, like he was lit up. The Silver Kid. The guy never looked around either; never even glanced over his shoulder.

From the east side of Collins, LaBrava shot him going into Eli's Star Deli. About fifteen minutes later he got him coming out. He got him going in and coming out of a dry cleaner's. Finally he got him going into the Paramount Hotel, just above Twentieth Street. LaBrava hung around about an hour. The bad part. But better than sitting in a car full of empty Styrofoam cups and crunched-up paper bags. At least he could move around.

He walked to the taxi stand on the southwest corner of Collins and Twenty-first and waited nearly twenty minutes for a red Central cab to arrive with the Nigerian, Johnbull Obasanjo behind the wheel, scowling.

"What's the matter?"

''Notting is the mattah.'' With an accent that was both tribal and British.

''You always look pissed off.''

''It is the way you see, not the way I look.''

There were parallel welts across his broad face, tracks laid by a knife decades ago that Johnbull, second cousin of a Nigerian general, told were Yoruba markings of the warrior caste. Why not?

''You're disappointed.''

''Ah,'' Johnbull said. ''Perhaps what you see is disdain.''

''Perhaps.''

''Mon say to me, the fare, 'Did you learn your English here?' No, in Lagos, when I am a boy. 'Oh,' he say, 'and where is Lagos?' '' Johnbull's twin knife scars became vivid, underlining the white-hot pissed-off expression in his eyes. ''When I am a child in school, for God sake, I can draw a map of the United States. I can show you where Miami is, I can show you where Cleveland is. But nobody here, they don't know where Lagos is, where you get the second most oil from any place in the world.''

''I'm looking for a guy,'' LaBrava said, ''who doesn't know where his ass is. Big blond guy staying at the Paramount.'' LaBrava handed Johnbull a ten-dollar bill. ''Watch for a black Pontiac Trans Am, late model. If it picks up the big blond guy, follow it. Then give me a call. I'll pay for whatever time you spend on it. If you have to leave, tell the other guys, I'll give 'em the same deal.''

''I want a picture for my mother,'' Johnbull said. ''This one smiling.''

''Let's see a big one,'' LaBrava said. He raised his camera and shot the Nigerian framed in his window, grinning white and gold.

The woman in the office of the Sharon Apartment-Motel said, ''Tell me you arrested him and you want Mr. Fisk to take a look it's the same one . . . Nuh, no such luck, uh? Oh well. Mr. Fisk is lying down he's so upset. Soon as the other police left he had to lie down. You know what he's worried you don't find him? What if he comes back?''

LaBrava waited.

Mr. Fisk came in, wary.

"You don't look like no cop to me, would wear a shirt like that. With a camera. What is this, you're on your vacation?"

LaBrava said, "We like to take a few pictures when we process a crime scene, Mr. Fisk. You by any chance speak to Sgt. Torres?"

"I don't know—they come in a car with the lights. You know how long it took them? Twenty-five minutes."

"See, they make out a U.C.R.," LaBrava said. "That's a Uniformed Crime Report. Then the Detective Bureau follows up. Did he give you his name? The big blond guy?"

"He showed me a gold star and the name of the company, something that says 'Private protection means crime prevention,' and his name printed there, typed. But I don't remember it. I should a wrote it down."

"What'd he say exactly?"

"I told the two other cops were here. I told them all that."

"In case you might've left out something important."

"Okay, he wants to sell me protection. What else is new? I tell him I don't need any, I tell him I've got the Miami Beach Police Department one minute away from here down the street. That's how dumb I am. I don't know it takes you to drive from First Street to Twelfth Street in a police squad car full speed with the siren and everything twenty-five minutes."

"How much did he ask for?"

"Five hundred. In advance, of course. He says for a year's protection guaranteed. Oh yeah? Next month he's back for another five hundred. I grow up, live forty years of my life in Crown Heights, I don't know this kind of business goes on?"

"He threaten you? Say what would happen if you didn't pay?"

"Get ready. You want me to tell you exactly what he said?"

Mrs. Fisk said, "We can't prove he said *any*thing. The policeman was here said unless the other places he did the same thing, we all speak up, then maybe."

"Tell me what he said, Mr. Fisk."

"He gives me the pitch, all this protection I'm suppose to get for five hundred dollars. I ask him, against what? What could happen to my place? The guy says, 'Well, let's see.' He goes over to the door, looks out. He says, word for word, 'Somebody could come around and take a dump in your swimming pool every night.' Wait. Listen. Then he says, 'That wouldn't be too nice, would it?' Not, he's gonna smash all my windows, he's gonna throw a bomb in, blow the place up, like they used to do it. Or even threaten to break my legs. No, this big blond-hair son of a bitch is gonna poo poo in my swimming pool."

LaBrava shook his head. After a few moments he said, "Would you step outside here, Mr. Fisk? Thank you. Over by the pool more. Yeah, right there. Now give me kind of a pissed-off, defiant look. If you would, please."

"Then the cop comes," Mr. Fisk said, "and what does the cop do? He takes my picture. I'm telling you . . ."

LaBrava passed up dinner with Jean and Maurice to spend the evening in the darkroom, watching Nobles appear in trays of liquid, pleased with the shots because they were clear and in focus. He liked the ones where there was motion in the foreground, out of focus, the top of a car as it passed, in contrast to the clarity of Nobles' confident, all-American boyish face. Hometown hero—the hair, the toothpick, the hint of swagger in the set of silver-clad shoulders. What an asshole.

How did they get so sure of themselves, these guys, without knowing anything? Like people who have read one book.

He hung Nobles up to dry and spent the next two and a half hours with Jean Shaw, in her apartment.

They did talk about Nobles, recapping, and he told her what Nobles had been up to and that he'd have prints in the morning, confirmation. She seemed fascinated. She sat facing him on the sofa and asked questions, probed for details, listening intently. Yes, it was fascinating—she used the word—that he could follow someone so closely, document the guy's activity, and not be detected. She asked him about the Secret Service and continued to listen until—

In one of her pictures, she said, there was a subplot about counterfeiting and they began to talk about movies and she told him what she hated most about making pictures: the two-shot close-up face to face with an actor she often couldn't stand. Nowhere but in the movies did people stand so close when they talked—and you'd get these actors with foul morning breath or reeking of booze—the two of them on the sofa getting closer and closer and that was fine, with confident breaths, good smells, aware of nature's horny scent in there, LaBrava ready once again to try for that overwhelming experience. He told her he wanted to see one of her pictures with her. She said she would get one; she was going home tomorrow to pick up some clothes, a few things, she's bring the tapes. He said he would like to drive her, see her place.

She said, "Spend the night with me. Tonight."

That sounded good.

She got a wistful look and said, "I need you, Joe."

And that didn't sound so good because—there it was again—it sounded familiar, and he had to tell himself that playing was okay, they were just having some fun. Except that she made it sound serious.

She said, "Hold me."

He did, he held her tight and she felt good. Before she felt too good he sneaked a look at his watch.

LaBrava was in his own bed when Johnbull Obasanjo phoned a few minutes past 2:00 A.M.

"I have been trying to call you, you never at home."

"I'm sorry."

"You tell me you want information—"

"I apologize."

"I accept it," the Nigerian said. "Now, you want to know where they went to in the black Pontiac sportcar, I tell you. They went to a place call Cheeky's. I know a man name Chike, he is an Ibo, but not a bad man. I don't believe this place, though, is of the Ibo. I believe it is for men who have pleasure in dressing as women. So they go in there."

"You saw the driver of the Pontiac."

"Yes, a Cuban man."

"What'd he look like?"

"I told you, a Cuban man. That's what he look like."

LaBrava wondered if Nigerians told jokes and if they were funny. "Was there anything different about him?"

"My friend, you have to be different to go in there. I told you that already."

"I apologize." Maybe they had a sense of humor if you got to know them. "You didn't by any chance get the license number of the Pontiac."

Johnbull Obasanjo said, "You have a pen? You have the paper, something to write on when you ask such a question?"

LaBrava turned the light on and got out of bed. Fucking Nigerian. The guy delivered, though, didn't he?

Five and a half hours later, still in bed, the phone again lay on the pillow against his face. He raised it slightly as Buck Torres came back on with his NCIC computer report.

"Cundo Rey. That's the owner's name. You got a pencil, I'll spell it."

"Please do."

"You ready?"

"Spell the goddamn name, will you?"

Torres spelled it. "You're a bitch in the morning, aren't you?"

"What else?"

"Cuban National, came from Mariel during the boatlift but wasn't processed. Arraigned for transporting a stolen motor vehicle, Volusia County, that's up north, no conviction. Assigned to Chatahoochee for psychiatric evaluation. He disappeared from there."

"Is there a warrant out on him?"

"Nobody wants him, figuring we got enough Cubans."

"You got his picture?"

"I can get it. Take a couple of days," Torres said. "He looks harmless to me. Refugee, fell in with some bad *hombres.*"

"Get the picture," LaBrava said. "I think you're gonna need it."

14

Nobles had half of a Debbie Reynolds to finish and a few half-done fries left. Little Eli could make a sandwich, *damn,* but he couldn't deep-fry worth shit. Nobles said to Cundo Rey, who was playing with his coffee spoon, "You do any good last night?" and took a big bite of his Debbie.

"I don't make so much in that place as a Ladies' Night place. See, they know I don't fuck the same way they do. I mean—you know what I mean."

"That's good to hear," Nobles said. "Jesus, but that place is scary, you know it? All them queers dressed up like girls. I had to get outta there."

"I thought you might see one you like to take out and rob him. That was a good idea."

"Yeah, but I don't believe I could touch the fucker to do it. I mean they are scary. How'd you make out?"

"I made a couple hundred. Man, I need money. I have to go home and get some."

"Pretty soon." Nobles shoved the rest of the Debbie Reynolds into his mouth. "You ready?"

"What?"

Nobles chewed and chewed. "I said, you *ready?* Get the wax outta your ears."

"I was ready before you start eating."

"Go on out. I don't want Eli to see us together when I talk to him."

"He already see us together, now."

"Yeah, but he won't remember you. All you boogers look alike. Go on outside, wait in the car."

"It isn't going to work."

"Go on. Scat."

Nobles walked over to the counter, laid his check on the rubber pad next to the cash register, fished a few toothpicks out of the tray. The man that owned the place, little Eli, came over wiping his hands on his apron, sort of a worried look on his face, or sad.

The Jew should shave and clean hisself up, Nobles thought, he'd feel better.

"Well, how we doing today, partner?"

Eli didn't answer him, eyes cast down. He rang up the bill, came back to the rubber pad and now had to look up, there was no money on the counter.

"Put her on account," Nobles said, "and tell me what you think of the deal I offered you."

The guy seemed afraid to move or speak.

"Hey, wake up."

What was the matter with him? He looked sickly. Refused to say a word, nod his head or blink. Nobles watched him turn to the counter behind him, move some stuff out of the way, a telephone book—the hell was he doing? The guy came back around holding up a photograph, holding it in front of his face, so that Nobles was looking at the picture and the guy's knuckles bony white pointing at him.

"Where'n the hell'd you get that?"

A shiny black and white shot of Richard Nobles coming out of Eli's Star Deli: so sharp and clear you could see the toothpick in the corner of his mouth.

The guy's shaky voice behind the shaky photograph was telling him to get out ". . . and don't ever come back again or I call the cops!"

It was getting scary. Sitting in the Trans Am with Cundo, hidden from humanity and street glare behind smoked glass, Nobles said, "You believe it?"

"I tole you it wasn't going to work."

"Guy holds it up—same kind of pitcher. That little fucker with the swimming pool, now this guy. What in the hell's going on? Somebody taking my pitcher . . . I gotta try another place. There's that dry cleaner up the street."

"I tole you," Cundo Rey said.

"You *told* me? What? You told me you saw this guy following me with a camera?"

"I tole you it wasn't going to work."

"You gonna keep saying that?"

"You want to work that kind of deal," Cundo Rey said, "you break the guy's window *first,* then you go in, sell him the protection. I tole you, it's how to do it."

"Yeah, well I want to know who's taking my pitcher."

"They hire somebody. They got more protection than you think."

"No, these people—what do you think they call 'em Jews for? They Jew you down, don't spend a dime less they have to. They ain't gonna hire a guy take pitchers."

"It couldn't be that girl," Cundo said. "No, it wouldn't be her."

"What girl?"

"She live over at the hotel where the woman is."

Nobles was half listening, staring at people going by on the sidewalk. Cundo began tapping his ring on the steering wheel and Nobles turned to him. "Cut it out."

"What am I doing?"

"I'm thinking." After a moment he said, "Oh, man, I don't know what's wrong with me. The dink I been looking for for Christ sake's a photographer. With a newspaper."

"You haven't seen him, have you?"

"I haven't seen *him,* but shit, he's seen *me*. It's got to be him."

"How could he know you down here?"

"He's *seen* us. How else you think, for Christ sake. He's seen *me,* anyway. Goddamn it."

"So, what difference does it make? Let's go see him, take his pictures away from him." Cundo paused, watching Nobles staring out the window. "What are you worried about? Take his pictures. Go in there, take the picture from the Debbie Reynolds guy. Get the picture from the swimming pool guy. Get all the pictures he has."

Nobles said, "I don't know . . ."

Cundo studied him. This Richard, most of the time you could read his face. Right now, though, it was empty, like he had been smoking some of the sky blue reefer from Santa Marta that paralyzed you, made you numb. Cundo said, "You know something? I haven' seen you hit anybody. Man, I even haven' seen you break anything. How come you not get mad?" He turned the ignition key, heard the engine come instantly awake, rumble and pop its muscle. He turned the radio on and heavy riffs filled the car, everything working now.

Cundo said, "Okay. We go see the guy."

LaBrava had taken the new issue of *Aperture* from his mail slot, opened it as he turned and got as far as the registration desk, held by a series of color photographs made by a painter, a fine artist, who shot into mirrors and got startling effects.

He had placed an envelope sleeve on the countertop. He laid the magazine over it, resting his arms on the edge, on cool marble, and wandered to the text to read that a still picture is more powerful than a motion picture, more memorable, that images from movies that stay with you are reasonably still . . . He would agree with that. Because the film pictures of Jean Shaw in his mind all seemed to be stills. Jean Shaw in black and white giving—he caught a glimpse of her giving Victor Mature the look.

Then saw her in muted color, a skirt, a top with a narrow belt, a straw bag, the real-life Jean Shaw coming off the elevator, not smiling, now trying on a faint smile as she saw him. She said, "What time did you leave?"

"It was about one-thirty. I couldn't sleep."

"Did you think about waking me up?" With almost a sly, bedroom look. But after the fact in a hotel lobby the next morning. He wondered what would have happened if he'd started in again, Jean drowsy, half awake, maybe less mechanical.

"I think the reason I couldn't sleep, I was expecting a phone call." And knew immediately it was the wrong thing to say. Giving her second billing.

She said, "Oh." Any hint of a sly look gone.

"It was important. The guy called about two."

She said, "Maurice wants to take me. You don't have to bother." Not icy, but not warm, either.

"I'd be glad to help."

"I'm just going to get a few things. Clothes, mostly. Maurice insists. I think he wants to talk." Her tone beginning to lose its stiffness. "What about the pictures?"

"Right here." He moved the magazine aside, brought the black and white eight-by-tens of Nobles out of the manila sleeve and laid them on the counter facing Jean.

She said, resigned, "Yeah, that's Richie. Are you sure he didn't see you?"

"I used a telephoto from across the street. The blur along the edge, that's a car going by. This one, I'm in a park across from the motel, the Sharon. No, I'm pretty sure he didn't see me."

Jean's eyes remained on the photos. "You're positive he's doing something illegal."

"He doesn't work for Star Security anymore," LaBrava said, "so he has nothing legal to sell. Even if he was still with them, they're not licensed in Dade County."

"But there's no way to prove he's doing something illegal, is that it?"

"Not till they catch him with a stink bomb, or breaking windows. Then they could get him for malicious destruction. But he's fooling with extortion. That's a tough one to prove."

Jean said, "If Richie knew you had these—" She shook her head slowly and seemed almost to smile.

"How about if he thought the police had a set? Would that shake him up?"

She looked at LaBrava, brown eyes wide for a moment. "Are they after him?"

"I haven't given them the pictures yet, but I think it might be a good idea. Before somebody gets hurt." He gathered the photos together, slipped them in the envelope. "So that's your friend Richie Nobles."

"The all-American boy," Jean said. "Can I have them?" When LaBrava hesitated she said, "For my own protection. In case Richie ever comes around again." She looked over as they heard the elevator land, the door open. "Let's tell Maury about it later, okay? Or I'll never get out of here."

Maurice was taking off his nubby silk jacket as he crossed the lobby. He wore a yellow sport shirt with long collar points, the top button fastened. "You think I need a coat?"

Jean picked up the envelope with her straw bag. "If it makes you happy."

"Nah, we're not going anyplace, are we?" He folded the jacket inside out and laid it on the counter. "Joe, lock it in the closet for me, will you? We're going up to Boca, get a few things of Jeanie's."

LaBrava said to her, "What about the tapes? You said you have a couple of your movies?"

She hesitated. "You really want to see them?"

"You kidding? With the star?"

"If you promise you won't fall asleep. We'll have to bring the VCR and plug it into Maury's TV."

Maurice said, "What? What're we talking about?"

"Jean's movies," LaBrava said and looked at her again. "What ones do you have?"

"Just the two available on tape. *Shadowland* and *Let It Ride.*"

"I can hardly wait," LaBrava said, not sure if he had seen either of them. "It's been a long time."

They'd crept past the Della Robbia, past the Cardozo to park across the street from the Cavalier, on the beach side of Ocean Drive. Nobles had curled his size into an almost fetal position in the front seat, face pressed against the inside edge of the backrest so he could stare out that smoky rear window and see the Della Robbia, the bunch of old ladies sitting lined up on the porch.

Cundo Rey said, "Man, we don't have no air. How about I open it just a little?"

Nobles didn't answer him. In a moment a draft of salt air touched his face and it felt pretty good. He reached behind him and opened the window on his side a few inches. Yeah, that was better.

"I don't want to see her just yet. Till we're ready. You understand?"

Cundo said, "Sure," even though he didn't. Why ask him questions? He was acting strange.

"What I'm getting at, I walk in there I'm liable to see her. Or be seen *with* her, I mean. You follow me? Best we wait for him to come out."

They had been parked here more than a half hour. Cundo couldn't believe it, Nobles becoming cautious, not wanting to go in there and get the guy's pictures, take the guy in his hands, throw him out a window if it was high enough. He would like to have a look at this guy in the light, see him good. The guy didn't seem to scare Nobles, no, but seeing the pictures of himself had changed him; he didn't seem to know what he was doing.

Cundo said, "If the guy works, then why would he be there?" Nobles didn't answer. He didn't know anything, so why ask him?

Cundo said, "I don't like that place I'm living, La Playa. I'm going to move." The reason they were at different hotels, Nobles had said they shouldn't be seen together too much. He had asked why and Nobles had said, because. That was his answer. Because.

"I'm going to find a good place, move my things down from West Palm. What about you? You want to move your things?"

Nobles wasn't listening, he was pushing up straight against the backrest, stretching his neck, saying, "Jesus Christ, there she is."

Cundo had to press his face against the side window, his neck twisted, to see. He said, "Tha's the movie star? Man, she look pretty nice. Who's that old guy?"

"Must be the one she's staying with, one picked her up." Nobles watched them cross the street like they were going to the beach in their good clothes, but now they stopped. He watched the old man pull open a car door and get in while Jean Shaw went around to the other side. They were going someplace. Just her and the old man.

As soon as Nobles had his idea he said, "They go by, you get out. I'm own take the car, meet you later on."

"You want to take *this?*"

Nobles' head turned with the Mercedes going past them. "Okay, get out."

"Man, this is my *car.*"

Nobles said, "You little booger—" Got that far.

Cundo saw the look and stepped out of the car saying, "Sure, please take it." Stood in the road saying, "Go with God," and watched until the insane creature from the Big Scrub turned left on Fifteenth Street.

Franny came out of the ocean like a commercial, body glistening in two strips of mauve material, Coppertone clean with an easy stride, letting her hips move on their own as she came up on the beach. It was empty in front of her, all the way to the park.

Where was Joe LaBrava when she needed him?

He was across the street, coming out of the Della Robbia with Paco's wheelchair, sitting in it now on the sidewalk, trying it out, talking to the old ladies leaning out of their chairs, reassuring them. By the time Franny reached the grass, he was wearing a plain, Beachcomber Panama with a curvy, shapeless brim, a camera hanging from his neck, waving to the ladies as he wheeled off.

Franny yelled his name. He looked over, made an awkward turn and stroked his wheels across the street.

"How do you get up curbs?"

She helped him, came around in front of him again and he was aiming a Nikon at her. *Snick.*

"I wasn't ready."

"Yes, you were. You look good. You're the first girl in a bathing suit I've ever shot."

"None of that commercial stuff."

He gave a shrug. "Maybe there's a way to do it."

"The bathing suit in contrast to something. How about sitting on a TV set?"

He smiled and she watched him reach around to the camera bag hanging behind him, watched him bring it to his lap, the hat brim hiding his face as he snapped off the wide-angle lens, put on a long one and aimed the camera down a line of palm trees to a group of elderly people sitting on a bench.

"What're you gonna shoot, the regulars?"

"Get 'em when they aren't looking."

"Why don't you come up after . . . do me."

She was serious or she was having fun. Either way, it didn't matter.

He said, "I don't have any color."

She said, "Whatever you want to use, Joe, is fine with me."

He remembered sore feet from all that standing around steely-eyed in front of hotels and at rallies and fund-raisers, protecting important people. A numb butt from sitting in cars for days doing surveillance. Tired eyes from reading presidential pen-pal letters. Not even counting protective-detail duty in Mrs. Truman's living room, a life that sounded exciting was 80 percent boredom.

It had certainly taken a turn lately.

He cruised Lummus Park in the Eastern Airlines wheelchair, using the Nikon with a 250-mm lens now to shoot across Ocean Drive to get porch sitters: panning a gallery of weathered faces, stopping on permanent waves, glasses flashing sunlight, false teeth grinning—peeking into their lives as he picked them off one at a time. Later on he would see their faces appear in clear liquid, in amber darkroom light, and would be alone with them again and want to ask them questions about where they'd been and what they'd seen. Raped by Cossacks, Franny said, or mugged by . . .

The Cuban-looking guy said, "What're you doing, taking pictures?"

His hair was slicked down across his forehead and he wore a gold earring. But even without it LaBrava would have known him. The way he moved, for one thing, the way his hand drifted up to touch the wavy ends of his hair.

LaBrava was happy to see him and gave him a smile and said, "Yep, that's what I'm doing, taking pictures."

"You down here on your vacation?"

"Just enjoying life," LaBrava said.

"That's nice, you can do that."

The guy wore a black shirt that might be silk and fit him loose. He was skinny under there, a welterweight with that high compact ass in his cream-colored slacks, the shoes white, perforated.

"Tha's a nice camera you have."

"Thanks. How about if I take a picture of you?"

"No, that's okay."

"I like to get shots of the natives."

"Man, you think I'm a native?"

"I mean the people that live here, in Florida."

The Cuban-looking guy said, "Tha's an expensive camera, uh?" He hadn't taken his eyes from it.

"With the lens it runs about seven and a quarter."

"Seven hundred dollars?"

"The camera cost me five hundred."

"Oh, man, is a nice one, uh? You let me see it?"

"If you're careful." LaBrava had to take his hat off to lift the strap over his head.

"No, I won't drop it. Is heavy, uh?"

"Hang it around your neck."

"Yeah, tha's better."

LaBrava watched him raise the camera, almost as though he knew what he was doing, and sight toward the ocean, the breeze moving strands of the guy's raven hair.

Lowering the camera, looking at it, the guy said, "Yeah, I like it. I think I'll take it."

LaBrava watched the guy turn and walk off. Watched the easy, insolent movement of his hips.

Watched him take four, five, six strides, almost another one before he stopped—knowing the guy was going to stop, because the guy would be thinking by now, *Why isn't he yelling at me?* Now the guy would be wondering whether or not he should turn around, wondering if he had missed something he should have noticed. LaBrava saw the guy's shoulders begin to hunch. Turn around and look—the guy would be thinking—or take off.

But he had to look.

So he had to turn around.

LaBrava sat in the wheelchair waiting, his curvy-brimmed Panama shading his eyes, the guy fifteen to twenty feet away, staring at him now.

"What's the matter?"

Holding the camera like he was going to take LaBrava's picture.

The guy said, "I have to ask you something."

"Go ahead."

"Can you walk?"

"Yeah, I can walk."

"There's nothing wrong with you?"

"You mean, you want to know if you took off could I catch you and beat your head on the pavement? There is no doubt in my mind."

"Listen—you think I was going to take this camera?"

"Yeah, I did. You changed your mind, uh?"

"No, man, I wasn't going to take it. I was kidding you."

"You gonna give it back to me?"

"Sure. Of course."

"Well?"

The guy lifted the strap, brought it over his head. "I could leave it right here." Stepping over to the low cement wall. "How would that be?"

"I rather you hand it to me."

"Sure. Of course." Coming carefully now, extending the camera. "Yeah, is a very nice one . . . Here you are," reaching sideways to put it in LaBrava's hand and stepping back quickly, edging away.

"What's the matter?"

"Nothing is the matter. No . . ."

"I'd like to take your picture. What do you say?"

"Well, I'm busy now. We see each other again sometime."

"I mean in my studio." Motioning, thumb over his shoulder like a hitchhiker. "Up the street at the Della Robbia Hotel."

The guy's reaction was slight, but it was there, in his eyes for part of a moment, then in his casual gesture, touching the curly ends of his hair.

"Tha's where you live, uh?"

"I've got like a studio right off the lobby. When you want to come?"

He hesitated now. "Why you want to take my picture?"

"I like your style," LaBrava said, not sure how many movies it was from. Ten? A hundred? "You ever do any acting?"

The guy was saying something. It didn't matter. LaBrava raised the Nikon and snapped his picture. *Snick.*

15

Maurice stood on the balcony that ran the length of Jean Shaw's tenth-floor apartment. The Atlantic Ocean was right there. All of it, it seemed to Maurice, the whole ocean from right downstairs to as far as you could see. It was too close, like living on a ship. He said, "I sat out here at night with that surf making noise, I'd drink too. It drive you crazy."

She said from the living room, "You know that isn't my problem."

"Yeah? Well, I would a thought I drank more than you do," Maurice said, "but I never threw a glass at a cop car."

"I didn't throw the glass. I explained that, I was in a funny mood."

"They laugh? You were a guy the cops would a beat your head in, for showing disrespect. You know what your problem is? Living in a place like this. There's no atmosphere. All you got is a view." He moved to the doorway, looked into the silvery, mirrored living room. Jean stood with two hanging bags draped over a chair done in white satin. "You got to be careful not to confuse class with sterility. Clean can be classic. It can also bore the shit outta you."

She said, "Well, you built the place."

"*I* didn't build it."

"You know what I mean. You've been into more developments like this than anyone I know . . . Living on South Beach like a janitor."

"Manager's fine. Don't put me down."

"What're you into now?"

"I'm resting my money, mostly tax-free bonds. We get a Democrat in there, everything'll pick up again."

"You still giving to thc Seminoles?"

"Miccosukis. Some of'em with runaway nigger slave blood in 'em. They appealed to my imagination."

"And your pocketbook."

"I made some good friends. Buffalo Tiger, Sonny Billy, they taught me to drink corn beer. We had some laughs, I got some good shots . . . And I don't *give* money to 'em. It's a foundation—send a few Miccosukis to school every year 'stead of selling airboat rides and shooting the heads off frogs. What's wrong with that?"

"Jerry thought you were crazy," Jean said. "I used to love to hear you argue. He couldn't believe it—all the money you were giving away."

"Yeah, well, I'm giving some to the whales, too. What would Jerry say about that, uh? I'd started a foundation for used-up lawyers he'd a loved it."

She said, "Well, Jerry wasn't the brightest guy I ever married." She sighed. "I thought he was going to be a winner, too."

Maurice said, "He stayed with the wrong guys too long, Jeanie, you and I both know that. They ate him up—used him, used his dough, he had no recourse. Who's he gonna go to, the FBI? He hadn't died of a heart attack, he'd a died a much worse kind of way, even *thinking* about pulling out. Up to Kefauver everybody's having a ball, nothing to it, you could deal with those guys. Frank Erickson, Adonis, any of 'em. After Kefauver, no way, they don't trust nobody."

She said, "Jerry was dumb. There's no other way to describe him."

"May he rest in peace."

"Yeah, wherever he is—died and gone to hell. But it doesn't help my situation."

Maurice said, "Jeanie, any woman I know would trade places with you in a minute. You got the looks, guys're attracted to you—sometimes the wrong type, I'll grant you. You got a nice life . . ."

"Go on."

"What's your problem? I know—don't tell me. But outside a money, what? You want money? I'll give you money. Tell me what you need."

She walked over to the television set, built into black formica shelves. "I don't want to forget the recorder." She picked up two tape cartridges in boxes. "Or the movies. You want to see them?"

"Of course I do. You know that."

She said, "Maury, I already owe you, what, sixty thousand."

He said, "You want to get technical we're up to seventy-two-five. But have I asked you for it?"

She said, "If I had money to invest, something working for me—"

"Jeanie. Have I asked you for it?"

"Or if you'd buy me out. Maury, I could pay you back, get out from under it."

"From under what? How many times have I said it? If you don't have it, you don't owe me. It's that simple. I buy you out, your share's worth about a hundred grand. Say a hundred and a quarter. You pay me back outta that, where are you? If I go, the hotel's yours. Don't worry about it, it's in the agreement. Until that happens—which is something I don't think about. I'm not afraid of going, it's gonna happen, but it's not something I sit down and think about. Until then, you need money, you let me know. It's that simple."

"Like an allowance."

Maurice said, "Sometimes—I don't know, Jeanie."

She put the videotapes down and seemed restless, though she didn't move. "I'm sorry, I didn't mean it that way. I'm not ungrateful, I'm frustrated. Maury, you're the best friend I've ever had. I love you, I love to be with you . . ."

"But what?"

"I feel useless, and it makes me mad."

"Then do something. Get back into acting."

"Maury, come on. I'm not going to play somebody's mother. And I'm not going to do the little-theater bit, work in a converted barn, wring my hands in *Fiddler on the Roof.* I've done all that."

"Big screen or nothing," Maurice said. "You know what I think of that particular kind of pride—from eighty-years experience, from knowing all kinds of successful people with all kinds of dough who are now dead or else in jail? I think it's a bunch of shit. Money and success've got nothing to do with making it on a day to day basis, and that's all that counts."

"I love rich old guys who say that—and don't have a worry in the world."

"Aw, Jeanie, come on"—he sounded tired—"you're smarter than that. Quit thinking, start doing something. Girl with your intelligence, your talent . . . I'm telling you, money ain't it."

"Joe thinks you're practically down and out."

"Let him think it. Either way, it wouldn't matter to him, he's an artist. He doesn't know it yet, but he is. He's gonna be a name."

She said, "Yeah, well, I wish him luck."

"Quit worrying, you get lines in your forehead."

"I always love your advice."

"Then listen to it. We ready?"

"I guess so."

"The suitcase and the two hanging bags—that's it?"

"If you'll take those," Jean said, "I'll bring the recorder. I'm going to drive, too. I want my car down there."

"For what?"

"Maury, let me feel at least a little independent."

The glare hit Nobles smack in the eyes coming up out of the Trans Am, had him squinting with a painful expression. Man, it was hot out. Walking toward the high-rise entrance he could feel the blacktop burning mushy under his cowboy boots, the heels sticking.

He had figured this deal wrong, but it was working out anyway. He believed the old man was taking Jean Shaw home, would drop her off and scat. But the old man was up there it seemed an hour—the black car ticking in the heat—then he had come out with a grip and what looked like her clothes and drove off with them.

Which meant she was going back to South Beach. Shit.

But if she wasn't home for good, least she was home now. Would she be glad to see him? He'd sure be glad to see her—thinking of words like *alone at last*. He could hardly wait.

Inside the air-conditioned elevator he pushed "10" and began to wonder what she'd say when she opened the door, what kind of look she'd have on her face.

Franny was still in the mauve string bikini.

She had a pinkish tan, freckles on her chest. She had a deep groove between her breasts, round bare hips and naked belly, like a young belly dancer on her day off—except for her round tinted glasses and that wiry hair; that hair was Franny and nobody else. She wasn't the least self-conscious. She poured wine, left the bottle on the glass table. She asked him if he was going to keep his hat on; he could if he wanted; she loved it, she thought it looked like Vincent van Gogh's a little, and didn't say much after that. She was quieter this afternoon.

He could hear the air-conditioning unit working hard. He was okay, he was just a little nervous, wanting to act as natural as this girl but knowing she had a lead on him, had not had to unlearn as many customs of propriety. He had decided she was going to fool around, make the moves on him and here he was, a guy who had gone to bed with a movie star, trying to act natural and not think of the movie star, not think at all. It wouldn't be cheating. How could it be cheating? He hardly knew the movie star. He felt he knew Franny longer, if he wanted to look at it that way. No, he was here because she'd invited him up . . . Franny wasn't sweating it. She'd probably decided it would happen or it wouldn't. No big deal. She was quieter though, at first.

Thinking about something. Rearranging the pillows, a pile of them on the daybed. She straightened and said, "Oh." Went into the bedroom and came out in less than a minute wearing a white cover, soft cotton, plain, that buttoned down the front and reached to her tan bare feet. She asked him if he wanted ice in his wine and after that began to talk. She asked how long his marriage had lasted.

"Thirty-eight months."

"You say it like that, it sounds like a long time."

"It was."

"Any kids?"

"No. How'd you know I was married?"

She said, "Maurice," and said, "What happened?"

"I don't know." He thought a moment and said, "Dames are always pulling a switch on you."

"Is that from one of your friend's movies?"

He shook his head. *"Laura."*

"Your friend's been married three times."

"How do you know that?"

"I talked to her. Showed her my wares. She uses a cream made from queen bee extract, turtle oil and seaweed."

"You talked to her?"

"She thinks it's great. I've got a book—a panel of doctors was asked their opinion of the queen bee cream and their answers were: No value, no opinion, a gimmick, quackery, and crap. She's had a tuck, Joe. Also a nose job. The nose when she was breaking into pictures."

"She told you all that?"

"Sure. Why not? She's nice, I like her."

"You do?"

"Very easy to talk to—doesn't give you any bullshit. I'd like to see one of her flicks." Franny paused. She almost smiled as she said, "Guess what I sold her?"

"You didn't . . ."

"Swear to God."

"Bio-Energetic Breast Cream."

"Listen, I showed it to her and she went ape-shit. 'Oh, for bounce and resiliency—really?' Trying to contain herself, act cool. It's about as effective as queen bee extract and turtle oil. You either have bounce, Joe, or you don't." She said, "Wait, I've got a surprise," and went into the bedroom.

In a few moments he heard soul music, a male vocal with back-up voices, a familiar melody but not a recent one. When she came out he said, "Who's that?"

Franny said, "You're putting me on. You haven't heard that a couple a hundred times?" She wasn't wearing her glasses now.

"Smokey Robinson?"

"Who else. And the Miracles. 'You've Really Got a Hold on Me.' " She came back to the daybed, her place on stage. "A big hit in Motown when you were a little kid, right?"

"I was in high school."

"See? I know all about you, LaBrava. Special Agent Joe LaBrava, United States Secret Service. I knew you were into something shady, at least at one time. So I asked Maurice. He says you're doing Murf the Surf now. I thought you were leaning more toward Iggy Pop, but you never know, do you. You quiet guys . . . Will you tell me some secrets, Joe?"

He said, "Former President Harry Truman's house has faulty wiring. You're watching a movie on TV, it goes off, comes back on, goes off, comes back on . . ."

She said, "Uh-huh, really interesting work, uh?"

"The lights would go off and on too."

She nodded, accepting this, said, "Well, you ready?" and began unbuttoning her cover, by the daybed piled with pillows, facing him.

He sat across the glass table from her in a wicker chair. There were two rolls of film on the table by the wine bottle. He raised the Nikon, made adjustments, lowered it and looked at her again.

Franny stood with her legs somewhat apart, hands on bare hips, naked beneath the cover held open behind her hands. She said, "How do you want me?"

He studied the pose.

She was playing. He hoped she was playing, giving him a line to come back to. Yeah, she was playing. Having fun. *How do you want me?* Except that her lavender eyes were serious and those big brown-tipped earth-mama breasts were serious and the belly rounding into the thickest patch of black hair he had ever seen in his life was as serious as can be. Well, you could be serious and still have fun. In fact, he believed it was the secret of a happy life, if anybody wanted to know a secret. *How do you want me?* And his line, keeping it low-key, soft, the sensitive artist:

"Just as you are."

After a moment she said, "Are you gonna take my picture?"

LaBrava said, in all honesty, feeling himself becoming more and more serious, "I doubt it."

Each time Cundo Rey thought about the guy in the wheelchair he would sooner or later see Richard driving his beautiful black car, and it was the last thing he wanted to think about.

See the guy, see Richard. Relating them, knowing he would have to do something about the guy.

Cundo sat in the lobby of the La Playa Hotel now waiting for Javier, fooling with his earring. Javier was from Cambinado. He was doing okay in his business. He had already offered to give Cundo whatever he needed.

What a place this was—the tile floor cracked and broken, pieces of it missing. He compared it in his mind to Cambinado del Este because the people who lived here reminded him of convicts. The difference, Cambinado del Este was cleaner than this place, it was still a new prison.

He compared it also to the National Hotel in Havana. The National Hotel was as dirty as this place, but instead of people who looked like convicts, there were Russians staying there, Russians smelling of garlic, talking in loud voices, complaining. They complained like children who didn't like their dinner. They didn't complain of things worth complaining about. What did they know? They didn't work on the housing brigade in Alamar twelve hours a day breathing cement dust. The Russian he had known was an engineer or a technician of some kind. In his room he had vodka, bars of chocolate, boxes of rubbers and dirty picture books he had bought in New York City. The Russian hated Cuba. Say *Cooba* with his garlic breath and spit on the floor. Cundo Rey, aching to leave, dying for the chance, defended his country because he hated the Russian and had gone back to the man's room late at night. He had almost wasted his life because of the Russian, using the Russian's own gun.

Thinking, Oh well, that was done.

Then thinking about the guy in the wheelchair again, because that wasn't done.

How many guys who lived in the Della Robbia Hotel took photographs of people from a distance, unseen, with a telephoto lens? Sure it was the same guy who had taken the photographs of Richard—oh shit, seeing Richard in his mind again . . .

And seeing a guy who was called David Vega coming into the lobby. David Vega had looked at him as though he knew him, but had never approached to speak to him. So he watched David Vega whenever he saw him.

When Javier came in David Vega was still in the lobby, drinking a Coca-Cola from the machine. So Cundo didn't greet Javier, pretending not to notice him. Javier would see this and do the same.

Cundo waited several minutes before going up to Javier's room. He accepted a glass of rum as a formality and listened as

Javier expressed his desire to move to South Miami. There was no hurry. Listening to Javier kept him from thinking about his car in the hands of Richard the swamp creature. Javier finished his rum before he brought the metal footlocker out of the closet, worked the combination and opened the lid to display his wares.

"Any pistol you want," Javier said, "wholesale price to a *Marielito*. Machine gun one-third off. MAC-10 cost you eight hundred."

"Something small," Cundo Rey said.

"You want a snubbie. This one, .38 Special, two-inch barrel. Same kind the Charlie's Angels use."

"Yeah?"

"Also Barney Miller."

"Wrap it up," Cundo Rey said.

16

Nobles had his grin ready. The door opened and he said, "Well, look-it who's here, huh?"

He'd decided she would be all eyes, surprised as hell. But she wasn't. Or didn't act it. She gave him a stare like she wasn't going to move.

He said, "Sugartit, I don't want to knock you down but I been in the car it seems like all day. I gotta go pee pee so bad I'm gonna be spitting in another minute. It just come on me."

So she had to get out of his way—it was a fact, he would have picked her up and moved her—had to let him through to run down the hall to her bathroom.

Nobles loved it in here, it was full of perfume bottles, bath oils and powder in pale-colored boxes, all kinds of good-smelling stuff. He would like to look in her medicine cabinet sometime, poke around and find intimate things. It was so *clean* in here, no rust stains in the toilet or the washbasin. He looked around at all her girlish stuff relieving himself, groaning sighs and finally shuddered. Oh man.

She was still in the parlor, sitting at one end of the sofa now, her straw bag on her lap, legs crossed to show him her knee above the chrome coffee table. She seemed calm now, not drilling him with her eyes, though not with what he'd call a sweet expression, either.

He said, "You glad to see me?"

Huh-uh, she didn't look too. She said to him, "Richard, what are you doing here?" Calm and patient, like she was talking to a child.

He said, "I missed you. Did you miss anybody?"

She said, "What am I going to do with you, Richard?"

That was better. He gave her a grin. "Well, let's see . . ."

She said, "You're just a big loveable bear, aren't you?"

He had never thought of himself that way. Shit—a bear. He said, "You got anything cold to drink? Man, I'm thirsty from sitting in that car." He started for the dining room, all shiny glass and silver in there, to go through to the kitchen.

When she said, "Richie?" and he glanced over, walking past her, he saw the pictures laid out on the coffee table, his own familiar self looking up at him and he stopped, not too thirsty anymore.

He put his hands on his hips. The first thing he thought to say was, "Man, I would like to know what's going on—this guy taking my pitcher." He squinted his eyes, looking up at Jean then. "Wait a minute. How'd you get 'em?"

Jean said, "Richard, you're priceless."

"I want to know how you got 'em."

"He gave them to me. How else?"

"What's he doing—he with a newspaper or what?"

"No, he's not with a paper. He goes out and takes pictures of people." She seemed to think about it a moment, not quite sure. Then nodded. "That's what he does."

"You don't have to get permission?" Nobles said, indignant now. "Just take pitchers of anybody you want?"

"Would you like to sue him? How about invasion of privacy?"

"Shit, it oughta be against the law."

She said, "You could go to the police . . ."

Wouldn't that be something. Get some cop he knew, like Glenn Hicks up in Boca, to come down on the scudder.

"Except they're going to find out about you anyway. He wants to give them a set of pictures."

Nobles had to squint again, trying to see this business in his head. It was a queer feeling to know somebody had been watching every move he made, like every time he stepped out of the daylight darkness of that black car. He was right back where he started, asking, "What in the hell's going on?" Asking, "Who is he, anyway?"

Jean said, "It's not so much who he is—his name is Joe LaBrava—but what he used to be. Joe was a Secret Service agent for nine years, Richard. He keeps his eyes open, doesn't miss a thing."

Nobles felt just a little bit relieved and said, "Hell, I know boys work as gover'ment agents. You help them out, they help you out. You work a deal."

She said, "Richie, do you know what you're talking about?"

He didn't like that bored goddamn ho-hum tone at all and she'd better watch it. He stayed calm though and listened. Heard her say:

"This man knows all about you. He knows you've been bothering me. He knows I can't discourage you, no matter how hard I try."

Learning amazing things from her now.

"Wait. You told him that?"

And saw her eyes catch fire.

"I *had* to, you dummy. He *saw* you. He asked me about you."

It stung him. But he kept his mouth shut and she seemed to settle back and it was quiet. He could hear the ocean.

She said, "Why you came to the clinic—God, I'll never know."

"I wanted to get you out of there."

She said, "Richard," her normal calm self again, "why do you think I got drunk? Why did I walk out of the bar? Do you know how long I had to wait for a police car? I thought I was going to have to go find one. Richard, before I left, what did I say?"

"The bar?"

"Before I walked out with the drink."

"What'd you say? You said a lot of things."

"I asked you not to drink so much."

"I was keeping up with you is all."

"I said trust me. Do you remember that?"

"Yeah, I remember."

"I wrote it on a napkin. *Trust me.* And told you to put it in your pocket. Trust me and wait, I'll call you. The police drive me to the place in Delray. I have them call Maurice and he comes immediately, anxious to take care of me."

"Yeah?"

"I stay with him. We talk. He feels even closer to me than before. He feels responsible for me. He wants to help me no matter what happens . . ."

"Yeah, but you didn't tell me any of that part—how you were gonna bring him in."

"If you trust me, Richard, I don't have to tell you anything . . . Do I?"

"Well, you could a told me *some*thing. Shit, I didn't know." He began to get tender feelings again, admiration. This little lady had put it all together, thought it up all by herself.

She said, "What did you do, the night at the clinic, start a fight? I was afraid you'd get into something."

"It was the *guy,* the one you're talking about. The scudder blindsided me while I'm talking to the girl there."

"Well, you picked the wrong guy, Richard."

"*I* didn't pick him—"

She said, "Listen to me. All right?"

She could be so calm no matter what, keeping her voice low and a little bit husky. He would look at her and get that tender feeling and not care how old she was. She was good looking, she smelled good, had nice legs—that knee looking at him, a little thigh showing . . .

"You've brought a man into it," she was telling him now, "who knows how to watch people, how to follow them. He was onto you for days and you didn't see him, did you?"

"I wasn't looking especially."

"Well, there's nothing we can do about it now. The police are going to get involved anyway, sooner or later, so maybe it doesn't make any difference. You're going to be the obvious suspect. Especially now. You've not only been bothering me, you've practically advertised—with pictures to prove it—you're into extortion, in one form or another."

"Hey, I was offering my service—"

"Richard."

"Yeah. Go on."

"They can't convict you with pictures. They've got to catch you in the act, destroying property, threatening someone. So I don't think the photographs are going to do us any harm. We have to have a suspect to make it believable and, Richard, I have to say, you're perfect."

He said, "I appreciate that."

"They might question you."

"I know it."

"They'll be convinced you're the guy."

"So?"

"It's going to be up to you, Richard, whether we succeed or not. You're the star."

"I am?"

"They could put a lot of pressure on you."

"I been in some ass-tighteners. Don't worry about it."

"And the guy who's going to help us," Jean said, "he'll have to understand a few things. At least he'll have to think he does."

"I know what you mean."

"You have someone in mind?"

"Already hired him. Cute little booger does anything I tell him. He's half queer, done hard time in Cuba—listen, you was to draw a picture of the one you got in mind, I'd turn this boy over and you'd say, that's him, don't let him get away."

"He's Cuban?"

"Pure-D. Listen, he told *me* a idea was crude, but didn't sound too bad. He's a nasty little booger. I wish you could meet him."

"I'm the victim, Richard."

"*I* know. I haven't told him any different. I'm just saying I think you'd get a kick out of him. Dances go-go when he feels like showing off. Wears a earring. Little Cundo Rey, the Cuban hot tamale. You know what they say the weather is down there? They say chili today and hot tamale."

He grinned, waiting for her to loosen up, but she was being serious about something and he could hear the ocean again.

In that quiet she said, "Why are there pictures of you and none of him?"

"I done the selling. I was gonna save Cundo for the dirty work."

"Did he like the idea?"

"Well, I wouldn't say he was real tickled. He believes you have to break the guy's window *first,* then sell him the protection. Maybe that's how they do it down in Cuba, I wouldn't know."

Jean said, "Richard, that's not unlike the way we're going to do it. Isn't that right?"

He had to think about that. "Yeah, sorta."

"Are you sure he'll do whatever you tell him?"

"No problem. The little fella's greedy."

She was staring at him now, hard.

When he'd decided she didn't intend to speak, Nobles said, "Listen, maybe we ought to get our heads together here," coming around the coffee table to ease down next to her, "get this deal fine-tuned." But he was no sooner down, she was up.

Going over to the television set with her straw bag, telling him, "Stay there, I'll be back."

Not sounding mad or anything, just peculiar. He watched her pick up a couple of video cartridges and shove them into the straw bag, a big roomy one. She dropped the bag over on a chair, like she didn't want to forget it when she left. Then she stooped down, opened the cabinet beneath the shelves and he stared at her fanny as she brought out a third video cartridge. This one she snapped into the VCR, the movie player, and turned on the television set, telling him he could carry the recorder down to the car after.

"After what? We gonna see a movie?"

"Part of one." She stepped away from the set.

Nobles laid his arm across the sofa's backrest, waiting for her, but she stood there watching the screen as music came on over the Columbia Pictures logo. The music quit. For a moment the screen was black. Then the picture's musical score began, dirge-like, a promise of doom, as the screen turned white and the main title appeared, a single word within a black border, *OBITUARY*.

"I saw this one."

"I want you to see it again. The first part."

"That's all I ever seen, like half of it. How's it end?"

"Be quiet," Jean said.

"There you are," Nobles said, reading the titles. "Starring Victor Mature. Jean Shaw. Victor Mature—yeah, I remember this one, he's the cop. Which one's Shepperd Strudwick?"

"My husband."

"Henry Silva. Which one's he play?"

Nobles looked up. Jean was walking out of the room. He said, "Hey, get us a cold drink, okay?" He wouldn't mind something to eat, either, and raised his voice. "You know how to make a Debbie Reynolds?"

No answer.

Maybe she'd surprise him. Yeah, he remembered this one. Starts with the funeral. Jean Shaw standing there dressed all in black with her husband, old enough to be her daddy, biting his lip, man with a nervous stability, rich but afraid of dying, having to leave the cemetery in a hurry. Running off to his limousine. There, going in close to Jean Shaw watching him leave. Looking through her veil at her eyes. Something going on in her head and not sweet affection for her hubby, from the look of it.

Jean came back in the room holding something in both hands wrapped in tissue paper he hoped was a snack of some kind. She sat down next to him on the sofa, close, and Nobles said, "What a we got there, hon?" She didn't answer. She unwrapped the tissue paper and handed him—Jesus Christ—a little bluesteel automatic.

"The hell's this for?" Nobles looked at it, read on the side *Walther PPK/S Cal. 9mm* and some words in a foreign language. It was a little piece, the barrel only a couple of hairs better than three inches long.

Jean said, "I want you to show me how it works. I used to know, but I've forgotten."

"Where'd you get it?"

"It was my husband's. Be careful, I think it's loaded."

"Hey, I know how to handle guns. What do you want this peeshooter for?"

"Just in case."

"We ain't robbing a bank, sugar."

She said, "Let's watch the picture. You can show me later."

Her tone sounded encouraging, soft and husky again. She could sound pissy one minute and like she was in heat the next. He brought his arm down from the back of the sofa and she snuggled right up against him. Yeah, she seemed to be getting in the mood herself, staring at herself in the moving picture. It tickled him to see her watching herself, hardly ever blinking her eyes, her mouth open just a speck.

He bent his head to whisper to her, "My but that's a cute-looking woman. I wouldn't mind loving her up some."

She said, "Shhhh," but laid her hand on his thigh, the red tips of her fingers touching the inside seam of his blue jeans. She began to pick at the seam as she watched herself. Pretty soon she'd begin to scratch him. He liked it when she scratched him. She was a good scratcher.

17

Franny said, ''Oh man. Man oh man.'' She said, ''I bet there's a guy somewhere right now—he's in Boston, but I forget what school it is—he's looking at a seismograph and he's going, 'Holy shit, look at this,' like he's got about a seven point five on his Richter and there's *got* to have been a major earthquake in the last five minutes or a volcano, another Mt. St. Helens, and this guy's seismograph is going crazy—a major disturbance, look, somewhere in Florida, and they narrow it down however they do it and the guy goes, 'Look, in South Beach. Ocean Drive and Thirteenth. Wait. Room two-oh-four, the Della Robbia Hotel. But what could it've been?' You know what it was? It was everything coming together—and I don't mean it that way, but that's true too, huh?—no, I mean everything, the light, the sepia tones, the room, the mood, Smokey and the Miracles, Marvin Gaye and then no sound at all, absolute silence right after. Did you notice?''

''You're saying you had a good time?''

''To feel my loins consumed by a scorching torrent of liquid fire? It wasn't bad.''

''You make a lot of strange sounds.''

''I know I do. I can't help it.''

''You talk, too.''

''Yeah, but I keep it relevant.''

''You keep it basic.''

''You make faces.''

''Out of control.''

''No, even before. But mostly you smile. You look a person right in the eye . . .''

''You want your wine?''

''Goddamn pillow. There's one that's digging into me . . . There. Next time however . . .''

''What?''

''I don't want to sound presumptuous.''

''Next time in the bedroom.''

''The next time you take my picture.''

"I'll shoot it now if you want."

"I have to tell you something, LaBrava. I love your name—I'm gonna call you LaBrava from now on. I have to tell you, there's no guy in New York I want to send a self-portrait to. I lied."

"Women who want to be shot in the nude, they want their picture taken. It's okay with me."

"That wasn't it. I wanted to go to bed with you. You know why?"

"Tell me."

"Because I knew it would work. I mean I knew it would be the complete, ultimate act, every part of it first rate."

"First rate—"

"Certain types, when you see the person you just *know*. You know what I mean? Also I like older guys. You're not that old, but you're still older. You've been to bed with the movie star, haven't you?"

"You can't ask a question like that."

"I know, but the reason I did—well, I'm sure you have, otherwise you'd have said no, you haven't. I think. But the reason I mention it—"

"This's gonna be good."

"If it was just for fun and not serious—I mean if you're not in love with her, and I don't think you are or you wouldn't be here. Some guys, it wouldn't matter, but not you. Anyway, if it was just for fun with the movie star, you weren't exactly disappointed, but it wasn't the big thrill you thought it was gonna be either. How do I know that? Because you like it sorta wacky, goof around and have a good time. I knew that just from talking to you. But she's too much into herself for that. I don't mean because she's especially proper or ladylike. I can tell she gets right down to business and it's more like jogging with somebody than making love. You know what I mean? Of course you do."

"You're sure of that."

"Oh shit—now you're mad at me."

"What'm I supposed to say?"

"What're you doing now, pouting? Christ—"

"I'm not doing anything."

"I'm sorry. I thought we were pals."

There was a silence.

"We're pals. Here's your wine."

"Thanks."

"You said you thought she was nice."

"I do, I like her."

"But you think she's too much into herself."

"I get the feeling she's always on stage."

"Not altogether honest?"

"No, I don't mean she's devious. It's just that she's never right out in front. Movie stars, they either seem to fade away or James Dean out, but Jean—maybe she's played so many different parts she doesn't know who she is anymore."

"She always played the same one."

"Well, there you are. What do I know."

"But you like her."

"Sometimes, that quiet way you have of sneaking up—you know what you sound like?"

"A cop?"

"You sound like a cop."

Nobles told her sometime he'd like to see how it ended, it was just getting good. She asked if he thought the beginning slow. He said no, he meant it was getting even better. It was a real good movie. It was fun to watch her put on that sexy look and work her scheme.

He said, "Just tell me, do they catch you or not?"

Jean said, "No, but something happens I never expected."

They had talked, going over the plan in detail. Now Jean had him sitting at her desk in what she called her study. It was full of books and framed pictures of guys Jean told him were famous movie producers and directors. Nobles did not know any of them or was able to read the names they signed. One guy, Harry Cohn, she said he'd owned a movie studio but acted more like a gangster than any real gangster she had ever known. She had told Nobles about some of the S & G Syndicate people her husband worked for and they hadn't sounded very tough to him. They sounded like any dagos that dressed up in suits and snap-brimmed hats and showed off by spending money. That wasn't being tough. Being tough was doing brutish work as a boy, getting into fights on Saturday night and drinking till you foundered. Being tough was going into dark places with a .357 and a sap and praying to Jesus some nigger would try to jump you. Being tough—shit, it was not poking your fingers at a typewriter that looked like a little toy one.

He'd told her he didn't know how to work it. She said he showed her how to use the gun, she'd show him how to use the typewriter. He was suppose to put what she dictated to him into his own words.

Like Jean said, very slowly, "You know what will happen to you now. You will die. If you don't—"

He said, "Wait, hold it." He kept forgetting to press down the key on the left side, hold it down, to make a capital letter. She told him to type the capital letter over the small letter. It would be all right if it was messy. Nobles said, "Neatness don't count in a deal like this, huh?"

"If you don't leave the money—" She stopped and said, "No, start over. In all capital letters—push the one right above it down and it locks. Here." She did it for him, leaning over him, giving him her nice perfume smell. "Now, the first line, all in caps, your life is worth six hundred thousand dollars. Go ahead."

He typed, *YOUR LIFE IS WORTH $—)),)))*

He said, "Shit, I can't type."

She didn't get mad. She pulled the sheet out and rolled in a clean one, regular tablet paper with lines, telling him not to touch it, and he decided schemers had to be patient so as not to seriously fuck up. She bent over the side of the desk and began writing in the tablet, printing the words faster than he had ever seen anybody write. She said, "There," when she'd finished, "that's what the note should say. But you have to put it in your own words."

He read what she had written and said, "This here looks fine to me."

She said, "Listen to yourself. That's what I want it to sound like."

It didn't make any sense to him that writing would sound like a person. Writing was writing, it wasn't like talking. But he did as he was told, fought that dinky typewriter and finished the note.

Jean said, "All right, read it to me."

" 'Your life is worth six hunnert thousand dollars,' " Nobles began, rolling the sheet up out of the typewriter, remembering not to touch it. " 'You have three days to get the money. It must be *used* money with nothing smaller than a twenty and nothing bigger than a hunnert dollar bill and don't say you can't get it. You are worth a sight more than that.' " Nobles looked up. "I added that part."

"Fine," Jean said. "Go on."

"Let see. 'Get four thousand hunnerts, three thousand fifties and twenty-five hunnert twenties.' " Nobles paused. "How you know the bag'll hold it?"

"It will," Jean said. "Go on."

" 'You are to put the money in a Hefty thirty-gallon, two-ply trash bag. Put this one in another Hefty trash bag of the same size and tie it closed with some type of wire. Hay-baling wire is good. You will be told where to take the money. If you do not do as you are told you will *die.*' I like that part. '. . . you will *die.*' Underlined. 'If you try any tricks you will *die.* If you tell the police or anybody you will *die.* Look at your car. You know this is not just a threat. You have two days to get the money and your car fixed. *I am watching you.*' Underlined. I said baling wire there, so it won't come undone. Is that okay?"

"Good idea," Jean said. She leaned close to him to look at the note. "You misspelled *baling,* as in *haybaling wire.*"

"Shit," Nobles said.

"That's all right, leave it," Jean said. "But if the police question you they might get tricky and pick up on that word, ask you how to spell it."

"Yeah?"

"There's no *e* in it. It's b-a-l-i-n-g."

"That's *balling,*" Nobles said and started to grin and said, "Hey, puss . . ."

"Richard, we have a lot of work to do and I have to get back."

He hunched in to look at the note with her. "Hey, what should we sign it?"

"Well, *Cordially,* would be nice," Jean said. "No, that's fine the way it is. Now we'll write what you're going to say when you call, so you'll have it word for word. You'll tell me to go to a phone booth, you'll call me there at a certain time." Nobles was shaking his head. She said, "What's the matter?"

"Nuh-uh, they're gonna have traps on the phone. Shit, I know that much. I seen the feds do it when I was on the Opa-locka Police, setting up drug busts. They can't prove what I write, but they can sure as hell get my voice print on a phone. You have to tell 'em where you're suppose to go, don't you? Make it look real?"

"Yeah, you're right."

"By the time you get to Boca they got a trap on the phone booth. It tells 'em right away what number I'm calling from. See, it's different from a movie. They got equipment now, shit, you don't have a chance of doing something like that. You might as well give 'em your phone number."

Jean said, "All right, we'll do it with notes. Instead of a call I receive a note at the hotel, telling me where to go . . ."

"Find it on the porch, say."

"I'll go to the phone booth in Boca, find another one—"

"Hold it there. I'm being watched how'm I gonna put the note in the phone booth?"

"I'll have it with me," Jean said. "Make it look as though I found it. Hello—what's this?"

"That'd work."

"The note tells me to go to my apartment." She gave him a wink. "Got it?"

"Gotcha."

"I find another note, slipped under the door."

"You have *it* with you too."

"Or we write it now and leave it here."

"Yeah?" Nobles was thinking. "You know where you go next?"

"Of course."

"Got the whole deal worked out, haven't you?"

"Every step. The only change, notes instead of phone calls. I like it even better—they'll be playing with all their electronics for nothing."

"They love it, the feds, all that technical shit. Where's my little Cuban come in at?"

"The next stop."

"You're still gonna have a tail on you, you know that."

Jean nodded, smoking a cigarette, blowing the smoke out in a slow stream. Boy she was calm.

"All I'll need is to be out of their sight for about twenty seconds."

"You got the place?"

"I've got the place. I'm pretty sure. But I'm going to look at it again when I leave here."

"Cundo's gonna take it from you by force."

"There's no other way," Jean said. "But I'll cooperate, you can be sure of that. Does he have a gun?"

"Doesn't like guns or rough stuff. Talks big but being half queer he's girlish."

Jean said, "Okay, we'll write the notes. We'll need three . . ." She paused. "You'll have to take the typewriter with you when we're finished here."

"Yeah, I guess I better."

"Drop it in the Intracoastal. That area just before you come to the Hillsboro Inlet, there're a lot of trees."

"It's a shame, it's a nice typewriter."

"Richard?"

"Don't worry, I'll get rid of it. Or I could sell it."

She said, "Oh, Christ."

"Just kidding. Don't you worry, it's good as done."

She was thinking or worrying about something though. This little schemer—boy, she was a sketch.

She said, "Does your friend Cundo know where you live?"

"You mean up here or down there?"

"In Lake Worth."

"Nobody does, 'cept you."

"You can't go there while you're being watched."

"I know it."

"Promise?"

Nobles said, "Hey, you think I'm stupid or something?"

She thought of handkerchiefs and how simply it was done in the movies: Henry Silva making phone calls with a handkerchief over the mouthpiece, in a time before electronic surveillance; the movie cop using a handkerchief to pick up the murder weapon. Henry Silva had used a second-hand typewriter and dropped it off the side of his boat on their good-luck cruise to Catalina, their last time together before her husband would receive the letter—*$150,000 or you're dead.* Impressive enough as a pre-inflation demand; today it would hardly be worth the risk. She remembered her line: "You can't come near the boat as long as the cops are tailing you." (Beat) "Promise?" And Henry Silva's line: "Do I look stupid?"

Some of it was different, some of it almost exactly the same. One thing she was certain of, it wouldn't end the way the movie did.

18

The old man said it was Joe Stella up in Lantana had given him this address, so he had come on down in his pickup truck. There it was across the street. It had dust-settle on top of that salt stickiness and he hadn't had no place to wash it, being too busy looking for his sister's boy, Richard Nobles. The old man said his name was Miney Combs.

His pickup was parked behind Jean Shaw's clean white Eldorado.

LaBrava told Miney yes, he had heard his name from Joe Stella.

The old man looked like he had lived outdoors all his life, the kind of man who knows where to fish and dig wells, how to fix pumps and tune his truck. He was heavyset with a belly; wore a John Deere hat, suspenders over his gray work clothes, long-sleeved underwear beneath, and carried about him the sour smell of aged sweat.

They sat on the porch of the Della Robbia talking, in the front corner section next to Thirteenth Street. The old ladies would bend forward to look over because the old man was using a snuff stick and they had never seen one before. LaBrava hadn't either.

It was like the man was brushing his teeth. The twig was about the size of a toothbrush, frayed soft on the end and stained the color of brown shoe polish from sticking it into his Copenhagen and then massaging his gums with it, sometimes leaving it in his mouth like a cigar. LaBrava went over to the Cardozo and brought back four bottles of cold beer. The old man sighed and his metal chair groaned as he settled in, resting his work shoes on the rail.

Miney said, "There's parts of that swamp you'd think nobody but Jesus would dare walk it. Richard, he'd go in there be right at home. Preferred it to his own home I believe account of the way my brother-in-law raised him. See, he believed you whupped boys you made 'em humble. Twist you a half-dozen lengths of hay-baling wire and whup 'em regular. See, my sister, what she did she run a grits mill. Had a old tractor engine tied onto the mill and would grind up was nothing but mule corn, hard as gravel, but it made pretty fair grits and she sold it, fresh grits. See, Richard worked there till finally he left to peck it out on his own, sport around in the swamp and hire out to take folks for canoe rides, so they could watch birds. You imagine? I said to Miz Combs, watch 'em do what? I heard it I wondered if they'd pay to watch me plow a field. First I heard of Mr. John after him was when he killed the eagle. Why did he kill it. Knowing Richard it was to see it done. All right, then here was these two boys working a still I heard from cane skimmings. But that couldn't a been, 'cause the first time they was brought up I knew the judge said it ought to be against the law to arrest anybody could make whiskey good as theirs. Then the second time, with our Richard testifying, swearing in court, they got sent to Ohio. Same as my boy and in the same court. My boy had done his time once. Yes, he bought weed from the shrimpers and sold it to college boys, but he never smoked it once. Now Richard come along and tells on him and some others to Mr. John—only the Lord Jesus knows why—and my boy is doing thirty–five years in a gover'ment lockup."

LaBrava said, "What do you want to do to Richard?"

Miney said, "What do I *want* to do? I want to put a thirty-ought-six in him, right here." Miney touched the bridge of his nose with a finger that looked hard as bark. "But what I am going to do is put him in the back of my truck rolled in a dirty tarp and take him on home. We'll decide fair. Maybe lock him in a root cellar for up to thirty-five years—how's that sound? Let him out when Buster gets his release."

That didn't sound too bad.

LaBrava said, "You think you can handle him?"

"He's big as a two-hole shithouse and I'm blocky," Miney said, "but once I lay my ax handle across his head I don't expect trouble."

"He's over at the Paramount Hotel on Collins Avenue," LaBrava said.

Nobles walked into the lobby, his head aching with images of things to come, little details he had to remember. Like—Jesus, *the typewriter!* Already he'd forgot one. He was suppose to have taken care of that on the way down. He saw himself in darkness dropping it off the MacArthur Causeway . . .

And saw his Uncle Miney in that same moment—Miney sitting asleep with a snuff stick in his mouth, right there in the Paramount Hotel lobby. Nobles felt himself yanked out of that future time and back into a Jacksonville courtroom past, Miney extending his arm, his finger, pointing the Last Judgment at him . . . He got out of that lobby. Ran up to Wolfie's on the corner of Twenty-first to phone Cundo.

But the little booger wasn't in his room.

Nobles didn't want to go over there. He didn't like the feel of the place, all the foreigners hanging around. So in the next couple of hours he killed time having snacks, corned beef sandwiches, and checking the lobby, each time seeing Miney sitting in the same goddamn chair like he would let moss grow on him if he had to.

Finally, when it was dark he drove over to the La Playa Hotel, checked to see if Cundo had returned—not yet—and sat outside in the car to wait, listening to the jabber of dagos passing on the street. Little fuckers, ought to be sent back where they came from.

Send Cundo back too when they were through with him.

He heard Cundo's voice before he saw him—like a dago prayer shouted to heaven. The next thing, Cundo was feeling his car, running his hands over it in the streetlight, asking had he hit anything, had he stripped the gears, had he got bugs on it. Try to get a word in about something important. Nobles had to wait and found it was worth it. For once Cundo saw his car was okay the little fucker was so grateful he nodded yes, right away, and kept nodding yes to everything Nobles told him.

Go see Uncle Miney and give him a story. Yes. Tell him Richard's moved and nobody knows where. "Convince him or he'll ruin this deal we got. You understand?" Yes, of course. "Send him on his way or he'll mess us up good." Don't worry. Still looking now and again at his black Pontiac.

"The woman's car's over there at the ho-tel. Eldorado parked on the street." Yes? "Smash the windows with something. Windshield, headlights, 'specially the window on the driver side." Yes, okay. "Later on tonight I'll tell you the rest, what you're gonna do, then we don't see each other for a while. You understand?'' Yes. ''You gonna miss me?'' Of course.

''Something else. Shit, I almost forgot. There's a typewriter in your trunk I want you to throw in the ocean, in Biscayne Bay. You hear me? Not in a garbage can or out in some alley, it's got to be sunk for good.''

Yes, of course. Not even asking why—the little booger was so grateful to see his car again.

Sitting in the middle of the sofa LaBrava would lose himself for a time, watching Jean Shaw on the television screen and feeling her next to him. He could turn his head and see her, right there, the same face in profile. In the darkness of the room the two Jean Shaws were nearly identical, pale black and white. But he would not lose himself for long, because Franny Kaufman sat close on his other side and he was aware of her too. He would hear her, soft sounds in response to what she was watching, and feel her leg and sometimes her hand. She was here because Jean Shaw had invited her. Maurice, in his La-Z-Boy, paid no attention to Jean's whispers to be quiet. If he felt like making comments he made them.

''I'm gonna tell you something. Guys that ran dice games never looked like Dick Powell.''

''Shhhh.''

''I never knew a good-looking guy ran a dice game. I tell you about a guy named Peanuts?''

''Maury—''

''Edmund O'Brien was starting to get fat even then, you notice?''

At one point Franny's voice in the darkness said, ''Hey, Jean?'' a tone of mild surprise. ''I've seen you before . . . I can't think of the name of the picture.''

LaBrava was aware of the silence until Maurice said, ''Jeanie, you still know how to deal cards like that?''

Cundo Rey said to the old man he understood from the guy over at the desk, the hotel guy, that he was looking for Richard. Cundo watched this Uncle Miney take the stick out of his mouth, almost gagging as he saw the dirty brown end of it.

"You a friend of Richard?"

Like he was accusing him. From the sound and the look of the man, another strange creature from the swamp, Cundo didn't believe he should tell him yes. He said he *knew* Richard, he had seen him around here.

The old man said, "Where?" He said, "Take me where I might find the son of a bitch."

They got in the old man's pickup truck and the old man began talking about Richard Nobles, saying he had "fell from grace once he got his ass up against hard work." Saying he had become nothing but a mean rascal who would sell his friends and blood kin to save his own hide, or maybe just for fun—Cundo understanding only some of what the old man said, but getting enough to hold his interest and want to keep the old man talking. Miney saying there was a time he himself was "wilder'n a buck and went looking for women and to do some drinking," but a man had to reach a point where he left that behind him. Richard's appetite was such he must be "holler to his heels." The old man said Richard—maybe what was wrong with him—had never looked up to nobody. He said to Cundo, "Who's you all's hero? People like you."

Cundo had to think. Fidel? No. Well, yes and no. Tony Perez? Of course. Roberto Ramos, if he was still playing in the big leagues. But he didn't know if the old man had ever heard of Tony Perez or Roberto Ramos, so he said, "The President of the United States."

Miney said, "Shit, that scudder—they's people eating nothing better'n swamp cabbage, he don't give a shit."

Cundo asked him what he wanted Richard for and Miney said, "You shake him out of the tree and I'll take care of the rest." Yes, as Nobles had said, it sounded like this old guy could make trouble for them. Cundo gave him directions. Take a left. Take another left. They were on Ocean Drive now coming up on the Della Robbia from the south.

Cundo touched the old man's arm. "You see that white Cadillac there? That's Richard's car."

Jean got up to turn the lights on. It was her show, she had insisted on turning them off. Maurice, trapped in his recliner, extended his empty glass, and LaBrava got up to make drinks, remembering a Bogart line to the question, "How do you like your brandy?" Bogart, as Sam Spade: "In a glass." In that frame of mind after seeing Jean's picture. Hearing Franny say, "Well. I loved it. I loved your part especially. Lila. She was neat. Wonderful situation, if she wins the money she loses the guy, but she has to go for it. Say the line again."

Jean: Let it ride?

Franny: Yeah. Like you did in the movie.

Jean: Let it ride.

Franny: Perfect. I love it.

LaBrava poured drinks with his back to the room, listening to movie voices.

Franny: I wasn't sure, but I had the feeling Lila was getting a little psycho.

Jean: No, not at all. It's more an obsession. She's in a hopelessly corrupt situation, she's disillusioned, but you know she has to play the game.

Franny: It's the lighting and composition—

Jean: That's part of it, the ominous *mise en scène.*

Franny: I mean if she's not psychotic then it's the look of the picture, the expressionistic realism that gives that feeling.

Maurice: You two know what you're talking about?

Jean: You do see a change. She's essentially content in the beginning, an ordinary young woman . . .

Franny: I don't know. I think subconsciously she's looking for action. Like in that other picture I saw of yours . . .

Jean (pause): Which one?

Franny: I only saw like the last half, but the character was a lot like Lila. Your husband's gonna die, he knows it and also knows about this shifty business you have going with the private eye—

Jean: Oh, that one.

Franny: So he kills himself, commits suicide—shoots himself and makes it look like you did it. I mean, what a guy. He was a lot older than you.

LaBrava turned with Franny's and Maurice's drinks. In almost the same moment, with the sound of glass shattering outside, he was moving toward the nearest of the front windows.

* * *

Cundo Rey used the blunt side of the ax head, smashed the windshield of the Eldorado first, hitting it three times thinking the whole thing would shatter, fly apart, but it didn't; the ax punched holes and the windshield looked like it had frost on it, ice. He smashed the headlights, one swing for each, and remembered Richard saying the driver side window too, 'specially for some reason. He swung the ax like he was hitting a line drive and that window did shatter, fly all apart.

"Let's go, man. Come *on*."

He had to shove the old man, still looking out the back window of the truck, to get him to drive off. "Left. This street, *left*. Keep going . . . Go past Collins Avenue. Go on, keep going." The old man didn't know what was happening.

"Somebody's gonna call the police."

Listen to him. "That's why we want to get away from here."

"That was Richard's car?"

"Yeah, see, now you know he isn't going to leave. He has to get it fix."

"But where's he at?"

"I'm going take you where I think he is."

"Why's he leave his car there?"

"He has a girlfriend, you know, live by there."

"Well, if his car's setting there—"

"No, he leave it on the street there." Jesus Christ. "See, is more safe for the car there than where he live. Yeah, he leave it there all the time."

"We going back to the ho-tel?"

"We going to another place where I think he is." Jesus, this old guy with his questions. "You know, where he like to go sometime. We maybe have to look for him different places."

The old man turned the snuff stick in his mouth as he drove. They went over Thirteenth Street to Alton Road, on the bay side of South Beach, turned left and drove in silence until Cundo told him to go slow, to turn right on Sixth Street and then left on West Avenue. "Right here. Stop," Cundo said. "The Biscaya Hotel. Yes, this is good."

The old man was looking up at the building enclosed behind a chainlink fence. "I don't see no lights on in there."

"Is nobody live there anymore," Cundo said. "Is all a wreck.

People go in there and wreck it. One time the Biscaya Hotel, now is nothing."

They got out and Cundo led the way through an open gate in the fence, in close darkness through rubble—just like buildings he had seen in Cuba in the revolution—through overgrown bushes and weeds choking the walk that had once led through a garden along the side of the hotel. There were rusted beer cans and maybe rats. As they reached the open ground behind the hotel, Cundo watched the headlights on the MacArthur Causeway off to the left, not far, the cars coming out of darkness from the distant Miami skyline. The old man was missing it. His head was bent back to look up at all those dark windows—hotel this big and not one light showing. He should go inside and see the destruction, like it was in a war.

"How come nobody stays here?"

"It's all wrecked."

"Well, how come it closed up?"

Cundo said he didn't know, maybe the service was no good. He said, "Come on, we take a look. Be careful where you walk, you don't hurt yourself," leading the old man through weeds, out beyond the empty building that seemed to have eyes, following a walk now that led down to the seawall—the old man turning to look up at the nine stories of pale stone, black windows, staring, like he couldn't believe a place this size could be empty, not used for anything.

"Some bums stay there," Cundo said, "sometime."

"What's Richard do around here?"

"I tole you, didn't I? He has a boat," Cundo said. "See, he like to go out in his boat at night, be at peace. When he come back he come here. See? Tie it there by the dock."

"Richard drives a boat?"

"Yeah, a nice boat. Look out there in the water. You see a light moving?"

"They's about five, six of'em."

"Those are boats. One of them I think is Richard."

"How you tell?"

"Well, he isn't no place we look and his boat isn't at the dock over there. Tha's how you can tell. Yeah, I think one of them is

Richard. Watch those lights, see if one it comes here. He would be coming pretty soon.''

Cundo pulled his silk shirt out of his pants, reached around to the small of his back and felt the grip of the snubbie, the pistol Javier had sold him for one hundred and fifty dollars. Man, that gun kept pressing into his spine, killing him.

Miney said, ''That's Miami right there, is it?''

''Tha's a island right in front of you,'' Cundo said. ''Way off over there, that's the famous city of Miami, Florida. Yes, where you see all those lights.''

''There's an airplane,'' Miney said. ''Look at it up there.''

''Take you far away,'' Cundo said. He raised the .38 Special and from less than a foot away shot Miney in the back of the head. Man, that snubbie was loud. He didn't think it would be that loud. It caused him to hesitate and he had time to shoot Miney in the head only once more as he pitched forward into Biscayne Bay.

There was something he was supposed to throw in there, Richard had told him. He was right here looking at the water, but he couldn't think of what it was.

19

Buck Torres said to the man who had waited in Mrs. Truman's living room for the mailman and in unmarked cars among empty paper containers, waited in Mrs. Truman's piano parlor watching movies and in more unmarked cars, "Wait while I talk to the Major."

So LaBrava waited. Holding the phone. Staring at a photograph of an elephant named Rosie pulling a cement roller over a Miami Beach polo field sometime in the 1920s.

Jean Shaw and Maurice waited, seated at Maurice's dining-room table where the note waited, open, out of its envelope but creased twice so that it did not lie flat.

Buck Torres was talking to his superior, the major in charge of the Detective Bureau, Miami Beach Police. When Torres came back on he said, "It wasn't mailed, right? She found it in her car."

"This morning," LaBrava said. "The windows were broken last night at ten past ten, that's the exact time. But the note wasn't found till this morning."

"You went out to the car last night . . ."

"We heard it, glass breaking. We went out, but didn't see the note. It was on the front seat. The car was locked, the guy had to break the side window to drop the note inside. This morning, when the lady went out to her car, she found the note."

"Nothing came in the mail."

"I just told you," LaBrava said, "it was in the car."

"This's the first one."

"Right."

"Nothing in the mail, no out-of-state phone calls."

"Look, it's yours," LaBrava said. "You want to bring the FBI in that's up to you."

"The Major isn't sure."

LaBrava shifted his weight from one foot to the other, looking at the elephant named Rosie pulling the cement roller. There were small figures, men wearing blazers and white trousers in the background of the photograph. He said, "Well, it wouldn't be a bad idea if somebody looked at the note. You know what I mean? Got off their ass"—getting an edge in his tone—"since it's a murder threat if the money isn't paid." He had to take it easy, stay calm, but it was hard. He knew what Torres was up against.

Buck Torres said, "How much was it?"

"I told you, six hundred thousand."

"I thought you said six thousand," Buck Torres said, calm, and was silent.

"You gonna choke?" LaBrava said. "If you're gonna choke then get some help."

"Take it easy," Torres said. "I'll be over in a few minutes." He paused and said, "Joe, don't let anybody touch the note."

"I'm glad you mentioned that," LaBrava said and hung up. He was on edge, out of practice. Or on edge because he felt involved in this, a personal matter. But he shouldn't have said that about choking, or any of the dumb things he said. He said to Jean and Maurice, looking at Jean, "They don't know if they should call in the FBI."

Jean straightened. She said, "Well, *I* do."

"Or if they should come here or you should go there." LaBrava said, approaching the dining-room table. "This's a big one and it caught them by surprise. I can understand that, they have to stop and think for a minute. But Hector Torres, I know him, he's very good; he's their star, he's closed homicides over a year old. He'll look it over and then decide about the Bureau, whether they should bring in the feds or not. But technically it's not their case—at least not yet. I think, the way Torres sees it, it would be better if he came here—and I mean without any show, no police cars—than if we went down to the station. In case the hotel's being watched."

Jean said, "Well, it's fairly obvious who to look for. It can't be anyone else."

"Last night," Maurice said, "I thought it was some kids got high on something. You see in the paper this morning, Beirut, they blew up a Mercedes this time with a car bomb. A white one. You wonder why they didn't use a Ford or a Chevy." He looked at LaBrava. "You didn't see anybody?"

"It was too dark."

"It's Richard Nobles," Jean said. "As soon as I read the note—I can hear him, the way he talks."

"The hay-baling wire," LaBrava said. "His uncle, Miney Combs, when I was talking to him yesterday he mentioned hay-baling wire. He said Richard's dad used to twist a few lengths of it together and beat him with it when he was a boy, to teach him humility."

"It didn't work," Jean said.

"I looked at the note, that word jumped right out at me," LaBrava said. "He doesn't know how to spell it though."

He leaned over the back of a chair to look down at the typewritten message, a man who had experienced a great deal of waiting, a man who had read several thousand threatening letters at a desk in the Protective Research Section, Washington, D.C. This one was typed single-spaced on ruled steno notebook paper, a vertical red line down the center of the sheet, the top serrated where it had been torn from a spiral binding. The type was elite in a common serif-ed face. There were typos, capital letters struck over lowercase letters, as in the words *Hefty* and *Hay*. Only the one word, *baleing,* was misspelled. The type was clear, without filled-in or broken letters, or irregularities; though the touch of whoever had typed the note was not consistent, there were dark letters and several very faint ones. The I.D. technicians would photograph the note, print blow-ups, then check for latents with an iodine solution that would stiffen the paper and turn it a tie-dyed purple.

LaBrava pictured Nobles hunched over a portable typewriter pecking the note out slowly, painfully, with two fingers. The message read:

YOUR LIFE IS WORTH $600,000

You have three days to get the money. It must be <u>used</u> money with nothing smaller than a 20 or bigger than a $100 bill and don't say you can't get it. You are worth a sight more than that. Get 4000 100s, 3000 50s and 2500 20s. You are to put the money in a Hefty 30 gallon 2-ply trash bag. Put this one into another Hefty trash bag of the same size and tie it closed with some type of wire. Hay baleing wire is good. You will be told where to take the money. If you do not do as you are told you will die. If you try any tricks you will die. Look at your car. You know this is not just a threat. You have 2 DAYS to get the money and your car fixed. I am watching you.

Buck Torres came with an I.D. technician, both of them in shirt sleeves, without ties, Torres with a jacket over his arm. The I.D. technician, young and respectful, brought their holstered revolvers out of a black athletic bag and they hooked them on—both at the point of the right hip—before approaching the note lying on the dining-room table, moving toward it almost cautiously.

LaBrava, waiting a few feet away, watched them read the note, neither of them touching it. Jean and Maurice watched from the living room. Torres—white Latin male, forty-three, with hard-boned, tough-guy features that made him almost handsome—appeared older today. Immobile, lit by the hanging dining-room fixture, his face was a wood carving for several minutes, a man looking into a casket. He brought a notebook out of his hip pocket, sat down at the table and copied the typed message word for word. Then said something to the I.D. technician who used the eraser end of a pencil to slide the note and envelope into a file folder. The I.D. technician opened his black leather bag and Torres said to Jean, "Miss Shaw, we have to fingerprint you, if you don't mind, for elimination prints." He said, "You understand, if you're the only person who's touched the note."

Jean said, "Joe made sure of that."

Torres looked at LaBrava, waiting. "I'm glad you were here."

LaBrava was glad too, about some things. He was glad he had felt this coming and had got the shots of Nobles and the boat-lifter. He was glad Torres was handling it; but he knew what was going to happen now and he wasn't glad about the waiting.

There was no way to hurry it. There was no way yet to pull Richard Nobles out of a hotel room and throw him into a police car. LaBrava thought only of Nobles at this point. He believed once they had Richard they would also have the boat-lifter, the *Marielito*.

The I.D. technician left. They waited for Jean to wash her hands, then waited again while she made coffee in Maurice's kitchen, LaBrava knowing he would keep his mouth shut through the next part and listen to things he already knew about.

For the good part of an hour then, Jean told Buck Torres about Richard Nobles, Torres waiting for long pauses before he asked questions, always quietly, never interrupting, taking only a few notes. She had the photographs of Nobles ready, the ones LaBrava had given her. Torres studied them and looked at LaBrava.

"The same guy?"

"He's at the Paramount Hotel on Collins," LaBrava said. "Or was."

While Torres was making a phone call LaBrava went downstairs to the darkroom. He came back with a black and white eight-by-ten of Cundo Rey standing on the beachfront sidewalk, one hand going up to his face, almost to his chin, his eyes alive, a startled expression, as he looked directly into the camera held by the guy in the curvy straw hat sitting in the wheelchair.

"He's at the La Playa on Collins," LaBrava said. "Or was. I almost made him last night busting windows, but I wouldn't tell it in court. You don't want him for busting windows anyway. I'll give you the negatives, both guys."

Buck Torres made another phone call. He came back and asked Jean about Cundo Rey. Jean shook her head. She stared at the photograph a long time but still shook her head. Finally Torres asked the question LaBrava had been waiting to hear:

"Why six hundred thousand?"

Jean didn't answer right away.

Maurice said, "What difference does it make? It's a nice round number with a lot of oughts."

Torres said, "So is five hundred thousand. So is a million."

Jean said, "I've been wondering about that. The only reason I can think of, my condominium is worth about six hundred." She paused, looked at Maurice as though for help, then back to Torres and said, "I hate to admit it, but I did tell him one time my apartment was paid for. Richard has a very . . . sort of homespun way about him."

He does? LaBrava thought.

"A country-boy charm."

He remembered her saying that, in this room, telling about Nobles that first time.

"He gives you the feeling you can confide in him, trust him," Jean said. "I think I told him the apartment was really the only thing I had, making a point that appearances can be misleading, that a lot of wealth down here is like a Hollywood set, a facade." She said, "Now that I think of it . . . I remember one day in the parking lot I ran into him. He mentioned a couple in the building had their condominium up for sale and were asking four hundred and fifty thousand. I told him they ran from about four to six hundred, as you go up. He knows, of course, I live on the top floor, oceanfront."

LaBrava listened to her quiet delivery, Jean Shaw being contrite, owning up. He wondered if it was hard for her to tell it.

"Obviously I misjudged him. As I told Maury, and Joe, you were there"—looking at him for a moment—"Richard comes on as a friendly, honest guy; so I was nice to him, I didn't treat him like one of the help."

"But he intimidated you," Maurice said. "Kind a guy, you give him a hand he grabs it, he wants more. What'd I tell you you first mentioned the guy? I said he's out for something, he's gonna take you for all he can get."

"You did," Jean said, "I know."

"I told you, guys like that, they been working Miami Beach since the day they built the bridge. Now they hop on the freeway, go up to Boca, Palm Beach."

Torres said, "Did he ever come right out and ask for anything?"

Jean said no. "But he seemed to take for granted he could stop by whenever he felt like it. After a while he became—the only word I can think of is possessive."

LaBrava remembered her saying, that first night, when she had told them about Nobles, *The way he walks around the apartment, looks at my things.*

But she didn't say it this time.

Torres said, "Have you seen him since you've been staying here at the hotel?"

"No."

"But he knows you're here."

She said, "That's fairly obvious, isn't it?"

Torres was thoughtful, arranging information in his mind and coming down to: "Six hundred thousand, it's a lot of money."

And LaBrava remembered her saying that first night, *Then there's nothing to worry about, because I don't have any.*

But this time she didn't mention that either.

In the afternoon LaBrava took Maurice's car and drove past the Paramount Hotel and the La Playa. The Miami Beach detectives were hard to spot using confiscated cars rather than the plain unmarked Dodge and Plymouth models they drove on duty. He made one cop doing surveillance in a red Chevy cab, No. 208, knowing that official Central Cab numbers were in the 1100s or higher. When he returned to the Della Robbia a Southern Bell truck was parked in front.

Torres was going according to the handbook: he'd got State Attorney OK for a wire tap on Maurice's line and was letting the telephone company do the installation. They would put a second phone in Maurice's apartment along with the tap. If a call came for Jean Shaw Maurice would use the second phone to call Southern Bell security and they'd trap Maurice's line to get the source of the incoming call. At the telephone switching office they would install Pen Registers on the lines of both the Paramount and La Playa hotels to record the numbers of all out-going calls; no court approval required. A police command post, with phones and a recorder, was located in an area that used to be part of the Della Robbia kitchen, next to the darkroom. LaBrava believed the taps and traps would prove to be a waste of time.

Torres knocked on his door a few minutes past six. Torres said they had the Eldorado towed to a Cadillac dealership, dusted it for prints and left it to have the glass replaced. For a while then they sat with cans of beer, Torres quiet, tired; LaBrava patient, still in his waiting period. He had resolved, as a civilian, not to ask questions or offer opinions unless asked. But when Torres said, "Well, all we can do now is wait."

LaBrava said, "For how long?"

"There you are," Torres said. "Do it right I need almost half the Detective Bureau, pull three shifts a day at three locations. They're sitting in cars, hotel lobbies—all the bad guys hanging out would love to hear about it. See, if it goes down soon, right away—get the money in two days, deliver on the third—we're all set. Otherwise I have to bring in the *federales.*"

"He's not gonna call," LaBrava said.

"You don't think so."

"He was a cop. He knows about traps and voice prints."

"Yeah, but he's strange," Torres said. "You ever hear of one like this? The guy wants a garbage bag full of money. He says, use hay-baling wire, it's good. Guy's right off the farm. Look how he tried to intimidate, use that old protection shit. Like he was trying to get caught."

"You know where he is?"

"Sure, he's at his hotel. He walks up to Wolfie's, walks back. Only place he's gone."

"You got a tap on his room phone?"

"His Honor the judge said no. So all we got is the Pen Register. He calls her we'll know it."

"What about the boat-lifter?"

"He hasn't been home."

"He check out?"

"No, he just hasn't been around. We had a guy owes us one go in and ask for him."

"Why don't you take a look in his room?"

"His Honor the judge said no."

"What about the boat-lifter's car?"

"Nowhere around. You can't miss that kind of car, but it's no place we've heard, Dade, Broward or Palm Beach."

"What bothers you the most?"

"About what?"

"The whole thing. How it looks."

"Is the guy this dumb? That's what I keep asking," Torres said. "You say he was a cop, he was a gypsy. Then a rent-a-cop, four bucks an hour. He's got a license for a three-fifty-seven, that's pretty interesting. But does he know how to work extortion or is he dreaming?"

"What else?"

"I don't believe he knows what he's doing."

"Thank you, Jesus—you hope and pray. Please let him fuck up, quick. What if nothing happens?"

"The Major says after three days we bring in the Bureau. Let the college boys run it. Send the letter to Washington, they analyze it sideways, upside down and tell us it's a Smith-Corona on steno notebook paper, done with a black ribbon. Oh, is that right? Hey, thanks. Let's go, boys, get out there and find that fucking Smith-Corona. The guy moves, Joe, or he's full of shit and he doesn't."

"Maybe waits till some other time."

"I got three days, that's all."

"He contacts her again. Then what?"

"She makes the delivery, we go with her."

"With the six hundred thousand?"

"There's no other way."

"You can cut up paper."

"What did the note say, Joe? *You try any tricks you will die.* We have to believe that. If we say, 'Oh, he's full of shit, don't believe it,' and it turns out the guy's crazy and he whacks her? We don't look so good. The woman, she looks terrible. Maybe the way it has to be, the way it turns out, he has to see the money before we can touch him. It has to look real. You know that. Long as we don't let the movie star or the money out of our sight. Then it's up to him, how good he is. But nobody's that good and can sound so fucking dumb."

"You ever see one of her movies?"

"I probably did, I don't remember. I know her name and she looks kind a familiar, that's all. Was she a big star?"

"No, but she was good. I mean she was good."

"I like to see her sometime."

"What about the money? Where's she getting it? Six hundred thousand in cash?"

"You kidding? Miami banks, they got that lying around in boxes. Same ones the dope guys used."

LaBrava didn't say anything for a moment. "She tell you she could get the money?"

"I asked her, I said I don't want to get personal, but are you able to put up that much? She said yes. She said since we know who it is she doesn't consider it much of a risk. Also, considering the fact the guy's a dummy."

"She said that?"

"Words, you know, like that. She seems pretty sure Richard's going to fuck up."

"But first she has to come up with the money," LaBrava said.

"Where she gets it," Torres said, "she could have it under her bed, it's none of my business."

"You're gonna copy the serial numbers."

"Photograph the bills. I assume at the bank, I don't know yet. But if the guy gets away with them, they're gone."

LaBrava was silent. He sipped his beer, looked out the window at the sky over the ocean, all that space in fading light; it was pure out there, nothing going on. Dirty ideas came about indoors. Now Torres looked out the window. He saw no answers there and turned back to LaBrava.

"What bothers you the most?"

"Same thing you're wondering. Is he that dumb?"

"I have to believe it."

"Or does he want you to think he's dumb?"

"He doesn't have to try very hard."

"But what if he's not the guy in charge?"

Torres had to think about that one. He said, "Who, the boat-lifter?"

"Cundo's been around a few days looking things over," LaBrava said. "The note's delivered, he drops out of sight. He gives you Richard to watch. Maybe to keep you busy while he operates."

"I wish we could check him out, see what he did in Cuba."

"He did time. According to David Vega by way of Guilli and Paco Boza."

"You got more informants than I do."

"I don't bust them."

"Maybe you can find out some more about the boat-lifter, what he did."

"Maybe all you have to do," LaBrava said, "is pick up Richard. Are you smarter than he is?"

"Jesus, I hope so."

"Put on a show, like you got hard evidence. Then tell him you'll trade off for the boat-lifter. Richard loves to make deals with policemen. Pick up the boat-lifter and put 'em in a room together. The one that comes out alive gets ten to twenty-five."

"Yeah, or they both walk."

"It's an idea."

Torres said, "You know what I get, listen to you say something like that? What I feel?"

"Tell me."

"You don't seem too worried about the movie star, her best interest."

LaBrava didn't say anything.

"I don't want those guys for 'Attempted,' I want them with the garbage bag in their hand. So what I have to do, I have to keep my eyes on her and on the garbage bag. Never let them out of my sight. That's the only thing I have to worry about. I don't want her to lose her life on account of me and I don't want to look bad," Torres said. "In that order."

20

It was like one of her movies.

It came into his mind at different times now because of what Buck Torres had said. "You don't seem too worried about the movie star."

He had to think about that, see if it was true. If it was true then it was because he was getting the two Jean Shaws mixed up. The real one and the one on the screen. He had never worried about the one on the screen because she could take care of herself, or because she wasn't a person who deserved a lot of sympathy. She was often the perpetrator, never the victim. But now she was in something that was like one of her movies and she *was* the victim in this one and not playing the part of the spider woman or the other woman or the girl with the greedy eyes. This time she was the good girl. Except that good girls were usually blond, wonderfully wide-eyed, fairly chaste, and ended up with Robert Mitchum, Dick Powell . . .

Victor Mature.

He could see her, a glimpse of her with Victor Mature in a room with barred windows. Blowing cigarette smoke in his face. (Good girls didn't blow smoke of any kind.) The bars casting striped shadows in the bare room. And Victor Mature making his jaw muscle jump but not blinking at the smoke. Not pissed off as much as disappointed. Near the end of the picture . . . She blows the smoke at him, walks into a courtroom and is sentenced to life in prison. For murder.

She screams at the judge, "I didn't do it! I swear I didn't!" And they lead her off as the newspaper guys are running out putting on their hats and Victor Mature is standing with the good girl now, the professional virgin, in the back of the courtroom, Victor clenching his jaw but with a wistful look in his eyes.

And he remembered Franny Kaufman saying to Jean, after they had seen *Let It Ride* and Franny was trying to identify another Jean Shaw picture, "Your husband commits suicide . . . what a guy . . . and makes it look like you did it." And Jean said . . .

Jean said, "Oh, that one."

And he had turned from Maurice's bar with a drink in each hand and heard Jean's car windows being smashed.

Like one of her movies?

The movie audience didn't worry about the girl who played Lila in *Let It Ride*. Poisoned her husband in *Nightshade*. Had her lover thrown off the Golden Gate Bridge in *Deadfall*. They could worry about the good girl if they wanted to, but the good girl always won out in the end. The good guy saying to her, "You crazy kid, don't you know it was you all the time? How could I ever fall for a dame like that?" And the dame, out of the picture, is saying, "Swell."

So he had to remind himself: she's the good girl in this one. But this one isn't a movie and doesn't have to end the way movies end. Okay. Except that when he thought of the real Jean Shaw he saw the same confidence, the same quiet awareness that he saw in the screen Jean Shaw. He had to somehow separate the two images in order to be able to worry about her. If there were background-music scores in real life it would be easier to identify her.

There she was in his mind again with Victor Mature. Blowing smoke at him. Bits of the picture coming back. He believed it was the same Jean Shaw picture Franny had seen and mentioned the other night.

Now it was the morning of the day after the note was delivered. He had not yet seen Jean or Maurice. He knocked on Franny's door, waited, went down to the lobby and there she was surrounded by Della Robbia ladies. At first he thought she was giving them a skin-cream demonstration, using one of the old ladies, Mrs. Heffel, who sat rigidly in front of her.

But she wasn't. Franny was sketching the woman in pastels. She looked up at him and said, "Well, say it, Joe."

He was surprised. "I thought you did hotels."

"Sit down, I'll tell you about it."

At this point he saw the cop across the lobby motion to him: a young, clean-cut guy in plainclothes standing by the alcove that led to the darkroom and the command post in the hotel kitchen. Walking away he heard Franny say, "Hey, Joe, what's going on?"

The young cop glanced around before saying, "Sergeant Torres, I'm suppose to tell you, wants you to meet him at the M.E.'s office, Jackson Memorial."

"For what?"

"They got a floater he wants you to identify."

"Why me?"

The young cop didn't know.

The body of Miney Combs lay naked, autopsied and closed, on a metal tray-table inside a refrigerated semi-trailer.

The Dade County Morgue, Jackson Memorial Hospital, had become overbooked since Miami's jump in population, the 120,000 who rode in on the Mariel boatlift. Some of them were now killing each other. So the Medical Examiner had rented the refrigerated semitrailer to accommodate the overflow. It stood behind the morgue and at one time had displayed the name *Burger King* on the side panels. But the words had finally been painted over and it was no longer something to write about in the paper.

LaBrava stared at the man's face, bloated, mutilated, no longer a face he would recognize, as Buck Torres told him about gunshot entrance wounds in the back of the head, one through and through, one hollow-nose .38 caliber slug deflected-hard-headed old guy—lodged within the frontal lobe of the brain. The old man's body had been picked up by the Coast Guard on its way out Government Cut on the tide. He had been in the water close to twenty-four hours. LaBrava was called because his name and address were found in Miney Combs' wallet, written in ballpoint pen on a five-by-seven memo sheet imprinted with the name *STAR SECURITY, Private Protection Means Crime Prevention*. The dead man's pickup truck had been found in front of the abandoned Biscaya Hotel.

His gray work clothes, work shoes, keys, a can of Copenhagen, wallet containing a driver's license and thirty-eight dollars, were in a paper bag wedged between legs that resembled marble tubes about to burst. A white tag was attached to the big toe of his right foot. Torres said no, they didn't find a snuff stick. What was a snuff stick?

LaBrava stared at the bulge of the old man's body, the crude incision from breastbone to navel, and again at the mutilated face.

LaBrava said, "He's Richard Nobles' uncle." He said, "I sent him over there, to Richard's hotel." After several moments he said, "Well, you have a reason to pick him up now, don't you?"

He could hear himself, his voice, amazed that he sounded as calm as he did. He was not calm inside his body. He felt his waiting period coming to an end.

He went home. Jean's car stood on the street, whole again. He wanted to see her, but he went to the darkroom instead and printed a set of Richard Nobles eight-by-tens. Then sat alone in his living room looking at the former rent-a-cop Franny thought was a hunk. A hunk of what? He wanted to say to Franny, "Look at him closely. Watch him move. Listen to him talk."

Could you lean on a guy like Richard? Scare him? Make him run?

Torres called in the late afternoon and said to stop by.

LaBrava walked down Collins. Was the guy dumb or not? When he reached the La Playa Hotel he hesitated. Was the boat-lifter running it or had he pulled out? LaBrava continued on to the MBPD Detective Bureau, the windowless stucco building built like a blockhouse on the corner of First and Meridian.

The squad room inside was like all the squad rooms he had ever seen in older police buildings: different types of desks and tables bunched in rows to conserve space, a few men at desks who might have been athletes at one time, solidly built, or had the look of career noncoms in civilian clothes. No one wore a shoulder holster anymore; they packed Smiths on their hipbones, short-barreled mags with big grips. In a corner of the room was the holding cell—and this was different than all the others he had ever seen—made of wrought-iron bars, the kind of ornamental grillwork you might find on a Spanish patio.

Buck Torres' desk was in the opposite corner, next to the door that led to the lavatory, the coffeemaker and the four-and-a-half by five-and-a-half interrogation room. LaBrava sat down and Torres pushed Richard Nobles' *Advice of Rights* toward him, the Miranda sheet.

"We interviewed Richie."

LaBrava saw Richard's initials after each statement on the sheet—the Buck Torres method of avoiding surprises in court. Interviewees read their rights aloud, initialed each one as they went along and signed just below the *Waiver of Rights* statement. The signature read *Richie Nobles.*

"You show him Miney Combs?"

"First, before we brought him here. Driving over to Miami he says, 'You guys are making a big mistake. You maybe think you have something'—called me *partner*—'but you can't touch me for nothing.' "

LaBrava listened to each word.

"We take him inside the truck over there. I'm going to tell you something," Torres said. "It was a shock to him. He wasn't acting, it was a shock."

"Is he dumb?" LaBrava said.

Torres hesitated. "He's not smart enough to fake it."

"You have to be smart to be an actor?"

"Joe, he wasn't faking it. He sees the old guy, he couldn't believe it."

"He identified him?"

"Sure, His Uncle Miney. Surprised. 'What is Uncle Miney doing here?' "

"So you sat down with him in the little room, the closet, and got intimate."

"He says he had no idea the old man was down here. Swears he didn't see him. The desk clerk at Richie's hotel puts the old man in the lobby a couple hours or more the evening of the day before yesterday. But he can't put Richie with him. He can put a little Latin dude with him . . ."

"Like a boat-lifter?"

"Like maybe a boat-lifter, guy with wavy hair and an earring. But he can't put Richie with him."

"You ask Richie if anybody he knows saw the old man?"

"Sure. He says no. Let's say the Latin dude is the boat-lifter. Okay, I can put him with the old man, but I can't put him with Richie. I want to, man, but I can't."

"You know Johnbull, drives for Central?"

"Guy, he's always pissed off about something?"

"That one. He can put Richie with the boat-lifter. Find out if Johnbull saw the boat-lifter's Trans Am at the hotel the same time the desk clerk saw the Latin dude and if they left together in the car."

"No, they must've left in the old man's truck, because it was sitting at the Biscaya and the old man had the keys. We got latents, all over that truck. Okay now, if it's the boat-lifter, this guy Cundo Rey, we got to get his prints from Volusia County, where they had him on possession of a stolen motor vehicle. That would be pretty nice if we can put him in the truck. Richie swears he never saw it."

"Maybe," LaBrava said, "but he knew the old man was looking for him. Talk to the guy, Joe Stella, at Star Security, Lantana, where Richie used to work. There's no way he can be clean. You're gonna find out he sent the boat-lifter to get rid of him. What do you think?"

"To kill him?"

"That's one way."

"Richie was shocked, Joe. I'm not kidding."

"How many floaters has he seen, gunshot? You can know a person's dead, but when you see him like that . . . You know what I mean."

"Joe, the guy let us look in his room."

LaBrava was aware of voices in the squad room for the first time, a telephone ringing.

"It was clean," Torres said. "Like he had the maid come in every hour."

"He show you his gun?"

"And his license. He hands me the piece, says, Here, you want to check it?' "

"Looking you right in the eye."

"He didn't do the old man, Joe."

There was a silence again, until LaBrava said, "You mind if I suggest something?"

"What?"

"Pick up a guy at the La Playa Hotel named David Vega, he's a *Marielito,* and ask him about the boat-lifter. See if you can find out if Cundo's got a gun and happened to buy any hollow-nose, steel-jacket thirty-eights. There's a guy at the hotel sells guns and ammo, anything you want."

"How do you know that?"

"I took his picture. Holding a sawed-off shotgun."

"Jesus Christ," Torres said.

"I asked him, 'You don't care who sees your picture?' He's stoned most of the time. He said, no, it would be good for his business."

"Jesus Christ," Torres said.

"David Vega's the guy you want. If he gives you the gun seller, do whatever you feel like, but ask him about Cundo first. If you can't find David Vega look for a guy named Guilli, he deals out on the Pier."

Torres said, "How do you know all these guys?"

"They like to have their picture taken. But let's get back to Richie. Was he nervous anytime?"

"Once we got here he was cool. Or he acted surprised at everything."

"Acted," LaBrava said.

"Eyes open real wide. Who, me? They all do that. But I think he was waiting to see if I'm going to mention a note or the six hundred thousand or if he knows a movie star."

"You didn't though."

"I can play dumb too. But he knows we know. Last night and this morning he's walking around Collins Avenue, Lincoln Mall, he goes in a place, comes out the back, or all of a sudden he crosses the street against the light. Bullshit stuff. He follows girls a lot, makes the moves, then looks around, wants to make sure he has an audience. He does everything but wave at my guys. I'm finished talking to him about the old man, he says, 'There anything else you want to ask me about?' You see what I mean? He knows. He's telling us he knows."

"You turn him loose?"

"What have I got? Man, if I brought in every suspect fits something like this I'd have to pick up half the neighborhood. I told him to stay close by."

"It didn't bother him?"

"He gives me some you-all shit, he be obliged we get the scudder 'at done it."

"Is he dumb?" LaBrava said.

"Guy's a showoff."

"But is he dumb?"

"I think it could be what you said before. The boat-lifter's running it and Richie's the beard."

"Put a clown suit on him," LaBrava said, thoughtful, wondering. "Got him in the trick bag and he doesn't know it. You think?"

"Could be."

"If he's dumb enough," LaBrava said. "It keeps coming back to that."

"And if the boat-lifter is smarter than he is."

"Or if there's somebody else smarter than both of them," LaBrava said. "Have you thought of that?"

"Maybe I should talk to the movie star again," Torres said. "See who else's been in her life since she became a widow."

"It wouldn't hurt," LaBrava said.

21

Paco Boza came for his wheelchair, a happy guy.

Lana was back with him. She hated Hialeah, it was like in the country and she was a big-city girl. She loved her photograph. She wanted LaBrava to send it someplace, some magazine, be a centerfold girl. It was early evening and they were out on the sidewalk, the street quiet, Paco wearing his straw hat cocked, about to take off in his wheelchair.

LaBrava said, "You know the big blond guy."

"The Silver Kid," Paco said, "of course."

"I want somebody to deliver a note to him, at his hotel."

"Sure."

"And write it."

"What does it say?"

"I want him to come to the park tonight, 1:00 A.M., across from the Play House Bar."

"Sign your name?"

"No, sign it *C.R.*"

"Just *C.R.*"

"That's the *Marielito,* the one with the earring."

"Oh," Paco said, "yes, I remember."

"But I have to make sure the big blond guy gets the message and not the police."

Paco said, "Man, you got something going on."

"If I can, I'd like to get hold of a baseball bat," LaBrava said. "But I think the stores are closed."

"You and this guy going to play ball? In the dark? Never mind, don't tell me," Paco said. "I got one for softball, you can use."

"I'll take good care of it," LaBrava said.

Nobles wished he had a car; he'd take the cops on a tour of Dade County, see if they were any good at tailing. Man, he would love to get them up in the Big Scrub, lose their ass in two minutes. This walking the streets, stopping at bars, was getting to be a bunch of shit. One more day he could take off. Tomorrow night sometime.

When he got back to the hotel, about ten, the desk clerk waved and held out a plain white envelope with his name printed on it in pencil. It was not only sealed, there was a hunk of pink chewing gum stuck to the flap. The desk clerk worked his eyebrows up and down as he said a girl delivered it, a little Latin mama. Nobles said, a girl uh? He took the envelope across the lobby, looking at his name that some kid or halfwit might've printed. The message inside, on plain white paper, printed in pencil, said for him to come to the park tonight . . . and *Do not bring police* and *Do not phone.* Signed, *C.R.*

It didn't make sense. Cundo was supposed to be long gone, hiding somewhere until it was his turn again. Unless something had happened to him or they were watching him.

But the cops didn't know anything about Cundo. How could they?

Maybe the little booger was sick.

What Nobles finally decided, he'd slip out of the hotel and go have a look. It would be like a dry run, disappear in the night. Then do it the same way tomorrow when he'd take off for good. He wondered if he should pay his hotel bill before he left. Shit, he needed money. The idea came to him then: long as he was out, going over to the park anyway, he could mug a queer and pick up some change. Queers—he couldn't imagine why—always had jobs that paid good money. Slip out like old Zorro used to do it with his mask and sword. Zip, zip, zip, mark a big fucking Z on the wall. Soldiers come busting in, old Zorro he's back sitting by the fire, pretending *he's* queer. There were enough real ones out there, hanging around the south end of the park, he ought to be able to cut a straggler. He wondered why he hadn't thought of it before. Man, he needed something to *do.*

At 1:05 A.M. Buck Torres got a call at home from one of his guys on the Paramount Hotel surveillance detail. Nobles had temporarily disappeared. Torres, lying in bed in the dark, said, "Temporarily. Oh, that means he told you he was coming back?" No, it meant he didn't have anything with him, any luggage. Torres said, "Oh, did he check in with luggage?" Then said, "Forget it, tell me what happened." Resigned himself and listened to the flat, boring tone of the guy's story: how Richard had walked out of the hotel at 12:32 giving them the same old shit, looking back every once in a while, walked south on Collins to Sixteenth, over Sixteenth to the St. Moritz, walked through the hotel to the beach and that was the last they saw of him. There was no way two guys could keep a subject under surveillance out on that beach, a beach that big, at night. You would have to stay within twenty feet of the subject and even then it would be almost impossible with just two guys. There was a moon but also clouds; it was supposed to rain tomorrow, intermittent showers until sometime in the afternoon. Torres listened to the weather report, his guy trying to give him at least some predictable information. Torres suggested they go back to the Paramount and wait. He called the Della Robbia command post and told them to keep their eyes open, Richard was loose.

Hell, he just waited till there was cloud cover, ducked over that hump of sand that was like a low hogback down the length of the beach near the water, kept to the smooth hard-pack where the surf was washing in and headed south. Nothing to it. Around Tenth Street he came up, crossed the beach to Lummus Park and had it made. From here down there was more vegetation—lot of screw pine and what looked like pitchapple, but was probably seagrape trimmed back; kind of dark, creepy place he was used to. Hardly any people. Pairs here and there on benches he'd pass and leave be. First rule of fairy-hawking, pick a stray. Let the sweet boy have the first word. *H'ar you tonight?* Just fine, h'ar you? *Beautiful night, ain't it?* Ain't it though. *Are you tired? Would you like me to give you a back rub?* No, but you can do old Hank the shank if you've a mind. Let the boy get down there and gobble, then as you feel the juice commence to flow, club that sucker with a right hook to put him away. Pick him clean as he whimpers and moans. Then walk, don't run. Only thing queers don't blow is a whistle.

There was one.

Sweet boy sitting on the wall with his hands folded.

But he'd better check on Cundo first. So Nobles walked out to the street. The Play House Bar was almost right across the way.

There didn't seem to be any little Cubans hanging around anyplace. Well, it wasn't one o'clock yet. He'd make a quick score and then look for him. So he cut back through the trees to where that boy was waiting, sitting on the low cement wall, waiting for a lover. Shit, guy like that, anybody'd do.

Sucker had designs—like big flowers, Nobles saw as he got closer—all over his shirt. No, they weren't flowers, they were palm trees and sailboats. Guy had trees and boats for Christ sake all over his sport shirt.

The guy looked up at him, just a few feet away, and said, "Richie, how you doing?"

Nobles had to take a moment. He said, "Je-sus Christ, look-it who's here. I been wondering what in the hell ever become of you, you know it? It's something, meeting like this again, ain't it?" Nobles glanced around, both ways. It was nice and quiet here.

He had time. He couldn't think of the guy's name now. Joe something, like a dago name. He sure did not look like any government agent Nobles had ever seen. It was in his mind to make a remark about that when he remembered just in time, shit no, he wasn't suppose to know anything about the guy or even he was the guy'd been taking his picture and was a friend of the cops. He had to realize all that at once now, try to play dumb and not make any mistakes.

What shook him was, thinking that, right *as* he was thinking that, the guy saying, "Are you dumb, Richard?"

He didn't know how to answer. The guy wasn't calling him dumb, he was asking him if he was, like he wanted to know. Then the guy was confusing him some more, saying, "Hay-baling wire is good."

Je-sus Christ.

"Your Uncle Miney said your dad used to whip you with it. Teach you humility."

Nobles stared at him.

"But that isn't something you need for extortion, is it? And if you're any good and get the six hundred grand, the last thing you're gonna be is humble, huh?"

"Oh my," Nobles said, "we sure think we're clever, don't we?"

"You're not supposed to know what I'm talking about."

Nobles said, "Mister, I'm gonna run my hands over you. I feel a wire, me and you are gonna say nighty-night. I don't, well, we can see where it goes. Stand up and turn around."

LaBrava got up slowly, raising his arms straight out to the sides as he turned, and Nobles moved in close to run his hands up to LaBrava's shoulders, took hold of the muscles close to his neck and began to pinch hard. LaBrava tried to hunch and twist free and Nobles grabbed him by the hair with one hand and punched him in the back of the neck with the other, jabbed him hard with the knuckles you use to knock on a door.

"So you're the blindsider," Nobles said, and rabbit-punched him again. "Huh, is that right?" Pulled up on his hair and drove those knuckles in again. "You the blindsider?" Rabbit-punched him again. Then punched him with shoulder behind it, letting go of the hair. LaBrava fell forward to hit the low wall made of cement and coral and had to catch himself, hold on with his thighs to keep from going over. He hung there, moving his head carefully from side to side, feeling pain, throbs of it up through his skull, and seeing black objects crawling around the edges of his vision. Nobles, behind him, kept at it. "Yeah, blindsider, they like to sneak up on you, hit you when you're not looking." LaBrava was looking down at sand on the beach side of the wall, close to his face, hoping for his head to clear. High overhead clouds moved and moonlight edged toward the wall—Nobles saying, yeah, goddamn blindsider, I love to get me a blindsider—and now LaBrava was looking at the softball bat lying in the sand, the bat the same color as sand. His hands, hanging over the wall, went to the handle right-over-left to bat right-handed. He was about ready.

When he came up with it he pushed off the wall with his knees, came around from the left and saw Nobles doing a quick backstep jig, right hand going into his silver jacket—LaBrava seeing it and believing in that moment he should be hitting from the other side tonight. But it was all right. Nobles brought up his left arm for protection, instinct jerking it up, and LaBrava found it between wrist and elbow with a bone-cracking, line-drive swing that brought a gasp from the big guy, and his right hand out of the silver jacket empty to grab hold of the broken arm. LaBrava came back for good measure with a left-side, cross-hand swing to pound shoulder and muscle, getting a grunt this time, Nobles covering his head with his good arm. So LaBrava hit him across the shins and that brought him down to the grass with a scream, trying to curl up, cover himself. LaBrava was finished with the bat. He dropped it as he straddled the big guy, yanked the .357 Smith out of his belt and worked the blunt bluesteel tip, once again, into Nobles' mouth.

LaBrava said, feeling he should tell him, "I think you're in the wrong line of work. You've got size and you look mean enough, but I believe you lack desire. Open your eyes."

Nobles had them squeezed closed and seemed in pain. LaBrava slipped the gun out of his mouth, barely out, laying the sight under the lower lip, and Nobles said, "Jesus Christ, I'm hurt. My goddamn arm is broke." He turned his head to look at it, outstretched on the grass.

LaBrava said, "I hope it is. But let me tell you what's more important, to your welfare as well as your health. You like to deal. I think you ought to make one, give the cops the boat-lifter."

"The what?"

"Cundo Rey, your little buddy."

Nobles stared at him, maybe thinking faster than he had ever thought in his life, but thinking within his limitations. He did appear dumb, the vacant look giving him away.

"Let the cops have Cundo . . . and whoever else you got. They'll make you a nice deal."

Look at him thinking. Now trying to show some pain, going for sympathy.

"The cops have you made, Richard. You know that. They can put Cundo with your uncle and you with Cundo."

"I never *saw* Uncle Miney. I told 'em that."

"Doesn't matter," LaBrava said. "You don't give 'em Cundo Rey they'll pick the little Cuban up—guy like him, he's hard to miss—they'll offer him the same kind of deal and he'll give 'em Mr. Richard Nobles. He'd be dumb if he didn't."

Nobles was listening closely to this.

"He gets something like five to twenty up at Raiford, you move up there for life. He'll do three out of the five, and if you don't get him in the yard, he walks.''

Nobles said, ''Wait a second. What one are we talking about?''

''Take your pick. Murder first degree or the threat of it, for money. Either one'll put you away.'' LaBrava paused, looking down at him. Big dumb blond-haired clown. He did look mean. But deep down where it counted, all he could claim to be was a snitch. ''Go make your deal and let the state attorney get you a lawyer. You'll come out all right.''

He was so quiet now, staring up, moonlight catching his eyes.

''First thing in the morning,'' LaBrava said. ''You don't want to spend the night locked up.'' Keeping his tone mild, almost soothing. What a nice guy. ''You want, I'll tell the lady never mind about getting the money, and the trash bag. Say you changed your mind.''

Those eyes staring up at him.

''You want me to tell her that?''

Those dumb eyes in moonlight began to change, trying for a different look, creasing, getting a crafty gleam.

Nobles said, ''I know who you are. You and all them other copsuckers, you're about to get the surprise of your life.'' That greasy tone sliding out and his mouth barely moving. ''Now get offa me or I'm gonna have your ass up on charges.''

See? Try to be reasonable what happens? He'd be talking about his rights next. Waving a Xeroxed copy of his Miranda sheet.

LaBrava cocked the Smith, for effect, for the sound of it, stuck the tip of the barrel into Nobles' mouth, hooking the front sight in behind his upper teeth and saw him gag as the gleam went out of his eyes.

He said, ''Richard, are you trying to fuck with me?'' Getting that flat, effortless cop sound. He believed in this moment he would have been a good one.

He said, ''Richard, I got the gun. You don't have it, I do. But you threaten me. I don't understand that. What'd you think I was gonna do?'' He drew the barrel out enough to lay it on Nobles' lower lip. ''Tell me.''

Nobles said, ''You don't have no right—''

See? LaBrava shoved the barrel back into his mouth. It was that goddamn Miranda thing. They packed, swaggered, picked on and scared the shit out of civilians, then ran and got behind Miranda.

He said, "Richard," wanting to make it clear but no big deal. "If I got the gun, asshole, I got the right." The way a Metro cop would say it. The one doing paperwork sniffing whiteout wanting to get back on the street so bad. He knew something the Metro cop knew. He could sit on Nobles' belly and feel him breathing in and out beneath him, feel the man's life between his own thighs, and be detached and deal with the man on a mutual basis of understanding. It was a strange feeling, but natural; like discovering something about yourself you never knew before. He felt that he could kill Nobles; in this moment he could. Pull the trigger. But he didn't know what he would feel the moment after, with the sound fading and hearing the surf again. Something was happening to him. The cop in him coming out. After all that waiting. Nine years or more of official waiting, hanging back steely-eyed and looking smart. He had heard Buck Torres say one time to a witness, pleading for information, "I give you my word as a man." Not as a policeman, a man. He would never forget that. It was what it came down to here, in this situation. Man to man he said to Nobles, "Bullshit time's over. Are you dumb?"

He eased the barrel out and watched that all-American face, pale in moonlight, move from side to side.

"I can't hear you."

"No, I ain't dumb. Jesus."

"How do you know who I am?"

"I don't."

"You said, a minute ago, 'I know who you are.' "

Look at him thinking, trying to be careful. LaBrava moved the barrel along the curve of Nobles' chin. "They wire your mouth shut for a broken jaw. Talk while you can."

"You already broke my goddamn arm!"

"See what I mean? . . . How do you know who I am?"

"I heard, around."

"Where?"

"On the street. I heard you live at that ho-tel."

LaBrava drew the barrel down the bridge of his nose. Look at those eyes, trying to be sincere.

"I heard you was a secret agent of some kind with the gover'-ment. Listen, I know some of those boys. Maybe're friends of yours. Up in Jacksonville."

"Who told you?"

"Nobody, I just heard. Was some guy, you know, in a bar."

"What's the surprise?"

"What?"

"You said, 'You're about to get the surprise of your life.' What's the surprise?"

"I was just, you know, talking. Jesus, my goddamn arm hurts something terrible."

"What's the surprise, Richard?"

"Nothing. I was talking is all."

See? It reached the point every time where you had to deliver or let the guy up. Tell him one time what you're going to do. Tell him twice, he knows you're full of shit. Once you started to lose it it was over. LaBrava leaned in closer, eye to eye, the gun barrel beneath Nobles' chin, raising it slightly.

"The surprise is how six hundred thousand dollars disappear. Look at me, Richard. The surprise—you see all the cops standing around scratching their head. You're undoing the baling wire, opening the garbage bag, taking out all that money. Look at me, Richard."

He did. Nobles met his eyes and said, "I ain't done nothing."

"What else do you see, Richard?"

"I ain't done nothing."

He was losing it.

"What movie did she show you?"

"What?"

"She said she showed you a movie."

He was getting it back. Maybe.

Nobles was thinking again. "She told you that?"

"What was the name of it?"

"I don't know, I forget."

"Who was in it?"

"You kidding me? Shit, I don't know."

"Where's your partner?"

"I don't know—I don't have no partner."

"The little Cuban."

"I met the booger one time, 'at's all."

"You came to meet him tonight."

"Shit, it was you. God*damn,* we're clever."

He felt tired knowing he was losing it. It was hard to keep it up unless you were honestly detached enough to go all the way and break the guy's jaw looking into his eyes. He could sit on the guy all night and threaten and never deliver and finally the guy would get tired of it. So who was full of shit?

He tried again, though, one more time. Said, "Richard, call it off."

Heard himself and knew it was over.

Nobles said, "Or what?"

See?

Nobles said, "I gotta go the hospital."

See?

"So get the fuck offa me."

Man, lost and gone forever. He would give anything to be able to bust the guy's jaw. He couldn't do it. So he reached out and hacked the gun barrel across that forearm—already broken—a gesture, for Uncle Miney if not his own peace of mind—and had to roll for his life as Nobles screamed and erupted beneath him, came up in a crouch holding his arm tight to his body, ran hunched into tree shadow a dozen yards away and must have felt protected. He took time to yell at LaBrava, back there on his knees, "You're crazy! You know it? You're fucking crazy!"

22

Buck Torres thought he was crazy, too. He didn't say he was crazy, he said, "You broke the guy's arm?" and asked if he was crazy; it was the same thing. He came at 7:30 in the morning to say Nobles had left his hotel during the night and never returned.

Once LaBrava told him to check Sinai and Jackson Memorial Out-Patient and look for a guy walking around with his left arm in a cast, he had to tell it all. He wondered if Torres was going to comment. He was silent for so long after, staring at him in the kitchenette pouring coffee for them. Finally, that was when Torres said it.

"Are you crazy?"

"I don't think so."

"What's the matter with you?"

"Maybe I'm a little crazy. But maybe you have to be crazy to make something happen or make it hard for them," LaBrava said. "Look at it. A note comes asking for money. Jean goes to the bank, picks it up. Another note comes, it'll tell her to take the money to a certain place and she'll do it." LaBrava paused and said, "Is it that easy?"

"We're with her every step, Joe."

"They know you're gonna be with her."

"We have to wait and see." Torres sounded helpless. "What else can we do?"

"You ever had one like this or heard of one?"

"Only dope, dopers trying to score off each other. The Major called the Bureau and they never had one like this either. They said, what is this? Your suspect is practically wearing a sign."

"The Bureau's in it now?"

"Miami office. They're busy on some Castro spy stuff they didn't care to discuss, but they took the note for analysis. They give us their R.A. in West Palm, the resident agent, and some words of wisdom. 'Don't lose the woman or the money or it'll fuck up your day.' "

Jean Shaw came into LaBrava's mind in black and white and then in color and then in black and white again. He brought the color picture back, saw her eyes looking at him and wanted to be with her, talk to her. He saw Richard Nobles' face now, in moonlight, and said, "The guy can't wait for it to happen. He tells us we're about to get the surprise of our life."

"He had to say something like that," Torres said, "you're sitting on him. It's like what a kid would say."

"The whole thing is like a bunch of kids made it up," LaBrava said. "Gimme the money or I'll kill you. Are you gonna play with them? You say you have to. All you've got is this six-foot-three-and-a-half blond asshole in a silver jacket waving at you, trying to get your attention."

"Not anymore we don't."

"He could've left anytime. He stayed around long enough so you notice him. Jean says, 'This guy's been bothering me,' and there he is, right there. That one. What does that tell you?"

"If he's running it," Torres said, "he has to be pretty fucking dumb."

LaBrava smiled, because he could feel they were looking into the center of it. He blew on his coffee and took a sip.

"Or somebody else is running it and using Richard," LaBrava said, "I like to think because he *is* pretty fucking dumb."

"Using him—who, the boat-lifter?"

"The boat-lifter and somebody we don't know about who's smarter than both of them." LaBrava paused and said, "What about the old man's pickup?"

Torres shook his head. "No boat-lifter prints; I couldn't believe it. We found any the Bureau was ready to put out a fugitive warrant. But . . . the way it goes."

LaBrava said, "Think about the boat-lifter and somebody else we don't know about who's using Richard. If they're gonna stand him out in the open and hang a sign on him . . . what does that tell you?"

Torres said, "They make it they're not gonna cut him in. They'd be dumb as him if they did."

"That's right," LaBrava said, "Richard's a celebrity now. The first twenty he breaks he's in jail. If he does it around here, and

I don't think he could wait. So if they don't give him a cut . . .''

"They have to dump him,'' Torres said.

"There you are,'' LaBrava said, and sipped his coffee. "Richard's a throw-away and doesn't know it.''

"You tell him that?''

"I hadn't thought of it yet.''

"You still have his gun?''

"He can get another one. I think he better.''

"Joe, come on . . .''

"Don't ask, you won't have to worry about it.''

"You don't carry a gun anymore, Joe, you're a civilian now. You and I can talk, I appreciate it; but you got to stay out of it when the time comes. You understand? It's not anything personal, it's the way it is.''

"I know that.''

"You don't want to get mad, do something dumb.''

"I'm not mad at anybody.''

"Yeah? How come you broke the guy's arm?''

"I didn't mean to. He raised it to protect his head.''

Torres said, "Oh, Joe. Man, come on . . . You're kidding me, aren't you?''

LaBrava said, "Yeah, I'm kidding.''

For a while last night he had become detached, able to respond impersonally rather than in a role with conditions. He felt this detachment again and liked the feeling, content to be a watcher, though not for too long.

Mrs. Heffel, the Della Robbia lady who picked up the envelope from the floor and placed it on the marble counter, said it was not so long ago that she found it. She put it there at once. She said she didn't open it and read it so don't accuse me. Maurice said, no one is accusing you; these gentlemen want to know what time it was and if you saw anybody in the lobby might have left it. Mrs. Heffel said, I put it over there, I minded my own business, so please don't accuse me, you don't know what you're talking about.

It was close to four o'clock by the time Jean and then Buck

Torres read the note lying open on the marble counter. It was typed on the same kind of steno paper as the first one and said:

> Here we go. Put the Hefty bag with the money in it in the front seat of your car and no place else. You are to drive ALONE north on I-95 to Atlantic Blvd, Pompano Beach. Go over to AIA and drive up to the market on the corner of Spring St. where you see the Coppertone sign (almost to the Hillsboro Inlet) and you will find 4 outside telephone booths. Wait at the second phone from the left as you face the street. Be there at exactly 6 P.M. ALONE. No cops. No tricks. Or you will be sorry. I am watching you.

LaBrava read the note and became an observer they let hang around.

He saw the plainclothes cops, Jean, Maurice, everyone in a hurry to do what was expected, hurrying to follow instructions. He wanted to talk to Jean, but it wasn't possible now. After he read the note, he went into the area of the hotel kitchen where the police had set up their telephones and recording equipment. A detective was talking to the resident FBI man in West Palm, requesting traps on the Hillsboro phones. Jean Shaw was unbuttoning her blouse. He watched Jean, he watched Torres, solemn, impassive, tape a GE body pack to her rib cage, close beneath the white bra cup covering her right breast. The pack was smaller than a package of cigarettes and contained microphone, battery and transmitter in one. She would be wired without wires. He saw her eyes gazing at him, solemn—everyone solemn—over Buck Torres' dark head bent close to her body, as though he might be listening to her heartbeat. She didn't say anything to him. She raised her eyebrows a little, resigned, that was all. She buttoned her blouse. Maurice came in with a detective carrying the Hefty trash bag that bulged out in a smooth round shape about half full; not heavy, the detective carrying it easily with one hand, holding it by the neck that was secured with a twist of baling wire. An I.D. technician came in and gave Jean and Torres each a handwritten copy of the second note. Jean went upstairs to get her purse. Torres spoke to the West Palm R.A. on the phone, giving him a description of Jean's Cadillac and the three surveillance cars they would be using. Another detective was talking to the Broward County sheriff's office. All of them serious, playing the game almost deadpan. The only evidence of emotion before they left: Torres wanted to get in the back seat of Jean's car, lie on the floor. She refused. He tried to insist and she said, then she wasn't going. She said, "It's my life, not yours," Torres gave in.

Maurice said, "Thank the Lord it's cocktail time," sounding more relieved than worried. He poured Scotch over ice at his credenza, brought one to LaBrava looking at a photograph on a wall of the living-room gallery, and climbed into his La-Z-Boy.

The photograph, a half century old, showed a bearded man in a dark business suit standing in sunlight at the brushy edge of a stream.

"Guy claims that's the site of the original Garden of Eden," Maurice said. "On the east bank of the Apalachicola River between Bristol and Chatahoochee, and you know the kind live up at Chatahoochee. Guy also said Noah built his ark right there, in Bristol. When the flood came he floated around about five months, landed on Mount Ararat and thought he was in West Tennessee. Kind a mistake people make all the time."

"Did you give her the money?"

"I loaned it to her. That would be ridiculous have to mortgage her condo. This guy, he don't know what he's doing, they'll pick him up. Guy's a clown."

LaBrava came over and sat down. "You went to your bank and drew six hundred thousand, just like that."

"Signed some bonds over to her. You want to know how much money I got? Don't worry about it."

"Can you afford to lose it?"

"Joe, I ran a horse book. Don't try and tell me anything about risk, what the odds are in a deal like this. It's a lot of money, but at the same time it's only money. I know what I'm doing."

"The cops think it's Jean's."

"They're suppose to. Jeanie doesn't want it to get out I'm the bank, give anybody ideas. So don't say anything, even to your pal."

"Jean's idea."

"We agreed it's the way to do it. I never went in for publicity like some guys. I don't say anything that ever gets on the financial page. I could, Joe. I could tell the experts a few things, where to put your dough while the government's fucking up the economy; but nobody asks me and that's fine."

"You don't seem too worried about her."

"Yeah, is that right? You know what I'm thinking?"

"She doesn't seem too worried either. Everybody's just sort a going along with it."

"Your experience, Secret Agent X-9, what would you do?"

"No—what I'm saying, it can't be this simple. There's gotta be a surprise . . ." LaBrava stopped and looked at Maurice. "You put real money in the bag?"

"You think we cut up paper? You gotta assume the guy's gonna look at it, whether he does or not."

"And he could take her along, couldn't he?"

"I worry the guy might be psycho, yeah, do something crazy," Maurice said. "I'll tell you, Jeanie gets into some situations. She's very bright, except she's not too good a judge a character—some of the bums she gets mixed up with, guys on the make. But she's a tough lady, she always comes out okay. Sees what she has to do . . ." Maurice looked over at the wall of photographs. "Like Noah . . . Guy says he built the ark out of Florida gopher wood and if you don't believe him look it up."

LaBrava had never heard of gopher wood. He said, "Has this ever happened to her before?"

"What?"

"Extortion. Somebody threatens her."

"Oh no, nothing like this. Couple of times she got in the hole gambling—she was in that movie she thinks she knows how. They threatened her, yeah, but they didn't have to. She paid. Another time she paid off a guy's wife was gonna drag her into a divorce action. She gets into these situations, she seems to have a knack for it."

"I thought she was smarter than that."

"She's smart. But like I've said, Joe, you gotta remember she was a movie star. Movie stars are different than you and I."

23

She had written a script once, walked into Harry Cohn's office at Columbia and handed it to him. In a bright red cover. He threw it on the desk, said, "Tell me what it's about in three sentences, and no cheating." She told him: smart, attractive girl is offered anything she wants by rich playboy who's nuts about her, furs, jewels, you name it. Harry Cohn said, "Yeah?" Girl turns him down because getting it that way is unsatisfying, too easy. Harry Cohn said, "She nuts? I never met a fucking broad yet'd turn down anything." Jean said, wait. The girl cons the playboy out of a lot of money and is happy because *she* did it, she earned it herself. Harry Cohn said, "You mean the broad wins?" She said, "You bet." He told her the idea stunk.

The pay phones, four in a row, were in Plexiglas shells mounted on metal posts. Jean stood by the second phone, waiting, giving it another minute. It was 6:12. Two of the police surveillance cars were across A1A at the Sunuco station; she didn't see the third one, or signs of any local police. Her purse rested on the metal ledge beneath the phone, open toward her. She might as well do it now. Sgt. Torres, his nose practically in her bra, had told her to speak normally, they'd pick up her voice. She straightened, getting ready, and could feel the tape pull against her skin.

Jean said, as though talking to herself, "If he doesn't call, what do I do? This has to be the right place." She waited a few moments, then took the folded sheet of steno paper from her purse.

Ready? With curiosity, then surprise:

"There's something . . . It looks like . . . My God, it's a piece of note paper just like the ones . . . It's sticking out of the phone book." She unfolded the sheet and looked at the note she had dictated to Richard. "It says . . . 'Go directly to your apartment. Now. Bring the money with you. Now. I am watching you.' "

She looked up, looked around for effect. She could see them, inside the cars at the Sunoco station. They started their engines. She said, "I'll leave the note here."

Victim eager to cooperate. Don't think. Play the part.

Seventeen minutes later, in the guest parking area of Jean Shaw's condominium on Ocean Drive, Boca Raton:

Torres sat in the communications surveillance car, a black Mercedes sedan that had once transported heroin, and watched Jean Shaw walk into the building, her upper body slightly twisted, using both hands to hold the trash bag bouncing against her leg.

Her voice said, "I don't see anyone." The sound thin, coming from a tunnel or from across the ocean. "Isn't someone supposed to be here? . . . I'm going to pick up my mail."

He had told her police would be in the building, never more than a few seconds away from her. The FBI's West Palm resident agent and people from the Palm Beach County Sheriff's. The West Palm R.A. would be up on her floor.

"I'm entering the elevator now."

Nearly thirty seconds passed.

"I'm at my apartment . . . I think there's someone . . . I heard the fire exit close, at the end of the hall. If it isn't one of ours you'd better get up here."

He liked her voice. No strain. Being transmitted from beneath those softly scented breasts. The tape had stuck to his fingers and he'd had a time trying to act natural, putting the body pack on her. She had a mole beneath her left breast, about an inch down.

Her voice said, "I'm in my apartment. Should I wait for a call? I don't see a note anywhere."

Torres picked up his Walkie and said to the West Palm R.A., a guy named Jim McCormick he had met for the first time at the Sunoco station, "Jim, she's in there. The door should be open. See how she's doing."

Almost a minute passed. Her voice said, "Do you think he'll call?" Torres could hear sounds, another voice. A couple of minutes passed.

The West Palm R.A.'s voice came on the Walkie. "Sergeant, we got another note. It was in with the mail."

Torres, feeling a degree of relief, said, "Then it's your case, man."

The West Palm R.A. said, "It wasn't mailed, it was stuck in the box, hand delivered."

Torres said, "Oh."

The West Palm R.A. said, "This guy thinks he's a joker. Now we go back. Ms. Shaw is to proceed to Fort Lauderdale, take I-95 to Sunrise. Proceed east to Northeast Twenty-fourth and turn right past Burdine's in the Galleria Mall. Turn left on Ninth Street and proceed to the end. You got it?"

"It's not clear," Torres said.

"Then write it down," the West Palm R.A. said.

"I did write it down. What else does it say?"

"I am watching you."

She liked the idea of leading a procession of law-enforcement officers—city, county, federal, losing some, picking up others as she left Palm Beach County and entered Broward—and not a soul through miles of freeway traffic knew it . . . all these people poking along, heading for their little stucco ranch homes and an evening of real-life nothing. She liked the idea of reaching Sunrise with the sun poetically down, to drive east toward a darkening sky, still in traffic, taking her time, wanting the light down fairly low for the last act.

She wasn't sure, at first, if she liked having the West Palm FBI guy along. Then decided she liked it, because he added a little class without being much more than an observer. She liked him for the same reason she liked Torres—good casting, big-city cop type with ethnic color—and liked having Joe LaBrava involved. Though she was just as glad he wasn't in the procession, noticing every detail; he could be scary. She liked them because working with professionals brought out the best in you; you could count on them for cues, sometimes inspiration. Whereas amateurs could ruin your concentration and timing, make you look awkward. She guessed she liked Joe LaBrava for a lot of reasons. He was imaginative. He acted without acting. Played a street character with marvelous restraint, a natural innocence. He was agreeable, understanding, sensitive. He liked Maurice a lot, a big plus.

Seemed to have an open mind. A fairly keen one. He certainly had a sense of the dramatic; look at his pictures. Finally, and it could be worth putting at the top of the list, he was a fan.

True fans understood and were willing to make excuses. If they had to. Joe was a fan for the right reason, he recognized her as an actress.

But, my God, he didn't miss a thing. Had even identified and photographed Richard's little helper—whom she was about to meet for the first time and had better get mentally prepared. She hoped he would have something heavy enough to break the glass. She hoped he would be reasonably calm but quick and, please, wouldn't have a gun.

The shopping center was coming up on the right. She had to assume there would be Lauderdale or Broward Sheriff's cops around somewhere. There was Burdine's, the name against the rising wall of the store. Just beyond were Neiman-Marcus and Saks. She approached the light at Northwest Twenty-fourth.

The instructions were intentionally vague from here, Twenty-fourth to Ninth Street to the end, because she wasn't going that far.

She would turn right onto Twenty-fourth, follow the street-level underpass to the rear of the mall and be out of sight of the surveillance cars for about fifteen seconds. No more than that.

The light was green. She turned, passed beneath the drive-through to Ninth and turned left. She was now approaching the only weak sequence in the script. Later, she would have to explain in detail why she suddenly left Ninth and turned into the parking structure instead of proceeding to the end of the street, according to instructions.

For the time being, she said to the mike beneath her breast, "There's someone waving!" Got some urgency in her tone, then doubt, fear, saying, "Is he one of ours?" and let it go at that.

They heard it in the Mercedes approaching Twenty-fourth. Torres said, "Go—" and the detective driving mashed the accelerator, then had to brake hard to make the turn. "Where are you?" Torres said, as they came out of the underpass and did not see the

Eldorado. "Say something." But there would be nothing for the next minute or so, until they heard the sound of breaking glass.

Cundo Rey watched the Cadillac come out of the underpass, dull white car way down there. Yes, the same one, the windows fixed now. He turned and moved down the nearly empty aisle to the ramp, where cars turned off at this level, and stood against the column with a brick in his left hand, a red brick with some mortar stuck to it. He wore white work gloves, new ones. He could hear the Cadillac, inside now, somewhere below him.

Richard said he didn't need to have a gun, she would be so scared she would let him have the money and not give him any trouble. He had the gun anyway, under his shirt hanging out. He didn't know this woman; what if *she* had a gun? He knew what he was going to do. Step out, raise his right hand . . .

Richard said don't say anything because the woman would have a wire on her. Richard, the creature, knew a few things, but not too many.

The car sounded like it was in a hurry, tires squealing in the turns. It reached the third level. Now it was coming, he saw the front end, coming up the ramp. The car got louder. He stepped out, extending his right hand, stopping the car like Superman, the fender coming to touch his hand gently, without a sound. There she was looking at him. He took the brick in his right hand, saw her turn away, bringing up her arm, as he smashed the brick through the passenger-side window, unlocked the door, opened it. Yes, she was a beautiful woman and very calm, her eyes looking at him. Taking the trash bag by the neck he had to say something to her, so he said, "Thank you very much, lady—" and ran for the exit sign above the door to the stairway.

He would go to the ground level and walk behind the stores to come out on Twenty-sixth Avenue where the new Buick Skylark, stolen this afternoon, waited on the street. Nothing to it. He wished he could take off in the Skylark, go to Georgia right now; but he had to go back to Miami Beach to get his car. Sure, he could buy a new one. But he loved that car too much. He felt good in that car. He said, "Yeah? Well, how does it feel to be rich?" He said, "You kidding me?"

She couldn't afford to wait too long—twenty seconds from the time the Exit door closed. She concentrated a moment, worked up a feeling of agitated fear, careful to keep it just short of hysteria, and shouted, "He's got it! He broke the window!" She paused, opened her door and heard tires squealing, more than one car, and pulled the door closed. "Will you please hurry? He's getting away!" Without telling them the direction he'd taken. A lapse she would attribute later to fear, anxiety, so much happening at once—wring hands and look helpless. The black Mercedes was coming off the third level, up the ramp now, followed closely by another car, then another. She could hear sirens outside. Torres was in her rearview mirror, running toward her with a radio in his hand.

She'd push the door open, come out with her big brown eyes glistening, pleading, and maybe even throw herself in his arms.

24

It was late now. Joe LaBrava sat alone on the porch of the Cardozo Hotel thinking about a zebra he had seen a few hours before. A zebra run to the ground by wild dogs, a dog with the zebra's upper lip clamped in its jaw, a dog hanging to its tail, dogs frisking, dying to join the dogs tearing open the zebra's loins from underneath, pulling out entrails. The voice of the narrator—an actor who played heavies but had hired on for this film as an animal behaviorist—said the zebra was in a state of deep shock and felt no pain. And LaBrava had thought, Oh, is that right? Look at the zebra's eyes and tell us what it's like to stand there and get your ass eaten out fucking alive.

He couldn't stop thinking about the zebra and the actor who knew so much about zebra anxieties and pain thresholds. What was the zebra thinking through all that? Torres came over from the Della Robbia, sat down at the table in the edge of streetlight and popped open one of the six cans of beer the waiter had left saying goodnight. Torres placed a tape recorder on the table, said, "This is at Hillsboro," and turned it on.

LaBrava listened to Jean Shaw's voice over the pictures he saw of her. He could see her very clearly, most of the pictures, new to him, composed in his mind in black and white.

"This is at her apartment."

LaBrava listened, seeing pictures of the zebra again among pictures of the movie actress, wondering what they were both thinking.

"This is the West Palm R.A., McCormick."

LaBrava listened.

"This is at Galleria Mall."

LaBrava listened, and when it ended he sat in silence looking at palm-tree silhouettes beyond the streetlights, stars over the ocean, the zebra gone. He picked up the recorder, pressed buttons and listened again to the last part, waiting for:

"Will you please hurry? He's getting away!"

Rewound, stopped and played it again.

"Will you please hurry? He's getting away!"

He could see her. Except that she wasn't in a white Cadillac in a parking structure. He saw an old picture of her in a black car, some kind of expensive long black car, at night. She looked scared as she called out, "He's getting away!" Then sat back and didn't look scared.

He rewound to the middle part, searched, found what he wanted and heard her say, "Isn't someone supposed to be here? . . . I'm going to pick up my mail." There was a pause. He heard her say, "I'm entering the elevator—" and shut it off. McCormick was coming up on the porch. McCormick said, "One of those have my name on it? Christ, I hope so." Sturdy, compact, in Brooks Brothers khakis, blue button-down shirt, beige necktie, the West Palm R.A.

"That is a very attractive, very intelligent lady," McCormick said. "I found out in about five minutes I wasn't gonna learn shit I didn't know or suspect going in, but I talked to her an hour and a half anyway. She is a sharp lady."

Torres said, "You're the first Bureau guy—you actually admit you didn't learn anything?"

"For two reasons," McCormick said. "One, it isn't my case, you poor bastard. Two, I'm gonna retire the end of the month and become a stockbroker, so either way I don't give a shit. It's all yours, man, and it's getting away from you by the minute. You've got nothing firm. No positive I.D. of the guy who grabbed the bag or the guy who waved to her to come in the garage. Never seen them before. I showed her the pictures of the two guys you like, Mutt and Jeff; wasn't either of them. I asked her why she went in there. She says she thought the guy who waved at her was a police officer, but even if he wasn't we were supposed to be right behind her. Where in the hell were we? . . . Outside of that there's only one part that bothers me." McCormick paused and then said to Torres, "You know what it is?"

Torres thought about it, looking off at the ocean.

McCormick poured a beer, began to drink.

LaBrava said, "Why did she stop to pick up her mail?" If he didn't say it, McCormick would. Or he wanted to hear himself admit what he was beginning to feel.

McCormick put his glass down. "You want a job? Uncle Sam can use you."

"He already did," LaBrava said. "You ask her?"

"She said habit. She comes in, she always checks the mail. I said even when you're carrying six hundred grand in a garbage bag?"

Torres said, "Wait a minute—"

"It probably doesn't mean shit," McCormick said. "It's like a reflex, she comes in, she checks the mail. Okay, she goes up to her apartment, she's in there a few minutes before I come from down the hall. She says to me, 'You think he'll call?' and starts looking through the mail. But what if she hadn't picked it up? The whole schmear falls apart. The other thing is the few minutes she's in there alone . . ."

Torres said, "You're making her a suspect. She's the victim, for Christ sake."

McCormick said, "At this point everybody's a suspect, I don't give a shit. I don't know for sure where she got the six hundred gees, do you? She said she cashed some bonds. Maybe she did. On the other hand maybe she borrowed it and she's gonna stiff the guy. I don't know this broad, but I'll tell you what you better do, to be safe. Tomorrow morning—in fact I'll do it for you, it's out of your jurisdiction. I'll go up to her apartment and take a casual look around for different items, trash bags, a typewriter . . . It happens all the time, you don't know shit till you open some drawers, feel under the undies, you can find things you didn't even know you were looking for." He glanced at LaBrava. "Am I right? I forgot there for a minute you used to be with Treasury."

"Cover your ass at all times," LaBrava said.

"Cover it first," McCormick said, "then worry about what people think of you, if you worry about such things. Next, get the Lauderdale cops to canvas the mall, see if they can get a lead on the two guys. They'll give you a lot of shit, but at least you tried. After that . . . what've you got? Nothing. I don't see the big blond guy in the picture anywhere."

"Richard—" Torres began to say.

"If those two guys have the balls to grab the bag, what do they want to cut Richard in for? What's he, their typist?"

"Listen, Richard—I didn't tell you," Torres said to LaBrava, "we found out was treated early this morning at Bethesda Memorial, compound fracture. The nurse said a cop brought him in."

LaBrava was wondering why he'd gone all the way up to Boynton Beach, fifty miles, as McCormick said, "Cop from where?"

"She didn't know where the cop was from," Torres said, looking at LaBrava again. " 'But a real one,' she said, not a rent-a-cop. We called every town from West Palm down. Nobody's got him or has a record of him."

"He has a friend who's a cop," LaBrava said, and could see Richard Nobles in the Delray Crisis Center flashing his badge and the slim girl standing up to him, Jill Wilkinson, and Richard saying he had a friend . . . either with the Delray or Boca police . . . the other girl, Pam, saying yes, she knew him. "I'll see if I can get his name for you."

He wondered if the slim girl was back from Key West.

McCormick said, "Let me take a look in her apartment tomorrow, maybe give you a better idea what you have to do next."

LaBrava said, "You gonna get her permission?"

"I could do that," McCormick said. "Or I could take a peek first. See, then if it looks interesting, get a warrant. Why bother the lady?"

"Get her permission," LaBrava said.

McCormick stared, smiled a little. "Well, now, what have we here?"

"Get her permission," LaBrava said.

"You don't," Torres said, "I bet you could open the door and get your arm broke."

Nobles could see without even trying there was no way he could get a uniform shirt on. The goddamn cast came all the way bent-arm to his shoulder. He ended up he had to cut the left arm out of his good silver jacket; put on uniform pants and the goddamn police hat to make him look at least semiofficial. No sense wearing the holster, empty.

It was too late to get another gun. It was too late to get anything to eat and he was hungry for a Big Mac and some fries. He thought about the snake eating the bat—the lesson there, be patient. He thought about—the idea he liked best—walking up behind that blindsider and tapping him on the shoulder. "'Scuse me." And as the blindsider comes around hit him in the face with the goddamn cast. Then say to him laying there on the ground . . .

He'd have to think of something good.

Going on 3:00 A.M. he hiked the two and a half miles from his dumpy place out Township, cut across the county airport past a lot of rich guys' planes, then over Lantana to Star Security, across from the state hospital. It was not luck he had kept a set of patrol car keys, it was using the old bean.

Going on 4:00 A.M. Nobles was down on Ocean Drive, Boca Raton, slow-cruising the beach condos like a regular security service car, except now he was looking for the law instead of boogers. He did not expect any sign of them. Why would there be with the horse out of the barn? He rode up to the top floor in that goddamn pokey elevator, went into her place with the key she'd given him and right away could smell her. Taking a leak he began to feel horny. She had yelled at him one time, "Close the door, you sound like a horse." And he had yelled back, "Puss? Come in here and help me hold this hog, would you, please?" They'd had some times. In her bedroom he was tempted to poke through her drawers, but knew he'd best take it and get.

It was in the walk-in closet. Lord have mercy, it actually was. Round fat garbage bag of money he and her had agreed to split two to one in her favor, which he believed was fair. Shit, $200,-000 he could buy any goddamn thing he wanted, starting with a pair of lizard wingtip cowboy boots he'd seen on Burt Reynolds one time up in Jupiter. Buy the boots, buy a 'Vette, buy some guns, have 'em in glass cabinets in his knottypine den . . .

He had to drive back to his place first, which had two rooms and not any kind of den, to store the loot. He had to drive back on over to Star Security and leave the car, shit, then hike the two and a half miles back home. It wasn't so bad though. He started out thinking of what he would say to the blindsider laying there on the ground.

"You mess with me, boy—"

''You fuck with me, boy—''

''You fuck with the bull, boy—''

He liked ''bull'' but he didn't like ''bull, boy.''

How about, ''Boy, you fuck with the bull . . . you see what you get.''

''You see what can befall you.''

Be*fall* you? He sounded like a preacher.

Saw the blindsider being struck by a bolt of lightning.

Saw him through a car windshield as he ran over the son of a bitch.

Then saw Cundo Rey, Lord have mercy, and felt tears come into his eyes it was so funny to imagine. The little booger opening that other Hefty bag. Sure, he would, set to skip with the whole load. The dink might even skip and *then* open the bag. Get to some motel up around Valdosta, open her up . . . The poor little fucker. He'd blame it on the law doing him a tricky turn, and there wouldn't be a goddamn thing he could do about it.

Cundo Rey woke up the next morning, 6:00 A.M., he didn't sleep so good, he opened his eyes he had a headache. Ouuuuu, he had a good one. He believed it was from not using his anger.

Anger was good if you could use it right away, let it pick you up and carry you. But if you didn't use it, then it passed and it left your brain sore. Like balls became sore if you were ready to make love but for some reason didn't do it. Like you had to get out of her house quick. Man, they ached. It was the same thing with the brain. He took aspirin and Pepsi-Cola. Pretty soon he was able to think. In time he began to wonder why he had got angry.

The creature had told him to get a good place close by to hide. He had found a perfect place, Bonita Drive, a one-block curve of apartments, cheap, between Seventy-first Street and Indian Creek Drive. Ten minutes from the action down on South Beach. One minute from the North Bay Causeway, shoot over to Miami, you're on the freeway. He rented the first floor of a two-story place for a month; it even had a garage to hide the car in.

He had given the address to the creature and the creature said good, here's what I do and here's what you do, and told him all the things he eventually did. Take the bag from the woman, who would follow a note to the car-park building. Run home and hide the bag. Get rid of the stolen car . . . Then after a week or so, when it was cool, the creature said he would come and pick up his half of the money and they would never see each other again.

But the creature never told where *he* was going to be hiding. The creature never called him a name and said, don't try to take the money for yourself or I'll find you and kill you. That should have opened his eyes. But his own greed, thinking how easy it would be to take it all, had perhaps blinded him.

So last night, 8:30, he came back from getting rid of the Skylark, a nice car; he opened the Hefty bag upside down, and for a long time he sat looking at the pile of cut-up newspaper on the floor, the *Miami Herald* and one called the *Post*.

What made him angry was thinking the cops did this to him. The cops not caring if it endangered the woman. The dirty cops, like all cops, full of cop tricks. He drank a pint of rum and a liter of Pepsi-Cola to become tranquil, but it didn't do any good.

This morning, a beautiful day outside, he looked at the pieces of newspaper he had kicked all over the living room, at the pieces of broken glass and dishes on the floor, and began to wonder different things.

Why the creature hadn't tried to frighten him: take the money, you die.

How the creature himself was able to put the note in the woman's car and in that hotel if the cops were watching. How he could do it, a man who always wished to be seen, and *not* be seen.

Why there were no cops in the car-park building if the note told her to go there. He had been very careful entering, looked in cars, all over.

Why, if the note *didn't* say to go there, she did.

It was getting good.

Why she seemed to be stopping the car—there was no sound of her car's tires—before he came out from behind the post.

Why she looked at him so calm and did not appear frightened. Like she expected him to be there.

He sat staring at the pieces of newspaper, thinking again of the notes the creature said he had written, wondering again how he could have given them to the woman, beginning to see the fucking creature was a liar—as a thought related to this lifted him out of the chair.

He went through the kitchen to the garage that was part of the building, and looked in the trunk of his car. There it was in a case—which he opened to make sure—the typewriter he had forgot to drop into Biscayne Bay. He touched the typewriter and the carriage slid out to one side and locked there; he couldn't get it back. So he left the case and took the typewriter into the apartment.

That typewriter got him thinking some more and he sat without moving, letting thoughts of Richard and the woman slide through his mind, seeing the two of them friends, good friends. Seeing the woman, again and again, stopping her car as though she knew exactly where he would be, almost smiling at him, so calm, knowing he wasn't going to hurt her, knowing he was taking pieces of paper.

He sat without moving and thought, Richard isn't coming. Of course not. It was Richard and the woman. He didn't know how. He didn't know why she would be stealing from herself, except that Richard was a liar and maybe she wasn't rich and it wasn't her money they were stealing. Richard was a liar and it was Richard and the woman.

Cundo sat without moving for so long that finally when he moved he knew he would keep moving and get out of here. What was he hiding for? He didn't do nothing. What did he steal, some pieces of newspaper? He didn't have to stay here, he could go any place he wanted . . .

Because if it was Richard and the woman they wouldn't want him to be caught and talk to the police. So she wouldn't look at pictures and identify him. Afraid he might tell the police about Richard. He would, too.

Uh-oh. It made him think of something else he had forgot about just as he had forgot about the typewriter.

What if it wasn't the woman and the creature stealing the money but the woman and the picture-taker?

He had forgot about that fucking picture-taker.

If he'd had the snubbie when the picture-taker sat in the wheelchair and took his picture . . . But he had bought the snubbie *after,* to use on the picture-taker, and then had become too busy preparing to steal a bag of newspapers cut in pieces. Oh, man . . . crazy.

And thought of the time he walked in the crazy-place in Delray naked, to get information. He had to smile. There was always a way to find out what you need to know.

Sure, call up the woman. Don't worry about the picture-taker, if he's in this or not. What difference does it make?

Call up the woman and ask her she wants to buy a typewriter, cheap. Only six hundred thousand dollars.

See what she says.

25

McCormick said he didn't want to bother her, he could get the manager, with her OK, to let them in. This was Bureau check-list routine, go over any area known to the suspect. Jean said no, it wasn't a bother—immediately establishing an attitude—she'd be glad to drive up and meet them; not asking, which suspect? In the car she tried on several attitudes from wide-eyed innocence to cold resentment, cutting remarks, but decided she'd been instinctively right on the phone: victim with a passive respect for authority was still the way to play it.

They were waiting downstairs when she arrived, Mr. McCormick and two officers from the Palm Beach County Sheriff's Department with their evidence kits; McCormick explaining they would like to pull a good set of Nobles' prints if they could, also look around in case he might've left something; Jean nodding, following every word, showing how fascinated she was; McCormick saying clues turned up in unexpected places; Jean saying yes, she imagined so; thinking, You sneaky FBI son of a bitch. Both sides buttoned up with respect.

Jean had to play it with a knot in her stomach at first—until McCormick came out of her closet; then, for a while, with mild apprehension. She could have overlooked something. A crumpled sheet of steno paper behind the desk, a scrap of newspaper in the closet. She had gone over the apartment thoroughly once the plan was set. There were no Hefty bags around. No Walther automatic to find unexpectedly. All old Miami and Palm Beach papers had been thrown out . . .

As apprehension eased, left her, McCormick became fun to watch. Neat but beefy in his seersucker suit, blue Oxford cloth button-down, beige and blue rep tie—he dressed like so many guys she used to know—glancing at his reflections in silver and glass, trying to remain offhand, polite. But losing it as he looked in or behind every closet, cabinet, piece of furniture and found nothing. He did come up with a pair of sunglasses she'd misplaced and her gratitude, at this time and somewhat overstated, apparently rubbed him. With suspicion in his eyes, quiet awareness in hers, he seemed bound to pull out something, if even remotely incriminating.

McCormick said, "I understand this place was bought for you."

Jean said, "That's right." Nothing to hide.

"But not by your husband."

"He died," Jean said. "A friend bought me the place."

"A boyfriend?"

"A benefactor." She loved the word, the prim sound of it. "You know what he paid? Less than a hundred thousand, back when real estate was relatively sane."

"I understand," McCormick said, voice flat, eyes watchful, about to ambush her, "he was a member of organized crime."

"A *member,*" Jean said, smiling. "As opposed to what, an independent contractor?" Turning the smile then gradually from shy to off. "That was so long ago." Getting a little sigh in her tone. "It was an exciting time and I'm afraid I was, well, impressionable, to say the least. If you will accept that, Mr. McCormick . . ."

"Jim—"

Wanting to add, Then you'll accept anything.

"But I'm positive this doesn't involve anyone I used to know, Jim . . . From out of the past." Starring Bob Mitchum; she'd really wanted the Jane Greer part. Giving him her aware brown eyes straight on. "Aside from Mr. Zola, of course. He's advised me all through this, suggested I cash in bonds rather than re-mortgage the apartment. I'm not left with much." Chin up, resolute, but eyes beginning to mist. "I'll make it though. I can always sell the place, move back to the Coast." Wistful hint of a smile. "I know, this is a coast too. But once you've been in film, Jim"—tough line—"there's really only one Coast."

"I understand," Jim said.

"I think you should put all your effort into finding Richard Nobles," Jean said, "though he's probably far away from here by now." Looking off, coming back suddenly then to hold his gaze. "He did mention once he'd love to go out to the Coast, try the movies. Like several hundred others who look just like him try every year, and maybe a couple of them make it in television, wrecking cars. The only thing I can suggest"—sigh, tired but still willing to help—"alert your office on the Coast, send them Richard's picture . . . and if I should think of anything else in the meantime, Jim . . ."

Jim told her that once Richard was established as a fugitive the entire Bureau would be on him from Seat of Government through every field office in the country, the case tagged a major.

"I'm flattered," Jean said.

"Maybe we can have a drink sometime," Jim said.

"I'd like that," Jean said. Pause. "I'd like that very much."

Not a memorable performance, but not bad. About average. Not nearly as difficult to make convincing as the love scene in *Treasure of the Aztecs*. God—telling Audie Murphy that neither the sacrificial dagger of Montezuma nor the conquering sword of Cortes could stop her heart, her *pagan* heart, from throbbing with desire, "my golden Lord." And Audie in his jerkin and codpiece squirming, eating it up. She wondered if she could update it and run it past LaBrava, just for fun.

She felt like performing . . . She could get on the freeway and be at Richard's house in about fifteen minutes; she'd memorized the directions. They had planned to wait at least a week, give the police time to relax. But she was so close and her mood was perfect.

She could hear the elevator door close across the hall, the elevator begin to descend with McCormick and the two Palm Beach officers.

It might be the best time of all. Richard would be surprised. Just in case he had ideas . . .

Coming away from the door Jean paused, looking at herself in the wall of glass behind the sofa. She smiled. Too much. Staring at herself she saw a worried expression now, with a smile trying to break through. "Richard, is everything all right?" Make it a little more personal. "Richard, are you all right?" Maybe even, "Richard, I couldn't wait to see you." Well—disarm him, but don't overdo it.

* * *

LaBrava stood by his window with the phone. He could see Franny in the park across the street, sitting at an easel in shade, painting one of the Della Robbia women who sat facing the ocean. When the slim girl, Jill Wilkinson, came on he said, "How was Key West?"

She said, "I love it. It's the only place I know you can rest and not get hit on all the time. I mean a girl. Wait a minute." She was gone several minutes. When she came back she said, "I'm sorry. We've got a guy took one of the panels out of the ceiling and crawled up into the overhead. He won't come down because he says the office is full of alligators. Keeps saying 'They's gators down there.' He's right, but we're not supposed to let on." He asked her the name of the cop Richard Nobles had mentioned that night, the one Pam said she knew. Jill said, "Hold on." He heard her call to Pam and ask her. Jill came back on and said, "Glenn Hicks, he's Boca P.D. But tell me about Richard. What's that subhuman piece of shit up to now?"

Franny looked naked at her easel; and her hair made her look like a little girl. The Della Robbia woman was getting up, walking around behind Franny to look at the painting. Watching them LaBrava phoned Torres and gave him the name of Richard's friend. Glenn Hicks.

He crossed the street from the Cardozo to Lummus Park, two ice-cold cans of beer in each of his hands. Boy, did she look good: the mauve bikini top with cutoff jeans, artist at work under a palm tree, very nice if you can get away with it, if you're any good. Artist concentrating, showing the tip of her tongue, touching up, canvas chair where the subject had been sitting, empty. Her weird hair moved, she was looking at him, waiting.

"Well, how're you doing?"

She said, "How am I doing. I went home for a wedding three days ago, you didn't even know I was gone."

"You got married? Here I've been looking all over for you."

"Why, were you horny?"

"Reasonably."

"You don't get reasonably horny, Joe, you are or you aren't."

"I was more than horny, I missed you." He handed her a can

of beer, then paused as he was about to sink into the canvas chair, looking at the easel. "That's very good. You know it?"

"Who is it?"

"It's Mrs. Heffel. Don't you know who you're painting?" He was pretty sure it was Mrs. Heffel.

"*I* know. I didn't think you did."

"Even without the nose shield. You know how I know her? I took her picture. She's got a little girl inside her that shows every once in a while, when she doesn't think people are accusing her of something. You caught the little girl. A glimpse of her." He sat down and popped a beer.

"You think so?"

He handed her the opened beer, took the one Franny was holding and popped it. "I think so. What happened to your hotels?"

"I like hotels okay, but hotels are things. I've decided my interests lie more in people. That's your influence, LaBrava. I look at your work, I want to see what you see."

"You do, you see things."

"I don't know. I see a certain thing in your work because you caught it, there it is. But I don't know if I'd see the same thing before. I don't know if I have the eye."

"You got Mrs. Heffel."

"I've been watching her for a week."

"You've got the eye. The secret is, don't look at everything at once, concentrate on one part at a time."

She said, "Maybe I'm doing it, I'll find out." She sipped her beer and said, "So what've you been up to while I was in New York having the time of my life with my relatives?"

He said, "Not too much. I've been trying to think of a movie I saw a long time ago."

"Don't tell me, starring Jean Shaw. You still have the hots for her? She's too old for you."

"As a matter of fact it *was* a Jean Shaw movie. You saw it too, because you mentioned it that night we saw *Let It Ride.*"

"What's the name of it?"

"*Obituary.*"

"The one, her husband knows he's gonna die of an incurable

illness so he kills himself, then makes it look like she did it because she and her boyfriend took him for a lot of money?''

''That one.''

''I didn't see it.''

''How much of it do you remember?''

''I think I saw like the last half.''

''She go to jail?''

''Yes, there's a trial, and she's found guilty, not for what she did but for killing her husband, which she didn't do. Heavy irony.''

''Who was the guy, the hero?''

''I don't know. He had sort of a chiseled face and the muscle in his jaw kept jumping. He had sorta wet lips too. The other girl, the good one, is the daughter of Jean Shaw's husband by his first wife. The daughter, when her dad starts getting his own death notices clipped from out-of-town papers, the daughter right away thinks Jean's doing it, but nobody believes her, including the cop.''

''Victor Mature.''

''Yeah, that's who it is. I forgot his name.''

''The husband's afraid of death anyway—''

''It petrifies him. Anybody mentions death, he looks like he's gonna throw up. Until near the end of the picture, when he finds out he's got this incurable illness and he really *is* gonna die, then he accepts it. His daughter gives him a talk about dying being part of living and he buys it. It's really dumb.''

''So they send the death notices to scare hell out of him, set him up . . .''

''Yeah, and then the death *threat,* pay up or you're dead. Jean, the wife, is not only in on it, it's her idea from the beginning.''

''She delivers the payoff?''

''Yeah, but not really. Let me think . . . They get a phone call to deliver the money to a motel somewhere, a certain room. She goes there, gets another phone call to go someplace else. But first she switches the suitcase full of money with a suitcase full of newspapers or something that's already in the motel room. You understand?''

''Yeah, go on.''

"So then she makes the drop. Along comes some guy her boyfriend hired, a weirdo with big eyes—"

"Elisha Cook."

"He swings with what he thinks is a suitcase full of money. He opens it, goes berserk when he sees newspapers and falls out his hotel-room window."

"He didn't know the wife was in on it."

"He didn't know shit, he's just sorta in the picture."

"Then what? The boyfriend . . ."

"The boyfriend goes to the motel and picks up the real stuff. He takes it to a cabin up in the mountains, opens the suitcase . . . You think Jean is jobbing this guy too, but it's all there."

"Henry Silva."

"Right, the same guy that played Mother in *A Hatful of Rain*. I just saw that one too."

"So after a while Jean arrives at the cabin . . ."

"She comes in with her own suitcase, an empty one."

"And what happens?"

"You're going west on Lantana, okay, you take a right just past the county airport and go on up," Richard had told her, "till almost you come to like a subdivision and you take a left onto Township, it's a dirt road, and you go on out till you see a whole bunch of scrub pine and this house setting by itself, cute little place used to be painted white."

No telephone, but it had propane gas and running water, inside toilet, stove, fridge, hundred a month, shit. Kind of place you think it'd been left to weather, no reason to go near it. Perfect spot, Richard said.

Poor Richard, peeking out the front door.

Jean parked in tree shade, left the key in the ignition and released the trunk. She did not look at the house now, knowing Richard was watching her open the trunk, lift out the tan leather suitcase. There was the sound of a light plane circling the county airport, the sound persisting, fading, coming back. There was dusty summer heat in the air, a depressed rural feel to the location; not anything like the cabin up near Big Bear. It had been cool, she'd worn a trenchcoat and a black beret. She had the line ready. "Richard, I couldn't wait."

But when he appeared in the doorway Jean revised it without thinking and said, "What happened to you?"

"I got my goddamn arm broke."

"I can see that. How did you do it?"

He was squinting at the road, in the direction of the airport. "You sure nobody followed you?"

"I'm sure."

"I wasn't expecting you for least a week."

"I couldn't wait, Richard." There, getting back to the script. But then forced away from it again with, "What happened to your arm?" Moving past him into the house, dim with shades drawn, depressing, a musty smell to the place.

"You want me to tell you? It was that goddamn friend of yours, that blindsider, same guy 'at hit me the time up in Delray, that place they took you."

They were way off the script and might not return for some time; but she had to sit down, stare at him and hear every word of this, Richard's version of what happened in the park: how he was struck from behind, arm broken before he even saw the guy, hit in the legs, the head; man was like he was crazy.

Jean said, "He brought you there . . ."

"He tricked me."

"To ask you questions?"

"I didn't tell him nothing."

She said, "Richard, how do you know you didn't?"

"I know what I told him. He didn't have no wire on him, I checked. Listen, with one hand 'fore we were through there I punched the sucker out and I told him, 'You got a surprise coming, asshole,' just that much, without telling him nothing. Shit, I wasn't gonna let the scudder get off."

Jean said, "Oh, Richard," her tone soft, almost loving. She sat in a wornout easy chair, her head back against the cushion, feeling the bristly mohair of the arms beneath her hands, damp with perspiration. Her straw bag was on her lap. She reached into it, found a pack of cigarettes and lighted one, inhaled, blew the smoke out slowly.

She said, "Well, it doesn't matter."

Nobles said, "Shit, no. We done it, didn't we? You haven't

asked did I get the sack or not. You ready to have a look, divvy up?''

''I guess I'm ready,'' Jean said.

Nobles walked into the bedroom and got down on the floor. She could see the bed from where she sat, blanket folded on a soiled mattress. He would try to get her in there, with sticky words, mouth curled. She watched him pull the Hefty bag from under the bed—each move separate, deliberate—rising to his knees, to one foot, standing, turning to come out . . . He sat on a straight chair facing her, the bag between his legs. Jean watched the fingers of one hand working to unwind the baling wire. She said, ''Richard, how did you get here?''

''I didn't know how I was gonna make it to the hospital, see. So I called this boy Glenn Hicks I know. I told you, he's with the Boca Police?''

''Yes?''

''He drove me to Bethesda, the one in Boynton 'cause he didn't know any others without going clear to Palm Beach.''

''Then how did you get here?''

''Yeah, Glenn drove me.''

She said it again, ''Oh, Richard,'' with that same weariness.

''Glenn's a good boy, does what I tell him. Don't you worry 'bout old Glenn.'' He held the Hefty bag open. ''Here, look-it in here. I want to see your eyes pop out.''

''Did you count it?''

''Did I count it?'' He grinned at her. ''I been counting it since I drug the sack in. It's fun, you know it, count money?'' He frowned then, reaching into the bag. ''What I couldn't figure out, what you put this in there for?'' His hand came out holding the Walther PPK, the little bluesteel automatic.

Jean raised her hand from the arm of the chair and Nobles hesitated, then shrugged, reached over, and laid the grip in her upturned palm. ''She's on safety. That's a cute little piece, but be careful now.''

Jean brought the gun up, looking at it. ''I didn't want to leave it at home, risk someone finding it. And with all those cops I didn't want to carry it, have someone pick up my bag, feel the weight.''

Nobles sat hunched over the Hefty bag between his legs. ''Lady carries around a suitcase full a money, she needs a gun. Keep the boogers off her.''

''That's it,'' Jean said. He was so close, hunched over, his cast resting on his knees. ''Aren't you going to offer me a drink?''

That got him up. ''Well, sure. You want a cold beer or a warm one?''

''Cold, please.''

Nobles went into the kitchen and was out of view. She heard the refrigerator door, heard the popping sound as he opened the cans. Henry Silva had poured Scotch, no ice, turned with a tall glass in each hand . . . She raised the Walther in her right hand, six rounds in the clip, one in the chamber, extended it toward the doorway to the kitchen and waited for Nobles to appear.

Both cans of beer were in his right hand; his left arm, in the cast, covered his stomach. So she aimed just above the cast. When he looked up, one stride out of the doorway, he paused, seemed to smile, trying to at least, and said, ''Hey, puss, be careful now—''

She shot him where she aimed, shot him again and shot him again, quickly, the sound so overpowering she missed details. Already he seemed in shock, pressed against the door frame, eyes glazed, the cast painted with blood. So much blood. Where were the beer cans? She had only a moment to notice effects. Henry Silva had touched the neat wound in his chest, looked at his hand with disbelief, looked up . . . She shot Henry Silva again and he did a slow movie die, reflecting betrayal right to the end. She shot Nobles again and he might have already been dead, sliding down the door frame to the floor.

LaBrava said to Franny, sitting in Lummus Park among palm trees, sipping cold beer, ''Then what happens?''

Franny said, ''Well, nothing happens after that the way it's supposed to.''

26

He saw only her eyes, her bland expression, and wondered who she was at this moment and if she was going to say anything, and after another moment if she was ever going to say anything. He watched her turn from the door without a word, hands coming away from the front of her robe, the robe falling open as she entered the bedroom.

So LaBrava went to the kitchen where an open bottle of Scotch and tray of melting ice cubes stood on the sink, decided, as he poured himself a good one, to let her lead; he'd catch on soon enough. He picked up the ice tray to put it in the refrigerator and hesitated—why should he?—then had to make another decision and did put the tray in the refrigerator and crossed to the bedroom with his drink.

Jean sat at the vanity in a halfslip doing her eyes, classic nose in the air, eyes indifferent, bare breasts indifferent, pale shoulders rounded in a slouch that described her attitude. He saw her drink waiting among cosmetics. She took time now to pick it up, her breasts rising as her eyes raised, two sets of brown eyes in the mirror watching him. He believed he could outwait them but would have to sit down. Tell Maurice they would be late for dinner, bring the bottle in here and then sit down. He had never played this game before. She was putting on eyeliner now. Then surprised him.

"Have you spoken to your friend McCormick?"

"About what?"

"I can believe he didn't report to you, since there was nothing to report. But you must've been curious enough to call him."

She sounded like his former wife, tone full of dry innocence, delivered deadpan. Taking the long way around.

He said, "Let's see. McCormick searched your place . . ."

"As you suggested."

He almost smiled. "He told you that?"

"Your words, according to Jim, 'Why don't you get her permission to have a look around?' I'd call that a suggestion."

"I'm surprised," LaBrava said.

"At what?"

"McCormick does care what people think. Wants you to like him." He watched her move to the other eye. "But he didn't find anything, uh?"

"Did you think he would?"

One way or another they were going to reach this point. It wasn't something he had to think about anymore. It would be good to get it out in the open. It was time.

He said, "Probably not, but there was always the possibility."

She paused, holding the eyeliner away from her, looking at him in the mirror. "You mean something Richard might have left behind? Fingerprints?"

"Something," LaBrava said, "either of you might have overlooked."

There was a silence. He expected it and waited, leaning in the doorway. It wouldn't be her style to let go, throw a jar of cold cream at him. She would adjust, making her own decision now, staring at him in the mirror, eyes telling nothing, eyes lowering then as her hand went to the vanity table. She picked up a pearl earring, cocked her head as her eyes raised to look at him again and a new Jean Shaw appeared, a playful expression in her eyes now, a glow of anticipation.

He said, "How do you do that?"

"How do I do what, Joe?" Her tone different, relaxed, ready to be amused. "How do I manage to . . . get by, survive? It ain't easy, kid. Learn to adapt, use whatever is at hand. I was just getting to like it here and now it's time to go home, or somewhere. I may go abroad . . . if anyone wonders where I am."

"If you think you can afford it."

Jean smiled, or seemed to. Her head turned slowly as she picked up the other earring, still looking at him. "Tell me what's bothering you, Joe."

"How you can do this to Maurice. That bothers me more than anything else."

"What am I doing?"

"It's *his* money."

Her hands came away from her face and she straightened,

looking at him directly. "Maury and I have known each other forever. You have to understand that first."

"Yeah?"

"He happens to love me."

LaBrava kept quiet.

"And knows I wouldn't hurt him for the world."

"How about for six hundred thousand?"

Jean got up from the vanity, moved to the bed where she picked up a white cotton shift, brought it carefully over her head, down past her hips. Standing erect, hands flat on her thighs, she said, "Do you think I need a bra?"

"You look fine."

"Not too flat? I've never had the nerve to go without one until lately."

"It couldn't have been lack of nerve."

"Modesty, then." She got her drink from the vanity, held his eyes as she came over. He didn't move. She turned to edge past him through the doorway, her body, her breast, brushing his arm, still looking at him and said, "You have to be very careful or people get the wrong idea, they think you're immodest."

"You haven't answered my question."

"So why ask?"

She took his glass and he followed her to the kitchen, wondering if he should put her flat on the floor, sit on her holding her arms, face to face, close. *You give?* And not let her up until she did.

She brought the ice tray out of the refrigerator saying, "I have a question. *Did* you tell McCormick to search my apartment?"

"What difference does it make?"

"My opinion of you, Joe. That's important to me."

"Look, one way or another, even if he had to get a federal warrant, McCormick was gonna search your place. I told him to ask you first."

"Why?"

"So you'd understand what you're into. You'd see these guys are serious, they're the pros and they've got you down as a suspect."

"Not anymore."

"Jean? . . . Listen to me."

She poured Scotch in their glasses before raising her eyes, mildly interested, patient.

"This isn't the movies," LaBrava said, "an hour and a half it's over." Using a quiet, confiding tone, one she might appreciate and believe. "This one doesn't end. Once they make it their case they'll take it all the way and sooner or later they bring in this guy, that guy, and your name comes up and they say, 'Oh, yeah, Jean Shaw, the movie star, what do you suppose she was thinking, dream up a scheme like that? Swindle six hundred grand from a nice old guy's supposed to be her friend.' And there's no way, I give you my word, it's not gonna happen."

In the silence she took time to sip her drink. She said, "What makes you think I did it?" with little more than mild curiosity in her tone.

"I *know,*" LaBrava said, still quietly. "It doesn't matter how or whether I can prove it or not. I *know.* And if I know then they're gonna find out. What you have to do is get the money. Now, as soon as you can. Give it back to Maurice before you do anything else—and you know what I'm talking about. If it's not too late I'll help you every way I can, see if we can cover it up and hope no one asks too many questions."

She said, "Would you do that for me, Joe?" Got sad stars in her eyes and said, "What a guy."

LaBrava had to take a moment. He wasn't sure if the line was familiar but it was her kind of line and her delivery. He paused to remember where he was, to bring Jean Shaw back into perspective and detach himself from reality. She knew what she was doing. Performing, but she still knew what she was doing.

With that easy delivery, looking at her drink now, she said, "It sounds like a wonderful part. Innocent woman unjustly accused, a wall of evidence against her. I'd love to play it."

"You did," LaBrava said, "in *Obituary.*"

She looked up at him abruptly.

"Don't you remember? I do. I can tell you the whole picture, beginning to end, and I saw it when I was twelve years old."

She said, "*Obituary,* yes, you're right," but sounded unsure, vague. "I wasn't only accused of something I didn't do, I was found guilty." Her tone picked up a little. "I had a wonderful courtroom scene. I lost my voice screaming—there must have been fifteen takes. But it was worth it."

He said, "Jean, where's Richard?"

She continued to look at him but seemed lost now. Her gleam had faded and he wondered if it might be gone forever, there was so little hope in her eyes.

She said, "Joe, were you really only twelve years old?"

He had to take another moment. She was serious now and he had to adjust. He said, "Jean, you're so good you could act your way out of a safe deposit box."

She seemed to smile. "Who was it said that?"

"I think it was James Garner doing Philip Marlowe. But it's true. You're even better now than you used to be, and you were my favorite as far back as I can remember."

She said, "Were you only twelve, Joe?"

"That's all. But I was horny as a grown man, if that'll make you feel better."

Maurice opened the door, a dish towel over his shoulder, a cooking spoon in his hand. He said to Jean, "Go pick up the phone, there's a call for you."

She walked past him, not asking who it was. LaBrava closed the door as Maurice said, after her, "Guy tried to get you earlier, I told him to call back around eight." He turned to LaBrava, extending the spoon. "Smell. We're having gumbo. Make the drinks while I go stir it."

Jean was at the desk in the living room, pulling off her earring as she raised the phone.

LaBrava said to Maurice, "Who is it, Torres?"

"Some guy with an accent. I don't know."

"You ask him his name?"

"Hey, go make the drinks, will you?"

He tried to read her expression. She stood holding the phone in both hands, listening. He heard her say, "What?" a sharp sound. She was about fifteen feet away from him. He could make her a drink and take it over. She said something else but he didn't hear it because Maurice was telling him to be careful if he opened the freezer, there was half a peck of okra in there he didn't want all over the floor. Maurice saying, "Come here and taste this," as he watched Jean speaking into the phone, a few words. He started toward her and Maurice was next to him with the big spoon, offering it, putting it in his face. "Taste it, authentic Creole gumbo, recipe I got from a lady brought it here from Gretna, Louisiana. Little broad, her name was Toddy, she wore those pinch-nose glasses, weighed about eighty-two pounds, and made the best gumbo you ever tasted in your life. I would a married her, I mean just for her gumbo . . . Hey, Jean? Where you going?"

She stood holding the door open. Then closed it as they watched her.

"What's the matter? . . . Who was that on the phone?"

"Nothing important. Somebody with the police."

"It wasn't Torres. I know Torres' voice."

"No, one of the other ones. He was just checking, see if I'm okay."

"Yeah? Are you? You look funny. You feel okay?"

"Well"—she hesitated—"I do feel a little . . . strange. I think I'll go get some air."

"All you been through," Maurice said, "I can understand it. Stick your head out the window."

"No, I think I'll go outside."

"I'll go with you," LaBrava said.

"No, please, stay here. I'll be all right. Maury, do you mind? I'm just not hungry at the moment."

"You sure you're all right? You want any kind of pills? Alka-Seltzer?"

"No, I'm fine. Really."

They sat eating. Maurice said, "Ordinarily I put crabs in it, with the shrimp, but I didn't see any I liked at the market. So I put in some oysters. It's good with oysters. Or you can put chicken in it. The secret is in the preparation of the okra. When you sauté it you have to keep stirring it, fast. Also you have to stir the hell out of your roux when you're browning it, have to stir it and stir it. You know what I'm talking about?"

LaBrava said, "Maury, who's crazy, you or me?"

"How do I know?" Maurice said. "Maybe both of us. Don't ask me any hard ones."

When the phone rang Maurice took his time, waving LaBrava

off as he started to get up. Maurice went over, answered the phone and laid the receiver on the desk.

"I should a let you. It's your friend Torres."

He said to her, "You might as well tell me."

They sat on the Della Robbia porch. He would look at her as she stared at the view that was every picture ever taken of a moonlit sandy beach through palm trees, ocean in background. The view did nothing for either of them.

He said, "All right, let me see if I can tell it. The guy in the movie who picked up the bag went out a hotel-room window, but this one didn't. He found out, somehow, you've got the money and he wants his cut instead of a bunch of old newspapers, and if you don't pay him he'll turn you in." LaBrava waited. "It isn't fun anymore, is it?" He waited again and said, "Just say it, you'll feel better. You don't say it, I won't be able to help you."

A car passed on Ocean Drive, shined in the streetlight for a moment and their view returned.

She said, "What would you do?" her voice clear but subdued.

"Get him off your back."

"How?"

"I don't know yet. I'll have to talk to him first."

"You know who it is?"

"The boat-lifter. Cundo Rey."

She turned her head to stare at him. "How do you know that?"

"I showed you his picture, didn't I? You use somebody you never saw before. That was your first mistake. No, it would be your second mistake. Richard was your first."

She was silent again.

"How much does he want?"

After a moment she said, "All of it."

"Or what?"

"He didn't say."

"Tell me what he did say."

"He asked me if I wanted to buy a typewriter."

There was a silence.

"Your typewriter?"

"Yes."

"It can be traced to you?"

"I think so. There's a little sticker on the back—the name of the place where I have it serviced. I forgot about that."

They all forget something. "How'd the boat-lifter get it? You didn't give it to him, did you?"

"No, someone else."

"You gave it to a world-class fuckup to get rid of and he gave it to the boat-lifter who probably sold it and then had to get it back, once he figured everything out . . . What else did he say?"

"He wants me to meet him, so we can talk."

"Where?"

"A bar on LeJeune, Skippy's Lounge."

"Skippy's Lounge. Jesus. Are you supposed to bring the money?"

"No, that's what we're going to talk about. Where we make the exchange."

"Where is it, the money?"

She paused. "In my apartment."

"You think the place is safe now because they tossed it?"

She said, "Joe, if you'll help me . . ."

He waited and she seemed to start over. She said, "You have to understand something. I love Maury in a very special way. I know him better than you or anyone else ever will, and he knows me, he understands me." She said, "Joe, I promise you, I would never do anything in the world to hurt him."

Something she had said before, but in real life, not in a movie that he remembered. He said, "That's nice but we're past that. Torres called. They found Richard."

She stared straight ahead.

"It wasn't a cabin up in the mountains. It wasn't even that far from other houses . . ." He gave her a moment, but she said nothing. "I told Torres to have a talk with Richard's pal, Glenn Hicks." She turned again to stare at him and he said, "You get the feeling I know more about it than you do?"

After a moment she looked at the view again and said, "Joe, you have to believe how I feel about Maury . . ."

"I thought we were on Richard now."

She said, quietly, "There is no way anyone can prove I killed him."

"I didn't even say he was dead. But I'm not gonna tell on you. You're grown up enough to do it yourself."

She said, "Does he really matter?"

"Not to me, no. But the state attorney, you hear him you're gonna think Richard was his kid brother. See, you shoot and kill somebody you have to have a better reason than for money."

She said, "You broke his arm. What if you had hit him in the head?"

"I had a chance to and I didn't. That's the difference. Richard could've brought me up if he wanted to, I accepted that possibility. You're trying, as they say, to get away with murder." He realized he was at ease because he was in control and it didn't matter what role she tried on him. The poor lady didn't know who to be, so she was playing a straight part for a change and not coming off anything like a star. She was beginning to look older to him.

The view was the same. It didn't change.

She started to get up and he said, "Where you going?"

"To buy a typewriter."

Good line. He liked the way she said it; it gave him a feeling for her again.

He said, "Put your bra on and relax. I'll go talk to him, see if he wants to turn himself in."

"Why would he?"

"It's better than getting shot . . . I'll need the key to your apartment, to pick up the money."

"Swell," Jean said.

"Save that one," LaBrava said. "It's not over yet."

27

It was Ladies' Night at Skippy's Lounge. *Ladies Only. Drinks two for one till 9 P.M.*

So LaBrava hung a Leica and a camera bag on him and told the manager he was doing a photo story for the *Herald's* Sunday magazine, "Tropic," and the manager said to be his guest—but don't shoot any housewives supposed to be at K-mart shopping and a movie after unless you get a release. There were about a hundred of them, all ages, crowded around the circular stage watching the all-male go-go show. LaBrava said, "Let me get one of you while we're standing here, Skip." The manager said, "I look like a Skip to you? Those assholes up there with the razor cuts and the baby oil all over 'em are the Skips."

Five of them plus Cundo Rey doing their show opener.

The five Debonaires wore wing collars with little black bow ties, cuffs with sparkly cuff links and black bikinis. Cundo Rey wore a leopard jock and cat whiskers painted on his face, streaked out from his nose to his ears. He was the one and only Cat Prince, extra added attraction, who hung back in the opening number and did not new-wave-it the way the serious all-white Debonaires did. It was their set, repetitious, robotic, each Debonaire dancing with his own ego, three of the five in front of the beat, stepping all over it; they ducked and hopped to *I Do* coming out of the sound system and set J. Geils back ten years.

Cundo Rey came on for his solo with his raven hair, his earring, his painted-on whiskers, with West African riffs out of a Havana whorehouse, and Cundo was the show, man turned on with flake and blood into the catstud prince come to set the ladies free; his body glistened, his moves purred with promise, said stuff a five into my polyester leopard-skin, ladies, and we'll all be richer for it.

Many of them did and Cundo followed the waitress to LaBrava's table counting his sweaty wet take. He eyed LaBrava, smiled at the camera, blinked in the flash.

"So, the picture-taker."

LaBrava lowered the camera. "The boat-lifter."

Cundo ordered a sugar-free soft drink from the waitress, slipped into a chair still glistening, smelling of cologne, cat whiskers waved by his smile. "So, you and the woman. Is all the same to me. I sell you the typewriter, a nice one. I think you have to give me the camera, too. Is it the same one?"

"A better one," LaBrava said. "Older but more expensive."

"That's okay, I'll take it."

"Why didn't you try to take the other one?"

"I didn't know it would be so easy like this."

LaBrava said, "Is it?" He pushed the camera bag toward Cundo, who leaned over the table to look inside. As he looked up, LaBrava pulled the bag back, closer to him.

"Tha's Richard's gun?"

LaBrava nodded.

"What happen to him?"

"He got shot."

"I believe it," Cundo Rey said. "Guy like him, he would get shot. Did it kill him?"

LaBrava nodded.

"That guy, he don't know what he was doing. I don't know what he was doing either. Or you, or the woman. But I know what I'm doing, man, I'm going to sell you a typewriter or that woman is going to jail. Maybe you going too."

LaBrava said, "What would you think—you give me the typewriter, then give yourself up?"

Cundo said, "Give myself to the police?" He sat back as the waitress, with dollar bills folded through her fingers, placed a glass in front of him and filled it from a can of Tab. She walked away and Cundo leaned in, frowning. "I look crazy to you?"

"I don't know you," LaBrava said. "You could be some broke dick going from failure to failure, never gonna make it. See, if you're like that maybe you ought to turn yourself in, they'll take off a few years. You go up to Raiford and do your go-go number they'll make you Homecoming Queen."

"Man, I don't steal nothing. Why do I want to go to jail?"

"For killing that old man, Richard's Uncle Miney."

"Man, what is this? Some shit you telling me. What we have

to talk about—you like to see that woman go to jail?''

''No, I wouldn't,'' LaBrava said, ''and I'll tell you why. I don't trust her. I think just for a kick she could put the stuff on us. I mean the whole thing with her is for fun. She doesn't need the money, it's for thrills.''

''For thrills . . .''

''You understand what I mean? She's a very emotional person.''

''Yes, I understand.''

''She borrows the money from the old guy that owns the hotel . . .''

''Yes?''

''Then steals it from him.''

''She's some woman.''

''Very determined. You know, hardheaded. She says she doesn't want to buy the typewriter.''

''She doesn't? Why?''

''Because of her honor. She won't be forced to do it. She doesn't think you'd give the typewriter to the police.''

''No?''

''No, because if you turn her in—she said for me to tell you—she'll give them your name. They already have your picture, your fingerprints . . . Is that true?''

''Yes, is true.''

''So if she goes to jail, you go to jail.''

''What about you, yourself?''

''What did I do?''

''You kill Richard?''

''I never said that. But I see what you mean. You got a point.''

''I do?''

''Yeah, she could lay Richard off on me. Try to.''

''So why don't you kill her? You want me to?''

''I don't think we have to go that far. But I don't think you should try and sell her the typewriter, either.''

''No?''

''See, if the cops even suspect her, they search her place and find it?''

''Yes?''

"She could be pissed off enough she'd finger both of us."

"Yes, so what do we do?"

"You give me the typewriter. I'll take care of it."

"Give it to you . . . What do I get?"

"Half the money."

Cundo had to bite on his lip and think about it. "Three hundred thousand dollars?"

"That's right."

"How would you do it?"

"No problem. She already gave me the money, to hide. See, in case they search her place. So I give half to you and you give me the typewriter."

"What does she do then? Her money's gone."

"Who gives a shit? The typewriter's gone, too; she can't even prove *she* did it. She tries to put the stuff on us, it's her word against ours. What can she prove?"

"Nothing."

"So, all you have to do is give me the typewriter."

Cundo thought about it again. He said then, "You give me half the money, okay, *I* get rid of the typewriter."

"If I knew you better," LaBrava said, "if we were friends it would be no problem. But I don't know you. You understand? You give me the typewriter, you get half the take, and neither one of us has to worry. What do you say?"

Cundo thought some more and began to nod. "All right, half the money. Keep your camera, I don't want it."

"When?"

"Maybe tonight. After I go-go."

"Why not right now? Three hundred thousand, you don't need to hang around here shaking your ass."

"I like to do it."

"Okay, then later on?"

"Let me think."

LaBrava let him. He looked at those cat whiskers painted on Cundo's face and said, "You know, one time I was as close to Fidel Castro as I am to you right now. It was in New York."

"Yeah? Why didn't you shoot him? Maybe I wouldn't go to prison if you did."

"What were you in for?"

"I shot a Russian guy."

"Just trying to hustle a buck, uh?"

"Man, is tough sometime. You got to think, is somebody want to kill me? You never know."

LaBrava, nodding, had to agree. "As Robert Mitchum once said, 'I don't want to die, but if I do I'm gonna die last.' "

The Cuban with the cat whiskers painted on his face stared at him and said, "Who's Robber Mitchum?"

Cundo Rey was back at the place on Bonita now.

The first thing he had decided: there was no sense in the picture-taker giving him half the money when he could give him all of it.

The second thing: he needed light to see it. Make sure it wasn't some money on top of newspaper; he had enough newspaper. He didn't want to go to the woman's apartment where, the picture-taker said, the money was still in the trash bag; he didn't want to go anyplace he had never been. He didn't want to go to a bar or a cafe or some all-night place where people came in. He didn't want to go outside, in a park, where there wasn't any light.

He went through all this before coming around to the place he already had, on Bonita, a perfect place. Nobody on the street knew him or maybe had even seen him. All he had to do was leave the picture-taker here, go over the Seventy-ninth Street Causeway to the Interstate, be in Atlanta, Georgia, tomorrow. Go anyplace he wanted after that with his bag of money. Somebody would find the picture-taker in a week, two weeks, they would smell him and call the cops and break into the place.

He couldn't get over the picture-taker being so simple and trusting. He had thought the country people recruited for the housing brigade in Alamar were simple. This guy was as simple as those people. Either he believed he could trade half the money for the typewriter, or he believed he could pull a trick, get the typewriter and keep the money. Either way he would be very simple to think he could do it.

Cundo could feel his snubbie pressing into his spine, silk shirt hanging over it. Let the guy come in. Make sure the money was in the bag—no newspaper. Then do it. No fooling around. Do it. Leave the guy. He could drive out maybe to Hollywood, California, see how things were doing out there. Sure, get some new outfits, go Hollywood.

He was getting excited now, looking out through the Venetian blinds to the street that curved past the apartment. Empty. It always looked empty, even during the day. He was getting anxious waiting for the guy to arrive here. He rubbed a finger under his itchy nose, looked at his hand and saw the black Magic-Marker on his finger, from his cat whiskers he had forgot to wash off, from being anxious and excited. It was okay. Take half a minute.

Cundo left the window, moved from the living room through the short hall to the bathroom. That snubbie was hurting him. He pulled it out of his pants, laid it on the toilet tank. Wrap a facecloth around it after he washed off his cat whiskers, try it that way stuck in his pants, so the hard edges wouldn't hurt . . .

A sound came from the front.

He ran into the living room, looked out through the blinds. The street was still empty. Right behind him then, a few feet away, someone knocked on the door and Cundo jumped. He moved to the door and listened. The knocks came again in his face.

"Who is it?"

"It's me," LaBrava said. "Guy with the money."

Cundo opened the door, stood holding it for the picture-taker and right away could feel a difference in him. Like a different guy . . .

Coming in like a Brinks guard, holding the round Hefty bag in his left hand and Richard Nobles' .357 Mag in his right, pointed down.

Cundo couldn't believe it. He wanted to feel the snubbie pressing into his back; it would have felt good now, but that fucking snubbie was in the bathroom. He said, getting amazement in his voice, "Man, what do you have that gun for?"

"Respect," LaBrava said. "You still have your cat whiskers on."

Cundo didn't like that big goddamn Mag. He said, "Listen, why don't you put that thing away?"

''Pull my shirt out, stick it in my pants?'' LaBrava said. ''Where've you got yours, in back? I know you bought one off Javier, he's a good friend of mine. Turn around.''

Cundo said, ''What are you doing?'' as he turned around, wanting to show he was a nice guy, cooperating. He felt LaBrava poke the barrel of the Mag against his spine and then run it along his belt.

''Where do you keep it?''

''Man, I don't have no gun.''

''What'd you shoot Miney with?''

''You mean that old man? . . .''

''Why'd you shoot him in the back of the head like that?''

''Why?'' Cundo turned and stared at him, frowning, because he couldn't believe this was the same guy. This guy didn't sound simple and trusting. He was calm, but sounded like he didn't care very much, without emotion. What he sounded like was a policeman. ''Who said I killed him?''

''Where's your gun?''

''I told you, I don't have no gun.''

LaBrava was looking around the room. ''You don't keep a very neat house. What do you—you don't like the news, you tear the paper up?'' Still looking around. ''Where's the typewriter?''

''All right,'' Cundo said, and motioned toward the kitchen.

LaBrava dropped the Hefty bag between the green arms of a vinyl living room chair and followed Cundo through the kitchen to the garage, where he got to the trunk of the Trans Am and said, ''Oh, I got to go back in and get the key. I forgot it.''

LaBrava slid the barrel of the Mag over Cundo's hip, over tight knit material to his right-hand pants pocket.

''What's that?''

Cundo didn't say anything. He brought his keys out and opened the trunk—a clean trunk, nothing in it but a typewriter case.

''Bring it inside.''

In the living room again LaBrava motioned and Cundo placed the typewriter case on the maple coffee table. LaBrava sat down on the sofa in front of the typewriter case and motioned again. Cundo moved back a few steps. LaBrava laid the Mag on the coffee table and opened the case. It was empty.

Cundo waited for LaBrava to look up. He said, "Somebody must have stole it." He began to turn then, carefully, saying, "Excuse me, but I got to go pee-pee."

He walked past the Hefty bag sitting on the vinyl chair, he walked through the short hall and into the bathroom, hand going out to that beautiful snubbie on the white tile of the toilet tank . . .

"Drop it in the toilet," LaBrava said from the doorway, "and put the top down."

Cundo turned enough to look over his shoulder. "Man, I just want to go pee-pee."

"Drop it in the toilet, go pee-pee and then put the top down," LaBrava said. "How's that sound?"

He brought Cundo, hanging his head, back to the living room. He lifted Cundo's face, the barrel of the Mag under his chin, stared at him with a deadpan eternal cop look and Cundo said, "Is in the closet."

LaBrava found the typewriter. He stuck the Mag in his waist, carried the typewriter over to the coffee table and set it into the case, then had to bring the carriage in line so the top of the case would come down and snap closed. He looked over to see Cundo sitting in the vinyl chair now, the Hefty bag on the floor in front of him. LaBrava sat down on the sofa; he had not yet decided how he was going to handle the difficult part: how to get out of here with the typewriter and leave Cundo, with the money, for the cops.

The cops would wonder what was going on, because Cundo would tell them a story and LaBrava would have to say to Torres, "Oh, you believe that?" The cops would give the money back to Jean and she would have to return it to Maurice and then answer all the questions about Cundo's story the cops would ask her at the station and all the questions the state attorney would ask her perhaps in a courtroom. He could protect her tonight; tomorrow she would be on her own.

LaBrava looked up as Cundo said, "Is this half or all the money?"

"All of it," LaBrava said. "Six hundred thousand dollars."

The Mag was digging into his groin. He pulled it from his waist and laid it on the typewriter case.

''Something is telling me we not going to do business,'' Cundo said.

He sounded tired, almost sad, and LaBrava said, ''You can look at it if you want. Imagine what it would be like.''

''Why not?'' Cundo said, and began unwinding the baling wire from the neck of the bag.

He could lock him in a closet, LaBrava was thinking, and call the cops. But he would have to stay here until just before they arrived or Cundo would bust out.

The boat-lifter was reaching into the bag now, feeling around. He brought out a handful of currency he looked at shaking his head very slowly. His hand went into the bag with the currency to stir it, feel it, sink his arm into it. His expression changed then, eyes opening a little wider. He drew his arm out and extended it toward LaBrava, his hand gripping a small bluesteel automatic.

''How do you think about this?'' Cundo said. ''You know, I say to St. Barbara I believe this is my day. Then I don't think is my day. Then I have to think, yes, it is my day. How do you like this, uh?''

LaBrava nodded—not to say yes, he liked it, but to confirm what he felt. See? He wasn't able to be detached, objective enough to take it all the way. When the boat-lifter reached for the gun in the bathroom that was the time to be detached and shoot the motherfucker and that would have been it; but he had even felt sorry for the guy, invited him to look in the bag . . . He had looked in the bag himself in Jean's apartment when he picked it up and had brought out a handful of bills, but it hadn't occurred to him to ask her what she did with the gun. He could pretend to think like a cop and he could put on a cop look with a gun in his hand, but he couldn't take it all the way.

Now it was turned around and now it was all right to be subjective about staying alive and having to shoot the guy to do it, *if* you could do it . . . with the .357 Mag an arm's length away on the typewriter case and the boat-lifter aiming the automatic from about eighteen feet away—LaBrava stepping the distance off with his eyes, less than six strides to the guy who had shot the old man in the back of the head, twice.

Cundo said, "You look at me like that . . . Now you don't have nothing to say."

"I got a question," LaBrava said.

"Oh, you want to make a deal now?"

"No, I was gonna ask, how do you know the gun's loaded?"

Cundo didn't answer.

"What is it, a Beretta?"

Cundo didn't answer.

"It's probably a Walther. Pray to St. Barbara it isn't a Saturday-night special and misfires on you. They always misfire."

Cundo, one eye closed, was trying to look at the gun and keep LaBrava in his sights at the same time.

"If it's a Walther you'll see some writing on it, in German. Unless it's a Czech seven-six-five."

Cundo was squinting, one eye closed, extending his head now, leaning toward the gun and turning it slightly to read the inscription on the side of the barrel . . .

And LaBrava thought, Jesus Christ, knowing he was going to have to take it all the way right now, before he started to feel sorry for the guy aiming a gun at him, if that was possible—right now all the way—and reached for the .357 Mag on the typewriter case, concentrating on picking it up cleanly . . . Cundo firing . . . and coming around and putting the Mag on him . . . Cundo firing . . . and squeezing the grip . . . Cundo falling back in the chair firing at the ceiling . . . squeezing the grip, squeezing the grip, and shot him three times up the center grove of his rib cage. After that, in silence, the little Cuban with the cat whiskers stared dead at him in the green vinyl chair and then hung his head.

LaBrava locked the Hefty bag in the trunk of the Trans Am, called the Miami Beach Police to report gunfire on Bonita Drive, just to be sure, and left with only what he had come for, the typewriter.

28

Now he would stay out of it as long as he could, or until it was settled.

He slept late. He didn't answer his phone. He kept very still when there were footsteps in the hall and twice during the morning someone knocked on his door. He did not look out the window at the view that was all ocean views. He did look at his photos and decided he didn't like any of them: all that black and white, all that same old stuff, characters trying to be characters. He said, Are you trying to be a character?

In the afternoon, which seemed like a long time after to him, there was a knock on the door and he opened it when he heard Franny's voice.

Franny said, "Where've you been? . . . Don't you know I miss you and hunger for you?"

He smiled because it didn't matter what kind of a mood he was in. When he saw her he smiled and knew he would not have to bother choosing an attitude.

Franny said, "What's going on? The cops were here again."

He told her he didn't know. He didn't want to learn anything from Franny that might be misinformation or only part of it or speculation. He wanted it to be settled and then learn about it in some official way, facts in order.

She said, "*Some*thing's going on and I'm dying to know what it is. I mean finally we get a little ac*tiv*ity around here. Live in a place like this, LaBrava, the high point of the day is some tourist comes in and asks where Joe's Stone Crab is."

"Or the mailman arrives," LaBrava said. "Let me take you to Joe's tonight, or Picciolo's, any place you want to go."

He put on the banana shirt after Franny left and looked at himself in the mirror. He liked that banana shirt. He looked at his photos again and began to like some of them again, the honest and dishonest faces, enough of them so that he could say to himself, You got promise, kid.

Who was it said that?

Who cares?

He took off the banana shirt, showered, shaved, rubbed in Aqua Velva—Maurice had told him, "Use that, you must have cheap skin"—put the banana shirt on again and picked up the typewriter case. It was now seven in the evening. It was time. So he went up the stairs to the third floor, walked past Maurice's door to Jean Shaw's, knocked and waited. There was no sound. He walked back to Maurice's door.

Maurice said, "The hell you been?" Wearing a white-on-white shirt with long collar points, a black knit tie; his black silk suitcoat was draped over a dining room chair.

Jean Shaw, in a black sheath dress, pearls, stood at the credenza making drinks. She was saying—and it was like a background sound—"Orvis, Dinner Island, Neoga, Española, Bunnell, Dupont, Korona, Favorita, Harwood . . . Windle, Ormond, Flomich . . . Holly Hill, Daytona Beach. There. All the way to Daytona."

"You left out National Gardens." Maurice winked at LaBrava standing there holding the typewriter case.

She turned saying, "Where does National Gardens come in?" Her eyes resting on LaBrava.

"After Harwood," Maurice said. "Look who's here."

"I see who's here," Jean said. "Is that my typewriter you're returning?"

"Sit down, get comfortable," Maurice said. "Jean, fix him one. He likes it on the rocks."

"I know what he likes," Jean said.

"Well, it's all over," Maurice said. "You missed Torres this morning. Go on, sit in my chair, it's okay. In fact, I insist." He waited as LaBrava curved himself, reluctantly, into the La-Z-Boy; being treated as a guest of honor. "There's a couple a discrepancies they can't figure out. Like Richard was killed with the Cuban's gun and the Cuban was killed with Richard's gun, only he was killed *after* Richard was killed," Maurice said, moving to the sofa. "Which has got the cops scratching their heads. But that's their problem."

Jean came over with drinks on a silver tray.

"The cops found the money, we got it back," Maurice said. "Far as I'm concerned the case is closed."

She handed LaBrava his and he had to look up to see her eyes, those nice eyes so quietly aware.

"The cops can do what they want," Maurice said.

She handed him his drink, Maurice on the sofa now, and sat down next to him, placing the tray with her drink on the cocktail table. LaBrava watched her light a cigarette, watched her eyes raise to his as she exhaled a slow stream of smoke.

"You can't have everything," Maurice said. "I told your friend Torres that, he agreed. You got the two guys you want, be satisfied."

Her gaze dropped to the typewriter case on the floor next to the recliner, lingered, came up slowly to rest on him again.

"Torres said they always thought there was a third one. Only why didn't he take the money? Unless he had to get out a there fast once he shot the Cuban and didn't have time to look for it. Richard's gun—you know where it was? In the toilet. Listen, there was even another gun in there, in the toilet, they find out shot somebody else. You imagine?"

LaBrava said, "Maybe the third one will walk in, clear everything up."

Jean was still looking at him.

"I told the cops, be grateful for what you have," Maurice said. "That third one, whoever, did you a favor. Any loose ends—well, you always got a few loose ends. Who needs to know everything? No, as far as I'm concerned—" He gave Jean a little nudge with his elbow. "What is it they say in the picture business?"

"It's a wrap," Jean said.

He nudged her again. "Should we tell him?"

"I don't see why not," Jean said.

Maurice got higher on the sofa, laid his arm on the backrest. "Well, we decided last night . . . Jeanie and I are gonna get married." He brought his hand down to give her shoulder a squeeze. "Look at him, he can't believe it. Yeah, as a matter of fact we start talking last night, we couldn't figure out why we hadn't thought of it a long time ago. Make life easier for both of us . . . We're tired a living alone."

LaBrava didn't say anything because he didn't want to say anything he didn't mean.

The former movie star in her fifties looked younger, much younger, sitting next to the retired bookmaker, natty old guy who didn't know he was old.

"I'm gonna take good care of her," Maurice said.

"And I'm going to let him," Jean said. She said then, "It's not the movies, Joe." Looking at him with those eyes. "Maury wants you to be his best man."

He wasn't going to say anything he didn't mean or cover up whatever it was he felt.

What he finally said was, "Swell."

Then gave them a nice smile: maybe a little weary but still a nice one. Why not?

CAT CHASER

For Katy Leonard

1

Moran's first impression of Nolen Tyner: He looked like a high risk, the kind of guy who falls asleep smoking in bed. No luggage except for a six-pack of beer on the counter and the *Miami Herald* folded under his arm.

He reminded Moran of a show-business personality going to seed. Long two-tone hair thinning fast, what was left of a blond pompadour receding from a sunburned peeling forehead. Moran could see dark roots that matched his dark, neatly trimmed mustache. The khaki shirt was neat too, freshly laundered, faded, the cuffs of the sleeves turned up once, shirttails hanging out, aviator sunglasses hooked to one of the flap pockets. Onetime dude over the hill at forty. Maybe half in the bag. Dreamy eyes looked up from the registration card to the calendar on the wall behind Moran, then half-closed, squinting.

"Is it October already?"

It was almost November.

He filled in another line of information about himself, looked up and stared directly at Moran, deadpan.

"This is the Coconut Palms Resort Apartments. Is that correct?"

"That's correct," Moran said, just as dry.

Nolen Tyner's gaze shifted to the inside window of the office that looked out toward the Atlantic Ocean, past the oval-shaped pool and empty lounge chairs. His sleepy eyes returned to Moran.

"Then why don't I see any palm trees?"

"Some bugs ate 'em," Moran said. "I had to have six trees removed."

"It doesn't bother you," Nolen Tyner said, "you call this place the Coconut *Palms* there isn't a single palm tree out there? Isn't that false advertising?"

"The high rise on the south side of us, nine stories, is called the Nautilus," Moran said, "but I don't think it's a submarine. The one on the other side, it's ten stories, is the Aurora. Tell me if you think it looks like a radiant glow in the upper atmosphere. That'll be thirty dollars. You're in Number Five, right next to the office."

Nolen Tyner continued to stare at Moran. He nodded. "Okay. How about if I sit out by the pool and drink my beer and I don't take a room? How much is that?"

"That's also thirty dollars," Moran said. "For the ambience and the music."

"I don't hear any music."

"I haven't turned it on yet," Moran said. "I'll tell you what though. You can take your six-pack up the road, you might find something more to your liking. Maybe even less expensive."

Nolen Tyner was looking at Moran's beard, his white T-shirt and cutoff jeans. "You work here or own the place?"

"Both," Moran said. "My desk clerk'd stand here and chat with you all afternoon, but he's off today."

"Being courteous to people who come in off the street," Nolen Tyner said, smiling a little, "I imagine that can be a pain in the ass at times, huh?"

"It can if you let it," Moran said.

Moran looked at the reservation card.

Nolen Tyner, 201 Alhambra Circle, Coral Gables, Fla. 33134. Make of car: '76 Porsche. No license number.

Written in an arty back-leaning style, half-printed. Give him an "A" for neatness but an "F" for lying about his home address, since 201 Alhambra Circle was a big glass building, the Ponce de Leon Plaza, where his former wife's lawyer had his offices. It wasn't more than a mile from where Moran had lived during the seven years of the marriage.

If Nolen Tyner did live in Coral Gables or had an office there and he liked to sit outside in the afternoon and drink beer, why didn't he go to Bayfront Park? Why come all the way up to Pompano, an hour's drive, pay thirty bucks for a room and then sit outside? Which the guy was doing now. Lying in a lounge chair on the afternoon shadyside of the pool. Holding a can of beer on his chest, moving it almost in slow motion when he'd take a sip. Wearing his sporty safari shirt, but also wearing, Moran noticed, very unsporty black socks with his open-toed sandals. If he wasn't meeting a woman here—and after about an hour and three cans of beer it didn't look like it—then he was either hiding or looking for action.

But if he was hiding he'd stay inside. Wouldn't he?

And if he was looking for action and had heard something about the Coconut Palms' SECRETARY SPECIALS—advertised twice a year in big-city papers up north—it was possible he'd come with the idea of picking up some poor secretary who was here by herself, bored out of her mind. Except that October was a very lean month for secretaries compared to February and March. And the guy had not said anything clever or hinted around about looking for girls.

So maybe he was looking for somebody in particular. And if that was the case, without checking the guest chart Moran knew who it would be. Not the secretaries from Dayton in Number Three. Not the ones from Fort Wayne in Four. Or the elderly couple who wanted Seven so they could keep an eye on their Buick parked on the street. No, it would have to be the afternoon lovers in Number One, the lower oceanfront apartment.

They had been meeting here every afternoon except the weekend for the past eight days: the young Cuban-looking guy who wore rings and chains, gold-rimmed sunglasses up in a nest of thick hair, and the stylish woman who was about ten years older than the guy and probably married to a Cuban businessman in Miami. The guy had signed in *Mario Prado* and Moran, taking in the guy's glistening hairdo, said, "Haven't I seen you on TV?" Mario Prado said yeah, he did guest shots on Tony Marvin's show; he was playing cocktail piano at the Sheraton in Palm Beach; his manner so bored, relaxed, Moran was afraid the guy might collapse, melt into a puddle of grease. Mario took Number One oceanfront for a month, paid fifteen hundred cash in advance, without Moran asking for it, and the mystery woman appeared a short time later. Mario Prado waited on the street, sunglasses over his eyes now, until the gray Mercedes pulled up. He took a case of champagne out of the trunk. After that they arrived separately each afternoon between one and two and usually left about five, not much later. Neither of them ever spent the night.

One time, a few days ago, the woman arrived on schedule, but the piano player failed to show. Moran watched her come out of Number One to stand by the low cement wall that separated the yard from the beach, the woman in a white sundress and heels, her dark hair shining in the sunlight, tied back with a violet scarf. She had her arms folded and seemed impatient, though she didn't move much. Moran went out in his T-shirt and cutoffs to get a look at her.

He said, "Mrs. Prado, how're you today?"

She appeared to be in her late thirties, about Moran's age, stylishly thin, holding a languid model pose now, wrist bent on her hip, as she studied Moran from behind big round violet-tinted sunglasses.

"That's not my name," the woman said, with an edge but only the hint of an accent.

"It's the name your husband signed," Moran said.

"My *hus*band?" the woman said. "You think that's my *hus*band?"

"Well, whoever you are, we're glad to have you," Moran said. "You like me to put some music on? We've got outside speakers."

"I like you to beat it and leave me alone," the woman said and turned to look at the ocean. She had a nice profile, thin, straight nose, her hair pulled back tight to show round white earrings.

"Well, enjoy your stay," Moran said and got out of there. He couldn't imagine her being much fun. Maybe that was why they brought all the champagne, get her loosened up. Lula, Moran's part-time maid, would come out of Number One in the morning with a plastic bag of trash and give him a report. "'Nother dead soldier and the brandy's near touching bottom. Should see how they tear up a bed." Moran never went into occupied rooms out of curiosity, to see how people lived or what they'd brought with them; he respected their privacy. But he did consider sticking his head into Number One, some quiet evening after the lovers had gone. Inspect the setting on the off chance it might reveal something about them. Still, it had to be a purely sexual relationship, and if that was the case then what would he be looking for, pecker tracks? He could think of a lot more important things to do—if he put his mind to it.

The day following the brief meeting with the woman the piano player came into the office, his pink shirt open to show his chains and said to Moran, "I understand you try to make the moves on the lady with me. I'll tell you something, man, what's good for you. Stay away from her. You understand?"

At this point the piano player and the woman had used up only about two hundred of the fifteen-hundred-dollar advance. The numbers registered in Moran the innkeeper's mind as he considered grabbing the piano player by his pink shirt and throwing him out on the street, and the numbers gave him pause. It wouldn't hurt to be polite, would it?

Moran said, "I'm sorry if I gave Mrs. Prado the wrong impression. I didn't much more'n say hi to her."

"You ask her if she want to dance with you."

"No, I'm not a dancer," Moran said. "I asked if she wanted me to turn some music on." He grinned in his brownish beard. "I suppose a lady as attractive as your wife has guys hitting on her all the time. I can see where she'd become, well, defensive." Which was not an easy thing for Moran to say. Now if the piano player would accept this and leave . . .

But he didn't. Mario Prado spread his ringed and lacquered fingers on the counter like it was a keyboard, like he was going to play Moran a tune, and said, "I hear you go near her again you going to be in deep shit, man. You got it?"

Moran said to him, no longer grinning, "Mario, there's a certain amount of shit you have to put up with in this business, but you just went over the limit. You want, I'll give you the rest of your money back. But if I do I'll probably pick you up and throw you in the swimming pool, and with all those fucking chains you got on you'll probably sink to the bottom and drown. But it's up to you. You want your money back?"

The piano player squinted his dark eyes and got hard drawn lines around his nostrils. This, Moran assumed, was to indicate nerves of ice banking the Latin fire inside. Moran wondered if the guy practiced it.

The piano player said, "Just wait, man. Just wait."

That was a few days ago and Moran was still waiting for the Cuban's revenge—the guy and the woman in the apartment right now doing whatever they did. While Mr. Nolen Tyner reclined in a lounge chair on the shady side of the pool, beer can upright on his chest, as though he might be sighting the beer can between the V of his out-turned sandals, aiming his attention directly at oceanfront Number One. Keeping an eye on the Latin lovers who, Moran had decided, deserved one another.

Wait a minute. Or was Nolen Tyner watching out for them, protecting them? Hired by the piano player.

Christ, he could be keeping an eye on *you,* Moran thought. It gave him a strange feeling. It reinforced the premonition he'd been aware of for a couple of weeks now, that he was about to walk into something that would change his life.

Except that it wasn't time for Moran's life to take another turn. He was thirty-eight, not due for a change until forty-two. He believed in seven-year cycles because he couldn't ignore the fact that every seven years something happened and his life would take a turn in a new direction. Only one of his turns was anticipated, planned; the rest just seemed to happen, though with a warning, a feeling he'd get. Like now.

When he was seven years old he reached the age of reason and became responsible for his actions. He was told this in second grade, in catechism.

When he was fourteen a big eighteen-year-old Armenian girl who weighed about thirty pounds more than he did took him to bed one summer afternoon; she smelled funny, but it was something, what he learned the human body liked.

When he was eighteen he misplaced the reason he had acquired at seven and joined the Marines, Moran said to get out of being drafted, to have a choice in the matter, but really looking for action. Which he found.

When he was twenty-one, back on the cycle and through with his tour, he left the Marines and his hometown, Detroit, Michigan, and went to work for a cement company as a finisher, to make a lot of money. This was in Miami, Florida.

When he was twenty-eight Moran married a girl by the name of Noel Sutton and became rich. He went to work for Noel's dad as a condominium developer, wore a suit, bought a big house in Coral Gables and joined Leucadendra Country Club, never for any length of time at ease in Coral Gables high society. He couldn't figure out how those people could take themselves and what they did so seriously and still act bored. Nobody ever jumped up and said, "I'm rich and, Christ, is it great!" Moran knew it was not his kind of life.

And when he was thirty-five Noel, then thirty, divorced him. She said, "Do you think you can get by just being a hunk all your life? Well, you're wrong, you're already losing it." Answering her own question, which was a habit of Noel's. Moran told her answering her own questions was a character defect. That and trying to change him and always being pissed off at him about something. For not wearing the outfits she bought him with little animals and polo players on them. For not staying on his side of the court when they played mixed doubles and she never moved. For "constantly" bugging her about leaving her clothes on the floor, which he'd mentioned maybe a couple times and given up. For drinking beer out of the can. For not having his Marine Corps tattoo removed. For growing a beard. A lot of little picky things like that. He did shave off the beard, stared at his solemn reflection in the mirror—he looked like he was recovering from an operation—and immediately began growing another one. Henry Thoreau had said, "Beware of all enterprises that require new clothes." Moran believed those words ought to be cut in stone.

The divorce was not a bad turn in the cycle. Moran had never been able to say his wife's name out loud without feeling self-conscious or thinking of Christmas. So that was a relief, not having to say her name. Also, not having to look bright and aggressive when he was with her dad. Or look at beachfront property and picture high-rise condominiums blocking the view.

He had certainly been attracted to Noel, a petite little thing with closely cropped dark hair and a haughty ass: she seemed to be always at attention, her back arched, her perfect breasts and pert can sticking out proudly; but he wasn't sure now if it was love or horniness that had led him to marriage. In the divorce settlement Noel got the house in Coral Gables and a place her dad had given them in Key West and Moran got their investment property, a twelve-unit resort motel in Pompano Beach, the Coconut Palms without the palm trees.

Sort of a U-shaped compound, white with aqua trim. Two levels of efficiencies along the street side of the property. A wing of four one-bedroom apartments, two on each level, that extended out toward the beach. The apartment wing was parallel to a white stucco one-bedroom Florida bungalow that also faced the beach. And the oval swimming pool was in between, in the middle of the compound.

Moran moved into the bungalow and found he liked living on the beach and being an innkeeper, once he'd hired a clerk-accountant and a part-time maid. He liked meeting the different people. He liked being in the sun most of the day, doing odd jobs, fishing for yellowtail and snapper once a week. Renting the efficiencies for fifty a day in season and the apartments for seventy-five Moran grossed around eighty thousand a year. Taxes, utilities, upkeep and salaries ran thirty-five to forty, so Moran wasn't exactly socking it away. Still, it was a nice life and he was in no hurry to change it.

Then why did he feel it was about to take another turn on him?

He was planning a trip next week: fly down to Santo Domingo in the Dominican Republic, a vacationland Moran had invaded with the Third Battalion, Sixth Marines in 1965 when a revolution broke out and Johnson sent in Marines and Airborne to safeguard American lives and while you're at it run out the Communists. "I'm not going to have another Cuba in the Caribbean," the president said. In his thirty-day war Cpl. George S. Moran, Bravo Company, Third Platoon, a First Squad fire-team leader, shot a sniper, was wounded, taken prisoner by the rebels, got a Purple Heart and met a Dominican girl he would never forget. He wanted to walk those streets again without sniper fire coming in and see what he remembered. He might even look up the girl who had once tried to kill him. See if she was still around.

Maybe it was the anticipation of the trip that Moran mistook for a premonition of something about to happen.

But maybe it was something else. Something winging in at him out of the blue.

2

The following afternoon at the municipal tennis courts, Moran worked his tail off to win two hard sets, hanging in there against a kid with a vicious serve and a red headband who'd try to stare him down whenever Moran called a close shot out of bounds. Moran was only in doubt about his calls a couple of times. He dinked the kid to death with left-handed backspin junk, sliding the kid around on the clay, until the kid threw his racket at the fence and dug out a ten-dollar bill folded to the size of a stamp. Moran said to him, "You're all right, kid. Keep at it." He had always wanted to call somebody "kid" and today was the first time.

When he got back to the Coconut Palms there was Nolen Tyner out by the pool with a six-pack.

Jerry Shea, sitting at the office desk with a pile of bills, was whistling as he made entries in the ledger. Moran never knew the songs Jerry whistled. He asked him today, what's the name of that? And Jerry said, "This Year's Crop of Kisses." Jerry was a retired insurance salesman, sixty-seven, who cocked his golf cap to one side, slapped his broken blood vessels with Old Spice and went after lonely widows who'd invite him up to their condominiums for dinner, happy to cook for somebody again, have some fun. Moran pictured withered moth-eaten flanks, or else globs of cellulite getting in the way. Jerry said there was more active poon around than you could shake a stick at. With the fat ones, you rolled them in flour and looked for the wet spot.

Moran said, sitting down, taking off his tennis shoes and socks, "That guy out there drinking beer—"

'Mr. Nolen Tyner," Jerry said. "Works for Marshall Sisco Investigations, Incorporated, Miami. Actually their office is in Coral Gables."

"He told you that?"

"Ask a person what they do, they generally tell you," Jerry said. "Especially since I recognized the address. We used to use Marshall Sisco on insurance investigations from time to time; it's a good outfit. Nolen says he's been with them a year, but I think he's part-time help. Before that played dinner theaters up and down the coast and says he's been in movies. He was an actor."

"I think he still is," Moran said. "He checked in yesterday about two and left at six, didn't use the room."

"Well, when he come in today," Jerry said, "he took it for a week. Number Five. I asked him was he taking some time off and he says well, you could say that. Sort of combining business with pleasure."

Moran got up and turned to the window to look at Nolen lounging in the shade. The two secretaries from Fort Wayne had their recliners on the cement walk out by the wall, aimed at the sun that soon would be hidden behind the condo next-door, the Aurora. Moran's gaze moved from their pink corrugated thighs to Number One.

"How about the lovers?"

"They're in there." Jerry swiveled around from the desk. "The woman got here first for a change. Then, when the piano player come, Nolen Tyner got up and went over to say something to him. They talked a few minutes, the piano player goes on inside Number One, then comes out again and has another talk with Mr. Tyner."

"Arguing?"

"I don't believe so. A lot of nodding, both of 'em, getting along fine. Then the piano player goes back inside and Mr. Tyner returns to his beer."

"This is a nice quiet place," Moran said. "I don't want some husband coming here with a gun."

"Maybe they're friends," Jerry said. "Or she's a rich woman and Nolen Tyner's her bodyguard; why he thinks it's pretty good duty, combining, as he says, business with pleasure."

"Maybe," Moran said. "But I better find out."

He didn't want to talk to the guy in his sweaty whites, barefoot; it wasn't his natural image. It reminded him of the country club, standing around in whites in polite conversation, waiters coming out with trays of tall drinks. Moran followed the walk to his bungalow, passing behind the figure reclined in the lounge chair, waved to the two 40-year-old secretaries from Fort Wayne and went inside. He drank a beer while he showered and changed into jeans, a T-shirt and dry tennis shoes, old ones that were worn through and he slipped on without socks. He got a fresh beer from the refrigerator, then on second thought another one and took them, one in each hand, out to the Marshall Sisco investigator lying in the shade.

"You must like the place you sign up for a week."

Nolen Tyner opened his eyes behind the aviator sunglasses, startled, about to rise, then relaxing again as he saw Moran extending the beer.

"Cold one for you," Moran said. "Yours must be pretty warm by now." Four empty cans stood upright on the ground next to the lounge chair with two full ones still in the cardboard casing.

"That's very kind of you," Nolen said. He jerked the backrest of the chair up a notch and reached for the can of beer that was beaded with drops of ice water. His sleeve rode up to reveal a bluish tattoo on his right forearm, a two-inch eagle with its wings raised.

While on Moran's left forearm, also extended, was his faded blue Marine Corps insignia.

They looked at each other. Nolen said, "From the halls of Montezuma, huh?" Smiling, popping open the can of beer.

"And I take it you were airborne," Moran said. "Not by any chance the Eighty-second?"

"That's the one."

"Second or Third Brigade maybe?"

"Third. You're leading up to something, aren't you?"

"As a matter of fact," Moran said. "I wonder if you were in Santo Domingo sixteen years ago. Sitting on the bank of the Ozama River by any chance?"

"Sitting high on the east bank, up on the grain elevators," Nolen said, smiling some more. "You don't mean to tell me you were there?"

Moran pulled a recliner over with his foot and sat down, straddling the leg rest, now eye to eye with Nolan. "You had a weapons squad up there, didn't you? Up on the silos, or whatever they were. With a one-oh-six recoiless rifle?"

"We had a bunch of 'em up there."

"And one day you're using your one-oh-six trying to hit a

sniper, firing across the river at this *one* guy. He was in a building the corner of Isabella Catolica and Luperon.''

Nolen raised his eyebrows. ''Marines weren't ever that close to the river. Were they?''

''I got excited,'' Moran said. ''The heat of the chase.''

''You mean you fucked up,'' Nolen said. ''Got suckered.''

''The dinger would fire a round, then disappear,'' Moran said. ''You never knew where you'd get shot at from next.''

''I remember snipers,'' Nolen said. ''Yeah, and I remember the troopers talking about they took this guy out. Little fucker with an M-one.''

''It was a medium-size fucker with an M-fourteen,'' Moran said. ''It was *me* they got. We're chasing the dinger, I run upstairs, he's gone. I look out the window and a fifty-caliber tracer round nearly took my head off.''

Nolen was nodding again. ''Fired from the spotting rifle.''

''I *know* what it was fired from,'' Moran said. ''Followed by a screaming one-oh-six. I had a mitt I could've stuck my hand up and caught it.''

''Didn't kill you, huh?''

''It took out the back end of the third floor and the stairs. I got hit here, below my flack jacket and down my leg. Fifteen pieces of iron they dug out and gave me a Heart,'' Moran said. ''So you were Airborne. What'd I bring you a beer for?''

''You felt something, a kinship,'' Nolen said, ''one grunt sniffing another. I'll tell you what. Even if it wasn't me I'll buy you a drink later on. Make it up to you.''

''I'm going down there next week,'' Moran said.

''Where?''

''Santo Domingo.''

''Jesus Christ, what for?''

''Walk my perimeter, see if it looks the same. Stay at the Embajador—we were bivouacked right there. Maybe look up some people. There doesn't seem to be anything going on; now it's El Salvador.''

''If there's any place down there we can go in and fuck things up,'' Nolen said, ''Reagan and Haig'll find it, don't worry.''

''You been back to the D.R. since?''

''I ate that chow just one time and got Trujillo's Revenge,''

Nolen said. "I partied with *one* girl, *one* and took home a dose. I take a vacation, man, I go to Las Vegas where everything's sanitary."

They took a sip of their beers. Looking at Moran Nolen Tyner said, "Well, well . . ."

"I'm not gonna say it's a small world," Moran said, easing back in the recliner to get comfortable, crossing his sneakers, the strings hanging loose.

"You want to know how small it is," Nolen said, looking across the pool. "You got a couple Dominicans right in that end apartment. The piano player and the broad, the lovers. Though my sheet says the piano player might be Puerto Rican."

"I thought they might be Cuban," Moran said, "all the Cubans in Miami. "Your sheet—what do you mean by your sheet?"

"The IDs of people I got under surveillance. The broad, for example. She's married to a guy by the name of Andres de Boya. Miami big bucks, I mean big."

"Wait a minute," Moran said. "The woman in there?"

"They got a house on Biscayne Bay looks like that Polynesian restaurant in Lauderdale, the Mai Kai, only bigger."

Moran agreed, nodding. "That's right. But the woman isn't Mrs. de Boya."

Nolen gave him a funny look, guarded. "How would you know?"

"Mrs. Andres de Boya's from the same place I was originally," Moran said. "Detroit. And she's no more Dominican than I am. She's a very nice-looking woman. In fact she's . . . well, she's a nice person."

Nolen was looking at the holes in the toes of Moran's sneakers, the left one larger than the right. He didn't seem too sure about Moran.

"Maybe it's a different de Boya, a relative."

"How many Andres de Boyas are there?" Moran said. "He was in Trujillo's government, something like twenty years ago, right up to the time Trujillo got shot on the way to see his girl friend."

"Twenty-seven times they hit him," Nolen said. "A prick like that, I guess you have to be sure."

Moran was patient. "De Boya came to Miami—I imagine with

a few million he'd scored. He was a general in charge of something or other . . ."

"Something or other—try head of the secret police," Nolen said, "the Cascos Blancos, the white helmets. You're a poor Dominican you see a guy wearing a liner painted white you run for the fucking hills."

"I thought he owned sugar mills," Moran said.

"That's how he got rich. Trujillo used to pass out sugar mills for good behavior. Three days after the old dictator's killed, de Boya's on his yacht bound for Miami. With all the U.S. dollars he could get his hands on." Nolen was looking at Moran's sneakers again; his gaze thoughtful, still somewhat skeptical as it raised to Moran's beach-bum bearded face.

"How do you know him?"

"Leucadendra Country Club. I played golf with him a few times. Actually it was twice," Moran said, "in the same foursome. That was enough."

"Too rich for your blood, uh, the bets? Little Nassau?"

"No, the guy cheats," Moran said. "You believe it? Guy that's worth, easy, forty fifty million, he cheats on a hundred-dollar round of golf and all the clucks, the guys that play with him, know it. I couldn't believe it. They not only pay up they go, 'Gee, Mr. de Boya,' give him all this shit what a great game he plays."

Nolen said, "Yeah?" Still a little hesitant. "What about you? You pay him?"

"No, as a matter of fact I didn't," Moran said. "My father-in-law at the time, I thought he was gonna have a stroke. 'You out of your mind? You know who that is, for Christ's sake?' I said, 'Yeah, a guy that cheats. Fuck him.' My father-in-law goes, 'A hundred bucks, Christ, I'll give you the hundred.' I tried to explain to him that wasn't the point, but my father-in-law was nervous because de Boya was putting money in his condominium developments and I worked for him, my father-in-law. So he was afraid it would look like he was siding with me, not making me come across. I told him that was too bad, I wasn't gonna pay any tinhorn hacks his way out of the rough like he's cutting weeds, three-putts the hole and says he took a five. Bullshit."

"You belong to Leucadendra?" Nolen's tone of skepticism was giving way to mild surprise.

"Not anymore," Moran said. "De Boya tried to get me blackballed. He not only didn't like the way I played golf, he hinted around I was trying to hit on his wife."

"Were you?"

"No. I told you, she's a very nice person. Her name was Mary Delaney, worked for de Boya's lawyer before they got married."

"Change her luck and marry a spic, uh, with fifty million. Shit, I'd marry him too."

"Be careful," Moran said.

Nolen grinned. "Got a little soft spot there? I won't say another word."

"De Boya didn't get me blackballed," Moran said, "but it didn't help my standing at the club any. Then when my wife divorced me for not playing the game, her dad helped give me a shove and there went the club membership. Which was fine, I never liked golf that much anyway."

"So you were married to bucks, too."

Moran shrugged. "It might've worked, it didn't, that's all. The last time I saw de Boya—he came by here about six eight months ago like nothing had happened, like he hardly knew me, and offered to buy the place, build a condominium."

"What'd you tell him?"

"I turned him down. I got real estate people calling here every week. They're trying to build a solid wall of condos from Key West to Jacksonville."

"I won't ask you the last time you saw his wife." Nolen grinned to show he was kidding around.

Moran didn't grin. He said, "Good. We leave her out of this." He said, "I understand you had a talk with the piano player today."

"You got eyes even when you're not here," Nolen said. "Yeah, actually I felt sorry for him. I told him I had him under surveillance with a woman he wasn't supposed to be with. Then, before he started to sweat I told him he was perfectly safe, I wasn't gonna turn him in. Even though I was taking a terrible risk."

"You made him understand," Moran said, "the risk ought to be worth something."

"Like fifty a day. Why not."

"And you don't even give 'em clean towels," Moran said. "What do you do when you're not hanging out?"

"I rest," Nolen said. "I got rid of my goals, decided to take it one day at a time. Don't overdo it, never drink more than a case of beer or a fifth of booze in any given day. Unless there's a party."

"I've always admired restraint," Moran said. "Not overreaching your capabilities."

"There you are," Nolen said. "I was an actor for twenty years. Well, ten years professionally. Some film work in New York, mostly dinner theater down here. You're trying to act, the audience's sitting there trying not to break wind out loud. They want to leave, go home, but not any more'n I do. I played either the lead guy's buddy or the broad's brother. You know, just a straight asshole type of guy, wrings his hands a lot, opens his eyes real wide: 'Gee, Scott, I don't know if I'd do *that.*' Doesn't ever know what the fuck's going on. I start playing the guy as a drunk, give the part a little dimension. Or I'd play it, give it just a hint the guy's homosexual. But the asshole directors on that dinner circuit, to get any respect from them you had to be Forrest Tucker . . . Doug McClure. You know what I mean? That type."

"I imagine it's tough," Moran said, "when you think of all the Doug McClures out there." He saw Nolen eying the two Fort Wayne secretaries, their chairs backed up to the low cement wall, the high-rise shade now up to their knees.

"I'm at a motel in Golden Shores," Nolen said, looking at Moran again. "It's not bad, three bills a month, it's fairly clean. The thing is, I'd like very much to give you the business—"

"I think you are," Moran said.

"But even your off-season rate, thirty bucks a day, and you know, come on, that's not only steep it's unrealistic. Maybe not for transients, no. But what I'm offering you is the assurance of a permanent tenant."

"How permanent?"

"What have you got? With the lovers and the secretaries you got about four units out of twelve rented, am I right? And it's like that I bet eight nine months of the year. Okay. For a fair rate you'll have guaranteed occupancy of Number Five the year 'round. I'll even help you out keeping the place up. Skim the pool, cut the grass—''

''We don't have any grass.''

''Feed the chickens—I don't know what you do around there. You tell *me*.''

''Six hundred,'' Moran said.

Nolen said, ''George, six hundred, I can get a furnished two-bedroom apartment for six hundred.''

''Maybe over at the Seminole Indian Reservation. Not on the beach you can't.''

''How about three? For old time's sake, the Dominican Republic,'' Nolen said. ''I'll entertain the secretaries, teach 'em how to sit up and roll over. Listen, I'll even sign a year's lease.''

And leave in the dead of night, Moran thought. But what would he be out? He liked Nolen. He didn't trust him especially, but he didn't have to. Moran said, ''Okay, but no smoking in bed. You promise?''

Saturday Nolen Tyner moved into Number Five with everything he owned. Two old suitcases and several cardboard boxes loaded with magazines, letters, glossy photographs of himself in different outfits and poses, a hair dryer. A liquor case that held bottles of scotch, vodka and rum, most of them nearly empty. A lot of clothes, soiled-looking, out-of-style shirts, trousers and sport coats doubled up over bent hangers. A big Northern tissue box of sporty shoes, tan ones and white perforated ones that caught Jerry's eye and Nolen told him he could have any pair he wanted if they fit. The man's life was in cardboard boxes he carried from one motel to another.

Jerry left with his shoes and Nolen poured Moran and himself a scotch to mark the occasion.

He said, ''You're right, that Dominican broad is not de Boya's wife.''

''You find out who she is?'' Moran sat at the Formica table with his drink.

''She's de Boya's sister. I see the address, Bal Harbor,'' Nolen said, ''I guess I assumed they're separated and she moved out. So this morning I ask Marshall, 'Why'd you tell me it's the guy's wife?' He goes, 'I didn't tell you that. I told you her name's Anita and who the client is, that's all. You musta decided she's his wife.' Marshall's one of those guys, he's never wrong. He gives me the information on the back of an envelope."

"His sister," Moran said. "I didn't know he had one."

"Anita's forty-two, divorced for the third time." Nolen poured himself a little more scotch. "She starts fooling around de Boya calls Marshall. 'Anita is doing it again with somebody.' De Boya protecting the family name. 'Find out who she is fucking and let me know.' This's been going on for years. One time he follows her all over Miami, she keeps giving him the slip. Marshall's sitting in his car in front of a place over on Collins Avenue, a store where he *knows* she went in. He looks in his rearview mirror, Christ, here she comes up behind him in her Mercedes, slams into the ass-end of Marshall's car, backs up, doesn't give a shit her grille's all smashed in, and gives him the finger as she drives past. Gives him the old finger. . . . Another time, Anita starts out she's balling this jai-alai star in Dania. Right in the middle of the investigation, Marshall's moving in, getting the goods, she switches over to a bongo player with some reggae band doing a gig on the Beach. This broad, she's got gold fixtures in her bathroom, I mean *gold,* man, and she's fucking this guy wears a wool cap pulled down over his dreadlocks out in the sand. They don't even get a *room.*"

"Love is funny," Moran said.

Sunday night Moran saw lights on in Number One and checked with Jerry. Jerry said it was the Latin lovers, they'd paid for the place they could come anytime they wanted, couldn't they? Moran was always patient with Jerry; he said yeah, but why at night all of a sudden when up till now they'd only come afternoons from one to five? Jerry said, don't ask me; those Cubans, you never know what they're up to. Moran checked with Nolen and Nolen said the piano player was off Sunday and Monday. Moran said well, maybe they were seeing what it was like at night, like regular folks. He wouldn't worry about it.

3

Moran was watching Monday Night Football on television, Detroit Lions and the Chicago Bears fighting it out for the obscurity award, Moran trying to decide if he'd rather be a wide receiver or a free safety . . . whether he should have another beer and fry a steak or go to Vesuvio's on Federal Highway for spaghetti marinara and eat the crisp bread-sticks with hard butter, Jesus, and have a bottle of red with it, the house salad . . . or get the chicken cacciatore and slock the bread around in the gravy . . . The phone rang.

Moran got up out of his chair and walked barefoot across the vinyl tile floor. It felt sticky and he thought again of carpeting the living room, redecorating the place and getting rid of the dumb furniture that was here when he moved in: the jungle floral print, black and pink and green, curved bamboo arms on the chairs and sofa. He could hear the wind outside, that overpowering ocean pounding in out of the night. Sometimes it made him feel daring to live on the edge of it, fifty yards away watching a professional football game in color. The phone was on the end of the high counter that separated the kitchenette from the rest of the room. He said, "Coconut Palms. . . ." and expected to hear the voice of a secretary calling from up North somewhere.

Jerry said, "George, could you come in the office a minute, help me out here?" Then a silence, waiting.

It was Jerry's voice but it didn't sound like him. His tone was quiet, cold sober and that wasn't Jerry's sound after six in the evening, even when he was doing the books.

Moran said, "What's wrong?"

Jerry said, "There's a party here looking for somebody. I don't know they're registered or not."

There was an innocence in this voice that was not Jerry. Jerry knew everything.

Moran said, "Hang on, I'll be right there."

Outside he felt the wind through his T-shirt and looked for stars. There weren't any. Tomorrow it would continue to blow and the secretaries would moan about the weather. Their apartments were dark, only the amber porch lights on. Number One showed light behind draperies drawn closed. It surprised Moran. The second night in a row for the lovers. Here all night—they'd left sometime this morning and were back at it. Couple of alligators. Moran couldn't picture them saying romantic things to one another. He imagined the woman scowling, impatient with the piano player, telling him what to do as the poor guy tried to service her. Moran walked past the warm underwater glow of the swimming pool and approached the office. Through the window he could see Jerry behind the registration desk that was like a narrow counter, Jerry shaking his head, saying something past the two men who were leaning on the counter close to him, not meeting their gaze, nervous, evasive, not like Jerry.

Both of the men wore lightweight jackets with open sport shirts, the collars folded out flat. One dark, with thick hair and Latin features, a mustache that curved down around the corners of his mouth. The other older, pink-skinned, heavyset going to fat; he wore dark-framed glasses and pushed them up on the bridge of a pug Irish nose as the door opened and he turned from the desk.

Moran's first-glance impression: Miami Police.

Jerry was tense, frowning. He said, "George, do we have a guest name of Prado staying with us?" He had a stack of reservation cards in his hand. "I don't recall that name. Less they checked in on my day off."

"Let me see," Moran said, coming around the counter now, playing the game with Jerry for whatever reason he was doing it, but knowing one thing for sure, before they said a word: They weren't police. Jerry and the police were buddies. Moran took the guest cards and started going through them. They were old ones, from last season.

The Latino younger guy was staring at Moran, weighing him and apparently not impressed. He said, "Come on, what is this?"

Moran said, "What was the name, Bravo?"

"*Prado.*" The younger one reached across the counter, held his arm extended and snapped his fingers.

"Give me those. Come on, let see what you got."

Jerry said, "I told him, George, they're private property. I'm not supposed to show 'em."

The heavyset Irish-looking guy put his hand on the younger one's outstretched arm. The arm went down to the counter and the heavyset one pushed up his glasses again. He said, "George, we're not getting anywhere fast here, are we? Looking through cards—what've you got, maybe two units rented, three? You got five cars outside counting mine." He turned to the windows that looked out on the courtyard and the illuminated pool. "You got lights on in one unit I can see. Maybe they're in there watching the ball game, which I wish I was home watching right now myself. But I know this fella we're looking for doesn't care too much about the NFL or who goes to the Super Bowl next January, so he's probably doing something else in there. We can go down and knock on the door. We can knock on every door you got here, but I don't want to disturb any your guests might be sleeping. Cause a commotion, give the place a bad name. That's where I stand. What I want to know, George, is where you stand, why you're being uncooperative."

Moran didn't say anything. He was trying to think of the phone number of the Pompano Beach Police.

"He owe you rent money?"

Moran still didn't say anything.

"That's a pretty easy question, George. You don't have to scratch your head on that one, do you?"

The Latino one said, "Come on, George, cut the shit. What room is he in?"

The heavyset one turned to look at the Latino. He said, "Corky, go on outside, okay? Go on, I'll take care of it."

The Latino took his time, reluctant, but went outside toward the pool.

The door closed and the heavyset Irish-looking guy said, "Fucking spic. Somebody told 'em they have hot blood, they have to live up to it. Don't worry about Corky, I'll put him on a leash I have to."

"Or I can call the cops," Moran said.

The heavyset man sighed. He dug into his rumpled size-44 jacket, brought out a business card and laid it on the counter.

"Jiggs Scully. I used to be a cop myself. City of New York, borough of Manhattan, George. I bet I can talk to 'em better'n you can."

Moran picked up the card. "Business Consultant . . ."

"That's correct," Scully said, "I'm a consultant. See the address? New World Tower, Biscayne Boulevard. I advise people on business matters, act as a go-between, bring people together that want to make deals . . . things like that. You want to know any more, come by my office we'll have a coffee sometime. Okay? Right now I'm going down to see Mr. Prado. Where you come in—I'm gonna knock on his door, he don't open it then I might have to kick it in. I mean the business I got with him is that pressing. So you can give me a key and maybe save yourself a door. What do you think?"

Moran said, "You can knock on the door. But if he doesn't open it you don't go in. You can talk to the cops and we'll see how good you are."

"Oh, man," Jiggs Scully said, sounding tired, leaning on the counter again. "I notice that thing on your arm. Once a Marine, always a Marine, uh? Gonna stand your ground. Okay, pal, he don't open the door I'll go home, watch Monday Night Football. How's that sound to you?"

Jerry stayed inside by the window, within reach of the phone. Moran would give him the high sign if he had to use it. Right now it was quiet out there. The two men had gone down to oceanfront Number One, knocked, waited, knocked again and the door opened. Now they were inside. Jerry looked at the clock. Twenty past ten. They'd been in there only a couple of minutes. Jerry opened the office door now. He called out in a low voice, "George?"

The figure near the shallow end of the pool didn't move; he was watching the end apartment. Beyond it was darkness and the ocean. Jerry stepped outside. He closed the door behind him quietly and crept up to Moran.

"You able to hear what they said?"

Moran shook his head.

"That wind out there, you can't hear yourself think," Jerry said. "The piano player opened the door, then seemed to step back, didn't he? Like he was inviting them in?"

Moran didn't say anything. He wished Jerry would go back inside.

"Maybe they're from the finance company, gonna repossess his car. I didn't like 'em at all. That type," Jerry said, "they come in a place, you know they're gonna take whatever they want. First I thought it was a stickup."

"You better stay by the phone," Moran said. "You look up the number?"

"Seven eight five . . . seven eight five two nine . . . Or is it nine two one one?"

"I don't know what it is," Moran said, "but you better be sure." He saw the door open. "Jerry, they're coming out."

Jerry hurried off.

Moran watched the younger guy, the Latino named Corky, appear, then the piano player and the woman. The Irish-looking guy, Jiggs Scully, closed the door and turned the knob to make sure it was locked. They came in single file now along the front of the apartment wing, heading for the alcove next to the office where the Coke machine and ice maker were located. They could go through the alcove to the street. They were about twenty feet away, passing him now.

Moran said, "Mrs. . . ." He didn't know what to call her. He said, "Is everything all right?"

Jiggs Scully, a barrel shuffling along, bringing up the rear, looked over. "Everything's lovely, George. Go on back the ball game."

Moran said, "Mr. Prado?"

The Latino guy, Cooky, said something in Spanish and laughed. Jiggs Scully said, "George, you're paid up, you got nothing to worry about there. We're gonna go out have a few pops. We'll see you later. Have a nice evening."

Moran followed them as far as the alcove. He watched them walk past the line of angle-parked cars, past the woman's gray Mercedes, Nolen's rusting-out blue Porsche. He didn't see the piano player's car. All four of them got into a two-tone red and white Cadillac and drove away.

Moran had to go to the office to get the key to Number Five. Jerry said, "Nolen's in there. He's been in there all evening."

"I guess he's asleep," Moran said.

"But why would he know anything about them?" Jerry said.

Moran didn't answer, already going out the door. He stepped over to Number Five, listened—there were faint sounds coming from inside. He knocked hard, three times. When nothing happened he used the key to open the door. The place smelled like a bar.

The TV was tuned to the football game. Nolen sat in the room's one comfortable chair facing the set, eyes closed, head lying on his shoulder, snoring a little. Moran shook him, taking the empty glass he held in his lap.

"Hey, Nolen?"

He woke up right away. "What's the matter?" He rubbed his hand over his face and saw Moran placing the glass on the table, by the scotch and the box of crackers. Moran came back to the chair.

"Two guys came in. Looking for the piano player."

Nolen didn't say anything.

"You hear what I said?"

"What time is it?"

"About ten-thirty. They came out with Prado and Anita, said they're going to have a drink, but I don't think so. They put 'em in a car and drove off. A red and white Cadillac."

"There you are," Nolen said.

"What do you mean, there you are? They took 'em somewhere."

"Forget about it," Nolen said. He still hadn't moved, sitting low in the chair.

"One of them, his name's Jiggs Scully. The other guy was Cuban—I don't know, Latin."

"The guy told you his name?"

"He gave me his card. Jiggs Scully."

"You believe him?"

"He gave me his *card.*"

"You're paid up," Nolen said. "Forget about it."

"You sound like the guy Jiggs," Moran said. He turned around and walked out.

When he got the key to Number One Jerry wanted to go with him, but Moran told him he'd better stay in the office in case there was a call. He didn't want Jerry along. He was afraid he'd see something in the apartment and Jerry would ask questions and he'd end up telling Jerry the woman was Andres de Boya's sister and then Jerry would ask more questions and Moran would have to stand there saying, "I don't know," over and over, Jerry driving him nuts. It was true, he didn't know what was going on. They could be good friends and the guy was kidding about kicking the door in. The woman hadn't yelled. She could have run or at least yelled out when she saw him standing by the swimming pool.

He had a funny feeling going in the apartment, the wind blowing, then quiet as he closed the door—the place empty but all the lights on, every one of them.

It still surprised him the woman hadn't yelled something. A woman like that, she would have demanded help if she needed it, then complained if he didn't jump right away.

The apartment seemed in order, music playing softly on the radio. If they didn't turn the radio or the lights off, that could mean something. Forced to leave without any fooling around. Or it could mean they didn't worry too much about bills from Florida Power. People who owned places along the beach were always comparing their electric bills. An ashtray was full of long cigarette butts. A few Coconut Palms illustrated postcards lay on the desk. There was an empty champagne bottle in the trash can. He didn't see the brandy bottle, the one Lula said was down a couple inches every morning when she cleaned. Lula said they tore the bed up; but both double beds were still made. A pink negligee hung in the bedroom closet. Moran wondered if he should take it; he was pretty sure he would never see them again. There didn't seem to be anything that belonged to the piano player. Moran turned off the radio and the lights before he left.

* * *

They didn't come back during the night. When Moran walked out to the street, early, before seven, he saw the woman's gray Mercedes was gone. He thought, Well, that doesn't mean anything. All of them still could be friends. They got back late and the woman decided to go home; the lovers never spent the night anyway. Maybe they'd be back at it this afternoon . . . Just about the time Moran would be at Miami International boarding the Eastern flight to Santo Domingo.

He waited until after nine before calling the number on the business card that bore the name *Jiggs Scully* and *Consultant* beneath it.

A woman's voice said, "Good morning, Dorado Management."

Moran said, "Mr. Scully, please."

The woman's voice said, "Mr. Scully?" As though she didn't recognize the name. "Just a minute." There was a silence on the line for about ten seconds. The woman's voice came back on and said, "I'm sorry, sir, there's no Mr. Scully with the company."

Moran said, "I've got his card. Your phone number's on it."

The woman's voice said, "I'm sorry, sir, there's no one here by that name," and hung up.

Moran didn't see Nolen until ten-thirty. He came out to the cement wall with a beer in his hand, stringy hair blowing in the wind, and raised his face, eyes closed, to the overcast sky.

"Beautiful morning."

Moran said, "They didn't come back last night."

"They never do."

"I called the guy's number. Scully? There's no one there by that name."

"He lied to you," Nolen said, "didn't he? But, in any event, the lovers will come back sometime or they won't. What else can I tell you, buddy?"

Moran was ready to jump on him. "You can cut the buddy shit and tell me what's going on. Why'd Anita and the piano player pick this place? There a thousand motels they could've gone to, they pick this one. Why?"

Nolen took a drink of beer without opening his eyes. "It's halfway between them—I don't know."

"But you were told to come here, weren't you? You didn't follow them here."

"Marshall gave me a postcard picture of the place, when it had palm trees."

"De Boya gave it to him?"

"I guess so."

"He tell his sister to come here? Good place to shack up? Come on . . ."

"Maybe she saw the postcard at her brother's house," Nolen said, in pain, persecuted. "She tells the piano player to meet her here 'cause it's the only place she can think of. How's that?"

"Something's going on," Moran said, "and I'm standing in the middle. Does de Boya think I know his sister? I invited 'em here?"

"I don't know," Nolen said, "I really don't. I was hired to watch Anita." He sucked in fresh ocean air, still not looking at Moran. "And sort of keep my eyes open."

"For what?"

"See who comes to visit you." Nolen glanced at Moran and could not have liked the way Moran was staring at him. "Marshall said—you want his exact words?—he said keep your eyes open for a broad."

"Go on."

"With sort of blond streaked hair, good-looking."

"About thirty-two?"

"Yeah, he said around thirty."

Moran kept staring at him. "What else you do for money? Anything you're told, huh?" He walked off toward his bungalow.

Nolen said, "George?" and waited for him to look around. Nolen raised his beer can. "You got any cold ones?"

Moran looked tired. He said, "Come on," with a halfhearted wave of his hand.

Nolen followed him inside.

Jerry Shea watched the black Cadillac pull up in front. At first he thought Moran had called for an airport limo. But then realized this car wasn't any ride to the Miami airport. This was the real thing, a personal limousine with no-glare windows that were almost as black as the car and a driver who wore a buttoned-up dark suit that could pass for a uniform.

Jerry Shea said, "Oh, my God," out loud.

The driver was the Latino guy who was here last night, the one the other guy had called Corky. Now he was a chauffeur. He stood holding the handle of the rear door, ready to open it.

Now the other one, Jiggs Scully, who had given Moran his card, came out of the passenger side of the front seat. He wore a dark suit and stood pulling up his pants and sticking his shirt in, adjusting himself.

Jerry picked up the phone but didn't dial.

The driver, Corky, was opening the rear door.

A man about sixty got out. A man with a broad, tight expanse of double-breasted gray suit that he adjusted smartly, pulling the jacket down to appear even tighter. The man was Hispanic but very light and had a certain bearing, immovable, built like the stump of an oak tree cut off at about five nine. He reminded Jerry for some reason of a labor leader, a guy high up in the Teamsters, a Latin Jimmy Hoffa. Though this guy was more polished. That word was in Jerry's mind because the guy looked like he darkened his hair with black shoe-polish, the way it was shining in the sun, like patent leather.

The man was taking a pair of sunglasses from his inside pocket as he looked up at the Coconut Palms. He didn't seem too impressed.

Moran was half-dressed, packing his canvas carry-on bag. Two pair of pants, five shirts, a couple of light cotton sweaters . . . he wasn't sure how long he'd be down there. Four or five days maybe. When the phone rang Nolen looked up. He'd been sitting with his beer, grateful, not making a sound. He heard Moran say, "They're back?" Then heard him say, "Jesus Christ, yeah, that sounds like him . . . It's okay, Jerry, I'll see what he wants." Moran was looking toward the side window as he hung up.

Nolen said, "What's going on?" Watching Moran pull on a dark blue sport shirt and move toward the door.

"Stay where you are," Moran told him. He swung the door open and stopped.

The Irish-ex-cop-looking guy, Jiggs Scully, was standing outside the door, pushing his glasses up on his nose. He said, "George, how we doing? Your team won last night, uh?"

Moran stepped out, pulling the door closed behind him. He started past Scully and stopped.

"Which one was my team?"

Scully gave him a wise grin. "The Lions. You're from the Motor City, aren't you?"

"What'd I do?" Moran said.

"I don't know, George, you tell me. Or tell Mr. de Boya there. He wants to ask you something."

Moran moved past Scully, buttoning his shirt, approaching Andres de Boya now who stood near the far end of the cement walk, looking out at the beach with his hands locked together behind his back. He turned to watch Moran coming, then squared around again to face the beach as Moran reached him.

"How much frontage you have?"

It stopped Moran for a moment. He opened his beltless khaki pants and tucked in his shirttails, zipped as he said, "The same I had the last time. Was it a hundred and twenty or a hundred and thirty feet? I forgot."

"You're talking about a difference of two hundred thousand dollars," de Boya said to the ocean. His voice was soft, but with a heavy accent.

"Numbers aren't my game anymore," Moran said. "How's your golf?"

De Boya didn't answer or move a muscle.

Moran wondered what would happen if he kicked the guy ass-over the cement wall into the sand, and walked away. He attempted again to nudge him with, "If you're looking for your sister, she isn't here . . . You already know that, huh?"

Hard-headed guy, he refused to come to life.

"Am I getting warm?" Moran said. "I'll tell you something. If you think I had anything to do with her coming here, you're wrong. I never met your sister before the piano player and I've only talked to her once, if you could call it that."

"How much you want?" de Boya said, out of nowhere.

"For what? My place?"

"I give you . . ." de Boya paused. "Million six hundred thousand."

"You serious?"

"How much you want?"

"The real-estate guys that call about every week now are up over two million."

"I give you two million and two hundred thousand."

De Boya's gaze came past him and Moran smiled. Was he serious? The man's gaze continued on, sunglasses like a hooded beacon sweeping the beach; black hair parted in a hard line, showing his scalp.

Moran said, "You want me to go away, Andres? Come on, what's your game?" He wanted to keep it light and not let the guy get to him. "Whatever it is, the Coconuts isn't for sale." And looked out at his beach, at the surf pounding in. "I like it."

"Why?"

Moran waited; he wanted to be sure.

"I ask you why."

The man had turned and was almost facing him now. He had asked a question that had nothing to do with real-estate value or numbers and seemed interested in getting an answer.

"I live here," Moran said. "It's my home."

De Boya looked past him, toward the stucco bungalow. "You live in that?"

"I live in that," Moran said.

"How much you make here?"

"A lot," Moran said.

"How much? A few thousand?"

Moran said, "I don't know your sister and I haven't seen your wife in over a year. I want you to understand that. I never made any moves on your wife. Never."

De Boya seemed to be staring at him, though might have been sightless behind the sunglasses, the wax figure of a former general.

He said, "Get three offers on real-estate letter paper. I give you a hundred thousand more than the best one."

Moran looked at him closely. Maybe you had to hit him on the head with a hammer to get a reaction. Moran imagined taking a ball peen and the man's plastic hair that covered his one-track mind flying in pieces.

He said, "You serious, Andres? You want to build?"

"Of course, build," de Boya said, more animated than before. "What else do you think?"

And maybe that's all there was to it, though Moran still had his doubts.

He said, "Well, we could sure use another condominium," turning to look at his property. "There's room for forty units you go up ten floors. Sell them for around three and gross twelve million. Cost you about eight and a half to build it, say two for the property, add on this and that, cost of tearing down the Coconuts, you net maybe a million, million and a half. I could do the same thing. But it seems like a lot of trouble to go to. I mean what do I get out of it? Pay half to the government. I'm the owner so I live up in the penthouse with a great view of the Atlantic Ocean but have to take an elevator anytime I want to go outside." Moran nodded toward his bungalow. "I already have a view of the ocean. I got a living room, a bedroom. I got a color TV . . ."

The Dominican former general, cane grower, head of the secret police or whatever role it was that made him rich, stared at Moran. Maybe he understood; maybe he didn't.

But either way, Moran thought—packed, ready to take off on his adventure—what difference does it make?

He said, "Andres, all I'm trying to say to you is, there's no place like home and no friend like Jesus."

Moving away Moran's gaze came to the two figures standing at the opposite end of the walk, in front of the bungalow, Nolen and the Irish-looking guy, Scully. As Moran got closer he saw they were each holding a can of beer, *his* beer; Nolen acting, telling a story, Scully grinning, getting a kick out of it.

There you are, Moran thought. You gonna worry about these people?

4

All over the world, Moran decided, the past was being wiped out by condominiums.

There were condos now on the polo grounds west of the hotel, where Amphibious Task Force helicopters had dropped off Marines from the U.S.S. *Boxer,* the grounds becoming a staging area for Marine patrols into the city. There were condos and office buildings rising in downtown Santo Domingo with the initials of political parties spray-painted on fresh cement, PRD and PQD; but only a few YANQUIS GO HOME now, on peeling walls out in the country, old graffiti Moran had noticed coming in from the airport.

There were young wives of ballplayers sunning themselves at the hotel pool—where the Marines had set up their water purification tanks—the young wives talking about housing and travel while their husbands, down here to play winter ball, took batting practice and went off for a round of golf.

There were no open fields near the hotel now. The gardens were gone, where the first group of Marines had dug in. The Kentucky Fried Chicken place on the corner of Avenida Washington and Socorro Sanchez was gone. The mahogany trees on the street south of the U.S. embassy were still there; the trees looked the same.

They had gone up this street beneath the arch of trees, wide-eyed in the dark, all the way to Nicolas Penson in a war where the street signs were intact and they found their way with a Texaco road map. In the morning they saw people in the streets, crowds of people lining Washington along the oceanfront, like they were watching a parade. They were—waving at the tanks and amtracs. Even with the FUERA YANQUIS signs painted on houses most of the people seemed glad to see them.

The next day, filing back to the embassy, a Marine walking point was shot dead by a sniper; Item Company, at Checkpoint Charlie north of the embassy, drew heavy fire and soon there were snipers working the whole neighborhood, what was supposed to be the International Safety Zone, using bazookas as well as small arms, even old water-cooled 30s that pounded out a heavy sound and at first were thought to be .50-caliber. The Marines moved crosstown, east, establishing a Line of Communication with the Eighty-second Airborne troopers coming into the city across the Duarte Bridge. The LOC held the rebels cornered in the old section of the city and kept the loyalists from getting at them. But it didn't stop the snipers.

A battalion officer told them, "You got your Friendlies and you got your Unfriendlies." He told them most of the snipers were hoodlums, street gangs who'd armed themselves when the rebels passed out guns the first day. These people were called *tigres* but were not trained or organized, not your regular-army rebels. The *tigres* were out for thrills, playing guns with real ones. "So don't fire unless you're fired on." That was a standing order.

Wait a minute. You mean there're *rules?* Somebody said, "We're *here,* man." Two Marine battalions and four Airborne. "Why don't we go downtown and fucking get it done?"

The question was never answered. By the end of the first month of occupation nineteen U.S. military had been killed in action, one hundred eleven wounded.

Moran said to his driver today, in the early evening sixteen years later, "I have a friend who was here with the Eighty-second, the paratroopers. He believes we could have gone into the rebel area, the old section, and ended the whole thing in about fifteen minutes."

"Yes, I believe it, too," the driver said.

"You were here?"

"Yes, I always be here."

"What side were you on?"

"This side." The driver, who was an old black man with Indian cheekbones that looked as though they had been polished, tapped his steering wheel. "Three taxicabs ago, the same Number Twenty-four. Chevrolet, but not new like this one." They were in a '76 Chevrolet Impala, Moran in front with the driver, the windows open, Moran now and again smelling wood smoke and the smell would take him back to that time.

"You were glad to see the Marines?"

"Yes, of course. To have peace. I drove pressmens from the United States. Yes, we come to a corner, a street there, we have to go fast or those rebel fellas shoot at you. One time the bullets come in this side where you are, they hit here"—he slapped the dashboard—"and go out this way past me, out the window." The driver's name was Bienvenido. He was born in 1904 and used to Marines from the United States. He said to Moran, "You want to see where Trujillo was killed, yes?"

"Tomorrow," Moran said.

"And the old quarter, Independence Park."

"Tomorrow," Moran said. He was silent a moment and then said, "Do you know a woman by the name of Luci Palma?"

The driver thought about it and shook his head. "No, I don't think so. Luci Palma . . ."

They followed the drive into the grounds of the Hotel Embajador, past the front lawn where the American civilians had waited with their luggage to be evacuated. Moran said, "Will you do something for me?"

"Yes, of course."

Moran took a piece of notepaper from his shirt pocket and unfolded it. "I want this message put in the newspaper. In *Listin Diario* or *El Caribe,* I don't care, whichever one you like better. All right? Tell them to put it in a box. You know what I mean? With lines around it. So it'll stand out. Okay?"

"Yes, okay."

"In English."

"Yes, in English."

"Just the way it's written here. Okay? See if you can read it." He handed Bienvenido the piece of notepaper with the hand-printed message on it that said:

CAT CHASER

is looking for the girl who once ran over rooftops and tried to kill him. Call the Hotel Embajador. Room 537.

Moran waited for the driver to ask him a question. Bienvenido stared at the notepaper, nodding, his lips moving.

"You understand it?"

"You want a girl to call you?"

"The girl I met when I was here, before."

"Yes."

"She'll recognize 'Cat Chaser.' If she sees it."

"Yes."

"That was the code name for my platoon. When I was here. I was Cat Chaser Four, but she'll know who it is. I mean if she's still here." It didn't seem enough of an explanation and he said, "This girl shot at me, she tried to kill me. I don't mean it was anything personal, it was during the war. Then, I was taken prisoner by the rebels and I got a chance to meet her . . . You understand what I'm saying?"

Bienvenido was nodding again. "Yes, I understand. You want this girl. But if you don't find this girl, you want another girl?"

Mary de Boya watched Moran enter the lobby. She watched him pick up his key at the desk and cross to the elevators. She was aware of an instant stir of excitement and in her mind, concentrating hard, she said, *Look this way.* She said, *Moran, come on. Quick. Look this way!*

The elevator door closed behind him; he was gone.

Maybe she was expecting too much. It was dark in the hotel cocktail lounge. Even if he'd looked over he might not have been able to see her. Or their telepathy was rusty.

A few years ago Mary de Boya could stare across the lounge at Leucadendra and make Moran feel her eyes and look at her. Moran could do the same. In the dining room or the club grill she would feel it. Raise her eyes to meet his and something would pass between them. Not a signal, an awareness. They could smile at each other without smiling. Raise eyebrows, almost imperceptibly, and make mutual judgments. Aloud they could make comments removed from reality that would whiz past her husband, his wife, and they would know things about each other that had nothing to do with their backgrounds, both from the same city. That was a coincidence, nothing more. Though it was handy if needed, when Andres drilled her with his secret-police look and wanted to know what they'd been talking about. "Detroit." When in fact they'd been talking about nothing in particular, nothing intimate, nothing sane, for that matter, "Detroit" was the safe answer. "We just found out both of our dads worked at Ford Rouge, but George lived on the northwest side and I lived downriver, in Southgate." The look between them had remained harmless. Still, each knew it was there if they wanted to make something of it.

Mary smiled thinking about it now, realizing she missed him. It didn't seem possible to miss someone you saw only once or twice a week over a period of a few years; but she had continued to picture him and think about him and what she felt now was real. You know when you miss someone.

Before today she hadn't seen Moran since his divorce. Since his father-in-law drummed him out of the club, ripped the crest from his blazer. Mary saw it that way in fantasy, in flashes: Moran standing at attention in his beard and sneakers, expelled for refusing to wear white patent-leather loafers with tassels, and matching white belt. Out. Refusing to talk about real estate, grain futures, tax shelters, more real estate. Out.

She should have jumped up and yelled and run across the lobby. Nine hundred miles from home . . .

Call his room.

An outfielder with the Cincinnati Reds' Triple-A farm team came over to where Mary sat at the first table inside the lounge and asked if she'd have a drink with him. Good-looking, well built, at least ten years younger than she was. Mary smiled and said, "I'd love to. Sit down."

Giving her something to do, so she wouldn't have to make an instant decision. For all she knew Moran was meeting someone, a girl . . .

They talked about the World Series in New York and Guerrero, the L.A. Dominican, hitting the home run Sunday, the outfielder telling how everybody in the lounge watching it on TV had practically freaked out, their boy coming through. She flirted with the outfielder a little, because she could see he was taken with her and it made her feel good. The mysterious American woman in expensive casual silk, alone in Santo Domingo. The muscular, curly-haired outfielder sat with his big shoulders hunched over the table eating peanuts one at a time, holding back.

Mary de Boya, at thirty-four, was quite likely the best-looking woman the outfielder had ever seen in real life. Her blond honey-streaked hair fell in soft waves to her shoulders framing delicate features, a fine mist of freckles, startling brown eyes.

She asked the outfielder what it was like to stand at the plate and see a hardball coming at you at ninety miles an hour. The outfielder said it didn't matter how fast it came, you had to stand in there, you couldn't give the pitcher nothing. He said it was the curveballs that were more apt to do you in. Curves low and away. The outfielder asked Mary if she had ever been down here before. She told him a few times, for polo matches at Casa de Campo. He said oh, was that what she was down for this time? Mary paused. She said no, she was meeting her lover. The outfielder said oh . . .

"Now I've got to run," Mary said, and left the outfielder half in, half out of his chair. At the front desk she asked for Mr. Moran's room number.

The clerk said, "Mr. Moran," and looked it up. "Five three seven."

"How long is he staying?"

The clerk had to look it up again. "The twenty-ninth. Four days."

Mary turned part way, paused and turned back to the desk again. "I think I'd like a room."

"Yes," the clerk said, "we have a very nice room. Or we have a suite if you like a sitting room, too."

"That's fine," Mary said, though she didn't seem quite sure about something. "I don't have my luggage with me." She looked at the clerk now for help. "It's at Casa de Campo. If I give them a call, can you send someone to pick it up?"

"Yes, but it's seventy miles there," the clerk said. "I don't know how rapidly they can do it."

"Do the best you can," Mary said. She filled out the registration card using her maiden name, Mary Delaney, and an address in Miami Beach off the top of her head, committing herself now, beginning to make her move, thinking: If you're meeting someone, Moran, I'll kill her.

The view from Moran's room was south, past the swimming pool area directly below and down an abrupt grade to a postcard shot of white colonial buildings and palm trees on the edge of the Caribbean. In this time when dusk was becoming night, color gone from the sky, he could hear voices, words in clear Spanish and bikes whining like lawnmowers: the same distinct, faraway sounds they listened to sixteen years ago in tents on the polo fields. The sounds of people doing what they did despite the other sounds that would come suddenly, the mortar and rocket explosions, five klicks removed from the everyday sounds, off somewhere in the city of Santo Domingo. He didn't like those first days, not trusting the people, not having a feel for the terrain. He studied his Texaco map by flashlight and memorized names of the main streets, drew red circles for checkpoints, Charlie and Delta, the embassy, the Dominican Presidential Palace, the National Police Barracks. Take Bolivar to Independence Park, where burned-out cars blocked intersections, and duck. Beyond this point you could get killed. He liked it once he had a perimeter and was able to tell his fire team what they were doing. None of them had been to war.

He would walk those streets tomorrow . . . and hear the voices again on the field radio . . . "Cat Chaser Four, you read? Where the fuck are you?" . . . And the girl's voice coming in. "I know where you are. I see you, Cat Chaser . . . Hey, Cat Chaser, come find me . . . You no good with *tigres.* All you know how to hunt, you Marines, is pussy. Come find me, Cat Chaser Four, whatever your name is . . . This is Luci signing off."

Luci Palma, the sixteen-year-old girl who gave them fits with an M-1 carbine from World War Two. The girl who ran over rooftops . . .

The room-service waiter came with a bucket of ice that held three bottles of El Presidente beer. Moran signed, gave the waiter a peso and said, "Were you here during the revolution?"

The waiter didn't seem to understand.

"*Hace dieciséis años,*" Moran said.

"Oh, yes, I was here."

"What side were you on?"

Again the waiter hesitated.

"Que lado? Los generales o los rebeldes?"

"No, I don't fight," the waiter said. "I like peace."

"No one I've talked to was in the war, the *guerra,*" Moran said. "I wonder who was doing all the shooting."

The phone rang.

"I was in Samaná," the waiter said.

"Everybody was in Samaná," Moran said. "Thanks." He walked behind the waiter going to the door and stopped by the nightstand next to the bed. As the phone rang for the fourth time he picked it up.

"Hello."

The voice instantly familiar said, "Moran? What're you doing in Santo Domingo?"

He said, "I don't believe it. Come on . . ." grinning, sitting down on the bed. "What're you doing here?"

"I asked you first."

"Where are you?"

"About twenty feet above you. Seven thirty-five."

"I don't believe it." He sat up straight and wanted to make his voice sound natural, casual, as he said, "Mary? . . . Is Andres with you?"

"He can't come back here, George. He's afraid somebody'll shoot him."

"Gee, that's too bad. I mean that you couldn't bring him." He heard her giggle. "Well, who're you with?"

"Nobody. I'm all alone."

"Come on . . . I don't believe it."

"Why're you so amazed?"

"You kidding? I don't believe *this.* I'm not sure I could even imagine something like this happening."

She said, "Are you alone?"

"Yeah, all by myself."

"I mean are you meeting anyone?"

"No, I'm alone. Jesus Christ, am I alone. I don't believe it," Moran said, getting up, having to move around now, excited.

"You know I recognized your voice right away? What're you doing here?"

"I saw you in the lobby. A little while ago."

"Yeah? . . ."

"If you're not busy, you think we could have a drink?"

"If I'm not *busy?* Even if I was . . . Listen, I've got three cold bottles of El Presidente sitting right in front of me, unopened."

She said, "Why don't you come up and see me, George? Bring your beer with you."

"Right now?"

"I'll have the door open."

She did, too.

Waited just inside the sitting room for him so that when he appeared in the doorway and entered the short hallway past the bathroom and closet he would have to come to her and she would open her arms . . . Except that he was carrying the ice bucket in front of him with both hands and when she raised her arms he didn't know what to do and they stood there staring at each other, anxious, aching, until she said, "Make up your mind, Moran. Are you going to hold the beer or me?"

He hurried past her into the sitting room, placed his bucket on the coffee table next to hers that held a bottle of champagne. Now they could do it. Now as he turned she came into his arms like it was the most natural thing in the world, wanting to hold and feel each other close after only looking at one another for all those years and keeping a distance between them, sometimes inches, but always a distance. There. It felt good, better than imagined, and from that moment something more than two old friends meeting. Their mouths came together, unplanned, but this too seemed natural, their mouths seeking, brushing, fitting softly as their bodies relaxed and began to blend. . . .

Abruptly, without a flicker, the lights in the room and in the hall went out.

They pulled slightly apart, still holding each other. Moran said very quietly, "We must've blown a fuse. Generated too much electricity."

"I'd believe it," Mary said, "if I hadn't been here before. They run low on power and have to black out parts of the city.''

''For how long?''

''I think fifteen or twenty minutes. Didn't you notice a candle in your room?''

''No . . . Where you going?''

''To find the candle. I saw it somewhere . . .''

''I can't see you.''

''I think it's in the bedroom.''

He followed the sound of her voice, moving carefully now in total darkness, hands ready in front of him. His shin hit the coffee table and he heard the ice bucket rattle against glass.

''Where are you?''

''I'm in the bedroom,'' Mary said. ''I think.''

He moved in that direction, around the coffee table, and came to a doorway that seemed darker than the dark sitting room. Entering cautiously, a room he'd never seen, with nothing to picture from memory, Moran extended his arms like a man sleepwalking. He caught the scent of her perfume, moved a cautious step and felt her hair brush his face. She was between his arms and he closed them around her now, feeling her hands slide up over his ribs.

He said in almost a whisper, ''You find the candle?''

''No. It must be in the bathroom.''

He said, ''Do we need it?''

He felt her hands, her breath—this slim girl, not as tall as he'd remembered her, the image of her across a room. He felt the silky material covering her bare skin, the skin smoothly taut, her body delicate but firm pressing into him, their mouths brushing, finding the right place again, and this time drifting into a dreamlike kind of consciousness, Moran aware but not seeing himself, Mary moving against him, moving him, guiding gently, and Moran knew where they were going, feeling the foot of the bed against his leg and it was all the bearings he needed. They bailed out in the dark and fell into the double bed in the excitement of each other. She said, ''You don't know how long . . .'' He said, ''I know.'' Barely moving their mouths apart to speak. She said, ''God, I want you.'' He said, ''How do you get this off?'' He said, ''Shit, I tore it.'' She said, ''I don't care, tear it,'' pulling his belt apart. He said, "Can you wait, just a second?" She said, "No." He said, "I can't either. Jesus." She said, "Don't talk." He said, "One second . . ." and got on his knees and pulled off her sandals and slacks and somehow got out of his pants, pausing then, catching his breath to pull his shirt over his head and when he sank down again into the bed they were naked, with nothing to make them hold back all that longing they could now release. The lights came on as they were making love, a soft bedroom glow that was just enough and could have been cued as Moran said, "Oh, man," and had to smile as he saw Mary smiling. Now they could see each other and it wasn't simply an act of their bodies, they were identified to each other, finally where they wanted to be more than anywhere. Moran's urge raised him stiff-armed, raised his face to the headboard, to the wall above them and he groaned, letting go that was like, "Gaiii-yaaa!" and brought Mary's eyes open, but she closed them again, murmuring, moving, and remained in iridescent sparkling dark as he came back to her again, winding down, settling.

She felt moisture on his back, his shoulders. She said, "Oh, God," as though it might be her last breath. Then opened her eyes to study his face in repose, his eyelashes, his eyelids lightly closed.

She said quietly, "Well . . . how have you been?"

"Not too bad."

"Do you always do that?" Her words a soft murmur.

"What?"

"I thought you were in pain."

"I was, sort of."

"You really throw yourself into it."

"That was the first time I ever heard myself do that. It just came, so to speak." He opened his eyes. "You do an analysis after?"

"No, but I've always wondered about you," Mary said. "Do you know how many words we've spoken to each other, counting today?"

"We didn't have to use words. That was the spooky part about it. I always had the feeling we knew each other when we were little. Little kids who played together, then didn't see each other for about thirty years."

"I'm not that old."

"You're old enough. You know what I mean," Moran said. "I don't have to explain anything to you."

"No."

"Boy, you are really something."

She said, "There's more to it than that, isn't there?"

"There's way more," Moran said. "I don't mean just in bed. Will you tell me what you're doing here?"

"I came down with some girls from the club. Polo buffs. Or that's their excuse to get away and party, maybe play a little tennis. Actually they came down yesterday, but I couldn't make it till today."

Moran said, "Yeah, I ran into them at the airport. They looked sort of familiar—one of 'em's name is Philly?"

"Right, Philly, Marilyn and Liz, my old tennis court buddies."

Moran said, "You're staying here, this place? I don't think it's very *in*."

"No, what happened," Mary said, "my friends drove in from Casa de Campo to meet me and go to a cocktail party at the Santo Domingo Country Club. Mostly embassy people."

"Yeah? . . ."

"Then I was supposed to drive back to Casa de Campo with them later. The polo matches start tomorrow." Mary paused. "But I left the party."

"Why'd you come here?"

"Well, you told Philly you were staying here . . ."

"Yeah? . . ."

"I thought I'd stop by and say hi."

Moran said, "Really?" And began to smile. "You came to the hotel just to see me?"

"You want the truth?" Mary said. "I came to Santo Domingo just to see you."

"But you said—"

"I lied," Mary said. "I didn't plan to make the trip. But then Philly called last night to coax me, tell me about the embassy party and happened to mention she saw you at the airport." She said, "There, I've bared my soul to you, Moran."

"It's a nice one," Moran said, "I'm getting excited all over again. But what about the polo matches?"

"I think polo's boring," Mary said. She smiled and he smiled. "I sent for my bags. For the time being I don't have any clothes."

Moran said, "You don't, huh?" Still smiling.

5

She said, "You're getting tired of me already."

"What, because I said we ought to go out? Room service is okay, but it's still room service."

"I have to admit, George, you're a lot more romantic than I thought you'd be."

"I hear myself sometimes," Moran said, "I sound like I'm about seventeen."

She said, "You don't look much older, except for the beard. I love your beard. I love your body."

Even after he had told her why he was here and she was fascinated and wanted to walk the streets of his war with him, they remained in the hotel for the next two days. They needed the intimacy of being alone together, to look at each other with no one watching now and realize, no question about it, they were right. Boy, were they right. Meant for each other. They could say it and it sounded fine. They could say, I love you, earnestly, though so far only in the midst of love, perspiration glistening on their bodies, and I love you sounded pretty good, too. They lay in the sun at the hotel pool, a breeze coming off the Caribbean. She touched him and told him he could be one of the winter ballplayers. He told her she was way better looking than any of the young baseball wives, looked around, realized it wasn't even a contest and widened the scope to include all the girl movie stars he could think of. He believed it. They talked, never having to think of things to say, and were at ease with each other in silence.

"I remember times at the club I'd see you staring off in space," Mary said, "like you were planning to go over the wall."

They lay side by side at the deep end of the pool, facing the afternoon sun, their lounge chairs touching.

"I got pardoned," Moran said. "If I hadn't, yeah, I would've done it. I could feel it coming."

She said, "Can we get a few things out in the open?"

"It's all right with me."

"Okay. Why'd you marry Noel?"

"I think it was her heinie," Moran said. "That high, insolent ass, like it's got a personality all its own."

"Are we going to only say nice things?"

"Well, you know her as well as I do. Sometimes the things that attract us are the things that sooner or later turn us off. I should've looked at her stuck-up ass and known."

He turned his head to see Mary's slender body in the yellow bikini, the delicate line from armpit to breast, her belly a shallow basin between the small-bone mounds of her hips. He wanted to jump on her.

"You asked me because you knew I was gonna ask you. Where you stand."

"I suppose."

"Okay, where are you?"

"Well, not too long ago I almost asked Andres for a divorce. I had the words ready, exactly what I was going to say . . ."

He was aware of his instant reaction: *great*. He didn't tighten, begin to feel trapped. No, he liked what she was saying.

"But I chickened out."

"How come?"

"Well . . . I felt sorry for him."

Moran didn't say anything.

"Or I felt sorry for myself—I don't know. I thought, if I'm gonna leave, I should be going to something I want to do. But even if there *was* something, I don't want to just walk out. I want to talk to him, so he'll understand how I feel. But we don't talk. In the six years we've been together"—she turned her head to look at Moran—"if there's a gale blowing out of Biscayne Bay in the hurricane season we might get in a good exchange about the weather. We don't even see each other that much. We have dinner together about three times a week. Half the time he doesn't get home till late, or we meet at the club."

"What'd you marry him for, his money?"

"I might've."

"I was kidding."

"No, you weren't. But that may be the real reason, security," Mary said. "At first I was fascinated by him. General Andres de Boya. In a way I thought he was cute."

"Jesus Christ," Moran said.

"I did, at first." Mary pushed up on her elbow, getting into it. "Usually—well, you know—he's very formal, he's the boss, you have to do things his way. But then when you see a vulnerable side, just a glimpse, you realize he's a person like everyone else."

"Regular guy," Moran said.

"No, he's not a regular guy. That's what I mean. He was a soldier in the Dominican army, worked his way up to general, then lost everything. He came to Miami with practically nothing and did it all on his own."

"I heard he escaped with a fortune."

"You heard wrong. He put fifteen thousand down on an apartment house in South Miami and that was everything he had."

"You stick up for him."

"George, what do you want to believe? That story—he came with millions on a private yacht, that's baloney. He escaped with his life, very little else. But I know one thing, if he ever has to make a quick exit again he's gonna be ready."

"He keep his money under the mattress now?"

Mary paused. "It sounds funny, but to Andres it's real life. He thinks there's always somebody out to get him, so we have full-time security guards, armed. They never smile."

"Well, I guess you were head of secret police for Trujillo," Moran said, "and now you're sitting on all that dough . . ."

"That was political," Mary said, "we're talking about the man now."

Moran could argue the distinction—the man was still responsible for a lot of people dying—but he let it go.

"All right, you're telling me why you married him."

"I'm trying to think of a good reason," Mary said. "I was twenty-eight and all the good guys were taken. And he talked me into it."

"I hope you can do better than that."

"I was ready to get married. I didn't like what I was doing. My dream, always, was to get married some day." She paused, thinking. "He's not bad-looking really, and he's very romantic."

"Jesus Christ," Moran said.

"Well, he thinks he is, but most of it's in Spanish. He's very, you know, serious, a heavy breather."

"I'm not gonna say anything," Moran said.

"On the other hand he's extremely cold, aloof," Mary said. "Sometimes smirky. If I want to see him I practically have to get an appointment. But he's a rock, George."

"I won't argue with you there."

"He's absolutely reliable. If Andres says he's going to do something, believe it. Whatever it is."

"He wants to buy the Coconuts," Moran said. He had told Mary about Andres's sister and the piano player, without going into much detail. "He came—I was gonna say yesterday, but it was three days ago. Anyway he made an offer and I said, 'You trying to get rid of me, Andres? Come on, what's your game?' "

It brought her upright. "You didn't. What's your *game?*"

"Listen, the other day I beat a guy playing tennis, a young hotshot, I said to him, "You're all right, kid.' I'm starting to say things I've always felt like saying. But try to get anything out of your husband—I think you could punch him, he wouldn't make a sound," Moran said. "Maybe when you married him you thought you could change him. Turn him into a teddy bear. He's not at all cute, I'll tell you, but you thought you could make him cute."

"No, you're wrong," Mary said. She eased back to lie flat on the lounge again. "I was working in that law office typing one profit-sharing plan after another, pages and pages of figures, pension plans, trust funds, all due at five o'clock, always, and I had to get out. Andres came along—it was his lawyer I worked for. He'd divorced his first two wives. He has four grown children, a girl who's married and lives in California, three sons in Madrid who're in business together—those are the legitimate ones. He let his mistress go . . . I think. And I decided he was fascinating. I thought the difference between us might make it all the more interesting, maybe even fun. I thought, well, assuming there's a person under that cold, formal exterior, why don't I try to bring him out?"

"How'd you do?"

"Well, the only thing I can figure out," Mary said, "he puts on the front so no one will know what a real asshole he is."

"So walk away," Moran said. "What's the problem?"

"I told you, I want him to understand why I'm leaving. I don't want him to think it's for any other reason than we shouldn't have got married in the first place. We made a mistake and I want him to realize it."

"What other reason is there? You don't like him, that's all."

"There's a good one," Mary said. "I signed a prenuptial agreement. I didn't want to but Andres insisted. In the agreement it says if the marriage ends in divorce, for any reason, I'm to be given a flat settlement of two million dollars."

Moran said, "You didn't want to sign it?"

"I felt like it was an inducement. I didn't want to make a *deal* with him. I wanted to marry him. I might've been dumb, but I was sincere."

"Well, it was his idea," Moran said. "But if you're worried about what he thinks—I mean you want to prove you're still sincere, then don't take the money."

"Yeah, except that I like being rich."

Moran studied her face, the fine bone structure, the delicate line of her nose, knowing the face would change and he would still want to look at it for a long time to come.

"You got a problem," he said.

They were silent now. His gaze moved past her to the shrubs that bordered the south end of the hotel grounds. After several moments he said, "My first night here, I slept in a hole. Right over where that hedge is. . ."

6

The afternoon of the fourth day. The Chevrolet Impala moved in low gear through streets that were like alleys, past stone structures with wooden entranceways, tenements that dated only a hundred years—new housing in a town where the son of Christopher Columbus had lived in style. Mary stared at scarred walls. They could be in San Juan or Caracas. The heat pressed motionless in the narrow streets. She searched for something to hold her interest as Moran spoke to Bienvenido in English and pidgin present-tense Spanish. The oldest buildings of all, she realized, the ones that dated to the early sixteenth century, were the newest in appearance, clean, reconstructed among recent decay, with all the charm of Disney World.

When they left the car to walk, Moran would nod to people along the street and in doorways staring at them, staring longer at the blond-haired woman than at the bearded man.

Mary said, "You're sure we're all right."

Moran's gaze came down from the upper floors of a building to the narrow shops on the street level. "They look at you and it's instant love. Blondes have some kind of magic." His gaze lifted again. "Up by that corner window—those are bullet holes. My fire team came along this street . . . We shouldn't have been anywhere near this area."

"What's a fire team?" She pictured firemen.

"A third of a squad. Two riflemen, an automatic rifleman and the fire-team leader. Thirteen men in a squad, forty-eight in a platoon. The platoon was Cat Chaser. After we lost our sergeant I was Cat Chaser Four—if anybody wanted to call up and say hi."

"Mister!"

Moran turned to see the dark face close to him, teeth missing and brown-stained eyes smiling, the man holding up lottery tickets. Moran waved him away, moving past.

"You the Marine, uh?" the man said, stopping Moran again in his tracks. "I hear it on the radio, the marine looking for his girl. You the Marine, yes?"

"I was a Marine," Moran said.

They were standing now, people gathering around. Mary saw the eager expression on the man's face as he said, "This is the Marine!" Excited. "You looking for the girl Luci Palma. You find her?"

Mary watched Moran shake his head, with the same eager expression as the man's. "You know her?"

"No, I don't think so." The man turned to the other people and began speaking in Spanish.

Moran took Mary's arm. They continued up the old street past lingering people, piles of trash, children following them now, the children and the lottery-ticket man's voice raised, telling everyone something in Spanish, with feeling, like he was telling a story.

"What's he saying?"

"I ran an ad in the paper, looking for somebody," Moran said. "Evidently one of the radio stations got hold of it."

"Looking for somebody," Mary said.

"Someone I met after I was taken prisoner. One of the snipers."

"A girl?"

"She was about sixteen. Luci Palma."

"That's why you came here? To see her?"

"No, this is why I came. What we're doing now. But I was curious."

"I'll bet you are."

"She was a skinny little kid."

"She won't be now, though," Mary said, 'will she?" Have you seen her since then?"

"This is the first time I've been back," Moran said. Coming to a corner he was looking at the upper stories again. Mary watched him turn to look off in the direction of the river. "There the grain elevators I told you about. See? Ten stories high. The Eighty-second sat up there with their cannons. Up on top."

Mary stared at the cement cylinders standing about a mile away, on the opposite bank of the Ozama River. She felt Moran's hand on her arm and they continued across the intersection. Behind them, Bienvenido's Impala came to a stop. Moran was pointing now. "That's the building. The one on the corner. Where I chased the sniper."

"The girl?"

"No, it was a guy in a green striped shirt. Green and white." Moran turned, looking at the side streets again, thoughtful. "They'd hide a gun in an upstairs room, take a shot at you, come out, walk up the street to an apartment where they had another gun stashed and let you have a few more rounds. You see how narrow the streets are, you have to look almost straight up. You feel exposed, looking up, trying to spot the window, the guy's already someplace else, drawing a bead on you . . ." He turned slowly back to the building on the corner and stared, squinting in the sunlight. "I stuck my head out of that third-floor window, right there. . . ."

It was the girl, Luci, who had brought him here, this far, and got him in a lot of trouble, though she was not the one he had chased. A sixteen-year-old girl playing with him, now and then taking shots at him. That was the trouble with the whole deal: After a while it was like a game and he would get excited and lose his concentration. He got chewed out for it more than once by the platoon sergeant who told him he was going to get fucking killed and go home in a bag.

A lot of it was boring and a lot of it was fun. More exciting than anything he had ever experienced before. Hugging a doorway under fire, then stepping out, seeing them running across the street down at an intersection and squeezing off rounds at them. Hearing the voices then laughing and calling you *hijo de puta,* son of a whore, that was the favorite; learning what it meant and yelling it back at them, though "motherfucker" remained the all-time any-situation favorite. (Ham and lima beans: ham and motherfuckers.) "Hey, motherfucker! Come on out of there! Where's your balls!" Kids playing. Working a street and finding a *cantina* open, Christ, and stopping for a beer in the middle of a firefight. Or stopping to let the trucks go through with sacks of rice and powdered milk, the U.S. military feeding the people they were fighting. Did that make sense? None of it did. That's why you might as well accept this deal as being pretty weird and have some fun. Though it wouldn't be fun now.

* * *

Mary walked back to the taxi. Bienvenido got out. He opened the door for her and she said, "I'll wait. Thanks." She watched Moran, on the other side of the intersection, then said to Bienvenido, "Do you remember General Andres de Boya?"

Bienvenido said, "Oh my. Oh my, yes. General de Boya, ouuuh, he was a devil, that man."

"Why do you say that?"

"Because he kill people with his *Cascos Blancos.* Everyone the enemies of them. They kill more people than the malaria fever."

Mary said, "Oh . . ."

"That fella was a devil. Yes, we very glad he's gone from here."

Mary got in the car. She sat in back, staring through the windshield at Moran across the street.

Once Luci picked up their radio frequency she kept cutting in on them. They didn't know what she was using and they didn't talk to her at first. They'd switch frequencies and there she'd be like Tokyo Rose, giving them the business. "What you doing here, Marines? You come to kill us? Why? We haven't done nothing to you. You afraid of Communists? We not Communists, but you turning us into Communists you stay here." Political at first, till she got to know the Cat Chasers that patrolled along Independencia as far as La Carreras in a jeep with a 50 mounted on it. He spoke to her a couple times, asking her name and if she'd have a beer with him. She said sure, come over to Conde Street, she'd meet him. Conde, where rebel headquarters was located.

They were almost ambushed and got in a firefight at the corner of Carreras and Padre Billini; the Cat Chasers gave chase, in and out of the buildings, and that was when he finally saw her the first time, running across a rooftop with her carbine.

He saw her from a window across the street, the window a story higher than the roof she was on. He put his M-14 on her and began to track and saw her look back, laughing, yelling at somebody, waving then, *Come on!* Then she was looking this way, surprised, and he saw her face clearly. There was a burst from a submachine gun. He saw a guy on the same roof now, a guy wearing a baseball cap, a pouch of magazines slung over his shoulder, the guy aiming at him. Moran hung in and squeezed off and the guy spun, grabbing at his side above the left hip, and went down behind the cornice of the building. The girl disappeared. They went up to the roof but all they found was some blood and a few 9-mm casings. The next day, over the radio, the girl's voice said, "You so slow, you Cat Chasers. You tired from chasing *putas*." She didn't mention the guy who got hit.

The second time was after the 106 fired from the silos across the river almost put him under, tore his leg up with shrapnel and he had an awful time getting down from the third floor with the stairway blown to hell. He should have stayed up there. He climbed through the rubble, slipped out the back thinking he was pretty cool and walked right into them. A gang of guys in sport-shirts carrying old M-1s and Mausers. He'd always remember how they grinned at him. The fuckers, they weren't even soldiers.

They blindfolded and quick-marched him to a house he'd never have found again even if he could have seen where they were going; gave him a bucket of water and a dirty towel to do something about his bleeding and locked him in a room. Every once in a while the door would open and some more of them would look in to see the prize, laughing and making, no doubt, insulting remarks in Spanish. He told them to get fucked but they just laughed some more. When the girl came and stood in the doorway he knew who it was right away. Maybe it was the carbine she had slung over her shoulder, though he told himself later it was her eyes, the way she looked at him like they had met before.

She was skinny, without any breasts to speak of, but had beautiful eyes and chestnut brown hair.

He said, "Well, Luci, how you doing?" Taking a chance and hitting it on the head. She smiled. She looked like she'd be a lot of fun just to be with. She wore a T-shirt and jeans that were patched and faded. She left the carbine outside, came in and closed the door.

She said, "You're the Cat Chaser." Her whole face smiling.

"I'm one of 'em."

"You catching much lately?"

"Well, I didn't do too good today, I'll tell you."

She liked that; she smiled and went out and came back with a bottle of El Presidente and a dressing. She fooled around with his leg while he drank the beer, the leg not hurting yet, though it looked a mess. He asked about the guy he'd shot and she mentioned the guy's name, which he forgot, and said the guy was not hurt bad but had quit the war. She asked him where he lived; he said Detroit and she told him she had stayed in Miami, Florida for two months, visiting. She told him she loved Miami, Florida and wanted to go back there sometime. She asked him if he liked the Beatles or did he prefer the Rolling Stones? Everyone, she said, was in love with the Beatles. They discussed the Supremes, Freddie and the Dreamers, Sam the Sham & the Pharaohs, the Righteous Brothers, Herman's Hermits . . . She did not care much for the Beach Boys or Roger Miller. He said he didn't either. Her favorite of all was Petula Clark. She sang a little of "Downtown" in English, snapping her fingers; she knew more of the words than he did.

When they took him out and put him in the panel truck she was there. He told her to take care of herself. She gave him a look that was sad and sort of longing and told him to take care of himself, too. She said, "I won't shoot at you no more." Some war.

They told him see, we're not bad guys; we're good to you. It's your government, your President Johnson we don't like. They handed him over to a Marine patrol on the west end of Independence Park. The Marines looked at him like he was some kind of weird freak and drove him to the field hospital at Haina.

It was the end of Moran's war.

Mary was patient because she enjoyed watching him and could feel the enthusiasm he tried to keep inside him. Like a young boy. Excited but self-conscious at the same time. It gave her a feeling about him that was tender and made her want to touch his face. But maybe she simply liked to touch him; she would watch him asleep, breathing softly, and the same feeling would come over her.

When he returned to the taxi and got in next to her, she said, "That's where you were wounded?"

He nodded slowly, several times, then cocked his head, looking out the windshield. "It seems bigger. You go back to a place where you lived or spent some time and it always seems smaller. But Santo Domingo seems bigger."

"It probably is," Mary said. "It's grown. A million people live here."

"I don't mean that way," Moran said. "I guess I mean it isn't as easy to understand as I thought it would be. Things aren't black or white, are they?" He shrugged and said, "Maybe it's me. I see it differently now."

With feeling, Mary thought. How many people did she know who spoke or looked at anything with genuine feeling? Without being cynical, on stage, trying to entertain. Without puffing up or putting down. She wanted to know what he felt and, if possible, share the feeling.

"What happened then?"

He hesitated for a long moment. "I was taken to a field hospital. Five days later I was evacuated. Home."

They returned to the hotel along the broad expanse of Avenida Washington with its tall palms, its view of the Caribbean on one side and the facade Santo Dominog presented to the world on the other: sun beating on walled colonial buildings and straw markets, the old giving way to solitary glass structures rising in the background. Mary said, "This is one section that's never blacked out." She told of a Dominican couple she'd met at the country club who paid twelve hundred dollars a month for electricity. Moran said it would be something to tell his neighbors in Pompano; they were into electric bills and loved to compare them.

He asked Bienvenido about the radio broadcast. Was it true, what the lottery-ticket man had said?

Bienvenido said, "Yes, all day it's on the radio about you. You don't hear it?" He began switching dials on the car radio, getting static and rock music until he found a voice speaking dramatically in Spanish. "There," Bienvenido said. "Listen."

"What's he saying?" Moran hunched over the front seat rest, laying his chin on his arm.

Bienvenido was leaning toward the car radio. "He say . . . the American Marine who fell in love with the girl name Luci has returned."

"What? Come on—"

"For many years since the way Captain Morón has been thinking of her, missing her . . ."

"*Cap*tain?"

". . . with his heart breaking, until now he has returned to find her."

"Jesus," Moran said, "They're making it up. I hardly even knew her." He turned to glance at Mary who sat composed. "They're making all that up."

"He say . . . if anyone knows where to find Luci Palma, tell her that the Marine, Captain Morón, is here who loves her very much and wants to take her to the United States to live. He is at the Hotel Embajador."

"I don't believe it," Moran said. "How do they know all that? I mean my name. I didn't give anybody my name."

"Captain Moron?" Mary said.

"Morón," Moran said. He poked Bienvenido's shoulder. "How do they know about me? What'd you tell the newspaper?"

"What you told me, only. I think the radio station call the newspaper and maybe the hotel," Bienvenido said, "talk to some people there. I don't know."

"But it isn't true. None of it." He turned to look at Mary again. "Do you believe it?"

Mary gave him a nice smile. She said, "I can't wait to meet Luci."

There were a dozen or more Luci Palmas scattered about the hotel lobby, some with relatives, mothers and perhaps fathers; several more were in the cocktail lounge talking to winter ballplayers, doing all right, forgetting why they had come here. There was no announcement. It was like a celebrity, a movie star, arriving. A bellman nodded, holding open the door, and all the Luci Palmas converged on the bearded man with the stylish lady, who was maybe his aide, his secretary. They called out to him, "Captain! Here I am!" They said, "Oh, it is so good to see you again!" They said, "My Marine, you have return!"

Moran said, "Wait a minute! . . ."

The bellman said, "Can I assist you, Capitano?"

Mary slipped through the girls crowding in, walked over to the front desk. She watched from here, standing with a travel group of Chinese from Taiwan who nudged each other, staring. Mary said, "It's George Moran, the American film star," and some of them raised their cameras and began taking pictures.

She watched Moran in a much different role now, but the same Moran, surrounded by girls with silky dark hair and woolly Afros, girls in dresses and girls in tight jeans, girls with imploring eyes trying to make themselves heard in both Spanish and English—Moran in the middle, hands raised close to his body, trying not to touch them. He was working his way out of the pack now toward the front desk, his eyes with a helpless look finding Mary. She smiled at him.

Reaching her he said, "What do I do?" And looked at the desk clerk who stood composed, almost indifferent.

"Will you tell them I'm not the one?"

The desk clerk raised his eyebrows. "You are Captain Morón."

"I'm not a captain. I never was."

"I don't believe they care you aren't an officer. You are Mr. Jorge Morón, are you not?"

"They're not old enough," Moran said.

The desk clerk seemed surprised. "You like them to be older?"

"They're not old enough to be Luci Palma. It was sixteen years ago. There isn't one of them over thirty."

"Take a good look," Mary said. "There isn't one of them over twenty-five."

Moran said to the girls, "Wait, stand still. Be *tranquilo,* okay? I'll ask each of you one question, *una pregunta,* all right?"

"I'll be in the bar," Mary said.

"Wait. Help me, will you?"

"You're doing fine, George. Ask your *pregunta.*"

Walking away, working through the girls pressing in, Mary heard him say, "All right, I'm gonna ask you how old you are. *Comprende? Quantos años tiene?* . . . You first. Hi, how're you doing?"

She was aware of the tender feeling again: a comfortable feeling, even as she realized there was much more to Moran than a natural, easygoing manner. At times he seemed almost naive; yet he continued to surprise her.

* * *

She chose a table on the far side of the lounge, away from the entrance and the ballplayers at the bar, and ordered a scotch. The chair felt good; it was low, with soft cushions and casters; she crept it closer to another chair at the table and put her feet up, stretching her legs, brushing at the wrinkles in her beige slacks. When the waitress brought her drink she looked up to thank her. The waitress moved off and a man was standing at the table.

"If you'll permit me . . ."

"To do what?" Mary said.

"Speak with you, please." His manner was pleasant, unhurried. "You're the friend, I believe, of the Marine."

Mary nodded. "We're buddies."

The man's dark eyes relaxed in warm creases. He looked to be in his early thirties with a trimmed mustache and hair styled by a hotel barber, swept straight back from a high forehead: the look of light-skinned Dominican aristocracy, Mary judged. He wore a tailored white cotton shirt that hung free of his trousers like a light jacket, open enough to show some of his chest hair.

He said, "I like to have a woman who is a buddy. I didn't know it was possible."

"Why?"

"I don't know, I suppose the way we are, men and women, uh? The difference between us."

"How do you know the Marine and I aren't married?"

"I find out those things." He smiled.

More than pleasant, his manner was instantly familiar, confident, the Latin lover come-on. Mary sipped her drink; she'd been there several times.

"Excuse me. My name is Rafael Amado." He paused, giving Mary a chance to introduce herself, but she passed. "I think your friend should know that none of those girls could be Luci Palma."

"He knows," Mary said. "He's just having a little fun."

"Yes, that's good. . . . My name is Rafael, but by most people I'm known as Rafi."

"That's cute," Mary said.

The Dominican smiled. "You like it? Good. I wonder if I may join you." He brought over a chair without waiting for permission and eased into it, careful of the press in his black trousers. "Thank you. May I buy you a drink?"

Mary raised her glass. "I'm fine."

He looked up, snapped his fingers and said something in Spanish that was abrupt, without the pleasant manner, though it returned instantly as he said to Mary, "If I may have one with you."

She wished Moran would hurry up. She wanted to see the look on his face, coming in and finding her taken care of. It might tell her something. Then immediately doubted it. Moran wouldn't make assumptions, waste time being jealous. If he were to hesitate, appear to be just a little awkward, that would be good enough.

Rafi said, "When I heard on the radio about the return of the Marine I thought, Could it be? Then in *Listin Diario* I see the message, Cat Chaser is looking for the girl . . . and I thought, It is, it's the same one."

"The message," Mary said, "I haven't seen it yet."

"In the newspaper personal column," Rafi told her. "Cat Chaser is looking for the girl who ran over the roofs of buildings and tried to kill him. Call this hotel. It's very clever the way it's said."

"The girl named Luci tried to kill him?" Mary straightened in her chair, bringing her legs down.

"Well, she try different tricks, you know, to lure him."

Mary wanted to be sure. She said, "To *lure* him?"

"To bring the Marines where they shouldn't be. Trick them. But that was a long time ago. It was the war."

"You said you were sure then he was the one. What one?"

The waitress appeared with Rafi's drink. He took it from her without a word, then leaned toward Mary, his expression grave.

"I was with Luci Palma. In the group of partisans with her. I was on the roof with her." He continued to stare at Mary before easing back in the chair. "He didn't tell you? The Marine?"

"What? I'm not sure."

Rafi placed his hands on his chest, fingers spread, an amber stone with a dull gleam on his little finger.

"On the roof," Rafi said, his expression still grave, "I'm the one he shot and almost killed."

7

All those white teeth flashing at him, different scents of perfume, a couple of the Luci Palmas taking his arm and rubbing against him. At some other time in his life, not too long ago, Moran would have asked them more than how old they were, might have staged a mini—Miss D.R. pageant and chosen a winner.

Going into the lounge he was thinking of something to tell Mary—that he was getting out of the motel business to become a movie producer; at least a casting director. He saw Mary's hair and a guy in a white Dominican dress-up shirt and took it a little easier going over to the table. The Dominican guy saw him now and was getting up.

Mary said, pleasantly enough, "How did it go?"

"Well, it was different."

"If you're through casting . . ."

It amazed him, how well she knew him already.

". . . this is Rafi. I'm sorry I didn't hear your last name."

"Rafi Amado. I'm very pleased to meet you." Extending his hand across the table. "I'm honored."

Mary was looking up at him. "Really? . . . And this is Jorge Morón, Rafi. The infamous Marine."

Moran glanced at her, taking the Dominican's slender hand, the grip not too firm.

"What did I do?"

"On your last trip it seems you shot somebody on the roof of a building," Mary said. "Well, Rafi's the one you shot."

Moran stared at him now, not sure what to say, the Dominican giving him sort of a guarded look, like he wasn't sure what to expect.

Moran said, "You're the one?" He seemed awed now.

"I believe so," Rafi said. "A house on Padre Billini near Carreras? Up on the roof? I was with Luci Palma."

Moran said, "Boy . . ." He moved his hand over his beard, still not sure what to do in this situation. He said, quickly then, "Sit down, please. What're you drinking?"

"I have one. Thank you."

They sat down and Moran ordered a beer. It gave him something to do, time to settle, get used to the idea that he was looking at a man he had once tried to kill.

"You had an automatic weapon. Like a grease gun."

Rafi was nodding. "Yes, I forgot what kind. They gave out all types of guns the first day of the revolution, in the park. I had different weapons."

"You tried for me first," Moran said. He held up his hand. "I don't mean that the way it sounds. But I remember you fired a burst. I was in a window across the street."

"I believe so," Rafi said, "but I don't shoot too straight. Which is good for you."

"Listen, I'm really sorry," Moran said. "Were you hurt bad?"

"No, not seriously. You like to see it?" Rafi leaned forward unbuttoning his shirt, pulling it open now and thrusting out his chest, giving Mary a sly glance. He brushed at the hair covering his left breast to reveal several inches of white scar tissue. "The bullet went this way, across me, instead of *in*to me, which was good, uh? It took off the nipple," Rafi said, "but I wasn't using it, so it doesn't matter."

He chuckled and Mary smiled, seeing him glance over again. Mary said, "You're a good sport, Rafi."

Moran said, "I thought I hit you lower and more in the side. Down around the belt."

Rafi pressed his chin to his chest looking down, feeling his mid section as though to make sure.

"No, I don't think so. It seems all right."

"We went up on that roof," Moran said. "You were gone."

"Yes, I hope so. Luci help me to get down. Maybe without her, I don't know, I may not be here. She was the one take me to the hospital."

The waitress brought Moran's beer, half the bottle poured in a glass with a foamy head. He said, "Thanks," still looking at Rafi and let the glass stand on the table.

"You know where she is?"

Mary's eyes, mildly curious, moved to Moran and waited for his reaction as she heard Rafi say, "Luci? I didn't see her after that war. But, I didn't hear anything happen to her either."

Moran seemed to accept this calmly enough. Mary had thought he'd be sitting on the edge of his chair. He said, "You knew I was taken prisoner."

Rafi hesitated, somewhat surprised. "Is that so? No, I didn't know that. And they release you?"

"The same day," Moran said. "I found out later a guy from the Peace Corps worked it out."

"Ah, that was good."

"But I got a chance to talk to her. It's funny, I remember I asked about you."

"Me?"

"She said you were alive and would be okay. She told me your name . . ."

"Yes?"

"But I forgot it. She brought me a beer . . ."

Rafi seemed to relax. "Yes, she was very thoughtful of people. And very brave." He sipped his drink, placed it on the table again as though in slow motion, a thoughtful expression on his face. "You come all the way here to find Luci Palma?"

"No, not really," Moran said. "I wanted to see Santo Domingo again. As a tourist this time."

"It's much bigger now," Rafi said. "You live where, in what state?"

"Florida. Pompano Beach. It's about fifty miles north of Miami."

"Pompano," Rafi said. "Is a nice place?"

"George owns the Coconut Palms," Mary said, "a very exclusive resort."

"Yes?" Rafi appeared thoughtful again, nodding. "I think I heard of it. Like the Fontainebleu in Miami? Very big place, uh?"

"Not as big," Mary said, ignoring the look Moran was giving her, "but much classier, if you know what I mean."

Rafi brightened. "A swanky place, uh?"

"That's it," Mary said. "It's got a lot of swank." She gave Moran, shaking his head slowly, a look of wide-eyed innocence.

Rafi was saying, "Perhaps I can be of help." It brought them back. "Find out for you where Luci Palma is."

"Well, I doubt if she's still here," Moran said.

"Yes, if she's still here in Santo Domingo she must know about you. Everyone seems to," Rafi said. "So I think she live someplace else. La Romana, Puerto Plata . . . There isn't much mobility among the Dominican people. I can find out for you."

"I don't want you to go to a lot of trouble though," Moran said. "I'm curious about her, that's all. She seemed like a nice girl. Very eager, you know, full of life. I hope nothing happened to her."

Rafi looked at his watch. "Let me make phone calls, see what I can do."

As he finished his drink and got up Moran said, "Really, it's not that important to me."

Rafi said, "Put it in my hands," gesturing, glancing at his watch again. "Now I have business to do. I'll call you later." He gave Mary the hint of a bow. "And I hope to see the buddy of the Marine again. It was a pleasure."

He was walking off. Moran rose. He said on impulse, "How about dinner later? If you're free . . ."

Rafi made a circle with his thumb and index finger. He waved and was gone.

Moran sat down.

Mary said, "I'm surprised he didn't click his heels."

"Your Dominicans are very polite people," Moran said.

Mary gave him a look. "Tell me about it."

"That's right, you have one at home, don't you? You see his Rolex?"

"He'd like you to think it's a Rolex, but it's not."

"How do you know?"

"I know gold, George. I have some of that at home too."

He sipped at his beer in silence.

"If she's in Santo Domingo, fine. But I don't want to go chasing all over the country."

"Then don't."

"Yeah but, what if he busts his ass, goes to a lot of trouble, finds out she's in Puerto Plata . . . I don't want to go to Puerto Plata. I'm really not that hot about taking him to dinner."

"But you don't want to seem ungrateful."

"You shoot a guy's left nipple off," Moran said, "I think you ought to buy him dinner, at least. Especially if you're the owner of a swank resort."

"I couldn't help it," Mary said. "Are you mad at me?"

"The Fontainebleu. Jesus, can you see me running a place like the Fontainebleu?"

"You can't say he wasn't impressed."

"That's what I'm afraid of. I'm his new buddy."

Mary waited a moment.

"You don't seem to be as anxious about finding Luci. What happened?"

"Nothing. It was an idea, that's all," Moran said. "Something that happened a long time ago. Sixteen years." He looked at Mary. "What were you doing sixteen years ago? . . . What were you doing last week? The week before? . . . What're we doing sitting here?"

Rafi said to the desk clerk in English, "Let me see it again. The woman's."

The clerk looked past him at the lobby before taking out the registration card and laying it on the counter.

Rafi studied the card without picking it up. "I don't know if that's a one or a seven, in the address."

"*Siete,*" the clerk said.

"All right, take it. I'll fix it up when you want to score, man. Let me know the room and what time."

"Speak so I can understand," the clerk said.

"I'm practicing my American," Rafi said.

He walked past the uniformed guard into the hotel casino where there were players at the first roulette table and at several of the blackjack tables, though not much of a crowd this early in the evening. Rafi nodded to the young American in the three-piece gray suit, pointed to the telephone on the stand by the entrance and the young American, the casino assistant manager, gave him the sign, okay, though he seemed to hesitate and have doubts. Rafi picked up the phone and told the hotel operator the number he wanted, then turned his back to the room, hunching over the stand that was like a podium.

"It's Rafi again." He spoke in Spanish now. "Mary Delaney. Seven hundred Collins Avenue, Miami Beach."

The woman's voice on the phone said, "Wait."

Rafi turned to look over the room, though with little interest; he drum-rolled his fingernails on the polished wood of the stand. The woman's voice came on. "Rafi?"

"Yes." He turned his back to the room again.

"It's a jewelry store, that address, and there is no Mary Delaney in Miami Beach."

"Hiding something," Rafi said, pleased. "Can you look her up some other way?"

The woman's voice said, "I have directories—what do you think I am, the FBI?"

He could see the woman, imagine her sitting in her room that was like a gallery of photographs of important people: some of the pictures framed and enscribed, "To La Perla, with love," or "fondest regards," though most of the pictures, the ones in color, had been cut from magazines twenty or thirty years ago. La Perla had written about parties and scandals and was said to have been an intimate of Porfirio Rubirosa, the world's greatest lover. Now she sold pieces of her past and somehow remained alive.

"You have to see this one," Rafi said. "Anyone who looks like she does has to be somebody. I think I've seen her picture, but I'm not sure. I don't have your memory, like a recording machine."

"What does she look like?"

"An ice cream. I had a spoon I would have eaten her," Rafi said. "Listen. Be at Mesón de la Cava, nine o'clock, you'll see her."

"You're taking me to dinner?"

"Sit at the bar. Look at her and tell me who she is."

"I have to take a taxi there, five pesos," the woman said, "for you to buy me a drink?"

"I'll pay for the taxi," Rafi said. "You can have two drinks."

"I hope I don't become drunk," the woman said.

"Tell me what would make you happy," Rafi said.

"I want three daiquiris, at least," the woman said, "and I want the large shrimp cocktail."

"If she's somebody, you can have a flan, too. Nine o'clock," Rafi said, looking at his watch. He hung up and walked over to a blackjack table where the dealer, a light-skinned Dominican who wore the casino's gold jacket and vacant expression, stood alone waiting for players. Rafi hooked his leg over a stool and gave the dealer a ten-peso note for ten pink chips. As they began to play Rafi touched his chin and worked his jaw from side to side.

"My face hurts from smiling."

"All the sweetness gone out of it," the dealer said. "You want a hit?"

"Hit me . . . That's good." He watched the dealer turn over his cards, totaling fifteen. "Take one yourself."

"I know how to play," the dealer said, putting a card down. He went over twenty-one and paid Rafi his chips.

"I'm letting it ride," Rafi said. "Deal." They continued to play, Rafi winning again. "You think of her husband's name?"

"Who?"

"Who have we been talking about? Luci Palma."

"I still don't remember it," the dealer said. "They live in Sosua. That's all I know."

"I don't like her having a husband," Rafi said. "She have a good-looking sister?"

"Some brothers."

"Pay me again. I'm letting it ride," Rafi said. "I know she has brothers. Hit me. It was a brother I talked to. He knew the one who was with her that the Marine shot. I think I need a younger sister if I don't find a good Luci Palma."

"You're crazy," the dealer said, paying him for thc third straight time.

"How do you know? Have I told you anything?"

"I don't want to know," the dealer said.

"Hit me," Rafi said. "Does the Marine come in here?"

"I haven't seen him."

"Again . . . What about the woman that's with him?"

"I don't know his woman."

"You haven't seen her? Once more. You're missing it. She's an ice cream. Butter almond. I look at her . . ."

"You wish you had a spoon," the dealer said.

"I think I need a girl about twenty. Very beautiful, very innocent. I mean with the appearance of innocence. I don't have that in my stable right now."

"Your girls look like the hotel maids," the dealer said, paying Rafi for the fourth straight time.

"I'm riding one hundred and . . . seventy pesos," Rafi said, holding out his original ten. "If I win this one then I'm going to win something else very big, maybe the jackpot of my life . . . Come on, give it to me."

The dealer gave him an ace and a queen. Blackjack.

"There," Rafi said, like there was nothing to it.

He watched the dealer turn up his own cards. Another ace, another queen. The dealer raised his eyes.

"The thing about it is," Rafi said, "you have to know what is a sign and what isn't. You can be wrong about signs, sometimes interpret them the opposite of what they mean."

"You're still crazy," the dealer said.

Rafi used restraint. He said, "Am I?" and left the dealer with that, a secret smile that told nothing because it had nothing to tell. At least for the time being.

He would have to be more attentive in reading signs.

The Cat Chaser's notice in the paper and the business about it on the radio had alerted Rafi, immediately captured his interest. He talked to people who referred him to others who had taken an active part in the rebellion and there it was, once he put the pieces of the story together: an approach, a way to play a feature role in this, using an old knife scar to represent a bullet wound. He saw in his mind a crude scenario that went:

RAFI: I'm the one you shot sixteen years ago.
MARINE: Oh, I'm so sorry. What can I do to make amends?
RAFI: Please, nothing.
MARINE: I insist.
RAFI: Well, as one businessman to another (assuming the marine was now a businessman), I could tell you about a most unusual investment opportunity. . . .

Something, in essence, like that. Make it up, get his check; gone. But now the mystery woman had entered the picture and the scenario was changing before Rafi's eyes, the woman the Marine called Mary emerging to become, possibly, the key figure. So far it was only a feeling Rafi had. But to a man who lived by signs and instinct, what else was there?

8

They descended a spiral iron stairway fifty feet into the ground to dine in a cave, a network of rooms and niches like catacombs where tables were set with candles and white linen and Dominican couples danced to the percussion sounds of *merengues*. The old city and this place, no Coca-Cola or Texaco signs, Rafi said. This is Santo Domingo.

He told them he had begun to make inquiries about Luci Palma, but so far had learned nothing. It might take a little more time.

Moran tried to convince him it wasn't important, but Rafi insisted; he was curious about Luci now himself. What could have happened to her? He ventured the possibility she had become a full-time revolutionary and fled the country. Like Caamaño, who had led the revolt in '65; he left the country, returned and was shot. It happened.

They talked about that time sixteen years ago, the situation. Moran said it had been impossible to understand, being here in the middle of it. The rebels kept saying to them, "Can't you tell your government we aren't Communists?" It didn't begin to make sense. Almost all the people were friendly; still, guys he knew were getting killed. He read about the situation later and decided they had helped the wrong side—just as they'd been helping the wrong side in Latin America for eighty years. Like Nicaragua, helping that asshole Somoza against the Sandinistas, the good guys. Except look at the good guys now. They just shut down a newspaper for criticizing them; they were doing the same thing Somoza did. What happens to good guys once they get control?

Mary said they have the right to make mistakes like anyone else. Don't assume anything; don't label people. She said, What if a skid-row bum asks you for a handout? Are you going to qualify him, give him the money only if he promises not to spend it on booze? No. Once you give him the money—and it's your choice whether you do or not—then it's his, with no strings. He can spend it on anything he wants. He can screw up or not screw up, that's *his* choice. Unless you're buying him. That's something else.

Wine with dinner conversation: a bottle of red with the *sopa Dominicana* that was like beef stew with noodles; white wine with the sea bass simmered in a peppery tomato sauce . . . Rafi hanging on every word: Moran's basic sympathy with the underdog, the revolutionary, maybe with a few minor doubts; while the woman's analogy said don't expect too much, don't be surprised. Interesting; what Rafi considered the usual man-woman positions reversed. The woman using reason—at least, he assumed, until one got inside her pants. The man asking questions of what he's learned—but essentially, typically, an American bleeding heart.

Yes, it looked good.

Rafi excused himself. He visited the men's room, came out and entered the bar area that was set apart, like a passageway in the cave, only a few couples here having drinks. At the far end of the bar was La Perla with her daiquiri, holding the big snifter glass in both hands beneath a pink glow, staring into the glass, an old woman in theatrical makeup, amber costume jewelry; a gypsy fortune-teller, a magic act waiting to go on.

"Tell me," Rafi said, tense now, expectant.

"Yes, I have her picture."

"I knew it! Who is she?"

"You don't know anything," the woman, La Perla, said. "We have to negotiate this some more. The shrimp cocktail isn't going to do it."

Now Rafi had to decide whether to give in to his impatience or play with the old woman, croon a few false notes to her, put his hand on the curve of her narrow back. But he was tired and he didn't care to feel old bones. He said, "Buy your own rum," and started away.

"She comes to Casa de Campo . . ."

He paused. "Yes?"

". . . for the polo. But without her husband."

"Ah, she's married; I knew it. And he's rich, uh?"

"I'm starving," La Perla said. "I want the entrecote, asparagus with hollandaise . . ."

Rafi raised a hip to the empty stool next to her, her perfume overpowering him as he leaned close.

"Why don't you order whatever you like."

"I still want the large shrimp cocktail."

"You should have it," Rafi said. "Who's her husband?"

"You won't believe it when I tell you."

"I promise I will," Rafi said.

"He's Dominican."

There was a pause between them; silence.

"But he can't come here with her," La Perla said.

"Why is that, if he's Dominican?"

"Somebody would shoot him. *Many* people would shoot him if they could."

It was a game. Rafi tried to think of names—expatriates, political villains—anxious now, trying too hard, as though a buzzer were about to go off and he'd lose.

"He's rich, isn't he? He has to be, with an American wife who likes the polo."

"You won't believe it when I tell you," the woman said again. "I think I want a bottle of wine also. A full bottle of Margaux."

"When you tell me who it is," Rafi said, "have whatever you like. With my love."

The woman tapped the bar, rings rapping on the varnished wood. "Put the money here for my taxi and my dinner," she said. "But keep your love. I don't want to destroy my appetite."

There was not a noticeable change in Rafi when he returned to the table; they talked about Reaganomics and taxes and the price of automobiles. In Rafi's own mind, though, he was at once more cautious, even more observant. If the woman had turned out to be a film star or an international jet-setter he would be coming on to her now with subtle masculine moves, signs that he was available, a man who viewed pleasure as a way of life; far more sensitive than this former Marine who wiped his salad plate with his bread. Take him on *mano a mano* and go for the woman with nothing to lose.

But this woman was a celebrity in a much different light. Married to a man who was at the same time rich and a son of a bitch, accredited in both areas; a man responsible for the deaths of hundreds of people, perhaps thousands. (How many were thrown from the cliffs during Trujillo's time? The sharks still came to Boca Chica.) Married to the butcher and having a love affair with the bleeding heart.

Rafi was quiet now, cautious, because he saw himself in the presence of his future, the opportunity of a lifetime. Here you are. What can you do with this situation? The obvious, of course. But wait and see.

Though not for long. The conversation wound down and the woman covered yawns, smiling at the Marine with sleepy bedroom eyes, the idiot Marine sitting there fooling with his coffee spoon. In these moments, in the Mesón de la Cava, Rafi began to feel contempt for the Marine; he should take the woman away from him. A lovely woman wasted on a man like this was a mortal sin. Move in . . . She'll buy you gifts.

But on the other hand . . .

It was an either-or dilemma. Go for the woman, get her to turn those eyes on him and have her. Or, use the affair with the Marine to score far more in the long run.

Or do both. Was that possible? Bleed the bleeding heart. Yes? And *then* take the woman? It was a shame she wasn't married to the Marine and having the affair with de Boya. As it was there were interesting possibilities to think about.

Rafi cautioned himself again to go slowly and said, "I think I should see you two back to your hotel." There was no argument. "I'll call you tomorrow if I learn anything, all right?"

What else? It seemed enough for now. Don't be eager. At least don't appear eager.

They got into bed in Mary's suite and held each other in silence, tired and wanting nothing more than this closeness, until Mary said, "It's coming to an end. I can feel it."

He said, "Are you a worrier?"

She said, "No, not usually."

He said, in a soothing way, "You know what's coming to an end and what isn't. I don't think we have a choice, we're stuck with each other. But it's gonna be a lot harder for you than it is for me. I mean if we plan to see each other."

"We have to," Mary said.

"Good."

She said, "I've never done anything like this before. Have you?"

"When I was married? No."

"Did you ever have an affair with a married woman?"

"No."

"Then you've never done it either. We're amateurs. I've never even thought about it." She paused. "No, that's a lie. I used to look at you and think about it a lot."

"I did too."

"I used to stare at you and when you'd look over I'd say let's get out of here and go somewhere, be together."

"I would have gone."

"Would you?"

"I wanted to."

"Boy, we've come a long way." She said then, "Where will we meet?"

"You can always come to the Coconuts. Andres's sister and her boyfriend love it."

"We're not like that, are we?"

"I was kidding."

"We're not shacking up . . . Are we?"

"No, there's a big difference."

"God, Moran, I'm gonna have trouble handling this. Sneaking around, not telling anybody. I've got to get it settled with Andres, but I don't want to involve you."

"He was suspicious before he even had a reason."

"He's not dumb. But I've got to make him understand why I'm leaving and that it's got nothing to do with you."

He said, "What about your friends at Casa de Campo?"

She said, "Oh, my God."

"You forgot to call them."

"I haven't even thought about them. When I left the embassy party I said I might change my plans and Marilyn, one of the girls, gave me a look—ah-*ha,* have fun. I'm pretty sure they have an idea what's going on, but you're right, I ought to call, get our stories straight."

''Are they close friends?''

''Not really, but we get along, play tennis a few times a week.''

''They wouldn't call your home—I mean to see if you're there.''

''No, but I'd better let them know where I am.'' Mary said then, ''Shit. They went home today.''

''Is that a problem?''

''I don't know. I hope not.''

''Call one of them tomorrow, at home.''

''I'd better. How long are we staying?''

''You mean it's up to me? You don't sound too worried.''

''I am though. I'm starting to get nervous. And this is just the beginning, isn't it?''

Moran went to sleep; maybe for only a few minutes, he wasn't sure. Lying on his side he held Mary's back curled into him, his knees fitting into the bend of hers. He said, ''Mary?''

''What?'' She was close to sleep.

''Rafi's left-handed. You said tonight you were sitting with two southpaws and he didn't know what a southpaw was.

''Remember?''

She didn't answer.

Moran opened his eyes to see the balcony in sunlight, the sheer draperies stirring, puffing in the breeze. Facing away from Mary he felt her move and get out of bed saying, ''Yuuuk, I drank too much wine.'' Moving toward the bathroom her voice said, ''What time is he going to call?''

''I don't know, maybe he won't . . . Mary?''

''What?''

''The guy I shot was right-handed.''

She said, ''You can remember that?''

He heard the bathroom door close. He lay staring at the clear sky framed within the balcony, hearing the water running in the bathroom, thinking of the swimming pool then and winter ballplayers. The bathroom door opened again and Mary's voice said, ''I forgot. I brushed my teeth and drank the water.'' She came into his view, her slim body in the nightgown clearly defined against the sunlight. ''If I'm gonna die I don't want it to be from drinking water.''

Moran said, "I can see him holding his weapon and he was righthanded. Somebody shoots at you you can close your eyes and see it anytime you want. He wasn't that far away."

She turned from the sunlight, eyebrows raised in question, her face clean and alive.

"He was wearing a Cincinnati Reds baseball cap," Moran said, "an old one. I can still see him."

In Boca Chica, twenty miles from Santo Domingo and twenty years ago, the home of a wealthy family close to Trujillo was confiscated soon after his death, turned into a clubhouse by the sea and passed along to a succession of young men who drank rum and looked for girls and sold goods on the black market. The house now stood in an old section of the resort community that was decaying, losing itself to debris and tropical vegetation. Nearby was a beachfront café that had once been a gas station but now seemed dirtier with its litter of paper cups and ice-cream wrappers that were never picked up. There was blue Spanish tile in the men's room where, to Rafi's recollection, the toilet had never flushed. Late in the morning he would walk from the house to the café for his coffee or sometimes a Coca-Cola and sit outside beneath the portico at a metal table. He made phone calls from the café and brought girls here that he picked up on the beach, to buy them treats and eventually talk business. In an informal way the café was his office.

This morning he was interviewing a girl by the name of Loret. She was seventeen and had some good points, some not so good. She was attractive, she seemed intelligent enough—at least not out of the cane—but she was sullen; her normal expression was a frown, almost a scowl.

"Smile," Rafi said.

Sitting with her can of Seven-Up, Loret bared small teeth. Her smile seemed defensive.

"Relax and do it again . . . That's better. Now relax your smile very slowly . . . There. That's the expression you want on your face. Very nice. And sit up straight; don't slouch like that."

For a girl so small her breasts seemed to fill her T-shirt and pull her shoulders forward with their weight.

"What do you use on your hair?"

"A rinse, I make it lighter." It was a shade of henna, too bright for her tawny skin.

"Maybe we'll put it back the way it was."

"I like this," Loret said, touching her wiry hair. "I don't want to look Negro."

This increased her sullen expression and Rafi told her, again, to smile. "You want to be rich, you have to learn how to smile."

"What do I get?" the girl asked him.

"The world," Rafi said.

She could have it. He'd settle for a home in the embassy section of town, a few servants, an armed guard at the gate he'd present with a cigar each evening as he drove out in his Mercedes.

Rafi had been hustling since he was seventeen years old, since working the *aduana* trade during the revolution of '65 when they looted the customhouse and the docks along the Ozama and sold everything on the black. TV sets, transistor radios, tires, Japanese bikes. It had been a training ground: learning how to get ahead when you begin with nothing. But he was up and down, spending half what he earned on his appearance, to look good in the hotel lobbies, and he had nothing of substance to rely on for a steady income. The few girls he managed worked when they felt like it and cheated him when they did. He'd threaten to cut them with a knife and they'd give him big innocent eyes. Loret's look was more sulk than innocence.

"Push your lower lip out a little more."

"What do I get for this?"

He loved her more each time she said it. It was a sign she was moved by greed.

"Push the lip out . . . Yes, a nice pout, I like that. Aw, you look so sad. Let me see a little more—you're filled with a great sorrow . . . Yes, that's good. Begin to believe you're very depressed. You feel lost."

She said, "You better tell me what I get."

"Tell me what you want," Rafi said. "But not yet. You're too depressed. Something terrible happened to your sister that you loved very much . . ."

He cocked his head at different angles to study the sad little girl. Not bad. The breasts were a bonus. She would have to be rehearsed, of course; still, he knew he was very close to what he needed. Work with Loret the rest of the day. Present her sometime tomorrow.

In the meantime he should pay his respects. Call the Marine and tell him you're onto something but don't tell him what. You'll get back to him later this evening. Yes, you want to look industrious. You don't want to seem to be just hanging around.

He called the hotel and asked for 537.

When there was no answer he got the operator again and asked if Mr. Moran had left word where he would be.

The operator said, "Mr. Moran has checked out."

"What do you mean he's checked out? Give me the desk." He was sure there was a mistake. But when he spoke to the clerk he was told, "Yes, Mr. Moran has checked out." What about Mrs. Delaney? "Yes, she also."

Rafi said, "Did Moran leave a message—I'm sure he did—for Rafi Amado?"

The desk clerk said, "Just a moment." He came back to the phone and said, "No, there's nothing for you here."

9

He talked to Jerry for a few minutes, left him whistling "Zing Went the Strings of My Heart" and as soon as he was in the bungalow Nolen's smiling face appeared at the door.

"You're home. When'd you get in?"

Moran said, "When did I get *in?*" He dropped his bag on the kitchen counter. "You're watching me get in." He had left Mary exactly fifty minutes ago at the Miami airport where they stood holding, kissing in a crowd of people, as though one was seeing the other off. She got in a taxi and Moran wandered through the parking lot looking for his car, the white Mercedes coupe he'd owned for seven years.

Nolen said, "You wouldn't have a cold one in that fridge there, would you?"

"If you left any," Moran said. "Take a look." He wanted him to leave so he could call Mary. It could be the wrong time to call but he missed her and he couldn't imagine de Boya answering the phone himself; a servant would answer. And pretty soon his voice would become familiar to the help. Here he is again for missus. He'd have to make something up, give himself, his voice, an identity.

Nolen uncapped a couple Buds, placed one on the counter for Moran and slipped up onto a stool.

"I skimmed the swimming pool."

"Good."

"Didn't find any used condoms or anything. No alligators. The two broads from Fort Wayne left and the old couple with the Buick. In fact everybody's gone. We had a couple broads from Findlay, Ohio, work for Dow Chemical, they were here for three days. I asked 'em if they heard the one, the salesman from New York who's in Findlay, Ohio, on business and runs into a foxy broad at the Holiday Inn? One drink they're in the sack, it's beautiful. But this guy's a good Catholic so he looks up a church right away, goes to confession and the priest gives him five Our

Fathers and five Hail Marys for his penance. He leaves for New York, meets another good-looking broad at La Guardia. They drive into town together, go to her apartment and jump in bed, it's beautiful. But now he's got to go to confession again before he gets home. He goes to St. Pat's, tells the priest what he did and the priest gives him a rosary. The guy says, 'Father, I don't mean to question you giving me a rosary, but I went to confession in Findlay, Ohio, for the same thing and I only got five Our Fathers and five Hail Marys.' The priest looks at him and screams, 'Findlay, *Ohio!*' Like he can't believe it. 'Findlay, *Ohio*—what do they know about fucking in Findlay, Ohio!' . . . Otherwise," Nolen said, "there's nothing new."

"How about old business?" Moran said, taking clothes out of the bag. "I'm a little more interested in what was going on when I left."

"The lovers?" Nolen said. "They broke up."

"And when we last saw the guy who broke them up," Moran said, "you were treating him to one of my beers."

"Jiggs," Nolen said. "He's all right, a nice guy."

"Yeah, good old Jiggs Scully," Moran said, "hands out phony business cards for laughs, but as it turns out works for de Boya."

"I'm gonna have to explain a few things to you," Nolen said.

Moran picked up his clothes and dropped them in a wicker basket. "Will it take long?"

"George, that's not nice . . . See, you'll be interested to know that Jiggs doesn't exactly work for de Boya. De Boya borrows him from time to time, for heavy work."

"The piano player, Mario, that's heavy?"

Nolen shook his head. "De Boya didn't hire Jiggs for that one. The sister did, Anita."

"I see," Moran said, telling Nolen he didn't see at all.

"You know the song 'Breaking Up Is Hard to Do'? It's like that," Nolen said. "Anita doesn't want to go through a lot of shit with Mario, she just wants to cut it off clean. So she hires Jiggs. The piano player thinks her brother sent him and he's not gonna have a tantrum or argue with the brother and get his legs broken, he wasn't that deeply in love. I said to Jiggs, 'You ever hear the guy play? You gonna break anything break his fingers.' But evidently the brother *did* find out about it and he sent Corky along. You got it now?"

"Have I got what?"

"Corky is Corky Corcovado. He's Dominican, he works for de Boya. But Jiggs, Jiggs you call when you need him."

"Not the number on the card he gave me," Moran said.

"As a matter of fact," Nolen said, "that *is* his number. But the girl on the switchboard won't admit it if she doesn't know who you are. You call him, you have to be a regular."

Moran thought a moment. "She said Dorado Management."

"Yeah, it's sort of a euphemism. She said Ballbusters Incorporated it would've been closer, but that doesn't sound right on the phone, it's too graphic."

Moran waited, letting Nolen talk. The guy was on stage.

"Dorado either manages or controls all the businesses—the restaurants, the furniture stores, dry cleaners—that were into them for shylock money and couldn't make the payments. We're talking about the wise guys. You understand?"

Moran nodded. "Yeah, go on."

"So Dorado, the wise guys, foreclose and take over the business. All I'm saying is things like that go on, you know that, Miami's very heavy into all kinds of shit. It doesn't have anything to do with what we're talking about, nothing. Except I want you to appreciate where Jiggs Scully's coming from, his background. He's like a bill collector. He's on call. Dorado has an outstanding debt or, say, they believe one of their drug dealers is skimming they call Jiggs and he straightens it out. De Boya is something else entirely. I assume he's been into deals with Dorado Management and that's how he got to know Jiggs. But I don't know anything about the deals and I don't want to know. Forget I even mentioned it."

Moran said, "What're you getting into?"

"I'm not getting into anything."

"You gonna start wearing a black overcoat. Pack a gun?"

"They don't wear overcoats down here, George. I'm telling you who's who, that's all. You want to know who Scully is, I'm telling you."

"You think he's a nice guy."

"I think he's funny," Nolen said. "He says funny things." Nolen grinned. "He says, 'Something's wrong, what they teach you in school. How come, I'm an altar boy, I go to mass and communion every morning of my young life, I end up working for the fucking guineas, the fucking spics, carrying their bags?' "

"That's pretty funny," Moran said.

"You have to hear him, the way he says it."

"Well, it wouldn't bother me too much I never saw the guy again," Moran said. "And if you'll excuse me—I want to rest and get cleaned up."

"Hey, that's right—how was the trip?"

"I'll tell you about it later." Moving Nolen to the door.

"Yeah, good. You gonna be around?"

"I don't know yet. I might go out." Practically pushing him through the door.

"I want to hear all about it, George. What was your platoon down there? Ass Chaser? You get much this time?"

"Get out of here," Moran said and closed the door on him.

She had told him her phone number and he'd memorized it on the spot. He dialed and waited, standing at the counter, anxious, without a story for the maid or whoever answered. A woman's voice with an accent said, "Yes, may I help you?"

"Mrs. de Boya, please."

"May I say who is calling?"

Shit . . ."Tell her Mr. Delaney." When she came on he said, "Mary?"

She said, "Who're you supposed to be, a relative?"

"Do you have any?"

"Not around here. They're all up in Michigan."

"Then I'm visiting . . . I miss you already."

"I do too. I ache."

"Can you talk?"

"Not comfortably. He's home."

"Where are you?"

"I'm outside on the deck, having a glass of sherry. I'm nervous."

"I can hear a boat," Moran said. "Have you talked to him yet?"

"I just walked in the door."

"I mean have you seen him."

"Yeah . . . we said hello. That was about it."

"Did you kiss him?"

"On the cheek."

"I'm not good on the phone. I miss you."

"I miss you more. God, I miss you. Let's go back."

"Tomorrow?"

"Let's meet somewhere."

"I'll pick you up."

"No, let me think . . . Do you know where Matheson Hammock is, the park?"

"Yeah, just south of you, on the bay."

"Drive out to the point. To the left of where you go into the beach."

"I know where it is."

"I'll meet you there tomorrow at . . . what time?"

"Six A.M."

"How about noon?"

"I'll be there."

"I love you, George." She hung up.

He had to pace the room a few times before settling down, getting organized. Through the window he could see Nolen sitting by the pool, alone with his beer. The bit actor, part-time private eye who thought Jiggs Scully was funny. Turned on by the guy's deadpan involvement with businessmen who hired him to break legs and collect the vig on money owed. Moran moved from the window.

He had all he could handle for the time being. Nolen Tyner would have to look out for himself.

From the sun deck she could see the park and tropical gardens, a peninsula of jungle extending out of the coral shoreline a half mile to the south, where she would meet him tomorrow. The sky, streaked red above the jungle and fading, darkened as her gaze moved east into the ocean, to the faraway Cape Florida light at the tip of Key Biscayne. Looking at the ocean made her feel safer, above suspicion to anyone in the house watching her. Resting after a two-hour flight and the usual airport hassle. Innocent. Though not eager to talk to a husband she hadn't seen in five days. If not innocent at least honest. What was there to talk about? Andres made statements, issued commands, grunted . . . breathed through his nose when he made love, finished and left her bedroom. He might come to her tonight.

On the lawn that extended to the seawall a figure moved out of shadows, a stand of young acacia, crossed open ground to the dock where the de Boya cruiser was moored, then continued on in the direction of the swimming pool, secluded among tropical palms. Day and night armed guards moved about the property: either Corky or one of several serious young Dominicans Andres employed. More security guards than household help: millionaire self-sufficiency and thoroughly modern, from the weapons the Dominicans carried to the video scanner mounted above the front door.

Altagracia, their maid, served dinner: chicken breasts glazed with fruit flamed in brandy by candlelight, the shadow of Altagracia moving across polished wood, soundless. Mary said to her, "The next time I go down give me your mother's number and I'll call her. If you'd like me to."

Altagracia said, "Yes, señora. But she don't have a phone."

Mary said, "Oh." Altagracia finished serving them and left. "We haven't made plans to go back, but I thought if we ever did . . ." Mary let her voice trail. She raised her eyes to the candlelight, watched for a moment as Andres ate with his shoulders hunched over the table, lowering his head to the fork barely lifted from the plate—the can cutter who had become a general. "We had a wonderful time."

She could hear his lips smack. When they were first married she had enjoyed watching him eat, even to the way he sipped his wine with a mouthful of food, sipped and chewed; there was something romantically hardy and robust about it, for a time.

"The weather was perfect. A few afternoon showers, but they didn't last." Mary tried hard to remember more about the Dominican weather.

Andres said, "That friend of yours, the fat one with hair like a man. I saw her."

It was coming now. Mary sat very still, then made herself reach for the salt. He was watching her now.

"You mean Marilyn? She was with us." Bold now, getting it out in the open. "When did you see her?"

"Yesterday. I was going in the club."

"Then she told you I was staying an extra day."

"She told me nothing about that."

Mary could see his eyes in the candle-glow, age lines making him appear tired, less rigid, the look of vulnerability she had mentioned to Moran. But it was the lighting, she realized now, that softened him, not something from within.

"She told me about polo. But she doesn't sound like she ever saw it. She doesn't know who was in the tournament."

"Well, I guess what we like," Mary said, "is the atmosphere more than anything else. Watching the people. Everybody all slicked up in their polo outfits."

"You see anybody you know?"

It startled her. He had never asked a question like that before; he had never seemed interested enough.

"Philly got us invited to a party at the Santo Domingo Country Club. Mostly embassy people. A few I'd met before."

"Did you see anybody from here?"

"Outside of our group? No. I told you, didn't I, I was going with Marilyn, Philly, Liz? . . ."

"You didn't see—what is his name, he used to belong to the club. The one from your city." He seemed to stare now, as though daring her to say the name.

"Who, George Moran?" Once she said it she had to keep going. "What would he be doing in Santo Domingo?"

"You said you were at Casa de Campo."

"I thought you meant at the embassy party." Then, trying to sound only mildly interested: "How do you know he was there?"

Andres said, "How do I know things. People tell me. Or I want to know something I find it out. He was there the same time you were, but you say you didn't see him."

Mary took a breath, let it out slowly as she picked up her wine. She wanted to begin now, say something that would lead to a confrontation, without involving Moran. She said, "Andres . . ."

but felt Moran's presence already here and lost her nerve.

He said, "Yes?"

She hesitated. "Do you know why I stayed an extra day?"

"Tell me."

"I toured Santo Domingo. Saw all the old places."

"Yes, did you like it?"

"My driver told me about the war . . ."

"Oh? What war is that?"

"A few years after you left, the revolution."

He seemed in no hurry now as he ate, his eyes heavy lidded in the candle-glow, watching her.

She said, "I remember vaguely reading about it, seeing pictures in *Life* magazine. You were here then, but you must have followed it closely."

"I know all those people."

"So you must've leaned toward one side or the other."

"Did I lean?" Andres said. He held his fork upright, his arms on the table. "Do you know the difference between a loyalist and a radical insurrectionist?"

"Well, the driver explained some of that, but his English wasn't too good."

"Or your Spanish wasn't good enough."

"You're right. I shouldn't blame the driver."

"You want to know about it, ask your friend George Moran," Andres said, watching her in the candle-glow. "He was there with the United States Marines. Didn't he tell you that?"

She managed to say, "I can't recall he ever mentioned it. Are you sure?"

Andres seemed to smile. "Why would I say it if I'm not sure? The first time I met him, we were playing golf, he told me that. Very proud of himself. I bought a drink for him, because at that time he was on the side of the loyalists. Maybe he didn't know it, but he was. Now I think loyalty doesn't suit him. He believes only in himself."

Mary waited, not moving. She watched Andres raise his glass, a gesture, a mock salute.

"Good luck to him. May he become loyal again."

* * *

In darkness she pictured the drive from Cutler Road into Matheson Hammock Park, through the dim tunnel of mangrove to the booth where you paid the attendant a dollar and went on, suddenly entering the cleared expanse of crushed coral that reached to the ocean. She saw their cars standing alone at the edge of that open space, as far as they could go, cut off; one way in, one way out.

It was close to two in the morning when she called Moran, heard him answer sleepily and said to him, "He knows."

There was a silence and when he spoke again he was fully awake though his tone was subdued. "What did he say?"

"He knows you were down there."

There was another silence before he said, "The day Andres was here, I was packing to leave."

She said, "We can't meet at the park. It's too out in the open."

He said, "But I can't wait to see you. I can't sleep."

She smiled at that. "Yeah, I could tell." She was within the sound of his voice and for the moment felt secure, as though they could go on talking and say whatever came to mind. "I'll think of a good place and call you tomorrow, before noon."

"Why don't you come here?"

"I'm afraid to. Not yet." She lowered her voice to almost a whisper. "I've never done this before, George. I don't know the ropes."

"How's it going otherwise?"

"I'll tell you tomorrow. Go back to sleep."

She hung up and lay back on her pillow in the dark, beginning finally to relax as she listened and heard only silence. She needed to see Moran, his face with the soft beard, and feel his arms around her. Just being held made everything else go away.

She called at eleven-thirty and said, "The Holiday Inn on Le Jeune Road. Do you know where it is? This side of Flagler."

He said, amazed, "The Holiday Inn?"

She said, "I've already made a reservation under Delaney. Okay? I'll see you about one."

It made him think of Nolen's salesman, scoring at the Holiday Inn in Findlay, Ohio.

But he told himself it wasn't like that and when he got there and he was holding her, moving his hands over the familiar feel of her and saying how much he missed her, barely bringing their mouths apart, he was sure it wasn't anything like Findlay, Ohio. They made love and drank iced wine in bed, in the stillness of the room. Touching each other. Looking at each other. Gradually getting to things they needed to talk about.

He said, "Come live with me. It doesn't matter what he thinks."

She said, "Why didn't I tell him before this? If I bring it up now he's gonna blame you, because you're on his mind. He *knows* we were together."

"All right. What do you want to do?"

"Wait a while."

"How long?"

"I don't *know* how long."

He eased off. "I'm sorry. You have to do it your way. I understand that. I'm anxious, that's all . . ."

She said, "God, I don't want to lose you . . . But I have to wait for the right time. A month ago I felt sorry for him. Now I'm afraid of him—I don't know how he'll react. But I know if he wants to make it difficult . . . well, we have to be very careful." Her tone was thoughtful as her mind sorted through images of her husband. "The right time will comc. I don't know when but I'll feel it and I'll ask him for a divorce. I'll *tell* him I'm gonna get a divorce . . . or if he wants to file, that's fine, if it's a pride thing with him. He'll understand if I do it right, if I can keep you out of it." She gave him a weak smile. "I don't want to beat this to death, but more than anything I want you to understand."

He held her in silence.

"What're you afraid of?"

"*Him*. I don't know what he'll do."

"Do you sleep with him?"

"I don't know how to handle that either. Not since we got back," Mary said. "But do I lock my door? We've never even had an argument; but how can we if we don't talk? Do you see what I mean? I want to be fair."

"Don't be too fair."

She pressed against him, trying to get closer. "I don't know what's gonna happen."

He said, "Well, you walk out with a two-million-dollar settlement, you'll still be one of the richest ladies in Coral Gables—including wives and girl friends of dope dealers. You're not gonna have to get a job as a waitress."

"That's been on my mind too," Mary said. "I don't think I should take the money. Assuming he'll still offer it."

"You've got a signed agreement, haven't you?"

"I don't think that would bother Andres too much."

Moran raised her face to see her eyes, dark, questioning. "I was rich once. I thought it was more of a pain in the ass than anything else. As a matter of fact the beer at the club never tasted right."

Mary said, "George, ten years ago I was making a hundred dollars an hour modeling." She gave him a quick couple of fashion-model expressions, mouth and eye movements from smile to pout. "All that high-fashion New York—beautiful-people bullshit. I did lipstick, perfume, eye-makeup; I was gone before designer jeans. I quit and didn't look at myself for two years. I thought about going to law school until I worked for a lawyer and got pension plans up to here. I don't know what I want as far as a career goes; but the best thing is to just be rich and not worry about it."

He said, "Are we gonna get married?"

She raised her face, her turn to search his eyes.

"I don't know. Are we?"

"It's okay with me."

She pulled away from him. "What do you mean, it's okay? You just go along? You're not obligated, Moran. You can do whatever you want."

He brought her back to him gently, moving his hand over her, down her arm to the curve of her breast, soothing.

"Don't think so much. Let it happen. We'll know what to do when the time comes."

They met at the Holiday Inn each afternoon for the next several days, tried the Castaways on the Beach and went back to the

Holiday Inn because it was familiar and they felt at home. Mary came in her tennis warmups. (Nolen Tyner asked Moran where he went every afternoon. Moran told him visiting. Then Nolen got a surveillance assignment and Moran wondered if he was the subject; but it had to do with a child-custody case in West Palm.) They booked the Holiday Inn room for another week and brought wine and fruit. They talked about playing tennis sometime. They didn't talk about Andres or when or what if. They were together and it was enough. Mary said maybe being rich wasn't that important. Moran said not as long as you can afford motel rooms. But it was a shame to pay when he had an entire motel going to waste, the place empty except for one guy and he wasn't there during the day. Mary finally said all right, she'd come to the Coconuts. Tomorrow.

She came at one o'clock in her warmups carrying her yellow bathing suit. Moran introduced her to Jerry and showed her around; it took about five minutes. Mary said she loved it. They went into Moran's bungalow and he told her not to pay any attention to the tropical floral-print upholstery and the curved bamboo arms on the furniture, he was going to redecorate one of these days. Mary told him to forget it, his decor was back in. He showed her the bedroom next, where she could change, put on her bathing suit.

They were still in there a little after two when Jerry called. Jerry said, "There's a gentleman and a young lady here to see you."

Moran stood holding a towel around him.

"Who are they?"

Jerry said, "His name's Rafi Amado. He says he's from Santo Domingo."

10

Mary watched them from a side window: Moran standing with his thumbs hooked in the low waist of his cutoffs, the bearded innkeeper, gesturing then, yeah, this is it. How do you like it? She could almost read his lips.

The red-haired girl seemed, if not impressed, at least satisfied by what she saw. A strange-looking little thing, attractive, but all her colors wrong.

Rafi, in a shiny black business suit, was squinting, cocking his head as he inspected the Coconut Palms' center court—doors to a dozen rooms in a plain white facade with aqua trim facing the small swimming pool—as though if he caught the right perspective the Coconuts would become the Fontainebleu, a place with real swank.

It's your fault, Mary thought, but had to smile. Rafi was nodding, trying to look impressed. The red-haired girl would roll her lower lip, then lick it and roll it out again. Very strange. She wore a blue and yellow flowered-print dress—giant mutations that might be daisies—the dress tight in the bust but several inches too long, below her knees. Miss Sugarcane.

That's not nice, Mary thought.

But did she have to be nice? Moran seemed to be handling the amenities, making them feel at home, inviting them now to take a lounge chair. He came toward the house as they sat down, Rafi with a stern expression saying something to the girl.

Moran came in and closed the door.

"Not a soul here, the guy shows up all the way from the Dominican Republic."

Mary came away from the window. "Who's the girl with him?"

"Loret. That's all I know." Moran went to the refrigerator. "She wants a Seven-Up."

"Are they staying?"

"He says he's got something to tell me. Like bad news, the way he said it . . . I don't have any Seven-Up. I knew I didn't have any, I don't know why I'm looking."

Mary said, "Should I come out?"

Moran brought two Cokes and a bowl of ice from the refrigerator and closed the door. "Whatever you think."

"Aren't you a little surprised to see him?"

"I'm very surprised. He says, 'And how is your buddy, Mary?' and gives me a wink. I said you're fine."

"You didn't tell him I'm here?"

"No." Moran was at the counter now mixing a rum and Coke for Rafi. "I've still got a funny feeling about him. In fact I've got more of a funny feeling than ever."

"Do you think he knows who I am?"

"It wouldn't surprise me."

"Should I come out? I've got to go home pretty soon."

"Shit," Moran said. "The one time I don't have anybody here. Maybe I can get rid of them."

"No, you can't do that," Mary said. "Assume he's straight, but keep your eyes open. I think I'd better just slip out."

"You can go around the other side to the street."

"I'd better. Unless you want me to help you entertain." Mary smiled. She walked over to him, raising her arms. "Our time will come, George. Hang in."

Rafi said, very quietly, "I like Loret to tell you if she can. She has trouble not only with the words but"—he gestured, touching his chest—"because of the way it makes her feel."

She didn't seem too troubled to Moran: leaning over to slip her sandals off, the bodice of the dress opening to give Moran a peek at her full breasts. She sat back wiggling her toes. They looked dirty.

"But let's see," Rafi said, his sad eyes moving to the girl. "Loret? Tell him who you are."

The girl looked at Rafi and immediately her expression clouded, her lower lip came out and her chin seemed to tremble. Rafi gave a small nod toward Moran. The girl turned to him, raising her head proudly.

"I am the sister of Luci Palma."

Moran said, "Well, I'll be." The girl looked nothing like the Luci Palma he remembered. He said, "You're a lot younger."

"Yes, twelve years," the girl said.

"Well, how is Luci these days? Where does she live?"

"She's dead," the girl said. She seemed to glance at Rafi before placing her glass of Coca-Cola on the ground and covering her face with her hands.

Moran heard muffled sobs. He looked at Rafi.

"She's dead?"

Rafi nodded. "I found it out the day you left. I spoke to someone who told me of Loret and I went to see her."

"How did she die? Was she ill?"

Rafi looked at the girl. "Loret, tell him how she died."

Her hands came away from her face; her eyes seemed glazed now, red with sorrow.

"She was kill."

"She was killed," Rafi said. "Shot to death."

Moran said, "During the war?"

"Loret," Rafi said, "he asks when she was killed."

"Four years ago," the girl said, "but I think it was yesterday. She was so good to me. I live with her and she send me to school, but now I got nothing. I live in a terrible place by the Ozama River. It's very terrible."

"Loret," Rafi said. "Tell him how she was killed."

"Yes," the girl said, "they took her from the house at night, beating her and put her in an automobile and took her away."

"Tell him who did this," Rafi said.

"The men of the government. Like soldiers."

"Regular soldiers?"

"The bad ones, the det squad."

"The death squad," Rafi said. "Continue."

"They took her out in the country and shot her twenty times. She was like my mother . . ."

"Someone found her and told you?" Rafi said.

"Yes, and then I went out there and she was dead. They rape her too. It was like I loss my mother. Now I'm alone."

"Tell him why . . ." Rafi began.

"They kill her because she was, she belong to the New Revolutionary Party . . ."

"The NPR," Rafi said.

". . . which she join because she want to do something for the poor people, but they kill her and do terrible things to her." Loret's chin trembled. "She was my sister. I love her and miss her so much I don't know what to do."

Moran watched her cover her face again and begin to sob. He reached over to touch her shoulder. He wanted to say something, but felt Rafi watching him and wondered what he would say if Rafi—frowning, shaking his head in sympathy—wasn't here.

"She misses Luci very much," Rafi said. "Their mother died and Luci became the mother for her. But Luci"—Rafi sighed—"you know how she was, the spirit she had as well as kindness. When the revolution failed she began again, working for the new party . . . She wanted to go to Nicaragua." Rafi shrugged, weary. "It's a shame, a fine girl with spirit."

"Was she married?" Moran asked.

"Loret," Rafi said.

"No, she never get married," the girl said.

"Do you know why?" Rafi asked.

Loret paused. Then looked at Moran. "She never marry because, well, I believe she was always in love with you."

Moran said, "What? Come on—I hardly knew her."

"She told me," Loret said to Rafi, who gestured toward Moran with a quick movement of his head. "She told me," Loret said, now to Moran, "she had a feeling for you in her heart. She want to write to you but was afraid."

"Afraid of what?" Moran asked.

"I think she didn't want to bother you. You happy living in the United States with everything you want. You don't need a poor girl to be crying to you."

She began to sob and Rafi gave her the handkerchief from his breast pocket. He said to Moran, "She becomes very upset with the reminding of it."

Moran was silent. He wanted to put his arm around the girl, comfort her, wipe the eye makeup smudged on her cheeks. She reminded him of a little girl playing dress-up in her mother's clothes . . . Except for those breasts that seemed to have a life of their own. And except for Rafi sitting in his business suit prompting, making sure she told it all, holding his drink in his left hand, sipping, taking small hesitant sips in the presence of sorrow.

It gave Moran a strange feeling, to be moved by the girl's performance while knowing it was part of Rafi's scam. The two of them working so hard but so obvious about it; amateur night at the Coconut Palms.

He asked Rafi, "Where're you staying?"

"We have no place yet. We came from the airport."

"Well, you've got a place now."

"No, I have friends in Miami if I can find them," Rafi said. "I don't want to inconvenience you."

Moran said, "How can you inconvenience a motel? We're not the Fontainebleu, but . . ."

"No, you're not," Rafi said.

Moran called Mary at 10:30. She answered and he said, "Can we talk?"

"The great stone face went out in his boat. He takes business people out, entertains them."

"Do you ever go?"

"No, I think he entertains with girls. I'm hoping he falls in love with one of them . . . How did it go?"

He told her Loret's story, the way Loret recited and Rafi prompted. "But I really felt sorry for her."

"Do you cry in movies, George?"

"I choke up now and then."

"Where are they now?"

"Well, I told them they might as well stay here. Rafi wants to look up some old friends in Miami. I still don't know what he does for a living."

"Are you charging them?"

"Well, the place's empty anyway."

"You already bought him dinner. But that was for shooting him, right?"

"*If* I shot him. I bought another dinner tonight and found out Loret doesn't like Italian."

"That's a shame," Mary said. "Has Rafi made a pitch yet?"

"He's working up to it. But you know what?"

"You feel sorry for him."

"In a way, yeah."

"He's gonna try to take you, George."

"I know . . . but the poor guy, he's working his ass off and you can see it coming a mile away."

"Well, have fun. Are you gonna show them the sights tomorrow . . . while cute little Loret shows you hers?"

"No, I was planning on being at the Holiday Inn in Coral Gables at one. I feel horny."

"God love you," Mary said. "Stay that way."

Moran was watching the late news when Nolen stumbled at the door and almost came through the screen. Moran said, "Wait and I'll open it, it's easier."

Nolen made himself comfortable and Moran handed him a beer. Nolen said, "Well, if you insist." He drank the can down about a third and said, "That broad in the pool ain't from Fort Wayne or Findlay, Ohio, I know that much. She's got a pair of lungs on her she could float across the ocean on 'em."

"That's Loret," Moran said. "I didn't know she was a swimmer."

"She isn't, she's a floater. Fernando Lamas was nervous, kept telling her to get out, but she wouldn't. I think she told him to get fucked in Spanish."

"That's Rafi Amado."

"Yeah, he says you shot him one time. He showed me."

"What'd it look like to you?"

"It looked like he had one tit."

"The scar."

"It looked like somebody cut him."

"Yeah, and I hit him lower. You hit somebody at about thirty meters you remember it. You can play it back and look at it."

"What's he want?"

"He comes all this way—I don't think just so I can meet cute little Loret. He tell you about her?"

"I wasn't paying much attention; I was watching her float. She's the sister of the girl you went down there looking for and life's been dumping on her and he thinks you're a swell guy. Something like that. What else?"

"I'm waiting for the rest of it."

"So you don't trust this boy."

"Not too far."

"There's somebody doesn't trust you either," Nolen said, giving Moran a sly look. "The old Cat Chaser."

"What're you talking about?"

"Gimme another beer I'll tell you."

"You got one."

"Time you pop another it'll be gone."

Moran walked around the counter into the kitchen and got the beer rather than take Nolen by the throat and choke him. It seemed easier; the man was half in the bag and had something he wanted to tell. Moran came over with the can of Bud to where Nolen was sprawled on the sofa, neck bent against the cushion, his legs sticking straight out. He was wearing a pair of old curl-toed cowboy boots. Nolen handed Moran his empty and took the full one.

"Who is it doesn't trust me?"

"Well, Jiggs Scully wants to know—as Jiggs says, 'Tell me. Your buddy Moran, he working over in Coral Gables at the Holiday Inn there?' " Nolen raised his eyes, holding the beer can at his chin. "Sound like him?"

"That's very good," Moran said. "What's he following me for?"

"He isn't following you, he's following de Boya's wife. He sees her go in the Holiday Inn, he sees you go in the Holiday Inn. She comes out, you come out. Scully wants to know if it's a coincidence or what. He doesn't know what to tell de Boya."

Moran stared at Nolen for a moment, Nolen waiting with the sly look, then went to the kitchen and poured himself a scotch with one ice cube. He stood at the counter now looking across the width of the room at Nolen.

"Scully says he'd rather talk to you than de Boya. He doesn't like de Boya."

"How much does he want?"

"He's not shaking you down, he wants to talk."

"About what?"

"He's an interesting guy. I think you ought to listen what he has to say."

"Yeah, about what?"

"I'm not at liberty. At this point it's strictly between you and him."

"How long's he been following Mrs. de Boya?"

Nolen grinned. "We're very formal, aren't we? I knew something was going on. Back when the guy's sister was shacking up with the piano player—the way you mentioned de Boya's wife, like she was up for canonization, and all the time the old Cat Chaser's meeting her on the side. Jiggs says you have to have very large balls fool around with the wife of a guy like de Boya. He says you mention Andres de Boya to people that know anything about him it shrivels their balls right up."

Moran sipped his drink.

Nolen was comfortable, having a good time.

"You're not saying, uh? Well, I don't blame you. Afraid you'll get your laundry scattered all over. But I think you should talk to him, Jiggs. It might be, you find out it's in your best interest."

Nolen wouldn't say any more than that.

Pulling into the Holiday Inn the next day, driving around to the side, to 167 at the rear of the building, Moran didn't see Jiggs Scully's two-tone red and white Cadillac or anyone sitting alone in the few cars that were parked here. He pulled in next to Mary's Mercedes, both cars white, his old Mercedes next to hers giving a before-and-after impression. He hadn't decided how much to tell her.

And for a while it wouldn't have mattered if de Boya himself were parked outside; they were together and there wasn't anything else, only faint street sounds they might have heard but were removed and had nothing to do with them. They lingered, making it last, until the present began to seep back and sounds outside became images of two-tone Cadillacs and limousines; with awareness came apprehension, waiting for something to happen.

She said, "What's the matter?" When he didn't answer she said, "We don't have to do this."

"Yeah, we do," Moran said. "We're way past that. We could say we're not gonna see each other, but we would."

She said, "He hasn't mentioned you since the day we got back. I've been rehearsing my lines, I'm almost ready to corner him." Her tone softened. "I'm not dragging my feet, I'm just scared."

He said, "I know."

She said, "You're off somewhere."

"No, I'm here. I'm resting."

"Tell me what's going on."

She wanted to know about Loret. He told her the story again in detail and the parts that bothered him: the twelve years difference between Luci and Loret, no mention of brothers and sisters in between; that wasn't a Dominican family. The revolutionary party Luci joined; he didn't believe it existed; the political situation there had been quiet for years. And the way Rafi put words in her mouth, prompted so she wouldn't forget anything.

Mary said, "And are they having fun at the Coconuts?"

He had put them up in oceanfront Number One and Number Two. He told Mary that Jerry said he was crazy, giving them a free ride and now he'd have to get Lula in to clean. Jerry called them "boat people," like the Cubans from Mariel; pretty soon they'd be taking over.

Mary said, "Bighearted George. Well, as long as you know what you're doing."

"But I don't," Moran said. "I'm not sure what's going on. But he makes a pitch I can always say no, right?"

"I don't know, George. Can you? You know they want something, but you're still moved."

The afternoon went too fast; it always did. Mary slipped into her warmups. They said goodbye, holding onto each other for several minutes and almost went back to bed. Moran waited then by the door as Mary got in her car and drove off. Still no sign of a two-tone Cadillac.

Moran got in his car and drove out toward the front of the Holiday Inn. He saw Mary's car turn south onto Le Jeune. Then saw a familiar car come out from the portico in front of the building, out of the shade, and turn onto the street after her. An older-model, faded blue Porsche. Nolen Tyner's car.

Moran followed, seeing faint bursts of colorless smoke coming out of the Porsche's tailpipe as it accelerated. There was no doubt in his mind it was Nolen. He hung back, keeping the oil burner in sight, then caught the light at Miracle Mile and had to sit there as both cars continued on, disappearing in the southbound traffic.

He took his time now, worked his way over to Granada and followed the road through Coral Gables to the country club to see if she might have turned in there; but there was no sign of either car. He passed the street where he had lived for seven years, drove through caverns of tropical trees to streets that branched off into fingers of coastal land, the houses built on a network of free-form canals and hidden by walls of stone and vegetation, stands of sea grape, hibiscus, jungles of orchids and acacia trees. He came to Arvida Parkway and rolled slowly through the gloom of foliage, catching flashes of Biscayne Bay in the late afternoon sunlight.

The de Boya home stood on a spur of land that curved out a few hundred feet into the bay, the peak of its roof ascending steeply against the sky like a tor, a landmark from the bayside but from inland only glimpses of bleached wood and glass. Moran had called it Polynesian contemporary, the home of a South Seas potentate. Mary said, "If not a very successful cocaine dealer." She called it bastard modern, neo-nondescript. The entire house, she said, could only be seen from the dock at the edge of the front lawn. Otherwise, and especially from the road, only an idea of its astonishing angles could be seen beyond the iron pickets mounted to the low cement wall and through the forest of poinciana and acacia that sealed off the front of the property.

Stone columns marked an entrance to number 700. The driveway circled into the trees and came out again at another pair of columns up the road, without revealing the front of the house or cars that might be parked there.

All he could do was assume Mary was home now and Nolen had passed this way a few minutes ago. What would happen if he pulled into the driveway? What was he doing there if de Boya came out?

Moran took the freeway north out of Miami thinking of the afternoon motel room and the warm awareness in Mary's eyes as she called him bighearted George, touching him, understanding him. Good, that part was good. But his own image of a bighearted George was not the bearded guy in the motel room. Or the cement-finisher working in the sun. Or the fire-team leader in the narrow streets of Santo Domingo. Not the fantasized seventeen-year-old lover either. The bighearted George he saw in his own mind was a dreamer, the ideal dumb-guy mark. He caught every light in Pompano Beach going toward the ocean and the bridge raised across the Intracoastal; it was all right, he was patient now as he realized he was out of patience, tired of waiting, accepting, listening to people like Rafi and Nolen, with their angles.

There was no faded blue Porsche parked in front of the Coconut Palms, no sign of Jerry anywhere, no one sitting by the pool. Lula came out of Number One carrying dirty towels and a plastic trash bag. Moran waited for her, looking out at the beach, empty with the sun gone for the day though it was still light.

"That girl in there," Lula said, "nobody musta taught her to pick up after herself. She got clothes, and they pretty things, all over the place."

"Leave 'em," Moran said, "you're not her maid."

"She messy. Dirty all the dishes—they been cooking in there. It don't smell bad but it makes a mess."

"They'll be gone soon."

Lula cocked her head, frowning. "I still got that, like a night-gown the woman left? You can see through it."

"You want it?"

"Honey, I can't even get one arm in it, or nobody can I know. It's hanging in the laundry room."

"I'll take care of it." Moran looked over at Number One. "They both in there?"

"She's in there eating potato chips," Lula said, "getting 'em all over everything. That's all I seen her do is eat. The man, I don't know where he is."

Moran got a beer and came back outside with a canvas deck chair he sat in to look at the ocean, his feet on the low cement wall. He'd get things settled with Rafi before the day was over, put him against a wall and pull his pockets out . . .

Nolen said, "You drinking without me?"

He came up next to Moran running a hand through his thinning hair as the wind whipped it across his forehead. He raised the can of beer in his other hand.

"I got my own. I bought four six-packs today; two for you, two for me."

"You doing a little surveillance this afternoon?"

"No, I was off today. Listen"—he sat down on the cement wall hunching in close to Moran, anxious to tell something—"that broad, your little pal from Santo Domingo, she comes up to me—no, first she has her swim, her float. She gets out of the pool, comes over and sits down next to me in this little string number, her lungs about to come tumbling out—you wonder if the straps can hold all the goodies in there. She's sitting there—Isn't it a nice day? Get all that over with. You like Florida? Yes. She's sitting there very quietly for a couple of minutes, she goes, 'You want to have a party?' I ask her what kind of party. She goes, 'You know'—and looks around to see if anybody's watching——'do it, man, have a good time. Me and you.' I go, '*Do* it?' Like I just got in from Monroe Station, some place out on the Tamiami. 'What do you mean, do it?' She gives this surprised look and says, 'What do you think? Half-and-half for fifty dollars. Okay?' . . . That's your little orphan."

Moran said, "You do it?"

"I told her it had to be for love. I'm gonna catch her later. Little broad—she isn't eighteen years old she's a pro."

"When'd all this happen?"

"Couple hours ago. Before I went to the store. I bought her some potato chips. She can't get enough of 'em."

"Where else did you go?"

"No place. What is this? I told you, it's my day off."

"I didn't see your car out front when I got home."

"No, I loaned it to your buddy Rafael Amado. The guy's a hustler, you know it? He comes on with the manners like he's the chief of protocol, but just the way he asks if he can use the car, buy the gas, all that, you know he's a hustler. So be careful. He wants to sell you something, tell him no, you got one."

"When'd you give him the car?"

"This morning, around noon. He left almost the same time you did," Nolen said. "He was right behind you."

11

The shock of seeing him was instant, even before he called her name. She had just now arrived home. Turned from the front door to see Corky hurrying toward the blue car in the driveway, Rafi getting out, smiling—*there,* at that moment—knowing who it was before she saw his face clearly but recognizing something about him, Corky shoving him then, keeping him against the car, and Rafi was calling, "Mary, help me!"

Beaming then, all a joke, with a few words in Spanish for Corky and he was coming to her with outstretched hands—to do what, put his arms around her? She took his hands, managed to smile and said pleasantly, with a note of surprise, "Well . . ." It was the best she could do.

"Mary, Mary, it's so wonderful to see you again!" His head darted and he kissed her, almost on the mouth, before she could pull back.

Mary said, "Well . . ." She said something that sounded like, "What a surprise."

Altagracia served them chilled white wine on the sundeck. Rafi made a show of raising his to the fading sun and came close to rejoicing over the red hues reflected in his glass. He wore his tailored white Dominican shirt, the squared-off tails hanging free of his trousers.

"It's lovely," Rafi said then, "everything, your home, your—how should I say?—your taste in decorating, it's as I imagine it would be."

Mary said, "I didn't think you knew my name."

His gaze came away from the view, the boat dock, the sweep of lawn, smiling with that air of familiarity, confidence, she remembered from the first time they met.

He said, "Mary, a woman of your beauty begs to be identified."

She said, "Rafi, knock it off. Get to the point."

"I'm sorry," he said. "What?"

"Who told you my name?"

"You're well known, Mary. The wife of a man who was once very important in our government. You come to Casa de Campo . . . You're the buddy of a man who was a celebrity in Santo Domingo for a day or two, looking for his lost love." He stopped. "I can't imagine that, why he would look for someone else if he has you."

"We're friends," Mary said.

"Yes, I notice. Very good friends."

"Have you called him since you got here?"

"Who, Moran?" This brought a new depth of enjoyment. As his smile began to fade a trace still lingered. "You just left him, Mary, at, I believe, the Holiday Inn? Didn't he tell you I'm staying with him?"

Mary had stopped smiling some time ago, seeing it coming. And now here we are, she thought. She was ready and said very quietly, "How much are you asking for?"

Rafi seemed hurt, furrowing his brow. He said, *"Como?* How much do I *ask* for?" Overdoing it. Then let his expression relax, though still with sensitivity, misunderstood. "You don't believe I intend to make something of this, do you? Your affair with Moran? I think it's beautiful. I admire both of you very much."

Past Rafi's shoulder, far out in the bay, a powerboat was trailing a curving wake, coming in toward shore. Mary saw it and recognized *El Jefe,* the de Boya sixty-foot yacht, vivid white against the darkening ocean.

She said, "why did you bring the girl?"

"Loret? He's looking for her sister." Innocence now in Rafi's tone. "But she's dead. Gave her life in a cause, and now poor Loret has no one to take care of her. I tell this to Moran because of his feeling, if he wants to give something to Loret for her future, her education, something to help the poor girl. It's up to him."

"And how," Mary said, "do you put the bite on me?"

"That sounds good," Rafi said, "whatever it means. I'd give you some nice bites, Mary, if we were more than friends. But"—he gestured, a sad smile now—"what can I do? I'm not your lover. I can only approach you as a friend. Ah, but there, perhaps I can suggest a very profitable business investment in Santo

Domingo that might interest you. Something you can come down to see from time to time. I show you and we watch it grow. Maybe something like that?''

''How much?'' Mary said.

''The investment? I don't know, I have to show you the papers.''

''Would you like to show my husband?''

''He has his investment, uh?'' Rafi said. ''You have yours. What's the matter with that? I wouldn't wish to take his valuable time, a man like your husband . . .''

''He's coming,'' Mary said, nodding toward the bay. ''Tell him about it.''

Rafi turned to see the prow of the boat approaching the dock, a heavy rumbling sound reaching them.

''I think you misunderstand me.''

They could hear the boat's exhaust clearly as the white hull crept toward its berth and a deckhand jumped to the dock with a line.

''Really,'' Mary said, ''tell him about your profitable investments.''

''Well, I'd be happy to meet your husband, of course . . .''

''You don't sound too sure.''

''General de Boya. Every Dominican knows of him. It would be an honor.''

''He's not a general anymore,'' Mary said. ''He's . . . I'm not sure what he is. Ask him.''

Rafi had lost some of his confidence. He seemed apprehensive, watching de Boya, in a business suit, coming across the lawn toward them, and looked at Mary quickly.

''I don't want to take his time.''

''He won't let you take his time if he doesn't want you to,'' Mary said. ''Tell him whatever you like.''

She glanced at Rafi preparing himself, squaring his shoulders; then waited until her husband was mounting the steps to the sundeck. He was wearing sunglasses, his grim expression in place.

''Andres, I'd like you to meet a fellow Dominican, Rafael Amado.'' And told him they had met at the Santo Domingo

Country Club on her last trip. "Rafi's in investments. You two should get along fine."

She watched Rafi step forward and bow, eyes lowered, as he took her husband's hand, a commoner in the presence of royalty. But it was her husband's reaction that surprised her more. His posture seemed to be not the stiff formality he reserved for strangers, meeting someone for the first time, but the more guarded sense of suspicion he usually reserved for her. She wondered if he knew who Rafi was. They spoke in Spanish for less than a minute while Andres eyed him and Rafi looked off nodding, trying to maintain a thoughtful, interested expression; until Andres gave him a stiff nod for a bow, looked at Mary briefly as he excused himself and walked into the house.

Rafi now seemed dazed. He said, "I've met General Andres de Boya."

"And he didn't take you out and shoot you," Mary said. "He must like you."

It was as though Rafi took her seriously, his expression numb, a glazed look in his eyes.

"When I was little," he said, then paused. "Perhaps I shouldn't tell you. It might seem offensive to you."

Mary shrugged. "No more than anything else you've said."

Now he seemed wounded. "Have I hurt you?"

"When you were a little boy," Mary began. "What?"

"My mother would threaten me," Rafi said, "as many of the mothers of small children did at that time. She would say to me, 'If you're not good, General de Boya will come and take you and we'll never see you again.' " Rafi gestured with a weak smile. "That's all. As you introduced me to him I thought of it again."

"Well, it sounds like something to keep in mind," Mary said, "no matter how old you are."

There had been a list of POOL RULES on a board nailed to a palm tree, put there by the previous owner. *No running . . . No splashing . . . No swimming without showering first . . . No glass objects allowed on the patio . . .* A list of negatives Moran never cared for. So when the palm tree died and was removed the POOL RULES went with it. He did set an example, though, and when he switched after two cans of beer to scotch he poured it into a plastic party glass with ice and took his drink outside to sit in his deck chair and wait for Rafi.

It was dark now though still early evening. He had not seen Rafi all day. When he saw him again it would be for the last time. He did not have to prepare a speech; what he had to say was simple enough. Get your ass out of here.

He told himself he shouldn't let things get out of hand like this. He should never wait for things to happen and then have to clean up after. Maybe he should have put the POOL RULES up somewhere. But then he thought, no. Even if you said *No glass objects* people could still bring a glass out and break it; they could still cut themselves and sue you. No, rules were cold, unrelenting. You had to handle people individually, take each situation as it came. Just don't let them talk you into something you don't want to do.

He wished Mary were here looking at the ocean with him. Looking at the ocean at night made him think of himself in a quieting way. He felt the breeze with a smell of salt in it and thought of turning on some music. Start with Placido Domingo doing love ballads. She said he was more romantic than she'd expected and he told her he felt like he was seventeen. He did. Thinking about her now mellowed him. Start with Placido and work up to J. Geils.

So that when Rafi showed up, coming across the patio from the office, Moran waved—"Hey, I want to talk to you"—and walked toward the swimming pool where Rafi stood in the green glow of underwater lights.

"What'd you lay on Mary?"

"I'm sorry . . ." Rafi began, not understanding.

"I am too," Moran said. "Never buy a guy dinner until he proves you shot him." Rafi still looked puzzled—real or acting, it didn't matter to Moran. "You weren't on that roof with Luci anymore'n that little broad's her sister. So let's cut the shit. I don't care if you own up or not, long as you're out of here tomorrow."

Rafi seemed hurt now. "George, what is it? Why you saying this?"

"You can try it out on me," Moran said, "it was kind of interesting, see how you handle it. But you go for my friend, the fun's over. Take your little hooker and get out of here."

Rafi said, "My hooker?"

"Your *puta*. She's over there waiting for you." Moran nodded toward Number One, at the figure of the girl in the doorway, and it took him by surprise; the classic pose, the girl's body outlined in a soft glow of lamplight, inviting without making a move.

Rafi said, "George, you heard her story . . . I swear to you on my mother's honor . . ."

"You better keep your mother out of it," Moran said, "unless you want to hear some street Spanish about where you came from. You *comprende, pendejo?* Let's keep it simple. You brought the girl along so I'll feel sorry for her and you can make a pitch. Something for poor little Loret, living down there in the slums. And if I get your meaning you don't have to hold anything over my head. Then what? You parade her in front of Mary? . . . You knew who she was when we were down there, didn't you? Must've lit your eyes up. What'd you say to her today?"

Rafi took his time. "George, part of what you say is true. Yes, I recognize Mary. But I don't say anything because I don't want to . . . surprise you and you think the wrong thing."

"Bullshit, you had to come up with a scheme. You followed me today, you followed her . . . You tell her how much you want or you haven't made up your mind yet?"

"George, what do you think I want?"

"Not *what,* how much. I know what you want. Christ, the way you do it, you might as well wear a sign. You're a fucking lizard, Rafi, that's all I can say."

Rafi gave himself a little time. He sighed. "You make it sound ugly, George, I'm surprise. A man like you, run this kind of place." Rafi looked about critically in the glow of the swimming pool, unimpressed. "You want me to believe it's very swank. But soon as I come here I realize something, George. You see a good thing you go for it. You accuse me, but, George"—with a smile to show patience and understanding—"I'm not the one fucking General de Boya's wife, you arc."

Moran hammered him with a straight left, aiming for the grin that vanished behind his fist and Rafi stumbled back, over the side of the pool. He landed on his back, smacking the water hard, went under and came up waving his arms, gasping. Moran stood on the tile edge watching him. Rafi was only a few feet away but struggling, fighting the water, still gasping for breath. Shit, Moran thought.

He yelled at him, "Take it easy! Hey—put your head back, you won't sink."

Rafi was trying to scream something in Spanish, taking in water, gagging, going under again.

"Relax, will you. Take it easy."

Moran glanced around to see the girl, Loret, next to him now, calmly watching Rafi in the water.

"Can't he swim?"

"I don't know," the girl said. "It don't look like it."

"Shit," Moran said. He pulled his untied sneakers off, hesitated, took his wallet out of his pocket, dropped it behind him and jumped in the pool.

As soon as they got him in the living room of the apartment Rafi slumped into the sofa, his Dominican shirt sticking to him, transparent. Moran yelled at him, "Not on the couch!" and grabbed an arm to pull him up. Christ, the guy was making a survivor scene out of it, saved from a watery grave, the girl bringing a blanket she'd ripped from the bed. Moran held her off and pushed Rafi toward the bathroom. "Get in there. You ruin my furniture I'll throw you back."

Nolen was standing in the doorway holding the screen.

"What happened?"

"Asshole fell in the swimming pool."

"He all right?"

"Who gives a shit," Moran said. He started out, then looked around at Loret. "Give me my wallet."

She hesitated, then reached behind her and brought it out of the waist of her jeans. "I holding it for you."

"Thanks," Moran said. "Now pack. You're going home tomorrow." He took his wallet and left.

Nolen watched Moran cross to his bungalow and go inside. For several moments Nolen stood with his hands shoved into his back pockets, looking about idly.

"Moran hit him then save his life," Loret said.

"Funny guy," Nolen said. He came in now, moved through the

living room to the kitchenette, snooping, looking around. "What do you and Rafael drink for fun, anything?"

"They some wine in the refrigerador."

"I'll be back," Nolen said.

Loret began in Spanish and Nolen had to tell her to talk English or shut up. He listened to see if she had anything of value for him, but all she was doing was bitching at Rafi.

"I don't know why I come here with you. I learn what you tell me, I say it perfect."

"You don't say it perfect," Rafi said.

"I say it so good I begin to cry myself and he touch me. You see that. He reach over and touch me. I did it perfect. But you—you sav something he push you in the *piscina*." She looked at Nolen sitting forward on the sofa, pouring himself a drink from the bottle of Scotch he'd placed close by on the coffee table. "You know how much money I didn't make since I start being with him? I'll tell you—"

Rafi said something to her in Spanish that shut her up.

"It's okay," Nolen said. "How much?"

"Two hundred dollar a night—all those nights I have to spend listening to him, it come to *dos mil,* two thousand dollar I don't make," Loret said. "Maybe more than that."

Nolen was getting up, hands on his thighs like an old man. "You're a cute little girl," he said to Loret, taking her by the arm, leading her to the bedroom, "but you talk too much. Stay in there and be quiet." He pushed her into the room and closed the door. When she pounded on it and began yelling in Spanish Nolen opened the door a few inches and pointed a finger inside. "I said be quiet, you hear? Or I'll have to get rough with you and I don't want to do that." He closed the door again and went back to the sofa. Easing himself down he said to Rafi, "I recited that line every night for two and a half months. 'Be quiet now, you hear? Or I'll have to get rough with you . . .' Oh my, where were we? That's right, we haven't started yet, have we?"

Rafi sat quietly in a straight chair turned away from the desk. He seemed drained of energy after his ordeal, his hair still wet, flat to his skull, his body wrapped in the comfort of a brown velour robe.

"First, you didn't do it right," Nolen said. "You come rolling in like a medicine show, got your little helper with you. Fine, except every guy to her's a trick. You see it in her eyes, she can't wait to get your fly open. Second, you picked the wrong guy. I don't mean because he doesn't have any money, I'm not talking about money. And I don't mean he's the wrong guy in that you ever leaned on him seriously, spoke right out and tried to blackmail him, he'd beat the shit out of you. That's nothing. You've been cut, you know what I mean. You get over it. No, I'm talking about you picked the wrong guy from the standpoint you didn't pick the *right* one. Are you following me?"

Rafi was moving his tongue over his teeth or touching his mouth gently with the tips of his fingers.

"You paying attention?"

Rafi didn't say. He seemed to nod.

"I'm not telling you this," Nolen said, "because I think you need counseling. You're no more fucked up than the rest of the pimps trying to get by, but you're not a pimp."

"I was never a pimp," Rafi said, as indignant as he could sound with a sore mouth.

"I mean you don't have the right stuff to be a good pimp," Nolen said. "You're not only about thirty years behind in your style you're playing the wrong part. You come on like a young Fernando Lamas when another type entirely, today, is selling tickets."

Rafi said, "What tickets?"

"Just listen," Nolen said. "What's going down in the Caribbean, in Central America, El Salvador now, ever since Cuba? Revolutions, man. They've always been big down there, but now they're getting more notice because they seem closer to home. Only an hour, two hours across the friendly skies and it scares the shit out of people. It's going on right in Miami with the Cubans, the Haitians, Colombians that come to visit—you got dope and international politics all mixed up with terrorists that use pipe bombs and automatic weapons, man, it's real and it's right here. You understand what I'm saying to you? You want to score today you got to get into the action that's going down, you got to spread a little terror."

Rafi was listening. He said, "Yes? How do I do that?"

"I'm glad you asked," Nolen said. "You've got the background, the hot blood, all that shit. I think with a little direction, a good slogan, you could make a pretty fair revolutionary. *Viva Libertad*—you know, get excited."

Rafi frowned. "You want to start a revolution?"

"No, you do," Nolen said. "You want to make it look like you're part of a wild-ass revolutionary movement. You're an ace terrorist come here to do a job. You're a fanatic, man, you can't wait to blow somebody away. But, you want him to know it first. You want to make him believe he's got this fucking movement coming down on him, not just some muggers—you know what I mean?—some real gung-hoers, man, fire-eaters."

Rafi said, "What guy?"

"I thought so," Nolen said. "Right there in front of you and you don't even see it. You go after Moran and his girl friend . . . what about the girl friend's husband? He's the guy with the prize, not Moran. Moran's one of the good guys."

"Wait," Rafi said. "You have to explain this to me."

"In time," Nolen said. "First we got to think of a good slogan, something to get the guy squirming—he doesn't know what's going on, where it's coming from, but it looks like some pretty heavy shit coming down."

"An *eslogan? . . .*"

"Not a slogan—how do you say it?—a *grito de combate*. A battle cry."

"Yes? To say what?"

"How about *Muerte a de Boya?*" Nolen said. "That's got a pretty nice ring."

Rafi had stopped touching his sore mouth. He stared at Nolen, interested but uncertain, trying to put it together in his mind.

"You asking me to kill him?"

"Would you like to?"

Rafi didn't answer.

"I want you to think about it," Nolen said, "get a feel for the part. You're Rafi Amado, the man from Santo Domingo, a no-shit revolutionary full of zeal, revenge, whatever revolutionaries are full of. You understand what I mean? Get in the mood and we'll talk about it some more."

12

Jerry was reading the *Sun-Sentinel.* He held it up as Moran came in the office.

"You see this? Right up at Hillsboro. Guy walks out of his condo, he's taking his morning exercise, look what he finds right out in front of his place." The headline of the newspaper read:

33 HAITIANS DROWN IN HILLSBORO SURF;

SURVIVOR'S STORY DOUBTED BY OFFICIALS

The photograph that ran the full width of the page and was about five inches deep showed four naked swollen bodies lying on the hard-pack sand at the edge of the surf in early morning light. A Coast Guard helicopter hovered about twenty yards off shore.

"I'm telling you," Jerry said, "it's getting out of hand. People up there, they invest a lot of money in their retirement homes—this's what they got to put up with."

"What's the story the officials don't believe?"

"That they came all the way from Haiti in this rickety boat, sixty-something people. If they're not coming from Cuba it's Haiti now, we don't have enough Latins here, we got all this extra welfare money laying around. Oh . . . there was a phone call for you. You know how many Cubans they got in Miami now?"

"Who was it called?"

"Two hundred thousand. Over half the population. Some woman . . . she didn't leave her name. Plus a hundred and twenty-five thousand boat people, for Christ sake, half of them out of the Havana jails and insane asylums. They send'em here for us to take care of . . . Here's the number."

It was Mary's.

"When'd she call?"

"Few minutes ago. We're different, we got us a couple Dominican freeloaders. Where you going? You just got here."

"I'll be back."

Moran shoved the slip of notepaper into his jeans and walked out into the sunlight, back toward his house. He was anxious.

Nolen, coming out of Number Five, stopped him.

"George, can I talk to you?"

"I got to make a phone call."

"Just take a minute." Nolen, his shirt open and hanging out of his pants, got to Moran at the shallow end of the pool. "I got a request. How about letting your buddy from the D.R. stay a couple more days? He's afraid to talk to you."

"I hope so," Moran said.

"He's sorry. He said he made a mistake."

"I made the mistake," Moran said, "ever talking to him." He started to move away.

"George, he can't hurt you. Let him stay a while."

Moran stopped. "Why?"

"Why not? He's all right, just a little fucked up. He's an interesting type, I can study him."

"I know what you want to study," Moran said.

Nolen shrugged. "I think I can get a freebee, a libretito." His hair hung oily looking, he needed a shave, he looked terrible, forlorn, standing barefoot with his hands in his pockets. "She wants me to show her Miami Beach, all the beeg 'otels."

"Good," Moran said. "You take her down there we'll probably never see her again. Look, I don't have time right now. Tell her to clean up the kitchen before you go and tell Rafi he'd better stay away from me, not that I'm pissed off or anything."

"I'll keep 'em in line," Nolen said, "no problem." He watched Moran hurrying away. "Hey, one other thing . . ."

"Later," Moran said. He ran inside his house and locked the door.

Moran waited. As soon as he heard her voice on the phone he said, "What happened?"

"He's still here but he's leaving. Going out on the boat."

"Should I call back?"

"No, it's okay, he's outside. I can see him."

"What's the matter?"

"He told me this morning he doesn't want me to drive anymore. I can't go anywhere alone in the car. If I go out, Corky's supposed to drive me."

"Why?"

"Because he knows. Or he thinks he does—it's the same thing."

"What'd he say?"

"He said he wants me to take the goddamn limousine, but if I insist on using my own car Corky's still going with me."

"I mean what reason did he give?"

"Crime in the streets, the high incidence of muggings and holdups. It's for my own safety. I told him there aren't any muggings at Leucadendra or the Dadeland shopping mall, but you don't argue with him. I told you, he's a rock."

"Can he order you like that?"

"If I get in the car, Corky gets in with me. That's it, or stay home. What're we gonna do?"

"You got to get out of there, that's all."

There was a pause. "I had sort of a talk with him."

"Yeah? What happened?"

"Not much. I'll tell you about it some other time, not now," Mary said. "God, I'm dying to see you."

"I'll be over in a little while."

"You can't come *here.*"

"I've got an excuse. I'm gonna return something."

"What is it?"

"I'll be there in about an hour. Why don't you invite me to lunch?"

"God, Moran—hurry."

Nolen caught him again, coming out of the laundry room holding a grocery sack, the top rolled tightly closed. Moran was wearing a sport coat and good pants. Nolen looked him up and down.

"The casual Holiday Inn attire?"

"There times you can say anything you want," Moran said. "This isn't one of 'em. I'm in a hurry."

"Jiggs wants to talk to you."

"You told me."

"Give him the courtesy—what've you got to lose?"

"My good name, being seen with a kneecapper. There isn't anything he can tell me I need to know."

"I'm not asking you to go out of your way."

"I hope not."

"I'm not suppose to say anything," Nolen said, "but I'll give you a hint. It's got to do with freedom of choice and self–respect. Like not having to sneak in the Holiday Inn anymore."

"What I have to say to that," Moran said, "has to do with self-control. How I'm learning to stay calm, not pop anybody in the mouth, dump 'em in the swimming pool every time I get a little irritated. But it's hard."

"I know, stay out of your personal affairs," Nolen said. "But I feel I owe you something. You've been a buddy to me, even after we tried to blow you away with a one-oh-six. I mean it might've been me, though I hate to say it."

"Let's let bygones be bygones," Moran said. "Long as you pay your rent on time. I'll see you."

Nolen said, "Hey, George?" And waited for him to stop a few feet away and look back. "You're a beautiful guy. I just don't want anything to happen to you."

"Jesus Christ," Moran said, "leave me alone."

"Only three nights I got to recite that line," Nolen said. "You can see why the fucker closed."

He liked the trees in this south end of Coral Gables, the quiet gloom of the streets; the trees belonged and were more than ornamental. It was old Florida, the way he felt Florida should still look. No way for a one-time cement-finisher to think, or a man partly responsible for a half-dozen king-size condominiums with majestic names. Maybe it was guilt. Or maybe he simply liked a tangle of ripe tropical vegetation. What was wrong with that? He told himself not to argue with himself; he was one of the few friends he had. He didn't care for what he was doing right now. It was like going to the dentist when you were in love with his nurse, but it was still going to the dentist. He turned off Arvida Parkway into the drive marked 700 on a cement column and this time followed its curve up to the house.

Mary was waiting outside. She brought him past the three members of the home guard who stood in the driveway and seemed disappointed. Moran recognized the one with the mustache. Corky. The one trying to look mean.

From the front steps Moran said, "Keep an eye on my car, okay?"

Mary took him by the arm. "Get in here." And closed the door. "What's in the bag?"

Moran opened it and brought out a pink negligee. "You like it? Anita de Boya's playsuit. She left it."

"He's not gonna believe that's why you came," Mary said. "Anita lives in Bal Harbor."

"Do you want me to care what he believes?"

"You're right, it doesn't matter," Mary said. Tense today, inside herself.

She led him from the hallway that was like an arboretum of exotic plants and trees, past an almost bare living room that resembled a modern-art gallery, through a more lived-in-looking room done in rattan and off-white fabrics and out to the sundeck with its several-million-dollar view of Biscayne Bay and the Atlantic Ocean, what Miami money was all about.

Moran was impressed; but he could be impressed by all kinds of things and not have a desire to own them; he considered himself lucky. He took in the sights, the empty boat dock, the stand of acacia trees, then back again, across the sweep of lawn to the swimming pool, designed to resemble a tropical lagoon set among palm trees and terraced flower gardens. Clean that setup every day, he thought. But said, "I like it."

"I don't," Mary said. "I've got to get out of here."

She stood at the rail with him, wearing sunglasses now, looking out at the water. When she turned away he followed her to a half-circle of chairs with bright yellow cushions. On the low table in the center was a white telephone and the morning paper headlining the dead Haitians.

"Why don't you leave now? With me," Moran said. He sat down. Mary remained standing, tan in her white sundress, silent, her slim legs somewhat apart, folding her arms now; protective or defiant, Moran wasn't sure.

She said, finally, "Rafi was here yesterday."

"I know, I had a talk with him," Moran said. "If that's what's got you clutched up, don't worry about it. Rafi comes on strong, but he's a twink at heart, he caves in."

"What did he say?"

"He's not our problem. There's a guy that works for your husband on and off, Jiggs Scully. You know him?"

"I know who he is."

"He's been following you. He knows what we're doing and wants to talk to me."

"Oh, God—"

"Wait. Nolen Tyner—I told you about him. He says Jiggs doesn't have his hand out, he wants to discuss something else entirely, but I don't see any reason to talk to him. Do you?"

"I don't know." Mary was wide-eyed now, gathering it all in. "If he saw us together and he works for Andres . . ."

"Nolen says he hasn't told Andres. You know why?"

"No."

"He doesn't like him. I feel like we're back in the eighth grade. Here's a guy—" Moran stopped. "Well, that's beside the point. What Jiggs and Nolen are up to's none of our business. I hope. But I don't want to see us get dragged into it. We got enough going as it is."

"Dragged into what?"

"I don't know, but it's got to have something to do with your husband and they either want to use me—I'm guessing now, you understand—or they want some information from me, or they want me to get it from you."

"Oh—"

The way she said it, like an intake of breath, surprised him. She was thoughtful now, staring. Then took several steps without purpose, moving idly, though he could see she was concentrating, looking down at the boards as she paced toward the railing, aimless, and came back. As she turned again he stopped her.

"You have an idea what it might be?"

Mary sat down now. She eased back into the chair next to him.

"Money. What else?"

"I had that in mind," Moran said. "But what kind of money?

How do you rip off a guy like your husband? I mean it's not like going to the bank, make a withdrawal. How do you get it? Extortion? They have something on Andres? It's a feeling I've got more than anything else. I think Nolen and this guy Jiggs are putting something together. But it wouldn't be a holdup, anything as simple as that. Nolen's not, well, he's a little shifty, but he's not an armed robber. I don't think he'd have the nerve to walk in with a gun. So it would have to be something he thinks is clever or he wouldn't be doing it. *If* they've got some kind of scheme in mind."

"There's money in the house," Mary said.

Moran waited a moment. "Is that right?" He waited again and was aware of the silence. "You mean a lot of money, huh?"

"Quite a lot," Mary said.

Moran looked out at the bay, at the dark shape of Key Biscayne lying five miles off, on the horizon.

"Is it money he has to hide? I mean, did he get it illegally?"

"I assume it's from his business. Andres's investments net, before taxes, three to four million a year."

Moran waited. If she wanted to tell him more he'd let her, up to a point.

Mary said, "Remember in Santo Domingo we were talking about Andres? You'd heard he came here in Sixty-one with a fortune. Everyone thought so—he was a millionaire general with a sugar plantation and God knows what else. But he lost all that. He had to run for his life and he came here with practically nothing."

"I remember."

"And I think I said something about he's never gonna let that happen again. Have to run and leave everything behind."

"You said he'd be ready next time," Moran said. "But I would imagine he has money in a Swiss bank or the Bahamas, one of those numbered accounts."

"I'm sure he does," Mary said, "but if for some reason he's not able to leave the country or he has to hide . . . All I know is he's got quite a chunk of quick-getaway money right here . . . in the house."

He could see the two of them at the deep end of the hotel pool

. . . the wives of the winter ballplayers in a group . . . "I asked you, where's he keep it, under the mattress?"

Mary was looking at him. She didn't speak right away; she didn't have to. Finally, in the silence, she said, "You want to guess how much?"

"I've got a feeling I know too much already," Moran said. "We've got to get you out of here. Why don't you pack a bag and leave him a note."

"Not yet. I'm gonna talk to him, George, if I have to hit him over the head. Last night, I had all the words ready. 'Andres, listen to me, okay?' Like talking to a child. 'This isn't a marriage. I'm not happy and I know you're not.' And that was as far as I got. He gave me papers to sign. 'Here'—like he hadn't heard a word—'read these and sign them.' "

"What kind of papers?"

"Business. I'm part of his corporation, one of them. He made a business transaction out of the marriage with that prenuptial agreement and that's all it is, a deal. I'm a member of the board."

"Resign," Moran said.

"Now he's trying to use the agreement to threaten me. He'll amend it so there won't be a settlement if I walk out. I told him fine, I don't care. I said, 'I just want to talk. I want you to understand how I feel.' "

"That didn't impress him?"

"I'll tell you, George, I'm scared to death. You know that," Mary said. She seemed to clench her teeth. "But I'm also getting mad, goddamn it."

"Good," Moran said.

"I'm gonna write it down, everything I want to say. Then I'm gonna try once more. If he still won't listen then I'll hand *him* the papers this time and that's it, I'm through."

"You promise?"

"You have my word," Mary said.

"Stay mad."

"I *am*. I don't owe him a thing."

"If anybody owes anybody," Moran said, and let it go at that. It would be nice to sit with tall drinks and talk about nothing and enjoy the million-dollar view. But his presence was making her nervous. He said, "Write your letter." He touched Mary's shoulder as he got up and left his hand there until she put her hand on his. She was looking up at him through her round sunglasses. More than anything he could think of he wanted to touch her face.

He walked away.

Jiggs Scully was in the road next to his two-tone red and white Cadillac, the car standing within a few yards of the driveway. So that when Moran swung out onto Arvida he had to brake to a stop or run into the Cadillac's rear end. Jiggs came over to him.

He said, "George, how we doing? If you don't have a pair of the biggest ones in town, come right to the man's house there, I don't know who does. You getting reckless or you just had enough of this sneaking around shit, going the Holiday Inn?"

Moran didn't say anything. He wondered if Jiggs had slept in his seersucker coat. He wondered where Jiggs lived and wondered what he thought about when he was alone.

"I'm gonna buy you a drink, George. How about the Mutiny up on Bayshore? You know where it is there? Cross from the yacht basin."

"Okay," Moran said. The room was still nearly full in the early afternoon, the tables occupied by men in disco sport shirts with dark hair and mustaches, a few in business suits, some of them wearing their sunglasses, some talking on phones brought to the tables. The waitresses, moving among them in skintight leotards, were experienced and familiar with the patrons, calling them by first names or the names they were using.

"You think it looks like a jungle, all the plants and shit," Jiggs said, "it *is* a jungle. This's where all the monkeys hang out. Jack a phone in there and make a deal, talk about the product; it's always the product now, and how many coolers it'll cost you. Use clean new hunner-dollar bills, George, a hunner K's maybe twelve inches high, little less. Put a million bucks in a Igloo cooler you look like you're going the beach. These guys kill me, all the hot-shit dealers." He was looking over the room, pushing his glasses up on his nose. "About every fifth one you see is making believe he's in the business and about every tenth one's a narc. The mean-looking ones are the narcs, with the hair and the bell-bottoms. Fucking bell-bottoms're out of style, they don't know it. Little guy there looks like he repairs shoes, he's the biggest man in the room. Looks like the Pan-American games, doesn't it? Spic-and-span. They're the spics, George, and me and you, we're the span." Jiggs raised a stubby, freckled hand from the table, fingers spread, and looked at it. "Distance between the tip of your thumb to the tip of your little finger, that's your span." He looked at the back of his hand, then turned it over and looked at the palm. "But I don't see nothing in it, do you, George? No, it's empty. The spics, they got the product, they got all these coolers we hear about. But we're sitting here with our fucking mitts empty. Why is that? They dont' work any harder'n we do. Is it we let 'em have it cause we're kindhearted or what?"

A waitress with a blond ponytail brought their beer and asked Moran what his sign was. He told her Libra and she said, "I was right," not telling him if she thought it was good or bad. She gave him a look though and he smiled.

"You got a nice way with the ladies," Jiggs said. "I admire that. You're quiet, you mind your own business, don't you? Till somebody pushes you. I notice that the night I came by your place, run the piano player off. You stood right in there."

"I'm going," Moran said, "soon as I finish this beer."

Jiggs grinned; his teeth were a mess. "I get talking to my own kind I run off. You talk to these monkeys they stare at you. Subtle—you try and say anything subtle to 'em you get a blank stare. You get what I'm saying but you don't make a big deal out of it. I don't think anything I might say to you would even shock you; I think you been around a couple times. Tell me what you think I got in mind. I'd like to know."

"If it's a payoff so you don't tell de Boya," Moran said, "you're out of luck."

"Come on, George, give me some credit. That's pussy, that kind of deal; I never stooped to that in my life. Jesus, I'm surprised at you, George."

"Forgive me," Moran said.

"What I do when somebody's paying me, I don't even think about it," Jiggs said. "But when it's my deal I try to be a little selective, stay away from the shlock. You have to understand there's all kinds of opportunity out there, George.''

''I'm not looking for work,'' Moran said. ''I've got all I want.''

''All right, let me tell you a quick story.'' Scully hunched in, planting his arms on the table. ''Not too long ago I'm out at Calder with Mr. de Boya and a gentleman by the name of Jimmy Capotorto, you may've heard of. He runs Dorado, very influential guy, does a little business with de Boya. Jimmy Cap'll send some cash over there, get it cleaned and pressed in some condo deal, but nothing big. We're at Calder. We're watching the races up in the lounge. I'm placing bets for 'em, getting drinks when the waitress disappears. I'm the gofer, you might say, I'm not sitting there in the party too much. De Boya wins a couple grand, it's on the table there, and Jimmy Cap asks him what he does with his winnings, his loose cash. They start talking about the trouble with money like a couple of broads discussing unruly hair'r split ends, Jimmy Cap saying in Buffalo he used to have a vault in the floor of his basement, but there aren't any basements here. De Boya says you don't need a vault, there a lot of places to hide money it'll be safe. Oh, Jimmy Cap says, like where? De Boya says oh, there lot of places. Jimmy Cap asks him what he needs to stash money for, he's a legitimate businessman, he doesn't deal in cash, what's he trying to do, fuck the IRS? De Boya says no, he always pays his taxes. Then he says, quote, 'But you don't know when you have to leave very quickly.' Jimmy Cap says use a credit card. I miss some of the next part, I'm shagging drinks. I come back, de Boya's saying, 'If I tell you, then you know.' Jimmy Cap says, 'You have my word.' The guinea giving the spic his word. But it's good. That's one thing I have to hand 'em, George. They give their word you don't need it written out and signed. De Boya says then, ''Put away what takes you a year to make and have it close by, so you can take it with you.' Jimmy Cap says, 'That the rule of thumb?' Like getting back to our span, George.'' Jiggs looked at his hand again. ''How much does it hold? How much does a guy like de Boya put away in case he has to slip off in the night and show up in Mexico as Mr. Morales? You follow me?''

''I don't know,'' Moran said, ''how much does he?''

''Later on I'm talking to Jimmy Cap,'' Jiggs said, ''I ask him out of curiosity how much does he think de Boya makes a year—all the condos, all the land deals. Jimmy Cap says, 'Net? Couple mil, easy.' "

Jiggs waited.

"What do you want me to say?" Moran said.

"Tell me where he keeps it."

"How would I know?"

"You could find out. Ask his missus."

"Why would she tell me?"

" 'Cause she thinks you're cute, George. 'Cause she thinks her husband's a bag of shit. 'Cause she'd like to dump him and play house with you. 'Cause if I knew exactly where it was I could be in and out of there in two minutes and your troubles'd be over."

"Why would they?"

"Because Andres de Boya would be dead, George, and you and the missus could sail off in the sunset."

Moran actually saw a picture of a red sunset, sky-red night . . . but put it out of his mind as he said, "What about Nolen? Is he in it?"

"I tell you the deal, Nolen dresses it up, adds a little inspiration. He's like my p.r. man, George, get you interested. It's the only reason I talked to him."

Moran said, "You've been thinking about this for some time, uh?"

"Walking around it," Jiggs said, "scratching my head. Then you come along and I think, here's a chance to do something for the happy couple. If they'll do a little something for me."

"I think you're crazy."

"I know you do, George, at the moment. But what you got to do is examine your conscience. You Cath'lic?"

"Sort of."

"You remember when you go to confession you examine your conscience? Let's see, I had five hundred impure thoughts and I entertained the idea of killing Sister Mary Cunnagunda. Examine your conscience, George. Go ahead, and tell me if you're doing anything wrong. It's in the intention where the guilt is. Your intention is to give me information. What happens after that is out of your conscience and into mine and I think I can handle it."

"You might be from New York," Moran said, "but you didn't learn to think like that at Fordham."

"No, I never quite made it, George. But the inference there, what you're driving at—well, you want to get philosophical and discuss whether a blow job from a married woman is the same as committing adultery or you want to make your life easier? I can get the guys and go in with blazing six-guns and tear the place up, we'll find it. But that's the hard way and I can't be responsible if an innocent bystander, if you understand what I mean, gets in the way. Or we can make arrangements, do it quietly. It's up to you."

"Why're you telling me this?"

Jiggs was patient. He sat back, pushed his glasses up, then hunched over the edge of the table again. "Geroge, correct me. Didn't I just tell you?"

"I mean how do you know I won't go to the cops?"

"With what, a story? Come on, George, whatever way this goes down, you think I'm gonna be a suspect? Guy like de Boya, you make it look political. Write on his wall 'Death to Assholes' and sign it the PLO or some spic revolutionary party, that's the easy part."

"He's got armed guards," Moran said.

"This town you better," Jiggs said. "No, that's something you take into consideration. But he's only got one guy dumb enough to stand in there with him, young Corky, and I'm taking that into account."

Moran sipped his beer, making it last. Maybe he had time for one more. Carefully then, thinking of what he was saying: "If this money de Boya's got, it's like an emergency fund?"

"Right, case he has to bail out in a hurry."

"Well, if he's ready to do it like at a moment's notice," Moran said, "why don't you spook him? Turn in some kind of false alarm."

"Yeah?" Jiggs said.

"He runs with it and you're waiting for him. Saves tearing his house apart."

Jiggs didn't say anything for a moment.

"That's not bad, Geroge. That's not bad at all. Sounds to me like you're in the wrong business."

"Or maybe I could tell fortunes," Moran said. He picked up his beer glass and gazed at it. "I see a guy murdered in his house. I don't see anything about him being robbed, no money in the picture. But wait a minute. I see the police have been given information about a suspect. Ah-*ha,* guy runs a motel and is a good friend of the victim's wife." He looked at Jiggs. "That how it works?"

Jiggs said, "Geroge, I offer you the stairway to happiness and all you gimme back're ideas. I'm telling you, you're in the wrong business."

13

Sometime between 12:45 and 1:00 A.M. an explosion blew the boat dock at 700 Arvida Parkway into Biscayne Bay.

The charge took out the wooden surface of the dock, the heavy planks, the steel davits, ripped out a section of the cement retaining wall, sheared off the pilings to leave splintered stubs that barely cleared the surface of the water, and shattered a sliding glass door on the sundeck of the house. Fortunately Mr. de Boya's $350,000 yacht, *El Jefe,* was moored at Dinner Key where Mr. de Boya had picked up guests, business associates, earlier in the evening and had returned there to drop them off at the time of the explosion. It was heard in downtown Miami.

Coral Gables Police called Dade County Public Safety and a bomb squad was at the scene by 1:30. They picked up pieces of wood and metal strewn over the lawn and would find out through gas chromatograph tests of residue the explosive used was C4 plastique. A Coral Gables detective said, "The fuckers are at it again." He put 700 Arvida on the computer to see if it was a hot address, if it had ever been used as a "safe house" where marijuana and cocaine were off-loaded, and found no reference. Andres de Boya's name went into the computer and came out clean. They didn't notice the graffiti, spray-painted in red on the cement pillars in front of the property, until daylight. They thought about calling in the Bureau but decided to wait. Dope or political, it was still within their jurisdiction and the graffiti could be either. Some kind of Latin dramatic effect that said, on all four of the cement pillars:

MUERTE A
DE BOYA

When Corky pulled up to the Jordan Marsh entrance to Dadeland the doorman was on the spot. He offered Mary his hand and slammed the door as Corky said, "Wait! . . . Mrs. de Boya?" She stooped a little to look at him through the dark glass, almost invisible behind the wheel of the Cadillac. He was gesturing as he said, "I'm suppose to go in with you. Wait, please. I have to park."

Mary said, "That's all right. I'll see you here in about an hour."

She heard Corky say, "What? Wait, please!"

"Tell him, will you?" Mary said to the doorman. She tried not to run entering the store. But once inside restraint gave way to eager expectation; it hurried her through Jordan Marsh and down the length of the Dadeland Mall to an entrance near the east end. She sprinted now, out into sunlight, saw the old white Mercedes waiting and almost cheered.

"I'm late," Mary said, catching her breath now, inside the car, as Moran drove through the crowded parking area toward an exit.

"Five minutes. Boy, you look great."

"I'm perspiring."

"Good. We'll take a shower. You know we haven't taken a shower yet?"

She seemed surprised. "Where're we going?"

"A new place. Change our luck."

They drove up Dixie to the University Inn across from the U of M campus where Moran had already got a room and iced the wine, just right, waiting for them. He poured glasses as she slumped into a chair, legs apart, flattening her tan skirt between her thighs on the seat.

"Here."

She took the hotel-room glass of wine and drank half of it down before her shoulders sagged and she began to relax.

"You better love me, Moran."

"Look at me, I'm dying."

"I mean you better *be* in love with me."

"I *am,*" Moran said. "Listen, if it was just getting laid there a lot easier ways." He'd better soften that and said, "You bet I love you. Boy, do I."

She said, "Do you, really?"

He wondered how a woman like Mary could have doubts about herself. He came over in the pale light and pulled her up gently, wrapped bare sun-brown arms around her and told her how good she made him feel and how he thought about her and couldn't be without her. She said again what she had told him before, "I don't want to lose you." He told her it wasn't possible. He told her they couldn't lose each other now. He paused. Was he holding back? No, he was running out of words. He told her they couldn't be pried apart with a crowbar or cut apart, they were sealed together for good. He believed it with the feeling she did too, now. Everything was all right; even with Corky waiting they could make slow love and lie in silence after, looking at each other. Save conversation. What more was there to say?

They talked while they were getting dressed.

She told him the police were in and out of the house all day yesterday investigating the explosion, questioning her, the help, Andres, mostly Andres. Their tone wasn't suspicious but their questions were, trying to find out what Andres was into, if Dominican revolutionary or anti-government factions had ever threatened him before. Moran let her tell what she knew, Mary standing at the mirror brushing her hair.

Then he told her about Jiggs Scully in the Mutiny Bar, and she put the brush down and stood very still. Moran ended with a flat statement.

"He knows Andres has at least a couple million hidden in the house. He wants us to tell him where it is. If we do he'll go in, take the money and he'll kill Andres, as a favor."

She said, "A *favor,*" wide-eyed.

"We sail off into the sunset and live happily ever after."

The room was as silent as he could remember a room being silent, going back to when he was a little boy lying in bed during his afternoon nap, wide awake. Mary walked to a chair but didn't sit down; she turned to Moran again. He was sitting on the side of the bed with a tennis shoe in his hand.

"I have to tell him," Mary said.

He gave her time.

"You understand that, don't you? I have to."

"The only thing I'm sure of," Moran said, "somebody's trying to use us. A guy talks to me out of the side of his mouth like I'm one of the boys. Why? As far as he knows I'm a decent, law-abiding citizen. It's true you and I happen to have something going—''

''That's quaint, George. Something going.''

''Something special, soon to be—you know—out in the open, above board. Let me just tell you the rest, okay? The question is, first, why would he think we'd go along?''

''That's right, he'd be taking a chance,'' Mary said.

''A big one. But let's say we do. We tell Jiggs where the money's hidden and close our eyes. What happens then?''

''You just said—he'll kill Andres.''

''Are we positive?''

Mary frowned, shaking her head. ''I don't understand.''

''What if the whole thing's your husband's idea?''

She hesitated now. ''You think Andres is using Scully?''

''You go to your husband and tell him his life's in danger. What's the first thing he asks you?''

''God, you're right.''

''You didn't hear it at the Dadeland shopping mall. But say you tell him,'' Moran said, ''and now it's confirmed, Andres knows we've been seeing each other. What does he do then?'' He saw a different look come into Mary's eyes. ''You know him better than I do, but he doesn't seem the type that loses gracefully. What does he do to you when you tell him?''

Mary's reaction surprised him: the look of calm that came into her eyes as she listened.

''You're right, it sounds like him. It's the roundabout way he thinks . . . the son of a bitch.'' She sat down in the chair, thoughtful.

''But we aren't sure,'' Moran said. ''There's the matter of your dock blowing up. Would Andres go that far?''

Mary shook her head. ''No, he's not gonna do something that makes him look vulnerable. Unless—why would it have to be part of Andres's scheme?''

''All I know is,'' Moran told her, ''Jiggs said he'd make the hit look political. Like some revolutionary group out to get your husband . . . But why does he tell me all this if there's a good chance I'm gonna tell you and you're gonna tell Andres?''

She said, ''He must be awfully sure we'd go along. Or it's worth the chance. He can always deny it. Which brings us back to the only question that means anything. Do I tell Andres or not?"

Mary looked like a young girl sitting in the chair, biting her lower lip now, though more preoccupied than frightened: an imaginative girl wondering how to tell her parents she was pregnant.

She said, "If something did happen to Andres . . ."

He said, "Mary, we don't need help. We don't have to hope he gets a heart attack or falls off his boat. All we have to do is walk away."

She said, "I know. I'm not hoping for anything like that," and looked at him with clear eyes. "But it would be nice, wouldn't it?"

14

Nolen and Rafi had been drinking the better part of two days and were both drunk when Moran found them in the early evening. Nolen was keeping it going. Moran saw it right away: Nolen had to stay up there because if he came down now he'd crash and burn.

They were having a private party in oceanfront Number One with scotch and rum, Coke cans, a bowl of watery ice and potato chips on the coffee table and the smell of marijuana in the room. There was no sign of Loret. They were wound-up drunk: Nolen bare to the waist, stoop-shouldered skin and bones, his slack cheeks sucked in on a joint; Rafi wearing a scarf rolled and tied as a headband, the ends hanging to his chest, his sporty Dominican shirt open all the way. Nolen was calling him Ché.

''You meet Ché? George, shake hands with Ché Amado, one of your premier fanatics, brought here by special request to combat the toadies of oligarchic imperialism, but don't ask me what it means.''

''You didn't know that,'' Rafi said to Moran. Rafi sat slumped in a plastic chair, feet extended in glistening, patent-leather zip-up boots. ''You think I come here to bite you for money. It work pretty good, didn't it? I had you fool.''

''You had me fool, all right,'' Moran said. ''I thought you were just a pimp. Which one of you did the job on the boat dock?''

''That was him,'' Rafi said, ''he's the powerman.'' He squinted up at Moran and said, ''What did you say before it?''

''That's powderman,'' Nolen said, ''in the trade,'' and gave Moran a sly look. ''I hear we're in business. Is that right? I heard it from a certain party, but I'd rather hear it from you . . . Where you going?''

Moran got a glass from the kitchen and came back to sit at the opposite end of the sofa from Nolen. He poured himself a scotch; he would probably need it.

''You're over your head,'' Moran said. He drank the scotch and poured another one.

Nolen was grinning. "So what else is new?"

"Stick to acting."

"It's what I'm doing, man. What's the difference?"

Aw shit, Moran thought.

He wondered why he'd ever had a good feeling about Nolen, why he'd been comfortable with him and went for that grunts together, old war buddies grinning their way through life bullshit; he wasn't anything like Nolen. Nolen was pathetic trying hard to be tragic and any more of him, Moran knew, would be a bigger pain in the ass than he could bear. He wanted to hear about it though, what they were into. He would hardly have to encourage them and it would come sliding out of their mouths with alcohol fumes.

"What'd you use," Moran said to Nolen, "on the boat dock?"

Nolen said, "On the dock?" focusing his eyes. "I was gonna go with ammonium nitrate and fuel oil, little dynamite, and light up the sky. But if these people're suppose to be pros, I thought no, you gotta go with a nonhydroscopic plastique, you dig? Slip in there in a Donzi, half-speed all the way. Me and my shipmate, this spic that steared—excuse me, Ché—guy was wearing sunglasses at night. You head due south from near Dinner Key where we launched till you get the Cape Florida light off your port bow, then hang a right and there you are. Drift in . . . I've already run the det-cord through the blocks, they got adhesive backing on 'em now, stick 'em flat under the boards but use a linear-shape charge on the pilings so it'll cut 'em off clean. Twelve pounds of plastique, could've done the house. I'm scared of timers, so we drifted down by Matheson Hammock and I blew it remote control." Nolen made an elaborate exploding sound on the roof of his mouth with his jaw clenched. "The dock's gone."

Moran said, impressed, "You remember all that from your paratrooper days?"

"No, I did a bit in *A Bridge Too Far* and hung around with the special effects guys. It's all make-believe, George."

"What'd you blow it for?"

"Show him somebody means business."

"Who did the lettering?"

"Ché. Right, Ché?"

"*De nada,*" Rafi said.

"Don't put yourself down," Nolen said. "You did it, man. Our silent partner goes, 'What's he gonna write?' I told him don't worry about a thing, this man's been writing on walls all his life, *fuera* or *muerte* to whoever happens to be around that pisses him off. The man's ace of the spray paint. You see his work?"

"Your silent partner," Moran said. "Who you talking about, Scully?"

Moran saw Nolen's fuzzed gaze shift to Rafi and return to stare at him. Nolen shook his head from side to side. The drunk being secretive. But Rafi was even drunker and didn't notice; he was eating his ice. Nolen pulled himself out of the sofa, took Rafi's glass from him—Rafi still holding his hand up, cupped—fixed another rum and Coke and put the glass back in Rafi's hand. Nolen stumbled sitting down. They were both in bad shape.

Moran could not see Jiggs Scully bringing these two into the game. Unless he had a special use for them.

"We're gonna publicize Mr. de Boya's past sins," Nolen said and gave Moran a stage wink, obvious enough to be seen in the back row, "unless he comes across with a generous piece of change . . . Isn't that right, Ché?"

"Less he pays," Rafi said.

"Tell George what the man did," Nolen said, "when he was in charge down there."

"What he did?" Rafi said. "He was the head of the Cascos Blancos, he sent out the death squads to get people he don't like or people who talk against Trujillo. He take them to La Cuarenta in Santo Domingo for the torture. Sometime he take them to Kilometer Nueve, the army torture place at San Isidro."

"Tell him what de Boya did to people," Nolen said.

"Well," Rafi said, "he like to sew the eyelids to the eyebrows and put them in a light. He like to beat them with Louisville Sluggers. He like to put acid on them sometimes. He like to castrate people. He like to take the nipples and pull them out and cut them off with scissors."

Moran said, "Is that what happened to you?"

"No, no, he do that to girls. Cut the nipples off. Men he cut everything off with—how do you say it, these big *tijeras?*"

"Shears," Nolen said.

"Yeah, chears. Cut off your business with them. I had a uncle that happen to. Then when General de Boya finish with them he have them killed and thrown from the cliff into the sea to be eaten by the sharks. You want to find out what happen to somebody, you ask, nobody knows. They say he's gone to Boca Chica to visit the *tiburones,* the sharks. Or sometime to Monte Cristi. That was twenty years ago—the sharks still come looking for General de Boya to feed them. He like to put ants on people, too."

Rafi rolled his eyes back.

"I don't like to think about it."

"Have a drink," Nolen said. The answer to most things.

Rafi took a drink. "I don't feel so good. Maybe I go lie down; I'm feeling tired." He stood up unsteadily, spilling some of his drink.

Moran watched him. He wanted to get up but didn't have the energy; the scene was depressing. He watched Rafi shuffle into the bedroom, Nolen calling after him, "Don't throw up on the floor, Ché. You hear? Go in the *baño.*"

He said to Moran, "I don't know what it is about them, partner, those people just don't hold the juice."

Moran watched Nolen pour himself another scotch.

"What're you gonna use him for?"

"He's our spray painter, man. You see his work?"

"But he doesn't know Scully."

"Jiggs wants to see how he works out first. So I told Rafi we got a guy on the inside, but he doesn't want his identity known just yet."

"I don't imagine he would," Moran said. "All right, what's the deal? What're you going after?"

"Jiggs says he told you."

"Come on, this isn't your kind of a thing."

"Is that right? Tell me what I'm saving myself for. It's the best part I've read for in ten years. Shit, I don't even have to act tough."

"He's using you," Moran said.

"Jesus, I hope so. I need to be used, man."

"You know what he asked me to do?"

"I sent you to him, didn't I, for the interview?"

"Come on—you know what he wants?"

"Yeah, he wants you to ask your lady where her husband hides his cash. What's hard about that? Shit, call her up right now."

"Jesus Christ," Moran said. He drank down his scotch and sat back. "How does he know . . . Hey, you listening?"

"Yeah, I'm listening. What?"

"How does Jiggs know she won't tell her husband what's going on? How does he know *I* won't tell him?"

"Well, shit," Nolen said, "because I told Jiggs you're my bud, we see eye to eye. I said sure, George's the old Cat Chaser, we served down in the D.R., man. I told him it was me almost put out your lights with the one-oh-six and Jiggs got a kick out of that. He sees the humor in life, everybody busting their ass trying to score off each other. I told you he's a funny guy and I was right, huh?"

"Yeah, he's funny," Moran said. "But I still don't understand. Why would he trust me? Tell me a story like that?"

"I just told you. And you want the husband out of the way, don't you? Jesus Christ, or else I came in late and missed something."

"Look," Moran said, trying to keep Nolen's attention. "You listening to me?"

"Yeah, I'm listening." Pinching the roach, sucking his cheeks in with a sound like the north wind.

"I'm not in it," Moran said.

"What happened?" Nolen grunting the words as he held his breath. "You change your mind? There's nothing to be scared of."

"I never *was* in."

Nolen expelled smoke in a long sigh. "Well, Jiggs says you gave him a hell of an idea. He told me. Make the man run and head him off at the pass. I said to Jiggs, I told you he's good, he's a fighting leatherneck. Jiggs says he didn't think much of the idea at first, frankly, 'cause what if the man took off in his boat? Jiggs doesn't like to have anything to do with boats. He goes, 'I don't want no parts of them fuckers.' He gets seasick he goes out. But then, hey, with the dock gone the man can't bring his boat in, can he? He runs, he's got to go by car. And when he does, Jiggs says he'll be way ahead of him . . . He likes you,'' Nolen said.

Aw shit. Moran felt heavy, out of shape, and the scotch wasn't helping at all. He said, ''Nolen?''

''What?''

''I'm not in. I didn't give Jiggs anything. You understand? What he's doing, he's using you. I don't know for what, but when he's through he'll dump you. He can't afford not to.''

''We made a pact,'' Nolen said. ''Us against them.''

Moran tried again. He said, ''You told me who he works for, what he does for a living, right? He leans on people. He breaks their bones. Isn't that right? That's what you told me.''

''He used to.''

''Okay. But does he sound like the kind of guy you can trust? You can put your life in his hands?''

''Jiggs says we're his kind,'' Nolen said. ''He's sick and tired of the guineas and the spics raking it in, taking everything, guys like de Boya sitting on top. Look at the guy. He's a fucking death squad all by himself. And he's married to your lady. What more like incentive you want, for Christ sake?''

''Don't call her my lady, all right?''

''What should I call her?''

It annoyed him, ''my lady.'' He never liked the expression; but that was something else. ''Think a minute,'' Moran said. ''What if somebody else put Jiggs up to this and he's playing a game with you?''

''That's it, man, a game.'' Nolen was half-listening. ''It's us against them. Shirts against the skins, man. They're swarthy fuckers, but they got white legs . . . if you know what that means on the basketball court can figure it out.'' He gave Moran a feeble grin. Then came alive again. ''We'll get little Loret some pom-poms, she'll be the cheerleader *Muerte a de Boya*. Fight! The old locomotive. M-U, M-U, M-U-E-R; T-E, T-E . . . What do you think? Get her a short little red and white pleated skirt . . .''

''Where's Loret?''

''Jesus, that's right. She hooked up with some guy at the Fontainebleu, guy in the lounge smoking a cigar. She gives him the eye, says excuse me, going to take a leak and I haven't seen her since. I know, you told me. But don't say it, all right? I hate guys like that. Have to rub it in."

Moran said, "What am I gonna have to do to get you to understand something? You dumb shit."

Nolen grinned, eyes out of focus. He held up the dirty stub pinched between his fingers. "How 'bout a smoke? Good stuff."

"It makes me hear tires squeal when I'm barely moving," Moran said. "No, this'll do me." He raised his glass. "Like it's doing you in. I don't want to sound preachy—"

"Then don't."

"But I got to tell you. You're in a no-win situation. The best you can get out of this if you're lucky, I mean if you come out alive, would be something like fifteen to twenty-five at Raiford. Hard time."

"Don't sweat it," Nolen said. "I'm having fun."

Moran stared at him before easing back in the sofa. All right then. Okay. . . .

He was tired.

He saw Mary in his mind, in the room in the University Inn, her hands between her legs on the chair cushion and could see the line of her thighs beneath the tan skirt. He saw her looking at him with her look of quiet awareness, waiting. What did he need to talk to this shithead for?

Corky came out to the red and white Cadillac in the drive. He asked Jiggs, getting out of the car, then reaching in to punch the headlights off, what he wanted. Jiggs said, "If I thought I had to tell you, Corko, I'd be in pretty bad shape. Tell Mr. de Boya I'll be around back where you used to have a boat dock somebody took out while you're keeping an eye on it." And walked away.

He was inspecting the splintered stubs of the pilings, barely visible in the dark water, when de Boya came out to him. Jiggs turned very carefully on the crumbled edge of the retaining wall and stood with his back to the tide breaking in below him, giving de Boya a casual, death-defying pose.

He said, "Seems you got a problem here," with a grin of sympathy. "Jimmy Cap says take a look. He don't care to see any his friends get fucked over by parties unknown. Jimmy says it's like they're doing it to him."

De Boya was looking down at the water now, at the stump remnants of his dock.

"How do you think of it?"

Jiggs took cautious half-steps from the cement edge until he felt the safety of grass underfoot. "Well, my first thought when I read about it in the *Herald,* I think to myself, some dopers're having a disagreement and one of 'em sends his guy to the wrong address. '*Seven* hundred Arvida. Oh, I thought you said six hundred. Oh well.' "

De Boya's reaction: nothing. Like a statue with clothes on.

"But then I started asking around."

"Yes? What did you learn?"

"You understand we got contacts in Little Havana," Jiggs said. "I first come here they're referring to it in the company as Sowah Seda. This girl Vivian Arzola used to work there says, 'Go on over to Sowah Seda,' I'm supposed to see somebody over there. I ask her where Sowah Seda is. She says, 'Sowah Seda, Sowah Seda.' Finally it dawns on me. Oh, Southwest Eighth Street. She says, 'Yeah, Sowah Seda.' Well, I talked to a guy down there this time name of Benigno, runs a tavern, if he's heard anything. What's this shit, a man's dock getting blown up? He looks around see if anybody's listening. They got the salsa on so loud I can't even hear Be*nig*no. He says it's the work of the FDR I said FDR? Franklin D. Roosevelt? You said that name to my mother she'd genuflect. Christ, she'd have left home, all the kids, for FDR, he ever wanted to get it on. But, it turns out, Benigno says it stands for Democratic Revolutionary Front."

"It's Salvadoran," de Boya said. "It has nothing to do with me."

"That's what Benigno says, they're from El Salvador. But evidently these people, your different revolutionary groups, are getting together, helping each other out. They don't give a shit you're Dominican, you're Nicaraguan, you come from the ruling class you're one of the bad guys. What do they call it? The oligarchs. You're one of them and they're all working for Castro anyway, they don't give a shit. See, he's sending 'em here to spread a little terror."

"For what purpose would that be?"

"I check around, hear it from some other sources there," Jiggs said. "These people with little bugs up their ass, they come here to cause trouble, score a few big names."

"What do they destroy the dock for?"

"Get your attention," Jiggs said. "So you know it's coming. Like toying with you. Little terrorist foreplay. You go to the cops for protection you're all right for a while. Then when you aren't looking—whammo. They hit you a good one, for real this time and get their initials in the paper."

Jiggs felt de Boya studying his face in the dark, probably trying to look in his eyes, the truth test. De Boya said, "Yes, and what do you do for me?"

"Well, are the cops helping any?"

"They say they keep an eye on my house. They drive by."

"You hire any more people?"

"Not yet." De Boya turned abruptly. "We go inside."

"I know you like Corky, but get rid of the rest of 'em," Jiggs said, following de Boya, "and I'll send you over a couple guys, couple heavy-duty Cubans worked for the CIA when the CIA had a hard-on for Castro. Now these guys're free-lance. Jimmy Cap says take care of you, that's what I'm doing."

"It's kind of him," de Boya said.

They went up on the deck, through the two-story hallway filled with plants and young trees like a path through the jungle, and into de Boya's study. Jiggs liked it, the oak paneling, the gun cabinet, the framed photographs of people in military uniforms all over the walls. There was a big one of Trujillo himself in a white uniform full of medals, shots of de Boya with different people, another one of de Boya in what looked like a German SS uniform, de Boya nonchalantly holding an old-model Thompson submachine gun. Jiggs paid his respects to the photographs, nodding solemnly, while de Boya went around behind a giant oak desk and sat down. There was a tape recorder on the desk, a tray that held a brandy decanter and glasses.

Jiggs finally took a chair. He said, "I wanted to ask you. I locate any of the party responsible, General, you're gonna want to prosecute, I take it."

"In my own way," de Boya said.

Jiggs said, "That's how I'd feel about it myself. You have 'em arrested they're back on the street in twenty-four hours." He said then, "I understand, what I've heard, you were the expert at getting people to tell you things they didn't want to. Back in the old days."

"Really? I'm surprised you hear anything about that," de Boya said.

"You kidding?" Jiggs said. "General, there certain areas you're a living legend among people that know anything about or appreciate the fine art of interrogation. It used to be, when I was a youngster on the Force in New York, we could use our own resources, so to speak, in extracting information. Now, the guy doesn't even have to tell you his name his lawyer isn't present. Fucking Miranda changed everything." Jiggs shook his head, began to grin a little. "Wasn't like that where you come from, I don't imagine."

"You say to get information?"

"Yeah, interrogate a suspect."

"The trick," de Boya said, "when you question someone is not to ask a question."

Jiggs maintained a pleasant expression. "You don't ask 'em anything?"

"No, never. You take the person's clothes off. Always you do this, strip the person naked, and sometimes it's enough. Or you subject the person to an unpleasant experience, increasing this gradually," de Boya said, giving his recipe. "The person wants to tell you something, but you still don't ask him. He pleads with you, he begins to say things, to ask the questions himself, yes, and then answer them, he's so anxious to please you if you'll stop the unpleasantness."

"The unpleasantness," Jiggs said, his face creased in appreciation. "That's not bad, general."

"But the information," de Boya said, "that isn't the important reason for interrogation."

"It isn't?"

"What do you wish to know?" de Boya said. "Where someone lives? Where they hide arms? Something they're saying about you, the government? No, the purpose of interrogation is preventive. What you do in the secrecy of the act always becomes known to others, to the ones against you."

"And it scares the shit out of 'em," Jiggs said, nodding. "I getcha."

"I like to think it gives brave men pause," de Boya said. "Remember, fear is of more substance than information."

"Yes sir, that's a good point."

"Information, it has degrees of importance at different times," de Boya said. "But fear, you can use fear always."

"Keeps your people under control," Jiggs said.

"Yes, they don't know what to do, so they do nothing." De Boya began to nod, a pleasant expression masking his thoughts, his pictures from another time. "I always do a good job at that." He gestured with his hands. "Well, it was my especiality, of course."

A few minutes past midnight Moran's phone rang. He turned off Johnny Carson and got to the counter, knowing it was Mary, feeling wide awake now.

She said, "Jiggs Scully was here, earlier this evening. They were in Andres's study with the door closed for almost a half hour."

Moran said, after a moment, "I know what you're thinking . . . But I talked to Nolen and now I'm leaning the other way, back to Jiggs."

"You think the whole thing's his idea?"

"I'm pretty sure. If Andres wanted to get the goods on us there's got to be a simpler way than all this."

"Then why did Jiggs come here? He must be working for Andres."

"For him and against him. Listen, you got to get out of there."

"I will, soon."

"Have you written down what you want to say?"

"I'm working on it."

"Does Andres know I was there today?"

"He didn't mention it, but I'm sure he does. He got home late." Mary paused. "Wait a second, okay?"

"What's the matter?"

"I heard something. Hold on."

Moran waited, standing straight up now. He heard it then, away from the other end of the phone connection, sounding like shots, glass breaking. He pressed the phone to his ear and heard a voice far away, someone shouting. He heard Mary's voice, closer, call out, "What is it?" Then nothing. He waited. He heard jarring sounds close, as though she might have dropped the phone picking it up. Now her voice in the phone was saying, "I'll call you back."

"Wait a minute. Are you all right?"

Her voice came as a whisper now. "I'm fine, but I can't talk now."

"What's going on?"

"Andres is upstairs."

"Just tell me what happened."

But she'd hung up.

15

Mary didn't call back during the night.

Moran phoned her in the morning. The maid with the accent said Mrs. de Boya was not at home. It was only nine o'clock; Moran didn't know what to say next. He asked what time she was expected. The maid said she didn't know. He asked then, "Is Mrs. de Boya all right?"

The maid, Altagracia, said, "Yes? I think so."

He took a chance and said, "What was all that noise last night?"

The maid hesitated. She said, "I don't hear any noise."

He tried again a little after ten.

A recorded voice answered to say, "The number you are calling is temporarily out of service. Please try again later." He dialed again to be sure and heard the message repeated.

What in the hell was going on?

He got the number of the Coral Gables Police from Information, 442-2300, dialed and a male voice answered. Moran said, "Hey, what was all the noise over on Arvida last night? Up at the end of the street."

The male voice said, "Who is this speaking, please?" Moran said he lived in the neighborhood and was just wondering . . . The male voice said, "Could I have that address and your name, please?" Moran hung up.

He knocked on the door to oceanfront Number One, waited and banged on it. Then got the key from Jerry, Jerry in a light-hearted mood whistling "I'm Going to Live Till I Die," and went back to let himself in.

The apartment was empty, still a mess from the night before: the bottles standing on the coffeetable, the bowl of water, bits of potato chips all over. The bed Rafi had slept in was unmade, the light spread and sheet in a tangle on the floor.

Nolen, in Number Five, was popping open a can of beer. He said, "Stand back. Don't say anything yet."

Moran waited in the doorway to watch.

Nolen poured a good four or five ounces of Budweiser down his throat. When he lowered the can and looked at Moran with grateful wet eyes he said, "Oh Jesus. Oh my God Almighty." He raised the can again and finished it in two tries.

"I'm gonna live."

"Till you die," Moran said. "Jerry'll whistle it for you while you're going down the tube."

"Fuck you," Nolen said.

"If you know you're gonna be hung over—"

"And if *you* know I'm gonna be," Nolen said, going to the gas range where a saucepan of chili with beans was starting to bubble, "what're you asking me for? You want to be useful, open a couple of beers."

Moran sat with Nolen while he ate his breakfast, chili laced with catsup to sweeten it and drank several ice-cold beers, the sorrow in his watery eyes giving way to a bleary expression of contentment.

Moran commented. "You having fun? You dumb shit."

"Don't judge," Nolen said, "till you walked a mile in my moccasins."

"Few weeks you'll be down to Thunderbird."

"Or Chivas. I'm making my run."

"Bullshit, you'll be down making love to the toilet bowl."

"I never throw up, George. I value my nutrition."

"What time'd you go to bed?"

"I watched black and white TV, you cheap fuck, and hit the sack early."

"Where's your pal Ché?"

"Who?"

"Rafi, your spray painter."

"He borrowed my car to go look for Loret."

"He expect to find her, Miami Beach?"

"Rafi expects—Jesus, this hits the spot, you know it? I doubt Rafi's expectations have anything to do with the real world. He's a twinkie."

"You finally realize that?"

"I've always known it. But he's got to learn on his own, right? I'm not gonna lead him by the hand."

"You bring him into the deep end, now it's up to him to get out, huh?"

"It's hard out there," Nolen said. "You can strike it rich or break your pick. It's up to you."

"That from a play or a movie?"

"It's an outtake. I'm on cutting-room floors at all the major studios. So I'm going into a different field."

"You remember anything I said last night?"

"Every word. I never experience blackouts."

"But you don't want to talk about it."

"I don't care. Get me a beer, I'll listen."

"Jiggs was at de Boya's last night." Moran waited.

Nolen spooned in bright red chili, his face down close to the bowl. "Yeah?"

"Why do you think he went there?"

"I think to tell de Boya some dirty Communists want to kill him. Also set the stage for what's coming up in the next couple of days. Time's getting short, George. Then you know what I think he did?"

Moran had to ask because he didn't expect all this.

"What?"

"Then I think he gave this crazy Cuban—the one drives his Donzi at night with sunglasses on? I think he gave the Cuban five bills and a twenty-two rifle and told him to take a run past de Boya's house and see if he can bust a few windows, then throw the twenty-two over the side, deep-six it, whether anybody comes after him or not. That's what I think, George. What do you think?"

He thought of Mary, little else. He went back to his house, called Leucadendra and had her paged in the grill and at the tennis courts, knowing she wouldn't be there. He thought about calling the Holiday Inn in Coral Gables; but would that make sense? He tried anyway. There was no Delaney or Moran registered. In the afternoon he tried her home again and listened to the recorded voice tell him the number he was calling was temporarily out of service. He thought about driving over there but knew he'd better wait. Mary would get in touch with him when she could.

It was a dismal, overcast day. The surf came roaring in making a spectacle of itself, but failed to interest him. Grocery-shopping at Oceanside didn't either. Until he was putting a six-pack of Bud in his cart and remembered something Nolen had said. Something about setting the stage for the next couple of days . . . time getting short. Christ, were they ready to move? He'd better put Nolen against the wall and get some facts.

But by the time Moran got home Rafi had returned and Nolen was gone.

Rafi said, "No, I didn't find her. But I went in the Fountainebleu and let my eyes see the most beautiful hotel in the world. I think I like to stay there before I go home."

Moran said, "There's a Miami to Santo Domingo at one tomorrow afternoon, they give you your lunch. Why don't you get on it?"

Rafi said, "Oh, am I being ask to leave? You have so many people staying you don't have room for me? Certainly, I'll be happy to leave a place where they don't want me."

Moran said, "Rafi, you're full of shit, you know it? . . . Where'd Nolen go?"

Rafi said he didn't ask him and if this was the way Moran felt he would leave as soon as he made arrangements to move to a resort that suited him. In the meantime, because Loret had taken his money, could he borrow a few dollars for something to eat? Moran gave him a ten and checked with Jerry, just before Jerry left for the day, to see if he'd had any calls.

None. He tried Mary and got the recorded message again. All right, he'd wait until later tonight—after the maid was in bed and hope de Boya didn't answer—and if the phone still wasn't working he'd drive over there, or drive past at least; he wasn't sure what he'd do. He fixed half of a yellowtail with tomatoes, onions and a touch of garlic for dinner, sauteed it, trying to keep busy, looking at the clock. He read. He watched a little TV. He read the latest on Stevie Nicks and an interview with Lee Marvin, former U.S. Marine, in *Rolling Stone.* Still looking at the clock. Anxious. Looking at it a few times each half-hour, waiting to call about eleven. It was the reason he would remember Jiggs Scully came at exactly 9:40.

Moran opened the door and Jiggs said, "You not doing anything I'd like you to come see somebody.'' Moran stood with his shirt hanging out, barefoot. When he didn't say anything Jiggs said, ''Mr. de Boya wants to have a word with you.''

Moran said, ''You serious?''

''Put your shoes on. I'll take you, bring you back.''

Moran said, ''What about?''

Jiggs said, ''George, come on. We get there you can play it any way you like. But don't try and shit a shitter, okay?''

Moran put on his sneakers and stuck his Hawaiian shirt into his jeans. He walked with Scully in silence across the patio and through the dark office to the street. Corky was waiting by Jiggs's two-tone Cadillac. Corky got in back as he saw them coming.

Walking around the front of the car, Jiggs said, ''Sit in front.''

Moran had the door open before he saw Rafi in the back seat with Corky, Rafi hunched forward. He said, ''George? I don't want to go nowhere.'' Trying to sound calm but scared to death. ''George? Tell them, please.''

Jiggs said to Moran, ''It's okay. Get in the car.''

The servants would be speaking to each other in Spanish and stop when Mary entered the room. They always did this; but today, for some reason, it had an air of conspiracy. The phone would ring. Altagracia would tell Mary it was someone for Mr. de Boya. Only once did she call Mary to the phone. She spoke to a man from the company replacing the window panes, half-listened to an involved tale of glass availability, why they couldn't come out until later in the day. Twice she tried Moran's number and got no answer.

And after that, for no apparent reason, the phone went dead. She called the telephone company on Andres's private line, in his den, with Corky standing by. Several times she returned to the den to try Moran again and each time there would be Corky. Finally she said, ''Excuse me, will you? I have to make a call.'' But he didn't move.

Corky said, ''I have to stay here if Mr. de Boya wants me. He say not to leave for any reason.''

She said, ''It'll take me two minutes.''

He said, "Yes, please," offering the phone. "But I have to stay here until the other phone is fixed."

She said drily, "Mr. Corcovado, if he can't reach you while the line's busy, why do you have to stay here?"

Corky said, "It's what he told me."

Is this your house? Mary thought. She said, "Well, in that case I'm going out. Do you stay by the phone or do you have to drive me?"

He said, "I'm sorry, Señora. Mr. de Boya say we not suppose to go out. Because what happen last night."

She said, "That's not the reason."

Mary went into the kitchen to speak to the cook about dinner, tell her not to bother, and came face to face with two men she had never seen before. They sat at the butcher-block table having coffee. Hispanic, confident, shirts open beneath summer jackets, both wearing strings of red and white beads. They looked her over but did not get up. Mary left the kitchen.

She felt she was in someone else's house. Corky, sitting behind Andres's desk now, told her the two were the Mendoza brothers, Chino and Nassin. They had been hired to replace the two Mr. de Boya fired after the boat dock was exploded. He told her the Mendoza brothers were Cuban and only one of them spoke English, but not very much.

Mary said, "Do they know who I am?"

Corky said, "Yes, of course."

"Who was it shot at the house last night?"

"We don't know that. It happens."

"And cut the telephone line?"

"The repairman tell the Mendozas he think it was a storm."

"There was no *storm*."

"Yes, then maybe it broke itself."

"Why can't I make a phone call in private?"

"I don't know." Corky shrugged; he seemed to be getting used to her. "Why don't you ask your husband?"

She mixed a vodka and tonic and took it out to the sundeck in the early evening, the sky clearing now that the day was almost past, the wind down to a mild breeze stirring the acacia trees. The two new ones, the Mendozas, watched her from the seawall, where the dock had been. They moved off in opposite directions still looking toward the house. Mary felt a knot of anger. She wanted to scream something as she sat ladylike, yell at the Mendozas, "What're you looking at!"

And waste it, she thought, on bodyguards who wouldn't understand or care if they did. Save it for Andres. The hell with writing down what she wanted to say—writing neatly in her precise up-and-down script. Let him have it with simple truth, you're leaving and that's it. Tell him right out, face to face. If he asks if it's because of Moran say *yes.* Absolutely. She was in love with Moran. She was so in love with him it didn't matter what other reasons there might be. Right now Moran was the reason. And Andres would say . . . The hell with what he'd say! Tell him and get it over with. Andres would think what he wanted to think anyway.

Which was pretty much what she had done six years ago. Talked herself out of all her misgivings, talked fast with the lure of everlasting security in the back of her mind and rationalized up front, telling herself marriage to Andres would be—God help her—fun. If she had known Moran then—if they'd been simply good friends, which would have been impossible, but just say they were—and she had announced she was going to marry Andres, Moran would have said . . .

With a straight face he would have said, "You're gonna marry a general, uh?" That's all.

And that would have done it.

She wanted to keep her anger intact, ready to level it at Andres when he got home. But she couldn't think of Moran and stay mad. She smiled to herself for a time. She looked out at darkness smothering the sunset and felt the smile dry up within her.

Fear was something else.

She'd have to ask him: Can you be afraid of something you think is absurd? No, she wouldn't have to ask, she knew the answer. If the thing that's scaring you doesn't know it's absurd you can laugh all you want, that won't make it go away.

Mary was upstairs when she heard the double horn beeps: Andres's way of announcing, when he drove himself, he was home. She went into Andres's bedroom, the lights off, and looked out a front window to see his immaculate white Rolls in the drive below. Andres was already out of the car talking to the two Mendoza brothers. She didn't see Corky with them. After a few moments they walked off toward the side of the house. It surprised her at first; then decided Andres was showing them around the property. But where was Corky? She hadn't seen him in some time.

Sitting in darkness her gaze moved to the massive shape of Andres's king-size bed mounted on a marble pedestal and remembered her reaction, the first time, sitting on the edge—a *waterbed?*—trying not to smile. And Andres's serious expression, Andres saying to her, "It's more than a bed . . ."

The bed delighted him without altering his expression. He came to her sitting on the bed, raised a knee awkwardly and pushed her back. His face close to hers he murmured, "We make love on millions of dollars," and finally smiled. But it was morning before he explained what he meant. *Making love on millions* . . . talking to his new bride in a boastful way, playful for Andres, but not failing to impress it was their secret, uh? His lidded gaze staring into her eyes. "No one else must know." She wondered now if his words had implied a threat. Or if making love on millions was still possible to do.

She would make love to Moran on cement. On nails.

And began to think of another bed not so large . . . the lights going out in her hotel suite, Moran calling to her in the dark, finding her as she slipped into his outstretched arms. She thought of them falling into the bed together, Moran trying to get their clothes off as she held onto him . . .

She saw the beam of headlights in the trees and moments later Jiggs Scully's Cadillac roll up the drive toward the house. It came to a stop behind Andres' car and the inside light went on as the doors opened.

Her breath caught as she saw Moran get out.

Now the others came out of the car. She recognized Rafi. The car doors slammed and they were in darkness. As Mary watched, the four figures moved off toward the north side of the house. But why? The gravel path on that side led through the garden to the swimming pool.

* * *

"He asks you," Moran said, close to Rafi, "you don't know anything, what he's talking about."

"All I did," Rafi said, his whisper hoarse, straining, "I write something, that's all."

"No, you didn't. You don't know *any*thing."

Corky was waiting for them at an opening in the hedge and Moran shut up. He could hear Jiggs Scully behind them on the gravel. He wasn't worried about Jiggs. It had been a quiet ride all the way and there was no reason to start talking now. Past the hedge they followed patio lights that were hooded and eerie in the close darkness, dull spots of yellow, misty in the tropical growth. The path brought them to the swimming pool, illuminated pale green among ledge rock and palm trees, the man-made filtered lagoon that looked to Moran like a movie set. Though the figures standing at the end of the pool were real enough, de Boya and two men Moran had never seen before. The two, the Mendoza brothers, came this way as Corky turned and gestured to Rafi, saying something to him in Spanish. Rafi didn't move.

Scully was next to Moran now. He said to Rafi, "I think Mr. de Boya wants to ask you something; that's all."

Rafi looked around, helpless, as though in pain.

One of the Mendoza brothers gestured now, pointing, and Rafi moved away from Moran to the edge of a curved section of the free-form pool, the water clearly illuminated to its tiled depths. Rafi looked down, then across the curved corner to de Boya who stood with his hands in the deep side pockets of a linen jacket.

His voice low Moran said, "Giving us the stare."

"That's what it is," Jiggs said, barely moving his mouth, "the old Santo Domingo stare. Suppose to, you look at it long enough, shrivel up your balls."

Twenty feet away de Boya stood without moving, the pale reflection of the pool lights shimmering on his white jacket, part of his face in shadow.

It began to look like the village players to Moran. Were they serious? He said, "Hey, Andres, what's going on?"

De Boya didn't answer.

If he gave a nod Moran didn't see it. He was looking at de Boya in the same moment one of the Mendozas stepped in behind Rafi, gave him a hip and Rafi went into the pool screaming a sound or a word in Spanish. He came up flailing the water, gasping, trying to scream, his eyes stretched open. Moran was yelling now, "He can't *swim.*" trying to get to the edge of the pool, but both the Mendozas turned to hold him off. He yelled again, "He can't *swim,* goddamn it!" and tried to get through the two Mendozas with shoulders and elbows, grabbing at a shirt and feeling a string of beads come apart in his hand. As he tried to lunge past the other one stuck a gun in Moran's stomach. He felt the barrel dig in as he saw Rafi struggling with his head thrown back, helpless, going under and coming up, going under again. Moran saw Andres watching, Corky watching, the two Mendozas turned from him watching. None of them moved. When Rafi's arms stopped flailing and he began to sink deeper they continued to watch in silence, without moving, staring at the string of bubbles coming out of Rafi's mouth, his body settling to the bottom now, rolling gently from side to side, eyes sparkling in the pool lights, eyes looking up at them sightless as the last air bubbles rose from his open mouth.

Moran listened to the sound of a single-engine plane in the night sky, the sound taking forever to fade. He didn't try to think of anything to say. He felt a hand touch his arm. He saw de Boya staring at him. He heard Scully's voice very quietly say, "Come on."

He saw de Boya staring at him.

He felt the hand grip his arm tighter. "George? Let's go." Still looking at de Boya staring at him. He was thinking now, Yes, he'd better go; turned and walked off with Scully, Scully saying, still quietly, "Let's take it easy now, George, not do anything you be sorry for, okay? Let's just get out of here before you say anything. Then you can say anything you want, that'll be fine, George, but not right at the moment . . ." Scully's voice soothing him, talking him all the way out to the car.

They were on Interstate 95, heading north to Pompano before Scully spoke again. He said, "That little spic makes a point he makes it, don't he?"

Moran was thinking of things he might have done or tried to have done. He was thinking of Mary in that house. He was thinking of what he would say when he called the police. He remembered the number, 442-2300. He wondered if the same impersonal voice would answer and if the voice would change, indicate a person inside, when he said he wanted to report a murder.

Jiggs said, "George, don't do what you're thinking. They get those funny calls all the time. Sergeant puts his hand over the phone. 'Who knows a guy name Moran? Got a swimming pool murder.' No, George, our friend Rafi Amado's on his way to the Gulf Stream right now and I don't mean the racetrack. The cops go to Seven hunner Arvida Parkway, nobody knows what you're talking about there. 'Somebody drown in the pool? Well, the pool's right outside here, officer, you want to take a look.' "

Moran said, "Tell me something."

"What's that, George?"

"How'd he know Rafi couldn't swim?"

Jiggs took a few moments. He said, "George, in the light of eternity, what difference's it make? The guy comes flying in from Santo Domingo with the hot setup, he's gonna try to make a score, right? It's called to my attention and I think to myself, What is this? This guy know what he's doing?"

"And you hired him," Moran said.

"Well, actually I never met the guy in my life till tonight. He was Nolen's boy."

"You're using Nolen," Moran said. "What's the difference?"

"George, you got a suspicious mind and now you're getting off on something else," Jiggs said. "What we're talking about here, all the guy does is spray-paint some bullshit on de Boya's gate-post. It doesn't matter the guy can swim or not, what I want you to look at here is the way de Boya handled it. He call the cops? It's an act of vandalism, you get a fine, maybe ninety days chopping weeds for the county—uh-unh, de Boya believes in capital punishment."

"You delivered him," Moran said.

"You want to look at it that way," Jiggs said, "I offered him up, like a sacrifice so you can see where we're at here."

Moran opened the car door.

"George, just a minute. Let's consider the documented fact you got something going with the guy's wife."

Moran slammed the door closed and Jiggs raised his hand, a peace sign.

"I'm not questioning your intentions, George. Where I live down on the South Beach—Hotel Lamont, sounds like class, uh? You should see it—down there you fall in love with some old Jewish broad on food stamps or you go uptown a mile and find a hooker. No, true love is beautiful, George; but in seeking it you got to be sure and keep your nuts outta the wringer." Jiggs paused and the inside of the car was quiet except for a faint ticking sound, the engine cooling down. "I'll bet you asked his wife—I'll bet it came up in conversation and you asked her where the general keeps his going-away money. Am I right?"

Moran opened the car door again.

"The only point I want to make about this evening, George—de Boya does that to a spray-painter, what's he gonna do to a guy he finds out's been jazzing his wife, room one sixty-seven the Holiday Inn? He's already pretty sure. The man'll believe anything I tell him."

Moran got out of the car this time. He said, looking in at Scully, "You want to tell him, Jiggs? Tell him." He swung the door closed and walked off toward the motel office.

Maybe it was the only way. Let it happen.

16

Trujillo had said he was riding a tiger and if he ever fell off the tiger would devour him.

"Please don't talk like that; put it out of your mind," Andres had told the old man, the Benefactor, who not only ruled his country for thirty years he owned it and was worth—with his sugar, his rice, his sisal, cattle, cement, his tobacco—some $800 million the day he fell off the tiger and was devoured.

Andres had tried for the next few days to transfer bank accounts and titles to property, searching for people he could trust to help him, and finally had to run for his life to Miami by way of San Juan with less than twenty thousand in cash and a cardboard box of photographs.

They hung in his study, all that was left of that time. Photos in black and white of Andres with Trujillo, with Peron, with Batista, with Anastasio Somoza, with Pérez Jimenez of Venezuela. A photo with U.S. Marine officers taken when U.S. Marines maintained tranquility and could be trusted. There was the photo of Andres holding the submachine gun that belonged to Trujillo's brother, Arismendi. They would go out on Trujillo's yacht—Andres and Arismendi, who was called Petán—and fire the submachine gun at the sharks off Monte Cristi, the sharks gorging on the rotten meat the sailors threw over the side, the two of them having a splendid time blowing the man-eaters to pieces.

Here it was another kind of boat-ride with a different species of shark circling, waiting for the boat to tip over. Riding this boat or riding a tiger it was the same end if you weren't careful. Trujillo had got old and failed to listen, failed to keep his enemies frightened of him. Which was easy enough to do.

Choose one from a group of suspected enemies and shoot him. Or drown him, it didn't matter. The others would look at the ground or close their eyes, not wanting to meet the eyes that would choose the next one.

But he had stared at Moran and Moran had not looked at the ground or at the man drowned in the pool. Moran had stared back at him. Perhaps he should have given Moran to the Mendoza brothers to be taken to sea with Rafi. It was possible Moran was not involved in the plot, but Jiggs Scully had made a point saying, "Either way you got to do Rafi. So let Moran watch and have second thoughts in case he *is* involved. Give him pause, as you say." Jiggs said he had questioned Rafi and there was nothing to learn from him, he was a "third stringer." Whatever that meant.

Jiggs said he had discovered Rafi through informants and was closing in on the others. Jiggs saying so much, Jiggs finding out about this plot and the people taking part in it. Jiggs giving, he said, all his time to it. But not saying anything about being paid.

Andres, the day before, had called Jimmy Cap to discuss this with him, to say he appreciated Jimmy Cap's concern, sending Jiggs to help. See if he had actually sent him. But Jimmy Cap was in Buffalo for several days and could not be reached.

So now late at night Andres sat behind his seven-foot desk drinking Cognac, staring vacantly at his past life in photographs, wondering what was taking place in the present.

Trying to see it clearly without interruptions.

First Corky. Corky in the doorway, a manila envelope under his arm, saying the business with Rafi Amado was finished. Then, remembering the manila envelope, coming into the study only far enough to place the envelope on de Boya's desk next to the brandy decanter, Corky reaching out, not wanting to intrude himself. "It came today from Marshall Sisco." The door closed. Andres picked up the envelope marked PERSONAL & CONFIDENTIAL.

Almost immediately the door opened again and Andres put the envelope down.

Now Mary stood in a white dressing gown that reached to the oriental carpet. She said, "Who was here?" She said, "Andres, what's going on?" Curious, perhaps alarmed.

But not without insolence. The way she always stood with her thin legs apart, one foot pointed out, shoulders slightly drooped. Demonstrating the bored insolence of American women as she asked her insolent questions. "Will you please tell me?"

He walked over to her.

"Andres—"

And closed the door in her face.

He returned to his desk trying to remember at what point he had left his mind, interrupted—ignoring for the moment the envelope Corky had brought—yes, he remembered now.

The cartridge was already in the tape machine on his desk, the recording of a phone conversation made earlier this evening at his office in the Biscayne Tower. A conversation with an old friend, Alfonso Silva, who was Cuban and zealously anti-Castro, a survivor of the Bay of Pigs, a former agent of the CIA and member of Leucadendra Country Club. Andres pushed the ON button, listened patiently to their voices, sipped cognac, then began to stroke, gently, his dark cap of lacquered hair as he heard:

ANDRES: You know the one named Scully who works for the Italians. Tell me again what you think of him.

ALFONSO: He does what we have spoken of before. Anything you want. If you trust those people you trust him. It's a decision you have to make.

ANDRES: But his appearance . . . How is he able to get information on the street? He's not one of us.

ALFONSO: With money. How else? Miami is a city of informants. What do you want to know?

ANDRES: He sent me two brothers, Mendoza . . .

ALFONSO: Ave Maria.

ANDRES: You know them? He said they worked for the CIA.

ALFONSO: They went to Cuba to do some work and were arrested and put in prison. Now they come back on the boatlift from Mariel. They wear red and white beads?

ANDRES: Yes, I believe so.

ALFONSO: To protect them from police. They belong to Changó, a cult of bandits and convicts, very bad men. They believe they have a dispensation to kill, given them by African gods.

ANDRES: Can I trust them?

ALFONSO: They're not of the revolution; there's no money in it, thank God and His Mother. They work for the one who pays the most.

ANDRES: I want to know about someone else. George Moran. He was a member of the club at one time.

ALFONSO: Moran . . . let me think. Is he the one you believed wanted your wife?

ANDRES: I want to know if he's active in a cause.

ALFONSO: I hear nothing of him.

ANDRES: Rafael Amado, a Dominican.

ALFONSO: No, I don't know him. But the one named Moran . . . I hear something in your voice. What is it now, still the wife? You get something in your head, Andres. . . .

He turned off the recorder, poured himself another Cognac.

It was more than something in his head, his imagination. It was Moran coming here. It was Moran calling his wife on the phone. He had instructed Altagracia, finally, to tell him his wife wasn't home. Then, mysteriously, the telephone was dead, the outside wire damaged. Security men on watch and something had happened to the wire. He questioned the Mendoza brothers and one of them said it must have been caused by the shooting the night before, a bullet struck the line and weakened it. Or it was old. The Mendoza brothers said they had no knowledge of telephone wires. They said the man from the telephone company who came fixed it, but didn't seem to know much himself, how it could break.

He had not told Alfonso Silva any of that. He could phone him now, tell him Rafi Amado had gone to sea and was no longer a problem. He could tell Alfonso how Moran stared back at him, not looking at the ground or closing his eyes. Ask Alfonso if that was something in his head.

He opened the manila envelope marked PERSONAL & CONFIDENTIAL, feeling the tape cartridge inside, letting it slide out on the desk, but in his mind still seeing Moran staring back at him. Andres snapped the cartridge into the recording machine—a conversation with Marshall Sisco the investigator, remembering some of it from two days ago—ran the machine forward and stopped, listened; ran it forward again until he found the part that began:

MARSHALL: . . . answer to your question, no. The latest report, I don't see any radical affiliations, any close friends of Hispanic origin. Guy worked for a cement company before he went with Sutton Developments. Now he runs his motel and that seems to be all he does. His credit's not bad and neither Broward or Dade have ever issued a warrant on him, even a misdemeanor.

ANDRES: He has affairs with women . . . married women, doesn't he?

MARSHALL: If he does he's superdiscreet about it.

ANDRES: When he was in Santo Domingo . . .

MARSHALL: Yes sir, I've got that right here. Stayed at the Embajador. Got his name in the paper as a war hero looking for a girl he fell in love with sixteen years ago, the time Johnson sent in the troops. They got very excited down there about him looking for the girl, but evidently he didn't locate her. Her name's Luci Palma. He was seen in the company of an American woman staying at the hotel and returned to Miami with her on the same flight.

ANDRES: What's the woman's name?

MARSHALL: Guy I talked to wouldn't say. You want it documented I'll have to send somebody down, spend a few bucks.

ANDRES: Do it. I want to know exactly . . .

Andres turned off the recorder. He picked up the manila envelope again and brought out a sheet of *Marshall Sisco Investigations, Inc.* letterhead that bore a handwritten note Andres didn't bother to read. Folded inside the sheet was a photocopy of a hotel registration card.

The name on the card in block letters read MARY DELANEY. The signature, very clear, precise, familiar, also read *Mary Delaney*.

Andres poured another Cognac. From the middle drawer of his desk he brought out a typewritten sheet that bore his attorney's letterhead, the sheet stapled to several copies of a legal-size document. With a paper clip he attached the photocopy of the hotel registration card to the legal papers.

Before getting up from the desk Andres sipped his Cognac and sat for several moments looking at the photograph of himself with Petán's submachine gun, the old Thompson. He had loved that gun, the feel of it jumping in his hands, hearing Petán's hoarse laughter, the sharks thrashing in a frenzy as the water turned a rust shade of red . . .

Mary's eyes came open with the sound of the door banging against the wall. Andres was at the bed, a shape outlined in the light from the hall, ripping away the sheet before she had time to move. As she tried to roll away from him his hand caught the back of her nightgown, tore it from her body and pulled her by the hair from the bed to the floor.

Mary screamed his name, once. Then silence. She could hear his breathing, grunts of effort.

She came to her feet submissive, looked in his face and cracked him as hard as she could with an open hand, seeing only his face, a flush of color rising, the moment before he hit her with a fist, drove it hard into her mouth and she saw pinpoints of light explode, falling, and felt him pull her again from the bed, locking an arm around her neck as she tried to butt him and dragged her naked from the room, across the hall and into his bedroom. The door slammed. Lights came on. When he threw her at the bed her knee struck the marble pedestal and he had to lift her, breathing through his nose, getting a knee between her bare thighs and now threw himself with her onto the bed, pushing to his knees to open his clothing, Mary feeling the wavy movement of the water bed beneath her, still aware of it, sinking without sinking, his weight pressing down on her again. He smelled of brandy, breathing through his nose, getting all of him between her thighs and using his hand, his fingers to pry and push himself into her, her legs stretched aching with the grinding of his hips. Now face to face as Andres levered his body to look at her, Mary staring back, dull eyes locked like arm wrestlers, Andres breathing with the labor of his body; and when he pressed his mouth against hers, when he gasped, sucking his breath in, she smelled his brandy with the taste of her own blood, felt it slippery wet on her face against his until his face slipped from hers to the pillow. He lay on her without his arms beneath him now, dead weight. Mary didn't move. She waited and would wait as long as she needed to. It was over now, there was nothing more he could do. She turned her head and saw their reflection in the wall of mirrors that covered the doors to Andres's closet. Saw her face strangely painted, blood-smeared. Saw her thigh upright against the mass of his pale naked hips. Saw the hem of the bedspread hanging and the marble pedestal that had the appearance of a solid block beneath the water mattress. *Making love on millions* . . . now raped on millions to mark the end of a marriage, Andres having the last word. Let him.

When he pushed up, throwing her leg aside as he got off the bed to stand with his clothes open, wiping a hand over his face, he looked at her and said, "Whore. Does he do that to you?"

She got up and walked out of the room, aching, feeling her front teeth, testing them with her fingers. In her bathroom she turned the light on to stare at her reflection, slipped on a terry-cloth robe now as she studied a face she had never seen before. God, she was a mess, mouth swollen, teeth aching with a dull throb. She bathed her face with warm water. It surprised her to realize she was alert, more relieved than resentful, a feeling of confidence giving her new energy. Then jumped in spite of her calm as Andres's face appeared behind her in the mirror.

"I'm not finished with you."

He gestured to her to come with him. When Mary hesitated he took her by the arm through her room and across the hall into his bedroom again. "Goddamn whore," he said, "go over there," and pushed her toward a bank of low dressers. She saw the legal papers, a gold ballpoint pen. "Read them or don't read them, I don't care," Andres said, "as long as you sign."

She saw her name in block letters on the copy of thc hotel registration card, knowing at once what it was, feeling some of her confidence slip away. She picked up the photocopy and looked at it, remembering the moment—standing at the desk and writing in "700 Collins Avenue, Miami Beach," making up an address but using her actual maiden name—thinking of Moran in the same hotel five floors above her. Thinking of him now . . .

"Sign it."

Andres was coming out of his walk-in closet carrying luggage, a full-size Louis Vuitton fabric suitcase in each hand. He swung them in Mary's direction to drop in the middle of the floor.

"Sign each copy. Then pack your clothes, everything you own, and get out." He turned and went back into the closet.

Mary picked up the legal papers, saw the heading, *Amendment to Prenuptial Agreement,* and glanced through the typewritten page, familiar with the legal terms, the ponderous sentence structure. She looked up as Andres came out of the closet with a second pair of Vuitton suitcases.

"These I give to you," he said, dropping the luggage. "There are more in the closet, all you need. Take them and get out."

"Let me be sure I understand this," Mary said, with cold composure, nothing to hide now, nothing to lose. It had begun as a business deal and was ending as one. "The divorce settlement is now an option?"

Andres was moving toward her. "That's correct." He picked up the pen from the dresser.

"And it's up to you whether you want to honor it or not."

"Yes, I have the privilege of not paying a wife who whores with other men."

"Before, it didn't matter," Mary said, composed, but with an effort now. "You insisted on a two-million-dollar agreement, regardless of what might cause a divorce."

"Now I change my mind," Andres said. "You get nothing in settlement, you get nothing in my will, no matter when I die. So if you're plotting my death with your lover you been wasting your time."

The words stunned her, yet were believable coming from Andres. She could study him six more years and still not understand the twists and turns of his mind, the man refusing to accept reality, or still living in another time.

She said, "You've got a lot of class, Andres. You know how long I've been trying to talk to you?"

"I would believe," Andres said, "since you began fucking in hotel rooms."

God—she wanted to hit him and tried to, bringing up her hand, but he caught her wrist and slapped her hard, slapped her again and forced her over the dresser, face stinging, eyes blurred, and worked the pen into her hand.

"Now sign it!" Holding her head bent with his fist tangled in her hair.

She wrote her name and he turned to the first copy.

"Sign it!"

She signed twice again, writing *Mary de Boya* in a scrawl that seemed as unrelated to her as the name itself, *Mary de Boya,* signing an identity that was no longer hers.

Once she finished he was finished. Andres pulled her upright, his hand still knotted in her hair, and threw her to the floor, discarded. He walked over to his closet, threw out another suitcase, then went through his dressing room to his bath and slammed the door closed. Within a few moments Mary heard the shower running.

She lay on the floor among several thousand dollars worth of matched Louis Vuitton luggage, eyes level with the pedestal supporting the king-size bed. She moved, pushing up on her elbow, and saw her shadow move on the dull sheen of Italian marble. She was aware of a faint ringing sensation, a feeling of pressure within her head.

But her mind was clear. A deal was a deal.

17

Moran walked the beach in a fine mist of rain, sky and ocean a blend of the same dismal gray, the day showing in faint streaks of light but not promising much. It was all right though. The solitude was like a vacuum, seamless; he could stand in the middle of gray nothingness with his mind at rest and soon a burst of revelation would come to him. Enlightenment. A cosmic reaction to his panting neurons. He waited, looking at nothing, trying hard to think of nothing. He waited and waited, calm. Still he waited. Then raised his face to the rain, to the murky wash of light, and yelled against the moan of the wind as loud as he could, "Fuck!"

After, he felt some relief but not much. It released maybe a few pounds of frustration and was better than slamming his fist into a wall, though the wall was still there and he'd be god-*damned* if he could see a way to get through it. All he wanted to do at this moment was talk to her.

He'd phoned at eight and the maid, Altagracia, had said, "I'm sorry, Mrs. de Boya is not here. She out for the day." Moran had said, "Please, okay? She wants to talk to me." And the maid had said again she was sorry. . . .

His sweater and jeans were soaked through, hair matted to his head. He had been wet before. He had come up against walls before. Had learned patience, he believed, in the Marines and could wait sitting on his seabag when there was purpose in waiting. He had learned about frustration in his war in the D.R. trying to tell Friendlies from Unfriendlies and it had been, up to now, the most gut-twisting time of his life—yes—frustrated on the one hand and set up and sucked in on the other, just like now, and he'd hacked and stalked his way through it—that's what you do. (Was it his revelation, the answer right there inside him all the time?) Yes—you don't think, you *do!*

Moran left the beach and went in his bungalow tracking sticky sand to the counter and dialed Mary's number. He felt pumped up. When the maid with the immutable tone said, "I'm sorry—"

Moran said, "Listen, you put her on the phone right now or I'm calling the police." Which made no sense to him but maybe it would to her.

Altagracia said, "A moment, please."

Moran said to himself, *Do,* don't think. But when de Boya's voice came on he was stopped. De Boya said, "Yes? Who is this?"

"Andres, it's George Moran. I'd like to speak to Mary."

"She's busy," Andres said.

"Would you ask her to call me?" Christ, saying it to her husband.

"You going to be busy too, very soon." Andres hung up.

For the second time since waiting for his revelation Moran felt a slight lessening of pressure. Mary was home. At least for the time being. All right. All he had to do was go get her. Then wondered what de Boya meant: he was going to be busy, soon.

Jerry, the morning paper under his arm, got his key out and unlocked the door to the office. He noticed the trunk of Nolen's car raised, then saw it go down and there was Nolen holding a grocery sack. Jerry watched in wonder because he had never seen Nolen up and about before 10:00 A.M. Jerry said, "I didn't know the liquor stores were open this early."

Nolen raised the sack. "Lemons."

Jerry said, "You gonna make lemonade?"

"I'm gonna squeeze all the vitamins out of 'em," Nolen said, "and make whiskey sours."

Jerry made a face as though he might be sick. At this point he saw the two Latins get out of a car across the street and start this way, one of them carrying garden shears.

Nolen had already seen them. He was moving Jerry into the office. "Call George. Hurry."

Jerry didn't understand the note of urgency. "I can tell 'em," he said, "we don't need any trimming done. The hell they want to work in the rain for?"

Nolen said, "Goddamn it, gimme the phone. He dialed the number looking out the window and said, "George, run. I mean *quick.*"

* * *

Moran put the phone down. On an angle through a side window he saw the Mendoza brothers coming through the corner alcove past the icemaker and Coke machine, coming toward the bungalow. Both were wearing wool knit watch caps and leather jackets, one of them carrying a large pair of pruning shears with rubber grips. Moran got back to the phone. He said, "Call the cops."

Now Jerry was on. He said, "What do they want, George?"

"They want *me*. Call the cops—tell 'em it's an emergency." He hung up. Christ—he had to get something on; he'd showered and dried himself but wasn't dressed. Moran pulled on jeans, got a sweater out of the closet. He needed a weapon, a club. He didn't want a knife, he didn't know how to use a knife. Now they were banging on the door. He had to get out of here. They were banging on the door again. The side window was stuck, it was always stuck. But he strained and raised it enough to slip through the opening. He was walking away from the side of the house when the two Mendozas appeared, coming around from the front. They waved.

The one with the shears said something in Spanish. The other one said, "Come here. We want to go inside."

Moran's ears strained for the sound of a siren. He picked up the ten-foot aluminum pole that was used, with an attachment, for vacuuming the pool.

"Got to work, *trabajo,*" Moran said.

The Mendoza brother who had spoken English held his palms up to the rain. "You don't work today, man. We go inside, out of this, the *tiempo*."

"I work every day," Moran said. "I love to work. Got to get it done."

He glanced around, saw Nolen coming up on the other side of the pool. Nolen was looking at the Mendozas, saying, "Hey, you got the wrong guy. This is a friend of Jiggs Scully, his *amigo*."

Moran said across the pool, 'These guys work for *Jiggs?*"

Nolen gestured, minimizing. "I think so . . . Hey, we're *amigos* of Jiggs. You *sabe* Jiggs? Go call him on the *telefono,* he'll tell you. You got the wrong guy."

The Mendozas didn't seem to understand or didn't want to. The one who spoke English had the end of Moran's aluminum pole now. He tried to pull it hand over hand toward him, but Moran tightened his grip and they tugged back and forth for a moment about eight feet apart. The other one stood with the shears in both hands now, the blades pointing up.

"We go in the house," the one holding the pole said. "You suppose to give us something for Señor de Boya." He repeated it, Moran believed, in Spanish and the one with the shears laughed and continued to grin.

"You think I'm going in the house with you," Moran said, "you're outta your mind." He raised one hand to indicate the motel units. "There people here, they're all watching. You *sabe* witness? Shit, what was the word? *Testigo. Muchos testigos* in all the *ventanas.*"

"Come on, we go inside," the Mendoza holding the end of the pole said, and gave it a quick jerk, almost pulling it away from Moran. But he got both hands on it and jerked back, his hands slipping on the wet metal, pulling, having a tug-of-war in the rain. When finally he heard the first high-low wails of a siren coming very faintly from Atlantic Boulevard, hearing it because he was listening for it, he let the Mendoza holding the pole pull him closer hand over hand until Moran was in reach, the Mendoza still gripping the pole when Moran let go and slammed a hard left hand into the astonished Mendoza's face; the man sat down, stunned. With five feet of aluminum pole in front of him now, the rest dragging, Moran drove at the Mendoza with the shears and caught him in the belly—the siren wail much louder now—and jabbed at him until the shears came clanging against the pole; but Moran was going to get in and not let this man alter his life and when he caught the Mendoza's throat with the pole it stopped him, brought him up, and Moran was able to step in and belt him with a left and another left that brought blood from his nose, the Mendoza wobbly but trying to stick him with the shears. Moran gave him a head fake and went in high, got inside those jabbing blades, grabbed hold and drove. They went over the cement wall to land in wet sand, Moran on top, getting a hand under the wool cap now to grab hair, twist the guy's head face-down. He heard words snapped in Spanish above him. The other Mendoza had a knee on the cement wall, pointing a blue-steel revolver . . . But now a voice called out in hard Anglo-Saxon English telling the Mendoza to freeze, called him an obscene name and that was it for the Mendozas. The two Pompano Beach officers came hatless looking like young pro athletes with nickel-plated Smith & Wessons gleaming wet and it was clear they would use them.

Moran said yes, he would sign charges, assault with deadly weapons or assault to do great bodily harm, whichever was worse, and if the officers could think of anything else put it down. This kind of thing, Moran told them, was not good for the tourist business. He didn't tell the police he knew the Mendozas or that he had seen them assist in murder last night; he'd save that and maybe tell them another time. One of the cops said, "Well, you sure handled these fellas."

Moran said, "I was protecting something more valuable to me than I can tell you."

From his bathroom—cleaning up, changing his clothes again—he heard a familiar voice in the front room and walked out through his bedroom to see Nolen talking on the phone. Nolen raised his hand. On the counter was a pitcher of what looked like French-vanilla ice cream, melted and watery.

"Jesus, make yourself at home," Moran said and went back into the bedroom. Putting on a clean pair of jeans and a dark blue pullover sweater, he heard Nolen say "Jiggs" a couple times. When he went out again Nolen was off the phone, pouring the mixture in the pitcher into two glasses. He offered one of them as Moran came over.

"Breakfast," Nolen said. "Fresh lemons, bourbon and four eggs. A little powdered sugar. You don't provide a blender, I had to beat hell out of it by hand."

Moran took the glass Nolen offered and drank it, not to be sociable but because he needed it. It wasn't bad.

"So, they work for Jiggs."

"Listen, he's very apologetic," Nolen said, seated at the counter now, cowboy boots hooked in the rungs of the stool, starched safari shirt hanging out. For a change Nolen didn't appear sick this morning. "Jiggs sent 'em over to de Boya, like to help out with that piss-poor security he's got, but actually to help Jiggs, get the master plan rolling."

"You mean those guys are your partners?"

"Naw, they don't know anything. You wind 'em up and pay 'em, they do whatever they're told. Like yank out de Boya's telephone line. Screw up his head, he thinks the terrorists are closing in."

"Well, you know who they're screwing up," Moran said, "while I'm trying to get his wife out of there."

Nolen poured a couple more sours. "You got time."

"Is that right? Tell me about it."

"That was Jiggs, I phoned him. He says de Boya sent the Mendozas over cause he found out about you and his wife and had a fit. *Not* from Scully, from somebody else."

Moran said, "Wait a minute—put the goddamn glass down." He gave himself a moment, Nolen telling him it was okay, take it easy, but he could feel his heart beating against his chest and he didn't know how to slow it down or if he wanted to.

"He's kicking her out of the house," Nolen said. "You got no problem."

"When?"

"Now, today. He told her to pack and get out."

"How does Scully know? De Boya tell him?"

"Scully gets pieces and puts 'em together. The Mendozas hear something from one of the maids—they're sitting around the kitchen—about the wife getting beat up and they call Scully—"

Moran stopped him. "Wait now. Andres beat her up?"

There was a look coming into his eyes Nolen had never seen before and hoped it wasn't for him.

"Take it easy, okay? She's fine."

"He hit her?"

"They had a heavy argument with some pushing and shoving, that's all. The Mendozas tell Scully and he goes over to check, feel his way around; he doesn't want any surprises when the time comes. He get there—no Mendozas. De Boya'd sent them here. They're suppose to bring your shlong back in a Baggie so he can give it to his wife. Weird, but it's like what Rafi was telling us, they do it with shears, man. Jesus, I get goose bumps thinking about it. The Mendozas, they don't give a shit they're not actually working for de Boya, it sounds like fun. Scully says it was a misunderstanding and he says he hopes you're okay. I told him the two guys're in the Pompano city jail and Scully says that's all right, he was through with them anyway.'' Nolen raised his glass. ''So here we are.'' He drank down his sour. ''And I might add, today's the big day.''

Moran walked away, Nolen's voice following him now into the bedroom. ''You gonna ask me what's happening?'' From the dresser Moran got his wallet and car keys, returned to the front room and kept walking toward the door.

''Where you going?''

Moran said, ''Where do you think.''

''Wait now, you don't want to go over there. Let her come here. Call her up.''

''I'm through calling.''

''He sees you he'll get a gun. Honest to God, I mean it. He'll kill you.''

Moran was still doing rather than thinking, more pumped up now than he was earlier; but Nolen's words and grown-up wisdom stopped him with his hand on the door. He looked back at Nolen.

''What happens today?''

''We hit de Boya. That's what happens.''

Moran came back to the counter. Nolen seemed to straighten on the stool.

''Your idea—flush him, make him run.''

''How're you gonna do that?''

''Bomb scare.''

''A real one?''

Nolen shook his head. He had Moran's interest now and could take his time. ''One was enough. He saw his dock blown to hell, the man's a believer. Jiggs'll ask him about the telephone line being cut and who came to fix it. Is he sure they were from Southern Bell? Give him doubts. So when he gets a call his house's been wired to go up he grabs his money and runs.''

''How do you know he will?''

''Because he's been looking over his shoulder for twenty years half-expecting something like this. I mean what's getaway money for otherwise? The man doesn't have to get hit over the head. He's ready to jump."

"Maybe," Moran said, "but he could be way ahead of you, have an idea what you're doing."

Nolen was shaking his head.

"Why not?"

"What convinces him it's real is who the call comes from." Nolen winked, feeling frisky. "The Coral Gables Police." He grinned at Moran. "Like it? I'd think you'd wish us luck anyway, clobbering the son of a bitch."

"That a line from a movie?"

"This is real-life drama now, George."

"You missed the big scene last night."

"Well, that was unfortunate, but guys like Rafi, that can happen. He overreached and didn't look where he was going."

"You used him."

"I had nothing to do with that."

"Are you drunk?"

"This's what I've had, right here. One beer when I got up."

"You were drunk I could understand you," Moran said. "Rafi was used and you're next, you don't even know it."

"Unh-unh."

"What's your part in it?"

"I make the anonymous call to the cops. Ready to go off around seven this evening. We want to wait'll the rush hour's over on the freeway."

"Then what?"

"I wait for Jiggs to call me. Bar out by Ninety-five."

"Go on."

"I meet him, wherever he's got de Boya."

"You mean wherever he's killed de Boya. Nolen, you dumb shit, he's not gonna let him live. You either. He'll take the both of you, fifty miles over to the Everglades, you're never seen again. Just tell me, is that a possibility?"

Nolen pretended to think about it, nodded once and took a drink.

"Well?"

"There's a certain risk," Nolen said, "I know that. But there's no payoff in this kind of action without risk, is there? See, I'm aware of that. You think I'm dumb. Jiggs, he uses me, yeah, for what I can do. But you're forgetting one thing." Nolen reached around behind him, dug under his shirttail and from the waist of his trousers brought out a Colt .45 automatic, winked at Moran and laid it on the counter.

"I was Airborne."

Moran saw Nolen's gleam, wet and bloodshot but still a gleam. He said quietly, "Nolen, that was sixteen years ago."

Nolen said, "I've jumped out of airplaines, George, and I've shot at the enemy. I've been to war. Tell me this is different."

"I'm going," Moran said. "I've got to get out of here."

He was at the door, pushing it open when Nolen said, "George, tell me something else and be honest."

Moran looked around. "What?"

"Tell me you don't want to see the man dead." When Moran didn't speak Nolen said, "See? It's why I can tell you about it and expect best wishes. I know where your heart is, buddy. I'll tell you something else too and put money on it. Here . . ." He dug into his shirt pocket and laid a folded bill on the counter. "Here's ten bucks says if you go to that man's house you're gonna get shot in the head way before I ever do . . . Come on, put up."

For another few moments Moran stared at Nolen hunched over the counter, the morning drinker with his bloodshot gleam and his slick-combed hair. He said, "Nolen, you don't have one chance of making it."

18

Three Louis Vuitton full-size suitcases—brown fabric bags that bore the LV crests like a wallpaper design—stood in the upstairs hall, at the head of the stairway.

As Mary came out of her bedroom Altagracia was mounting the suspended stairway, ascending out of the forest of plants and small trees that filled the front hall, the maid frowning now as she saw the luggage.

"Señora, you going on a trip?"

"I hope so," Mary said.

"I take these down."

"*No.*" She snapped the word and had to pause to regain her composure. "It's all right, I have to call a cab first, a taxi." She didn't want the luggage standing in the downstairs foyer, waiting. "But if you'll do me a favor—watch in front. The moment the taxi comes would you let me know?"

The maid nodded solemnly, "Yes, Señora," and said then, hesitant, "That man call and I lie to him again that you not here."

"It's all right," Mary said, "I understand."

"I didn't want to, you been very kind to me. You go to trouble to make my work easy and then I lie against you." Altagracia looked at her with sorrowful eyes.

"I understand," Mary said, both touched and surprised. It was the first time Altagracia had confided, revealed a personal feeling.

"Does your face hurt?"

"No, it's fine." Surprised even more.

"Your mouth look a little swollen is all. I'm very sorry it happen. If you go I hope you come back."

My God, she sympathized. Mary could see genuine concern in the woman's dark eyes. She said, "I appreciate your saying that. Thank you."

"If I can do something for you . . ."

Mary was already thinking. "Do you know where Mr. de Boya is?"

"Yes, Señora, in his study. A man came to see him. The one, the fat one, his shirt comes out."

"Mr. Scully."

"Yes, I think is his name. He just come."

Mary hesitated a moment. "Maybe it would be all right if you took the bags down now. But not to the front hall, all right? I think—why don't you take them the back way to the garage? Then when the taxi comes I'll have the driver pick them up there, it'll be easier for him." Offhand about it. "All right?"

"Whatever pleases you, Señora."

For several moments Mary watched Altagracia, a suitcase in each hand, descend the stairway that seemed to hang in space above treetops—moving so slowly—Mary wanting to hurry her, half-expecting Andres to appear in the hall below. She went into her bedroom, dialed Moran's number and asked for him.

A voice she has never heard before said, "He's gone . . ."

"Do you know where I can reach him?"

". . . probably never to return."

"Please," Mary said, "it's important."

The voice changed, brightening. "Oh, is this Mary? . . . Mary, Nolen Tyner. How you doing? We never met, have we?"

"Nolen, can you tell me where he is?"

"Yeah, he's on his way to your place."

"He can't come *here.*"

"Almost my exact words," Nolen said, "but you know George, that quiet type. You get him riled he's a hard charger. Listen—"

"I have to go," Mary said.

"Okay, but when we have some free time let's all get together. How's that sound to you?"

Moran jumped lanes, cutting in and out of the freeway traffic poking along in the rain, took 95 all the way to the end, followed the curve into South Dixie and didn't stop till he got to Le Jeune, where he turned into a service station. The attendant was sitting at his desk inside.

"Fill it with regular, okay?"

The guy was adding or entering credit-card receipts, taking his time.

"No, make it ten bucks," and added, to get the guy moving, "I'm in an awful hurry."

The attendant, an older guy in greasy coveralls, said, "Everybody's in a hurry. Slow down, you'll live longer."

Moran said, "If I had time I'd explain to you it's just the other way around." It amazed him that he was fairly calm. *Doing*. The guy gave him a strange look as he went out. Moran stood at the pay phone. He knew the number by heart, 442-2300. Then wondered if he should call 911 instead, the emergency number. Which one would an anonymous caller dial? Moran wasn't sure. The idea had come to him on the freeway—suddenly there in his head without any hard thinking—and it was a zinger: a way to spring Mary without a confrontation with Andres and a way to blow Nolen's plan at the same time. Christ, and now he wasn't sure which number to call. He said to himself, *Just do it*. And dialed 442-2300.

The male voice said, "Coral Gables Police," and a name that sounded like "Sergeant Roscoe speaking."

Moran said, "Sergeant, I want to report a bomb that's gonna go off."

"Who is this speaking, please?"

"It's an anonymous call, you dink. The bomb's at Seven-hundred Arvida Parkway; I think you better get over there."

"Sir, may I have your name and number, please?"

"Where the dock blew, asshole. The house's going next."

There was a pause at Coral Gables Police Headquarters.

"This bomb," Sergeant Roscoe or whatever his name was said, "can you tell me what type it is and where it's located?"

"Jesus Christ, the fucking house is going up, people're in it and you're asking me where the bomb is! Get over there and find it, for Christ sake!" Then added, for a touch of local color, *"Viva libertad! Muerte a de Boya!* You got it?" And hung up.

Jiggs Scully got a kick out of these guys that displayed pictures of themselves taken with politicians, celebrities, dignitaries—showing you the class of people they hung out with. Jimmy Cap did the same thing. The only difference, his pictures were taken with stand-up comics in golf outfits, horse breeders and a couple famous jockeys, five-eight Jimmy Cap with his arm around the little guys' shoulders. Jiggs noticed that Latin-American military gave themselves height by wearing those peaked caps that swooped way up in front, even higher than the ones the Nazis had worn; which showed you even your most hardassed rightwingers had some showboat in them.

He said to de Boya, "I was you, general, you have a sentimental attachment for your pictures there, I'd pack 'em away till we clean this business up."

"I don't see how anyone can get inside," de Boya said, sitting behind his big desk, all dressed up in a gray business suit.

"They don't have to get *in,*" Jiggs said. "That's why I want to take a look around, see how many wires you got leading to the house and where they go. The word on the street, the house's next."

"I question that," de Boya said.

"I know you do, but what if that repair guy wasn't Southern Bell? It don't mean anything he showed a card, you get those printed ten bucks a hundred. No, the vibes—you know what vibes are, general? Like an itch, a feeling you get. The vibes tell me we're sitting on a ticklish situation here without much in the way of protection. I send you a couple of pros and—I don't mean to sound critical, general, you're the man in charge, but they aren't doing us much good in Pompano Beach."

The general looked like he had a bad stomach, bothered by gas, and the present situation wasn't going to relieve it any. A very emotional people. He saw de Boya look up: somebody all of a sudden rattling off the Spanish. Jiggs looked around to see Corky, mouth going a mile a minute, telling de Boya something that pulled him right out of his chair.

Altagracia appeared in the bedroom doorway, timid, not certain if she was announcing good news or bad. She said, "Señora, he's here," and now was startled and had to get out of the way.

Mary was moving as the maid spoke, out the door past her into Andres's bedroom, past the two suitcases she hadn't used, still lying on the floor, to the front window.

Moran's old-model white Mercedes was in the drive, behind a red and white Cadillac and Andres's Rolls. Mary pressed closer to the window, the glass streaked with rain, blurred, and saw Moran out of the car, Corky moving out from the house toward him.

Mary left the window; she dodged past Altagracia again in the hallway and stopped.

''My bag, the small one.''

''I get it,'' the maid said.

It gave Mary the moment she needed to take a breath, collect herself. She would be forthright about this final exit, walk out with style in beige linen and if Andres said anything she might give him a look but no more than that. Altagracia came out of the bedroom with her white canvas tote. Mary slipped the strap over her shoulder.

She heard Altagracia say, ''Go with God.''

Damn right. With her head up, a little haughty if she had to be. Then hesitated.

Andres appeared in the hall below, moving with purpose toward the front entrance. She saw his back and now Jiggs Scully shuffling to catch up, recognizing the man's shapeless seersucker coat.

They were outside by the time Mary reached the foyer, on the front stoop that was a wide plank deck, low, only a step above the gravel drive. She saw Moran in a dark sweater in the fine mist of rain, Corky raising both hands to push him or hold him off. *Now,* Mary thought. And walked out the door past Scully, bumping him with the tote hanging from her shoulder, not looking at him or at Andres as she stepped past them to the gravel drive. Corky turned, hearing or sensing her. But she was looking at Moran now less than ten feet away, his eyes calm, drops of moisture glistening in his beard. She wanted to run to him and see his arms open.

Andres said, ''Stop there.''

But he was much too late. Mary walked up to Moran and said, ''Boy, am I glad to see you,'' in a tone so natural it amazed her.

His gaze flicked past her and back, still composed. ''You ready?''

''My bags are in the garage. The door that's raised.''

He looked over at the garage wing, an extension of the house, three of the doors in place, one raised open to reveal gleams of chrome and body metal in the dim interior. Moran took his time, listening, hoping to hear sirens coming for him twice in the same day—his first success giving him faith to try it again—aching now to hear squad cars screaming down Cutler Road toward Arvida; Mary looking at him like he was crazy. What was he standing there for?

"Mary." It came as a de Boya command. He stood with hands shoved deep in his coat pockets. "Come inside."

Moran said, "Stay where you are," touching her arm. He moved past her a step and said to Jiggs, "You tell him yet?"

It caught de Boya's attention. Jiggs didn't say anything; perhaps the first time in his life.

"I'll tell him if you won't," Moran said. "Hey, Andres?"

Jiggs said, "George, you got a problem?"

There it was in the distance, that sorrowful wail not yet related to them here, but it was coming fast and Moran hoped he had enough time to say what he had to say and get out.

"Andres, this guy's out to take you."

Maybe it was already too late. Jiggs was looking at him, de Boya staring off, frowning. Was it the wind in the rain, a police siren, what? Jiggs heard it without letting on. He said, "George, you been drinking?"

Now a yelp-type siren chasing the wails, coming from beyond the mass of Florida trees bunched along the road.

Moran said, "Andres?"

He got a glance, still with the frown.

"Jiggs Scully'll kill you if he gets the chance."

De Boya's glance came again, like Moran was the distraction and not the shrill sounds piercing the rain.

"I don't know why I'm telling you, but if he asks you to go anywhere with him, tell him no."

There. For what it was worth. He'd lost the attention of Jiggs and de Boya now, both listening, heads raised to the cool mist as the sirens wailed closer. Moran turned to Mary, saw her eyes. "You have to get in my car. Right now."

She moved without pause, not even a questioning look and he could have taken the moment and kissed her.

Squad cars were coming up both ends of the drive now, gumballs flashing, electronic sirens on high, some wailing, some yelping, giving the scene the full emergency treatment. As quickly as they arrived doors winged open and the police were on the scene, approaching the house.

Andres seemed bewildered.

But Jiggs was staring at Moran.

And Moran had to stare back at him, letting him know without saying a word who'd brought all this down on him.

A uniformed lieutenant was saying to Andres, with that impersonal deadweight of authority, "Sir, I'm gonna ask you to evacuate these premises. I want everybody out of that house."

Jiggs still hadn't moved, staring at Moran.

Moran smiled in his beard. Maybe Jiggs caught it, maybe not; it was time to go.

Mary was behind the wheel. She revved as he jumped in and pulled smoothly around Jiggs's car and the white Rolls. Squad cars coming with headlights on had to swerve out of the way as she pointed toward the garage and braked the old Mercedes to a skid-stop in the gravel. "My bags," Mary said.

The three matched pieces stood at the edge of the dim interior. Moran was out again, collecting the luggage, shoving it into the back seat. He took time to look toward the front of the house, the entranceway.

De Boya was holding the police back with his iron will, resisting, objecting, pointing a finger in the lieutenant's face. No one was entering his house without his permission and he obviously wasn't granting it. Except to Corky now. De Boya said something to him that sent Corky running inside.

"Moran, will you come on!"

He turned to look at Mary. "Drive out to the street before you get boxed in. I'll meet you out there in a minute . . . Go on!"

She gave him a look with her jaw clenched and took off, horn blaring now, swinging out on the grass to get around the squad cars stacking up in the yard. There were cops with dogs now heading for the garage.

Moran moved to the off side of a squad car, its lights flashing, radio crackling in a dry female voice on and off. He watched de Boya head to head with Jiggs now. They looked like they were arguing. De Boya at first standing firm, but Jiggs beginning to get through to him. De Boya, impatient now, gestured toward the garage. When de Boya turned and hurried into the house, Jiggs stood watching. Though not for long. Jiggs was moving now, running with a surprisingly easy grace toward the garage. He went in through the opening and Moran's gaze returned to the front entrance, the cops milling around, servants coming out now with umbrellas. When he glanced toward the garage again there was Jiggs framed in the dim opening.

Jiggs holding a telephone, its long extension cord trailing into the garage, talking into the phone with some urgency as he watched the police in front of the house. Jiggs stepped back into the garage and reappeared without the phone, pushing his glasses up on his flat nose. He took the glasses off now, standing in the rain, pulled out part of his shirttail and began wiping the lenses. When he put the glasses on again, still intently watching the scene, the shirttail remained out, forgotten.

The slob. But look at him, Moran thought, fascinated. The guy was improvising, trying to put his act back together. He could hear Jiggs saying to him in the Mutiny Bar, 'Gimme some credit, George,'' with that street-hip familiarity, his disarming natural style. He was fun to watch—as long as you didn't get too close.

Moran wanted to see de Boya again, but knew it was time to go: Mary waiting for him, anxious, Mary dying to get out of here. He moved down the line of squad cars looking back past Fireball flashers revolving slowly, the scene on hold for the time being. At the point where the drive curved into the trees he looked back one last time, hoping, deciding then to stretch it, give himself another minute, and saw de Boya coming out of the house:

De Boya hurrying to his Rolls followed by Corky and one of the maids, Altagracia. De Boya with a briefcase waving now at Corky who was carrying two suitcases to hurry up. Jiggs there now saying something to de Boya and de Boya shaking his head, Jiggs still trying, de Boya turning away as the maid came with a cardboard box in her arms, framed pictures—they looked like—sticking out of the open top, the maid waiting now to hand the box to Corky as he put the suitcases that were exactly like Mary's into the trunk of the Rolls.

Where was Jiggs?

Moran saw him then, getting in his Cadillac.

De Boya and Corky were in the Rolls now, the car starting up, coming this way across the lawn and Moran stepped into the trees.

19

"I told him, I said don't go with him," Moran said. He wanted to believe he had warned de Boya and wondered if he would have to repeat this to himself from time to time.

"You don't *tell* him anything," Mary said, creeping the car toward a police officer in a rain slicker waving them to come on, come on, move it out. They turned off Arvida Parkway onto Cutler Road and the feeling of being released came over both of them at the same time, brought smiles and inside the old Mercedes was a good place to be with the windshield wipers beating and the tires humming on wet pavement. The weather was fine. They passed the fairways of Leucadendra and tennis courts standing empty, left the country club behind with a feeling of starting fresh, on a new adventure. Though Moran's thoughts would turn and he would see de Boya coming out of the house—"Spook him and make him run," he'd said to Jiggs in the Mutiny and it was happening.

He said, "If he lets Jiggs follow him or take him somewhere he's crazy. I told him. You heard me, you were standing right there." He had to stop thinking about Andres. But then asked, "Where do you think he'll go?"

"Well, he owns property all over. Apartment buildings, even farms, land he'll develop someday. He could go down in the Keys, anywhere." Mary glanced at Moran. "If you're worried about him, don't be. Andres takes care of number one, the son of a bitch. And if Corky has to give his life Andres will let him."

Right, it wasn't something new to these guys. Moran looked at her staring straight ahead at the windshield wipers sweeping, clearing the glass every other moment. He loved her profile. He could see her as a little girl.

"You're a good driver."

"Thank you."

"How's your mouth? Is it sore?"

"Not bad."

"The way your lower lip sticks out, it's kinda sexy."

"You want to bite it?"

"I believe I might. Did you hit him back?"

"I hit him first. It only made him madder."

"There you are," Moran said. "The first rule of street fighting, never throw a punch unless you can finish it."

Mary said, "What are you, Moran, my trainer or my lover?" She felt wonderful and wanted to say corny things about being free at last and tell him something that would bring amazement and he'd say "I don't believe it" in that way he said it. But that could wait.

De Boya sat half-turned in the front seat holding his briefcase on his lap. He would look back through the mist the Rolls raised in its wake and see Jiggs Scully's car holding the pace, less than a hundred meters behind. They were on the freeway northbound, passing the Fort Lauderdale airport off to the right, a jumbo jet descending out of the gray mass almost directly in front of them.

Corky said to the rearview mirror, "I can put my foot into it and leave him."

"No, we bring him along," de Boya said. "He knows something." They spoke in Spanish.

"You're sure of it?"

"We'll find out. He wanted to take me to Boca Raton. He tells me a very safe place. I'm supposed to say yes, of course, and put myself in his care."

"He has little respect."

"That's the least of it." De Boya watched the green freeway sign gradually appear. "Eighty-four, that's it, to the New River Canal Road."

Corky followed the exit ramp, his eyes on the mirror. "He's coming."

"I hope so," de Boya said.

They drove west for several minutes past fenced land that was desolate and seemed remote, resembling an African plain. There were no houses in sight until they got off on a dirt road turning to muddy pools, passed through a stand of pine and tangled brush to arrive in the yard of a cement-block ranch painted white, flaking, lifeless in its dismal setting. De Boya had bought the house furnished, as is, surrounded by ninety acres of scrub; the house would serve as a jump-off if needed, close to the Lauderdale airport; the property could always be developed some day, turned into a retirement village.

"He's coming," Corky said, steering toward the garage that was part of the house.

De Boya looked back to see the red and white Cadillac creeping into the yard. The car stopped and Jiggs got out to stand looking around, hands on his hips. The rain didn't seem to bother him.

"Stay with me," de Boya said.

He got out of the Rolls with his briefcase and approached Jiggs who was moving to the back of his car now, looking at his keys as though to open the trunk, then glancing at de Boya.

"This is it, huh? General, I got to tell you you'd be a lot more comfortable this place in Boca. Belongs to Jimmy Cap. Got a sauna, everything." He was bending over the trunk now.

"What do you have in there?" de Boya asked.

Jiggs straightened. "I got a forty-four Mag and I got a twelve-gauge pump gun, a Browning. I got flares and a five-gallon can of gas. What else you need?"

De Boya motioned to him. "Let's go inside."

"I thought you'd want some protection."

"Get it later," de Boya said.

As they started for the house Jiggs said, "You want me to help with your bags?"

"No, we'll get those later, too."

Jiggs said, "I was gonna say, General, I don't think you needed to pack those grips. Bomb squad'll take the day—we shouldn't be gone more'n one night. We can call 'em now you got a phone, see what they found."

"Yes, we'll do that," de Boya said.

"I wondered, the cops say who called 'em?"

"They don't know," de Boya said. "What I don't understand is what Moran was doing there. What was it he said? That you want to *take* me?"

Corky moved ahead of them to unlock the door.

"That's what it sounded like," Jiggs said. "Only thing I can figure out, he was trying to confuse you, General, get your head turned around so he could run off with your wife. You want me to I'll go pay him a visit."

"That would be all right with Jimmy Cap?"

"Jimmy said help you out anyway I can."

"But I learn he's out of town, uh? Has been gone for a week or so."

Corky held the aluminum screen door for both of them, de Boya first, Jiggs saying, "General, I hope you're not doubting my word," his tone offering a strong measure of injured pride as he gave the place a quick look: a living room that had the flavor of a hunting cabin, knotty pine walls, maple furniture, a poker table, Indian blankets. Jiggs pulled his shirttail out to wipe off his glasses. "I'll give you a number you can reach Jimmy Cap or they'll tell you exactly where he is. You don't mind, I'd like you to talk to him and get this straightened out." Very serious about it.

"Yes, I would too," de Boya said. "Let me have the number." He handed Corky his briefcase.

Jiggs put his glasses back on. His hands went to his breasts in the loose seersucker jacket and gave them a pat, then touched his right hip. "Yeah, I got it. In my wallet. General, let me go the can and take a leak first, I can almost taste it." He moved off toward the hall where he saw the bathroom door open, green tile inside.

De Boya watched until the door closed, then extended a hand toward Corky and snapped his fingers, twice.

Corky was opening the briefcase on the poker table. He brought out a Walther P.38 automatic and handed it to de Boya. Now he took off his suit coat. From a shoulder holster snug beneath his left arm Corky drew a revolver, a Colt .38 with a stubby snout, and followed de Boya to the hallway. There was a bedroom at each end, doors open to empty rooms, neat twin beds with chenille spreads. The bathroom stood in between, its door closed.

They waited to hear the toilet flush, raised their pistols and began firing point-blank into the center of the door, the reports earsplitting in the confined area. Then silence. Corky turned the knob carefully, opened the door a crack, stepped back and used the sole of his foot to bang the door completely open.

Jiggs came out of the shower stall arms extended, holding a

blue-steel automatic in both hands, ignoring Corky to level it straight at de Boya's face. He saw those ice-water eyes wide open for the first time.

"Something I learned a long time ago, General, never take your joint out with guys you don't trust. Specially you hot-blooded fellas like a lot of noise, shoot the place up. Come in here. Come on," Jiggs said, stepping back on broken glass and bits of porcelain to let them come in past him. "Drop the guns in the toilet . . . That's the way. You too, Corko. What's this a truss?" He snapped the elastic strap of Corky's shoulder holster. "You got a hernia? That's it, in the toilet. Now I want you to take your clothes off. That's what you do, right. General? Strip 'em down bare-ass."

As he began to undress de Boya said, "I pay for my life, uh? How much I have to pay you?"

"Gonna make it easy," Jiggs said, edging past them to sit down on the toilet. "Only take your suitcases. Corky, gimme the car keys. I'll get 'em after."

"I begin to think it's what you want," de Boya said, "but I don't see how you know about it." He paused unbuttoning his shirt, occupied with his thoughts. "Unless it was my wife?"

"You told me yourself," Jiggs said, "talking to Jimmy Cap, that day out at Calder. All the rest of the bullshit is just bullshit, way to get you here." He said to Corky, "What're you looking at? Come on, get your clothes off." He raised the automatic in Corky's face. "Can't figure out what this is, can you? Looks like your standard nine-millimeter Smith Parabellum except for that hickey sticking out." Jiggs dug into his side coat pocket, brought out a five-inch gunmetal tube and screwed it onto the threaded stub, the "hickey" that extended from the muzzle of the automatic. "Factory-modified. They call it a Hush-Puppy. Come on, General, take it off. Take it all off—like the broad says with the shaving cream. You too, Corko, drop the Jockeys, but keep an eye on the general there he don't try and cop your joint . . . Shoes, everything."

He seemed proud of his gun and showed them the profile with the silencer attached.

"Got a slide lock here on the side. You fire once it doesn't eject, so you don't hear the slide click open. You don't even hear that *poumpf* you get with a silencer. You know why? I use a subsonic round, very low muzzle velocity. Take the lock off you hear the slide jack open and close as you fire, but that's all, just that *click-click* . . . You guys ready? Leave your clothes on the floor there."

De Boya said, "You're going to take our clothes?" He stood straight, shoulders back and seemed to be in good shape, heavy-set but not too much flab.

"I'll see they don't get wrinkled," Jiggs said. "Now get'n the shower. Go on, move."

"Both of us?" de Boya asked.

"Both of you the same time." Jiggs stood up now and motioned them into the stall. "Corky, watch yourself. Don't drop the soap." Corky was skinnier than he looked in clothes; chewing on that pussy mustache like he was going to cry. "Okay, turn the water on. Get it how you like it."

De Boya said, "What is the need of this?"

Jiggs said, "Just turn the water on, will you, please?"

He shot de Boya high through the rib cage with his arms raised to adjust the shower head, lung-shot him and shot him again in near silence as de Boya flattened against the wall and began to slide, smearing the tile. Corky was screaming now, hunching, holding his hands out protectively. He shot Corky twice in the chest through one of his hands, Corky's body folding to fall across de Boya curled up like he was trying to keep warm. He watched their heads jump with a final twitch as he shot them each again, watched the stream of water cleanse them, then pulled the shower curtain closed. He'd let the water run while he went out to get the suitcases.

20

The bar Jiggs had picked out for Nolen was on the corner of Atlantic and SW Sixth Avenue on the west side of Pompano, about thirty seconds from the freeway.

Nolen was wearing sunglasses and an old raincoat, creased with wrinkles, his cowboy boots hooked in the rung of the bar-stool that was as close to the phone booth as he could get: sipping scotch with a twist, fooling with the swizzle stick that was like a little blue sword. Four swords on the bar plus the one he was playing with. The bartender had tried to take them and Nolen told him no, he needed the swords to keep score. He was allowing himself six, no more than that. Just enough to keep his motor responses lubricated, idling. He didn't count the pitcher of sours; that was breakfast. It seemed a long time ago—still there in Moran's house sipping when he got the emergency call from Jiggs, Jiggs saying he was in de Boya's garage and the starting time had been moved up to right *now,* he'd call him at the bar when they got to Boca; only it might not be Boca, the general wasn't being very cooperative. All that at once while Nolen was trying to ask him what he was doing in the garage, for Christ sake, and what were all the sirens.

The place was dark and had a nice smell of beer, the bartender down talking to the one other customer that looked like a retiree with his golf cap.

They both looked up as the phone rang in the booth and watched the weird-looking guy in the raincoat and sunglasses almost kill himself getting off his stool, the seat of the stool next to him spinning, throwing him as he leaned on it to get up. The bartender said, "I sure hope that's your call."

Nolen waved at him, went in the booth and closed the door. As soon as he heard Jiggs's voice he said, "The hell's going on?"

Jiggs's voice sounded calm. Nolen listened, holding back on all his questions as Jiggs told him where to come, not Boca, but a place west of Lauderdale and not too far.

"Just tell me how it went?"

Jiggs's voice said it went fine, no problem.

"You got it?"

Jiggs's voice said he was going to get it out of the car right now.

"Where's de Boya?"

Jiggs's voice said he was in the bathroom. The voice stopped Nolen then. It said, "Nolen, you want to talk on the phone, shoot the shit, or you want to get over here and help me count?"

Moran said to Jerry, "Mary's gonna be staying with us maybe a few days. Oceanfront Number One."

Jerry took a moment to adjust before coming on full of cordiality. "Why sure, that's the one with the view. Except today. But the paper says it's gonna clear up by tomorrow." He got the key and said to Mary, "You like to register now? Or you can do it later if you want."

Mary held back. Moran said, "Jerry, she's not here. Okay?" He took the key and handed it to Mary. "If anybody asks."

"I never saw this young lady before in my life," Jerry said.

"I mean even if it's the police. All right?"

Jerry sobered. He adjusted his golf cap, resetting it in the same position, cocked slightly to one side. "Yeah, well I don't see any problem."

"We won't take any guests for a few days. Not that they're breaking down the door."

"Turn the No Vacancy on?"

"No, let's not tell anybody a thing. I appreciate it, Jerry."

"I know you do," Jerry said. He gave Mary a wink, getting the feel of his new role.

Moran opened the door to the courtyard and closed it against the rain coming in. "Jerry, how about Nolen? Is he around?"

"Got a phone call about an hour ago and left right after. Smashed as usual. I hope he don't get in a car wreck."

Moran went out with the bags.

Mary said to Jerry, "Nice seeing you again." Amazed at this natural response, her voice not giving her away. Outside, hurrying to keep up with Moran moving fast with the three bags, she said, "I don't believe it." Her voice raised in the wind. She said, "Remember how you kept saying that? When I called your room in Santo Domingo—'I don't believe it.' Remember?'' Talking out of a compulsion to hear herself and know she was in control. '' 'Come on, I don't believe it.' You said it about five times.''

Moran said over his shoulder, ''I believe it now,'' not stopping till they got to the end apartment off the beach, Moran hunching his shoulders against the rain coming in sheets off the ocean, Mary trying to hold her tote out of the way and get the door open.

They were soaked by the time they got inside and Moran let the bags drop. Mary closed the door and came to him, pressed her wet face against his wet shoulder, felt the familiar comfort of his arms come around her. It seemed late, so dark for afternoon. She pressed against him, hearing the wind moan out of the gray mass of ocean and felt an excitement that was hard to keep down. She said, ''I've done something else you're not gonna believe,'' raising her face to his.

Moran saw her expression, the grin she was trying to hold back. He looked at her with the innocence of a straight man waiting for it and said, ''Are you serious?''

She said, ''Wait till I show you,'' and saw his expression change, starting to grin but not sure he wanted to.

Nolen found 84 and turned off the freeway at the peak of his whiskey rush, the glow carrying him along with a feeling of effortless control, gliding in the high excitement of a rainstorm, clouds hanging close enough to touch. (He had come out of the bar with his sunglasses on and thought it was midnight.) Now it was that colorless nothing kind of time, the eye of the storm. He found the New River Canal Road, not another car in sight and kept pressing, riding the wind, the black overcast his cover, until he saw the stand of pines off to the north. He touched the right-hand pocket of his raincoat and felt the hard bulk of the .45. Here we go . . . turned in and rode the Porsche through pools formed in the ruts, hearing the wake washing aside, saw the house and two cars in the yard now, the wipers giving him quick glimpses. He rolled to a stop on the off side of the Cadillac and now considered—in spite of the charm he felt—the tricky part. Walking from the car to the house. He felt his mouth dry and wondered why he hadn't brought a bottle with him.

Well fuck it, he'd gone into houses on the east bank of the Ozama with cotton in his mouth and automatic weapon fire popping away and one place had found beer inside, not cold, but beer all the same and he hadn't gotten even a scratch in anger during that war and was subject to serious gunfire nearly every day and you know why?, because his life was being spared for something big if not fame that would come to him with more money than he could count on a rainy afternoon in Florida. You're goddamn right. He got out of the car and walked up to that house . . . saw the door open a crack . . . hesitated the moment he needed to clear the .45 and kicked the door in with a cowboy boot.

Jiggs sat in an easy chair that faced away from the front windows and the door, so that Nolen came in almost behind him. He saw Jiggs look him up and down, Jiggs just sitting there. Nolen looked past him at the two suitcases lying closed on a round card table. He turned and looked toward the hallway.

"Where's the general?"

"In the bathroom."

"Still?" Nolen looked at the suitcases again. "How come you haven't opened 'em?"

"They're open."

"Well, why don't you say something, for Christ sake?"

"I want to hear you," Jiggs said.

Nolen went over to the card table. He reached up to switch on the hanging fixture that was like an oil lamp with a glass chimney. He saw the suitcases were unfastened, unzipped, and looked at Jiggs again.

"Go ahead," Jiggs said.

Nolen lifted the flap of a suitcase and let it fall open. He saw newspapers. He saw the front page of the *Miami Herald* telling him Haitians had drowned in the surf at Hillsboro. He felt down under the papers. He threw back the flap of the other suitcase and saw more newspapers and felt through them all the way to the bottom. He looked at Jiggs, squinting at him.

"The general see us coming?"

"Nah, it wasn't the general."

"Well, did you have a talk with him? Christ!" Nolen whipped around, cocked his weapon as he stomped toward the hallway.

"I said it wasn't him," Jiggs said.

He waited, a clear picture of a rainy afternoon in his mind: Moran throwing the same kind of luggage into the back seat of a beat-up Mercedes, girlfriend who was way ahead of everybody behind the wheel of the getaway car. He heard Nolen scream:

"Jesus Christ!"

And waited for him to appear: barely moving in his shroud raincoat, gunhand hanging limp, like he'd been hit over the head and was now about to fall.

"It was your buddy," Jiggs said. "Son of a gun beat us to it."

"My settlement," Mary said, on the floor next to the open suitcase. "Now do you love me?" She had taken off her wet clothes, chilled, and held a cotton bedspread around her like an Indian blanket; a young girl at a pajama party eager to have fun. She said, "What's the matter, can't you say anything? You're looking at it, but you still can't believe it, huh?"

"I believe it," Moran said without emotion.

He sat in his shirt and Jockeys on the edge of the sofa, hunched over in lamplight to look at the stacks of currency, packets of brand-new hundred-dollar bills, rows of them filling the suitcase, remembering Scully telling him about the Igloo coolers and a hundred thousand stacking up to less than a foot high. He felt vulnerable and wished he had run across to his house to change first. He'd brought Mary here because of the three suitcases, because he thought she'd need more room for clothes than his house could offer.

He said, "All three are full of money?"

"No, two," Mary said. "I brought a few things, but I didn't want to load myself down."

"How much's in there?"

"I don't know exactly. It looks like a million one hundred thousand in each bag. But anything over two million Andres gets back. I only want what I have coming."

"You didn't count it?"

"George, this's the first time I've even seen it. I made the switch while Andres was downstairs in his den."

"The switch—you sound like a pro."

"No, it's my first job. I was gonna call a cab and then I found out you were on the way. My hero." She looked at him curiously, smile fading to a slight frown. "Does money make you nervous? What's the matter?"

He was looking at the scene on Arvida, flashing lights reflecting in the rain. "Andres and Corky came out with two suitcases, just like these."

"He has at least a dozen Louis Vuitton," Mary said. "I think he must have stock in the company. He kept two bags packed with his traveling money, always ready."

"Where'd he hide them?"

"You guessed it the other day and thought you were kidding. Under the bed."

"Come on—just sitting there? Not locked up?"

"Under two hundred and fifty gallons of water and inside a marble safe that looks like the pedestal of his bed. There's a tiny hole at the foot you can barely see. You slide in a magnetic key that's like a long needle and part of the marble slides open."

Moran said, "He trusted you?" and sounded surprised, thinking of her with Andres now rather than in the beginning.

"Why not?" Mary said, thinking of herself with Andres in that time before. "Something to impress the bride, a fortune under the marriage bed. Vanity, George. And if he hasn't trusted me lately, well, a cheater isn't necessarily a thief. He tends to sell women short."

"But what's in the bags Andres took? They weren't empty, were they?"

"No, I pulled out the suitcases with the money and then I thought, What if he gets suspicious when he sees me leave and runs upstairs to check? So I packed two other suitcases with old newspapers and shoved them under the bed. The worst part was carrying an armload of papers upstairs. I thought sure he'd see me and I couldn't think of a good story."

"You planned this? How come you didn't tell me?"

"I didn't plan it, I just did it."

Moran finally smiled; he couldn't help it. And for a few moments felt better about the whole thing.

"I was mad. My mouth hurt." Mary raised a hand to touch her

face and the bedspread slipped from one shoulder. ''Now, I can't believe I did it . . . Do you see a problem?''

Moran said, ''Do I see a *problem?*'' He reached over as if reminded and turned off the lamp. He could still see the neat stacks of currency. ''Mary, I don't think *problem's* the word.''

He was up now, moving to the window next to the door, parting the draperies to look out at the courtyard in a pale glow, a solemn stillness after the storm. It would be dark soon, dull light to dark without the color of sunset this evening.

She stared at his bare legs, shirttails hanging to cover the Jockey briefs. She thought about making a grab at him, get his attention.

''George, if Andres wants to fight about it, okay, we'll go to court. I'll bring the original prenuptial agreement—I hate that word—and the amendment he forced me to sign. It doesn't even look like my signature.''

Moran didn't seem to be listening.

He said, ''We've got to get out of here. I'm gonna run over and get some clothes on.'' He was still watching through the opening in the draperies. ''We could hide the money . . . No, we'd better just go, quick.'' He glanced at her now. ''Get dressed. And bring the wet things, don't leave 'em.''

She said, ''George, if Andres comes it's because he knows the money's here. We won't let him have it, that's all. I'll tell him to see me in court.''

Moran turned from the window now. ''And if Jiggs Scully comes, what do you tell him?'' He picked up his jeans from a chair, wet and stiff, and pulled them on as Mary watched, eyes staring wide now, holding the bedspread around her. He said, ''I'll be right back,'' and went out the door.

It gave her time to think, to relive the act, the awful anxiety of carrying an armload of newspapers up that open stairway, finding the key in the medicine cabinet of Andres' bathroom, down on the floor with her heart pounding pulling the suitcases out then retracing, replacing the key, taking the suitcases to her room, trying to compose herself, finally walking out past Andres . . . going through all that so she could give two million two hundred thousand dollars to Jiggs Scully? She thought, I've never even spoken to him.

It gave her a strange feeling because she could not think of a compelling reason to be afraid of Jiggs Scully, except that Moran was and Moran knew him.

She dressed in sweater and slacks and waited, sitting on the arm of a chair to look out through the draperies at the empty courtyard in the beginning of nighttime darkness, watching his house, waiting for some sign of him. Gone longer now than she'd expected. The door opened and she jumped.

Then let her breath out in relief. "God, you scared me. Where'd you come from?" He moved to the window without answering, parted the draperies to look out and she said, "We're too late, aren't we?"

"They're out in front," Moran said.

For several minutes they watched the courtyard in silence, until a figure in a long coat appeared out of shadow, walking toward the beach. He seemed uncertain, almost as though he were lost.

"It's Nolen," Moran said, but didn't move from the window.

21

Nolen reached the sidewalk facing the beachfront, looked around disoriented, hearing the ocean but no other sounds, missing something. That amber glow at the door to each of the units. No lights showed, not in Moran's house, the office, anywhere; it gave him a spooky feeling, like the place was closed, out of business. He walked over to Moran's bungalow, opened the screen and banged on the door three times, so he could say he did. Then walked around to a side window to look in the house. There was nothing to see. An empty pitcher and two glasses on the counter, in faint light from the kitchen window. It seemed a week ago, drinking sours with Moran. He felt useless, in need of a lift. In need of a guide, he thought, stumbling through the lounge chairs now to make his way around the pool. A beer would hit the spot. Christ, even a Coke. But he walked past the machine in the alcove, went out toward street-light reflections on empty cars and wet pavement. Jiggs stood on the sidewalk by the Coconut Palms office.

"They're not there," Nolen said. "Nobody home."

"That's funny, isn't it," Jiggs said, "with his car sitting there."

Nolen wondered if Jiggs was going to bust the door in. But Jiggs turned to look in through the dark office, through the windows on the other side, to study the courtyard in moonlight and he seemed calm. Never any different, Nolen reminded himself. Never upset, never excited about anything.

"How many units in there?"

"I think twelve," Nolen said.

"How many're occupied?"

"None of 'em. There's nobody here."

"They could be in any one of those rooms."

"I think they're gone," Nolen said.

Jiggs turned from the office window. "He picked her up, he was getting her outta there, that's all. They were going on a trip they'd be up around Orlando by now, or the car'd be at Miami

International. They're around here somewhere."

"Maybe they went to get something to eat."

"Stroll down the corner," Jiggs said. "That's what I'd do I thought somebody was coming after me."

Nolen said, "Yeah, but wait now, get in their head. They wouldn't know it's us coming anymore'n we know for *sure* his wife had the money when she left home. Maybe it's still in de Boya's house."

Jiggs was patient. He said, "De Boya thought he had it. If he didn't, who does that leave? You listening or you still smashed? Look, what I want you to do, Nolen, go in there in your room and keep your eyes open. Moran comes out, you been in a bar all day, you don't know anything what he's talking about. Stay awake till I get somebody to come over and take a look around. I'll try and get Speedy, but you got to stay awake till he comes."

"Who's Speedy?"

"For Christ sake you spent the night with him out cruising the bay. The guy Santos, with the Donzi. I want somebody check the place out isn't gonna fall over the furniture. I want to keep things as is for now so you can hit the sack and I can go up the corner, the Howard Johnson's and get my eight hours. Then in the morning, we need a couple more guys I'll get 'em. But you'll be awake, have your shower and shave by then, right?"

Nolen began to nod, concentrating, trying to get his mind working.

"No booze tomorrow, nothing," Jiggs said. He studied Nolen a moment. "You don't know what I'm talking about, do you?"

"I don't see where you need a lot of guys . . . or you have to hurt anybody," Nolen said. "Just take it, get out."

"Jesus Christ," Jiggs said, "you think I want to bring some guys in, *now,* we know where it is? I'm talking about a little surveillance, that's all. I want to know Moran and the broad're here and what room the suitcases're in. The sun comes out, looks like a pretty nice day—I want 'em to think, well, maybe we're okay, nothing to worry about, no reason to run or call the cops. It's not like hitting a bank, a liquor store; I don't do that. I want to come in here tomorrow have a quiet talk with 'em. Show 'em where we stand, say thank you and leave. I don't want a lot of confusion, somebody calls the cops, some old blue-haired broad up there in her condo. It's too hard to talk you know the cops're on the way. No, I want everybody to be relaxed, their heads clear, their hands away from the buzzer.

"Just talk to 'em," Nolen said.

"I think that's the way to handle it," Jiggs said, "don't you?"

Watching at the window reminded him of times in Santo Domingo during his war: a motel yard or a narrow empty street at night were much the same, waiting for the unexpected, trying to sense or anticipate a sign of movement. Not wanting to see that muzzle flash. The vital difference was he didn't have an M-14 in his hands. It would be an M-16 today or he would settle for Nolen's .45 with its stopping power at close range and feel much better about the shadows along the edge of the beachfront wall and over back of his house and along the motel units fronting on the street. Nolen had appeared and left. A figure—it became Nolen without his raincoat—appeared again in moonlight reflecting on the office windows and disappeared into shadow. It was nearly two hours later he saw the door to Number Five open and a light go on, Nolen again, a glimpse of him before the door closed. Nolen had finally ceased his wandering and was home. After that was only the sound of the ocean.

Mary said, "You saw Jiggs; you're certain that's who it was."

"I saw Nolen's car pull in," Moran said. "I was going to the office to leave Jerry a note, tell him I'd be gone a few days. I saw Nolen get out of his car as Jiggs pulled up in that red and white Cadillac, you can't miss it. They had to have seen my car. Then after that Nolen wanders around, probably checked the bar up on the corner—where am I? I've got to be here somewhere. But that doesn't mean they think you're here too."

"I left the house with you. Jiggs saw us."

"I could've dropped you off, taken you to the airport."

"He knows better than that," Mary said. "And if he thinks we have the money, well, the only way would be if he's found out Andres doesn't have it."

Moran said, "He might think Andres faked him out and the money's still at home."

She said, "Do you believe that?"

"It's possible."

"You wouldn't bet on it though," Mary said. "You don't want to come out and say it because if Jiggs opened Andres's suitcases the chances are Andres is dead. Isn't that right?"

In the dark of the room he didn't have to answer immediately. He assumed Andres was dead and realized, now, Mary accepted the possibility.

She said, "If I find out he is, I doubt if I'll feel much grief, and I'm sure not gonna pretend to. But I'll tell you something, Moran," her voice gaining a quiet force, an unmistakable edge. "I don't know Jiggs Scully, I've never even spoken to him. But I'll be goddamned if I'm gonna give him my money. It absolutely infuriates me, that he thinks he can walk in and I'll simply hand it over. I've been sitting here wondering, is Andres dead? I have a feeling he is. Then do I call the police? What do I tell them? 'I think somebody killed my husband, at least it's possible, and now he's after my boyfriend, my lover and me.' Do you like it so far? 'He's after us because we've got over two million dollars, *cash,* in a couple of suitcases . . .' And you know the first thing they'll ask?"

"Where'd you get the money," Moran said.

"Exactly. Then try to explain, beginning with Trujillo's assassination, why Andres kept two million dollars under the bed."

"First they check you out," Moran said, "see if you've ever been arrested for narcotics."

"Yeah, find out if I was using the dock that blew up to bring in cocaine and grass. 'No, I'm just a housewife—I mean a homemaker, officer. I play tennis and meet my lover at motels.' And after we get through with all that, maybe, just maybe they'll go after Jiggs and arrest him."

"For what?" Moran said. "He hasn't done anything we know of."

"That's right, we have to wait till he comes in and takes it."

There was a silence. Moran said, "I'll talk to Nolen. See what he knows."

"Now?"

"Tomorrow when he's hung over, in pain. Act like I don't

know anything and find out what's going on. I'll call your house, see if Andres came back . . . You stay here, out of sight and maybe it'll work. Jiggs'll sniff around and go away."

"I don't think I can do that," Mary said. "I know damn well if I see him I'll want to walk up to him and kick him right in the balls."

"You get mad, don't you?" Moran said. "You don't hold back."

"Why should I hide? I haven't done anything. How long do I stay in here? A couple of days? A week?"

Her tone was great; little jabs of anger that poked at Moran and stirred him, made him feel restless.

"You've got a point."

"Are you gonna bring me food every day? Wait till it's dark and sneak it in? While the police wait for Jiggs to do something, break a law? What is this, Moran? I've never hidden from anything in my life and it makes me pretty goddamn mad to realize that's what I'm doing."

"You're right," Moran said. Boy, she was good for him. "The hell're we doing sitting here?"

He moved away from the window, found the two suitcases in the dark and picked them up.

"Let's go over to my house and get a drink and something to eat. Christ, I'm starving."

"Now you're talking," Mary said.

22

It seemed like seven years ago, in another life, coming out to bright sunlight to see Nolen in a lounge with a beer can resting on his chest, sandals and black socks V-ed as though he was sighting on that tanker bound for Port Everglades.

Moran said, "Well, here we are."

Nolen said, squinting through his sunglasses, "You want me to go first? All right. I waited in the bar out by Ninety-five all afternoon and Jiggs never called, so I came home. That's my story and I'm sticking to it. What's yours?"

"I was wondering," Moran said, "if you had any lemons."

Nolen waited for that to make sense to him and decided it didn't matter. "Yeah, I got some lemons."

"And I've got a blender," Moran said. "You didn't know that, did you? I'll get 'em when I pick up your trash. But I'm not gonna make your bed." He walked off toward the office saying, "I don't do beds."

Jerry was behind the counter looking through the mail delivery. Moran came around and pulled a black plastic trash bag from a Hefty box, Jerry saying, "Well, look at this." He handed Moran a letter. "Notice the postmark. Sosua, Rep. Dom. Is that anybody we know?"

Moran put the folded trash bag under his arm and opened the letter with a strange feeling, knowing it was from Luci Palma, the girl who used to run across rooftops . . . one page of ruled paper neatly handwritten, though each line rose on a slight angle, up and away and he thought, She hasn't changed. He read it standing there and put the letter in his shirt pocket when he finished. The letter made him feel good and at another time he would have read it to Jerry. But not now. He said to Jerry, "You call de Boya's again?"

"He still isn't back. Maid says they haven't seen him since yesterday. I called the Coral Gables Police, but they wouldn't tell me anything. Kept asking who I was, so I hung up."

"They get a lot of calls like that," Moran said. "How about that Trans-Am?"

"Still parked down the street."

"Jerry, you don't have to stay around . . ."

He said, "If I thought coming here was work, George, I wouldn't be doing it. I'm your police contact, aren't I?"

"You sure are. You got the number handy?"

"I know it by heart."

" 'Cause I might only say 'Jerry' but that's what it'll mean. Call 'em quick."

"They know my voice," Jerry said. As Moran went out he said, "Take her easy now. Don't do nothing dumb."

Moran said, "I keep trying not to." Nolen took a sip of beer, turned his head enough to see Moran come out of the office unfolding a trash bag and go into Number Five with the passkey. Nolen yelled over, "In the fridge! Hey, and bring a beer!"

Moran came out within a couple minutes, the trash bag hanging weighted now with beer cans and whatnot, the sack of lemons and a cold one he handed Nolen. Nolen took it and popped it open to hold the two cans now on his chest, soothing the erratic action of his heart.

He said, "The last time I saw you, George, you stormed out of here, determination flashing in your eyes. I guess you didn't get shot, did you?"

Moran said, "No, but I bet somebody did. De Boya never came home. Hasn't been seen since he drove off in his Rolls."

Nolen took a drink of beer. "With police swarming all over the place."

"I thought you didn't talk to Jiggs."

"George, if I'm inconsistent, what's the difference? We're just gonna lie to each other anyway." He raised his head and took a long sip from the other can.

"You drink two at once? You been putting it away lately," Moran said, "haven't you?"

"Jesus, you sound like my wife."

"Is that right? I didn't know you were married."

"Three times. You sound like any one of 'em," Nolen said. "I got to win soon, man, get the fuck outta here. You make me nervous, feel like I'm being watched."

"Well, there could be truth to that," Moran said. "You know that Cuban you say wears sunglasses at night and drives a Donzi?"

Nolen squinted in the sunlight, adjusting his own glasses. "What about him?"

"Does he also drive a Trans-Am, black one with the hood flamed red and gold? He's parked in front of the Nautilus, next door, and if he isn't watching you then he's watching me." Moran half-turned to look toward the beach. "There's another one out there on an army blanket getting a Cuban suntan with all his clothes on. Your pal Jiggs doesn't care for 'em, but he sure uses 'em, doesn't he? Like the Mendozas, Rafi. He seems to use everybody he can."

"Don't," Nolen said. "You played that one to death."

Moran said, "Remember the day you came here? We started talking about the D.R. and how some trooper across the Ozama almost killed me with a one-oh-six?"

"It was the next day," Nolen said. "We didn't talk much the first day. I registered and asked you where all your palm trees were. You wouldn't give me a deal on a room."

"But I did right after. You were trailing Anita de Boya and the piano player."

"I wonder if she's getting much these days."

"You were making a halfway honest living."

"Not bad. But living by your wits gets tiresome."

"Then you met Jiggs Scully. He still as funny as you thought he was?"

Nolen stared for several moments. He said, "George, the last thing I want is to see you get hurt. Will you do me a favor?"

"Let's talk about it in the house," Moran said, "while I whip up some sours. What do you say?" He started to go and looked at Nolen again, taking the letter from his pocket. "Guess who I heard from? Here, read it." Moran walked toward his house with the lemons and the trash bags.

Nolen puts his beers down and opened the letter.

Dear George Moran (Cat Chaser!!!):

Was that really you who was in Santo Domingo looking for me? At first I thought it was a lot of far fetch to think you would come here but then I think no it is something the Cat Chaser would do. (I got your address from the hotel) I am married now and have five big childrens going to school. I bet you dont know who I married. He is the one you shot and became wounded on the roof of the building that time. His name is Alejo Valera. He is a salesman of insurance and is also the manager of the Sosua baseball team. After that war he went to the training camp of the Cincinnati Reds but came home to play baseball here. He is very good. He say to tell you he is glad you did not kill him or we would not be married together and have our family. Well I must close this letter. I wish I had seen you but maybe some other time when you come. I tell people I know you and how brave you were in the war. You did not sit behind the barricades. You came to find us. I am very glad I did not shoot you. Do you still like the Rolling Stones? I like the Moody Blues now very much. Please come to see us.

Affectionately,
Luci Palma de Valera

Nolen straddled a stool at the counter, comtemplating the foamy pitcher of whiskey sours, wiping froth from his mouth with the back of his hand. "Much better in the blender. All the difference in the world," he said and slid his glass toward Moran behind the counter for a refill.

"Tangy, isn't it?"

"Perfect," Nolen said, "for getting that morning goatshit taste outta your mouth. How many eggs you put in?"

"One to a blender," Moran said.

"Yeah, four makes it too heavy. I overdid it. Which is nothing new, I guess. I figure I've got about two years before I land in the weeds and have to join AA. You get to that point your choice is lead a clean life or die."

"Why wait," Moran said, "if you know it's coming?"

"I'm trying to get in all the fun I can."

"Yeah, I've noticed what a good time you been having."

"Well, shit, I try." Nolen thought of something as he took a drink and said, "Hey, that was a nice letter. Luci sounds like a winner. That part, she thought it was a lot of far fetch." Nolen grinning, nodding, being a regular guy. "That was a long time ago, wasn't it? Down there in the D.R. Not knowing shit what was going on. But I had a pretty good time, you know it? Even though I only got laid once and had to take penicillin for it. Come back with a dose and my trusty Forty-five. I used to fire it from up on that grain elevator. For fun, not hit anything."

Moran said, "How about if I buy it off you?"

"George"—Nolen took off his sunglasses to look squarely at Moran—"Now we get down to it. I started to say to you outside, do me a favor. Use your head before it's too late. You have de Boya's money? Leave it over there in oceanfront Number One where you got your lady hiding and take off. Get far away from here."

Moran said, "How'd you know she's there?"

"The guy in the Trans-Am, Santos, was into B and E at one time. He snuck around here last night listening at doors. It's my guess if he heard anything it was in Number One and I'm right, that's where you got her, isn't it?" Nolen seemed proud of himself.

"Jiggs's coming for sure, uh?"

"You bet he is."

"How much you want for the gun?"

"It's not for sale. I'm telling you—you know all about how to take it and run; well, this time you gotta leave it and run."

Moran opened a drawer on his side of the counter. He brought out a packet of hundred-dollar bills secured with a money strap, a narrow paper band, and placed it in front of Nolen.

Nolen said, "Jesus Christ," and seemed afraid to touch it. "How much is that?"

"Ten thousand," Moran said.

Nolen's gaze came up, a solemn expression, mouth partly open. "You did it, didn't you? Jesus, you really did it."

"If that isn't enough . . ."

Moran reached into the drawer again, brought out another packet of inch-thick hundreds and laid it on top of the first one.

"How's that?"

"You're crazy."

Moran reached to take back the money.

"I'll go get the piece," Nolen said.

"I already have," Moran said. "When I picked up the trash. It's loaded, isn't it? Full clip?"

"Yeah but . . . George, don't try and be a hero, okay? You wouldn't have a chance. That man's a pro, it's what he *does.*"

"It gives me a little more confidence," Moran said, "that's all. I don't feel so helpless."

Nolen was looking at the money again, almost in a daze. He said, "You really did it, huh?" A wistful tone, subdued. "Will you tell me something?"

"Maybe," Moran said.

"How much you get? Both suitcases."

"No, I'm not gonna tell you that," Moran said. "It isn't any of your business. It isn't any of mine either, when you get right down to it."

"Your lady walked out of the house with it, didn't she?" Nolen said, watery eyes showing the pleasure of it. "Where can I get me one like her? Walked right out past her husband, Jiggs, everybody. Of course with you there to help."

"I didn't do much," Moran said. "But I'm looking after her best interest now. You understand I'm not gonna see anything happen to her." He watched Nolen touch the packets, finally pick them up and feel them, fingers gracefully playing along the edges, riffling the stiff new bills. "Nolen?"

"What?"

"When's Jiggs coming?"

"He said around noon. He said he'd set things up then get his eight hours and have a late breakfast. Then he'll stop by. That's how he said it, like it's a business call."

"What're you supposed to do?"

"Act dumb. Tell you I don't know anything, where Jiggs is or what he's doing," Nolen said. "But if you look like you're getting ready to leave I'm supposed to tell you he phoned and wants to see you for a minute, have a quiet talk."

"What do you do when he comes?"

"Exit. He's on then."

"Nolen?"

"What?"

"Where's de Boya?"

Nolen took a sip of whiskey sour and said without looking at Moran, "He's dead. So's Corky." Nolen's gaze came up slowly now. "Jiggs made them take their clothes off and get in the shower, both at once. Then he shot them."

"Because they didn't have the money?"

"He didn't even know it till after. He was so sure."

"Were you there?"

"When he did it? No, I came later."

"Where're they now?"

"Still in the shower. Place west of Lauderdale, out in the country."

"You don't suppose he's looking to make a deal," Moran said, "when he says he wants to talk."

"No, that's not Jiggs," Nolen said. "But he does have to talk to you, find out for sure you have the money and where it is. After that he'll kill you. That's why I'm saying leave it, forget the whole thing. You run with the money—it wouldn't work, I'm telling you." Nolen was emphatic now. "A woman like Mary de Boya, where's she gonna hide? The cops, once they find her husband, they'll be looking for her anyway. You see what I mean? It doesn't matter where she goes Jiggs'll be hanging around, threaten her till she pays up. So get it over with now, leave it." Nolen looked at his watch. "We've got less'n an hour."

Moran said, "You on our side now?"

Nolen said, "George, come on. You know where I am. Nowhere. The idea, score off a guy like de Boya, it sounded great, worth the risk. But I saw him in that shower, man . . . I got sick and you know what Jiggs did? He patted my back while I threw up on two guns down in the toilet, telling me he'd take care of me. I wanted, today, I wanted to *look* like I was helping him but tell you to get out and then disappear, go to L.A. and get lost among the weirdos and hope to Christ I never make a name for myself. You said it the other day, George, I'm in a no-win deal."

Moran said, "What if we call the cops?"

"And what?" Nolen said. "He sees cops he waits. The only way, you'd have to have 'em hiding in the closet when he takes his gun out and then pray they're quick."

Moran thought about it, picturing Jiggs standing in the living room. "He sure likes to talk, doesn't he? Goes on and on."

"He puts you half-asleep," Nolen said, "telling you stories. Like a fucking spell he puts over you."

"No, he never rushes into it," Moran said, "he gives you time to think."

"This's the first time in my life," Nolen said, "I'm gonna suggest we leave what's in the blender and get the hell out."

Moran said, "Stay there," walked around the counter and said, "Mary?"

She came out of the bedroom, her expression composed, eyes moving to Nolen to see him getting off the stool, surprised. She said, "Can you tell me exactly where Andres is?"

Nolen said, "I thought you were over in Number One. You've been right here all the time?"

"I wanted you to feel free to talk, be yourself," Moran said. "You said the place was west of Lauderdale."

"Yeah, like a farmhouse. Off Eighty-four."

Mary nodded, almost to herself. "I think I know where it is. Near the airport."

Moran said, "Let's wait a little while before we tell the police."

"But if you can't deal with him," Mary said, showing concern now as she looked at Nolen. "Isn't that right?"

Nolen shook his head. "I wouldn't even think about it."

"I just want to ask him something," Moran said. "Alone."

23

Jiggs stopped at the flamed Trans-Am and stuck his head in the passenger side. Hunched over like that his seersucker coat parted at the vent to show the seat of his pants hanging slack, as though he had no buttocks and all his weight was in front. When he straightened, pushing his glasses up, the Trans-Am came to life, rumbled and moved off. Jiggs came on to the Coconut Palms straightening his blue-striped tie, smoothing the front of his shirt. Entering the office he said to Jerry, "Hey, how you doing? My pal George around?" He looked at one of the inside windows and said, "Yeah, there he is. Nice seeing you again," and left Jerry adjusting his golf cap, staring after him as he went out to the swimming pool.

Jiggs saw Nolen in a lounge. He saw Mary in an expensive-looking T-shirt and white sailor pants also in a lounge, both of them up by the oceanfront walk in the sun, and a silent alarm went off in his mind. *Setup.*

He couldn't believe it; Moran didn't seem that dumb. Unless the cops were here and had coached him. *Make it look natural. Like nothing out of the ordinary is going on.* Fucking cops. Like they knew what they were doing. He saw Moran coming across from the front of his house, white T-shirt and old work jeans, barefoot. Maybe—it surprised Jiggs—Nolen was better at this than he gave him credit. Maybe these folks were in for a surprise and he'd tell in about half a second—now—all of them looking this way now and, yeah, they did seem to clutch up and were motionless as he approached them.

Jiggs said, "Beautiful day, huh? You get one of those hard rains it's always nice the next day. You notice that? Mrs. de Boya, how you doing? . . . George? Nolen there, he looks a little hung over. You okay, Nolen? Have a beer you'll feel better. I just had a pot of coffee. I wondered"—looking around—"George, you got a toilet I can use?"

"In the house," Moran said.

Yeah, something was up: Mary trying to act natural as she

looked at Moran, Christ, gripping the arms of the chair. You'd have to pry her hands off. Moran walked over to the house with him and held the door open. Very polite this morning.

"It's through the bedroom."

"Thank you, George, I appreciate it. Be only a minute."

Moran walked around to the kitchen side of the counter. He moved the blender and the sack of lemons aside. Squared the telephone around on the end of the counter. He got a bottle of scotch from the cupboard. Brought a bowl of ice out of the refrigerator. Found two clean glasses. He poured about an ounce and a half of scotch into one and drank it down. He heard the toilet flush. He put ice in the glasses and was pouring scotch when Jiggs came out pushing his glasses up, buttoning his seersucker jacket and then unbuttoning it to leave it open.

"There he is," Jiggs said. "I had to take a leak, George, but I also hoped we'd get a chance to talk, just the two of us if that was possible. You understand, not get emotional about anything, right? Why do that? What I thought, let's lay it out, look over what we have here."

Jiggs stepped back from the counter and glanced around the room.

"You don't have a tape going, any of that kinda stuff, do you, George? I wouldn't think so, but somebody might've talked you into it." He was looking at the hi-fi system now.

"I can put a record on," Moran said. "You like J. Geils?"

Coming back to the counter Jiggs said, "George, I don't know J. Geils from jaywalking, which is about the only thing I never was arrested for. That's an exaggeration, of course, but the point I want to make—" He picked up the drink Moran set before him. "Thank you, I believe I will. Little pick-me-up. The point I want to make, I've been arrested, well, quite a few times, suspicion of this and that, I think on account of the people I been associating with the past few years. But I never in my life been convicted of anything. I'm cherry, George, as far as doing any time and I'm sure you can understand why. Because I'm careful. Because I don't go walking in someplace I don't know what's on the other side of the door. Entrapment don't ever work with me, George; because I don't partake of controlled substances, I don't fuck lady cops dressed up like hookers and I don't deal with people I don't know. So there you are. If you think you got me to walk into something here and you're gonna pull the rope and the fucking net drops on me, don't do it. Okay? Let's just talk quietly and make sure we understand each other."

"Fine," Moran said. "What do you want?"

"I want the two suitcases and everything was in 'em. You can tell me something first," Jiggs said, "cause the suspense is killing me. How much we talking about?"

"Two million two hundred thousand," Moran said.

"I'll tell you something. I enjoy talking to you, George, you got a nice easy style. I told you that once before. All right, how 'bout this? You keep the two hunner K, that's yours, for your trouble. You and the widow're gonna have more dough'n you'll ever be able to spend anyway. And you give me the rest. How's that sound?"

"What if we don't give it to you?"

"Then you got a problem. I put a lot of time in this, George. See, I don't have a pension plan, profit-sharing, anything like that. This's gonna be my retirement and if it doesn't come through I can't complain to some insurance company, can I? No, I got to take my beef to you and Mary and you know what I mean by that. See, I'd rather part friends, George. Maybe stop around and see you sometime in the future—how're things going? Shoot the shit about old times—by the way, something else I got to know. Where'd he keep it? The money."

"Under his bed," Moran said.

"Come on, you're kidding me. Guys like that"—Jiggs shook his head—"they're simpleminded, you know it? Under the fucking bed . . . Now where is it, under yours? I'd believe it. Jesus, I'd believe anything now. Whatta you say, George?"

"Mary says no," Moran said. "You don't get it."

"Yeah, but what do *you* say?"

"It's her money."

"I bet you can talk her into it, George. Lemme show you something." Jiggs got off the stool again and looked around the room. "What's that down there, top of the bookcase? Looks like a vase."

"It's a vase," Moran said.

"You buy that thing, George?"

"It was here when I moved in."

"Keep looking at it," Jiggs said. "Don't look at me, look at the vase. I'm gonna show you a magic trick I do." Jiggs moved back toward the front door so Moran would have to turn to face him, see what he was doing. "You looking at it?"

"I'm looking at it," Moran said, staring at the vase that was about twelve or fourteen inches high and glazed with the portrait of an old-fashioned girl holding a bouquet of flowers.

"You ready?" Jiggs said.

"I'm ready," Moran said.

The vase came apart, fragments of china flying outward with only the sound of it breaking, pieces hitting the floor.

Moran turned to Jiggs who was holding an automatic with a silencer attached that looked bigger than the gun.

"That's my magic act," Jiggs said. "Not a sound, not even that little BB-gun pop you usually get with a suppressor. Could be in a movie, out the track, you're walking up Collins Avenue, anywhere. You fall over. Person right next to you'd never hear a thing. What's this, a heart attack? . . . You understand what I'm saying? Could happen anytime, anywhere." Jiggs came back to the counter unscrewing the silencer. He dropped it into his coat pocket as he got up on the stool. "Or, you give me the suitcases, we part friends, wish each other luck."

Moran said, "Is that the one you used on de Boya?"

"George, you don't gimme any credit at all, do you? You think I'm gonna walk around with a piece they can do a ballistics on? I got I think four of these left now. Regular model Thirty-nine Smith only modified. Designed originally for the Seals in Vietnam. Guys'd slip ashore in the Mekong, take out some slopes and their buddies never hear a thing. You fire a subsonic nine-millimeter round. Notice the sights're raised so you can aim over the suppressor. Got a nice foam-rubber grip." He held the pistol up for Moran to look at closely.

"Pretty nice."

Jiggs slipped it into his right-hand coat pocket and picked up his drink to take a sip. "Have I made my point?"

"I believe you," Moran said.

"See, I was to demonstrate this in front of Mrs. de Boya," Jiggs said, "she'd be liable to come apart on me."

"I doubt it," Moran said.

"Well, playing it safe, I know I can talk to you, George. You got a nice even temper'ment." He laid his arms on the edge of the counter and took another sip of his drink. "Tastes pretty good. I don't usually drink during the day except special occasions. Last time I had a drink in fact we were at the Mutiny. Here we got another special occasion. So what do you say?"

"I just want to ask you something," Moran said and then paused. "Well, you've probably answered it."

"Go ahead, George, don't be bashful."

"Well, you wouldn't want to just walk away, forget the whole thing?"

"Oh my," Jiggs said, "I thought you were listening. What were you doing there, George, having dirty thoughts while I'm telling you my story?"

"I want to be sure I have it straight," Moran said. "You're saying if we don't give you the money you're gonna kill both of us. It's that simple, right? It might not be right now—"

"Probably wouldn't be," Jiggs said.

"But it could be anytime."

"I'm patient up to a point."

"Okay, that's all I wanted to know," Moran said. He reached over and picked up the phone.

Jiggs watched him.

Moran said, "Jerry, call the cops." He hung up.

Jiggs said, "George, am I hearing things? What're you gonna tell 'em? Some bullshit about I threatened you? I say I didn't, it's my word against yours, George, you know that." Jiggs seemed tired and a little upset. "There's nothing you can give the cops they can put on me."

Moran took his time. He said, "I didn't call them for you."

There was a pause. He saw Jiggs on the edge, motionless, between knowing and not believing.

Moran brought Nolen's .45 out of the drawer close in front of him and had time to rest the butt on the counter, the barrel pointed at Jiggs's striped tie. He saw Jiggs's right hand come up, clearing the edge of the counter with the Smith and couldn't wait any longer than that. He pressed down on the butt as he pulled the trigger, pressed and pulled the trigger and saw Jiggs blown from the stool, saw his expression in that moment, mouth opening, and the next moment saw him lying on the vinyl floor, head pressed against the base of the sofa. He saw the seersucker turning red, saw the hand holding the gun move and shot him again, the first explosions still ringing in his ears. Within moments he heard the door bang open, Nolen and Mary in the room and saw their eyes, a glimpse of the look in their eyes; but his attention was on Jiggs as he came around from behind the counter with the .45 leveled, pointed at a down angle, a thought coming into his mind that he might or might not tell Mary about someday; thinking as he saw the blood he was glad he had not had the tile floor carpeted.

He went to one knee, picked up Jiggs's glasses from the floor and carefully placed them on him, pushing the bridge up on his nose, looking at Jiggs's eyes staring at him, not yet sightless but lost beyond bewilderment. His mouth moving soundless. What was there to say? Moran stood up.

He heard a voice say "Jesus" that sounded like Nolen and heard Mary close to him say "Moran?" Not sure now when she used his first name and when she used his last, if it depended on her mood or if it mattered. He felt . . . well, he felt all right. He felt much better than he did after shooting Luci's future husband on the roof in Santo Domingo in 1965. Was that why he went back—the real reason—because he had shot someone he didn't know? He wondered. The more he became aware of what he was feeling the more certain he was that he felt pretty good. Close to Mary, looking at those eyes full of warm awareness . . .

He said, "I don't have a lawyer. You think I'm gonna need one?"

Mary was smiling now, trying to. She said, "I don't know, George, you do pretty well on your own."

Finally there was that high-low wail in the distance, listening for it like he was always waiting to hear sirens. Boy, what next?

SPLIT IMAGES

For Bill Leonard

1

In the winter of 1981 a multimillionaire by the name of Robinson Daniels shot a Haitian refugee who had broken into his home in Palm Beach. The Haitian had walked to the ocean from Belle Glade, fifty miles, to find work or a place to rob, to steal something he could sell. The Haitian's name was Louverture Damien.

The bullet fired from Robbie Daniels's Colt Python did not kill Louverture immediately. He was taken in shock to Good Samaritan where he lay in intensive care three days, a lung destroyed, plastic tubes coming out of his nose, his arms, his chest and his penis.

Louverture said he had an argument with the people who lived in the same room with him in Belle Glade. He paid forty dollars a week for the room and twenty dollars deposit for a key to the bathroom. But they had stopped up the toilet and it couldn't be used. They cleaned fish, he said, and threw the heads in the toilet. Speaking in a mixture of languages and sounds, Creole and Bahamian British English, he said, "I came here to search for my life."

The Palm Beach Police detective questioning Louverture that evening in the hospital looked at him with no expression and said, "You find it?"

Lying in the white sheets Louverture Damien was a stick figure made of Cordovan leather: he was fourty-one years old and weighed one hundred seventeen pounds the morning he visited the home on South Ocean Boulevard and was shot.

Robbie Daniels was also forty-one. He had changed clothes before the police arrived and at six o'clock in the morning wore a lightweight navy blue cashmere sweater over bare skin, the sleeves pushed up to his elbows, colorless cotton trousers that clung to his hips but were not tight around the waist. Standing outside the house talking to the squad-car officer, the wind coming off the ocean out of a misty dawn, he would slip a hand beneath the sweater and move it over his skin, idly, remembering, pointing with the other hand toward the swimming pool and patio where there were yellow flowers and tables with yellow umbrellas.

"He came out. He crossed the yard toward the guest house. Then, once he was in the trees over there I didn't see him for, well, for a couple minutes. I started across. Got about right here. Yeah, just about here. And he was coming at me with the machete."

They could hear the high-low wail of the emergency van streaking west on Southern Boulevard, a far-off sound, fading.

As Mr. Daniels rubbed his bare skin the squad-car officer would catch a glimpse of the man's navel centered on his flat belly, tan and trim, the cotton trousers riding low, slim cut down to bare feet that were slender and brown. The squad-car officer, twenty-seven years old and in pretty good shape, felt heavy in his brown and beige uniform, his gunbelt cinched tight to support about ten pounds of police gear. He was from West Palm and had never been in a millionaire's home before.

"Sir, you chased him out of the house?"

"No, I thought he was gone. I got the gun, came out to have a look around. . . . I see *him* coming out, I couldn't believe it. He was still in the house when we got home."

The wind had been blowing for several days, the sky overcast, an endless surf pounding in. Mr. Daniels said he hadn't heard the man, it was more like he sensed him coming across the yard, turned and there he was.

The squad-car officer wondered at first if Mr. Daniels was a movie star. He had the features and that kind of sandy brown curly hair some movie stars had and never seemed to comb. The few lines in his face disappeared when he opened his eyes that were pale blue and seemed amazed in the telling of how he had actually shot a man. Twice in the chest.

"Sir, how many rounds you fire?"

"I'm sorry—what?"

"How many times you fire your gun?"

"Twice."

"What was he about, twenty feet away?"

"Closer. Ten feet maybe."

"Swinging the machete."

"What? Yes, raising it."

"But he didn't get a swipe at you."

"No."

Mr. Daniels seemed surprised, or else he seemed dazed or preoccupied, thinking about it and the squad-car officer's question would bring him back to now. Otherwise Mr. Daniels was polite and seemed anxious to be of help.

People were always seeing movie stars around Palm Beach and Mr. Daniels mentioned George Hamilton twice. He mentioned Shelley Berman and he mentioned Burt Reynolds. Mr. Daniels and some friends had gone up to Jupiter to the Burt Reynolds Dinner Theatre, saw "God's Favorite" and came back, had a few drinks at Charley's Crab, then stopped by a friend's house to visit. He said he got home at approximately four-thirty, quarter to five.

Out visiting that time of the morning. The young squad-car officer nodded. He had seen a young woman down at the far end of the living room that was like a hotel lobby. Younger than Mr. Daniels. Light brown hair parted on the side, not too long; black turtleneck. Eating an apple.

"Sir, your wife was with you?"

"She's in Aspen."

That stopped the young squad-car officer. "Aspen?"

"Colorado. She's skiing. A houseguest was with me."

"Could I have that person's name?"

"Angela Nolan. Put down journalist. She's been interviewing me for a magazine, some kind of story."

"So she came in with you?"

"Yeah, but when I realized someone had broken in, the way the place was tossed, I told Miss Nolan, stay in the foyer and don't move."

The squad-car officer paused. One of Mr. Daniels's words surprised him, bothered him a little.

"Sir, you know what if anything was taken?"

"No, you'll have to search the guy. I didn't touch him."

"How 'bout the help? Where were they?"

"The servants? They came out after."

"Must've heard the shots."

"I suppose so."

The young squad-car officer had a few more questions, but a detective arrived with the crime-scene people and the squad-car officer was sent out to South Ocean Boulevard to wave traffic past the police vehicles lining the road. Shit, what traffic? He was curious about a few things. He wondered if the houseguest, Angela Nolan, had seen any of the action. He wondered if Angela Nolan was staying in the main house or out in the guest house.

The young squad-car officer's name was Gary Hammond.

On the third day a woman who worked in a shirt factory in Hialeah and said she was Louverture Damien's wife came to Good Samaritan to sit at the man's bedside while he died.

Officer Gary Hammond was stationed outside the Haitian's hospital door now—in case the poor son of a bitch ripped out his tubes, somehow crawled out of bed and made a run for it. Gary would talk to the woman from time to time.

How come if she was married to Louverture she was living in Hialeah? To work, the woman said. Well, how come her husband didn't work there? The woman said because her husband believed to work every day was a bad thing. "If work was a good thing the rich would have it all and not let you do it." Grinning then, showing her ugly teeth.

Jesus, the old broad was putting him on.

The woman was as skinny as the man in the bed. An old leather stick with a turban and nine strands of colored beads. She told Gary her husband had found nothing in his life worthwhile. She told him her husband was sometimes a thief, but not a dangerous one. He was too weak or cowardly to hurt anyone.

Gary said if he was harmless then what was he carrying the machete for, to get some coconuts?

The woman told him her husband had no *mashe.* She said her husband run. The man say to him to stop. Her husband stop. The man say to him to come back with his hands in the air. Her husband does this. The man shoots him and *li tomber boum,* her husband falls with a great crash.

Gary said, "You believe that?"

The Haitian woman said, "If he lie he could tell a good lie, he can tell grand stories. But I don't know." She said, "I go home tonight and fetch a white chicken and kill it."

Gary said, "Yeah? Why you gonna do that?"

The woman said, "Because I'm hungry. I don't eat nothing today coming here."

Gary said, "Oh."

He told the detective investigating the case the man had died. The detective said, well, there were plenty more where he came from. They stood between two squad cars parked near the gate entrance to the estate.

Eyes half-closed in cigarette smoke the detective said, "What do you think this place would sell for?"

Gary said he supposed about a million.

The detective said, "Try three and a half. You know how many rooms are in that house? How many just bedrooms?"

The young cop had a hard time figuring the house out. It was classic sand-colored Spanish with a red-tile roof, common enough in Florida, except it was big as a monastery with wings and covered walks going out in different directions. Hard to make out because of all the vegetation: the shrubs and sea grape, royal palms, a hedge of hibiscus full of scarlet flowers hiding the wall that ran about three hundred feet along South Ocean Boulevard.

The detective said, "Six bedrooms up, four more in the guest house not counting the servants' wing. The place will sleep thirty without putting anybody on the couch."

How'd he know that?

"Authentic iron hardware on all the doors, you can pick any lock in the place with a screwdriver. It's got a sauna will hold about twenty naked bodies of either or both sexes."

The detective had been a Detroit cop before coming to Palm Beach. Middle-aged stocky guy with short arms that hung away from his body. That shitty-looking thin hair greased back in a shark-fin pompadour the young cop bet would hold for days without recombing. The guy sounded a little bit like Lawrence Welk the way he talked, not so much with an accent, but seemed to say each word distinctly without running words together. He seemed dumb, squinting with the cigarette in his mouth to get a half-assed shrewd look. But the guy did know things.

The young cop was still wondering about the houseguest. Was she staying in the main house or the other one? He asked the detective if he'd talked to her. Angela Nolan.

Yeah, he had talked to her.

She corroborate what Mr. Daniels said?

The detective, with nineteen years Detroit Police experience, began to look at the young squad-car officer from West Palm a little closer, dumb-shrewd eyes narrowing.

Why?

Gary Hammond said he was curious, that's all. Was there something going on there? You know, hip-looking broad here, the guy's wife off skiing?

The detective said, "You mean you want to know do I think he's fucking her? Yeah, I think he's fucking her. I think he'd be out of his fucking mind if he wasn't. Robbie Daniels doesn't strike me as being double-gaited or having any abnormal ideas what his dick is for," the detective said. "I mean outside the popular abnormal ideas that're getting more normal all the time."

Gary said he was just wondering.

The detective was not on the muscle. Sounding a little sour was his everyday tone when he wasn't intentionally kissing ass for information or some other purpose. At those times he sounded appreciative, sometimes humble.

He said, "Did I ask him, you want to know, if he's dicking her? No, I didn't. Did I ask if they're tooting cocaine, maybe blowing a little weed? No, I didn't ask him that either. The man comes home to his residence, finds this Haitian in there in the dark. The Haitian comes at him with a bolo or some fucking thing and Daniels shoots him. Now, you want me to try and find some holes in that? You want to implicate the broad, the houseguest, like maybe she's in with the Haitian, left the door open? Or how about we take a look, see if Daniels has got any priors? That what you want?"

"Well, for one thing," the young cop said, "the Haitian told it different."

"I bet he did," the detective said. "I bet he said he was fucking assaulted. You been out to Belle Glade lately?"

''Sure.''

''You see how they jungle-up out there, how they live, you want to call it that? There's all kinds of work out there. Every day five, six in the morning the buses are waiting. No—this guy comes all the way from Belle Glade, stops by four-thirty in the morning see if they got any odd jobs, cut the grass or some fucking thing. Comes strolling up to the guy with a machete and the guy shoots him, you think something funny's going on.''

Gary Hammond was patient. He was going to say what was bothering him.

''He said something to me, Mr. Daniels. He said he come in—he realized somebody was there from the way the place was tossed.''

''Yeah? . . .''

''He used the word *tossed.*''

''So?''

''I don't know, it seemed weird. Like he used the word all the time, Mr. Daniels.''

The detective said, ''He say it was going down when he got home? How about, he looked at the guy but couldn't make him? TV—all that kind of shit come out of TV. They get to be household words. *Tossed,* for Christ sake.''

''What about the Colt Python?''

''Cost him four and a half. I told him I could have got him a deal in Detroit.''

''I mean is it registered?''

''Jesus Christ, get out of here, will you.''

''Okay, but can I ask one more thing?''

''What?''

''Robbie Daniels—he isn't a movie star, is he?''

The detective said, ''Jesus Christ, the man owns companies. He's got a big plant in Detroit supplies the auto industry with something or other. Has a development company owns land in seven states and down in the Caribbean islands. Resort hotels, condos, all that development shit. He's worth like in the neighborhood of a hundred million bucks—you want to know he's a fucking movie star.''

* * *

The detective, wearing a light blue wash-and-wear suit over a dark blue sport shirt and a cream-colored tie, the open suit coat tight around his arms and shoulders, waited for the young squad-car officer to drive off before he buzzed for somebody to open the gate.

Mr. Daniels wanted to talk.

The detective had not been told this. He knew it the way he would know from a woman's glance in a bar there it was if he wanted any. The only difference here, he didn't know what Mr. Daniels had in mind. The detective had already gone down the list.

He isn't gonna ask you you want to play tennis or fucking polo, anything like that. Ask you you want to join the Seminole Club.

He isn't gonna ask you who your stockbroker is.

He isn't gonna waste his time, chitchat about this and that. Though it would start that way.

What can you do he can't—outside of pressing two hundred ninety-five pounds straight up over your head? He thought about this following the drive that was lined with royal palms, but couldn't think of a good reason why the man would want to talk to him.

The detective's name was Walter Kouza.

''What's going to happen, not much at all,'' Walter Kouza said. ''They'll run it past a grand jury, Palm Beach County Criminal Court. They have to do that in the case of a homicide. The jury will practically be instructed to call it justifiable and that's it.''

''I have to appear, though,'' Robbie Daniels said.

''Yes, you have to appear, tell what happened. You're the only one knows, right? I take the stand, describe what the crime-scene people found—evidence of forcible entry, your gold cigarette lighter in the guy's pocket, Exhibit A, the machete—you'll be out in about twenty minutes.''

There would be a silence and Mr. Daniels would nod to himself, getting it straight in his mind. The detective was surprised Mr. Daniels didn't act bored or like he was better than anybody else. He seemed like a nice down-to-earth fellow. Sat with a leg hooked over his chair. White cashmere today against his tan;

faded jeans, gray and white Nike tennis shoes with the strings untied. The detective bet the guy never picked up his room when he was little or combed his hair. He still didn't.

He did kind of look like a movie star.

Or a cheerleader.

That was it. And the detective was the football coach. Big Ten. The two of them sitting around shooting the shit after the game. Only the coach called the cheerleader mister and maintained a pleasant expression.

Silence didn't bother the detective. He liked silence, waiting for the other fellow to speak. He liked the afternoon sunlight, the way it filtered through palm trees and filled the living-room-window wall twenty feet high. Sunlight made a silence seem longer because there was no way to hurry sunlight. You couldn't turn it off. He liked the cheerleader-coach idea too and thought of Woody Hayes. Woody Hayes had probably never spoken to a cheerleader in his life outside of get the fuck out of the way. But this coach would talk to this cheerleader, yes *sir,* and wait until spoken to.

What he didn't like was not seeing an ashtray around anywhere; he was dying for a cigarette.

"Will there be any problem with the gun?"

"The one you used? No, I don't see a problem. I assume, Mr. Daniels, the gun's registered."

The cheerleader nodded again, thoughtful. "Yeah, that one is."

That one. The guy still nodding as the detective waited, in no hurry.

"Hey, listen, why don't we have a drink?"

"Fine," the detective said, "if you're going to have one."

He thought a servant would appear and they'd have to wait around for the servant to appear again with his silver tray. But the cheerleader jumped up—let's go—and led the detective through a back hall, up a narrow spiral stairway to an oval-shaped castle door Mr. Daniels had to unlock. Not the wrought-iron crap, Walter noticed, but Kwikset deadbolt double locks. The door creaked. Walter saw shafts of light in narrow casement windows, an oriental carpet, bigger than any he'd seen off a church altar, books from floor to ceiling, inlaid cabinets. Spooky, except for the oak bar and art posters that didn't make sense.

Walter said, "You must read a lot."

Robbie Daniels said, "When I'm not busy."

They drank Russian vodka on the rocks, Walter perched on a stool with arms, Daniels behind the bar—long-legged guy—one tennis shoe up on the stainless-steel sink. Hardly any sunlight now: track lighting, a soft beam directly above them and the rest of the room dim. Walter wanted a cigarette more than ever. There was a silver dish on the bar, but he didn't know if it was an ashtray.

He said, "Detroit, I had a bar down in the rec room, all knotty pine, had these ashtrays from different hotels, you know, different places."

"That's right," Robbie said. "I forgot, you're from Detroit."

"As a matter of fact born and raised in Hamtramck," Walter said. "Twenty-three sixteen Geimer. Went to St. Florian's, Kowalski Sausages right down the street if you know that area, or you happen to like kielbasa. Yeah, my old man worked at Dodge Main thirty-two years. You know they're tearing it down. GM's putting up a Cadillac assembly plant, buying all that land around there from the city. The city tells the residents, a lot of them these old people, what they're gonna give them for their houses, that's it, take a hike. Ralph Nader, you say GM to him he gets a hard-on, he's mixed up in it now . . . Yeah, technically I was born in Hamtramck, been a Polack all my life." Walter Kouza paused. His eyes, deep beneath his brows, showed a glimmer of anticipation.

"You know who lived not too far away? John Wojtylo." He waited. "The pope's cousin. Yeah, you know. John Paul the Second?"

"Is that right?" The cheerleader gave him an interested little grin.

"Yeah, the cousin use to work over to Chrysler Lynch Road. He was a sandblaster. Only the pope spells it different. Wojtyla. With an *a* on the end 'stead of a *o*. He's a Polack too. Hey, and how about that other Polack, Lech Walesa? He something? Doesn't take any shit from the communists."

Walter's blunt fingers brought a pack of Camels and a green Bic lighter from his shirt pocket. "And you live, your residence is in Grosse Pointe, if I'm not mistaken." He looked again at the silver dish on the bar; it was within reach.

The cheerleader was nodding, very agreeable. "Right, Grosse Pointe Farms."

"I could never keep those different Grosse Pointes straight. You live anywhere near Hank the Deuce?"

"Not far."

"There Fords all around there, uh?"

"A few. Henry, Bill, young Edsel now."

"They got, in the barber college right there on Campau near Holbrook? Heart of Hamtramck, they got a chair Henry Ford sat in once, got his haircut. I don't mean at the barber college, when the chair was someplace else."

"That's interesting," Robbie said. He took a drink and said, "You mentioned the other day you were with the Detroit Police."

"Nineteen years," Walter said. "Started out in the Eleventh Precinct. Yeah, then I moved downtown, worked Vice, Sex Crimes, Robbery . . ." Walter lighted his Camel and pulled the silver dish over in front of him. Fuck it. "It was never boring, I'll say that."

"You ever shoot anybody?"

"As a matter of fact I have," Walter said.

"How many?"

"I shot nine people," Walter said. "Eight colored guys, one Caucasian. I never shot a woman."

"How many you kill?"

"I shot nine, I killed nine." Walter let himself grin when he saw the cheerleader begin to smile, eating it up.

"They were all DOA except this one guy, a jig, hung on three hundred sixty-seven days, if you can believe it. So technically his death wasn't scored as a hit. I mean he didn't dic of gunshot, he died of like kidney failure or some fucking thing. But it was a nine-millimeter hollow nose, couple of them, put him in the hospital, so . . . you be the judge."

"How about down here?" Robbie said.

"The guy was a quadriplegic, I mean when he died."

"Have you shot anyone down here?"

"In Palm Beach? I don't know if I tried to draw my piece it would even come out. No, I haven't, but the way things are going, all these fucking Cubans and Haitians coming in here . . ." Walter stopped. "I got to watch my language."

Robbie gave him a lazy shrug, relaxed.

Walter said, "Anyway, with the refugees coming in, lot of them jerked out of prison down there in Cuba . . . I know a gun shop in Miami I mentioned to you, guy's got three outlets, he's selling five hundred thousand bucks worth of handguns a *month*. Guy's making a fortune. He's got a range, he's teaching all these housewives come in how to fire three-fifty-sevens, forty-fives . . . Can you see it? Broad's making cookies, she's got this big fucking Mag stuck in her apron. But that's what it's coming to. It didn't surprise me at all a man of your position would have that Python. It's a very beautiful weapon."

The cheerleader was pouring them a couple more. "What do you carry?"

"Now? A Browning nine-millimeter." Walter laid his cigarette on the silver dish, raised his hip from the stool as he went in under his suit coat, pulled the weapon from the clip-on holster that rode above his right cheek and placed it on the bar, nickel plate and pearl grip sparkling in the cone of overhead light.

"Nice," the cheerleader said.

"Detroit I packed a forty-four Mag and a thirty-eight Smith Airweight with a two-inch barrel. But that's when I was working STRESS. As a matter of fact, eight of the guys I took out it was when I was with STRESS."

"I sorta remember that," Robbie said.

"Stop the Robberies, Enjoy Safe Streets."

"I'm not sure I ever knew what it meant."

"Yeah, Stop the Robberies . . . and so on. That was . . . let me see, I was on it back in '72, '73. We'd go in teams in a hot street-crime area, inner city. Dress like you live around there. One guy's the decoy, the target. Stroll down the street maybe act like you're drunk or you're a john looking for some quiff. The other guys lay back, see if you attract anything. See, we used teams of four. That would be your decoy, your backup, he'd be like another bum or civilian of some kind, then you'd have two more guys in the car, they covered you. We cut street crime way down, confiscated something like over four hundred guns. We had to shoot some people to do it but, well, it's up to them."

The cheerleader seemed to smile as he frowned, liking the idea but with reservations. "Isn't that entrapment?"

Walter said, "Hey, they named the game. All we did, we played it with 'em."

Robbie said, "May I?"

Walter said, "Sure." If the guy owned a Python he could handle a Browning. He watched Daniels heft the nickel-plated automatic, extending it now to take a practice sight. But then looked up, lowering the gun.

A woman's voice said, "Don't shoot. I'll leave quietly."

Walter made a quarter turn on his stool.

The houseguest, Angela Nolan, stood in the oval doorway. She was wearing a long navy blue coat with her jeans, over what looked like a workshirt and a red neckerchief. She said, "I'm on my way."

Robbie raised his eyebrows. "You're finished with me?"

"No, but . . ." the girl paused. "Could I talk to you for a minute?"

Robbie said, "Maybe some other time."

"I've got a plane. I just want to ask you something."

"Yeah . . . Go ahead."

"Could you come downstairs?"

"Not right now," Robbie said.

It was the girl's turn. Walter Kouza waited, feeling something now, a tension that surprised him: the two of them trying to sound polite, but with an edge, Mr. Daniels's edge just a hint sharper than the girl's.

She said, "Thanks, Robbie, I'll see you."

He said, "Angie? Don't go away mad."

The doorway was empty. Walter swiveled back to the bar as Robbie added, "As long as you go," and shook his head, patient but weary.

Walter said, "Gee, she walks out—I thought you extended her every courtesy. She's a writer, uh?"

Robbie was fixing up their drinks.

"Suppose to be doing a piece for *Esquire,* part of a book. At least that's what she told me. Like, 'The Quaint Customs of the Rich' or some goddamn thing. She tells me go ahead, do whatever I do, she'll *observe,* take some pictures and we can talk later. Fine. I'm on the phone most of the time I'm down here."

"I can imagine," Walter said.

"But then I sit down with her, she turns on her tape recorder—you know what she asks me?"

Walter shook his head. "What?"

"What's it like to be rich? Am I happy? She goes from that to, What do I think about abortion? What do I think about *busing* . . . I couldn't believe it. Or, If you can have anything you want, what turns you on more than anything? Another one, related to that. If you have all the money you could possibly spend in a lifetime, why do you keep making more? I try to explain that the money itself is only a way of keeping score, but she doesn't understand that."

Walter didn't either.

"But then if I don't have time to sit down and talk, she gets pouty. I couldn't believe it. Really, like I'm taking up *her* time. She seems intelligent, you know, has some good credits, but when a broad comes on like it's the Inquisition and then gives you that pouty shit . . . I said wait a minute. I agreed to be interviewed, yes, but you could get fucking washed out to sea tomorrow and I doubt anybody'd miss you."

"You told her that?"

"Why not? She came to me."

"Jesus, that's pretty nice stuff. I thought maybe she was like, you know, a girl friend."

Robbie said, "A girl friend? You look at her close? She's okay, but she's got to be thirty years old, at least. No, what she does, she gets you relaxed, talking off the cuff like she's your buddy, but what she's doing is setting you up. She's a ball buster," Robbie said. "I told her that. I said you don't care what I think. You interview somebody with a name, you just want to cut off his balls, make him look like a wimp. You know what she said? She said, 'I don't have to cut 'em, they come off in my hand.' I said well, not this pair, love. Go fondle somebody else.''

Walter Kouza said, ''Jesus.'' He never again thought of Mr. Daniels as a cheerleader.

He considered himself an ace at sizing people up:

A guy shoots and kills an intruder. The guy seems not exactly shaken but awed by it. A bright eager good-looking guy. Sort of a millionaire Jack Armstrong but very impressionable.

Yeah?

Walter Kouza would run through those first impressions again, then piece together step by step the revelations of that afternoon in Mr. Daniels's study.

He remembered Mr. Daniels, Robbie, opening the second bottle of vodka and going downstairs for more ice . . .

Yeah, and he opened another pack of Camels while Daniels was gone. Tore off the cellophane, dropped it in the silver dish full of cigarette butts, mashed Camel stubs. He remembered seeing words engraved around the rim of the dish he hadn't noticed before. *Seminole Invitational 1980* and the club crest covered with butts and black smudges. Shit. He got off the stool to look for a regular ashtray and almost fell on his ass. There weren't any ashtrays. He was standing there looking at the inlaid cabinets—beautiful workmanship—when Daniels came back in, closing the door this time, turning the lock, and said, ''While you're up, let me show you something might interest you.'' Took out a key and unlocked one of the cabinets.

There must have been two dozen handguns in there, a showcase display against dark velvet.

''Jesus,'' Walter said.

There were Smith and Wesson thirty-eights and three-fifty-sevens, in Chief Special and Combat Masterpiece models, two- and four-inch barrels. He had a Walther P thirty-eight, a Baretta nine-millimeter Parabellum. He had Llama automatics, several, including a thirty-two and a forty-five. A Llama Commanche three-fifty-seven, an Iver Johnson X300 Pony, a Colt forty-five Combat Commander, a Colt Diamondback and a Detective Special. He had a big goddamn Mark VI Enfield, a Jap Nambu that looked like a Luger. Christ, he had a ten-shot Mauser Broomhandle, nickel-plated, a Colt single-action Frontier model, a couple of little Sterling automatics. Walter's gaze came to rest on a High Standard Field King model, an ordinary twenty-two target pistol except for the barrel. The original five-and-a-half-inch barrel had been replaced by a factory-made suppressor, or silencer, that was at least ten inches long, fabricated in two sections joined together.

Walter pointed. "Can I see that one?"

Robbie handed him the twenty-two target gun.

"You turning pro?" Walter said and chuckled. He looked at the suppressor closely. "Jesus, Parker-Hale. You mind, Rob, I ask where you got it?"

"I'll tell you this much. The guy who sold it to me," Robbie said, "has a metallic gold-flocked sawed-off shotgun that matches his Cadillac."

Walter remembered saying, "Well, this little number right here," hefting the twenty-two, "this is the one the pros use, not to mention the CIA."

Robbie said, "Wait." He unlocked the cabinet beneath the handgun cabinet and said, "I've got some pieces here might surprise you, to say the least. The thing is, I'm not supposed to have them."

Even at this point he would seem naive and trusting, looking at Walter with his earnest nice-guy expression.

Walter said, "Rob, this is my day off. I don't run anybody in when I don't have to and I haven't been surprised at anything since I found out girls don't have weenies."

Robbie said, "I trust you, Walter," and brought out a forty-five U.S. Army submachine gun with a wire stock. He said, "M-three."

Walter said, "Jesus Christ."

Robbie was bringing out more submachine guns. "Sten, very old. Uzi, the Israeli number, needs some work but usable. German machine pistol . . . Ah, but here's my favorite . . ." It was MAC-ten with a thirty-two-round clip, all cammied-up for field duty. The compact little submachine gun was painted with free-form shapes in rose and dark blue on a light blue background, like a wallpaper design.

Walter stared. He took the weapon in his hands, caressed the pipelike attachment screwed onto the barrel stub.

"Silencer's bigger'n the gun, isn't it? Jesus. How much you pay for this?"

"Fifteen hundred," Robbie said, "in Miami."

"With the silencer?"

"No, the suppressor was five hundred extra."

"I could've got you the piece in Detroit for a K," Walter said. "The suppressor—yeah, that's about five anywhere you shop." Walter started to grin. "What're you doing, Rob, going to war?"

Robbie said, "Nothing that big."

Walter was sitting at the bar again when he explained about the trial coming up next month in Detroit: this family bringing suit against the police department and Walter Kouza for something like five million bucks. "Remember I said I shot a guy but he didn't die right away? . . . Rob?"

"I'm listening."

"Well, this was only a couple years ago, not when I was in STRESS. The guy I shot's got a brother was in Jackson, was in Marquette, and learned a few things there talking to the jailhouse lawyers. Comes out, he files this suit in his mother's name. Like by shooting her son I denied the family all the millions he would have made at the car wash, plus another few million pain and suffering, even though the guy's fucking paralyzed from the neck down, can't feel a thing. Me and the department, we denied the mother all the benefits she would have gotten if the asshole had not been shot. Yeah, they come all the way down here, give me a subpoena." He remembered saying, "Hey, come on, Rob, bull-shit. We're about as much alike . . . listen, I'll tell you something. I was six-two and had curly hair and I had a name like Mark Harmon, Scott Hunter . . . Robbie *Daniels,* shit, and I had *money?* I'd be fucking dead by now. I'd have burned myself out by the time I was thirty. No. I'm Walter Chester Kouza and there isn't a fucking thing I can do about it."

He said, "Can I drive a limousine? Rob, you drive a car you can drive a limo. I'll tell you what, though, I would never wear any chauffeur's uniform, fucking hat with the peak . . . Bodyguard, that's something else. Sure, I'd drive you though. Like around Detroit? Sure."

He remembered Robbie saying, "You sound like someone—yeah, you sound just like him. What's his name, you know . . ."

"Is this fellow, he's got an orchestra, he goes a-one and a-two and? . . ."

"Karl Malden. That's who you sound like."

Walter said, "Karl *Malden?*"

He could see Robbie over by a wall of books. Slim guy, standing hip-cocked. One hand, he's like rubbing his stomach underneath the white sweater, stroking himself. The other hand, he's pointing to different books, taking some of them partway out and shoving them back in.

Robbie saying, "A guy is hired to kill somebody, a woman, and falls in love with his intended victim. A man with no money, no known enemies, is murdered. Who did it?"

"Guy's wife," Walter said.

"Lot of who-done-its," Robbie, said, "But I'm not talking about that. Here's one. A famous hunter risks his life simply to put his sights on Adolf Hitler. Great book. Here, another one. The hired assassin is out to kill de Gaulle. This one, Winston Churchill. Here, the president's daughter is shot."

"His daughter?"

"Ah, but were they aiming at the president? Presidents are always good."

"Like Abraham Lincoln," Walter said. "Guy pulled that one didn't know what the fuck he was doing."

"Here, the victim's J. Edgar Hoover. This one, Martin Bormann."

Walter had never heard of Martin Bormann.

"An African dictator . . . A right wing newspaper columnist. Here, a guy *running* for president . . . Another African dictator. Dictators are fun. Murder in Moscow, a triple with the victims' faces removed. Beauty."

"Who's behind all this?" Walter said. "I mean in the books."

"Who's paying for it? Big money, big oil, the CIA. Self-appointed world savers . . ."

* * *

He remembered Robbie sitting next to him at the bar, in the cone of soft light.

Robbie saying, "I didn't say who do you think deserves to be killed. It's not a moral question I'm asking. I said who would you *like* to kill, anybody in the world, assuming you have the resources, whatever you need. You can go anywhere, hire anyone you feel can be trusted, like that."

"I already got one," Walter said, "the Ayatollah. What's his name, Asshollah Khomeini, take that sucker out."

"Not bad," Robbie said, "but I think we should be a little more realistic. I mean you land at Tehran, but where are you? I think it's got to be someone who's relatively accessible."

Walter thought some more, smoking, drinking his vodka. He wished he had a beer to go with it.

He said, "This is fun, you know it?"

Robbie grinned. "I thought you'd like it."

"Jesus—Fidel Castro!"

"You want a challenge, uh?"

"Slip into Cuba by boat," Walter said, "wait for the sucker to drive by someplace."

"I think you're into a storybook situation there," Robbie said. "You're right, there're some good ones. Yasir Arafat, the PLO guy. Qaddafi in Libya. I don't know what you might think of Ahmed Yamani." Robbie paused. "No, I guess Yamani's all right."

Good. Because Walter had never thought one way or the other about Ahmed Yamani in his life.

Robbie said, "But those are the kinds of names that are done in books and the situations are about as real as the heroes. You know what I mean? The hero's a superstar. Former Green Beret, CIA, KGB double agent, colonel in Army Counter-Intelligence. Can speak about seven languages including Urdu and Tamil. Expert with any kind of weapon ever invented and has a black belt in Tae Kwon Do. His hands are lethal weapons, ah, but manicured. You know the kind of guy I mean?"

"Sure, very cool. Has all these broads around—"

"But grim," Robbie said. "The serious type."

Walter was nodding. "Yeah, dedicated. Never looks around—

wait a minute, the fuck am I doing here? Like any normal person.''

''That's what I mean,'' Robbie said. ''Looking at it realistically . . . and we put our minds to it, decide to take somebody out . . . who would it be?''

''Somebody who's a real asshole,'' Walter said, thinking hard. ''In fact this fellow—tell me if I'm wrong, Rob—he's not only a rotten son of a bitch should be put away, he's fucking evil. Hey, and he can be dangerous. You don't just walk in and do him.''

Robbie was nodding. ''That's the guy.''

Walter thought some more; he looked up.

''You got one?''

''Well . . . I might.''

''Who is it?'' Walter waited.

Robbie smiled. ''Not yet.''

''Come on, Rob, you can tell me.''

Robbie said, ''I'm not even sure you want to make the move. You've been a cop a long time.''

Walter said, ''You kidding? I'll quit today.''

''What about your wife?''

''She can stay in Florida, get a job wrestling alligators. No—Irene'll be fine. Don't worry about it.''

Robbie nodded. For a moment there was silence.

Walter said, ''Come on, who is it?''

Robbie said, ''Walter, I'm gonna have to insist on a couple of things. First, no more Rob, or Robbie. From now on I'm Mr. Daniels. Is that understood?''

Walter managed to smile. ''No problem, Mr. Daniels. How's that?''

''The other thing,'' Robbie said, ''the day you come to work for me you're gonna have to quit smoking.''

2

Bryan Hurd watched Walter talking with his hands to his lawyer. They were in the hall outside the courtroom, tenth floor, Detroit City-County Building.

You could be wrong about him, Bryan thought.

Or maybe he's changed.

When Walter saw him he tucked his chin in like a fighter but grinned as he said, "There he is. Bryan, how the hell are you? Lieutenant Hurd now, uh? Homicide, getting up in the world. I was just saying to Eddie—Bryan, shake hands with Eddie Jasinski. Eddie's representing me in this deal. I was just saying to Eddie, you believe it? Secret Service're standing there, the guy squeezes off six rounds, empties the piece, then, *then* they're all over him. They all got a hand in there, all want to touch him, tell everybody how they grabbed the guy—what's his name, Hickle?—he's in there somewhere under this pileup, you can't even fucking *see* him."

No, he hasn't changed, Bryan thought.

"Then this other thing, Jesus Christ, the motive, thing with the broad? What's her name, Jodie Foster? Gain her respect and love—I never even heard of her. You can understand the guy wanting to make it with say, you know, Raquel Welch, one of those. I could even understand—no, I'll tell you the broad I'd kill for, Jesus, Norma Zimmer. But doing it for some teenage broad? Guy's got to be out of his fucking mind."

He hasn't changed a bit, Bryan thought. He was going to ask him who Norma Zimmer was, but Walter's lawyer was taking him aside, getting ready for the hearing.

Angela Nolan sat in the second row of the nearly empty courtroom, sunlight on pale varnished wood all around her. She began to write in her notebook, underlining key words or when she felt like it.

Wayne Circuit Court.

Pretrial *evidentiary hearing*. A motion by Kouza's lawyer to exclude Kouza's record as STRESS cop. Plaintiff's lawyer wants it in.

Judge. Robert J. Solner, 50s. Familiar with everyone. Goofs around with lawyers and witness (?). Tells story, lawyers laugh on cue, witness only smiles.

Defendant. Walter Kouza. Eats Certs like candy.

Def. Lawyer. Edward Jasinski, 50s. Expression of perpetual disbelief. Or fear.

Plaintiff. Ms. Jeanette Moore, 40s. Buddha in black dress and turban, white purse. Doesn't move or speak.

Plaintiff's son. Curtis Moore, 20s. Stud. Good moves, stage presence. Brother of *Darius Moore*, deceased—what it's all about.

Plaintiff's Lawyer. Kenneth Randall, 50s. Bill Russell in $500 gray suit, pearl tie. Cultured black cool.

Witness. Might be a cop. Or another lawyer. Nifty.

Angela looked up, glanced around. She wondered if Robbie would make an appearance, give his new bodyguard moral support. It wouldn't surprise her; strange things were happening.

Mr. Randall said, "Your Honor, we gonna be somewhat relaxed today, are we not?"

Judge Solner said, "What's the matter, you have a hard night?"

Mr. Randall said, "I hit my knee playing racquetball, Your Honor. Hit it with my own racquet, like a fool."

Walter Kouza and Edward Jasinski, sitting at the defense table, seemed lost, their heads turning in unison from the judge to Kenneth Randall, and back again, back and forth; spectators.

Judge Solner said, "Sounds like a good time to get you out on the court."

Mr. Randall said, "I'll stand up, Your Honor, you want me to. The pain isn't quite unbearable."

Judge Solner said, "It's all right, stay where you are . . . Mr. Jasinski, this is your motion, I believe."

"Yes, Your Honor"—rising briskly—"Your Honor, since the Detroit Police STRESS operation ended some eight years ago I see no reason to refer to my client's record as a STRESS officer, as exemplary as it may be, in any way, shape or form during trial proceedings."

Mr. Randall said, "What Mr. Jasinski means, the city's already paid out five, six million in STRESS-related damages. STRESS is a bad word and he doesn't want it mentioned in front of a jury."

Mr. Jasinski said, "Your Honor, this case has got nothing to *do* with STRESS!"

Mr. Randall said, "Same instability on the part of the police officer is involved. The point I want to make, Your Honor, is that Mr. Walter Kouza, based on his record with STRESS, should never have been allowed on the street. And if he hadn't, my client's baby boy would still be alive."

Veins stood out in Mr. Jasinski's neck. "The kid was nineteen years old! If he wasn't on probation he was in DeHoCo!"

Judge Solner said, "Mr. Jasinski, I didn't want you to have a heart attack in my courtroom. Calm down. Mr. Randall, save your act for the jury and tell the court how you want to proceed."

Mr. Randall said, "I'd like to call a witness, Your Honor, who was on STRESS back at the same time as Mr. Kouza and was also present—in fact it was his investigation—at the time the defendant shot Darius Moore. I'd like to call Lieutenant Bryan Hurd, Detroit Police Homicide, Squad Five."

Judge Solner did not say anything for several moments, his gaze not moving from Mr. Randall. He said then, "You represent the plaintiff and you're going to ask a police officer to describe the actions of a fellow police officer in a suit against the police department?"

Mr. Randall said, "Like expert testimony, Your Honor." And seemed to smile.

"Lieutenant, what was the purpose of the STRESS operation?"

"To interdict street crime in high-incident areas."

"Sounds like you're reading it," Mr. Randall said. "So you mingle with the civilians, pretend to be one of us?"

"That's right," Bryan said.

"Which suggests to me," Mr. Randall said, "an omnipresent, omniscient police force indistinguishable from the citizenry, ready to stop crime in progress or prevent its occurrence. Was that the lofty aim?"

Bryan said, "Or hold crime to acceptable limits."

"Now you sound like General Haig. That what the book says?"

"There is no book," Bryan said.

"Give you a gun, send you out to do the best you can, huh? . . . What kind of gun you carry on STRESS?"

"I carried a Smith and Wesson nine-millimeter."

"What else?"

"That's all."

"Didn't have another one down in your sock?"

"No."

"I thought STRESS cops carried two, three guns," Mr. Randall said. "Well, let's see." He looked at his file, open on the table, and said, "Lieutenant, I've got one, two, three . . . *four* incidents here in which Mr. Walter Kouza fired at fleeing robbery suspects after identifying himself as a police officer, killing all four of them. Tell me something. Why didn't he fire a warning shot?"

Bryan said, "Because a warning shot can kill someone blocks away, somebody looking out a window."

Mr. Randall said, "All right. What if you fire straight up in the air?"

Bryan said, "When the point man fires there's no way for his backup to tell a warning shot from any other kind. They could reach the scene and fire on a suspect who's already surrendered."

"Sounds very military," Mr. Randall said. "War in the streets. That how you feel about it?"

"No," Bryan said.

"I believe you quit STRESS after three months. Why was that?"

"I didn't like it."

"You're in Homicide now—you telling the court you don't like killing?"

"I thought it created more problems than it solved."

"Not to mention lawsuits," Mr. Randall said. "What did you think of Walter Kouza as a STRESS officer?"

Angela Nolan waited. She had underscored *black cool* in her Kenneth Randall notes and added: *Showboat, but fun to watch.*

Under *Witness* she had crossed out the line of notes and written in *Lt. Bryan Hurd,* as he spelled it for the court reporter. Now she underscored it and added *NIFTY* again in capital letters. She liked the way he sat straight but relaxed in his slim-cut dark navy suit and did not become indignant. She liked his hair and his bandit mustache, his hair long but not too long, not styled, and the way his mustache curved down and made him seem a little sad. She liked the way he looked directly at Walter Kouza as he answered Randall's question.

"I think he had a tendency to overreact."

Mr. Randall said, "Yeah, but isn't that the type volunteered for STRESS? All the gunslingers?"

Mr. Jasinski said, "Your Honor, I object to that." Sounding quite angry about it.

Judge Solner said, "So does the court. Mr. Randall, stand up to examine the witness. Maybe we'll get through this sometime today."

Pushing himself up with deliberation, his hands flat on the table, Mr. Randall said, "Yes, Your Honor . . . Lieutenant . . . let me see. How many officers did you have in STRESS?"

"I'm not sure," Bryan said. "Less than a hundred."

"Out of about five thousand. All volunteers, were they?"

"That's right."

"And how many people you boys kill?"

"Objection!"

"Let me rephrase that," Mr. Randall said. "How many suspects, directly related to the STRESS operation, suffered mortal wounds? . . . How's that?"

"I believe twenty-two," Bryan said.

"How many Walter Kouza kill?"

"I don't know exactly."

"We'll allow you to guess."

"Eight."

"Eight it is," Mr. Randall said, "but I'm sorry you don't win nothing. Your Honor, twenty-two suspects were killed and Mr. Kouza, alone, accounted for more than a third of them. I believe the court should consider the significance of that proportion and let a jury hear about it." Mr. Randall paused, referred to his notes and looked at Bryan Hurd again. "How many people—strike that.

In the death of how many suspects were you directly responsible, lieutenant?''

''While on STRESS? None.''

''Well, have you killed anybody lately?''

Yes, Angela Nolan thought. She could see him firing a gun as she might see it in a dream or a movie. She saw it again in slow motion, looked at it closely and saw his expression the same as it was now. He fit the role of homicide lieutenant in a filmic way, look and manner adaptable to motion pictures. And yet his manner was natural, almost boyish.

She was surprised then at Bryan Hurd's answer.

''No, I haven't killed anyone lately.''

''Homicide detective, you haven't had to use your gun?''

''The shooting's over by the time we get there.''

''How about when you make an arrest—you have your gun out.''

''Sometimes.''

''What I'm getting at,'' Mr. Randall said, ''you use your gun if you have to. Whereas another police officer might use his gun because he *likes* to. Is that a fair statement?''

''It sounds fair,'' Bryan said.

''So now,'' Mr. Randall said, ''tell us what you saw . . . No, first tell the court how you came to be at the Moore residence that afternoon.''

''A *capias* had been issued on a suspect in a felony homicide,'' Bryan said. ''He skipped bond . . .''

''Not Darius Moore or any member of the Moore family.''

''No.''

''The suspect, did he live at that address?'' Mr. Randall consulted his file. ''Seven-twenty-one Glynn Court?''

''No. The address came from a tip. Someone called it in.''

''Give you his name?''

''No, it was an anonymous call.''

''So you all mount up and ride out to . . . 721 Glynn Court to arrest this murder suspect. Tell me something,'' Mr. Randall said. ''Mr. Walter Kouza was not with Homicide, was he?''

"No. He was with MCMU at the time," Bryan said. "Major Crime Mobile Unit. We called them for backup."

"So how many people you have to make this arrest?"

"Three from Homicide, four MCMU officers."

"Feel you had enough troops for the job?"

Bryan didn't answer. He stared at Mr. Randall, waiting, and Mr. Randall said, "All right, now you're there. Tell us how Mr. Walter Kouza came to shoot Darius Moore, subsequently ending his life."

"Objection!"

Judge Solner said to Mr. Jasinski, "Counselor, try to keep it down." He said to the court reporter, a young woman poised over her machine, gazing off, "Helen, strike *subsequently ending his life.*"

Now Jeanette Moore, the mother of the victim, raised her voice without moving and said, "He died, didn't he? He wasn't cripple by the man he wouldn't have died. I know that much."

Her son, Curtis Moore, grinned and poked his mom on the sly with his elbow.

Mr. Randall leaned over to say something to the woman, putting his hand on her shoulder, while the son, Curtis Moore, stared up at the lawyer and began to shift in his seat as though he wanted to say something. Curtis Moore's hair was in tight cornrows; he wore a white T-shirt beneath a black leather jacket trimmed with bright metal studs and the words *Black Demons* lettered on the back in red.

Mr. Randall said, "I'm sorry, Your Honor . . ."

Curtis Moore said, "They kick in the door." Now Mr. Randall had to hobble a few steps to get his hands on Curtis's shoulders.

Bryan Hurd said, "We knocked several times. We could hear movement inside, voices . . ."

"Look like some gang out on the porch," Curtis Moore said, Mr. Randall squeezing his shoulder blades. "They come dress like some gang, they ought'n to make house calls."

Beautiful. Angela was smiling as the judge told Mr. Randall he'd be held in contempt, bad knee or no bad knee, if he wasn't able to control his clients.

She saw Bryan Hurd smiling, not giving it much, not enough to show his teeth, but smiling all the same. She saw him looking at her now, as though he were using the smile to bring them together. But as she smiled back she knew this was between the two of them and had nothing to do with anyone else or anything that was said. They continued to look at each other until Mr. Randall asked a question.

Bryan Hurd, said, "I went over to one of the front windows. That was when Walter, Mr. Kouza, kicked in the door."

"Yeah, then what happened?"

"Well, we went in."

"How many of you?"

"Sergeant Malik, Mr. Kouza and myself."

"Where were the others, the other four?"

"On the sides and around in back."

Mr. Randall said, "It wouldn't seem anyone could slip out, make an escape then."

Bryan said, "It wouldn't seem anyone could escape from jail, but they do."

"Got to watch myself with you," Mr. Randall said. "Go on, tell the court what happened then. Who was present in the house? You busted the people's door down, now you're in there."

Bryan nodded toward the plaintiff table. "Mrs. Moore was coming down the stairs at the time. Curtis was in the living room. Darius was in the dining room, directly behind the living room."

"What was he doing?"

"He started—it looked like he was going into the kitchen when Mr. Kouza yelled at him to stop."

"What did it *appear* he was doing when you arrived?" Mr. Randall asked. "In fact, the whole family. What were they doing?"

"I think they were getting ready to have something to eat. There was a pie and a bottle of Pepsi-Cola on the diningroom table. One of those big plastic bottles."

"So Mr. Kouza, he yelled at Darius, uh? What did he say to him?"

"He called for him to remain where he was."

"Yeah, but what did he say exactly?"

"He said, 'Freeze, motherfucker. Don't move.' "

"Like that?"

"Somewhat louder."

"Then what happened?"

"Darius turned and started back."

"Toward the living room?"

"That's right. But he was still in the dining room when Mr. Kouza fired."

"I thought Darius was shot in the spine," Mr. Randall said.

"He was," Bryan said. "From the front."

"Must have been a powerful weapon Mr. Kouza used."

Bryan didn't say anything.

"Was a *Mag*num," Curtis Moore said. He was standing now, Randall trying to get to him. "Was a big forty-four *Mag*num. Ask *me* what the motherfucker use. He want to shoot everybody, except this one"—pointing to Bryan Hurd on the witness stand—"stop him."

Mr. Randall had his hands on Curtis now, easing him down, saying, "Your Honor, please take into account this young man's emotional state, seeing his brother—" And stopped there.

Judge Solner said, "I've seen enough of Mr. Moore today. He can leave on his own or the court officer will throw him out. Right now."

Angela watched Curtis Moore stroll out of the courtroom in his black leather jacket and tight maroon trousers. All he needed was the Bee Gees playing behind him, his drag-step pace right on the beat. She wondered if any magazine would go for an interview with Curtis. Outside of *Easy Rider*.

Bryan Hurd was looking at her. He wasn't smiling now but almost. She looked at him with the same expression. She couldn't be cool with him. She didn't want to be. She wanted to make a face and see him smile, knowing he would. But the face would have to relate to something he would recognize. She knew him but she didn't know him.

Mr. Randall said, "I've only one more area to cover, Your Honor," and turned to Lieutenant Hurd again. "Was Darius, at the time he was shot, was he holding anything in his hand?"

"He was holding a knife," Bryan answered.

"What kind? Big butcher knife?"

"He was holding a silverware knife."

"Just a plain, ordinary silverware knife?"

"That's right," Bryan said. "With banana cream pie on it."

Twenty minutes later it was over. Angela watched Walter Kouza coming out, glancing back, blunt arms hanging rigid in his tight gray suit, buttoned, banging through the low gate to the aisle and glancing back again, livid, to say, "Thanks a lot, you son of a bitch."

Lieutenant Hurd was looking this way. He said, "Walter?"

But Walter was out the door.

Angela closed her notebook, slipped it into her canvas bag. As the homicide cop with the bandit mustache came through the gate she was ready.

She said, "Lieutenant? . . ." As he came over she said, "Bryan Hurd, is it?" Aloud for the first time, wanting to hear herself say his name. He was taller than she had expected. Younger looking, close.

He said, "Well, finally . . ."

They stared at each other.

He said, "You know how long I've been wanting to meet you?"

She said, "Wait a minute. How do you know who I am?"

He said, "I don't." Then said, making a statement, "You're not with one of the papers, are you? You're from somewhere else?"

"I'm on my own."

"That's what I thought. So am I, for the next ten days." He seemed to want to say something else, prevent a silence. "Actually I'm not off till Monday, then I've got the ten days . . . But see, I'm off this weekend, so it's like I'm off now." The silence began and he said, "Just stay with me through this part. I don't want to sound dumb and blow it, but you try too hard that's what happens . . . What's funny?"

"Nothing."

They stared at each other.

She said, "I should've washed my hair."

He seemed uncertain, or hopeful. Then began to smile and said, "You know what I'm talking about, don't you. You know exactly what I'm talking about."

"You haven't really said anything yet."

"That's what I mean. I don't have to say anything. You *know*. And your hair's fine. It's perfect."

She said, "Then I'm all set." And seemed confident again in her long navy blue coat, her jeans and cowboy boots. But she felt the need to say, "Boy, I don't know . . ."

They stared at each other again until Bryan said, "Let's get a drink and talk for a few days."

Neither of them spoke in the elevator going down.

3

Coming out of the City-County Building, walking east on Jefferson, they started over and spoke about the weather, looking off at the Ford Auditorium on the riverfront, the fountain misting in Hart Plaza, Bryan saying it was a little too nice, it wasn't like April, April in Detroit was miserable, wet and cold, with dirty snow left over from winter; Angela saying she lived in Arizona, Tucson, and didn't know much about weather, outside of weather in New York when you wanted a taxi; Bryan saying he thought that should about do it for weather, though he could tell her how muggy it got in the summer if she wanted.

Angela said, "Boy . . ." and shook her head in amazement.

"What?"

She said, "We know each other but we don't."

He said, "Maybe we're related. What do you think?"

She said, "I hope not." And was silent.

Bryan glanced at her. She was pulling in. But that was all right because she was still there. Her mouth and nose he had committed to memory and believed he could draw within a couple of tries with clean, simple lines. The awareness in her eyes . . .

"You have blue eyes, right?"

"Sort of blue."

"So're mine."

She said, "I know."

It made him feel good. Walter was a half-block ahead of them and he was pretty sure where Walter was going. Maybe he'd buy him a drink.

She said, "I think I'd like to do Curtis Moore sometime."

"I think Walter would too," Bryan said.

She looked at him now. "You know what I mean."

"I've interviewed him a few times," Bryan said. He told her the only way to get his full attention was to talk about bikes. Curtis had a big tricked-out scoot, a Harley, he kept in the house. He had a cane that telescoped out into a pool cue, with a grass pipe in the grip he smoked going sixty. Curtis painted a white girl brown one time and kept her a week.

Angela said, well, it was a thought.

He asked her how long she'd been writing. She said, making a living at it, just three years.

"You like to write?"

She looked at him. No one had ever asked her that before. She said, "I'm not sure. I've got a couple of problems. I don't know if I'm Oriana Fallaci or Studs Terkel. I'm serious. And I'm about to turn thirty and I'm having a little trouble with that, too."

He said, "I'll tell you how to handle the age thing. But why can't you be Angela Nolan?"

She said, "I don't know if pure Angela Nolan would sell."

He said, "Well, as long as you don't show off. What do you write about?"

"I do interviews. Not the usual type with famous people. Bum Phillips is the only one even remotely famous."

Bryan stopped.

"But why did you say that about not showing off?" Now Angela stopped and had to turn to look up at him. "What's the matter?"

"I read it. It was in *Playboy* and your picture was in the front part, right? With all the pictures?"

"Yeah, in the November issue. You saw it?"

"I cut it out," Bryan said.

"The interview?"

"No, your picture." He held up thumb and index finger about an inch apart. "It's that big."

"Come on—" She was smiling, amazed. "All the naked girls in there, you cut out *my* picture?"

"I'll tell you something else," Bryan said. "It's the first time in my life I ever cut out a girl's picture, naked or otherwise."

"But why?"

He said, "Why do you think? Why do you think we're here, right now?"

She said, "It's getting scary."

He said, "It's not getting scary, it's been. Ever since I saw you." They started walking again.

She said, "It's funny—watching you in the courtroom, you reminded me of Bum Phillips."

He almost stopped again. "You think I look like him?".

"No, I mean something he said." She delivered the line with the hint of a Western drawl: " 'I make decisions according to what's right and what's wrong, not to keep my job' . . . Even the judge was surprised Randall called you."

Bryan said, "Kenneth Randall—you ever get in serious trouble, hire him. He spends most of his time in Recorders Court, that's the criminal stuff; so I see him about once a week."

Angela said, "You didn't give him anything, but you didn't hold back either. I mean considering Walter Kouza's a fellow police officer. Isn't there some kind of unwritten law, you don't tell on each other?"

Bryan said, "He's not my fellow police officer. I don't need any Walter Kouzas."

Angela said, "He's a bodyguard now."

"Good," Bryan said. "Is that what you're doing, interviewing bodyguards?"

"I was interviewing the body Walter's guarding," Angela said, "Mr. Robinson Daniels of Grosse Pointe and Palm Beach? Daniels Fasteners. They make something for Chrysler."

"They make nuts and bolts," Bryan said. "Yeah, you see his picture a lot, Robbie Daniels. Or you see him at Lindell's with the jock sniffers. Every couple of years he offers to buy the Tigers and in between he buys 'em drinks. I hear he's a pretty nice guy."

Angela said, "That seems to be the word. At least from the gang down in Palm Beach. I haven't talked to anyone up here yet."

"What's he need a bodyguard for?"

"That's the first question I'm gonna ask, if we ever get back together."

"Did you ask Walter?"

"Walter says, 'Why you think? Rich guys need protection from the fucking kooks in the world.' "

"Well, it's not unusual," Bryan said. "Even if it's just for status. But, Robbie Daniels, he *is* pretty well known."

"I know, it's possible." Angela said. "Last week I was gonna drop the whole idea. It wasn't worth all the waiting around.

Either waiting for Robbie or waiting to see one of his friends and then getting the same old shit. Rich people don't think, they just assume things. They assume everyone thinks the way they do."

"You just said they don't think."

"Don't pick. You know what I mean," Angela said. "Then, when I'd finally get him to sit down and talk, he'd want to play around."

"Make the moves on you."

"No, not like that. The only time—when I met him the first thing he said to me. . . . I'm standing there, I've told him who I am, acting very legitimate and proper . . . he says, 'You know what I'd like to do, Angie?' And that's one thing I can't stand, I don't know why, being called Angie. He says, very straight, 'I'd like to tie you up and fuck your socks off.' "

Bryan said, "No hugs and kisses first, huh?"

"He was being cute. He says things with a straight face, then grins to show he's kidding. You're supposed to think he's a little off the wall but basically cute."

"You don't like him."

They were crossing Beaubien now toward Galligan's on the corner. Walter was already inside.

"I think he's an asshole," Angela said. "But I have a feeling there's another Robbie Daniels inside the cute Robbie and that one could be pretty interesting."

A young executive was holding the door open for two girls going into Galligan's, the girls smiling, touching the door, the young man finally letting go, giving the door to Bryan. He brought Angela past him into the foyer, touching her for the first time. She looked up at him. As the inner door opened, releasing voices and sounds, he said, "What's interesting about the Robbie Daniels inside the real one?"

She said, "I think he likes to kill people."

Walter threw his head back to drain the shot glass. He got his change from the bartender, checked it, picked up a draft beer and a straight-up martini and tried to narrow his shoulder as he came away from the bar, concentrating on the glasses. He looked up and stopped.

Angela was saying, "It's New York. Third Avenue." She saw

Walter a few feet away, holding the drinks, staring at Bryan.

Walter said, "You know what you did to me in there? I start to think about it, I don't believe it."

Bryan said, "Walter, I want to ask you something."

Walter said, "A knife is a knife. I don't care it's got blood on it, banana cream pie, what it's got on it. A fucking knife is a knife."

Bryan said, "Just tell me one thing. Who's Norma Zimmer?"

Walter said, "I ever say another word to you, long as I live, I hope I bite my fucking tongue off."

He walked away from them tight-jawed, concentrating on the glasses again as he moved between tables toward the booths against the wall. Now Owen Galligan was coming through the coat-rack hall from the back dining room, stopping at tables, the saloonkeeper officiating, getting the after-work crowd settled in. He saw the homicide detective and pointed to the first table against the brass railing that separated the tables from the bar patrons that were two deep, the young executives and clerks and lawyers who were checking out Angela now, rating her with cool deadpan approval.

"That's yours, Bryan, grab it. Quick."

Bryan said to Angela, "I come in with cops, I don't get this table. As a matter of fact I've never had it." He arranged the chairs so they sat with their backs to the bar and wouldn't have to look at the guys staring down at them. Angela looked the guys over, briefly, as she sat down, leaving her coat on, and that was that.

She said, "Don't you know Norma Zimmer?"

Bryan was looking for a waitress now. "The name's sorta familiar."

Angela said, "How about Alice Lon? Or Ralna English?"

Bryan was shaking his head.

"At one time or another," Angela said, "Norma, Alice and Ralna were all Champagne Ladies. They sang with Lawrence Welk. I tried to interview him once."

Bryan seemed relieved. "In court, I kept trying to think of who she was. Yeah, Norma Zimmer."

"You want to tell me why," Angela said, "or would you rather take a look at Robbie Daniels? He's in the last booth with Walter."

Bryan looked. He couldn't see much of Walter, but there was Daniels lounged against the wall, one foot up on the bench, his knee showing above the table. Daniels was wearing a beige tweed sport coat, white button-down shirt and striped rep necktie.

"He's got a nice tan," Bryan said. "He looks like a tennis pro. The tan and the hair."

"He's forty-one," Angela said.

Bryan's gaze moved to a waitress, tried to catch her eye and missed. "What're you gonna have?"

"I guess Jack Daniels on the rocks."

"Yeah? Is that what you drink?"

"Usually." Angela looked off again. "Robbie claims he runs six miles every day."

"I guess it's the thing to do," Bryan said. "Go over to Belle Isle, even during the week, it looks like they're holding a marathon. I drove around Palmer Park—I live out that way—and measured off a mile. The next day I put on the outfit—sweat pants, one of those knit caps, it was cold that day. I ran the mile, came home and threw up. I said to myself, you were right. It's not only boring, it makes you sick. So I quit jogging."

"When I'm home I like to hike in the mountains, Angela said. "Otherwise, I don't do much."

Bryan couldn't take his eyes off her. He said, "Well, you're five-five, you weigh about a hundred and two. I don't see that you have a problem."

She said, "You could work in a carnival."

"I do," Bryan said. "I guess weights, read fingerprints. Tell fortunes—tell some poor dumbhead he's gonna do mandatory life . . . but at least not the next ten days. I'm going down to Florida, sit in the sun and read."

"Mysteries?"

"No, I don't read mysteries. I'm gonna take the last twelve issues of *National Geographic* and read every word and look at the maps. Fall asleep on the beach reading. I like to wake up about five o'clock, there's nobody around. Then go in and get cleaned up . . . in the evening drink tall rum drinks and look at the ocean.

That's the first couple of days. After that I switch to bourbon and go to the movies."

She said, "Alone?"

Bryan smiled at her. He said, "Angela. I didn't think your name would be Angela. I don't know why, I thought it would be Sally or Nancy. I like Angela though, very much." He said, "Yeah, I'm going alone." He smiled at her again. "We have to know certain things, don't we? Before moving ahead."

She seemed hesitant now, getting to it. She said, "It isn't like meeting somebody at school; we've been out for a while . . . I was married when I was twenty, divorced, I was still twenty. It was really dumb. He was with a band and I was going through sort of a groupie period."

"I was twenty-four when I got married," Bryan said. "Divorced at, I was thirty-four or -five."

"How old are you now?"

"I'm forty."

"You don't look it. Do you have children?"

"No, but I'd like to. Unless it gets too late."

There was a silence. She said, "I'm gonna be thirty the day after tomorrow."

He said, "That's right, and you're having trouble with it."

She said, "It's not a major problem, I just have to get used to the idea. I know girls who panic and try to revert. They new-wave themselves over and look like clowns,"

He said, "You want to go to Florida next week?"

"Where?"

"Near Boca Raton."

She made a face that was an expression of pain or mild confusion. "I didn't mean *where*. I don't know why I said that." She looked serious now, intent. "I knew you were going to ask me, as soon as you said Florida, and I didn't know what I was gonna say."

"Let me build it up," Bryan said. "It's a nice place, the Ocean Pearl, right on the beach . . ."

She said, "I'm not like this. Why am I nervous? I keep saying the wrong thing."

"Just take it easy. Relax."

"That's what I'm trying to do." Gritting her teeth a little.

He said, "Soon as you *try*—that's what I was talking about before, in the courtroom, and I asked you to bear with me. We have to just get through this first part."

She said, "What I need is a drink."

"You *want* a drink," Bryan said. "You don't *need* a drink. That's like saying you need help, you can't handle it yourself."

"Jesus, you're full of advice, aren't you?" She was loosening up. "What do you read, self-improvement books?"

He held up his hand, looking off, and said, "Marcie, bring us a couple Jack Daniels on ice, please. Doubles." He said to Angela, "You want a double?"

She said, "Yes, I want a double. I don't need one, you understand. I *want* one."

"There," Bryan said, "you got that taken care of. What else's bothering you?"

She said, "I didn't think you'd be a smart-ass."

Bryan said, "Look, if you want, you sit here and I'll sit there. There'll be times when I'm a little tense and you'll give me a poke, straighten me out. It's like when you're taking yourself too seriously, catch yourself becoming indignant over little shitty things. You know what I mean? Or you get very dramatic about something. What do you do?"

"I don't know," Angela said. "What?"

"You give yourself a kick in the ass."

She said, "You're a lot of fun, Bryan."

He said, "You know the first thing I looked at as we came out of court? I looked to see if you were pigeon-toed. My wife was pigeon-toed. She'd walk around the house with this grim look on her face. By the time we knew we were splitting up, all she had to do was walk in the room, I had to get out. See, it wasn't that she was pigeon-toed, I don't mean to make fun of her. It was the tight-assed way she walked that to me represented her personality. She never came up for air."

There was a silence between them, an eye of stillness within the barroom's scattered bits of noise.

Angela said, "I feel a lot better, Bryan. I don't know what you're talking about, but I feel better."

He said, "Good. You want to go to Florida?"

She said, almost sadly, "I thought you were gonna be—this'll probably sound dumb—but I thought you were gonna be, well, romantic. I don't know why."

"I *am* romantic. Why do you think I'm asking you to go to Florida?"

She said, "God, a homicide cop. Why couldn't you be, I don't know, something a little more sensitive?"

"Because," Bryan said, "you came to me with a guy you say likes to kill people. If he likes it, he must've done it. So here you are. You take up with a homicide cop, that's what you get. Not much apparent sensitivity, but all kinds of expert advice."

She was stiffening as he spoke, looking right at him.

"I didn't *take up* with you."

"How about, sought me out?"

"It's not why I wanted to meet you."

"Your indignation is showing," Bryan said. "How many people has he killed?"

"Two that I know of," Angela said.

Robbie said to the waitress, "Darling, don't worry about it. Bring us another draft and a very extra-dry Beefeater and all's forgiven."

Walter said, "Hey, and a ashtray."

"One cigarette," Robbie said to Walter.

Walter looked puzzled. "I thought you meant while we're here. You said I could smoke, right?"

"Walter, you went through an ordeal today. You're a little uptight, okay, I said you could have a cigarette. One. And that's the last one I ever want to see you smoke."

Walter was holding the Camel close to his mouth. Christ, wondering now if he should wait. Drink half the beer first.

"Mr. Daniels, they got me by the balls. I need something like to hold onto. I can't just *sit.*"

"I understand that."

"Money I saved, took me twenty years—I'll flush it down the toilet before I give it to a fucking con." He brought out his green Bic and lighted the cigarette.

"Walter, I was there. I saw part of the show."

"You were *there?*" Exhaling cigarette smoke.

"The first thing you have to do is fire your lawyer."

"Eddie?"

"Walter, Eddie's pathetic. He should've objected to everything Randall said. I'm not a lawyer. I know that much. Walter, Randall and the judge play handball together at the DAC. Randall was the first colored guy I ever saw there as a guest. I looked, I thought one of the waiters was taking a shower . . . He even has a tan line."

Walter wasn't listening. "You were in the *court*room?"

"For a little while. I left right behind Curtis."

"I didn't see you."

"I know you didn't." Robbie looked toward the front, to the first table. "That homicide detective had your full attention. What I want to know is, what's he doing with Angie?"

"Mr. Daniels," Walter said, "the trial doesn't come up for a couple months. All right, I got some time. If you got another lawyer, or you have any suggestions at all, that's fine with me."

Robbie was thoughtful. "The mother could probably be bought for a few grand. But you've got Randall to contend with. He'll clean you out, accept a settlement for about a half-million from the city and take a third of it off the top."

"Jesus," Walter said.

"I told you before, your only alternative is to do something about the witnesses."

Walter squinted through his cigarette smoke. "I'm not sure what you mean, *do* something."

"I rode down in the elevator with Curtis. He doesn't say much, does he? Seems very distrustful."

"He's been in solitary half his fucking life. He doesn't know *how* to talk," Walter said, "till you get him in court. Then you can't fucking shut him up."

Robbie was looking toward the front again. "I'm sure a good defense lawyer can handle the STRESS stuff when it comes up. Make it sound like the homicide guy has some kind of a personal grudge. Discredit his testimony. But Curtis—especially if you have a predominantly black jury, which is quite likely—Curtis's something else."

Walter said, "You aren't kidding he's something else."

"What was he in Jackson for?"

"Shit, armed robbery, assault. Grand theft auto, I don't know how many counts they had. He was up for second-degree murder, shot and killed a guy in a bar, they send him to the Forensic Center. He gets cured of whatever suppose to be disturbing him, they let him out. He gets picked up on a gun charge and back he goes to Jackson for two years. He's a fucking nut."

"Now residing at 721 Glynn Court," Robbie said. "Member of the Black Demons, whoever they are."

"How'd you know that?" Walter seemed amazed.

"Walter"—like talking to a child—"I was in the courtroom."

"Yeah, that's right." Walter took a last drag on what was left of the Camel and stubbed it out. "I appreciate whatever you can do for me, Mr. Daniels."

Robbie said, "I've got to take care of you, Walter. I need you for the big one."

"Yeah, that's right." He sounded tired now.

Robbie studied him: heavy shoulders sagging, deep-set eyes staring at his green lighter. "Walter? Would you like one more cigarette?"

Walter looked amazed again, then grateful, little eyes glistening now. "You serious?"

"Hey," Robbie said, "I'm not such a bad guy to work for, am I?"

Bryan said, "Let me get it straight. The burglar was outside the house when Robbie shot him?"

"Yeah, out by the patio," Angela said. "But I don't think you'd call him a real burglar."

"No, I guess he had a few things to learn," Bryan said. He sipped his Jack Daniels. Angela gave him a look but didn't say anything for a moment.

"The second one happened nine years ago—I found out about it while I was researching him, getting some background. At a place called St. Clair Flats."

"That's not far from here."

"Robbie was duck hunting with an executive from one of the car companies, I think Chrysler . . ."

Bryan was nodding. "Yeah, I forgot all about that. Nine years ago, it seems longer. They were in a duck blind and the guy from Chrysler stood up when he shouldn't have and Robbie blew the top of his head off"—nodding again, remembering—"with a Browning twelve-gauge shotgun. Gold-inlaid, it must've cost him seven or eight thousand."

She said, "Were you in on the investigation?"

"No, that's a different county, out of our jurisdiction. I wasn't in Homicide then anyway."

"But you remember details."

He said, "I remember the kind of shotgun, but not the name of the guy from Chrysler." He tried to think of it, but finally shook his head. "Well, you've got justifiable homicide in one case, accidental in the other. What makes you think he likes it?"

Angela held her glass poised, off the table. She said, "Ask him. Here he comes." Robbie was making his way through the tables, glancing around at first, but now with a whimsical half-smile, head cocked, his eyes on Angela and no one else. Walter trailed behind.

Robbie said, "Could it be? It *is!* How're you, Angie? Good to see you, tiger." Extending his hand and holding hers as he gave Bryan a look of mild concern. "If this lady's interviewing you, lieutenant, let me give you a word of warning. Three words to be exact. Watch your ass." Then the grin. "Hi, I'm Robbie Daniels."

Bryan thought of a television commercial. "Hi, I'm Joseph Cotten." He didn't smile. He gave the handshake enough but not all he had. He liked the guy's sport coat. He didn't like his maize and blue Michigan tie, the way it was tied in a careless knot, the label side of the narrow end showing, *All Silk*. He had met millionaires before, when he drove for the mayor and wore black tie with the black mayor and stayed close to him at functions, Bryan slick and official in his city-bought tux. (A deputy chief called him sir at the benefits and openings until the deputy chief saw him at 1300, on the fifth floor, and found out Bryan was a sergeant on loan from Homicide.) He liked the mayor—enjoyed hearing him shift as smooth as a smile from street talk to official pronouncement—but had been indifferent to the indifferent millionaires he'd met. He would be indifferent to this one, too;

though not for the same reason. He resented this one, the uncombed hair, the careless tie, the patter, the same way he resented wavy-haired gospel preachers on television who never stopped smiling.

Robbie was acting but didn't know it, used to playing the role. Making everything look easy. Talking about George Hamilton now.

George Hamilton in town yesterday. Doing a Diamond Mortgage commercial.

George Hamilton's tan that you could kid him about all you wanted but was superb, 100 percent.

"Angie, I wished you'd called."

Angela said, "Why?"

"Hey, I've got to tell you this," Robbie said. Glancing around, "Walter, come here." Walter edging over, not looking directly at anyone as Robbie put an arm around Walter's rigid shoulders, a possession, though it was meant as an act of fellowship. "My star driver and head of security, Walter Kouza." Standing there in his gray double-knit suit, maroon shirt and tie.

Angela said, with innocence, "Why're you feeling insecure?"

"It's a long story," Robbie said. "I've had a couple of threats lately, in Florida. I didn't tell you about them, I don't think they amount to anything . . . But this is good. Walter's driving, we pick George up out in West Bloomfield where they're shooting—we're gonna have dinner at the Chop House and then drop George off at the Ponch. So we're in the car at least, altogether, forty-five minutes, right? We're talking, he's telling me about his new picture—it's about Zorro, but he plays him as a gay, if you can imagine a swishy George Hamilton who's had to have had more broads than any guy I know of"—his voice dropped—"with the possible exception of one guy." Robbie paused.

Bryan watched him; saw his expression go dead, then brighten again, immediately.

"You know, with the swords and all, the gay blade? We're talking about Hollywood, we're talking about Palm Beach, Dina, Bert . . . Angie, you know. We drop George off at the Ponch, we're pulling away and Walter goes, honest to God, 'Who was that?' " Robbie timed it, giving them a wide-eyed Johnny Carson look. "I said, 'That was George Hamilton.' Walter goes—are you ready? 'Who's George Hamilton.' " Still wide-eyed.

Then grinning, looking at Walter fondly as he gave the rigid shoulders a squeeze. "We're not laughing at you, Walter, it's just an improbably funny situation."

No one was laughing at anything. Walter tried to smile but failed. Bryan watched Robbie raise his arm over Walter's head and bring it down, saying he had to run. "But listen"—looking at Angela—"am I gonna see you?"

"I'll call you," Angela said.

"Okay, but better make it in the next few days or I won't be here. Do you need a car?"

"I'm just hanging out for the time being," Angela said. "At the Ponchartrain. Is that by any chance the Ponch?"

Robbie said, "What else? But if you need wheels, I mean even right now, I'm gonna be with my lawyers the next couple of hours, but Walter's free. He'll take you wherever you want to go. I *can't* see you tonight, Angie, but give me a call tomorrow."

Bryan said, "Would he mind driving us out to my place?" He felt the toe of Angela's cowboy boot poke at his leg. "I have to get my car."

"Sure, anywhere." Robbie gesturing, *why not?* Then frowning, puzzled. "Don't they give police lieutenants cars these days?"

"Not since the price of gas went up, " Bryan said. "No more driving home in blue Plymouths."

Robbie seemed interested. "How do you get around?"

"Well, I usually drive my own car down and park it," Bryan said. "This morning, one of my squad picked me up. We had to go to a scene."

Robbie was nodding as he listened. "Fascinating. You mean a murder scene. I'd love to watch an investigation sometime. Is that possible?"

"I suppose so," Bryan said, "if you're interested in homicide."

He felt the toe of Angela's boot again as Robbie said, "I am, indeed."

They rode in his Cadillac Fleetwood behind dark-tinted glass. Walter, silent, taking them north on Woodward Avenue. Angela looking at the city beyond downtown for the first time, not asking what's that or that until they passed between impressive stone structures, the main library and the art institute, and Bryan told her what they were, pointing out Rodin's *The Thinker* in front of the museum, saying that was it until they spotted the golden tower of the Fisher Building. Angela said, well, it's bigger than Tucson.

They didn't ask each other questions or loosen up and say all the things they wanted to say. Walter was right there: rigid, the man never moved, shoulders hunched over the wheel, shark-fin pompadour glistening, stray hairs standing like antennae.

Bryan said, "Walter, you like working for Robbie?"

Walter didn't answer.

"I drove for a guy one time. Followed him around, got to go to parties. You go to parties, Walter?"

No answer.

"I'll bet you see some interesting things, huh?"

Angela was making sad faces, in sympathy. She leaned against Bryan and whispered, "Leave the poor guy alone."

Bryan said, "I want to but I can't." His gaze moved to the side window. "You're in Highland Park now. Coming up on the old Ford plant."

Angela said, "Nice."

Bryan said, "Walter, I was wondering, how come you don't have on your chauffeur's uniform?"

Walter didn't answer.

"I forgot," Bryan said, "you had to go to court today. That the reason?"

Walter's hand moved, mashing the horn to blast a car pulling away from the curb.

Angela hunched her shoulders and Bryan poked her with an elbow. They could see Walter's hands, thick, padded, knuckles like smooth stones, gripping the steering wheel.

"Left before you get to Palmer Park, Walter. You got to go up past the light and come back. Then along the park over to Merton."

"It's looking better," Angela said as they passed Moorish and

Art Deco apartment buildings among lawns and old trees, Bryan hunching forward now.

"Up there on the left, Walter, the yellow brick with the front that looks like a mosque." He said to Angela, "Right across from the synagogue. We've got black people and gays of all colors. It's an interesting neighborhood."

Walter braked abruptly and sat looking straight ahead.

Getting out, Bryan said, "Walter, I'm sorry you feel the way you do. But I'll say this. You're a good driver and I think you'll always find work."

Walter waited until they were going up the walk.

"Hey, wise-ass."

Bryan touched Angela's arm. They looked back to see Walter with his elbow on the windowsill, a lone figure in that dark expanse of limousine. Bryan said, "You talking to me?"

Walter said, "I'll tell you something, wise-ass, you think you're so fucking clever. You're bush. Homicide lieutenant, all that goes with it, you're still bush. The biggest thing ever happens to you, some jig on Twelfth Street shoots another jig's been fucking his common-law wife, or you get a twenty-buck hooker slashed to death, tits cut off in some alley, all that street shit. Floater comes up at Waterworks Park, makes your fucking day. That's what you're in, buddy, and that's as class as it gets."

Bryan waited a moment.

"Compared to what?"

Walter hesitated, still aroused, almost eager, but holding back. "Get your head out of the garbage, maybe you'll see how it's done in the majors, wise-ass."

The limousine moved off abruptly, wheels throwing bits of gravel, engine revs rising, then fading down the street. They watched the car until it was out of sight.

Angela said, "I'm beginning to see through you, Bryan. You're not your everyday wise-ass; you use it with a purpose. Put the needle in and get 'em to talk."

They started up the walk again, Bryan taking out his keys. He felt pretty good: his interest aroused to speculate and wonder, without having to worry about it, feel a responsibility. He said,

"That's the first time in his life Walter's ever used any restraint, held back. What do you think he was trying to tell us?"

Angela waited as he unlocked the front door and held it open. "I think he was showing off, trying to one-up you. Behind the wheel of his Cadillac limo."

Bryan said, "I hope that's all he's doing."

4

Bryan was going through the stack of magazines on the toilet tank in the bathroom. *National Geographic, Smithsonian, Quest, GEO, Law and Order,* there, *Playboy*. But the wrong month. Two more *National Geographics,* another *Playboy*. Too recent. *Car and Driver* . . .

He heard Angela say from the living room, "What're these little marks in the wall?"

He looked out, through the hall and into the living room. She was standing to the left of the front door.

"Bullet holes."

And went back to sorting through the stack. An old *Newsweek, Atlantic, Monthly Detroit* . . .

"*Bullet* holes?"

Smithsonian, another *National Geographic, Esquire, Esquire* . . . another *Playboy* . . . November! He opened it, turned a page.

"Why're there bullet holes in your wall?"

"Somebody shot at me. I came in and turned the light on. Bang—a guy was waiting for me."

There she was: the nice smile, perfect nosc, the knowing eyes, soft hair slanting across her forehead, all within the square-inch or so border of the black and white photo. He got a razor blade from the medicine cabinet, sliced the picture out carefully and replaced the magazine, slipping it into the middle of the pile.

As he came out of the hall and crossed toward the kitchen, she saw him: in his shirt sleeves now, the grip of a revolver showing, the gun riding in the waist of his trousers, behind his right hip. It was unexpected and gave her a momentary shock. She said, "Were you hurt?"

"When?"

"When you were shot at."

"No, he missed. I think all I've got's Jim Beam."

"That's fine. What'd you do then?"

"What, with the guy? I took the gun away from him . . . Why don't you put on some music?"

In the kitchen he held the stamp-size photo carefully in the palm of his hand, looked about undecided, then opened the *Good Housekeeping Cookbook* lying on the tile counter and placed the photo inside. There. He turned to the refrigerator and brought out an ice tray.

In the living room Angela was looking through his record albums, a stack of them on the floor next to the Sears hi-fi system.

"All you've got is Waylon Jennings and Willie Nelson."

"No, there're some others. George Benson . . . Earl Klugh."

"You've got a *whale* record." She put on Bob James.

Lamplight softened the starkness of the room, laid flaring designs on the empty walls. The music helped too.

She said, "Did you just move in?"

From the kitchen: "Almost two years ago."

The room didn't reflect him; or anyone. Bare walls and shelves of paperbacks and magazines. A hanging fern, dying; a young ficus that wasn't doing too badly. Chair and sofa slip-covered in faded summer-cottage beige. It looked as though he could move out in less than fifteen minutes.

"When're you gonna fix the place up?"

"What's the matter with it?"

A grocery sack with a red tag stapled to it stood upright on the glass coffee table. It was open. All she had to do, sitting on the edge of the sofa, was pull the sack toward her to look inside. She saw a girl's hairbrush, a beaded purse, a rolled-up cellophane bag that contained marijuana, a packet of cigarette paper and book matches. She saw what looked like pink panties, sandals, a white T-shirt bunched at the bottom of the sack that showed part of a word in black.

She sat back as Bryan came in from the kitchen, a lowball glass in each hand. He said, "You can look at that stuff if you want."

"It belongs to someone, doesn't it?"

"Not anymore. She's dead." He placed the drinks on the table and started back to the kitchen. "I left in a hurry this morning, forgot to take it with me."

The T-shirt was soiled with what looked like coffee stains; black lettering on white that said

DETROIT IS FOR LOVERS

She dropped the T-shirt in the sack and sipped her drink, felt the warmth inside her as moisture came to her eyes. "You make a neat one," she called to the kitchen, relaxing, with a good feeling.

He came in with a bowl of dry-roasted peanuts. "I thought we had some crackers, but we don't." And went back out again.

"What're you doing?"

"We're having a party."

"Are we going to smoke at the party?"

"I quit."

"So did I. Why don't we start again and quit some other time?"

She heard him say, "Okay, but I don't have any."

She went into the sack and brought out the Baggie. The grass looked clean, just a few seeds and bits of stem, dark stuff with a green smell to it. She rolled a cigarette, lighted it and sat back again on the sofa. As Bryan came in, now with a plate of white cheese and celery stalks, she said, "Am I destroying evidence?"

He said, "Not unless you smoke the whole lid." When she offered him the joint he took it carefully. "It's been a while." Drew deeply on it and said, holding his breath, "The last time, I ate about five pounds of caramel corn."

She said, "Well, six feet, about one sixty. I don't see a problem that shows. When do you take your gun off?"

He brought it out, a revolver with a stubby barrel, and laid it on the coffee table. The grip, she saw, was wrapped tightly with rubber bands. He said, "I forgot something." And went back to the kitchen.

Angela drew on the cigarette, staring at the revolver, about to ask him about the rubber bands when he came back in with the *Good Housekeeping Cookbook* and handed it to her.

"You brought me here to cook, is that it?"

"No, look inside. There's something in there."

"What?"

"Just look. It might be in the chicken section."

Angela leafed through pages, came to *Poultry* and began turning pages one at a time, concentrating now, looking for some clue. Then stopped. She seemed awed by what she saw. "I don't believe it." She held up the inch-square black and white photograph of herself.

Bryan leaned over to look at the cookbook open on her lap and nodded. "Under chicken cacciatore."

She said with a softness he had not heard before, "You really did . . . I've got goosebumps."

Bryan said, "It is scary, isn't it?"

Patti Daniels stood against the open door to the study; arms folded, which told Robbie something when finally he pushed the off button on the remote-control tuner, the armed Secret Service agents on the television screen imploding to black and he looked over at his wife. She had asked him yesterday how many times he'd watched it—the video cassette tape of the Reagan assassination attempt—and if she wanted the latest tally he'd tell her: nine times so far this evening.

She said, "I don't get it."

He didn't feel required to answer. Comments would have to be put in the form of a question. He waited, fingering the remote-control device in his hand.

"How many times are you going to look at it?"

He hadn't anticipated that one. "I don't know."

"What're you looking for, blood?"

"There's not much of it to see."

She straightened, brushed at the loose sleeve of her lounging gown, refolded her arms and leaned against the door again. The hip line was provocative; but he knew better.

"Did you have dinner?" Patti asked him.

"Yeah, as a matter of fact, at the Renaissance Club. David and Roger. They're not doing an awful lot of business. I mean the club. All that new-Detroit bullshit—Cartier's moving out, right on the heels of your favorite shop. Walk through the RenCen, the only people you see're working there or wearing name tags. They don't even have full occupancy, they're putting up two more buildings."

Patti said, "I love to talk about economics."

"How 'bout the six hundred grand condo in Aspen? You'd hire an ad agency to sell me on that one."

She said, "The only reason you don't like it is because I do. I'm going back out for Easter."

"Your snooty pals are gonna miss you."

"Tell them I may come down for the polo matches. I'll see."

"The jock," Robbie said. "What've you got out west, another ski instructor?"

She stared at him, posed, pert blonde in folds of champagne silk by Halston, boat-neck design good on her for a few more years, flowing lines to conceal thick legs; in ski pants or tailored clothes, an aristocratic fragility above the waist, a peasant's big-ass sturdiness below: the halves of two different women in one.

She said, "Do you want to compare notes? How about your writer friend—she still around?"

"Angela? Come on."

"I forgot. She must be ten years over the hill."

"Maybe I'll go out to Aspen with you."

"I'm going to bed."

"Jealous husband shoots—what is he, Austrian? Swiss? . . . Jealous husband shoots ethnic ski instructor." Robbie grinned. "Wait a minute. You like that suave foreign type, what about Walter? You could have an affair with Walter, you wouldn't even have to leave the house."

She said, "Are you serious about hiring Walter?"

"Of course I am."

"The servants don't know what to make of him. They don't know which side he's on."

"I like him," Robbie said. "Walter's solid, good Hamtramck stock. Speaking of which, not only Dodge Main is no more, Lynch Road's gone. Chrysler's going down the toilet and Lee Iacocca hangs in there like a hemorrhoid. You see him in the TV ads? He's a fucking storm trooper. Buy a Chrysler product, you son of a bitch, or I'll kill you."

"Good night," Patti said.

"Wait a minute. There're some papers you have to sign, on the desk."

Patti straightened, moved toward the glow of the brass, green-shaded lamp. She seldom came into Robbie's study; it had all the hallowed solid-oak charm of the Detroit Athletic Club, where men in dark suits talked solemnly about ten-day reports and women were admitted through a side entrance. She looked at the pages of legalese and picked up Robbie's gold pen.

"What're we up to now"

"Some more of the liquidation," Robbie said. "Within four days a Jewish auctioneer will have wiped out seventy-five years of nuts and bolts for the automotive industry. And you know what the best part is? The goddamn Japs'll probably buy half the equipment. No more Daniels fascinating fasteners. That's not bad, I could've used that. I see things in headlines lately. Fastener firm finally says fuck it. Daniels—no. Foremost Chrysler ass-kisser closes its doors."

"Sells out," Patti said. "Buying the Cadillac was sort of a tip-off. Rolls and Mercedes don't count."

"Just sign the papers . . . I don't know why I stayed in as long as I did. He'd come down to the plant, his arm hanging, dragging his leg, he'd come down and sit among his bowling trophies and black-framed memories . . . Knudsen, Sloan, Tex Colbert, he even had Horace Dodge up there, Christ, while he stared at me through those fucking glass partitions. Go to Schweizer's for lunch. Dad went every single day for forty-five years. I'd say, let's go to Little Harry's for a change. No, Schweizer's. I'm never gonna eat another potato pancake as long as I live."

"Poor baby," Patti said.

"What I'm gonna do, sell every machine in the plant except one. I think a Waterbury Farrell Automatic Thread Roller, a big Number 50. Paint it black and stand it out on the front lawn with a plaque that reads: 'It's an ugly fucker, but it sure made us a pile of money' . . . I'd love to do that."

Patti said, "It's too bad you don't have the balls." She signed the papers and left.

"You lied to me," Angela said.

The first thing he thought of: you left the razor blade on the sink.

She had come out of the bathroom and was standing in the hall doorway, holding what looked like a magazine under her arm.

"You're not forty. You're thirty-seven or -eight. Which?"

He said, "I'll be thirty-eight in October," relaxing a little but still uncertain, until she held up, not a magazine, his high school yearbook.

"Western," Angela said, "nineteen-sixty-one . . ."

He'd taken it in there one morning weeks ago—saving time, looking up a familiar name, a robbery-homicide suspect he was pretty sure he'd gone to school with—and left the yearbook on the open shelf with the towels.

". . . 'Bryan proved his sterling character both in the classroom and on the Cowboy basketball court where he averaged fifteen points a game,' " Angela recited. "Sterling character, my ass."

"I averaged sixteen points," Bryan said.

"Why did you lie?"

"I'm not quite six foot either."

Angela waited.

He said, "Well, you were having trouble being thirty. So, I thought if I told you I was forty, and looked like I was handling it okay—you know, forty being worse than thirty—it might make you feel better."

"You did it for me?" Angela said.

"I guess so."

She was coming toward him with the warm look again.

"Sometimes," Bryan said, "I tell myself I'm forty. It makes me feel more—I want to say mature—but grown-up, anyway. See, I think you get over forty you're finally there, you're full-grown and it's easier to talk to people. Otherwise, I have the feeling everyone's older than I am."

"I do too," Angela said.

"So I pretend I'm older and it works."

"Are you shy?" She sank down next to him on the sofa and he handed her the joint, the second one she had rolled from the evidence bag.

"No, I don't think I am. Well, maybe a little."

"You weren't shy in court. But it's funny," Angela said. "In a way you seemed . . . not like a little boy exactly, but boyish. Natural. I wanted to make a face at you, like we were in grade school."

"Why didn't you?"

"I didn't know what kind to make."

"So you were feeling like a little girl."

"Yeah, but I wasn't aware of it till I started looking at you. See, I didn't analyze it *then,* at the time."

He said, "Why don't you put that thing down."

She said, "All right," and laid the joint in the groove of an ashtray that said *Carl's Chop House.*

He said, "Are you ready?" Touching her face with his palm as she turned back to him.

She said, "I'm ready."

They kissed for the first time, not rushing it but finally holding on and getting it all, not wanting to let go it was so good.

Bryan said, "That was the best kiss I've ever had in my life."

She said, "God, you're good. But don't say it if it isn't true. Okay?"

"No, I mean it. It was the best one I ever had."

"You're not lying . . ."

"No, it's the truth."

"Please don't ever lie to me, okay?"

"No, I won't. You a little high? I think I'm beginning to feel it."

She said, "It was the best one I've ever had, too."

He said, "Are you having fun at the party?"

Walter was wearing a raincoat over his pajamas because he didn't own a bathrobe. He was wearing black wing tips, too, but no socks.

He knocked and entered the study. It was dark: the only light coming from a green desk lamp on one side of the room and the TV screen on the other, where Mr. Daniels was sitting in a leather chair, his legs stretched out on a matching leather ottoman. The picture on the TV screen didn't move. It was like a color photograph of the Secret Service ganging up on the assassin, who was under the pile somewhere.

Robbie said, "Come on in, sit down."

Walter pulled a ladder-back chair closer to the TV set, sat down and hunched over with his elbows on his thighs.

Robbie said, "See the guy with the submachine gun?"

"Yeah, in the gray suit," Walter said. "It looks like an Uzi."

"That's what it is," Robbie said. "All right, watch." He began clicking the remote-control switch and the pictures on the screen backed up frame by frame. Then changed to another view of action. Then to an earlier, longer view of Secret Service agents and newsmen standing around, waiting. "There," Robbie said, "he doesn't have it." He moved the pictures forward and stopped on the Secret Service agent with the submachine gun angling up from under his right arm, his left arm extended, pointing; he was saying something. Robbie said, "There, he does. Where did he get the Uzi?"

"Out of a case," Walter said. "One latch open, the other one closed, with his finger on it at all times."

"How do you know that?"

"I just know, that's all," Walter said. "That's Quickdraw McGraw, whatever guy has that job, that's what he's called. Keeps within six paces of the president at all times. Maybe eight."

Robbie ran the sequence backward again and stopped on a frame that showed a hand holding a revolver in the right foreground, two bodies on the sidewalk, a policeman's hat, part of the president's limousine.

"What kind of gun is that?"

"No kind," Walter said. "Guy shoots the president of the United States with a fucking Saturday-night special."

"You feel he deserves better. I agree. This is how to do it if you're dumb but lucky," Robbie said. "You want a drink?"

"No, I don't care for anything. I was in bed."

"Two questions," Robbie said. "What did Angie and the cop talk about, the hearing?"

"No, just bullshit. He was pointing out to her some of the, you know, points of interest."

"Okay. The other thing, how do I get hold of Curtis Moore?"

Christ, try and keep up with this guy. "I don't know," Walter said, straightening, sitting back in the chair. "Call him, I guess."

"Incidentally," Robbie said, "you've got a new lawyer, Roger Stedman. He'll get in touch with you when the time comes."

"What do I tell Eddie Jasinski?"

"Tell Eddie he's fired," Robbie said. "I want to try to set up something with Curtis Moore either tomorrow or Sunday, preferably tomorrow. Where does he hang out?"

"You call him at home?"

"Several times, no answer. What about his motorcycle club? You must've dealt with them at one time or another."

"I don't know," Walter said, "they used to always be at a place on Jefferson, across from Uniroyal. Let me think." He looked around the semidark room, a study that was bigger than a parlor, Daniels staring at him, waiting. "Yeah, the Elite Bar, corner of Jefferson and Concord, across from where Uniroyal was. They sit out in front revving their machines. They don't go anywhere, just make a lot of noise, wake up the neighborhood."

"Call the bar, see if he's there."

"You serious?"

"Walter, the proper response is, yes, Mr. Daniels."

Walter sat at Mr. Daniel's desk, called information, then the Elite Bar, said, "What? You don't mean to tell me." Said, "Yeah?" a couple of times and hung up with an amazed look.

"You want to hear something? Curtis don't come in no more, he's working, parking cars at the Detroit Plaza Hotel. I never heard of any Plaza Hotel in town."

"In the RenCen. But why is that hard to believe?"

"You imagine giving your automobile to Curtis, hand him the fucking *keys?* That's what he used to do for a living, steal cars, all 'em for parts."

Mr. Daniels, sitting in the soft glow of the TV picture, didn't say anything for some time. He looked like he was falling asleep, while Walter rolled from one cheek to the other, trying to get comfortable on the straight chair. He said, "Mr. Daniels, you mind if I go back to bed?"

"No, I'll see you in the morning. I want you to pick up some people for me."

"Pick 'em up where?"

Robbie gave him a thin smile. "You've got to be the most, if not impertinent, the most informal driver I've ever had."

"I want to drive," Walter said, "I can drive my own car all I want. I didn't come up here to fucking drive around town. I thought I was hired for a deal you have in mind that I'm the man for it, not driving a limo or living with the help or taking a lot of shit from the cook who's supposed to be Ukrainian and can't even make pirogies, for Christ sake.''

''You're tired,'' Robbie said.

''I'll agree with you there,'' Walter said. ''I didn't hire on to drive any fink cops home to their doors either.''

Robbie was pulling himself out of the chair. Without a word he walked past Walter to the desk, took a key from his pocket and unlocked a side drawer.

''Come here.''

Daniels was taking a folder from the drawer now. He opened it and laid a large photograph, at least nine by twelve, on the desk beneath the lamp and looked at Walter.

''Here he is.''

It was a photocopy, Walter saw, of a photograph that had appeared in a newspaper or magazine, though there was no caption, nothing to identify the man sitting with the small boy perched on his lap, both posed, looking directly at the camera.

The man, who appeared to be about sixty years of age, was dressed in a formal military uniform laden with gold leaf and braid, rows of decorative medals with ribbons, and wore a fore-and-aft plumed admiral's hat.

Walter said, ''What's he in, Knights of Columbus?''

Robbie didn't answer, waiting for the right question.

The boy in the photo, with the same hint of Latin coloring as the man, wore a white double-breasted suit with short pants and appeared to be nine or ten years old.

Walter said, ''I give up. Who is he?''

''At one time,'' Robbie said, ''one of the world's foremost dictators.''

''I don't recognize him,'' Walter said.

''He died,'' Robbie said, ''exactly twenty years ago.''

Walter said, ''He's *dead?* Wait a minute. You mean you want to hit the kid?''

''The picture was taken thirty years ago,'' Robbie said. ''The kid isn't a kid anymore. He's a grown man, Walter. The guy we're looking for.''

Walter said, "Yeah?" Not too sure. The kid was a nice-looking kid. "This guy, he's pretty bad?"

Robbie said, "Walter, if I told you what a rotten prick this little boy's turned out to be"—Robbie paused—"Well, you'd want to fly down to West Palm tonight."

Walter straightened, eyes catching a gleam of lamplight. "You mean this guy lives down by you?"

Robbie said, "I don't want to get you all worked up too soon, buddy. We've got time."

"I'm ready right now," Walter said. "I'm not doing nothing."

Robbie said, "Yeah, but I am. Let me get some business out of the way, then we'll give it our full attention. How's that sound?"

"I'm ready," Walter said.

5

Angela woke up during the night and for a moment didn't know where she was. She had interviewed a woman who used to wake up at least once a week and not know where she was or who the guy was lying next to her; the woman had made a name for herself, subsequently, bringing people into Alcoholics Anonymous. Angela recognized Bryan and went back to sleep. In the morning she used his toothbrush, looked for a bathrobe and couldn't find one. Wearing her navy blue coat over bare skin she made coffee. The morning was bright, trees beginning to bud outside the window; but it was cold in the apartment. She went back into the bedroom, stood looking down at Bryan sleeping and kneed the side of the bed. He woke up, looked at her with instant recognition and a smile, a good sign, and said, "Well, here we are, huh?"

Angela, holding her wool coat closed but not buttoned, said, "I interviewed a Sicilian one time who married a girl in a big ceremony. This was in New York; they both came here from Sicily when they were kids. They're married, they fly down to Orlando, Florida, on their honeymoon to go to Disney World and that night he finds out his wife isn't a virgin. At least he's convinced she isn't a virgin and he has a fit. He calls up the girl's father and her uncle and complains, like they're responsible for giving him damaged goods. The girl, however, keeps insisting she's a virgin. So the guy takes her to a doctor for a virgin test and the doctor says, well, she might be a virgin, but then again she might not. Virgin tests are not all that conclusive. He takes her to two more doctors in Orlando. The first one throws them out. The second one gets the girl up on the table, feet up in the stirrups, takes a look—hmmm, everything looks okay to him; no hymen to speak of, but this doctor's an O.B. and he's not sure he's ever seen a virgin. The husband feels that if it's possible his wife isn't a virgin he isn't gonna go through life wondering about it, picturing her, as he says, with some Puerto Rican or worse. You're not part Puerto Rican, are you?"

Bryan moved his head back and forth, no, on the pillow.

"So the guy sends her home to her father and gets an annulment. The girl, virgin or not, feels the guy has ruined her reputation. Even back in Sicily, the village she left as a little girl, they're talking about it, shaking their heads, see, that's what happens when you go to the U.S. of A. So she brings a slander suit against her ex-husband for a million bucks. She's awarded two hundred thousand and the Appeals Court upholds it. When I interviewed the Sicilian guy he said it was not really her lack of virginity that turned him off. It was the fact on the honeymoon she deceived him. She had brought along a contraceptive device, french-kissed like a pro and had her hand on his joint before he'd even taken his coat off. He said, 'I should give a woman like that two hundred thousand dollars? I wouldn't even if I had it, and I don't.' What I'm getting at is, you can try hard to please somebody and in the end, nobody wins."

Bryan said, "That's an interesting story."

"I'm not a virgin," Angela said. "I was married; but even if I hadn't been, I still wouldn't be a virgin. I'm not giving up anything or making any kind of claim. I know what I want and I know what I don't want."

Bryan was lying on his back beneath the sheet and blanket, staring up at her, his hands behind his head now.

He said, "We haven't even done it yet."

She said, "Do you know why?"

He said, "I think I was asleep when you came out of the bathroom and you didn't wake me up."

"So it's my fault." Very dry.

"No, I held back, it was out of respect."

"Respect and dope," Angela said, "and a fifth of Jim Beam. I'll tell you what I *don't* want first, I don't want it to be a morning quickie."

Bryan said, "I don't either. I'm hoping it'll last a good ten minutes anyway. Why don't you open your coat?"

She did. Opened it and closed it, giving him a flash of suntanned skin, small pale breasts and slim white panties.

Bryan said, "You want to wait, huh? Little candlelight and soft music?"

She half-closed her eyes, a seductive, bored look, did a little one-two, one-two go-go step and flashed him again.

Bryan said, "Okay, tell me what you want."

Robbie left home at twenty past nine Saturday morning, came out on Lake Shore Drive and had to put his visor down at the spectacle of sun on water.

Both of his homes faced bodies of water. Not so much because he was drawn to the sight, but because people as rich as Robbie who lived in Palm Beach looked at the Atlantic Ocean and if they lived in Grosse Pointe, where there was less frontage, they caught glimpses of Lake St. Clair; one body of water reaching to Africa, the other, beyond the horizon, to Canada; one a deep blue, the other, green. At least today the lake was a summery green, though it lay flat and empty and it would be a month before the sailboats were out.

Lake Shore became East Jefferson, leaving behind Better Homes for a run through HUD country to high rises on the river and into downtown some twenty minutes later. Robbie turned his black Mercedes into the Renaissance Center—now the glass-towered face of Detroit in travel-magazine shots—bore to the right and came around to the entrance of the Detroit Plaza Hotel.

Now the tricky part.

Spot Curtis Moore. Time it so that Curtis takes the car and no one else.

Robbie nosed the Mercedes into the dim three-lane area beneath the port cochere, hung back to study the people standing around, the traffic flow, the procedure. Then moved up in the outside lane for a closer look. There was more activity than he thought there'd be this time of the morning: maybe a convention leaving or another group coming in. There were two doormen dressed as French policemen. Or redcaps. Two young black guys in red blazers handing out claim checks to the parking attendants who wore drab industrial-blue uniforms and were hard to spot in the half-light. They would give part of the ticket to the owner, jump in the car and take a sharp right down a ramp to the garage level, then reappear some minutes later, coming out a door that was off behind the cashier's window and marked *Authorized Personnel Only*.

Robbie had to leave his car and go over to stand near the door before he was able to identify Curtis.

No cornrows this morning, a moderate Afro. His movement, his walk seemed different too, less studied. He was offstage now doing his work . . . giving Robbie a look as he came past the cashier's window. Do I know you?

Robbie was wearing sunglasses, dressed in a gray suit and rep tie beneath a buttoned-up raincoat. He held out a ten-dollar bill.

"I think I'm next."

Curtis said nothing. He took the bill, went over to one of the parking maitre d's in the red blazers, got a ticket and came back.

"How long you be?"

"Couple of hours."

Curtis tore a stub off and handed Robbie his claim check. Now Robbie watched him slide into the Mercedes and take off as he slammed the door closed; gone.

Robbie waited near the cashier's window where several people stood with their backs to him. It would take a few minutes. There were no more than four or five parking attendants working, so three or four should come through the *Authorized Personnel Only* door before Curtis appeared again.

Well, you never knew. The door opened, a blue uniform appeared. The door closed and opened again within a few moments and there was Curtis. Out of order, out of character. It bothered Robbie, gave him a mild tug of alarm. Even a minor miscalculation would not do in this business; or else several dozen popular novels had given him the wrong information. But he had to proceed right now or throw out the plan and start over.

He held up his parking ticket, caught Curtis's eye.

"You just took my car down. I have to get something out of it."

Now the lassitude, the slow move, the look of indifference as Curtis shifted and got back into character, pleasing Robbie more than Curtis could imagine.

"What do you do in a case like this?"

"Want me bring your car back?"

"That doesn't seem necessary," Robbie said. "Why not take me down, show me where the car is?"

"Ain't allowed. Just the people work here."

Robbie showed him the folded ten-dollar bill he had ready. "What if I stand over there by the ramp? No one will see me. The next car you take down, stop for a second and I'll hop in."

"I don't have the key."

Robbie felt instant irritation. "You just took the car *down.*" It couldn't be this complicated.

"I put the key over in the cashier place"—Curtis pointed—"see, then I come out."

Robbie said, "Well, then get the key."

"I don't know I can do that."

Robbie brought his billfold out of an inside pocket. "I'll bet you twenty bucks you can."

Curtis went back in through the *Authorized Personnel Only* door. Robbie waited. Christ, complications. Curtis came back out.

"I get in a car," Curtis said. "Wait till you see the man owns the car goes inside the hotel. Or you see the dudes in the red coats looking? No deal, man. You understand what I'm saying to you?"

Robbie waited. He watched Curtis go over to pick up a gray four-door Lincoln Continental, watched him get in before he moved to the ramp opening, timing it, hearing the car coming and then a faint squeal of brakes. Robbie opened the door and slid in, the car moving as he slammed the door, down the right-curving chute, Curtis cranking the steering wheel, nicking the Lincoln's bumper along the cement wall.

Robbie said, "Where's Carlos?"

The flat tone was just right.

Curtis was holding the steering wheel cocked, tires squealing on the pavement. Now they were down, rolling along the aisle past rows of cars gleaming in fluorescent light.

Robbie said again, "Where's Carlos?"

Curtis braked abruptly. He said, "I seen you someplace. Else I don't know the fuck you talking about." He twisted around to look past the seats, backed the Lincoln into a space in one effortless move and pulled the keys from the ignition. He got out. Robbie got out.

Robbie said, "Whether you admit it or not, I know you're with Carlos." Staring at Curtis deadpan, the way it was done.

"I know I'm in deep shit you don't get out of here," Curtis said, handing Robbie his keys and then pointing. "Your car over there."

"You gonna wait for me?"

"I don't know you or what you talking about—fucking Carlo, whatever you saying." Curtis started to walk off. "I be back."

Robbie liked the way the Mercedes was parked, front end out. He got behind it and lifted the trunk lid. The canvas tool kit lay to one side of the spotless luggage compartment. He rolled it open, took out the frame of his High Standard Field King, then the ten-inch suppressor tube and grooved it onto the frame, hearing the click of the lock mechanism. The target pistol was ready, the clip fully loaded. He ducked down as a Seville came off the ramp and swept past. Robbie remained low. Another car came down. He listened to doors open and thunk closed. He listened to footsteps on the cement floor, heard voices yell back and forth, words that sounded to him like some Gullah dialect echoing through the concrete level, then laughter. Another car came down. He raised enough to watch the parking attendant get into a Buick Riviera and squeal off toward the exit ramp, following an arrow.

A green Chevrolet station wagon came down, Curtis Moore behind the wheel. Robbie unbuttoned the top half of his raincoat, slipped the target pistol that now measured close to sixteen inches in length inside the coat and held it there, like Napoleon. A car door slammed. Footsteps approached the Mercedes. Robbie moved past the side windows to the hood of his car. Curtis was across the aisle, coming this way.

Robbie said, "Curtis?"

Curtis looked up. "You got what you need?" Then stopped, looking right at Robbie. "Hey—how you know my name?"

Robbie wanted to hurry, but he had to play it out. Or else why bother? He said, "Because I know you work for Carlos."

Curtis was scowling, giving him a mean look. "Man, I work for the hotel's who I work for."

Robbie brought out the pistol, extending it like a blue-steel wand and began shooting Curtis, aiming high and seeing Curtis throw his head from side to side doing a backstep dance, the snout of the gun giving off hard punctuations of muted sound, casings ejecting, while off beyond were metallic pings and pops in the cement confines and the windshield behind Curtis sprouted spiderwebs. Robbie jammed the gun under one arm, got to Curtis, who was turning red, smearing chrome and sheet metal red, slipping off the red car fender, got to him and eased him down—eyes glassy, sightless—between the cars, careful not to get any of the red on his raincoat, then shoved Curtis with his foot, hanging onto a door handle for leverage, and got most of him hidden beneath the car. A sporty Chrysler LeBaron. Robbie liked it. It seemed an act of loyalty, the least he could do.

Driving up the exit ramp in his Mercedes he became inspired and saw a billboard statement in his mind, lettered in red:

"When it comes to hiding victims
I'll take a Chrysler every time!"

With his name beneath it in neat black type. *Robinson Daniels, well-known sportsman*. Hey, yeah.

Less than a minute later, at five past ten, the Mercedes turned the corner and pulled up in front of the main doors to the Renaissance Center, the area far less congested than the hotel entrance around on the side. Robbie, in his gray suit, maize and blue striped tie laid across his shoulder by the river breeze, stepped out of the car, stood in the V formed by the open door, waved toward the entrance and yelled out:

"Mr. Cabrera? . . . Here!"

The buyer from Mexico. A gentleman in a dark suit, followed by a young, darker-skinned gentleman in a dark suit, came out from the entrance shade nodding, smiling all the way to the Mercedes.

"Sorry if I'm a little late," he said now. "Hi, I'm Robbie Daniels."

"I hope there's a moral to this," Angela said. "I mean I hope you're making a point." With her dry tone.

"If I don't forget what it is," Bryan said. He was sitting up in bed now with his coffee, the covers across his waist. White skin, dark hair on his chest.

Angela sat in an unfinished rocker he'd brought back from Kentucky years ago, Angela still in her navy coat, legs crossed, letting him have a glimpse of tan thigh.

"Go on."

"Where was I? Yeah, Donnie and—I want to say Marie—Donnie and Lorie finally get married. But Margo won't leave."

"Why didn't they throw her out?"

"Well, for one thing it's Margo's house. The three of them're trying to get along the best they can, but Lorie says she can't take it anymore."

"Why didn't Lorie and Donnie move out?"

"Because nobody was working. They're living on food stamps. Donnie says you can't work full time and disco at night, it can't be done. See, his one ambition, he and Lorie, was to get on 'Dance Fever.' So he doesn't like Lorie working either. Margo goes out and hustles a couple nights a week and that's the only money they've got coming in. But, as you can imagine, Margo isn't too fond of the setup. She became, Donnie says, hateful and inconsiderate. And Lorie, meanwhile, every time she gets Donnie alone she tells him she can't live this way. If he doesn't get rid of Margo she'll leave him."

"I don't believe this," Angela said.

"It's true, every word." Bryan sipped his coffee. "Well, they finally work out a plan. They borrow enough money from Margo, like a hundred and fifty bucks, and take out a life insurance policy on her life, Margo's, for ten thousand. That part was Lorie's idea. Lorie keeps telling him, if you really love me you'll do it. Donnie would tell *me*—he'd get a sad, faraway look and tell me, 'I love that girl. I love her more than words can say.' "

Angela said, "Yeah," meaning, go on; interested.

"So finally one night the three of them have a party. They get Margo drunk on Scotch, Donnie takes her in the bedroom, gives her a last jump—"

"Come on—"

"It's what he told me. Then he holds a pillow over her face until she's dead."

"They murdered her?"

"They murdered her. Wait. Then they tie her to the bed, arms and legs outstretched. They ransack the house to make it look like it's been robbed. Then they set the house on fire, tie each other up quick and start yelling for help. Their story's gonna be a bunch of bikers broke in, robbed them, raped and murdered Margo. But Donnie gets trapped in his own fire. In fact he probably would've died if a cop hadn't come in through a window and saved him. The cop got a citation. We investigate—right away we don't like the looks of it. The way drawers have been pulled out evenly, left open. The sofa's ripped all to hell with a knife—for what? Who hides anything in a sofa? Nobody in the neighborhood heard any motorcycles that night . . . Well, Lorie confessed first, then Donnie, and both were convicted on first degree. But here's the thing. Donnie writes to me about twice a year. He's worried about what I think of him, my opinion. In the last letter he says—"

The phone rang in the living room.

"He says, 'I know there are a lot of ill feelings toward me—' "

The phone rang.

" 'so all there is left to say is, God help us fools.' " As the phone rang again he said, "Would you get that?"

Angela said, "It's gonna be for you, isn't it?"

Bryan said, "I don't have any clothes on."

Angela went into the living room in her navy coat. Bryan came out a few moments later with a bath towel around his waist. She handed him the phone and he said into it, "I'm on furlough." He listened for almost a minute, sitting down on the sofa, his tone subdued when he said, "What time did it happen? . . . You sure? . . . Who's on it, Annie? . . . See if you can get Malik, he's probably out on his boat. Doug'll be home in bed, Quentin, he'll be in bed too, somewhere . . . Good, Annie, I'll see you later." He hung up.

Angela was standing, hands in pockets holding the coat closed.

Bryan said, "So Donnie's in Jackson doing mandatory life and worried about what I think of him, all because he loved Lorie *more than words can say*. I finally wrote to him, I said, Donnie, why didn't you just give her some flowers and candy?"

Angela said, "Your compassion spills over, doesn't it?" She came to the sofa, sat down close to him and put her hand on his knee, moving the towel to touch his bare skin.

Bryan said, ''So the moral is, when you love somebody you better be able to say how much, in words, or you could get your ass in some deep trouble.''

Angela said, ''I'm not sure I'd kill for you, Bryan, but I'll buy breakfast.''

''Is that what you want more than anything?''

''I guess at the moment. It's not however the *big* thing I want more than anything.''

Bryan looked at her and moved his eyebrows up and down, twice.

''Macho man,'' Angela said. ''Guys kill me.'' She slapped his thigh, then leaned on it to get up. ''Let's go get some breakfast.''

''I'd like to,'' Bryan said, ''but I can't. Curtis Moore was shot and killed about an hour ago.''

6

He told Angela Police Headquarters was referred to simply as "1300" because it was at 1300 Beaubien and there the numbers were, in gold, above the entrance. Nine stories of Italian Renaissance gone to grime and without a vantage as the old Wayne County jail closed in from one side and a new jail facility rose in cement forms on the other.

He asked her if she was hungry yet, nodding to the Coney Island across the street where the fry chef in the window was grilling hot dogs. Angela said no, thanks. She could still see the blood smears on cement and chrome; all that blood from one person. They had stopped at a Koney with a *K* in the Renaissance Center and she smoked cigarettes, sipped black coffee, while Bryan had two with everything. Brunch. He told her outside Police Headquarters it was almost two-thirty. She said she still wasn't hungry.

Construction dust hung in the air, the sound of highsteel riveting and transit mixers grinding out cement for the new county jail addition going up behind 1300. Bryan said they wouldn't have to advertise, the new building would have full occupancy within a week of completion.

In the lobby past the snack bar were the names of police officers killed in the line of duty, memorialized in marble wall sections on both sides of the elevators. They had to wait, Bryan holding the grocery sack with the red tag. Police personnel came and stood by them. They moved into the elevator and Angela was aware of the size of the men; they reminded her of professional athletes.

Fifth floor. Directly off the elevator was Room 500. Bryan told her they had moved recently because they needed more space and got maybe an additional ten square feet. He kept talking to her. There was a hole in the laminated door panel that looked as though someone had tried to kick it in. Angela wondered about it. Why anyone would want to break into a Homicide Section squad room? Unless, on the other hand, the person had been brought in kicking.

There were sounds in the empty room. A phone ringing. A portable radio tuned softly to classical music. A walkie-talkie reciting code numbers, getting no response.

Bryan picked up a phone. Angela looked around, neither disappointed nor surprised, not expecting much in a sixty-year-old building that belonged to the city. Metal desks and file cabinets and a coffee maker against municipal green walls. About four hundred Polaroid mug shots mounted on a sheet of wallboard. A map of the city. Two windows that looked down on Beaubien and the Coney Island place. But an adjoining room the size of a walk-in closet that held a table with a typewriter and three chairs was painted pink. Bryan hung up the phone. He told her it was their interrogation room and the color was to relax suspects, make them more receptive to questions. Angela wasn't sure if he was kidding or not. She had questions of her own but saw they would have to wait.

Jim Malik came in. Back from the morgue.

Bryan seemed surprised. "They do a post on Curtis already?"

Just starting. But Malik had been there for someone else. A little girl, from what Angela could gather. Perhaps a previous murder. She realized they didn't finish one and pick up another, like piecework; the murders came in unscheduled. Malik seemed frustrated; a muscular forty-year-old with sandy hair and a Guard's mustache. Cordial, smiling as he was introduced to her, but on the hunt; a man who appraised women openly, making plans on glimpses of fantasy. Then it was time for Angela to listen and observe these people whose business was murder:

Malik saying, "The M.E. went all through her, twice. Peeled her throat, no sign of ligature. Laid open the lungs, nothing. No sign of hemorrhage, no indication of restraints on wrists or ankles. I mean he didn't find shit outside of some maggots ready to pop."

Bryan said, "Toxicology doesn't show anything?"

Malik said, "We don't have it yet. But no sign of trauma and they think she's too young to've O.D.'d. So they're making it indeterminate pending toxicology. If nothing shows up in the blood, they'll call it exposure."

Bryan said, "Her panties were rolled down."

Malik said, "I know they were."

The phone rang and Malik answered it. He said, "Squad Five, Sergeant Malik . . . Yes, ma'am . . . No, he's on the street right now." He hung up and said, "You know what I think?" The phone rang again. He picked it up and began talking to someone about a shooting.

Angela listened.

Bryan took off his sport coat. Gray tweed with cord pants that almost matched. She wanted to ask him about the rubber bands on the grip of his gun, but she wanted to listen to Jim Malik.

"The one in the bar? . . . Yeah, the thing is, Terry, usually that kind of a situation you ask who saw it and thirty people were out in the can at the same time taking a piss . . . Right, all at once. But this time they all go, yeah, they saw it. Was the big dude come at the little dude . . ."

Bryan asked her if she wanted a cup of coffee. Still listening, Angela said yes and watched him cross to the coffee maker that was next to a strange-looking box that held walkie-talkies in slots with small indicator lights on. She had the feeling Malik was aware of her listening to him. The soft strains of classical music were still coming from the portable radio sitting on a file cabinet.

"That's the way every one of 'em tells it. They go, yeah, the big dude—guy weighs about two fifty, two sixty—he comes at the little dude with a knife and the little dude gets this pistol from somewhere and pops the big dude through the left eye, that's it . . . Yeah. Terry? The evidence techs're through, the morgue guys, they have to get help the son of a bitch's so big. They lift him up to get him in the body bag, there's the knife. Pearl handle . . ."

Bryan was coming back with coffee in a Styrofoam cup. He said, "Tell him to forget it."

Malik was saying, "Well, that's up to you. *Maybe* manslaughter. But nothing you say is gonna stick with thirty eyeball witnesses looking at you . . . Seventeen, whatever. All you need's one . . . Terry, if you're hot for the guy try and stick him with the gun . . . Yeah, okay. Let me know." Malik hung up. "Prosecutor's office."

Bryan said, "They'll dismiss it at the exam and the gun'll never come up. Somebody shoved it at him. All of a sudden he looks down, there's a gun in his hand and this giant asshole's coming at him."

They spoke quietly while Angela felt excitement.

Malik said, "That's what I told him." He paused a moment. "Anyway, I think she pushed her panties down and put her hands in there to keep warm. I'm serious. Lividity shows she was lying on her left side on the back seat and she died that way, man, without any sign of a struggle, in that position."

Bryan said, "Her panties were rolled down, not pushed down." He began to tell Angela about the little girl, eleven years old, who had been dead two months when they found her in the back seat of an abandoned car inside an unused garage with *Somebody Please* written in the dust on a window.

Angela, nodding, trying to picture the little girl, said, "What did you mean about her panties?"

But the door opened and he was looking away.

Doug Parrish and Annie Maguire came in, both holding manila envelopes.

Bryan said, "Doug, Annie . . . Angela Nolan." Brief, but without trying to appear anxious.

A courteous pause. Nods. Glad to meet you. Annie Maguire somewhat shy about it, but a beautiful smile. That was done and Parrish was opening his envelope, dumping small shell casings and several bits of misshapen lead onto Bryan's desk.

Parrish said, "Curtis was done with a twenty-two. Guy hits him at least four times. Cracks a windshield, two slugs still in it. Ruins the finish on five cars. But, I would say professionally done." The old gray wolf speaking, adjusting metal-frame glasses that matched his full head of hair.

"But he wasn't close," Bryan said. "He didn't stick it in Curtis's ear, did he?"

"Look at the rounds," Parrish said, offering evidence. "What do you see?"

Bryan picked up a flattened chunk of lead.

"Stingers."

"Stingers and yellowjackets," Parrish said. "Hypervelocity, hollow-nose expanders. The guy knew what he was doing."

Malik said, "Kanluen, he took one look inside Curtis—they're just starting to do a post on him. He says it looks like Curtis was hit with forty-fives. The head, the face, in the chest, they tore around in there like in a pinball machine. The one in the head very much like that Reagan's secretary, what's his name."

"But he didn't get close," Bryan said. "What was he afraid of?"

"Well, nobody heard it," Parrish said. "What does that tell you? The guy used a silencer. And you don't get a silencer down at the corner."

"You have car noises in there," Bryan said.

"He fired ten rounds we know of," Parrish said. "He had a good suppressor it wouldn't been any louder'n a B-B gun."

Malik said, "I understand Annie isn't watching the autopsy 'cause Curtis didn't get hit in the privates. They still strip the guy down, Annie."

Angela watched Annie's reaction. A nice smile, not a trace of malice or resentment; probably used to Malik, something that went on between them.

Annie said, taking a handful of claim checks from the manila envelope, "I was busy learning the valet-parking business."

Bryan said, "Oh shit." Tired. He appeared to be dealing with several different thoughts at once, looking into the future as Angela watched him and smoked cigarettes. He asked when the parking guys were coming in.

Annie said around five-thirty.

Parrish said, "We're gonna have to run after one or two of 'em. I know goddamn well."

Malik said, "Or they walk in and start copping. Say homicide, they'll cop to whatever they think of first. Things we don't even know about."

Annie laid the claim checks on Bryan's desk and was taking out more as Bryan said, "Okay, we talk to everybody who parked there around ten o'clock. Hotel guests, visitors . . ." He picked up one of the claim checks. "It's on here. Time in, time out." And then said, "Shit, we have to find anybody who left about that time."

Malik said, "Get the license number off the ticket, the receipt."

Bryan said, "It isn't on here," and looked up. "Annie, how do they find a car if there's no license number written on it?''

The ticket indicates the section the car is parked in, Annie explained. And the ticket number corresponds with the other half of the ticket in the car, by the windshield. She said, ''We do have the license numbers of all the cars that were there when it happened.''

Bryan said, ''Except there was an empty parking space, wasn't there? Right across the aisle from where he was shot. Is that the section we're talking about?''

Annie said, ''I'm afraid so. You'll see all the ticket numbers are consecutive. The cars that came in after nine-thirty and were still there. And you're right, one ticket's missing and there's no receipt for it in the cashier's office.''

Bryan said, ''So a car was in that empty spot and there's no record of it. Did the guy drive down himself? That's against the rules, isn't it?''

''No one's allowed down there but the parking attendants,'' Annie said. ''I don't know how he could've gotten down.''

Malik said, ''The guy wanted to drive down, who's gonna stop him?''

Bryan said, ''Someone'd chase after him and not necessarily Curtis. We're not talking about robbery. If the guy wants Curtis he doesn't want to get in an argument first, with somebody else. He wants to deal with Curtis and only Curtis.''

Parrish said, ''Which gets us around to motive.''

Bryan said, ''Not yet.''

Saving it, Angela thought. The motive in killing a black-leather-jacket ex-convict parking attendant.

''Let's look at what we've got first,'' Bryan said. ''We get on the computer to Lansing with the license numbers, get the owners of the cars that were there when it happened. Narrow it down. Ask when they arrived if they saw a guy drive down on his own, or if they saw anything strange, guy getting into a car *with* a parking attendant. Okay. But what about the cars that *left* about the same time the guy who was in the empty parking place arrived, I mean upstairs at the entrance and might've seen him? Anybody waiting for their car to come up—how in the hell do we contact *them?*'' He said, ''Jesus.'' And then said, ''All right. We find out from the hotel who checked out between nine-thirty and ten and left in a car. That'll give us a few more names."

Annie said, "I think we'll have about thirty or forty counting check-ins and check-outs. But some of these aren't valet parking, they're people who're staying at the hotel. We won't need Lansing for them, the claim checks tell us who they are."

Bryan said, "How many parking attendants?"

"Four," Annie said. "I have their names and addresses if they don't show up."

Bryan said, "Okay, we start with them. First question. Did anybody see a black Fleetwood Cadillac over there any time this morning? Next question. If the answer's yes, then you ask if a black Fleetwood Cadillac occupied that empty space for any length of time. And if they say yes to that, we might have an arraignment first thing in the morning."

He had their attention: Angela, Malik, Parrish and Annie Maguire all looking at him, the three detectives with expressions of mild expectation, surprise.

"Or," Bryan said, and paused. "Where's Quentin?"

Malik said, "He's still at the morgue. Kanluen's opening Curtis up, Quentin goes, 'I wouldn't miss this for the world; the mother tried to shoot me one time.' "

"Maybe we can save ourselves a few hours," Bryan said. "Call Quentin and tell him to pick up Walter Kouza. I'll give you the address."

Malik said, "*Wal*ter? Jesus Christ, that's right. He might be dumb enough."

Parrish said, "Walter's never used a twenty-two in his life."

"I hope not," Bryan said. "But let's pick him up anyway."

7

Bryan finished off a pail of mussels, ordered crab-legs and potato skins and was content to wait with his glass of beer, believing he felt as good as he had ever felt in his life. Keyed up but in no hurry. It was his favorite time of the day.

Angela was working through a Greek salad with Jack Daniels on the side and whitefish on the way, no longer restrained. She had not seen the body, only the red traces that remained, but it had been enough to subdue her through the afternoon. She seemed aware again rather than preoccupied and would look around Galligan's at the after-work crowd with interest, then would look at Bryan again and ask a question. She asked a great many questions.

"Do you eat a lot?"

"I've had what, two hot-dogs all day."

"I just wondered. You don't look like you eat much."

"I wondered if you ever ate anything," Bryan said.

"I do when I'm not on police investigations," Angela said, "and have to go to murder scenes."

"I shouldn't have taken you."

"No, I wanted to go. In fact I'll go whenever you ask me." She took a big bite of feta cheese and tomato and made the act seem dainty. "I like to watch you, Bryan. I loved it in the squad room, watching you putting pieces together. You think the little girl was murdered, don't you? Even though there's no evidence to go on."

"Yeah, I think she was."

"What if you don't learn anything more?"

"Then I put it away," Bryan said. "Forget about it."

"Just like that."

"Well, try to forget about it."

She said, "I worked for a newspaper when I started out, but I never did police stories. What's a post? A post mortem?"

"Yeah, an autopsy. They have to determine the cause of death. Even when a man's been shot four times."

"It's so different than anything I've ever experienced—just listening to you," Angela said. "Everyone seems calm, but you know they're keyed up and they don't want to miss anything." The warm look was in her eyes again and she seemed keyed up herself. "You're a pretty earthy bunch, aren't you? Especially Malik."

"We work in the street, the street rubs off," Bryan said. "Malik has sort of an indifferent, tough-cop style, but you put him in the Pink Room with a suspect he'll get a statement. I don't mean with intimidation, Malik'll bullshit the guy, put him at ease."

"And Doug Parrish," Angela said. "Very firm in his convictions."

"He surprised me today," Bryan said. "You're right, Doug's set in his ways. He usually takes a more conservative approach. But if he's convinced the guy used a silencer then you can be pretty sure the guy used a silencer. He doesn't wing it very often. Annie's much the same, but her manner's entirely different. Annie, you don't even know she's there."

Angela said, "She seems too nice to be a homicide detective. I mean she doesn't seem the type."

Bryan said, "Well, you don't need muscle really, you don't have to smoke cigars . . ."

"The guys aren't inhibited by her?"

"No, Malik tries to shock her, but how's he gonna do that? She's seen everything. No, Annie smiles. She's a very easy person to be with."

"Have you ever . . . had a feeling about her?"

"No," Bryan said. "I've never kissed a cop or gone to bed with one. I kissed a girl writer once and went to bed with her, but nothing happened. She didn't want to rush into anything."

"I heard you blew it."

"Well, I know she didn't."

"Don't be crude."

"Can't I say anything I want to you?"

"I have another question," Angela said. "You don't really think Walter's the one, do you?"

Bryan looked at his watch. "Well, I'm gonna ask him in about an hour. Then let the parking guys take a look at him."

She said, "But he knows you'd suspect him. It would be so *dumb.*"

"I keep an open mind," Bryan said. "That way I never get too surprised. But yeah, I can see Walter doing it. I don't think intelligence is a factor. Look at what's her name, the head of the girls' school who shot the diet doctor. Jean Harris. She isn't dumb. You read the poems she wrote to him? Well, they were kinda sappy, I guess. But if anybody was *dumb* it's that skinny doctor. He didn't see it coming."

"I forget you're a psychiatrist," Angela said. "You read people and advise them."

"Only certain ones."

"You advise me, help me look at myself."

"You're easy."

"Okay," Angela said. "Do you know what I'm gonna do this evening?"

He felt a warning he didn't understand and now wasn't sure what to say. The waiter arrived and gave him time, serving Angela's whitefish, his crab-legs. A polite waiter in a black vest, anxious to please. He left them.

Angela said, "Well?"

He said, "For some reason I don't like the sound of it."

The waiter returned with potato skins, giving him a few moments more. He ordered another draft of Stroh's and a Jack Daniels for Angela. He liked the way she sipped it and seemed to enjoy the taste.

"All right. What're you gonna do this evening?"

"I'm going home."

He said, "You don't mean to your hotel."

"No. All the way home, to Tucson." She seemed to smile, a crafty look. "I thought you were never surprised."

"I was wrong," Bryan said. "Why're you going home?"

She said, "Well, I haven't seen my folks in a while, since last summer. I was away for Christmas and tomorrow's my birthday. So, I think it's a good time for a visit. I want to get a picture of you though, before I leave."

Bryan frowned, all this rushing at him at once. "Wait a minute. Are you coming back?"

"Sure. I'm still working on Robbie."

"Yeah, but he might be somewhere else."

"Well, you might be too. You're going to Florida, aren't you?"

"Not right away . . . You sound different. How long're you gonna be gone?"

"I don't know. A week maybe."

"And then what?"

He saw her shrug one shoulder in the navy blue coat and tried to remember her without the coat on.

She said, "I have to finish the piece for *Esquire*. That's Robbie. Then, there's a publisher wants me to do a whole book on rich people. But I don't know if I can handle it, or want to. Then, who knows?"

He said again, "You sound different."

"I'm not. Are you different?"

"No."

She said, "Aren't you hungry?"

"I don't think you're coming back."

"If I say I am but you don't think I am," Angela said, "then *I* think you're starting to choke up, Bryan. Maybe taking yourself a little too seriously. And you know what you do when that happens. Right?"

He said, "There a lot of things I want to say to you."

She said, "Good. Save them."

She took a picture of him outside, against Galligan's painted brick wall. She kissed him and said, "Don't I get a hug?" before she got in the taxi. He walked back to 1300.

In the hallway by the elevators Annie Maguire said to Bryan, "We had them down at Squad Six when Walter arrived, so they haven't seen him yet. They don't know what's going on. Walter doesn't either, for that matter. He's ready to go through the wall."

"Who's with him?"

"Quentin." Annie waited a moment. "Do you think this is a good idea?"

He said, "You want to wait for probable cause? Or you want to find out right now? Tell me how many times we get clear-cut probable cause?" Bryan entered the squad room.

Three of the valet-parking attendants were sitting next to desks like job applicants. The cashier was at Malik's desk and Malik was trying to get her to pose for a Polaroid shot. "Come on, smile now. Big smile." The girl was laughing, moving around. "I'm not shitting you," Malik said, "we're gonna send it in, Miss Black America contest." Parrish was watching, not saying anything.

Bryan opened the door to the Pink Room partway. Quentin Terry said, "Here's the man now, Walter. I told you he be here. You want cream and sugar?"

Walter said, "Cream, two-and-a-half sugars."

"Two-and-a-*half,*" Quentin said, getting up from the folding chair to edge past Bryan, rolling his eyes as he went out. Bryan closed the door. He could hear the girl, the valet-parking cashier, laughing.

Walter sat in the corner between the table with the typewriter and the wall, wedged in there and looking mean, heavy shoulders hunched, ready to come out of the chute.

Bryan said, "How do you like it?" Meaning the room, nodding then to the Miranda sign on the wall. "Your rights. There they are. Nobody can say we don't give you your rights. Read it, Walter."

"The fuck you think you're doing?" Walter said. "Bring me down here."

"I got to ask you some questions, Walter. Somebody did Curtis Moore."

In the silence that began to lengthen Walter said, "Come on," with reverence. "Come on, don't shit me."

"I'd never do that, Walter."

"Jesus Christ, you mean it? *Curtis?*"

"You didn't hear about it? It was on the news."

"How'm I gonna hear about it? I'm driving around the fucking limo all day. Pick these guys up, take 'em the plant. Pick 'em up again, take 'em out the airport. Listen, you find the guy did it let me know. I want to shake the fucker's hand."

"What plant?"

"Daniels. He's selling all his equipment. Got these buyers in from Cleveland, Indianapolis, Christ, Mexico, Japan. Couple

Japs, they come all the way over here to buy some machines that turn out nuts and bolts. Big fuckers—I mean the machines, like drill presses. Another guy don't speak nothing but Kraut, he comes all the way from West Germany."

"How about around ten this morning, a little before?"

"I left home quarter to ten, from Grosse Pointe. Eight-nine-nine Lake Shore. Ask the cook, he'll tell you. Fucking Ukrainian."

"Who'd you pick up at the Plaza?"

"What's that, the one at the RenCen? I never picked anybody up there."

"Didn't go near it, uh?"

"No, first thing I picked up these guys out at the airport. Fly in, fly out. Daniels had riggers there right at the plant. Some guys from the Teamsters, two-nine-nine. Give the buyers an estimate right on the spot, how much to haul the shit out. The auction isn't suppose to be till Monday, but Daniels, he can't fucking wait to get out of the nuts and bolts business. It was okay for his old man but Robbie, see, he's a friend of George Hamilton, whoever the fuck George Hamilton is. I met him, I still don't know."

"You drove the Cadillac?"

"What do you think I pick 'em up in, the fucking Omni?"

There was a yellow legal pad next to the typewriter. Bryan said, "Write the names on there and the approximate time you picked them up."

"I don't know their names."

"You can get them, can't you?"

"I don't know. I'll see."

Bryan opened the door several inches, glanced out and closed it again.

"Coffee's not ready yet. You want to wait?"

"You mean," Walter said, "do I want to leave now or do I want to wait till the *coffee's* done? Jesus Christ," Walter said, getting up off the folding chair.

Bryan pushed the door open all the way, caught Malik's eye and saw one of the valet-parking attendants look over his shoulder.

"Quentin's gonna drive you home."

"Tell that dinge I don't need any conversation this trip. Fucker never shuts up," Walter said, pulling down the sleeve of his gray suit, brushing at invisible dirt. He followed Bryan through the squad room now and out into the hallway to the elevators. Here, Walter narrowed his eyes, turned back to the squad room as Quentin came out putting on his suit coat, Walter catching a glimpse of the three valet-parking attendants looking this way. The door closed.

"Wait a minute," Walter said. "What's this shit going on?"

Bryan pushed the elevator button again. Quentin was adjusting his suitcoat.

"You brought me up here to get eyeballed, didn't you? Who're those guys. You try and put me in the Plaza today—that where they're from?"

"They park cars," Bryan said.

"Hey, I used to pull this kind of shit too, you know. You bring me up here, not a fucking shred of probable cause, hoping one of those monkeys'll cop on me, huh?" Walter stopped. He looked at the door again and said in a much quieter tone, "What'd you say they do?"

"They park cars," Bryan said, "at the Detroit Plaza Hotel. Where Curtis Moore used to park cars till somebody took him out."

"How?"

"We don't know yet."

"Bullshit—was he shot, stabbed, what?"

"Shot. Four times."

"What kind of gun?"

"That's what I meant, we don't know yet."

"The guys up in Firearms know," Walter said. "You telling me they haven't given you the ballistics yet? Bullshit."

Bryan said, "Thanks for coming, Walter."

When Quentin Terry got back from Grosse Pointe he met them at the Athens in Greektown, the cop bar. Parrish had gone home to watch "Hill Street Blues." Bryan, Annie and Malik were about ready to leave, having a last beer, picking over the information they got from the valet-parking attendants and the cashier, which amounted to almost nothing.

One of them didn't know Curtis had been working this morning. The others saw him, yeah, but didn't notice anything funny going on or Curtis talking to anybody in particular. The one who found Curtis's body said the blood led him to it; he thought at first somebody had spilled paint. The cashier remembered Curtis coming in, getting some keys from where they hung on hooks, Curtis saying a man needed something from his car; but people were at the window, she was too busy to notice anything. Except when the police came and she heard about Curtis, she remembered him getting the keys. No, there was nothing unusual about the keys that she remembered. Wait now—or did it have some kind of a charm or good-luck piece on it? She'd try to remember and let them know.

Quentin Terry said, "Walter didn't hardly open his mouth in the car. I told him a couple Polish jokes, the man didn't even smile."

Bryan said, "He ask you about the gun?"

"Yeah, he tried different ways," Quention said. "Especially interested if the gunshots were through and through. Wanting to find out the caliber."

"He was surprised when I first told him," Bryan said. "Couldn't believe it. The guy that did it, I think if he'd walked in Walter would've put his arms around him and kissed him."

Malik said, "Kissed him, he'd have blown him."

"But out in the hall," Bryan said, "he was different. You notice?"

Quentin said, "Like something begun to bother him."

"Not so much that we'd set him up," Bryan said. "It was when he found out those guys in there parked cars. Why would that bother him?"

He walked with Annie Maguire to the parking structure on St. Antoine, past the Saturday-night lineup waiting to get in the Hellas Cafe. She asked him where his girl friend was.

"I just met her yesterday, at Walter's hearing."

Annie said, "You have to start somewhere." She said, "I bet she's from a big family."

"I don't know. She didn't say."

"Haven't gotten into all that yet."

"Well, I don't know if we will," Bryan said. "She went home. Tucson, Arizona."

"She told you she'd be back, didn't she?"

"That's what she says, I don't know."

"Come on, don't play dumb, Bryan."

"I mean it. I don't know what she's thinking."

"Well, this afternoon," Annie said, "she took her eyes off you maybe once."

"Is that right?" Bryan said. "I didn't notice.

Annie stopped and looked around. "Isn't that your car back there?"

They had walked past Bryan's seven-year-old BMW. It was faded gray with rust spots along the chrome like sores. He said, "It looks like mine."

Annie said, "You need to get away, Bryan. Soon."

Daniels wasn't in his study when Walter got home and he couldn't go up the front stairs to look for him. He had to go through the pantry and the kitchen to the goddamn back stairs and go up that way if he was going to his room. The bathroom door was closed. Walter knocked. He heard the sound of the cook's voice give him a grunt. "Wash your hands when you're done!" Walter called through the door. Fucking Ukrainian. He went downstairs again to use the other john, the powder room in the front hall.

The black Mercedes sedan was gone from the garage. The yellow Mercedes convertible that Daniels called a drophead was there. The Cadillac was there and the Dodge Omni that nobody used was there. So Daniels could've taken the big Mercedes or his wife could've. Walter hadn't said two words to the wife. It was a fucked-up house. Nobody talked to anybody. Nobody even argued. The place was like a hotel where you passed people in the hall and everybody was polite but nobody seemed to give a shit about anything.

Walter heard a car; somebody dropping Mrs. Daniels off. She came in to find him sitting on the Queen Anne bench in the front hall, cocked a hip as she looked at him and smiled, sort of half-closing her eyes.

"You've been waiting for me, haven't you?"

Walter said, "Pardon?"

Mrs. Daniels seemed a little high. No question about it—all at once sinking down next to him in her lynx fur that Walter remembered from Robbery would run about eight, nine grand. She smelled of booze, but she smelled good too, leaning against him now. He didn't know what was going on. Her hair was in his face, but he'd have to touch her, hold her up if he tried to move. Now she was raising her face to look at him. He felt her hand on his thigh, trying to squeeze it but not able to get any purchase. He didn't know what was going *on*.

Mrs. Daniels said, "Can I ask you a question, Walter?"

He felt her hand crawl to his fly—Christ!—and probe until she found his member.

"What do you call one of these in Polish?"

Walter sat as straight as he could, not moving. "It's called . . . it's usually they call it a *hooyek*."

"A *hooyek*." Mrs. Daniels spoke the word lovingly. She let go, got up and crossed to the stairway, weaving just a little. A hand on the balustrade, she looked back at him. "A *hooyek?*"

"That's correct," Walter said. "H-u-j-e-k, *hooyek*."

"Thank you," Mrs. Daniels said. She went upstairs.

Walter fell asleep. He opened his eyes and thought the woman was back and got a shock when he saw it was Mr. Daniels sitting next to him now, in his raincoat. Daniels said, "What time's the next bus?"

It wasn't like a hotel, it was like a fucking state hospital—Ionia or the Forensic Center. It was in Walter's mind to go upstairs and pack, right now, get the hell out.

Daniels said, "You awake?"

His voice sounded all right. Walter was sure he'd been drinking though; he could smell it.

"Yeah, I'm awake."

"You don't have to wait up for me, Walter."

"I got to ask you something. In the study."

"There's nobody around."

"Your wife was here." Walter looked at his watch. "Jesus, almost an hour ago."

"Come on," Daniels said, getting up.

He poured himself a cognac from the portable bar next to the television set, rolled amber reflections in the snifter glass, raised it to his face, then seemed to remember Walter, fidgeting, moving about by the desk.

"You want one?"

"I want to know something," Walter said. "I want to know if it was you did Curtis Moore."

Daniels said, "The guy who was gonna testify against you and was shot and killed in the parking garage of the Detroit Plaza with a High Standard Field King twenty-two? No. It must've been someone else."

Walter sat down. "I knew it. They pick me up, bring me down to 1300, I'm wondering what the fuck's going on—it was you. I knew it, but I don't believe it."

"Good," Robbie said. "No one else will either." He sipped the cognac and rolled it around in his mouth now before swallowing. "Goddamn raw fish and seaweed. I should've taken them to the Chop House."

Walter said, "Mr. Daniels, I was a police officer twenty, almost twenty-one years. There is no way you can commit a homicide at a place like that, all those people around, and get away with it. There's no way in the world."

Robbie said, "Are you relieved, I mean that he's dead?"

"What I feel—yes, I am," Walter said. "But what I happen to feel has nothing to do with it. I appreciate your, well, your doing it for my sake. But, Mr. Daniels, I'm afraid you're gonna be in the worst trouble in your life. I can't believe it." He looked at Daniels with a vacant expression that said there was no hope, it was all over.

"Yes or no," Robbie said, "did Curtis deserve what he got?"

Walter nodded. "There's no question about that. Yes."

"You're enormously pleased he's out of the way?"

"Sure I am, but—"

"You were questioned by the police?"

"Bryan Hurd. The guy at the hearing."

"Did my name come up?"

"No, it didn't."

"Then I'm not a suspect, am I?"

Walter looked up. It did not occur to him until this moment that Daniels could possibly get away with it.

"Where did you tell them you were?" Daniels asked.

"At the time? Here. Or picking up the buyers."

"He believe you?"

"Yeah. I think he knows I didn't do it."

"Then what're you worried about?"

"What'm I worried about? *You.* What's your story?"

"What do I need a story for if I'm not a suspect?"

"Because it can get around to you," Walter said. "One thing leads to another. Pick up something here, pick up a piece of information there. Somebody saw a car. Next fucking thing they're knocking on the door."

"Well, I was with somebody too, if it ever comes to that," Robbie said. "I picked up some of 'em didn't I? The Japs."

"What time?"

"Walter, I just put the little guys on the red eye to San Francisco."

"They can be contacted by telephone, can't they?"

"I'm not gonna concern myself," Robbie said, "with something that's not likely to happen. We've got the big one coming up. Soon as I get those fucking machines out of there we head for Palm Beach and get on it."

"When?"

"Next week. And once we start—I forgot to tell you, you get an extra grand a week combat pay."

"Yeah? You never mentioned that."

"I think it's only fair. Pros get top dollar, don't they?"

"Hey, if you say so. I'll tell you, I like the idea of getting out of town. It can't happen too soon."

"How about a cognac?"

"Yeah, I'll have one." Walter was feeling a lot better. He said, "You know, they get somebody like Curtis as a homicide victim, they got to go through the motions. But they're just as happy as we are the fucker's out of the way. It's not like they got a hard-on to get a conviction, you know, where they're hot to get somebody. You understand what I mean?"

"Yeah, I can see that." Robbie came over with a snifter and

handed it to Walter. "Seventy-five years old. You've never had a cognac like that in your life."

Walter took the glass, put his head back and drained it. "Yeah, that's all right. Very good."

Robbie stared at him.

"But tell me the truth," Walter said. "Did you really do it for me, on account of the lawsuit?"

"Well, not entirely."

"I didn't think so. I figured there had to be some other reason, take a risk like that," Walter said. "You mind telling me why you did it?"

"Practice," Robbie said.

8

Sunday, Bryan spent part of the day at the Detroit Plaza talking to the doormen, the parking supervisors and several of the guests that had checked in Saturday morning. All it did was tire him out. He wondered if he was coming down with something, a virus. Very seldom did he feel this tired. He went home and watched a tennis match televised from Boca Raton. The weather looked good down there; though maybe boring, the sameness of it. He watched McEnroe put on one of his temper tantrums. The crowd booed and Bryan found himself siding with McEnroe, resenting the spectators in their sunglasses and resort outfits; outsiders looking in, not knowing shit what it was like. It surprised him, because he usually thought McEnroe was an asshole.

The phone rang and he thought of Angela.

He said, "Oh, hi, Peggy."

She said, "Well, what's the matter with you?"

"I was sleeping."

It was his former wife, who had got the house in Indian Village and was getting twelve hundred a month alimony, because at the worst possible time he had felt sorry for her: seeing her enter the lawyer's office, decoupage purse held in both hands, tiny pigeon-toed Capezios bringing her to the conference-table meeting that was as solemn as a Good Friday vigil; he would not have been surprised to see her genuflect and make the sign of the cross. His offense, his petition for divorce, was treated as a matter of faith and morals—even though there'd been no other women, no fooling around—while the settlement, like an atonement, was strictly in bucks.

Peggy said, "Well, I guess you've been hearing a few things, considering how people love to talk."

He told himself to sound concerned. "No, I haven't heard a thing. What about?"

"Well, I've been seeing someone," Peggy said.

"You mean a guy?"

"A man, yes. What did you think I meant?"

"Well, that's fine . . . Isn't it?" He wasn't sure yet what attitude to have. "He's not married, is he?"

"*No,* he's not married," Peggy said. "But people love to talk and they always will. I suppose it's human nature."

People. As in "People Will Say We're in Love." She had been cute Peggy Doran in her Junior Miss outfits, a little Doris Day doll who had turned Adult almost immediately following the ceremony. Serious. Responsible. Proper.

He said, "Well, Peggy, how you doing otherwise?"

She said, "I'm doing very well, if you'd like to know. Much better than I'm sure you ever expected."

Bryan said, "That's great."

"As a matter of fact, I'm getting married in August."

Bryan waited, cautious. Did she actually say it?

"I'm sorry. You're gonna do what?"

"I said I'm getting *married.*"

It was true. He heard the words clearly and they could mean nothing else.

"Are you still there? What's the matter with you?"

She always said, What's the matter with you? She had said he'd ruined her life, thrown away everything they had. (A world of Early Americana.) She had said she'd never marry again. Ever. Now she mentioned a name.

"In August, huh?"

But she was saying now, "You don't know him. He's in the insurance business. A very kind, considerate person."

"Peggy," Bryan said, "I think it's great and I want to wish you all the best." It was true! Christ, it was true! "And a lot of happiness." He couldn't think of what else to say. "I don't know him, huh?"

"No, and he's never heard of you. His name's Paul Scallen. He lives in Dearborn."

"That's great, Peggy. In August, huh? That's a good month, one of the best." Christ, only four more payments. May, June, July—maybe three.

She said, "I'm sure you're relieved. You won't have to pay alimony anymore."

Bryan said, "Hey, that's right . . ."

Later on he kept expecting Angela to call because he saw his luck changing right before his eyes. When she didn't, he pictured her mom and dad, nice people, asking questions about all the interesting places she'd visited. Maybe brothers and sisters around too. She had to have time with her family. She hadn't given him a phone number. He didn't even know their name, or if she was using their name or her married name or how many Nolans there were in Tucson. Well, he didn't feel tired now. Not at all.

Sunday turned out okay.

Monday was something else.

In the morning Bryan stopped by his inspector's office and brought him up to date with Case Assigned Reports, looked out the window at the county jail while Eljay Ayres skimmed through the yellow pages.

Ayres said, "Looks like you can close the little girl and the guy in the bar. They'll never bring him up."

Bryan said, "Let's keep the little girl open. We might learn something."

"Well, it's your time we talking about," Ayres said. "I thought you were on furlough."

"I'm supposed to be, yeah."

Eljay Ayres looked at him and than at the yellow pages again. "Curtis Moore . . . no big surprise to anybody."

There was an easy edge of authority in his tone. Eljay Ayres had been Bryan's counterpart, lieutenant of Squad Six until his recent appointment to inspector of the entire Homicide Section. He wore three-piece suits and a Smith and Wesson automatic tight in the waistband of his trousers, a street-hip black man who seemed wary of Bryan and addressed him at arm's length. Bryan wanted to tell Eljay he didn't resent his appointment, that he had no desire to move up into administration; in fact, if he had to stay at 1300 all day he'd probably find something else to do. A talk over drinks would come in time and both would feel better and relax. Right now it was business.

"How do you feel about Walter Kouza?"

"He didn't do it," Bryan said.

"The Polish Gunslinger. I don't know," Ayres said, "he could've been stewing over it, drinking booze. You check him out good?"

"Soon as I leave here," Bryan said. "Get the names of people he was with."

"Who else you got?"

"Nobody. You know Curtis, the people he ran with. One of his friends could't got tired of him. We inquire who he's been hanging out with; they ropa-dope you, tell you yeah, he's tight with Bicky, Micky, Kicky—nobody's got a real name."

"You don't close pretty quick," Ayres said, "who's gonna take the case?"

"Annie Maguire. She's got a few more people to talk to. There weren't any bikes around, nobody in club jackets. All we've got are a few hotel guests we haven't talked to yet. Ones that checked in about that time."

"Then I think," Ayres said, "you ought to forget Curtis, take advantage of the time you got coming."

Bryan said, offhand, a mild tone, "You trying to get rid of me?"

Ayres remained solemn. "I don't want you to overwork yourself, Bryan. There be plenty more when you get back."

The auction was underway at Daniels Fasteners: buyers and aides in business suits standing around with riggers in hard hats while the dressed-up auctioneer and his podium were moved along on a hand truck by assistants in red blazers. The procession passed beneath tired fluorescent lights to a machine that seemed to have no beginning or end and the auctioneer said, "Lot Number 35. We've got here, in excellent condition, a National three-quarter-inch double-stroke, solid-die and open-die, long-stroke Universal cold header. Who's gonna give me twenty thousand to open?"

Bryan said, "What I've always wanted." He stood in the dead factory with Annie Maguire, watching.

Robbie Daniels, followed by Walter, came up from somewhere behind them, Robbie saying, "And if you don't like that one I've got a Peltzer and Ehlers hot-nut former you'll flip over . . . Hi, I'm

Robbie Daniels,'' offering his hand to Annie as he glanced at Bryan. ''Lieutenant, good to see you again. But don't tell me this young lady's a policeman, please.''

Both Annie and Bryan smiled. He said, ''Well, I can't lie to you, Mr. Daniels,'' and immediately felt foolish. What was he doing? He caught Walter's eye, his serious expression staring back at him. Tense? It was hard to tell. In his tight suits Walter always looked a little tense. Daniels was saying to Annie, ''It's a pleasure. Do you know I've never met a policewoman before?'' As though it was almost impossible to believe. ''Come on, let's go up to my office. There's no place to sit around here.''

Bryan said, ''We just want to ask Walter something. Get some names.''

''Hey, that's right,'' Robbie said, ''you're investigating a murder, aren't you? Walter told me about it last night. Fascinating.'' He looked at Walter then. ''My attaché case?''

Walter said, ''What?''

''Remember? I left it in the car?''

Walter walked off. Bryan watched Robbie shake his head and thought he would comment but didn't.

He took them up a wooden stairway to the administrative offices that were divided by wood-framed glass partitions, the offices dark, empty except for bare desks and file cabinets, a few old-model typewriters under plastic covers. An oak desk and chairs remained in the spacious corner office that looked down on Franklin and Riopelle, on railroad tracks and warehouses and old brick factories extending to the riverfront, a setting left from the Industrial Revolution.

''Anyone who asks me why I'm selling,'' Robbie said, ''I tell them, would you rather come down here every day and look at this mess''—with a sweeping gesture, sport coat open, rep tie askew—''the backside of a dying city, or get down to the sunbelt where it's happening and invest in the future?''

Bryan thought, I got to get out of here. He said, ''I don't want to take up any of your time. If we could just have the names of the people Walter picked up . . .''

''That's right,'' Robbie said, ''you want some names.'' He turned to a thick file on the desk, opened it and began looking through company letterheads. "No—I thought so. These are today's. Saturday's are in my case." He walked to the windows now and looked down on Riopelle. "Come on, Walter, you're holding up the Police Department." Then said, "I can vouch for Walter. But from your point of view I can see why he's a suspect."

Bryan looked at Annie. He said, "Well, he isn't, really. We have to fill in some holes in the report."

Annie said, "He must've told you about Curtis's brother, the shooting."

"And a few others," Robbie said. "Walter doesn't know it, but he's a very entertaining guy."

Bryan looked at Annie.

"Here he comes," Robbie said, turning from the window now. "The ones he picked up Saturday had made firm offers. So I invited them in before the auction. Got rid of half the equipment. Guy from Mexico—he couldn't speak a word of English—even bought office fixtures. Right, Walter?"

He came in carrying an alligator attaché case. "What's that, Mr. Daniels?"

Robbie took the case and laid it on the desk. "I was telling them about the guy from Mexico who couldn't speak English."

"Only talked Spic," Walter said. "Used his hands all the time."

Robbie snapped open the case. He took out a High Standard twenty-two target pistol with a five-and-a-half-inch barrel and laid it on the desk without comment.

Bryan looked at Annie. Then at Walter, who was staring at the gun.

Robbie was taking out company letterhead sheets now, glancing at them, handing them to Walter. "These are the buyers you picked up, right?"

Walter looked at the first two or three. "I don't know, Mr. Daniels. I can't tell from just the names."

"Look at the cities, where they're from."

"I don't know," Walter said.

"Well, they're quite likely to remember you, Walter." Robbie glanced at Bryan. "Call 'em, if you want. But I'll take an oath

Walter left the house at nine-thirty and picked up these particular buyers."

"Quarter to ten," Walter said.

"All right, a quarter of ten."

"I didn't pick up any Jap. I know that."

Robbie said, "Sure you did. Namura. Little fella with horn-rim glasses and buck teeth." He looked at Bryan and grinned. "No, I'm kidding. He wasn't especially oriental looking."

Walter said, "I know I didn't pick up any Jap."

"Well," Robbie said, "I could be wrong. We were coming and going all day."

"I saw those two Japs here," Walter said, "but I know goddamn well I never picked 'em up."

"All *right!*" Robbie said.

Bryan looked at Annie.

"I think you've made your point," Robbie said. "Fine. You remember the ones you didn't pick up but not the ones you did. Anyway . . . take the letters and have 'em Xeroxed somewhere. I'd appreciate it."

Bryan said, "We can copy the names and addresses. Save some time."

It was all right with Robbie. "Fine, since you brought your secretary . . ."

"Miss Maguire's a sergeant." Bryan said, "A homicide detective."

Robbie grinned. "Well, Miss Maguire can get on my case anytime."

Annie said, "Okay," with a shy smile and looked at the twenty-two target pistol on the desk. "Do you keep that loaded?"

"Sure," Robbie said. "It's been lying around the office—I was taking it home. Since we're closing down. It's a nice little weapon."

Annie said, "It's a gun till you shoot somebody with it. Then it's a weapon."

"I never thought of it that way," Robbie said. He picked up the target pistol, touched the safety with his thumb to release it.

Bryan thought, It's a show. Why he brought us here. He watched the way Robbie held the gun.

Robbie was saying, "This was dad's office for something like a hundred years. He used to sit here and stare through the glass partitions at me. Past his secretary's office, his sales manager's office, to the one at the end, without the window. That was my office when I started out. In fact it was my office until he died, nine years ago." Robbie raised the target pistol as he spoke. "Dad would sit here and stare. He was partially paralyzed from a stroke and never seemed to move. Just stared, wondering what was gonna happen to the business, I guess. I couldn't read a newspaper unless it was the *Wall Street Journal*." He was sighting now through the glass partitions to the bare wall in the last office.

Bryan watched him.

Robbie fired.

Bryan saw the first glass partition drilled, cracks flowering out from the bullet hole. He saw Robbie fire again and fire again and all three partitions dividing the offices exploded, collapsed in the sound of shattering glass to leave jagged ends in the wood frames.

Bryan looked at the ejected casings on the carpet, green with a worn floral design. He wanted them.

Robbie said, "There." Then grinned. He said, "Before you call for an EMS wagon let me tell you I've been wanting to do that for as long as I can remember. There's something about those glass walls I've always resented . . ."

Bryan watched him stoop, pick up the ejected casings and drop them in his coat pocket.

"Like living in a goldfish bowl, someone watching you all the time." Robbie blew into the barrel of the target pistol for effect. "Well, they're gone now. In fact this whole goddamn place is gone, but I had to do it." Smiling. "I feel a lot better."

It was not something Bryan had to accept or believe at this moment. He nodded in sympathy and let it go at that. The man was putting on a hell of a show. They would review it later—once they got the spent cartridges, the bits of lead that would be flattened and imbedded in the plaster wall. But as he thought this he was startled by a realization that was as sharp and clear-cut as the broken shards of glass.

He wants you to have the bullets.

But not the casings.

It was a game that both sides had to play, or pretend to play. Walter was not involved. Walter seemed lost.

Annie said, "I wonder if you damaged anything. I noticed some office machines . . ." Annie knew something. Her eyes made contact with Bryan and moved away.

He said, "You've been looking for a used typewriter, haven't you, Annie?"

Robbie said, "We still have a few around. If the Mexican didn't get 'em." He was looking out at the empty offices, cooperating. "You see one you like, Miss Maguire, it's yours. But listen. I got to get back down to the auction and look interested. Okay? I'll see you a little later."

He's going to say *ciao,* Bryan thought.

"Ciao," Robbie said and headed for the stairs.

Annie walked out, began to roam after Robbie left. There were a few moments of silence before Walter said to Bryan, "The fuck you looking at me for?"

In the medium-blue unmarked Plymouth, moving up Riopelle to Jefferson, Annie opened her hand. Bryan looked from the windshield to the flattened bits of gray lead, three of them, in Annie's palm.

She said, "What do you think?"

He said, "I haven't finished yct. Ask me later."

Shc said, "You must know something I don't."

He said, "Well, I think you'd be safe in throwing those out the window. But let's get a comparison anyway."

"So you're sure it's not the same gun. Even though it's a twenty-two."

"No, but I'm pretty sure it's not the same barrel," Bryan said. "We could still make the gun if we had the casings, but he didn't let us have the casings, did he? He knows a few things about ballistics."

Annie said, "Wait a minute. Who are we talking about? I thought our guy was Walter. Like maybe he borrowed the gun and put it back and Daniels is a little weird but basically harmless."

"That could be," Bryan said, "but let's think it through again. After I make a phone call."

In the squad room he spoke to the Palm Beach chief of police, spoke to him for several minutes asking polite questions. He hung up and sat staring at nothing. Then rose to stand at the window, looking down at the Coney Island across the street, and began to feel tired again.

When Annie came in he knew by her expression what she was going to say.

"You're right. It's not the gun that did Curtis."

"At least not the barrel," Bryan said. "Though it probably doesn't make much difference. I just saw a hunch fly out the window. Palm Beach says the gun Daniels used on the Haitian burglar—justifiable homicide, the chief underlined that—was a Colt Python, three-fifty-seven."

"Maybe he has a collection," Annie said.

"That's a nice idea," Bryan said. "I like it."

She said, "I still think we should stay close to Walter. I'll call some of the people he picked up Saturday, if you want me to."

"Call the Japanese guy too."

"Walter said he didn't pick him up."

"But if the guy came halfway around the world—you know what I mean? Went to all that trouble, then somebody picked him up. And if we don't ask, Inspector Eljay Ayres is gonna want to know why, isn't he?"

Annie brightened. With her nice teeth and complexion she always looked clean, healthy; she responded to what she felt and looked you right in the eye.

"Maybe what's his name, the Japanese guy, stayed at the Plaza and Walter doesn't want us to know he was there."

"Maybe," Bryan said. If she wanted to bet on Walter he'd let her. In fact, he'd give her a little more to make it interesting and said, "I'll tell you something else. Down in Palm Beach, guess who investigated Robbie shooting the Haitian?"

Annie said, "No!" She loved it.

"Yes. And right after that Walter goes to work for Robbie. What does that tell you?"

Annie thought about it. "Not much, really."

She had a nice mouth too. Very expressive blue eyes. Bryan said, "Angela asked me if I'd ever made the moves on you."

Annie smiled but seemed embarrassed. "Did she? Why?"

"I think seeing us working together, the way we get along."

"Has she called you?"

"No."

"What're you gonna do about it?"

"Nothing. I'm going to Florida tomorrow. You guys are on your own."

Annie began to smile again. "But not the Ocean Pearl in Boca Raton this time?"

9

In the early morning old people walked the beach looking for shells left by the tide. The women, in sleeveless shirts and kerchiefs covering their hairdos, studied the sand and seemed to have purpose. The men followed, looking for something to happen. They wore adjustable nylon golf caps, many of them cocked in a recollection going back to world wars, sporty old guys who seemed lost. They poked at blue translucent balloons among the even line of seaweed washed up, dead Portuguese men-of-war, and that would be a high moment when nothing much was expected. There were people from Michigan, from Ontario, from Ohio and New York State. They wiped the sediment from their Buicks and big Oldsmobiles and talked about mileage; they went to the Early Bird dinner at five-thirty. There were not as many families with children as there used to be. Once in a while a girl with a nice body would appear way off coming along the sand and Bryan would wonder about her; but not long, not interested enough to put the *National Geographic* aside and push up out of the beach chair and go through the ritual of making the moves. Not this trip. He would look from habit or because the sight of a girl with the nice body was an element of pleasure in his picture of a beach on the Atlantic Ocean in season.

He went to sleep in the sun, lying on his side on a Woolworth blue and white beach towel and woke up in shade, his shoulder cramped, looking eye level at sandpipers running on their stick legs, nervous, afraid of everything. He would rather be a seagull and dive for fish. He wondered where birds went to die. There were billions of birds but you didn't see many dead ones. He was reading an article about cranes and egrets getting messed up in the oil along the Texas coast. It was cool in the shade; late afternoon now.

The lone figure way down the beach was still in sunlight. A girl coming along the edge of sand left glistening by the surf. A girl in twin strips of red cloth. She came gradually away from the waves rushing at her ankles and as she reached the shade the gleam left her body, her slender arms and legs turning a dusty copper, the patches of red cloth faded, though highlights and something white remained in her hair. She came across the empty sand looking at him through round sunglasses, past the line of seaweed and up the slight rise to his chair. The low chair with aluminum arms was all that separated them.

He pushed up to prop his cheek on his fist, looking at her sideways. The white thing in her hair was a barrette.

"I was gonna come up behind you," Angela said, "but you caught me."

He said, "What were you gonna do then?"

There was time to play around. No hurry now.

She said, "Lie down next to you. Blow in your ear. Feel you up. Have my way with you."

"Then what?"

"Have a cigarette. Did you bring any?"

"In the room."

"I didn't see them."

Bryan said, "Come on—really? What'd you tell Mr. Ocean Pearl?"

"I said I was your missus, what do you think?"

"You put your things in there and changed?"

"I was afraid you were gonna come in. Yeah, I changed and then walked down the road. Came back up the beach and made my entrance. Did you like it?"

"Soon as I saw you I knew it was you."

"Yeah—you thought it was some young girl. I mean you were hoping it was."

"Happy birthday. How're you handling it?"

"Well, four days into it, not bad. You're getting tan."

"How're your folks?"

"Okay."

"I thought you were gonna stay a week."

"I couldn't."

"Why, what happened?"

"Nothing. I missed you too much. So I called your office . . ."

"Well," Bryan said, "here we are."

They smiled, almost shy with one another. It was going to be something.

He said, "You want to be civil for a while or go crazy right away?"

She said, "Let's see what happens."

"Will you go with me to meet somebody at six?"

"Of course."

"Just for a drink. Then we're on our own."

"Fine."

He said, "Are we in the neighborhood of what you want most?"

She said, "We're right there. I think we've always been there, but I have to feel it. You don't have to say a word if I feel it."

"Start feeling," Bryan said.

They were in Number 1 facing the ocean, away from the rest of the units centered around the swimming pool and patio. Living room, bedroom, kitchen and the whole Atlantic right outside the windows.

Angela showered and he showered. She stood in the bedroom in white bra and panties. Every boy's dream. He got a glimpse as he poured bourbon over shaved ice packed in smoke-colored glasses. She came in to have her drink in a terry-cloth robe and that was fine. They'd see how long they could keep their hands off each other.

Gary Hammond, the Palm Beach squad-car officer, couldn't believe it when he saw them coming. The same girl, the houseguest; in a white sweater and slacks. She looked better than she had last month when it was cool and she wore the dark turtleneck. The Detroit homicide cop, Lieutenant Hurd, looked in shape. Not the big-city beer-gut dick he expected. Gary stood up, bumping the table and grabbing his glass of beer. He was glad he'd cleaned up, put on a sport shirt. The girl was smiling at him as they came in past the hedge to the sidewalk tables.

She said, "Well, it's nice to see you again," sounding like she meant it, and introduced him to the homicide lieutenant. Up close the homicide lieutenant made Gary think of a major-league baseball player; something about him. He looked like he should have a wad of tobacco in his jaw. Though he seemed very polite, soft-spoken. One of those quiet guys who looked at you and seemed to know things.

He asked if Gary would mind telling about Daniels shooting the Haitian, the circumstance and the investigation. Gary said, "Well, I'm glad *some*body's interested, except it's a closed issue." He told the story and the homicide lieutenant listened and did not interrupt once. Then he began asking questions. Good ones.

"You believe the Haitian—what's his name?"

"Louverture Damien."

"You believe his intent was burglary?"

"Yes sir, I'm pretty sure now."

"Why didn't you think so at first?"

"Well, it wasn't I thought he come for any other reason, it was just nobody looked to see if he might've."

Lieutenant Hurd seemed to like that. "Do you know where Daniels got the gun? Where he kept it?"

"No sir, nobody asked that either."

Angela said, "When I saw him in his study with Walter, the day I left, he had a gun in his hand. But it wasn't the one he used."

Lieutenant Hurd said, "Do you know if he has a gun collection?"

"Now that could be," Gary said. "I asked Detective Kouza if the Python was registered, the one Daniels used, and Detective Kouza made some remark like, you want to check him for priors, too? But at the hearing Mr. Daniels was asked that and he said yeah, he'd bought the gun from a reputable shop where he was known and often used their target range. See, like he'd been dealing there a lot."

Lieutenant Hurd said, "You think Daniels might've had the gun on him? Is that what bothers you?"

"No sir, it was his story about the Haitian coming at him with a machete."

"Whose machete was it?"

"There you are." Gary Hammond grinned. "The guy didn't come all the way from Belle Glade carrying a machete. His wife says he never had one in his hands. The first he heard about it was in the hospital, dying. So I say to myself either the Haitian's lying or Mr. Daniels, one. It turns out the machete was from the tool shed on his property. See, but how would the Haitian know to go in there and get it?"

"Was it locked?"

"I asked the gardener, he says no. I asked him was the machete, could it have been left out? He goes, hell no, I take care of my tools, put them away . . . and all like that."

"Was the machete checked for prints?"

"No sir. See, I got there—there was the Haitian on the ground, shot twice, bleeding all over the place, with the machete lying close by. But it wouldn't do no good to check it now. The gardener's probably been cutting scrub with it anyway.

"Did you ask Walter why he didn't have it dusted?"

"No sir, it was his investigation. I was mostly waving at traffic on South Ocean Boulevard . . . Hey, don't you all want a drink?"

Lieutenant Hurd said, "How about ballistics on the gun?"

"There was no need for it, nothing to prove."

"You keep the two slugs or did Walter throw 'em away?"

"No, they're in an envelope, in the file."

They sat back and talked about Palm Beach and the season, sipping bourbon, looking at the outfits in the cafe, trying to tell the tourists from the regulars, those who had money and those who didn't; Gary saying there wasn't much excitement other than stopping drunks and then you had to be careful who you pulled over. Palm Beach was a playground for the rich people and they okayed the rules. Place swung from Christmas to Easter, then rolled over and went to sleep.

Lieutenant Hurd said, "What do you think of Walter Kouza?"

Gary had to give that a few moments.

"Well, to tell you the truth, I thought basically he was dumb. I mean I don't think he was any good in school, if he ever went. But he knew things. We'd pick some guy up for vagrancy—Detective Kouza seemed to *know* if the guy had any priors and he'd usually get the guy to cop. We have a problem with vandalism, broken windows, something like that, I can't even get twelve-year-old kids to cop. Detective Kouza, he has 'em in the room there a couple minutes, they tell him whatever he wants to hear."

"What about when he left?" Lieutenant Hurd asked if Walter had said anything about what he'd be doing.

"He did and he didn't," Gary said. "He made it sound like foreign intrigue, like he was going to work for the CIA. But he really didn't say anything you could put your finger on. So I just figured, you know, it was bullshit."

"Trying to impress you."

"Yeah, he was always laying a trip on you, his twenty years experience," Gary said. "Like he had seen it all. I guess more than anything, Detective Kouza wanted you to think he was important."

Looking at the stars she said to Bryan, "I'd walk out in the desert—it's all open land back of their house, up in the Santa Catalina foothills. I'd go out just to be alone for a few minutes. And then I'd hear my dad. I mean I could sneak off, leave him asleep in his chair. The next thing, I'd hear his voice. 'See those lights over there?' " Her voice lower, a more serious tone. " 'That's the new Las Palmas condo development. Then over there you got Casas Adobes and Vista del Oro.' " She stopped and then said, "I'm putting you to sleep, aren't I?"

Bryan said, feeling as content as he could feel, having her right there and knowing she would be there for a while, "You were gonna tell me why you went home. The real reason."

She said, "All right. I didn't go home because it was my birthday."

He said, "You went home to see an old boyfriend. Look him over one more time."

"I don't have an old boyfriend."

"Since your divorce—what, ten years, you've never had a boyfriend?"

"You don't have boyfriends anymore. And I was never anyone's old lady."

"And nobody *dates,*" Bryan said.

"No, you don't date. I went with a guy who played with Frank Zappa and had known my husband. In L.A. It was kinda fun, but he was spacy."

"Not serious?"

"Never . . . You want to hear some music? I could go in and turn the radio on, open a window."

"I'd rather listen to you," Bryan said. "You can tell me anything you want."

He liked her voice, quiet and close to him, with the sound of the ocean breaking out of the darkness. He liked to sit and follow the specks of amber light that were ships in the Gulf Stream and seemed as far away as stars. People out there staring at shore lights. He looking at them and they looking at him, with fifteen miles between them. She got up and went inside. But no music came. She returned with glasses of cold Chablis, sat down in her deck chair—the arms of the chairs touching—and raised her legs to the low cement wall.

"Thank you . . . So you didn't go home to see your old boyfriend."

"No. I went home to see my dad."

When she paused he said, "Rich people don't say my dad. They say dad, like their dad is the only dad."

She thought about it and said, "You may be right. If I do the book on rich people I'll check it out."

"Go on about your dad."

"Okay. You reminded me of him quite a bit, as soon as we met. And I wondered if that's why I thought I knew you and felt good with you right away. I mean not only comfortable, I felt protected. Which could be a big mistake. Like giving me a false sense of security."

"Right. I'm not your dad."

"You sure aren't. And you're not anything alike, either. That's the amazing part. You might sound alike, a little. But your attitudes are so different."

"Does this turn out good?"

"There. That's the difference right there. He's serious about dumb things and you aren't. Of course it turns out good, because I think you're right. The way you look at things. You're not cynical especially, you're . . . I can't think of the word."

"Objective."

"No . . . Well, partly."

"Carefree."

"No."

"Romantic?"

"No!"

"Straightforward."

"Come on—"

"Erect."

She said, "Macho man returns." She looked off at the pinpoint glow of stars and running lights. She said, "Are you? Really?"

In the big double bed in darkness in the middle of the night she said, "God, I love you."

They could hear the surf through the open windows. No other sounds.

He could tell her. He could tell her a few things about how he felt. But he couldn't *hear* himself telling her. Not yet. He said, "We're there, aren't we?"

She moved her hand down to touch him and said, "You're not only not romantic you're not too erect anymore either."

He said, "Keep your hand there. Pretty soon we'll hear violins."

10

It was the next morning Annie called Bryan. She asked him how the weather was. Perfect, he told her. She asked if Angela had got hold of him. She certainly did, he told her.

Annie said, "The valet-parking cashier came through. Remember, she thought there was a good-luck piece or something on the keys Curtis took? She saw another one just like it, a circle with three spokes. A Mercedes insignia."

Now you're moving, Bryan told her.

Annie said, "Wait. I talked to the last of the hotel guests that came in that morning around ten or before. One of them was very friendly, I liked him. He checked into the hotel with his wife." Bryan said, yeah? "But he lives in Bloomfield Hills." Bryan said, oh. He said, well, the guy probably took his wife down for the weekend. Annie said, "He's a talkative type, sort of a bullshitter. At least he was at first. But as soon as he found out what it was about, he shut up." Bryan asked, then what was it she liked about the guy.

Annie said, "Before he shut up he remembered seeing a dark-colored Mercedes sedan. It was in front of him with the door open and he couldn't pull up to get past. But there was no Mercedes down in that area of the garage, near Curtis. So the question is, where did it go?" Bryan said, maybe the car only picked somebody up. Annie said, "That's possible. But I checked to see if anyone we know owns a Mercedes. And you know who does?"

Robbie Daniels, Bryan said.

Annie said, "You rat."

Bryan told her if she wanted him to be her straight man she'd have to set it up better. Or not sound so eager. What else?

Well, she'd finally got hold of the Japanese buyer. "But he didn't stay at the Plaza and Walter didn't pick him up."

Then why did Daniels make an issue of it? Why did he keep insisting Walter picked the guy up? Unless he wanted to confuse them, throw them off.

"I don't know," Annie said. "I did talk to a couple of buyers who remembered Walter, but they came in later in the day. I'm having trouble getting hold of the guy in Mexico City. Carlos Cabrera. Nobody at his company seems to speak English. But I'll keep trying if you think it's really necessary."

Bryan asked her how you could tell what was necessary from what wasn't until you did it.

Annie said, "As long as you're having a good time, Bryan, don't worry about it."

They hung up. About twenty seconds later Annie's phone rang.

"Annie, go out and have a talk with Daniels. Ask him who he picked up, if anyone. Fish around, see if he's hiding anything. Okay? And take somebody with you . . . Annie? What's the name of the guy's company in Mexico City?"

She told him Maquinaria Cabrera, S. A. And asked if he wanted her to spell it.

He said, "Maquinaria? If I can say it I don't need to be able to spell it." He wrote the name *Carlos Cabrera* on an Ocean Pearl postcard that showed the resort with palm trees on a perfect day. Then asked her for the phone number.

Anything else?

"Yeah," Bryan said. "Set Robbie up if you can. Look him in the eye and ask him if he was at the Plaza Saturday morning."

Angela, in the terry-cloth robe, sat at the breakfast table with the *Miami Herald*. She watched Bryan, in his bathing trunks, get up from the phone and begin to move around idly, looking out the windows, deciding something.

She said, "What's maquinaria mean?"

"Mah-kee-*nah*-r'yah." Bryan stopped to look at her. "Machinery." His bathing trunks, that he'd been wearing for ten years, were dark blue sun-faded to a washed-out purple. They reminded Angela, she had told him, of an old junk car, though she wasn't certain why.

She said, "You didn't learn to say it like that in Spanish class."

He said, "You go to Holy Trinity grade school for eight years with Chicanos and Maltese you learn how to pronounce all kinds of words. Some pretty good ones, too."

She said, "Let's get dressed and do our shopping now instead of later on."

"If you want."

"You need some outfits desperately," Angela said.

He didn't like the sound of that. He didn't like articles of clothing put together to make "outfits." He liked shirts and pants, sweaters, combinations that came together and didn't seem to mind, but were not thought out in advance.

"First," he said, "you have some pictures of Daniels, don't you? That you took?"

"Dozens."

"You have 'em here?"

"Yeah, in my case."

"I wonder if we could send a few to Annie," Bryan said. "Something she can show around."

Angela nodded, seeing some of the shots flash in her mind: Robbie in his thin sweater over bare skin scratching his stomach, Robbie grinning, Robbie gesturing; he could be a male model. She said, with hesitation, "Do you think he killed Curtis?"

"It's possible," Bryan said.

"But why would he?"

"You're backing off." Bryan said. "You told me, not too long ago, you think the man likes to kill people."

"Is that what I said?"

"Those were the words."

"Yeah, but . . ." It was different now, looking directly at the possibility. "Robbie seems so . . ."

"What, charming?"

"No—"

"Fun-loving?"

"Are we gonna play that again?"

"You're the writer," Bryan said. "What's the word? Robbie seems so . . ."

"Harmless," Angela said. "But weird."

"You were there when he shot the Haitian. You said there was something strange about it and you tried to talk to him after, later on."

"I did. I asked him, did you have to shoot the poor guy? It was the first thing I said to him after the police left. And Robbie said, very serious, 'You're writing about me and you have to ask that?' "

"Maybe blowing smoke at you," Bryan said. "I think he goes for dramatic effects."

"Or maybe telling the truth," Angela said. "As though he was saying, 'If you know me, then you'd know I had to shoot the guy.' After that, for the next few days, I tried to corner him to find out what he meant. But he avoided me—I mean to the point of being rude. He made excuses, never had time to talk. And he was strange. Off somewhere in his mind." Angela said then, "Do some people—have you ever met anyone who shot people for the fun of it? For kicks?"

"Whatever the reason," Bryan said, "yeah, there're people who like to shoot people. There're cops who look for an excuse. There're guys who get into armed robbery, I'm pretty sure, hoping they'll have to use their gun."

Angela was quiet for a moment. "At the hearing, the plaintiff's lawyer asked if you'd ever shot anyone."

"He asked if I'd killed anybody lately," Bryan said. "He knew. He was making a comparison, with Walter."

"Well, have you?"

"What, killed anybody? No, I never have. Or had the desire."

"What if you did have to, sometime?"

"Then I'd do it." Bryan said. "If there's no choice, I guess you do it."

Annie Maguire said to Robbie, "You've got an awfully nice house. It reminds me a little of where they signed the Declaration of Independence. The outside."

"It's comfortable," Robbie said. Leading Annie through the front hall to the study, his sneakers squeaked on the marble floor. He let her go in first, then rated her as she looked around the study. Nice can filling out the skirt of the beige suit. She wore a dark blue button-down shirt with it; a well-worn brown-leather bag hung from her shoulder. He wondered what kind of gun was inside. She wasn't bad looking at all: the clean, wholesome type. He imagined a spray of freckles over motherly breasts. There was that to be said of some older women: they offered a comforting, maternal sexuality that could be a nice change. Annie, he judged, was about thirty-four.

"You know who you remind me of? Julie Andrews."

Annie said, "Jim Malik—he's the one I told you on the phone was coming out with me? But something came up he had to do. Jim says I remind him of her too. Except I'm fatter and I don't talk funny."

"I certainly wouldn't call you fat," Robbie said. "In fact, the first thing that came to mind when I opened the door—you know what I wanted to do?"

Annie smiled. She said, "What?"

"Tie you up," Robbie said, deadpan, "and fuck your socks off. I've never slept with a cop before." He maintained his bland, almost melancholy expression, waiting for her reaction, ready to break into a grin.

Annie said, "Someone else said that to me one time." She walked past the big chair facing the television console and sat down on the couch of soft brown leather. "When I was working Sex Crimes."

Robbie didn't get a chance to grin. He said, "Sex Crimes?"

"We handled criminal sexual conduct. Rape, in varying degrees," Annie said. "That was before I got into Homicide."

"Sex Crimes," Robbie said again. It had a ring to it. He dropped into his chair, swung his sneakers, laces untied, onto the ottoman. The policewoman showed up very well against the rich brown leather. "How about a drink?"

"No thanks," Annie said. "Anyway, there was a guy we were after who came to be known as the Weekend Rapist. He'd go into a house Saturday or Sunday night—we'd find cigarette butts out by the garage where he watched the house until the lights went out. Then he'd go in. And always with a gun. He wasn't a cat burglar, the kind that sneaks in and out. This guy stuck the gun in their face, whoever was home, and took what he wanted. Mostly jewelry, valuables, things like that. Cash. And if there was a woman in the house he'd rape her. Actually he forced the woman to perform fellatio and then he sodomized her."

"Wow," Robbie said.

''Anyone else in the house—the husband, kids—he'd make them lie on the floor in the same room and cover them with a blanket so they couldn't see him. But they could hear, and this guy would give a blow by blow—''

Robbie grinned. ''If you'll pardon the expression, uh?''

''—of whatever he was doing. Though mostly what they heard was the poor woman crying. Then he'd *thank* her, take the stuff and leave.''

''What'd he wear?'' Robbie asked.

''Watch cap, dark sweat shirt with a hood and aviator sunglasses. He had a beard too.''

''Fascinating,'' Robbie said.

''But he didn't always say please and thank you,'' Annie said. ''Twice—and the women were alone both times—he put a pillow over their face, pressed a twenty-two revolver into the pillow and shot them in the head.''

''Unpredictable,'' Robbie said.

''In some ways,'' Annie said. ''In other ways, no. He always used his girl friend's car, as it turned out, and that led us to our suspect. A guy who was out on parole following a B and E conviction—there had been an attempted rape in that case too, but it was dropped in the plea bargaining. Anyway we brought the guy in—Dennis Kenzie, I'll never forget his name—and I handled the interrogation. Well, right away he started to come on to me, making sly remarks, saying what you said about tying me up.''

''Really?'' Robbie sounded disappointed, upstaged.

''We were pretty sure Dennis was our Weekend Rapist, just from little things he'd let slip. But we couldn't get a positive I.D. from any of the victims and we didn't have nearly enough to bring him up. But then,'' Annie said, ''he started calling me, asking me to go out with him. And he started hanging around. Twice I ran into him in Greektown. And finally I was pretty sure he followed me home. A few days later I came in the house—there he was waiting for me in his knit cap, his sunglasses, pointing a gun at me. He took my purse, pushed me in the bedroom and told me to take off my clothes. He'd even brought a rope to tie me up.''

''Jesus,'' Robbie said, ''what'd you do?''

"I reached under the mattress, pulled out my spare thirty-eight Chiefs Special and told Dennis to drop his gun," Annie said. "And when he didn't, I shot him."

Robbie liked it and began to smile. "Just like that. Did you kill him?"

"No, he survived. He's doing mandatory life," Annie said, "with a limp." She smiled back at Robbie now with that sweet-girl way that opened hearts and said, "Mr. Daniels, were you at the Detroit Plaza Hotel any time Saturday morning?"

His smiled remained, part of it, the smile becoming vacant with the effort to maintain his composure, giving himself time.

He said, "You know who picked up the Japs—after I accused Walter and we almost got in an argument over it? *I* did. We had so many buyers in that day . . . Well, everything's gone now, all the equipment . . ."

"Did you pick them up at the Plaza?"

"No, it was the Ponch. I'm quite sure."

"Did you pick *any*body up at the Plaza?"

He appeared to give it some thought. "I don't think I did. I know I dropped some people off there, later."

"What kind of car were you driving?"

"Saturday? . . . I had the Mercedes."

"What color is it?"

"Well, we have a black one and a yellow one, to go with whatever mood you're in. Saturday I was in something of a funereal mood, the end of an era, seventy-five years of nuts and bolts . . ." Robbie gave her a sly look and began to smile again. "You know, you're quite attractive. Were you ever a model?"

Annie said, "Are you serious?"

"Were you ever on television?"

"On the six o'clock news a couple of times," Annie said. "Walking a prisoner from 1300 to the Frank Murphy Hall of Justice."

"That's not all," Robbie said. He pushed up the remote-control box from the table next to him and pushed a button. "Watch."

Annie was looking at him and wasn't sure what he meant until he nodded toward the television console. She turned and saw herself on the screen, in color, walking toward the couch. She saw herself and heard her voice saying, "Someone else said that to me one time. When I was working Sex Crimes." She heard Daniels's voice, offscreen, say, "Sex Crimes?"

Angela had walked down to the beach while Bryan was on the phone again with Annie. She felt him near and opened her eyes. The hair on his chest moved in the wind.

He said, "Walter left yesterday with the Mercedes. Robbie's coming down tonight. How does he usually fly?"

"He hitches a ride on some company jet," Angela said. "Or he charters one. He very rarely flies commercial."

Angela waited. Bryan was looking off at the ocean.

"I think we ought to move to Palm Beach," he said. "You know of any places?"

"I know a Holiday Inn," Angela said. "I know many Holiday Inns, all over." She waited again.

"Robbie told Annic I should give him a call. He wants to play golf with me. You said he was weird," Bryan said. "I believe it."

"I also said he was harmless," Angela said.

"Yeah—we're not so sure about that part," Bryan said. "I would like to get to know him better."

Angela said, "Can I watch?"

The rental car was a Buick Century he could not say anything for or against. It was dark shiny brown in the hot sunlight. It took them north out of Boca on 95 while he told Angela about Annie's visit with Robbie.

"He doesn't *think* he picked up anyone at the Plaza," Bryan said. "Does that sound like him?"

"No," Angela said, "if anything he's Mr. Positive. But what he'll do, he'll look you right in the face and lie. Then have that little-boy impish grin ready in case you call him on it."

"The weird part, Annie said he videotaped her. He has hidden cameras mounted in the study and showed her a *movie* of herself on TV."

Angela was nodding. "The first time I interviewed him he played back the whole scene in living color."

"You saw the cameras?"

"Well, they're not exactly hidden, but they're not as obvious as the ones you see in banks or stores. He has the same setup in Palm Beach, also in his study."

"What is it, he likes gadgets?"

"That's what he claims," Angela said. "It's a toy. He had a surveillance system installed in his plant, got interested in electronics and bought much more exotic equipment for his homes. But just in his studies—I mean they're obviously not for surveillance. He doesn't touch a thing—the cameras pan with you when you move, zoom in for close-ups—I don't know how it works."

Bryan said it sounded like a pretty expensive toy. Angela said there was something like a hundred thousand bucks worth of videotape equipment in each home; but that was beside the point. Did Robbie play with his toy or use it for some other purpose? Bryan said maybe to keep from being misquoted. Angela said, or to record what some people might confide and then hold it over their heads . . . The son of a bitch.

"You don't like him," Bryan said.

"It's funny, I dislike him even more since I met you," Angela said. She was silent for several miles and then said, "Get off at Southern Boulevard. I'll show you where he lives."

They crossed the bridge over Lake Worth and came to Palm Beach. "Now right on South Ocean Boulevard," Angela said. "Just a little way. There. Pull into the drive."

Bryan could see only part of the house through the iron gate and the palm trees lining the drive. "Is that a house or a hotel?"

"Hacienda Daniels," Angela said. "Now we go north."

They backtracked, crossed Southern Boulevard on the beach road and Angela pointed to the Bath and Tennis Club. "From here up to Worth Avenue, about a mile or so, is the very *in* section, between the Bath and Tennis Club and the Everglades Club. If you know how much money you have you don't belong here. Robbie's a little pissed off because he's about two hundred feet *south* of being, quote, 'between the clubs.' The architecture is all either pseudo-Spanish or Mediterranean Mausoleum."

"I don't think you should write the book on rich people," Bryan said.

"Why, because I have a point of view?"

Bryan nodded toward a colossal, ornate structure with a slim minaret pointing to heaven. "What's that?"

"It's somebody's house," Angela said. "Shelter."

Bryan said, "I'd hate to have to vacuum and dust the place."

Angela said, "One old broad used to maintain a staff of fifty—count 'em—fifty servants. She also has eighty-six phones. One for each room. You have to know whose money it is, hers or his. See that house? *She* was once a baton twirler on the Sealtest Big Top Circus. But as the society writers say, 'She left show business behind.' That one, coming up, the old gal was a silent-film star who happened to marry John Paul Getty."

"You could be a tour guide."

"Yeah, stop the bus and everybody gets out and throws tomatoes."

Bryan said, "You don't sound upset, but you really are. I don't get it."

"I can point out a few hotbeds of fascism too," Angela said. "They're not all fascists, but when Jack Kennedy was shot some of the Old Guard actually threw parties."

"Who told you that?"

"A very reliable guy I know here. He writes for the local paper, the *Post*."

"Well, that was a while ago."

"Nixon was here last month. Greeted like a savior . . . That's Worth Avenue, where all the expensive stores are."

"Where the rich people shop?"

"No, where the tourists shop. Rich people don't spend their money, they invest it in real estate. That's the *in* thing to talk about at the clubs, real estate."

Bryan said, "Why do rich people make you mad?"

"They don't," Angela said. "I just feel that the way they live, their entire life-style, is irrelevant, it has nothing to do with reality."

"Because they have money and you don't?"

"No. Because their whole goddamn life is based on real estate. Owning things."

"You said that's all your dad talks about. Real estate. Is he rich?"

"No, he wears a string tie and a cowboy hat with his gold-frame glasses, drives a Cadillac, lives in Country Club Estates with a guard, a *guard,* Bryan, at the entrance and tries hard to sound rich. But he doesn't know how. That's what's wrong with them," Angela said, with her cool edge. "The rich people make their life look so goddamn good we all bust our ass trying to get the same thing."

Bryan said, "If the poor people suddenly became rich would they do it any different?"

"Probably not."

"Are rich people fun to watch?"

"Not especially."

"Fun to talk to? Interview?"

"Not at all. They don't *say* anything. They don't *know* anything that's going on outside their own walled-in life. They're completely out of touch with reality."

"I'll talk to you," Bryan said. "Soon as I think of something. But first, tell me where the Holiday Inn is."

"The one we're going to is in Palm Beach Gardens," Angela said. "About ten miles north of here."

"Palm Beach Gardens?" Bryan said. "I've never heard of it."

That was the first thing Robbie Daniels said, too, the next morning when Bryan opened the door of Room 205 and there he was, boyish as ever.

"Palm Beach *Gardens?* I've been here practically all my life, I've never even heard of it . . ."

11

The second thing Robbie said, looking over the room, the double beds, one made with its spread intact, the other torn apart, was, "You want to know something? This is the first time I've ever been inside a Holiday Inn. It's not bad at all."

Angela said to Bryan, "See? What did I tell you?"

She sat at the room-service table in her terry-cloth robe having breakfast.

Robbie said to Bryan, "Go ahead. I'll have some coffee with Angie while you get dressed."

"I am dressed," Bryan said.

"I mean for golf," Robbie said.

"I am dressed for golf," Bryan said.

Robbie looked at Bryan's dark blue T-shirt that had the words SQUAD 5 HOMICIDE stenciled on it in white. He looked at Bryan's faded gray corduroy pants and tennis shoes with four blue stripes on them—not three, *four*—and said, "Oh."

As they left Angela said, "Don't worry about me. I'll find something to do."

They drove off in Robbie's silver Rolls. Robbie said, "How is that, pretty nice stuff?" Bryan told him to be careful and Robbie shut up.

What Bryan did, he noted things he would tell Angela about later.

The Seminole Club. "Ben Hogan once said if he had to play one club all the time it would be Seminole," Robbie said. "Where do you play in Detroit?" Bryan said, "Palmer Park, mostly." A public course. "Oh . . . What do you shoot?" "Low eighties." "How about if I give you twelve strokes?" "Fine." Robbie gave him an entire yellow golf outfit. Yellow pants, yellow shirt with the little alligator on it, yellow silk sweater. ("I looked like the Easter Bunny.") White shoes with tongue flaps. Robbie gave him the twelve strokes—the son of a bitch, the sandbagger—and beat him by twenty-six. Bryan tried to cheat, moving his ball around in the rough, but the caddy kept watching him. He lost six golf balls, one in the Atlantic Ocean, but took a penalty on only two of them or else his score would have been one-oh-six. He wouldn't tell Angela too much about the game.

He'd tell her about the gingersnaps in the locker room. Strange. And the macaroni and cheese special for lunch; all the rich guys eating the macaroni and cheese they didn't get at home, eating it like they'd discovered it. He'd tell her about some of the rich guys he met—Angela was right—who talked about real estate in places he'd never heard of. And how he'd met the Chicano-looking guy named Rafael Fuentes who resembled Rudolph Valentino—he seemed to pose—and had a dry, almost bored way of talking with his Chicano accent that had some other accents mixed in, but seemed like a nice guy. Very well mannered. Robbie called him Chichi or Cheech and seemed on familiar terms. The thing was, the guy didn't seem to know Robbie. Robbie asked him, "How's the coke business, Cheech?"

Chichi said, "I no longer have the bottling plant. It was confiscated."

(Confiscated?)

And Robbie said, "Señor Slick. You know what I'm talking about, Chichi. A little *dulce nariz,* perhaps?"

Trying to show off. Literally translated, candy nose, but meaning nose candy. Cocaine.

Which Chichi smiled at in his bored cultured way, then snapped his fingers. "A party—where was that? Everyone wanted to escape, to fantasize."

Robbie said, "And you got caught in a cabana, I think it was, going down on the hostess."

"A lovely lady," Chichi said. Bony features creased in a smile of recognition. "Ah, Robbie"—pronouncing it Robie—"now I remember you. The Detroit industrialist with the delicacy of a drill press. Are you still seducing little girls?"

"Only when your sister's in town," Robbie said. "Nice seeing you again, Cheech."

"Nice seeing you, too," Chichi said. "By the way, I met your wife yesterday at Wellington . . ."

Got him. Bryan caught Robbie's instant look of surprise.

''Ah, you don't know she's here, uh? With that Polish count, what's his name? From Colorado. The one who dyes his hair white and wears the fringed jackets.''

Robbie said, ''What difference does it make?''

''I don't know,'' Chichi said, ''Patti is your wife, not mine. She and the count flew in for the polo. I wouldn't worry about it.''

Robbie said, ''Do I look worried?''

Chichi Fuentes took the question literally and studied him. ''No, you look more confused, I think. I told them, you want the best polo, go down to Casa de Campo; you want only to fuck, well, Palm Beach is all right.''

They *ciao*-ed each other with cold smiles and that was that.

Bryan would remember it as pussy time at Seminole: two grown men spitting at each other in the locker room. Was this the way rich guys had it out? He'd have to ask Angela.

But the most interesting part of the day came later. Robbie said why didn't they go to his place, kick their shoes off and have a few? Fairly offhand about it. Bryan said fine. He was already sure Robbie had something in mind and wanted to talk.

Bryan thought of a nun he had in the sixth grade at Holy Trinity whose favorite word was *gawk* and was always telling the class to quit gawking at the ceiling or gawking out the window at the new freeway excavation. Sister Estelle. She would not have been proud of Bryan Hurd as he walked through the Spanish mansion, through the living room that was larger than the Holiday Inn lobby, and gawked in every direction. Christ. People lived here. Two people. And some servants. He saw a maid in a white uniform and then a guy with his hair slicked back wearing an apron, in the kitchen talking to Walter. Arguing about something. Robbie entered and they shut up—Walter looking past his boss now to Bryan waiting in the hall. Walter staring, with almost a balloon coming out of his head that said, ''What's he doing here?'' Robbie spoke to Walter for several minutes, holding onto his arm; then came back apologetically, ''I'm sorry—'' and took the homicide detective upstairs to his study and unlocked the double bolts. ''I was interested—during Walter's court hearing that colored lawyer asked you if you'd killed anyone lately, you told him no,''

Robbie said, "and I wondered if in fact you *have* ever killed anyone."

Bryan said, "I remember reading about one of yours."

It caught Robbie by surprise. "The Haitian? That wasn't in the Detroit papers, was it?"

"The guy from Chrysler, in the duck blind." Bryan made a quarter turn on the bar stool, giving the room a glance. What looked like covered light fixtures high on the walls could be video cameras; he wasn't sure. The room was dim except for track lighting directly overhead. He wondered if there was a camera up there. He wondered when Robbie Daniels would get to the point.

"I forgot about Carl," Robbie was saying, standing behind the bar, a sneaker up on the stainless sink. "That was a shocking experience. But the Haitian, that was something else. Guy came at me with a goddamn machete."

"What'd you use?"

"Colt Python. It's my favorite, so I grabbed it. You want to see it?"

It didn't matter if he wanted to or not. Robbie went over and got it, left the cabinet open and came back hefting the big, three-and-a-half-pound revolver with the ventilated barrel. He seemed to enjoy holding it. When he offered the gun Bryan took it.

"What do you carry, lieutenant?"

"Regular thirty-eight Smith, Chiefs Special. I had a Colt automatic once, but I had to get rid of it," Bryan said. "I found out it wasn't authorized by the department."

"You found out?"

"Well, I didn't carry it much and I didn't keep up on all the regulations." Looking the Python over, extending it now, Bryan said, "He had a machete, huh?"

"Came at me swinging," Robbie said.

"So you had no choice but to shoot."

"None," Robbie said. "You've never been in that position?"

Bryan seemed to smile. "Not lately."

"I'm surprised, you don't seem interested in guns."

Bryan gestured, a small shrug. "No, not especially." He laid the Python on the bar and picked up his vodka over ice. Robbie hadn't asked him what he wanted to drink; he'd started pouring and that was it: a guy who had been drinking socially, semi-professionally most of his life and probably felt he could outdrink an Athens Bar city cop any day of the week. Maybe he could. The imported vodka was all right though. Bryan felt pretty good, his mind sharp and clear.

Robbie said, "You see this guy coming at you who obviously means business—what would you have done?"

"I wasn't there," Bryan said. "I guess nobody was but you. But if you say you had to shoot him, well . . ."

"All right," Robbie said, "how about—a different situation. You don't *have* to shoot, but you feel justified."

They were getting to it now. Bryan said, "Like some really bad dude, or somebody you're pissed off at?"

"Think of an individual," Robbie said, "you know the world would be a much better place without."

Jesus Christ, Bryan thought. "Like who?"

"Come on, you know the type I mean. An international purebred asshole of the first order."

"I don't know any," Bryan said.

"There are some fairly obvious ones."

"Well, I don't know how international he is," Bryan said, "but how about Howard Cosell?"

"Come on, I mean a real one."

"Two for one," Bryan said, warming up to it, "Cosell and George Steinbrenner. Or, I know a couple Recorders Court judges—but I think I'd rather catch 'em crossing a street and run over 'em with a car. Does it matter how you do it?"

"I'm serious," Robbie said. "Consider someone like—have you ever heard of Carlos?"

"Carlos," Bryan said. The name was familiar.

"Number one terrorist in the world today. Hijacks planes, kidnaps, murders—"

"You had a buyer from Mexico named Carlos," Bryan said, holding Robbie's gaze. "Carlos Cabrera."

It stopped Robbie. His smile was tentative, with a hint of suspicion. "How'd you remember that name?"

"I spoke to him on the phone," Bryan said. "Asked him if he remembered who picked him up that Saturday. He said you did."

Staring at Robbie, not letting him look away. "I asked him where he stayed. He said the Detroit Plaza."

Robbie moved around behind the bar again, giving himself something to do. "If Mr. Cabrera says I picked him up . . . Come to think of it I guess I did. But not at the hotel. No, he was waiting at the main entrance of the RenCen with his assistant. Right out in front." Now remembering details. "Did he tell you that?"

"He might've. But it's all the same general area, isn't it?"

"We're talking about an entirely different Carlos," Robbie said, breaking free and beginning to run now. "A Venezuelan educated in Moscow, trained in PLO *fedayeen* camps. Carlos has worked with both the Red Brigade and the Baader-Meinhof gang. He's the ultimate professional terrorist—kidnapped those OPEC guys in Vienna, he's murdered who knows how many people. His operating principle is from an old Chinese saying, 'Kill one, frighten ten thousand.' "

Bryan said, "You'd rather do Carlos than Howard Cosell, huh?"

"I'm serious, goddamn it!" Robbie took a drink to settle down and managed a weak grin. Serious but still boyish. "Sorry about that. Sometimes I get a little carried away."

Bryan, with all the time in the world, said, "You want to go out and shoot Carlos, is that what you're telling me?"

"Look at it this way," Robbie said. "All over the world people are shooting each other. Iranians and Iraqis, Russians and Afghans, Christians and Moslems in Lebanon. Look at Angola, Uganda, Cambodia, Chad—"

"Chad . . ." Bryan said. He had not thought too much about Chad lately.

"Ethiopia, Guatemala, El Salvador . . . People are shooting each other and most of the time they don't even know what side they're on. We look at those places, it's hard to tell the good guys from the bad guys. But there are other areas where we know goddamn well who the bad guys are."

"Wait a minute," Bryan said. There was something he wanted to do. He got off the stool, went over to the open cabinet and looked in.

The display of handguns was impressive, interesting: most of them high-caliber, high-velocity models that would be selected with serious intent. The twenty-two target pistol Robbie had fired in his office wasn't on display. He tried the door below the open cabinet but it wouldn't budge.

"I showed Walter my collection," Robbie said. "Walter goes, 'Christ, you could invade Cuba.' "

Bryan came back to the bar. "I don't know about Cuba, but it might get you through downtown Miami."

Robbie raised his eyebrows. "Speaking of which. You know the Cuban boat people, the ones that came from Mariel? Just in the past year something like eighty-five of them have been shot and killed."

Bryan settled into the stool. It was comfortable and things were moving right along. He didn't have to urge Robbie or lead him now.

"There's an outlet in Miami sells a half-million dollars worth of handguns a month, and that's only one place. We're into guns, man. Everybody is, the good guys now as well as the bad guys. And you know what it comes down to, the bottom line? Who shoots first."

Now he was trying to sound hip. He didn't know who he was. Or as Angela said, there was an interesting other Robbie inside the cute Robbie. The one in there was dying to pull the trigger and the present world climate was inspiring him, bringing him out on stage.

"You can wait for an intruder. Somebody breaks into your house, which happened right here. Or, if you have the wherewithal, the purpose, the ability, why not go out after the same sort of game? Only bigger?"

"Like Carlos," Bryan said.

"Like any number of individuals on the other side," Robbie said. "Carlos is an example. Maybe someday, down the road. A more realistic one might be . . . say, a big-time drug dealer that none of the government agencies can touch. A guy who's fucking up lives, kills people who get in his way and lives like a king."

Bryan said, "Well, you're looking for action you could join the Marines."

"Listen, a hundred and twenty years ago," Robbie said, "during the Civil War, gentlemen of means raised their own regiments. 'Bring your horse, a shotgun and a pistol and ride with Nathan Bedford Forrest.' You put a sign on a tree in the front lawn. Now you don't fight with armies; the sides aren't clearly enough defined. But, you don't have to raise a regiment to take out some of the bad guys."

He was serious. Listening to him was not exactly embarrassing, but close to it. The man didn't hear himself as he was. He was picturing himself in a role. With a sword. Born a hundred years too late. Maybe that was it.

Bryan said, "I notice you read some pretty exciting stuff. We can get all kinds of secret thrills from books, can't we? Especially in a nice comfortable study. Quiet, air-conditioned . . ."

"The star German terrorist Ulrike Meinhof," Robbie said, "refused to hide out in an apartment that didn't have central heating, or the usual comforts of home. He complained about the primitive conditions in PLO training camps, raised quite a stink about Al Halil, in Libya. Which incidentally got Qaddafi very pissed off."

"I guess what you're saying," Bryan said, "you don't have to be poor to want to kill somebody."

"You don't have to be a cop, either."

Bryan waited, letting the silence lengthen. "What's the matter, you bored?"

"Usually."

"Golf doesn't do it, uh?"

"There's very little competition."

"Well, now you're into a game I know something about," Bryan said.

"I'm aware of that." Robbie sipped his drink. "Except you haven't told me if you've ever killed anyone."

"Does it matter?"

"I don't believe you have," Robbie said, "and I think that's odd. I mean if I've killed and you haven't, who's the authority?"

"I think it might depend," Bryan said, "on who you've got in mind."

The curly haired smiler who owned a half-dozen cars, a couple of million-dollar mansions, property in seven states and was sometimes mistaken for a movie star looked at the thirty-grand-a-year homicide cop with the solemn mustache.

He said, "It's funny. You go to a club for a round of golf, you're asked what you shoot. But this kind of game you're asked *who* you shoot, or would like to. It's considerably more exciting, isn't it?"

"Only if you win," Bryan said. "You lose, you don't get off buying a round of drinks."

12

He groaned as he worked sore feet into his loafers, sat back and rested, then groaned again as he got up out of the Holiday Inn chair.

Angela said, "Sometimes you sound old."

She stood at the mirror over the bank of dressers, looking at his reflection across the room, the glass door to the balcony behind him in flat light.

He said, "I told you, I like to sound old."

"Not creaky old."

"I played eighteen holes on a ball buster. That'll do it to you."

Angela was adjusting the neckline of her dress, pulling it out and looking down inside. "But did he tell you *who* he wants to shoot?"

"He talks around it." Bryan moved to the closet, came out with his blue polka-dot tie. "If you could get rid of anybody you feel doesn't deserve to live—or the world would be a better place without—who would it be? I think some girl told him one time he's 'real deep' and he believes it."

"You know who might be a good one," Angela said. "Robbie."

"I thought of that," Bryan said, "after." He came over to the mirror to tie his tie, standing obliquely behind her. Angela's eyes raised to his reflection, his face already deeply tanned.

"Who did you suggest?"

"I gave him Howard Cosell. I didn't mean it though. I like Howard, he's all right."

"You like everybody."

"No, but when I think about it, I don't dislike as many people as I thought. I decided I like John McEnroe, for example. I'd take him for backup any time."

"How about Walter?"

"Walter's Walter. I think Daniels played the game with him and signed him up. Walter, I can see him, makes out a list of prospects and licks his thumb going through the pages. But I guess I didn't play it right. It was funny, I had the feeling, it was like I was waiting to get a bribe offer. If I said the right thing, showed some interest, he'd have offered me . . . I don't know. Shows me the exclusive club, his home—it was like, all this can be yours if you play along."

"The temptation of Bryan Hurd."

"Except he didn't offer me anything; so what was he doing? He tells me about an international terrorist as a likely target, a guy named Carlos. That rang a bell, so I told him I'd called that Mexican buyer, Carlos Cabrera."

"Did you?"

"No, I took a shot. I told him the Mexican said Mr. Daniels himself had picked him up. At the Plaza. And Robbie said, that's right, I guess I did. No argument. So he was there Saturday morning."

They thought about it separately, staring at their reflections, tieing a tie, pinning the front of a dress, wondering about a man who talked about killing people. She said, "Are you always this detached?" And thought of him in the squad room. "No, you're not. But you don't seem interested."

"I'm used to working from some kind of possible motive, and I don't see it," Bryan said. "Why would he kill Curtis Moore?"

Angela moved to the chair by the balcony and sat down, erect, knees together, as though practicing. She said, "You discussed it with him in the abstract, didn't you? When he talks about killing people, does he show any kind of emotion? Does he get excited?"

"He rationalizes. But when you begin with bullshit the conclusion you reach is still bullshit."

They were dressing to meet Robbie at the Everglades Club for cocktails and dinner. Angela had brought one dress, the beige wraparound cotton knit she wore. She wondered if it was dressy enough for the Everglades and had asked Bryan several times if he thought the neckline was all right. He'd said, "If you hold rich people somewhere below you, how're they gonna see down your dress?" She'd said she was asking what *he* thought, not anyone else, and made him feel like a smart-ass.

She would sit stiffly erect now, then bend forward from the waist, testing her moves as Bryan got into his dark blue Sunday suit.

"Did Curtis Moore come up at all?"

"No, but that's an idea," Bryan said. "Offer Curtis as a guy you'd like to shoot if someone hadn't already. See if he lights up."

"Would we be meeting him tonight if you weren't a cop?"

That was a good question. Or, would they have been invited? He sidestepped it and said. "I thought you want to see the Everglades Club."

"I do," Angela said. "How about when I bend over?"

"Nice . . . You don't have a bra on."

"Sure I do. See? But there's not much to it."

He said, "We've got a little time, haven't we?"

She said, "Now wait a minute. You know how long it took to get this pinned?"

He said, "We sound like we're married."

They looked at each other and then looked away. But there it was.

Walter got back to the house at ten minutes to seven, looked around and found Daniels out on the patio, all dressed up in a tan suit and red-striped tie, like he was going out. Except he was reading a book. Walter started his report: "You know how many Rolls—" But Daniels raised his hand, not looking up from the book. Walter had to wait for Mr. Cool to finish the page and bend the corner over.

"Now then."

"You said the guy had a Rolls. You know how many fucking Rolls are parked out at Seminole?"

"I told you it was a dark blue sedan."

"Well, it turned light tan since you seen it."

"Walter, did you follow him or not?"

"Yeah, I followed him. He went down to Hillsboro. That area there before you get to the inlet where you can't see the houses? It's all trees. He turned into a drive. I parked down a ways, came back. It's a big house made of like shingles. Right on the beach but back, you know? With all these sea-grape trees around it."

"Hillsboro." Daniels seemed mildly surprised, then pleased. "Go on."

"He picked up a broad. Skinny, but with great big ones, stuck out to here."

"How old?"

"Young broad, early twenties. Reddish hair with gunk around her eyes. Had on a lavender dress with little straps."

"What kind of shoes?"

"Sandals, like wedgies."

"Just teasing you, Walter." Robbie was in a good mood now.

"They got in the Rolls, took Sample Road over to the Interstate and went down to Miami, all the way to the end. Got off in Coconut Grove, that area there and drove over to a high rise on Brickel Avenue just north of the Key Biscayne Causeway. The place's got not only a fence around it, it's got bob wire on top the fence and a sign says beware of guard dogs. Fucking Miami, I'm telling you, the fucking natives're taking over."

"Between Brickel and Bay Shore," Robbie said. "You know what you can see from the penthouse of that condominium looking east?"

"I imagine you can see the whole bay," Walter said.

"Yeah, but in particular," Robbie said, "from twenty-six floors up you've got a clear shot of Government Cut."

"Yeah, I imagine you would."

"And the Coast Guard base."

"Now you're talking," Walter said, raising an arm as though he were making a muscle and pulled his shirt out from his armpit. "I was wondering what we're playing here. So the guy likes to watch the Coast Guard boats and he's not with the DEA, I know that, driving a fucking Rolls. So what's he handle, weed?"

"He doesn't *handle* anything," Robbie said. "He arranges for the importation of marijuana and cocaine, staying well above the action, and makes approximately, part time, two hundred thousand dollars a month . . . when he isn't inspecting embassies."

Walter said, "Wait. This is the same kid we been talking about? The kid sitting on the old man's lap with the Knights of Columbus outfit on only grown up now?"

Robbie paused, deadpan. He said, "Amazing," staring at Walter. "I'm the only person in the world would have any idea what you just said. To answer your question, yes, it's the same kid on the guy's lap with the Knights of Columbus outfit only grown up now."

"I think it was, with the Knights of Columbus outfit *on*. You left out *on,*'' Walter said and thought, Fuck you, too . . .

''Walter, why don't you sit down.''

''Yeah, I think I will. Thanks.''

''Okay. He went up to the penthouse, stayed about a half-hour. Right?''

''You followed him before?''

''Many times. Go on.''

''He was in the building twenty-three minutes,'' Walter said. ''The broad waited in the car . . . This kid comes along—listen to this. This kid comes along looking for his dog. He's calling, 'Here, Piper! Here, Piper!' ''

Robbie stared at Walter.

''The kid goes up the street. In a couple minutes here's this dog, this little white scottie comes along. The broad sees it, she opens the door, goes 'Here, Piper!' The dog hops in the car and she starts playing with it. The guy comes out, gets in the car—now you could see *him* petting the dog, playing with it. The broad goes to open her door, too late, he drives off, the dog's still in the car. The dog's got this little red collar on, you know, with the license hanging on it? Probably has the name and address. No, the guy drives off. He don't care if the dog belongs to the kid and it's gonna break the kid's heart, fuck no, take it. They drive off with the dog.''

Robbie waited, making sure there was no more to the story. He said, ''Walter?''

''Yeah?''

''Then where'd they go?''

''They went back up to Hillsboro, the broad's place.''

''How do you know it's hers?''

''I call the Broward County sheriff.''

''Walter, don't tell me that—''

''Mr. Daniels, what was I doing the past twenty-one years? I identify myself as an officer with Palm Beach County, give 'em a phony name, a badge number they don't know from shit and ask 'em to look up in their directory who lives at the address in question. I talk to a clerk, it took maybe a minute and a half.'' Walter dug into his back pocket, brought out a notebook that was limp, curved to fit his hip; he opened it, licked his thumb to turn a few pages and said, 3524 Ocean Drive. The deed to the property and the lots on both sides are registered in the name of Doris Marie Vaughn.

Robbie said, *"Dorie?"* Amazed. "She's a polo groupie."

Walter said, "I don't know what she does for a living, but she's got dough. That property in there with the lots'd be worth a couple million."

"Jesus," Robbie said, "Dorie Vaughn. Well, you know what he's doing, what he's using the house for."

"I got a pretty good idea what he's doing when I left," Walter said. "Even with the gunk on her eyes, that's a tasty broad."

"She's a good kid, but flaky."

"Well, nobody says you got to talk to 'em."

"I want to see the house," Robbie said.

"I thought—you're all dressed up you're going out."

"I've been waiting a long time for this kind of a setup," Robbie said. "Jesus, Hillsboro. It's perfect. Come on, I want to see the house."

Walter said, "I hope she knows how to take care of Piper. Knows what she's doing."

Robbie paused getting up from the chair, hands clamped on the arms. "Who?"

"Who we been talking about?" Walter said. "The broad."

Angela thought of an image. The tourists stroll past the expensive Worth Avenue shops. Near the end of the street they see any ordinary entrance gate, no sign, a pink facade, the unadorned back of a building. The tourists barely notice it. But its the rear end of the Everglades, one of the world's most exclusive clubs. And Worth Avenue is the *alley* that runs behind it.

"I thought of it coming in," Angela said.

Bryan said, "Then what happens?"

"Boy, are you a smart-ass."

"No, I think you should write your rich people's book. Get it out of your system."

"If I can do it without the usual knee-jerk attitude. It would have to be straight impressions without cute asides. And no adverbs." Speaking as her eyes wandered.

"You'd better close your mouth then, quit staring."

"I'm not staring."

He watched her gaze slide over the lounge that was like a formal living room. They sat in upholstered chairs, their drinks on a glass-top cocktail table.

"You are now."

She said, "My God. You know who that is?" Nodding to point. "The three ladies sitting together."

"That's all're in here. It's like a woman's club."

"The one with the pearls. That's Mary Sandford. Very close friend of Rose Kennedy. If you're putting on a charity you'd better have Mary Sandford or you're dead. I hear she's nice though."

"Are you from a big family?"

"Two sisters and two brothers. All older."

"And you had to wear your sisters' hand-me-downs."

"For about ten years. How'd you know that? . . . Damn it, I should've brought a copy of the *Social Pictorial*. Or the *Shiny Sheet*. The one's Mary Sanford. And I think the one next to her is Anky Johnson. That's Revlon money. But she usually wears a turban."

Bryan said, "How come you don't see any guys here?"

Angela's gaze began to move again, inching over the lounge. "They're all dead. Or they're upstairs playing dominoes. Or both . . . I hope we eat in the Orange Garden. I mean dine. That's *the* room here."

"We're gonna eat at McDonald's if Smiley doesn't show up."

"He's always late."

"Well, I read one time, a prompt man is a lonely man," Bryan said, "and it's true." He sipped his Wild Turkey. When they came in and sat down he was going to order their favorite, Jack Daniels, but he had said to the waiter, "While we're waiting for Mr. Daniels we'll have—" and paused awkwardly and changed the brand. Not wanting to call attention to himself. The homicide cop trying to act as though he belonged. Angela hadn't noticed.

She said, "Oh, my God," in a hushed tone. Then, without moving her mouth: "The one in pink, just coming in. The middle-aged Barbie doll. That's Robbie's wife. With the bald-headed guy with the white hair. And you know what? Robbie won't think a thing of it."

Bryan said, "The wild-west jacket and the hair, the guy looks like Buffalo Bill. I understand he's a count."

"He is? How do you know?"

Got her. "You hear things," Bryan said. "But how come, if his wife's here he doesn't know it?" He thought of his former wife, Peggy.

"Because," Angela said, "as Robbie puts it, 'Patti and I do our own thing.' "

"Why are they married?"

"Because it's too much trouble to get a divorce. Split up the fortune. If they can both do what they want, why bother? One of his girl friends—here's an example, a girl who thought he was serious about her came to the house one night. She got right to the point with Patti. 'When're you gonna give him a divorce?' Patti doesn't even know who she is. They go in and confront Robbie. He looks up from his book and says, 'Don't get *me* involved in this . . .' "

He thought of Peggy again. "My wife—I mean my former wife called last week . . ."

But Angela was watching the proceedings. "Now they're paying their respects to Mary Sanford telling her how wonderful it is to see her. Little hand-kissing there . . . Gushing now, it's always good to gush a little."

"You better not write the book," Bryan said. Then said, "Does Robbie have a girl friend now?"

"I don't know. He picks girls up." Angela thought of something and looked at him now. "It's funny, he talks about it, but he's not what you'd call a dedicated chaser."

"Maybe he likes guns better," Bryan said.

Robbie came out of the trees to the dead-end access road where Walter was waiting by the car, its front end pointing toward the beach, the silver Rolls ghostly in the early darkness.

Walter said, "He still there?" The words came louder than he'd expected and he half-whispered, "In the house?"

"His car's still there," Robbie said.

"You didn't look in a window?"

"When I get that close," Robbie said, "it's gonna be done. But we're not quite ready yet. Two things. I want pictures of the place—"

"What kinda pictures?"

"I'll show you the camera when we get home. I want movies. And I want you to watch the place for a few days. If he's bringing stuff in and out, and I'm sure he is, then I want to hit him when the stuff's here. You understand what I'm getting at?"

"You want the place put under one-man surveillance for a few days you say," Walter said. "*I* understand what you mean, but I don't think you do, if you don't mind my saying. The fuck'm I suppose to do, I came here twenty-four hours? Who relieves me? Right now a squad car comes along, we're parked here in the fucking trees, two guys, the first thing they think of, somebody's copping somebody's joint. This whole area, any place you got houses worth a million bucks you got more security'n in a fucking bank, and I'm not kidding."

Robbie said, "Walter, look at the house."

"I think I saw it closer'n you did."

"I mean—consider where it is. You can barely see it, even from the beach. Empty lots on both sides full of trees. You come out the driveway and walk across the road, there's the Intracoastal right there, almost in your backyard. And a dock. You notice the dock?"

"Yeah, I notice the dock?"

"Now we know little Dorie Vaughn didn't buy the house."

"All I know it's in her name."

"Walter," Robbie said, "a guy who makes two hundred thousand dollars a month on the side bought the house. Because it's exactly the house he wanted. He can take deliveries in front, right out of the ocean. Or he can come out the back door and pick up something left on his dock. A little watertight package that's worth around a million bucks. But *he* doesn't pick it up, the girl does; she's got to be good for something. Then, I'll bet you anything, you see a yellow van stop by the house. The same van you'll see down in Coconut Grove. The same guy driving it who lives in that high rise on Brickel Avenue. It's all coming together, Walter. All the work I've been doing on this project is finally paying off. But now we get to the tricky part. I don't want to have to buy some stuff and plant it on him. Christ, not when he's dealing in it. I want to get him, ideally, when he's in the house and there's a delivery sitting there. The police get an anonymous call, they find the son of a bitch, he's dead and it's obviously a dope-related hit. That's the way I want it to work and that's why I brought you in, Walter. Because you're a pro. You've forgotten more about surveillance than I could ever learn."

"Yeah, well I know surveillance," Walter said, "I've been on enough stakeouts in my life I should. But you got other people around here working not exactly surveillance but close to it. Security."

"Who, the police?"

"The police."

"Walter," Robbie said, "if you can buy a house, pick out a house and buy it because it's ideally situated for what you're doing—no matter what it costs—then, Walter, you can buy any fucking thing you want. Including police. A couple a bills a week to see that no Haitians break in . . . and not see anything else."

Walter rubbed his hand over his jaw. "You're talking about a lot of surveillance."

"Bring a cooler of beer and a pack of Camels." Robbie winked in the darkness. "Come on. I'm late."

They were on their third drink. Wild Turkey over ice.

Angela said, "Having fun at the club?"

Bryan didn't answer and they were both silent for at least a full minute, comfortable together if not with the waiting, neither good at small talk so not trying too hard.

"Would you rather belong here or Seminole?"

"If I had to play the same course every day, Seminole," Bryan said. "I like the macaroni and cheese."

"Did you try the gingersnaps?"

"I've never been in a locker room before where they serve cookies. Palmer Park doesn't have a locker room. You finish a round in the evening you walk across Woodward and have a drink with the hookers. Seminole, you talk about real estate."

"I told you."

"I met one guy who doesn't fit the mold. Chichi Fuentes. I

figured he was either a golf pro, a gigolo or an orchestra leader."

"I know him," Angela said. "In fact, if I do the book Chichi said he'll give me all kinds of trivia, for color. He knows everybody and everything that's going on in Palm Beach."

"He didn't seem to know Smiley."

Angela stared at him.

"Your mouth's open again."

"I just had a thought." One that seemed to disturb her. "What did Robbie say about him?"

"Nothing."

"He didn't tell you anything? Who he is?"

"No, but Chichi told Smiley a few things about his wife. That's why I know the bald-headed guy with long hair's a count. A Polish count."

"Chichi," Angela said, hunching closer, "is an international playboy from the Dominican Republic. You see him in *W* all the time."

"Wow," Bryan said.

"Listen. I'm serious. You remember Trujillo?"

"He was a dictator. Kind of a fat guy."

"God and Trujillo, that was his motto," Angela said. "Supreme ruler of the Dominican Republic for about thirty years, until he was finally assassinated in, I think, '61. Well, Chichi's one of Trujillo's illegitimate sons. He married a sugarcane heiress first, then a very rich American woman and then an Italian movie actress. Women adore him."

"Why?"

"Because he's charming. He's a lover." She groped and came up with another one. "He knows what women like."

"Did you read that or did he tell you himself?"

"Bryan—he's rich. He plays polo. He used to drive sports cars. He's held diplomatic posts all over the world. Chargé d'affaires in Paris, a lot of places. In fact, right now he's inspector of embassies for the Dominican Republic . . . I'm *serious.* He's single . . . probably the most eligible bachelor in Palm Beach."

"Robbie doesn't like him."

"You know why? Robbie would like to *be* him."

"Or George Hamilton. What else does he do?"

"Well, he's broken up a few marriages, once was named correspondent of the year. Let's see—over like a three-year period he collected seventy-seven parking tickets in Palm Beach County and was stopped something like twenty times for speeding. My friend at the *Post* did a story about it, how Chichi flaunts his diplomatic immunity and tears up tickets.'' Angela paused, thoughtful. ''There was something else,'' she said and paused again and began to nod.

Bryan watched her, used to waiting for answers.

''Yeah—he was called before a Dade County grand jury that had something to do with dope-related murders, I think in Miami. I read it when I was researching him, but I don't remember when it was.''

''What happened?''

''He refused to waive immunity, so they couldn't talk to him.''

''They didn't ask him to leave the country?''

''I don't think they wanted to indict him. Chichi was called as a witness. He had business dealings, I think, with whoever it was they were after.''

''Maybe he's a high-class smuggler,'' Bryan said. ''Uses his diplomatic pouch.''

''Cheech? I doubt it. He doesn't need money.''

''How do you know?''

Angela didn't answer.

''At the club, the first thing Robbie said to him was how's the coke business?''

''He did?''

''Then at his house,'' Bryan said, ''we're playing his game, who would you like to shoot? Robbie goes, well, there's Carlos the terrorist. Maybe someday. And then he said, 'But a more realistic one might be—' and paused like he had to think of one before it came to him—'How about a big-time dope dealer? Somebody who's messing up people's lives and the law can't touch him.' ''

''I can't see Chichi as a dealer,'' Angela said. ''He's the great seducer. He told me he hasn't slept alone since he was fourteen years old.''

''Maybe he's afraid of the dark.''

''I can't see him bothering with something like that, smuggling. He's not the type.''

''Maybe not,'' Bryan said. ''But Robbie didn't offer the drug dealer as an example. I think the idea appeals to him. Somebody bad who's close by."

Angela said, "Does Chichi look like a bad guy to you?"

Bryan said, "Does Robbie? . . . When I first mentioned Chichi you got a funny look on your face and you said, 'I just had a thought . . .' "

"I wasn't thinking about dope."

"No, it was before we got into that."

"Oh—" Angela came alive. "You said he didn't seem to know Robbie and I thought—right away I thought, what if Chichi's the one he wants to kill?"

"Why would he?"

"That's the trouble, the motive's so flimsy—"

"Because he doesn't like him?"

"Sort of, but more because Chichi never remembers Robbie's name," Angela said. "Does that sound dumb?"

Ruth May Hayes, thirty-seven, was tied by the neck to the rear bumper of her boyfriend's car and dragged in circles over a field until she was dead. Robert Jackson, thirty-four, and James Pope, thirty-five, died in a gunfight that developed when Jackson put his cigarette out in a clean ashtray. Sam James, thirty-five, told his wife their twelve-year-old daughter's shorts were too tight; an argument followed and James was stabbed to death. Paul Struggs, twenty-nine, was shot to death by his girl friend. Richard Scott, twenty-three, was shaking hands with people he'd been arguing with at a party when someone struck him from behind with a baseball bat and killed him. Myros Cato, forty-seven, was shot to death by his wife following an argument. James Ware, sixty-five, was shot to death by his son, a psychiatric patient at Veterans Hospital. Charles Roby, thirty-two, got in an argument with his girl friend over a pack of cigarettes and she stabbed him to death. Gloria Glass, fifty, told James Lindsey, fifty-six, they were through; Lindsey shot and killed her. Betty Goodlow, thirty-two, was beaten, doused with paint thinner and set on fire by her boyfriend. Michael Kirby, twenty-five, got into an argument with the babysitter, who stabbed him in the head, then shot him with a rifle. Geraldine Phillips, thirty-five, told her boyfriend she was going to jog around the block; he became enraged and stabbed her to death. Marvin Rife, nineteen, was throwing bottles at a neighbor's house when the neighbor came out with a shotgun and killed him. Benny Vann, forty-one, was shot to death by his girl friend because he'd dated her sister. Larry Young, sixteen, pulled a toy gun on his friend and said, boom; his friend, twenty-three, pulled a real gun and killed him. George Peterson, fifty-one, came out of a bar and mistakenly got in someone else's car; he was pulled out by the car's owner, identity unknown, and kicked to death. Cecil Castner, twenty-five, swiped at Delois Tanksley, twenty-one, with a knife; she hit him with a chair, got a handgun from the bedroom and shot him in the back of the head; she was convicted of careless use of a firearm resulting in death and drew eighteen months probation. Joseph Vennie, fifty-five, was angry when L.C. Ford, forty, locked out of his car, woke Vennie up and asked him for a coat hanger; Vennie struck Ford over the head with a gun; Ford took the gun away from him and killed him with it.

There were approximately six hundred seventy additional homicides, not unlike these, that had taken place in the Detroit area during the past year and were familiar stories to Bryan Hurd.

He said to Angela, "I can tell you how people kill each other and sometimes why and you tell me if any of the motives make sense."

She said, "So it doesn't matter if the reason sounds weird."

He said, "To tell you the truth, killing someone who doesn't remember your name makes more sense than most."

She said, "What do we do now?"

He said, "Let's get out of here and have a Jack Daniels someplace."

13

Bryan made phone calls most of the morning with the yellow pages open in front of him and by two that afternoon they had moved from the Holiday Inn in Palm Beach Gardens to the Villas Atlantis in Lake Worth, on the beach and only about five miles south of Robbie's home on South Ocean Boulevard.

"I didn't come thirteen hundred miles to sit by a swimming pool," Bryan said. "I like the ocean."

Angela said, "Uh-huh." She was sure they'd moved to be closer to the action, to keep an eye on Robbie.

Except that Bryan didn't contact Robbie. He wasn't kidding, he sat on the beach. He did make phone calls home from their Atlantis villa that was actually an efficiency and talked to Annie Maguire or Malik, keeping in touch. But most of the time for the next two days he was out there in the sun with his *National Geographics*. He told Angela interesting facts about owls, kelp life and jackals.

She said, "Nobody even knows we're here."

He said, "Good."

"Aren't you gonna *do* something?"

Bryan said, "You asked me—I told you I was going to Florida to sit on the beach and read and you asked me if I read mysteries? I said no. I don't read mysteries for the same reason I don't involve myself in homicide investigations when I'm on furlough. That's the whole idea of a furlough. Get away from it."

"But if you know someone's gonna get killed . . ."

Bryan said, "I know of, I bet, five hundred people in Detroit who could very likely kill each other or somebody else in the near future. I don't know how to prevent homicides. I go in after and clean up."

She said, "At least tell him you know what he's doing."

"Who, Robbie? He told *me*."

"Then we should tell Chichi . . . *some*thing."

"If he's in drugs he's watching his ass very carefully. You don't have to tell him a thing."

"But we don't know he is, for sure."

Bryan closed the *National Geographic,* got up from his beach chair, went into Villa Number 16, the third one back from the beach in the line of cement bungalows and made a phone call while Angela stood watching him in her red bikini and he watched Angela. He called young Gary Hammond of the Palm Beach Police.

Angela could hear the sound of Gary's voice but not what he was saying. When Bryan hung up she pounced on him. "What did he say?"

"Wait."

They had a glass of orange juice in the air-conditioned efficiency. Gary Hammond called back and Bryan listened; he said uh-huh several times, he asked Gary how he was doing, asked what was a good place to eat on a cop's pay, said great, I appreciate it and hung up.

He said to Angela, still waiting, "Chichi's the source for the Palm Beach crowd, the swingers who've moved up from Cuba Libres to just plain coke. He passes out weed gratis. He's small potatoes locally but a name in Miami. He's sort of an importer-broker. He doesn't deal directly, he makes phone calls and goes to Bogotá or Santa Marta a few times a year. And because he's in the diplomatic corps they can't touch him."

"Exactly the guy," Angela said, "that Robbie proposed to you. The untouchable asshole, the ideal target." She was silent for several moments, thoughtful. "You know what? I'm doing the wrong story."

Bryan watched her move to the closet now and come out with white pants that were like string-tied pajama bottoms and a T-shirt.

"Where you going?"

"Do some research," Angela said.

Walter spent the first day thrashing around in the scrub without getting even a glimpse of Chichi Fuentes. Hotter'n a son of a bitch in there. He could hardly breathe. Trying to swat bugs and work the goddamn Jap camera, the goddamn equipment, the videotape recorder and the battery pack, hanging by straps around his neck, either strangling him or banging his knees or getting tangled up in the brush.

"That's right, I forgot to tell you," Robbie said. "Afternoons Chichi's either at Seminole or Palm Beach Polo in Wellington." He said, "Sorry about that, Walter."

Walter said, "You know how many different kinds of bugs're in there, just counting the tuckers you can see and maybe you can kill if you're fast enough?"

"How many?" Robbie said. "No, I'm kidding, Walter. I'm sure you're doing a hell of a job. You do have something on the tapes though, don't you?"

"Yeah, I got him, finally. I got something else too."

"What?"

"Let me wash up, put something on these bites. My wife's got some stuff—she's always getting bit. I don't know why—I mean I don't know how a bug'd land on her, Jesus, and want to take a bite. Or maybe there're more bugs over in West Palm than come to the beach."

"I'll give you something," Robbie said. "Come up to the study."

He had the ointment sitting on the bar next to an ice-cold vodka and tonic with fresh lime. Walter came in and drank it down. Walked in wearing a clean shirt, new Bermudas that covered his knees, new sandals made of straps and buckles and brass rings that couldn't be much lighter than combat boots, put that frosted glass to his mouth and didn't take it down till he was sucking air. Robbie made him another one while Walter dabbed ointment on his arms and legs and they were ready.

"Showtime," Robbie said, sitting down before the television console. Walter remained at the bar, the bottle of vodka handy.

The picture came on.

"Okay, there's the house from the north side," Walter narrated. "Notice there's no doors. The only doors're in the front and in the back . . . Okay, there's the dock . . . Boat going by on the Intracoastal . . . Another boat . . . There's one going the other way . . . Okay, this is approaching the house from the other side. Notice, as I said, there's no doors."

Robbie said, "Christ, Walter, it's a four-thousand-dollar camera. Couldn't you hold it a little steadier?"

Walter said, "You try it. The fucker sitting up there on your shoulder."

"I gave you a tripod."

"How'm I gonna use a tripod? I get set I got to move. I look like those assholes on eyewitness news except I'm in a fucking jungle, fucking bugs eating me up, the VCR, the battery pack, the fucking cables—try lugging all that shit around and hold the fucking camera still."

"That the patio?"

"Okay, that's the patio. That's—see, there's Piper over there chasing something. Look, driving him crazy. Probably the fucking bugs . . . Okay, here she comes. Bugs don't bother this broad."

"Dorie," Robbie said. "Very nice tan. Well, hey . . ."

"Hang onto your pecker," Walter said, "the show's just starting . . . Takes the top off . . . You ever see anything like that in your life? Defy the laws of fucking gravity. Look at that . . ."

"No tan lines," Robbie said.

"You aren't kidding no tan lines," Walter said. "Now, hooks her thumbs in there . . . You got any music? We should have some music go with this. Boom. Da-da da-boom. Off comes the little panties. Look at that, the red hair and the black bush. She could have quails in there, hiding."

"Hasn't started to sag yet," Robbie said.

"That's how you tell if a broad dyes her hair, look at her bush."

Robbie said, "Is that right?"

"What I can't figure out," Walter said, "the fuck she put the bathing suit on for she's gonna come outside and take it off?"

"Why didn't you zoom in?"

"I zoomed. You think I didn't zoom, for Christ sake? Wait up. I almost zoomed out of the woods and jumped her . . . There's your zoom."

"Very tight."

"How would you know?"

"Your zoom . . . You're pretty steady now, Walter. You're getting better."

"You bet your ass I'm steady. I got it homed in now. Locked. You'd have to break my arms. That broad can't move, I'm on her. Look at that, scratching her puss . . . Now she gets on the lounge.

I kept thinking, like trying to give her mental telepathy, roll over, roll over, you don't want to burn your buns."

"What's this?"

"We're in the woods again. I heard a car so I moved a little toward the back of the house . . . Okay, there's his Rolls Royce. You notice it's light tan? The Datsun Z's the broad's. Okay, the guy's already inside."

"Chichi?"

"Yeah, it's about five o'clock now. But the day before it was closer to six."

"What's he do when he comes?"

"The fuck you think he does? . . . Now we're in the woods again . . . Coming out . . . I'm almost on the beach now. Notice the level, I'm practically lying down."

"There he is."

"Yeah, he comes out on the patio. See Piper? . . . Look at that, runs over to him . . . The broad rolls over . . . there she is, her puss winking at the guy he's playing with the fucking dog. I like dogs, don't get me wrong, but Jesus Christ . . . Now they're chatting. You have a hard day at the office, dear? About right there I had something hard I could've showed her . . . Playing with the dog again. Hi, Mr. Piper. You're a good little doggie, aren't you? You miss Coconut Grove and your little friend? Tough shit. Now they're looking out at the ocean. I thought maybe something was gonna happen here . . . There, shot of the ocean. Nothing. Back to the show . . . Broad gets up, stretches, he goes right on talking. Stands there like a pimp. I mean he doesn't even *touch* her."

"That's about what he is," Robbie said, "a pimp. He uses women."

"Well," Walter said, "if you use 'em for the right thing and they like it, that's different. She bends over now to pick up the suit. Look at that. Taking my picture with her brownie . . . They bullshit for a minute or so and go in the house. That's it. Beginning of the next tape'll show him coming out with the broad about twenty minutes later, then some more boats going by. No boats stopping, no yellow van."

Robbie didn't move, staring at the empty television screen.

"You want to see it again?"

"I think so," Robbie said with a thoughtful tone. "I want to study the layout a little closer."

"I know what you want to study," Walter said. "But hey, it's okay with me. You're the boss, Mr. Daniels."

Angela believed the shiny brown thing that had run out of the bathroom was a palmetto bug. Bryan told her she didn't want to think of it as a roach because of the connotation, but that's what it was, a cockroach.

They were in the Buick Century driving north into Palm Beach; seven-thirty and still bright, though the sun was gone, off somewhere behind condominiums.

"It was probably a German cockroach," Bryan said, "but it could've been a Madeira. They're both that shiny light brown. They'll eat anything, soap, paper . . . glue. I saw two of them when I went in there to take my shower. I thought it was one long one at first, but they were like butt to butt. I think they were getting it on."

"Palmetto bugs fly," Anglea said, bringing it up from some early recollection.

But no match for Bryan. "A lot of different species have wings, they're still cockroaches."

"I like your owl facts better."

"Roaches're ugly but you got to admit they're quick," Bryan said. "You know how quick an American cockroach is?"

"You're gonna tell me anyway," Angela said.

"An American cockroach—you roll up a newspaper and try and hit him with it, the American cockroach can take off in fifty-four thousandths of a second."

"Almost as quick as Chichi Fuentes," Angela said.

"So you didn't just buy a new dress today. Where's the place we met Gary?"

"Go up Royal Palm to County and turn right. It's on Poinciana."

"I'm glad you know your way around."

"That's not all I know," Angela said.

They sat back of the hedgerow, outside but in shade, among the tourists in their resort outfits, everyone drinking, finished with one part of the day and beginning the fun time. Bryan said, "You see cowboy hats all over now, don't you?" Angela told him the polo crowd was gradually going western; you saw cowboy hats at Wellington, even more at Royal Palm and Gulfstream. He told her he missed her today. She looked at him with her warm glow and said, "Did you, really?" He said, "I miss you when you leave the room to go to the bathroom."

She said, "When you were reading about roaches, was there anything in there about the Santo Domingo variety La Cucaracha Fuentes? I'm finding out what a beauty he is."

They sipped bourbon collinses from tall frosted glasses, Bryan in a blue-orange-yellow Hawaiian shirt, playing the role of tourist, enjoying it; Angela crisp in a white linen sundress, brand new, more conscious of an image.

"He procures girls for stag parties on yachts."

"I was in Vice," Bryan said, "but I never raided a yacht. I hung out mostly in public toilets."

"You're in Palm Beach now, boy," Angela said. "The toilets are Italian marble and Chichi will get you anything you want for a price. I talked to my friend at the *Post* and he sat me down with a society writer who's got a chart of who's sleeping with whom plus a list of the young single girls. The ones that come up from the minors and hang out at the polo clubs and the *in* bars. Chichi is hot right now for a girl named Dorie Vaughn. He's supposed to have her set up in a house somewhere."

"You mean a whorehouse?"

"No, for privacy, to get away. She's not in the phone book. I checked the County Clerk's Office and there's nothing registered in her name, so I tried Broward County. Drove all the way down to Lauderdale and what do you know? Dorie Vaughn has a home in Hillsboro."

"Where did that get you?"

"To Hillsboro, where do you think. I drove past and took a peek, just from the driveway. Little Dorie's got a place that's worth at least a million, maybe more."

Bryan said, "I mean where does it get you in the end? You know the guy's in dope. What else you want to know?"

Angela said, "I want to know about the scene here. I want to know if rich people get high like everyone else."

"Talk to the feds, they'll give you all the information you want."

"I don't want facts, Bryan, I want color. I want to get next to Chichi and get him to tell me some stories."

"I think you should stick to your rich people's book."

"Should," Angela said. "Do you say *should* a lot? I hadn't noticed."

"I don't know, but I think we should eat," Bryan said, "before I take a bite out of you."

They drove to Chuck's Bar-B-Que Pit on Federal Highway, a place Gary Hammond had recommended, where the light fixtures were wagon wheels and Charlie Russell prints hung on the walls. Angela said, "Oh, my God—never ask a cop where to eat." But it wasn't bad. They had ribs and a pitcher of beer in the rustic lounge and would remember Linda Ronstadt singing "It's So Easy to Fall in Love."

Bryan saw familiar cowboy hats come in. Two of them. The same two that had walked past the sidewalk cafe and eyed them.

Angela said, "Why don't you want me to do one on drugs?"

"It's been done."

"What hasn't? If cockroaches've been done, everything has."

The two cowboys came to the table that was between the bar and the booth where Angela sat close to Bryan, eating ribs with her fingers, busy talking and not worrying about her new white sundress. The two cowboys made a production of standing at the table and surveying the room, their gaze coming around to Bryan and Angela before they eased down and drew chairs up for their boots. Their big scoop-brim cowboy hats remained squared over their eyes. Angela was saying it was the point of view that was important; you could still make it interesting with a fresh slant. The two cowboys were telling the waitress they wanted a pitcher of beer.

Bryan felt tired. He asked Angela if she'd bought her new dress on Worth Avenue.

She said, are you kidding? She said the idea would be to describe the traditional Palm Beach setting, the island of conservatism, the last bastion of Old Guard ideas, beginning to gently sway to a new wave, the groovy Young Guard making its move.

''Cowboys at the polo clubs,'' Bryan said.

''Exactly. That's one indication. A shit-kicker informality seeping in.''

Both scoop-brim hats were funneled this way. One of the cowboys said, ''What did she say?''

Bryan said, ''Where else did you go today?''

''Well, I had lunch at Two Sixty Four, very lively place, with my newspaper friend and the society writer. She works for the *Shiny Sheet.*''

''And you were discussing Chichi . . .''

''Yeah. I told you that. Then I stopped by his apartment—it's at the corner of Worth and South Ocean Boulevard, the ultraexclusive condominium. But he wasn't home. The doorman said he was playing golf.''

''You talk to the doorman a while?''

''For a couple of minutes. Doormen like to gossip.''

''You asked him a few leading questions.''

''A few.''

There you are, Bryan thought. She talked to Chichi's doorman and the doorman picked up the phone and called somebody. His fingers were greasy. He glanced up to catch the waitress, get some clean napkins and took a look at the two cowboys staring at them: giving them their tough-hombre movie-cowboy stares that wouldn't have been worth shit without the big hats. They were both in their twenties, shirts open, straggly hair coming out of their hats. Not powerfully built young men—thank God—but that dirty mean type Bryan had been sending to Jackson for the past sixteen years. He would bet they had put in some hard time at Raiford or maybe a federal lockup. They wore pass-the-time tattoos on their arms, the coarse designs of prison artists.

One of them said, ''Hey, lady . . .''

And Bryan thought, Here we go.

Angela was saying, ''You have to be excited about what you're doing. If you don't have enthusiasm then your words are gonna just sit there. That's the problem I was getting into with Robbie. My angle was flat.''

''Hey, lady, what're you doing with that old fart?''

Bryan looked at them now straight on. He might as well.

Angela said, "What? Are you talking to me?"

"You aren't married to him, are you?"

"Shit, he's too old for'r," the other one said. "Come on over here, talk to us."

Angela said, "Are you serious?"

Bryan liked her tone: quiet, matter-of-fact, but with a put-down edge to it.

The one cowboy raised and recrossed his run-down boots on the chair in front of him. He said, "What you want an old fart like him for? Can't even get it up."

"I like old farts," Angela said, a little more tense. "Leave us alone."

"My, my, my, my," the first cowboy said. "you got a tongue, haven't you? Stick it out, let's see it."

The other cowboy said, "I got something she can tongue."

The first cowboy said, "What's the matter with your old man? He don't say nothing . . . Mister, you mind we take your girl out the van? You stay here, drink your beer."

Bryan edged out of the booth to stand up. He felt Angela's hand touch his arm.

"Bryan . . ."

"It's all right."

"*Bry*-an? That your name?" They thought it was pretty funny.

The second cowboy said, "Oh, Bry-an, Bry-an . . . Where you going, Bryan? You nervous, gonna go take a piss?"

"He's gonna complain to the management," the first cowboy said. "We ain't doing nothing."

Angela watched the Hawaiian shirt cross to the hallway where a sign read *Rest Rooms * Telephone*. The two cowboys stared at her now. She looked past them. Bryan was gone. The waitress came over with napkins; she said, "Will there be anything else?" Angela told her no, just the check, please. The two cowboys stared at her.

One of them said, "Who's the guy you're with?"

"I don't believe this," Angela said.

"Where you staying?" the same one said now. 'We'll come visit . . . You like weed? What do you like? How 'bout ludes?" His tone was different: intimate, coaxing. "Get rid of the old man we'll see you later, have some fun."

Angela picked up a napkin and concentrated on wiping her hands.

"You tight with that fella? He don't look like he knows where it's at." A confiding tone. "Some guy you picked up? Girl, you can do way better'n that tourist. Where's he from—up north?"

The other one said, "He come down here in his motor home?"

Angela saw Bryan coming back now, taking his time. She watched him walk over to the waitress at the service section of the bar and stand there while she totaled their check. She watched him take money out and pay her, the waitress laughing at something he said as he waited for his change.

"Tell him you're going with us. What do you say?"

Bryan was coming from the bar. Angela couldn't believe it: he was carrying a pitcher of beer.

"You don't want to tell him don't say nothing, we just walk out. The fuck can he do about it?"

She watched him come past their table to the booth. One of them said, "Well, here's Bry-an back, Hey, Bry-an, you thirsty? He must be thirsty."

Bryan said to her, "I'll see you outside." When she hesitated he said, "It's okay, I'll be right out."

He turned and placed the pitcher of beer on the table between the two cowboys. She was out of the booth now. She heard one of them say, "What's this?" And the other one say, "Trying to suck up, so he don't get hurt." She walked away from the booth. She saw the waitress watching. The waitress and a couple at the bar with serious expressions. The juke box was playing a Willie Nelson piece, "On the Road Again." She looked back and saw Bryan standing above the two cowboys. He was watching and nodded to her. She continued on to the double-door entrance but that was as far as she was going. She saw Bryan turn to the two cowboys.

They were looking up at him with keen expressions at this point, curious, the fresh pitcher of beer between them.

Bryan said, "Can I sit down?" He took hold of the chair where crossed boots rested and pulled the chair out from under the boots, carefully, the cowboy having no choice but to lower his feet to the floor. Bryan said, "Thank you," and sat down.

In a pleasant, normal tone he said, "Fellas, I'm down here on my vacation . . ."

He looked at their showdown stares waiting, those big, sweaty hard-rider hats pointing straight at him and he started over.

He said, "Fellas, let me put it another way," still with the nice tone. "I don't want to see either of you cocksuckers in my sight ever again. I'm telling you the truth. If I do, I'm gonna kick the shit out of you, sign a complaint you tried to assault me or sell me a controlled substance. Then I'm gonna see you get sent back to wherever you got those ugly fucking tattoos." He paused before getting up. "Are we of one mind on this?"

Angela watched him leave the table and cross toward her. She saw the two cowboys looking at each other, starting to move. Bryan didn't look back. He reached her, put a hand on her arm. Willie was still singing. She would remember that and remember going out the door into soft evening light and seeing the gumball on top of the squad car turning without sound, Gary Hammond coming out of the car.

Bryan said to him, "You got a stick?"

Gary said, "I got a flashlight."

Bryan said, "Let me have it."

Gary reached into the squad car. He tossed the flashlight underhand, arching it flat, the chrome catching light. Bryan swiped it out of the air the way you catch a baton and turned to stand squarely before the entrance to Chuck's Bar-B-Que Pit.

Angela was next to the car in the first parking place, looking at the back of Bryan's Hawaiian shirt. She saw one of the double doors bang open and saw Bryan step in and sidearm the flashlight at the first one out, slamming it into him to send his big hat flying and the cowboy stumbling back, grabbing hold of his head. She saw Bryan swipe the other one across the face and saw the flashlight come apart, batteries spilling out. She saw the two cowboys as though they were dancing, the one trying to hold up the one with blood on his face. Gary Hammond came past her, looking at Bryan cop-to-cop, asking no questions, a hand behind him working the cuffs from the back of his belt.

Bryan said, "It's okay. It was a misunderstanding." He said to the cowboys, "That's right, isn't it? You thought we were somebody else?"

They sat in the rented Buick and watched the yellow van pull out onto Federal Highway followed by the squad car. Angela let her breath out in a sigh. Bryan lighted a cigarette and handed it to her.

She said, "You called Gary?"

"I had him radioed—talking fast." He said, "Did you learn anything?"

"I'm shaking."

"But did you learn anything?"

She said, "For a quiet evening, go out with cops."

He said, "I didn't bring them. When you ask questions about people in that business they want to know who you are, look you over."

That brought her eyes open wide. "Those two work for Chichi?"

"Or somebody close to him," Bryan said. He started the car. "If it was me I'd fire them, get somebody can do the job."

In the night she said, "Does everybody have another person inside them?"

They had both been awake for some time, though not speaking. He said, "What if you saw me shoot someone?" And turned to see her staring at a shape on the ceiling, a reflection of the window.

"I've pictured that. I can understand that. Having to shoot somebody," Angela said. She was silent then.

He said, "But hitting the Miami cowboys seemed what? Vicious, unnecessary."

She remained silent.

He said, "Maybe it wasn't necessary. But I thought it was. I had to give them a reason to stay away from you while I'm gone." He felt her turn to him. "I want them to think about it and take their time and by then I'll be back. Unless you want to go with me."

Her head turned on the pillow, looking at him. "You have to go home?"

"Annie called today. They've got a witness in the Curtis Moore shooting, but the guy's holding back, won't tell everything he knows."

"When're you going?"

"Tomorrow sometime. I want to talk to Walter first, if I can. Walter could be the key to the whole thing." There was a silence again. He felt alone: the same feeling he'd had when she told him she was going to Tucson, the feeling of losing her. He wished she would say something without having to ask her a question first.

He said, "With the two cowboys—maybe I was showing off a little, too."

After a few moments she said, "Maybe I can help you with Walter." Giving him something, but not as much as he wanted.

14

When Bryan called Walter's wife in West Palm, Irene Kouza said, "Walter? Walter who? I don't know anybody by that name."

Bryan said, "Mrs. Kouza, we met at Lieutenant Daugherty's retirement dinner at Carl's about three years ago."

She asked him if he was down here on vacation. He said yes. Was he having a good time? Yes, a very nice time. She said, then what did he want to talk to Walter for and spoil it? She was way ahead of him and it took Bryan the first couple of minutes to realize it.

Bryan said, while he was down here he was hoping he could stop in and see Walter, say hello. Irene Kouza said both their daughters were down with their husbands on vacation and Mr. Big Shot hadn't even bothered to call yet, her dry tone becoming abrasively cute. Anybody who wanted to talk to Mr. Big Shot had to call over there to the beach and leave their name. She began telling Bryan the cost of lawn service for the tiny yard they had, seventy-five dollars to trim a hedge because Mr. Big Shot didn't have time no more, he was too busy—and Bryan got off the line as quickly as he could without sounding rude, feeling like he'd made an escape.

The idea had been to catch Walter at home or arrange to meet him there: try to pry open the old Walter in a familiar setting. But Walter was staying clear of West Palm. Bryan had seen it before. A man able to kill other men, but scared to death of his wife.

Angela said, "Let me try something."

She called Walter at the Daniels place and invited him to lunch. She needed a little help with the piece she was doing on Robbie Daniels, an insider's view of how rich people lived. Walter said, certainly.

She said to Bryan, "Charley's Crab at noon. See? You need me."

That was all it took. He felt inspired again.

* * *

A light blue suit coat straining, stretched across heavy shoulders—there he was, hunched over the bar with his shot and a beer and a pack of Camels.

Bryan said, "Like getting ready for the second shift, Dodge Main."

Walter turned to him, pompadour rising. "The fuck *you* want?"

"Angela's gonna be a little late. I told her I'd buy you a drink." It was ten to twelve. Bryan watched the bartender, good-looking young guy, serving customers on the other side of the bar pen, giving them draft beers to go with buckets of clams. The hostess was seating others in the near room among planters and plain-wood decor where young girls in black vests took over with smiles. Everything nice on a sunny day in season.

"Walter, what's he want to shoot somebody for?"

"You talking about?"

"He gave me the same routine he gave you. He shows me the guns, he says Walter took one look—he goes, 'What're you gonna do, invade Cuba?' "

"Guy's a collector, he likes guns," Walter finished the bottom of his shot and picked up the glass of beer. He said to the bartender, "Hey, buddy, Do it again."

Bryan ordered a draft. He waited for it to be placed in front of him, gave Walter time to pick up the new shot and sip off half of it.

"He's got some beauties. His gun collection."

Walter salted his beer and pushed the shaker toward Bryan.

"He showed me the Python he used on the guy that broke in." Walter didn't comment. "What I can't figure out," Bryan said, "is how you can have all that money, can do anything you want and still be bored. Christ, we'd think of something to do with it. You imagine?"

"Who says he's bored?"

"He did. He told me. What's he, a little fucked up?"

"He's a very educated man," Walter said. "Guy reads all the time."

"Yeah, but what does he read? All his books're about the same thing. People getting taken out. He says to me, 'Who would you pick? Some universal asshole who deserves to die.' "

Walter said, "What's hard about that? Christ, the way the world is today? Take your fucking pick. There's Castro. You got any number of dictators, shit. You got your PLO assholes, fucking Arabs. Your Cubans, your Haitians coming in, taking over. Go out to Belle Glade and warm up. 'Cause pretty soon everybody's gonna be packing. You won't have no choice, you want to stay alive you better fucking know how to shoot."

There were more sounds in the restaurant now, Palm Beachers coming in for lunch, though most of the places on this side of the bar remained empty.

"I talked to Irene this morning."

"Jesus Christ." Walter came around on his stool. "The hell you trying to do?"

"I was looking for you, I thought you might be home. Then Angela said she was gonna see you . . ."

Walter stared at him before turning back to his beer. He shook more salt into the glass and watched the dissolving crystals rise like foam.

"She says you don't cut the grass anymore."

"Three bills a week I give her, she can have it done."

"She says you've changed."

"Cut the shit, okay?"

Bryan sipped his beer. "She says if I see you, remind you your daughters're down for a visit."

Walter said, "Look, I don't ask you if you're fucking that girl writer. Mind your own fucking business, okay?"

"Okay," Bryan said, "I was just telling you what Irene said." He took another sip of beer, nursing it along. "So, I gather you like your job. Seeing how the other half lives . . . I wondered how much dough he's got in that gun collection."

"Don't worry about it," Walter said. "Guy can pay fifteen bills for a Mickey Mouse piece, he's not worrying about it, so don't you."

Fifteen hundred.

"What, a shotgun?"

Walter looked at him again. "I thought he showed you his collection."

"We didn't get into prices." Bryan waited. "I didn't see the High Standard. The one he had in his office."

Walter remained hunched over the bar on his arms. He pulled out a cigarette without picking up the pack and lighted it.

"I wonder where he keeps it," Bryan said.

Walter exhaled smoke, staring across the bar. He said, "You know who that is over there? The gray-haired gentleman, combed back?"

"Who is it?"

"That's Tony Marvin," Walter said. "He's down the beach at the Hilton. Has a show there."

"Tony Martin, the singer?"

"Tony Marvin. *Marv*in. Used to be with Arthur Godfrey. He was the good-looking dark-haired guy."

"Oh," Bryan said, "the announcer. With the voice."

"Yeah, Tony Marvin," Walter said. "I see him quite a bit, different places."

Bryan said, "Walter, get me that High Standard. For one day."

Walter said, "You're outta your fucking mind."

"One day," Bryan said.

"I should've known," Walter said. "All the chitchat, bunch of bullshit."

"Walter, you were a cop for twenty-one years."

He came off the stool brushing past Bryan, pushed his way between an elderly couple coming in the door and was gone.

The bartender said, "Your friend left his cigarettes."

Bryan paid for the rounds. Waiting for his change he put the half-pack of Camels in his pocket.

The routine was established. Robbie would sit back with his drink and his peanuts. Sometimes he'd say, "It's showtime." Sometimes he'd say, "Roll it." And Walter would drop the cassette into the recorder and turn on the TV console.

"Okay, boat coming along the Intracoastal. Okay, the patio. I'm waiting for somebody to come out." Slow minutes of stationary shots followed by abrupt jumps to something else, sky, trees, lots of trees, then back to the waiting shot of nothing. Like an Andy Warhol film.

Robbie said, "It reminds me—you've seen those security guards looking at their monitors, a whole row of TV screens. Looking at the lobby. Looking at any empty hallway. Looking at the parking lot . . . And nothing ever happens." He was bored.

"Here she comes now," Walter said.

"Little T and A for our viewing pleasure . . . You're good whenever Dorie shows up, Walter. Old steady-hands . . . What's this?"

"I hear a car," Walter said, "so I go back the road to check. It was the guy. You'll see him in a minute."

"Jesus, I almost forgot," Robbie said. "Guess what washed in out of the ocean? I found it this morning on the beach. A whole bale of grass. Goddamn thing must weight two hundred pounds."

"Waterlogged," Walter said. "Yeah, there's a lot of that. When I was with the cops here we'd find it up and down the beach. The stuff they throw over the side when the Coast Guard's bearing down on 'em. So, you want to use it?"

"Why not? Then we won't have to wait for somebody to make a delivery. I'd rather catch him with coke, but pot's okay."

"What'd you do with it?"

"I had the gardener put it in the garage."

"The *gard*ener?"

"I told him I'd talk to the police about it . . . Well, look at old Cheech."

"Looks like the fucking Shah of Iran," Walter said, "with the robe."

"Gold lamé," Robbie said. "They going swimming?"

"Skinny-dipping," Walter said. "You leave that stuff in the garage, somebody's gonna say something. The help could cop on you, that fucking cook you got."

"After we're finished here, put it in the Mercedes," Robbie said. "If you can lift it."

"What, two hundred pounds? I can lift more'n that."

"Even if it's half water," Robbie said, "dry it out you'd have, say, a hundred pounds of good Colombian worth on the street about . . . four sixes're twenty-four, four ones're four, carry the two, sixty-four, that's six hundred and forty times a hundred . . . say it's worth sixty grand at least. That should be plenty. You find that in a guy's house, he's a dealer . . . Where are they?"

"See their heads? They're out'n the ocean."

"Frolicking," Robbie said. "I never thought of Cheech as a frolicker."

"I'd frolick her," Walter said.

"Like a shot at that, huh?"

"They're coming out now. Fucking Adam and Eve."

"You zoom in?"

"Zoom in for what? They're coming out. Little grab-ass on the way. The guy knows how to live, I'll say that for him. Plays golf, goes swimming. Never has to work . . ."

Robbie leaned forward in his chair, toward the television set. "He's not hung at all." Sounding surprised. "I thought he was supposed to be hung."

"The guy just come out of the fucking ocean," Walter said. "What do you expect?"

Robbie was squinting at the set. "He's got one of those brown ones. But there's nothing unusual about it. Would you call that a big shlong?"

"I never measured any," Walter said. "That what you guys do, compare 'em? Maybe when I was about eight years old we did that, but not since then . . . Okay, grab their robes, go in the house."

"What's this?"

"I'm moving up on the house around the side. See if I can get a shot through a window."

"Nothing's happening."

"I left the camera, went up to check it out, but it was too dark. I'd have to use some lights."

"You need a gaffer," Robbie said.

"The fuck's a gaffer?"

Robbie was staring at the house on the screen. "Did you see anything?"

"You mean when I looked in? Yeah, Jesus, they were going at it. On the floor. They got this thick white carpeting."

"What were they doing?"

"They were doing it," Walter said.

"I mean *how* were they doing it?"

"Like you do it," Walter said. "You mean *how* were they doing it? Don't you know how to do it?"

"I mean were they just . . . doing it?"

"I'll tell you something," Walter said. "All the things you hear these days—I been wondering whatever happened to just plain fucking. Well, that's what they were doing."

"Amazing," Robbie said.

As far as Bryan was concerned it rained and turned dark at the wrong time. If it had rained and turned dark right after they came up from the beach and were alone in the room, then they could have used the mood of the rain and the dark and they would have gone to bed. By the time they got out of bed they'd be back together and doubts would have vanished. But when they came up from the beach it was still bright hot and he could hear kids playing in the swimming pool and a couple of the maids arguing in Spanish outside Number 15. When Angela was silent, Bryan was silent. He said, what's the matter? And she said, nothing. They could do that forever.

In the car going to the airport he began with, "You're different." She said, "No, I'm not." And he felt dumb, awkward. He said, "Why're you so quiet?"

She said, "I'm trying to figure out what to do with Robbie. I can't make it just another dopey interview. Not if he's got all those guns and he seriously intends to use them . . ."

A Mickey Mouse piece—it went through Bryan's mind, words without anything to picture—*a weapon worth fifteen hundred dollars.*

"Can I? I don't want to throw away what I have," Angela said, "so maybe I begin like it's another dopey interview, then throw Chichi at him and see what happens. But I know I have to talk to Chichi if I want any kind of emotional angle, a point of view, because Robbie's such a cold fish. He thinks he's Mr. Personality, but he's basically a very dull person. Do you see my problem?"

"Is that what you've been thinking about?"

"It's what I do, Bryan."

It got dark and began to rain as they drove through West Palm. She said, "I'm not moody. When I'm in my head I'm working.

I don't stew. If something bothers me I tell you.'' Her tone softened. ''And then you straighten me out. Right?''

He said, ''I never worried before this. I'm thinking too much because I don't want anything to happen to us.''

She said, ''Bryan, I think you're the niftiest guy I've ever known. I love you and all I see are good things happening.''

She said it so easily.

He said, ''I love you, too.''

It hung there inside the car with the sound of the windshield wipers going and the windows steaming over. He felt her hand touch his face, the tips of her fingers gently stroking. He heard her say, ''Bryan, don't worry about us, we can't lose.''

When they were inside the garage Daniels said, there it is. The bale of marijuana was wrapped in a big gunnysack and stood chest-high on Walter. Daniels told him to put it in the ''boot'' of the Mercedes.

The boot. T and A. Gaffer. Another one he used, ''dailies,'' referring to the videotapes. The guy loved to use words nobody knew what they meant. The guy had a lot of show-off in him and maybe he should have been an actor, as someone had suggested one time. The guy didn't even help him.

Walter struggled with the load himself and got the front of his shirt and pants messed up. He patted his pocket for a cigarette and remembered leaving them on the bar at Charley's Crab.

''I saw Hurd today,'' Walter said. ''He told me you showed him your guns.''

''Some of them,'' Robbie said. He brought the trunk lid down firmly, pushed on it again to be sure it locked and remained bent over, looking down. ''What's that?''

''Where?'' Walter said.

''It's a bumper sticker.''

Walter looked at it now. The bumper sticker said, *Real Americans Buy American Cars.*

''That's been on there. Probably somebody in Detroit put it on.''

''Christ,'' Robbie said. ''Well, get it off.''

''When I'm on surveillance or when I'm showing you movies?'' Walter said. ''Or when you're showing your guns to a police lieutenant investigating a homicide you happened to have committed?''

''I thought they'd gone,'' Robbie said. ''I called the Holiday Inn the other day, they'd checked out.''

''Well, he was still here today. He said you give him the same routine you used on me. Like he knew all about it.''

''Sounds like he was fishing,'' Robbie said. ''No, I was very careful, gave him only hypothetical situations. I was playing with him, Walter, that's all.''

''I think he makes you nervous,'' Walter said. ''I think you don't know whether to try and buy him off or take a crack at him, which'd make you feel better.''

''That's your expert analysis?''

''I know him,'' Walter said. ''He comes on like he's so straight he wouldn't even fucking jaywalk. But the son of a bitch—you give him any indication of probable cause, he'll throw the book away and come at you. I've seen it.''

''I know him better than you think,'' Robbie said, ''I played golf with him. And you're right, he cheats. But then, who doesn't? Would you feel better if we waited till he went home?''

''I get excited about it, I get all ready,'' Walter said, ''then we sit around. We gonna do it or not?''

''Well,'' Robbie said, ''I've got a late golf match tomorrow. How about the day after?''

15

There were pickets in front of the General Motors Building with signs that read GM HAS NO HEART . . . GM'S TAKING OUR HOMES . . . WAR! GM INVADES POLETOWN! . . . The little guy taking on the big corporation over a land dispute: a neighborhood the city had bought, condemned and already partly razed to make room for a new Cadillac assembly plant.

Bryan said, "Dodge Main's gone, what do they want, a house or a job?"

Annie Maguire said, "If you lived there you might feel differently about it."

Bryan said, "I might and I might not."

They got out of the blue Plymouth parked in the no standing zone and walked past the pickets, Bryan carrying a thick manila envelope, saying, "Maybe they don't have anything else to do," and into the GM Building, Annie saying, "I'm never sure what side you're gonna be on." Bryan saying, "Why do I have to be on either side?" Annie saying, "Ralph Nader thinks they're getting dumped on." And Bryan saying, "Who asked him?"

"You're in a terrible mood today."

"I'm not even supposed to be here."

"The guy we're seeing's name is Bill Fay. He's a nice guy. Try not to bite his head off."

Bryan said nothing, making no promises.

He followed Annie out of the elevator on the second floor to the end of the corridor and into a wing of glass-partitioned offices intersected with hallways. Bryan saw executives, some in shirt sleeves, each sitting between a worktable and a desk; he saw wallcharts and graphs, photos of wives and kids, draperies in some offices, venetian blinds in most. They entered an office where a pair of middle-aged secretaries presided, bore left, and Annie told the lady studying them, "Hi, Mr. Fay's expecting us." Bryan could see him through the glass in a gray pin-striped suit with a maroon handkerchief in the pocket, talking on the phone, gently swiveling from side to side in his executive chair. He looked up and waved them in with an alert eager expression and was off the phone, on his feet, by the time they entered.

"Miss Maguire, gee, it's good to see you again. How're you doing?" Then to Bryan, "Hi, Bill Fay . . . It's a pleasure. Lieutenant, this is some gal you got here. She knows her stuff, I'll tell you. Sit down . . ."

There were Chevrolet magazine ads, mounted and matted, covering most of one wall. A display line in bold, cursive lettering, off by itself, read:

SEE THE EIGHTY-ONE-DERFUL CHEVROLET TODAY!

The line held Bryan's attention. He thought of 1982, new models coming out in the fall . . .

He heard Bill Fay saying, "I'm afraid I'm gonna have to make this one short," and turned to see him shoot his cuff to look at his watch. "I've got an ad meeting in exactly . . . four-and-a-half minutes. *But,* I know your work is as important to you as mine is to me. I know you have to keep going back over the same territory, make sure you don't miss anything . . . But, hey, I had an idea. I wondered, what if you displayed your phone number in the paper? You know, anyone who was around there and just might have seen something strange going on, please contact us at this number. What do you say? I could have the agency speedball you a nice layout. Maybe put a gun in it? Hey, I love it."

"Newspaper stories usually include our number," Annie said. "What we were wondering"—she rose, taking the manila envelope from Bryan—"if you'd mind looking at these photographs again. Just on the chance one of them, you know, might ring a bell."

As Annie pulled the photos from the envelope Fay was studying Bryan, the beginning of a smile in place. He said, "Boy, all the legwork you have to do, huh? Sure, I'd be glad to look at them again," helping Annie now spread the black and white shots of Robbie Daniels over the glass-top surface of his desk. "This is your suspect, huh? He looks familiar."

Annie said, "He's not a suspect exactly, but we're curious

about him. We know he *was* in the vicinity of the Plaza that morning.''

''Oh?'' Bill Fay seemed a little surprised. ''Is this a new development? As I recall, you weren't that sure before.''

''He was there,'' Bryan said.

Fay waited for him to say more. Finally his gaze dropped to the photos and Bryan watched his demonstration of interest, row by row, studying all the Robbies, the on-camera shots, smiling, winking, the laid-back, heavy-lidded Hi-I'm-Robbie-Daniels shots and the true candid shots that caught him unprepared, or caught angles that emphasized his posture, his hip-cocked stance, the hand beneath the cashmere sweater.

Bryan said, ''Mr. Fay, you checked into the Plaza about nine forty-five Saturday morning?''

''Yeah, about that.''

''You told Sergeant Maguire you noticed a black Mercedes sedan.''

''It's funny, driving down,'' Bill Fay said, ''my wife and I were talking about foreign cars, particularly the Japanese imports taking close to twenty percent of the market. She was saying they shouldn't be allowed in the country, especially with the economic situation the way it is, and I said, wait a minute, just a darn minute, we got a free-enterprise system here. You don't make it, you pack your bags. It's rough out there, I kid you not. Though I believe there's room for some kind of quota system, yeah, for the time being—''

Bryan said, ''You did see a black Mercedes?''

''I'm coming to that. I said, you don't see, really, that many foreign cars in Detroit anyway. I mean it's not anything like L.A. . . . we're pulling into the Plaza, you know, underneath by the entrance, and she goes, 'Oh, then what's that?' '' Bill Fay grinned. ''Here's a four-fifty SEL Mercedes right in front of us. But wait, here's the kicker. On this big piece of German iron there's a bumper sticker that says, *Real Americans Buy American Cars.*'' Fay sat back for reactions, grinning.

Bryan said, ''Did you notice the license number, or any part of it?''

''No, I didn't. And I didn't *see* anyone because the car was empty. I remember the door was open. We had to wait before we could pull up. Then we had to stand around there a while waiting for a parking ticket."

Bryan leaned over the desk, pulled out a shot of Robbie wearing a suit and dropped it in front of Fay.

"Nope." He shook his head.

Bryan looked over the selection, found one that showed Robbie in a raincoat, an angle on him going into what was probably his home in Grosse Pointe.

"No," the GM executive said, but kept looking at it.

"Maybe," Bryan said, "if we showed the pictures to your wife . . ."

And Bill Fay said, "No, no, no—she didn't see anything. I know, I discussed it with her. As a matter of fact she went inside right away. She wasn't even there."

Bryan said, "What do you mean, *there?*"

"When I was waiting for my ticket."

"There's still a chance," Bryan said, "she might've seen him before she went in."

"There was nobody there before. I know—she didn't see a thing. We've gone over it and over it."

Bryan said, "Mr. Fay, was your wife with you that morning or was it someone else?"

The executive said, "Now wait just a darn minute. I hope I didn't hear an insinuation of some kind."

"You didn't," Bryan said. "I asked you in plain English if you were with your wife or someone else. You checked in at nine forty-five and checked out at four P.M. It's none of my business what you were doing there or who you were doing it with, but if you saw this man at the hotel, I want you tell me about it."

Bill Fay looked at his watch again. "Listen, we're gonna have to continue this some other time."

Bryan said, "Can I use your phone?"

Fay was putting some papers together, starting to get up. "Sure. Help yourself."

"What's your home phone number?"

Fay held onto the papers and eased down into his chair again. He straightened the papers now against the glass top of the desk and placed them squarely in front of him, preparing himself, getting ready. He said, ''Lieutenant, I can tell you in all honesty she did not see a thing. I'll swear to it.''

Bryan said, ''Tell me in all honesty if your wife was with you.''

''Does it matter?'' Fay said. ''I mean if she didn't see him it doesn't matter *who* didn't see him, does it?''

''But you saw him,'' Bryan said. He waited. ''The whole thing is, you don't want to be a witness and have to appear in court . . . Where did you tell your wife you were?'' He waited again.

''If I told you anything at all''—saying this carefully—''I *would* have to appear, wouldn't I?''

''I don't know,'' Bryan said. ''Your testimony would place him at the scene, but that's all. We'd need a lot more to get a conviction. The murder weapon, for example, and a positive ballistics test. If the suspect's lawyer sees we've got a case then he might enter a plea and there'd be no trial. You're off the hook. I can't promise you anything; but if you tell me he was there, then we can narrow it down, concentrate the investigation, get something that'll stick.''

Fay raised a hand to his forehead, spreading his fingers to massage his temples. He wore a diamond on his little finger, his nails were manicured and glistened with colorless polish.

''You saw him there,'' Bryan said. ''The reason you remember him, you know who he is. You saw him walk down the ramp or you saw him enter that area . . . he went down to the garage and shot a parking attendant five times, probably killing him instantly. We don't think, no matter who he is, he should be able to take another's man's life and get away with it. Do you?'' Bryan waited.

''He was wearing a raincoat,'' Bill Fay said. ''He walked into the entrance to the ramp. A gray Lincoln Continental turned in and stopped. I could see the rear end sticking out. Then the car continued on, but he didn't come out. So I assume he got in the car and went down.''

''Thank you,'' Bryan said.

''But I won't appear in court,'' Fay said. ''In fact, if you ever again ask me if I was even there, I'll deny it.'' He paused. ''I told my wife I was going to Cleveland.''

Bryan looked at Annie. She got up and began gathering the photos and he looked at Fay again.

"Do you know who that is?"

"If it isn't Robinson Daniels, it's somebody who looks just like him."

"Do you know Daniels?"

"No. I see him at the DAC every once in a while. And I've seen his picture. But why would he want to shoot a colored parking attendant?"

"Why would he want to shoot anyone?" Bryan said.

He got up and waited for Annie before moving to the door. Then looked back at the display of magazine ads and the theme line, *See the Eighty-one-derful Chevrolet today!*

He said to Fay, "What you might say next year—how about, See the Eighty-two-rific Chevrolet today?"

Bill Fay began to nod. He said, "That's not bad," and was making a note as Bryan and Annie left.

Outside, walking past the pickets, Bryan said, "How come they're marching around here instead of looking for a place to live?"

"You're all heart," Annie said. "I'll bet you don't even feel sorry for Mr. Fay."

"He should've gone to Cleveland," Bryan said.

They drove downtown and had to park two blocks from 1300 with the construction of the new county jail wings clogging the side streets with trucks and heavy equipment. Bryan could hardly wait to get upstairs. The first things he did, waving off Malik and Doug Parrish, he placed a call to the Atlantis Villas, Number 16. The phone rang nine times. He was ready to hang up, frustrated, when Angela's voice turned his mood around.

"You just come in from the beach?"

"No, I was washing my hair. How's it going?"

"I'm through. We're gonna have a meeting and that's it, I'm coming back tonight. In fact, if I get the five-thirty Delta flight I'll be there around nine."

"I'll meet you."

"You don't have to do that."

"Are you kidding? I can hardly wait."

"I'm not sure what time it gets in."

"I'll find out. If you miss it and have to take a later flight I'll wait for you. Just come."

"What're you doing?"

"I'm washing my hair."

"I mean outside of that."

"Oh—I called Chichi. Finally got hold of him."

"Yeah? . . ."

"I told him I need some color for a magazine piece I'm doing on Robbie and he said, 'You want some good stories?' He said, 'I've got some you'd never be able to print.' "

"Angela? Why don't you wait till I get back?"

"It's all arranged, I'm meeting him at six."

"Where?"

"The place in Hillsboro. I told him I knew where it was. He said, 'So you're the one.' I told him, don't worry, I'm a user not a snitch."

"Angela—"

"If I don't get him now I may never. But I'll be at the airport, don't worry about that."

"That's not it—"

"Bryan, what about the little girl?"

"What little girl?"

"The one—you found her body inside the car, with her panties pushed down?"

"Rolled down. Nothing. We don't know any more than we did," Bryan said. "Angela," he said then, "why don't you wait?"

"Bryan, who took care of me before I met you? I gotta go. I love you and I'll see you tonight."

She was gone.

16

The Palm Beach realtor that Robbie was to play golf with phoned at two-thirty to say he was terribly sorry but there was no way he could make it this afternoon; he was showing a Saudi's place to a West German, Christ, middleman in an Arab-Kraut deal and hoped to God he came out of it in one piece.

Robbie said, "You'll come out of it with about a hundred grand, Tony. But don't ever ask me to play golf with you again. Is that understood?"

The realtor said, "Hey, Robbie—"

And Robbie said, "Get fucked, Tony," and hung up.

He found Walter in his room and brought him up to the study along with two cold bottles of Heineken.

"Change of plans. We move today."

"How come?"

Jesus, everybody was giving him a hard time.

"Because I want to do it today," Robbie said. "I'm ready. I want to walk in there and do it. Is that hard to understand?"

Walter had to see it clearly in his mind. He took a big swallow of beer and wiped his mouth with his hand.

"How we know the guy's gonna be there?"

"He comes every day between five and seven, doesn't he?"

"Almost every day."

"Okay, if he's not there, we don't do it. We do it tomorrow. There's not that much to plan, Walter. I'm gonna use the MAC-ten with the suppressor. We walk in—"

"What do I use?"

"We walk in," Robbie said, "I open up with the MAC and you open up with the Hitachi."

"The *camera?* You're kidding me."

"I told you that, didn't I? I want to see it, I want to study it—same way a football team studies game films. I want to get it down right, Walter, so when we go for the big ones"—he snapped his fingers three times—"it works like that, like the pros do it. You have a team operation you better have split-second timing or else you're gonna blow it. And when you blow the big one, Walter . . . that's it. No more."

Walter said, "I'm gonna be standing there with the fucking camera on my shoulder—"

"This time you are. I want to *see* it, Walter."

"You're the star—that what you're saying?"

"I'm not gonna be in it—"

"Big movie, Assassination of an Asshole, starring Mr. Robinson Daniels. You want George Hamilton to be in it, too?"

"Walter, you don't shoot *me*. I'm not in it. I want the camera to follow only the guy. I want to see how he reacts, I want to see everything he does."

Walter was silent a moment. "What about the broad?"

"Who, Dorie? . . . We get her out of the way. Lock her in a closet."

"Jesus Christ," Walter said, "I thought you knew what you're doing. Lock her in a closet—the cops let her out, they take hold of her finger, this one. They say okay, you know who did it? Point 'em out."

"We cover up," Robbie said. Goddamn dumb Polack. "Wear masks or something. Ski masks—no, we'll tie bandanas around, you know, just our eyes showing and wear sunglasses."

"Jesus Christ," Walter said, "Butch and fucking Sundance. Broad looks at you, hears your voice, or she happens to look out the window, sees a Mercedes and a fucking silver Rolls Royce . . . I think, Mr. Daniels, I'm gonna pass on this one. What I ought to do, get my ass outta here right now."

"Finish your beer," Robbie said quietly. He walked away from the bar, stood with his hands in the pockets of his chinos, then drifted back, taking his time.

"Walter? . . ."

"You're not ready," Walter said. "You haven't thought it out. We went out on a STRESS operation—before we hit that street we knew every fucking move we're gonna make and what we do if different various situations come up."

Robbie said, "Okay, we don't want a witness, there won't be a witness. If Dorie happens to be there, well, that's too bad."

Walter said, "Oh no, uh-unh. The broad's got nothing to do with it."

"She works for him—what's the difference? She's part of an illegal operation."

"She puts out for him," Walter said. "That's all she does I know of or seen her do. I don't want no parts of shooting broads. I told you that a long time ago, I never shot a broad in my life and I hope to God I never get in a position I have to. You're telling me about all these assholes—were there any broads on your list? No. Broads might *be* there, yeah, but that's all. They're like on the side, what broads do, they hang out. No sir . . ."

Robbie said, "Okay, we call her up. Give her a message to meet Cheech at the polo club. Five o'clock. Which means we got to move."

"Wait a minute," Walter said. "Wait a minute. You got the phone number?"

"Not yet."

"You think it's in the book? Narcotics drop, they got it under N?"

"You can get the number, can't you? Call the Broward County Sheriff's Office. Like you did before."

"What if Drug Enforcement's got a tap on the line?"

"You're somebody from the polo club," Robbie said. "Chichi asked you to call her for him. You're not gonna leave your name, Walter."

"They might not have the number."

"They can get it, can't they? Or you call the telephone company. Tell them you're with the Palm Beach office of the DEA. You know people there, you know the routine. Walter, this is your end of it. You know how to do all that kind of stuff. But we've got to *move*."

"Yeah, but what if they want to talk to my superior, something like that?"

"You're the superior, Walter," Robbie paused. "You're the star. For two grand a week, including your combat pay, it doesn't seem like much to ask. A couple of phone calls? Come on . . ."

Walter walked over to the narrow casement window that looked down on the swimming pool and the patio with its umbrella tables. He stared at the immaculate blue, green and yellow orderliness of the scene, the arrangement of color reaching to the ocean. If the guy wanted to he could have the grass painted red and dye the water in the swimming pool purple or cover the whole setup with a golden dome. The guy could do anything he wanted. Easy. It came down to a simple question. Would you rather be inside pissing out, or outside getting it all over you?

Walter came away from the window. "Okay, I'll try the phone company, give 'em some bullshit. But when I call her, I don't think it should be a message from the guy. It's gotta be somebody else, 'cause what if he happens to call her? It's gotta be somebody offering her a deal, like something she can't pass up."

Robbie was sitting at the bar now. It seemed to come to him almost immediately, the way his expression brightened.

"Dorie thinks she's an actress. She does get a few small parts at dinner theaters, the maid, maybe a couple of lines. But how about—tell her they need somebody right away up at Burt Reynolds's place."

"Where, Jupiter?"

"Yeah, it's perfect. By the time she gets there and gets back, it's done."

Walter drank his beer. It sounded pretty good. He looked at Robbie sitting like *The Thinker* now, fist supporting his chin, weighing something heavy.

"What's the matter?"

"Nothing," Robbie said. "I'm trying to decide what to wear."

Angela wore the new white-linen sunback, feeling and looking good; but more for Bryan, later, than any effect it might have on Chichi. Cheech would probably try something just to test her availability—out of habit, part of his nature—come on with some kind of slippery Latin routine and she'd tell him to knock it off and he would. That's what she told herself. The alive feeling of expectation was something else. She didn't want him to make the moves, but at the same time she wanted to see him at least try. After all, how many internationally famous great lovers did you come across when you knew you were looking good and certain you could handle the situation? She hoped.

Then an anxious feeling of impending disappointment: following the gravel, coasting the Buick through the clumps of sea grape to find the circular drive empty; the cement apron in front of the three-car garage empty. The house with a closed, empty look. The son of a bitch.

Dorie, barefoot in bra and panties, a hairbrush in her hand, opened the door and said, "Hi," and disappeared.

Angela entered cautiously, through a hallway past kitchen and den to the spacious front room. A little white dog sniffed her but ran off as she reached to pet him.

"Sit down if you want."

Angela turned to see the red-haired girl halfway up the staircase. The little dog was with her, looking out through the balusters.

"I love your dress. I wear white, I look like some Appalachian kid in a CARE package dress. You know what I mean? I look dumb in plain white things, like they're wearing me. I have to wear something busier so it all like blends together. You know what I mean?"

Angela said, "Is Chichi here?" She held up her slim reporter's notebook, a credential. "I've got an appointment to interview him."

"Good luck," Dorie said. "Listen, I gotta get ready. Unless you want to come up."

"Do you expect him?"

"Cheech shows up or he doesn't. If he told you he'd be here—"

"At six."

"Well, he still shows up or he doesn't. God, is it six already?" She disappeared, the little dog hopping up the stairs after her.

Angela moved to the French doors, looked out at the patio and pool, the stretch of beach beyond. This had to be the most secluded place on the coast; almost as though the great real estate rush had passed it by. There was enough property here for a good-size condominium.

Dorie's voice said from the top of the stairs, "I don't think I know your name. Do I?"

"Angela."

"I'm Dorie and I've got a problem." Still in her bra and panties, pulling the brush through her hair. "You wouldn't do me a huge favor, would you?"

"Sure. If I can."

"I've got a chance to do a walk-on tonight at the—are you ready?—the Burt Reynolds Dinner Theatre. I don't even know the name of the play, I'm supposed to be there practically right now and my fucking car's at a gas station in Deerfield, getting fixed. Actually it's done. I thought Cheech would be here to drive me, but the son of a bitch, you can't rely on him."

"You need a ride just to Deerfield?"

"God, if you would."

"I'd be glad to," Angela said. "But hurry, okay? I'll leave him a note in case he comes—" and looked up as she heard the door open.

Chichi, in person.

In golf clothes and a linen sports jacket over his shoulders, the sleeves hanging empty. Angela watched his entrance, coming in to see two women waiting for him—one in a white sundress, one in a bra and panties—the inspector of embassies showing mild surprise one moment, a gesture of inevitability the next, no more than his due.

Then coming alive. "Angela!" Coming toward her, both hands extended, limp—the sports jacket somehow clinging to his narrow shoulders—to touch her gently, to kiss both of her cheeks . . .

Dorie said, "Cheech! I'm in a play tonight!"

He turned to look at her with genuine concern. "Ohhhh, Dorie, you're leaving us? . . . And Mr. Piper . . . How are you today, Mr. Piper?"

Dorie left in the rented brown Buick, not trusting herself in Chichi's Rolls. The Buick would be at the Mobil station in Deerfield. Then, later on, Chichi would drop Angela there on his way back to Palm Beach. No problem.

"Alone at last," Angela said, playing the game, smiling to show him she was playing.

"I'm going to bathe," Chichi said, holding his dog, trying to hold Angela's hand, drawing out his exit, "and change into something comfortable."

"After a hard day at the club," Angela said.

Chichi's eyes smiled. "You've had your bath."

"Yes, I have."

His eyes smiled and smiled.

She would make a note that they "flashed and danced" and see if she could work up an analogy to Caribbean moonlight, reflections on tropical waters—if she could do it unpretentiously and if Bryan didn't think it was dumb.

Walter had said, "First, we want the cars turned around so they're facing out, you never know. But that road's too narrow, all the trees and shit, to turn around once you're in there. So you have to back in from Ocean Drive. Wait'll you don't see anybody coming. You go in, I give it a couple minutes, then I go in."

This is where they were, on the access road to the beach, about a hundred yards from Chichi's house.

Over his jeans, a dark cashmere and the Colt Python in a shoulder rig, Robbie wore a light canvas shooting coat with deep pockets. He was hot, but needed a good deep pocket for his extra ammo clip. He wore a blue bandana rolled and tied around his forehead like a sweatband. (Walter had said, "You gonna blacken your face, too?") Walter wore his wing tips, his light blue suit pants and a dark blue poplin jacket that covered the Browning nine-millimeter holstered on his right hip.

He hung the VCR, the tape recorder, over one shoulder and crossed the strap holding the battery pack over the other, each one as heavy as a dictionary, and hefted the video camera to his shoulder—like a goddamn native ready to follow the white boss—the white boss in his commando outfit and tennis shoes half inside the "boot" of the Rolls now putting his submachine gun together. The "fag gun" Walter called it, all cammied up in shades of blue and rose. Robbie was screwing the suppressor onto the barrel stub, the silencer bigger and longer than the gun itself. Then fitting the thirty-two-round clip into the slot on the underside, just behind the trigger. If you couldn't hit one guy with thirty-two rounds you weren't going to hit him and you might as well take off the coat and leave the extra clip in the car. But Daniels was going in like it was a fucking assault on enemy headquarters—the guy probably sitting in there in his underwear, scratching his ass.

Robbie came out of the trunk. "Ready?"

"Okay," Walter said. "Just his car's there when we drove by. But we got to check, be sure nobody else's come in the meantime. We don't want no surprises. We stay in the trees and shit till we get to the house. Only the one car's still there we go in through the back, I'm right behind you. Do it, then we come back, get the grass out of the trunk."

"I don't think there'll be enough light inside," Robbie said, looking up at the sky that was pale gray-blue, without glare.

"Let's wait and see," Walter said. "We stand here we're not gonna have any light anywhere."

"I think I'd like to get him out by the pool."

"You might not have any choice," Walter said. "The guy makes a run, you have to drop him. I mean that's why we're here, right? You see him, you hit him, no fucking around, give him a chance to get away."

"Yeah, but I want to see him fall in the pool," Robbie said. "He's running—give him a burst, he falls in the swimming pool and you see him floating there, face down, the water turning red . . ."

"Jesus Christ," Walter said, "let's get it done."

Chichi called down from upstairs, "I won't be a minute. I hurried, so, I didn't have a chance to shower at the club . . . Why don't you make yourself a drink?"

"I'm fine."

"Well, sit down. Watch the telly if you like."

Angela looked about the sitting room that resembled a Cape Cod summer home more than it did a place in Florida. The sofa and chairs, slipcovered in a beige fabric, reminded her a little of Bryan's apartment. Comfortable, but indifferent to fashion. She was gathering impressions. The side-table bar offered a skimpy selection of several brands of whiskey, one gin and a blue siphon bottle. Now the room looked English. A cottage in Brighton. Apparently there was no ice. But she didn't want a drink anyway.

Angela looked up toward the top of the stairway as she said, "I'll be outside . . ."

Bryan was put on standby for the five-thirty Delta flight to West Palm. He told the ticket lady behind the counter he had to make it. "I'm getting married." The ticket lady glanced up at him and said, "Congratulations." He told her he was also a police officer—"See? My shield"—working on a very important case that was taking him to Florida and that's why they were getting married down there. The ticket lady looked at him again, into his solemn unwavering blue eyes. He would tell her anything.

All that, his stomach in a knot, then hearing his name called and grabbing his canvas bag.

He sat in the back of the plane and smoked cigarettes, drinking down the first bourbon over ice then sipping the second one, trying to make it last.

He would tell her about his former wife about to get married. It had nothing to do with them, yet somehow it did, because it relieved him and gave him no more reason to look back or think of reasons to feel guilty. He could concentrate on Angela. Tonight they'd have dinner in a dark place and go back to the Villas, sit by the seawall alone and look at the ocean and touch her and feel the familiar feel of her hand that was like no other hand and feel her arm, the soft hint of down, and feel her face—later, lying down, feel her face and trace the delicate line down her nose to her mouth and feel her breath. Jesus. He said, I love you. He said it again and then again, trying the emphasis on a different word each time. He said, I'm in love with you. He said, God, I love you. He said, I love you so much that . . .

She would know.

She had said, "You don't have to say a word if I feel it."

And he had said, "Start feeling."

But he would tell her so she would be absolutely sure.

They crossed a strip of lawn from the trees to the back of the house, Robbie running with his head down, shoulders hunched, the flowery submachine gun at port arms—the way it was done. Walter carried the video camera in front of him, using his arms beneath it for support. He didn't hoist the curved, saddlelike support to his shoulder until they were in the entranceway.

Robbie said, over his shoulder, "The door's locked."

Walter said to himself, Get out; right now. He said, "I 'magine it is. Kick it open."

"It's too heavy."

"Okay, you got a credit card?"

"Christ," Robbie said.

"Come on, gimme a credit card, I'll see what I can do."

Robbie gave him his gold American Express card from his wallet and held the camera while Walter tried to work the card into the crack between the door and the molding and slip the lock. It wouldn't budget.

"We'll have to go around the front," Walter said.

Robbie gave him the camera back and they moved along the north side of the house, pausing to look in a window at the empty living room. At the front corner of the house, Robbie raised his left hand to hold up his troops. He crouched, his gaze scanning the patio and pool area, then out to the empty stretch of beach. Rising now, Robbie moved around the corner. Walter lifted the camera to his shoulder again and followed his leader across the brick patio and in through the French doors.

Robbie stood in the middle of the room, the machine gun held close to him, the silencer pointing up past his head. He glanced at Walter and swept his left hand toward the back of the house.

Whatever the fuck that was supposed to mean. Walter said, "He's upstairs. You hear the shower?"

Listening, Robbie shook his head.

"It stopped," Walter said. "Get back in the hall there, wait for him."

They crossed quickly. Robbie poked his machine gun into the kitchen first, then looked in the den to be sure and shook his head at Walter.

Walter said, "I just told you, he's upstairs."

They waited in the hallway.

When Chichi appeared, coming from the right into his frame of vision, Robbie was looking at the man's back, at a gold lame robe, the skirts hanging nearly to the floor, a little dog running to keep up with him. He could hear Chichi's slippers slapping his heels as he crossed the room, approaching the bar now, rubbing his hands together. Chichi selected a bottle, stooped to bring out a leather-covered ice bucket from underneath. It was when he straightened, coming around, that he saw Robbie holding the gaily colored submachine gun and the heavyset man with the camera mounted on his shoulder, the man moving carefully to the side now, his face pressed to the eyepiece.

Chichi said, "Robbie—what are you doing, making a film? Can I be in it?"

"You're in it all right," Robbie said. "You're the star."

"You know, I did appear in a film once when I was married to Valaria," Chichi said. "I seduced her in the first reel and I was shot in the second reel by that weight lifter, very popular with the Italians. Muscular young man—I can't think of his name. Steve something . . . What's this picture about, Robbie?"

Walter kept the gold robe in the center of the viewfinder that was like a tiny television screen in front of his eye. The camera whirred in his right ear. He heard Robbie say something.

"Death."

Then Chichi. "The film is about death?"

The gold robe on the little screen was turning to the bar again. "Should I ask whose?"

"Yours," Robbie's voice said.

"You wouldn't prefer a drink, would you?" Chichi's voice said.

Son of a bitch—the gold robe was moving again. Walter heard the popping sounds like a heavy automatic B-B gun firing and saw the bottle on the side-table bar shatter. He saw the stunned expression on the guy's face for only a split moment—beautiful, got it—but now the guy was moving and he heard the hard popping sounds again and the little dog barking and saw the guy stumble like he was tripping over his robe and several panes in the French door exploded.

Angela heard glass breaking.

She was coming back from an anxious walk that had taken her a little way down the beach—carrying her sandals—restless now, feeling she was running out of time and wanting to postpone the meeting, put Chichi aside for another day—Bryan was right, he was always right—and get out to the airport. Be there waiting. Her mind wasn't on this at all. The ocean was even different, oily, uninviting. She didn't want to be here.

She heard the sound of breaking glass in a lull, coming clearly and by itself as the heavy sound of the surf receded and was still for a moment.

She came away from the ocean, crossing the littered sand, looking down to avoid patches of tar and seaweed, then looking toward the house again . . . at a figure in gold coming out. The Great Lover. God, in a gold bathrobe. He seemed drunk. She was halfway there, between the ocean and the grounds. She saw him coming out toward the swimming pool, staggering, the little dog coming with him. How could he have had that much to drink? He was fine when he came in. She saw two more figures, one of them carrying something on his shoulder. She moved toward them but not hurrying now, not understanding what was going on, but beginning to think now, to realize there were people associated with this man, like the two in the restaurant . . . She saw the other figure raise something in front of him that began to jump up and down as he held it and tried to control it and she saw Chichi in the gold robe running, stumbling, the thing still jumping in the other man's hands and she could hear it now, hard little muted pops, as Chichi staggered and went into the pool. She stood still. She saw the figure looking this way. She saw his arm extend, pointing directly at her. Angela dropped her sandals and began to run.

Walter said, "Who was that?"

Robbie was sweating. "Christ, I don't know." Concentrating, squinting at the section of beach in front of them, empty now, as though if he looked hard enough the figure in white would reappear. "Come on." He started off.

"Was that a broad?" Walter said.

Robbie reached the edge of the sand and looked back. "Whoever it was—we were *seen*. You understand? That's a witness."

"Was it the broad?" Walter said, his eyes open as wide as they would open. "It looked like it might be the broad."

"It was a *witness,*" Robbie said. "Will you get it in your goddamn head? Come on—I want you to shoot it, whoever it is"—slipping as he started off in the sand—"shoot it, goddamn it!"

Walter started after him, then stopped. He'd better change tapes, shove a new cassette into the recorder. He saw Robbie look back and yell at him again as he pulled out the first cassette and slipped it into his jacket.

Walter used to believe in always carrying a knife. You shoot fast in a street situation, okay, and you find out the guy wasn't armed or he was only reaching for his I.D., you put the knife in the guy's hand and you swear to God at the hearing the son of a bitch was coming at you and you had no choice but to shoot. You had to protect your ass. You had to protect it from people claiming to be witnesses, too, who were just as bad as the people you had to shoot. What was the difference? You gonna go up because somebody that works for him, just as fucking bad as he is, saw you do it and copped? He wants you to shoot it, Walter said, getting the goddamn camera on his shoulder and moving now, heading for the trees, then shoot it. Get it done.

He went into the scrub—almost used to it now, with the knack of moving without getting his straps and cases tangled up. He told himself not to think about whoever it was. Anybody goes to work for a guy like that guy in the pool, tough shit, that's how it comes out. It's your ass or the other person's. You going up for some fucking hooker? You bet he wasn't going up. It was no different here than on the street.

He saw her then. He saw something white. Moving along the beach at the edge of the trees. Crouched down now, trying to hide. Robbie would be coming up on her. She heard him, it looked like. She was coming into the scrub now, looking back but coming this way.

Walter snugged the camera to his shoulder, pressed his eye to the viewfinder and turned it on. He heard Robbie yell something. Robbie had spotted her. The white figure was in the sea grape, moving across Walter's tiny rectangular field of vision from left to right, looking back as she angled toward him head turned the other way. He panned the camera on the white figure. He heard the hard little pops of sound, Robbie opening up. He saw leaves flying apart. He saw the figure in white closer, looking back, no idea where she was going, then looking this way and he saw the awful expression of terror on Angela Nolan's face—not the other one, *Angela*.

It was like he was looking through the slit window of a tank and she was out there and wanted to get in, coming toward him to get inside with him where it was safe. He saw her face and heard those hard grunting pops and saw leaves flying, snipped off, and that was the end of it for him. Walter raised the camera in both hands above his head and threw it as far away from him as he could. Threw it and turned to get out of there and felt the cables still attached to the camera pull tight and now he was dragging the camera, unable to detach himself from it until he untangled the equipment straps, lifted them over his head. Robbie was calling something now, but he couldn't see him. Walter dropped the battery pack and the VCR. Then stopped and went back to hunch down over the recorder and yanked the cassette out, wanting it and not wanting it and not having time to think. Reacting then, rather than making a decision, he threw the cassette away from him hard overhand, and began running again—past the swimming pool. Where the little dog sat at the edge and the gold robe floated in the water, stretched open like wings, ran into the scrub on the north side of the house, all the way through the trees to the access road. Walter got in the Mercedes and took off.

He was on Sample Road moving west toward the Interstate before he realized he had a cassette in his jacket. The first one, the one that would show Chichi Fuentes in his robe. Walter pushed a button. The window next to him slid down into the door. He drove perhaps another mile staring straight ahead at the road. He pushed the button again and the window slid closed.

Give it a little more thought. Soon as it was dark enough he'd stop somewhere and dump the bale of wet grass. But the tape of the rich guy doing the playboy—that was something else.

17

She wasn't at the airport to meet him.

He hung around the front of the Delta terminal, walked over to Eastern and looked around there just in case, head raised moving through the crowd, all the last-minute vacationers down for Easter, then walked back to Delta. He had to keep moving. Goddamn it. He wasn't mad at her. He was mad at standing here watching people throwing their arms around each other, pretty soon standing alone with his canvas bag but without a sense of the policeman's patience. He wasn't aware of being a policeman. He wasn't too aware of himself, for that matter. He wanted the sight of her. He was on the edge of feeling what he would feel when he saw her, ready to turn it loose, and she wasn't here.

The taxi took Southern Boulevard over, followed the right-hand curve coming to the beach and passed along the wall of the Daniels estate. It was dark. The place felt dark. Bryan sat in front with the driver but they didn't talk much. Big cars poked along in front of them. There was nothing you could do.

Finally Bryan said, "There it is. On the left."

The driver said, "Villas Atlantis," like he was making an announcement.

They had to wait for a stream of oncoming cars. As the last of them crept past and the taxi turned in Bryan saw the police car. He paid the driver and got out. He didn't see the brown Buick Century anywhere in the parking rows.

The Palm Beach City police car was parked in front of the first unit, the office, where a neon sign said *No Vacancy*.

He went up the walk with his canvas bag, past the swimming pool where the underwater lights were on and kids were splashing around, their parents sitting with drinks, watching. They said good evening leisurely, with all the time in the world, waiting to see if he would stop and talk. He had never seen them before. He nodded once and said good evening. He kept walking, the line of cement villas leading to the ocean. Anywhere along here he could cut through to Number 16, over in the third row of villas. Or he could go all the way up the walk to the seawall . . .

He saw the uniformed officer, hatless, coming across the front walk from the left, out of darkness. He knew the uniform would be brown and beige when they were closer, when they met at the point where the walks intersected . . . But the uniformed officer was shortcutting, not hurrying, almost taking his time, but still he was shortcutting across the grass now, past the aluminum lawn chairs in a row, coming toward him at a slow walk.

He knew who it was.

''Lieutenant? . . .''

Bryan said, Oh, Jesus . . .

He knew who it was and knew what his expression would be like. From the tone of that one word he could look at the ocean or up at the sky and he would still see that solemn-neutral cop expression and know what it meant.

''Lieutenant? . . .''

See? Nothing else. Nothing more to expect or hope for in just that one word.

He said, ''Gary, get away from me. I mean it. Get the hell away from me.''

Bryan refused to look at him. He kept his eyes on the impersonal ocean and continued to the end of the walk until Gary was no longer in his vision.

Gary Hammond followed as far as the pipe railing. He put his hand on it and watched Bryan go down the seawall steps to the beach, becoming a small dark figure out there alone. He watched the figure walk into the surf to stand where the ocean reached land and came exploding around him. He heard him scream something. He heard the homicide cop standing out there in his good suit scream something that was maybe a word, two words. But he wasn't going to outscream the ocean. Nobody was going to do that.

18

Gary Hammond picked him up the next day. They drove down to the Broward County Sheriff's Office in Fort Lauderdale. They wanted to ask him a few questions and show him something. He had already identified her body.

There were people here from the Florida State Police and the Drug Enforcement Agency as well as Broward deputies, most of them in plainclothes. The meeting was in a cement-wall conference room with fluorescent lights above a long table. A television set had been placed at the end of the table away from the door; a videotape recorder was hooked to the set.

A girl by the name of Dorie Vaughn was here when he arrived but left shortly after. She was the one who had discovered the body of Mr. Rafael Fuentes in the swimming pool and called the operator who contacted the Broward County sheriff. The Palm Beach Police were alerted because Mr. Fuentes lived in their city. In the meantime the Broward crime-scene people had discovered a second body, a camera bag full of blank video cassettes and, partly hidden in the scrub among the matted, dead leaves, one video cassette with something on it. No weapon or videotape equipment was discovered at the scene, but it became obvious both had been used. The crime scene people collected seventeen nine-millimeter shell casings which they believed had been fired from an automatic weapon. Very possibly a submachine gun.

And once again Bryan thought of the Mickey Mouse gun that might cost fifteen hundred dollars. He said nothing about it to the law-enforcement officers.

He was asked to describe Miss Nolan's activities in Florida; they wanted to know specifically what she had been up to. He told them she was writing an article on rich people and had gone to see Mr. Fuentes to interview him.

A DEA agent lounged half-sitting against the conference table, wearing a straw cattleman's hat over his eyes, a creased, outdoor look about the man, asked Bryan if Miss Nolan knew Chichi Fuentes was a drug dealer. Bryan said yes, she did.

Roy Spears was the DEA agent's name. He said, when you run with that crowd anything can happen to you.

Bryan told him she wasn't running with anybody, she was on an assignment.

Well, how come they didn't meet at one of his clubs or some Palm Beach cocktail lounge? Roy Spears asked. How did she know about the place in Hillsboro? That was supposed to be a regular love nest, he'd heard, where Chichi kept his broads and they had all kinds of orgies there and apparently, it seemed, shot some pretty weird films. Was that a possibility? If she was that close to Chichi, Roy Spears wondered if she might not've been working for him, or at least fucking him.

Bryan hit Roy Spears across the table. He went after him but the Florida cops came alive, swarmed all over Bryan and finally sat him down. They helped Roy Spears out of the room to have a paramedic look at his mouth. They remained cordial to Bryan and seemed more relaxed after Spears was gone. One of them leaned close to Bryan and said don't worry, enough guys here would swear Roy Spears provoked him, if it ever came to that.

They asked him if Miss Nolan had contacted or interviewed anyone else in Palm Beach. Bryan said none that he knew of. He gave Gary Hammond a look.

They said they would inspect her personal effects later on. Bryan nodded. He had already gathered her notes, her typewritten sheets and her cassette interviews with Daniels and put them in his suitcase.

They said they were sorry they had to show him the one videotape they'd found; it wasn't pretty. But since he knew her, and especially since he was a police officer, maybe it would tell him something that would be of help to them. They turned on the machine.

The picture on the TV screen was of trees, dense growth, brief glimpses of the beach and the ocean, the picture jumping erratically as it moved, a camera looking for something but without a plan, never holding still.

Until Bryan saw the white linen sundress, not seeing it at first as a woman in a dress but knowing it was and who it was.

He saw her twisting through the trees like someone in pain and realized she was barefoot. He saw her clearly now. He saw her eyes pleading. He saw her eyes close and open, her expression change, her mouth stretch open in a silent scream and saw the red splotch appear on the front of the white dress. He saw another red splotch and another red splotch and another red splotch and another red splotch and red strings coming out of those red splotches pulling her, yanking her off her feet, and then leaves flashing across the screen round green sea-grape leaves filling the screen and then a pattern of mechanical lines jumping until the screen went gray and then went black.

They waited.

They said, Lieutenant Hurd?

He shook his head.

They asked him if he would look at it again.

He shook his head. He got up and walked out without saying a word, without ever mentioning the name Robbie Daniels.

He accompanied Angela's body to Tucson, remained for the funeral and flew home to Detroit that evening.

Annie Maguire called him the next day. It was in both papers, a two-column story with a smiling shot of Chichi, "the playboy of the western world," and a brief reference to the other victim of the apparent drug-related double homicide. Annie said everyone was worried about him and stumbled over her words until Bryan said he wasn't going to talk about it right now if she didn't mind. He would, pretty soon, but not right now.

19

Walter stayed at his sister's house on Belmont in Hamtramck. For three days he didn't leave the house. He drank. Finally he got in his sister's Monte Carlo and drove over to a bar on Jacob just off Joseph Campau. Lili's.

He wanted it to be like a homecoming. Walk in and the guys at the bar see him. "Hey, look who's here!" . . . "Walter, where you been? How the fuck are you?" And he would see if he could slip back into another time, back around '57, '58 when they'd come in after a softball game, CYO League or Catholic War Vets—fast pitch, none of this blooper-ball shit—and drink Stroh's and play the juke box and argue about American League batting averages and ERAs. Now there was a kid named Art he had never seen before working the bar and Lili wasn't around. Four o'clock in the afternoon Art said she'd gone to have her dinner. Her dinner? What was going on here? The place had a strange feel to it. It was different. The only thing that hadn't changed, Kessler's was still fifty cents a shot. Walter said they used to call it Polish Canadian Club. Art said they still did.

"Don't anybody come in here no more?"

Art looked at him like, what kind of a question is that? Though right now there were only two others in here, an older couple at the other end of the bar. Art said, "We do more business'n this place ever did since it opened."

"Everybody must be out taking a leak," Walter said, " 'cause I don't see 'em."

"Stick around," Art said.

Walter wasn't going anyplace. He ordered up-and-downs, Kessler and Stroh's, looking at all the strange fruit-flavored brandy on the back bar, the—Christ—egg-nog punch. He sat sideways to the bar, comfortable, looking around and not remembering much. The place seemed darker: a long narrow storefront-type bar with windows painted over and a small neon *Lili's* the only identification. He had been drinking all day for three days. He might be shit-faced, but he was vaguely confident he had his head on straight.

On his way north in the Mercedes Walter had stopped off in Deltona, Florida, to visit the sister he hadn't seen in about five years. He sat down as long as he could, talking about Irene and how much she liked West Palm, before asking his sister if he could stay at her house a few days, while he wound up some business in Detroit. His sister kept asking him questions. Wasn't he working for this Mr. Daniels? Living—I mean to tell you—in Grosse Pointe? No, he was quitting, getting into something else—Christ, having to explain everything until he thought he was going to have to take the goddamn house key off her. His sister would call Irene, there was nothing he could do about that; but he'd be out of her house in about a week. Once he contacted Robbie and made the deal. He had dropped off the Mercedes the first day. Robbie wasn't back yet. Or his wife. The maid didn't seem to know anything about them.

Walter would wake up hungover, the top of his spine like a spike sticking up through his head, still half-drunk, jumpy and in pain, with urges to look in the empty rooms. He'd have a couple of cold ones to settle him, fry some eggs and sausage, then spend about an hour in the can with the door locked, even though he was alone in the house. Mornings he had to keep moving, walk through the dark rooms with the shades drawn, figuring out where he stood and what he was going to do with the video cassette that showed the death of Chichi Fuentes—and a little more. So far he had hidden it in three different places. It was in a good place now, protected.

Coming here, staying here, was to settle him down. Look out a window and see a street that could have been back in '57, '58, or before that. The row of straight-up-and-down two-family houses with their imitation brick facings, grillwork guarding the porches and postage-stamp front lawns. They belonged to people who were proud to live in Hamtramck with a church around the corner, football games at Keyworth Stadium, "Home of the Cosmos," and doing a job at Dodge Main along with about eighteen thousand hourly working three shifts when you couldn't buy a better car for your money and the fucking Japs were still making birthday-party novelties and toys that fell apart. No more. People were moving to Warren and out to Sterling Heights. Well, you could still drink Kessler's for four bits and could listen to Johnny Shadrack's Polish-American Matinee, WMZK, and still hear in this hotshit new age "The Beer Barrel Polka" once in a while. But that was about it.

At least he felt safer in the bar than at his sister's house, in there in the dark waiting for the phone or the doorbell to ring. Darker than in here even. He felt pleasantly numb after the painful morning.

He felt like everything was going to work out.

He felt like talking.

He felt he knew the guy coming in now. And when he found out he was right he didn't know what to feel.

It was Bryan Hurd.

Bryan took the stool next to him and placed a flattened pack of Camels on the bar. He said, "You left these, Walter, in Florida."

"How'd you find me?"

"I'm a policeman," Bryan said. "You used to be a policeman. You remember that?"

Walter had too many words in his mind at once and it was hard to pick the right ones. He tried, "I read about it, I want to tell you I was shocked, I couldn't fucking believe it." He tried, "Jesus, you never know, do you? You get mixed up with—you get like involved with these people you're writing an article about, I guess it can happen, being at the wrong place, you know, at the wrong time. It's a shame, an innocent person. But you got a job, what can you do? You can't sit home. Right?"

Walter stopped. The way Bryan was looking at him all he could see were Bryan's eyes, the eyes not saying anything, except every time he looked away and looked back there were the fucking eyes, the eyes fixed on him. He wanted to get it over with. If Bryan was going to say something he should say it.

Walter thought of something else. "You want a drink? Art, fix us up here. Kessler and whatever the lieutenant wants." He said to Bryan, "Fucking Kessler's still four bits. You believe it?" It gave him an opening. "The only thing in this town hasn't changed. I used to live over by Geimer, when I was growing up? The house's gone. Hamtramck High School, where I went? Gone. Not a trace of it. Dodge Main? Fucking gone. There's a couple brick walls standing there I think was the boiler room, it's got so much steel in it they can't fucking knock it down. Kowalski's still there. St. Florian's still there. St. Florian's, you'd have to shoot the priests and blow it up. But Immaculate Conception? It's not in Hamtramck but it's close enough, right there. GM's tearing it down. Sure, taking all that land there and where Dodge Main was for a new assembly plant. Cadillacs in Hamtramck, for Christ sake. Everything's changed. I mean everything. Go over look at the juke box. They got on there The Mutants, the Walkie-Talkies, Adam and the fucking Ants. What else? The Fishsticks. The Plastics. The In*fec*tions, for Christ sake. What's going on? Look—picture of the broad over there on the wall?'' He pointed to a poster shot of David Bowie. ''You know who she is? They got Iggy Pop, all this shit, they got *one* Frank Sinatra on there, on the juke box.''

Walter thought as fast as he could to come up with something else, to fill the silence beginning to settle.

Bryan said, ''Walter, I want the gun Robbie used. I don't want a stroll down memory lane. I want the High Standard twenty-two and I want the suppressor that goes with it.''

Walter looked away and back again, knowing he had time and knowing what he wanted to say, the one word, the key word, *gun,* giving it to him.

He said, ''Bryan, I don't know if you're a Catholic, but how about the pope, uh? You believe it, somebody would shoot the fucking pope? John Paul the Second, best pope we ever had. Yeah, hey, his cousin use to live right over here on Mt. Elliott. You know that? You knew he was Polish, right? Educated—shit, he can speak seven languages, goes all over the world, seen by millions of the faithful and where is he? He's home, he's in St. Peter's Square, this Turk pulls out a Browning starts popping away. Fucking Turk.'' Walter stopped, a dramatic pause.

''Bryan, it was a Browning nine-millimeter, the exact same fucking gun I've been packing the last, what, three, four years. And you know what I'm gonna do with the gun, Bryan? I mean my gun. I'm gonna drive over on the Belle Isle Bridge, I'm gonna get out of the car and I'm gonna throw the fucking gun in the fucking Detroit River. I'm gonna tell you something I haven't told nobody at all. You think I'm in the fucking bag and I'm drunk, but I promise you that's what I'm gonna do. Throw the gun away and never pack again as long I fucking live and that's a promise."

Bryan said, "I want that High Standard, Walter, and whatever barrels go with it. I want you tell me where it is."

It didn't sound right to Walter. He said, "The twenty-two? He didn't use the twenty-two."

He saw Bryan's eyes fixed on him again and tried to remember—shit—what he had just said. He said, "Wait a minute . . ."

But it was too late. Bryan said, "You want to talk about Florida, Walter? You want to get into that?" Bryan unbuttoned his sport coat and held it open with both hands. "You notice anything different, out of the ordinary?"

Walter shook his head. "What?"

"I don't have a gun on me," Bryan said. "You know why? I was afraid I saw you the first thing I'd do, I'd stick it against your head, Walter, and pull the trigger. I thought about it a long time and then I put it out of my mind and stopped thinking about it. You understand? I'm not talking about Florida, I'm talking about Detroit. Curtis Moore. I'm not gonna give him to anybody in Florida. I want him here . . . You listening to me?"

"Yeah," Walter said, "Curtis Moore. Was shot with a High Standard twenty-two. Got a big fucking suppressor on it."

"That's the one," Bryan said. "Listen to me."

"I'm listening."

"Robbie's due back sometime tonight."

"How do you know?"

"Just listen. Sober up. Go in there and find the gun before he gets back. Don't touch it, leave it. Then call me and tell me where it is. When I go in I'll have a warrant, but I want to know where to look."

"You getting me into this?"

"If you're in it, you're in it."

"I didn't know he was gonna do Curtis. Honest to God, he never said a fucking word. He just pulls this cool shit and does it."

"He told you about it after?"

"Like that night."

"But you didn't tell anybody."

"Somebody was gonna do Curtis sooner or later," Walter said. "What's the difference? Go down the morgue, see all the fucking Curtises they got there."

"Walter? Call me at 1300 soon as you know where the gun is. I'll talk to you later about a statement."

"What statement?"

"Whatever he told you. Write it down and sign it."

"Not without immunity."

"I'll see what the prosecutor says."

"What about the other deal?"

"Walter," Bryan said, "if you're talking about Florida I'm gonna give you one more chance to keep your mouth shut. Don't mention it again, okay? Don't say one fucking word."

Walter got as far as saying, "I think you're imagining things that happened—"

Bryan hit him, spinning him off the stool. Bryan stood over Walter and said, "I saw it. I don't have to imagine anything, I saw it."

Art had to come around to help Walter, straining to get him on his knees and his arms over the side of the pool table—like a sack of cement—so he could pull himself up. Then had to help him away from there so he wouldn't be sick on the table. Walter looked awful, staring out bleary-eyed.

"Where'd he go?"

"Your friend?" Art said. "He left. What'd he hit you for?"

"It's okay," Walter said. "He's pissed off about something."

Malik and Doug Parrish were waiting in front of the General Motors Building, watching the pickets who were trying to convince everyone that GM had no heart and that GM was taking their homes. New signs today read:

DON'T TAKE OUR CHURCH!
SAVE IMMACULATE CONCEPTION—PLEASE!

Parrish said, "Wait a minute. If the archdiocese thinks it's a good idea, they sell the land the church's on to the city and the city sells it to GM, what're they bitching at GM for?"

Malik said, "You asking me? Ask the cardinal. These people're parading around trying to save their church hardly any of 'em go to, he's out at Gucci's, some shoe store, blessing the grand opening. They open up a new Thom McAn he sends an altar boy."

Parrish said, "You got that from the *Free Press,* the guy on the back page. I read it."

Malik said, "So? He got it from somebody else. What's the difference?" He nodded toward the blue Plymouth pulling in behind the blue Plymouth already in the no standing zone. Then watched Bryan closely, the way he moved as he came past the pickets to join them.

"What's the matter with your hand?"

"I'm trying to keep from killing people," Bryan said, "and I'm having a hard time."

Malik and Parrish looked at each other. As they walked into the building Parrish said, "How do you want to handle this?"

"I want a statement," Bryan said, "I hope without hanging the guy out the window. Stare at him and crack your knuckles, I don't know . . ."

It was past five and they were moving against a rush of people coming out. On the second floor, down the glass hallways, nearly all the offices were empty, desk tops cleared. Bill Fay's secretary had gone. He looked out from his desk with a weary grin, extending his hand as he got up, shaking his head, and Bryan knew he was rehearsed, ready. Not that it mattered. There would be no handshaking or introductions.

Malik and Parrish came up to the desk one either side of him as he said, "I'm gonna have to have a statement from you, Mr. Fay."

Bill Fay smiled and frowned, made several faces as he thought it over and finally said, "I'm prepared to say, from now on, I don't know what in the hell you're talking about."

Bryan picked up the phone and began dialing a number, paused after three digits, looked up and said, "Eight-five-one, seven-one-three-one?"

Fay said nothing, holding on.

Bryan finished dialing. He held the phone out so Fay could hear the rings.

"All right, put it down."

"You'll give me a statement? Everything you saw?"

The phone continued to ring. A woman's voice came on, a pleasant tone. "Hello?"

"Yes!" A half-whispered hiss. "Put it down!"

Bryan said into the phone. 'I may call you back in a minute," and hung up. He watched Fay sink into his chair and begin to swivel slowly from side to side.

"You seem to be experienced in ruining marriages," Fay said. "What's the least destructive way to do this?"

"I want a signed statement," Bryan said, "a positive identification of Robinson Daniels, what you saw him doing, the fact you saw him go down to the garage."

"I didn't actually see him go down."

"Tell what you did see."

"This is under duress, you realize."

"If you think I'm forcing you, don't do it."

"What else do you call it? You think I'd freely sign a statement?"

"It's called good-citizen cooperation," Malik said.

"Can I tell my wife that?"

"Tell her you just wanted a strange piece of ass," Malik said. "It might work."

Fay wrote his statement with coaching, editing help from Bryan. When he had finished and signed it, Bryan gave him some hope. He said, "Don't tell her anything yet. You never know what might happen between here and the Frank Murphy Hall of Justice."

It was dark, early evening, when Robbie got home. He left the front door open and walked into the hall yelling, "Hey! Where is everybody? Come out, I won't hurt you—I'm a friend!" He'd had four first-class Delta martinis on his first commercial flight in years.

A maid appeared, hesitant. Robbie couldn't remember her name.

"Where's Walter?"

He wasn't here. He *was* here a little earlier, but he wasn't here now. Greg talked to him.

Robbie went through the dining room and kitchen to the back stairway and called up, "Greg, where are you? I need you, Greg!"

The cook came down the stairs slicking his dark hair back with his hands, wearing his white shirt and his black pants. "Yes sir." They went into the kitchen and Robbie got a bottle of white wine out of the refrigerator while Greg quickly washed his hands at the sink. When Robbie couldn't find a glass Greg got one out of the cupboard, an everyday glass, and Robbie told him to bring one for himself.

"You see Walter?"

"As little as I can," Greg said. Greg was about thirty-five and looked to Robbie like a day laborer, but he could cook.

"I got to find him."

"He was here," Greg said. "He went in your study and I told him hey, you don't work here no more, what are you doing in there? The other day he brings the car back he says he quit."

"He was in my study?"

"About, well a few hours ago he was here."

"Where'd he go, do you know?"

"No sir. I could care less."

"Care," Robbie said, "just for a minute. I thought you two were from the same neighborhood. Hamtramck, right?"

"That doesn't give us anything in common. You know what he does all the time? He bitches . . ."

"It's a trait," Robbie said.

"He comes in here for a beautiful meal cost him twenty dollars outside, he starts bitching. Beef Wellington, he says take the fucking bread off. I fix veal Oscar you like? He want golabki, pirogies, he wants placki for breakfast. All the time telling me I don't know how to cook."

"He's a rustic at heart," Robbie said, not having any idea what Greg was talking about. "But where can I find him? You know any places he goes, where he hangs out?"

"I don't know if he goes, I know what he talks about, over there."

"Over where?"

"He talks like Hamtramck was Grosse Pointe, like Under the Eagle was the London Chop House. He don't know anything."

"Under the Eagle?"

"Yeah, I used to eat there sometime, till I learned how to cook. You go in there and get fat."

"Call the place up, see if anybody's seen him. You know any other spots?"

"Couple of bars maybe."

"Call 'em. See if he's been in lately, the past couple of days." Robbie started out of the kitchen with his wine glass, paused and looked back at Greg. "There's a footlocker out on the front steps the goddamn cab driver wouldn't bring in the house. But make the calls first, okay?"

Goddamn Walter. Robbie walked through the marble front hall to his den, flicked the light switch on and the switch next to it off as he went in.

The room seemed in order, everything in its proper place. No—some books were pulled half out of the shelves and the cabinet doors were open behind the desk. The dumb shit. Looking for the gun. That had to be Walter's purpose. Walter the cop turned driver-aide turning snitch. Scared to death. Or blackmailer, that was a definite possibility.

Robbie sat down in his chair with his glass of wine, picked up the TV remote control gadget and pressed the on button.

"It's showtime . . ."

He watched Walter appear on the television screen, Walter coming into the lighted room, looking around, weaving a little as he moved to the desk, placed his hands on it flat and leaned heavily, resting. He was drunk! Unbelievable. The guy comes in to burglarize the place smashed. Walter was groping around now, edging his way to the cabinets behind the desk while those sneaky cameras that resembled light fixtures followed every move. He'd even explained to Walter how the surveillance cameras worked, these particular ones programmed to look on a subject and follow until the subject left the camera's scan and walked into the field of another, the cameras activated when a light switch was turned on. But Walter was drunk, or wouldn't have remembered anyway. Walter's attention span was about from A to B. He desperately needed someone to wind him up and point him in the right direction. Walter stumbled around, going over to the bar now . . . standing there trying to decide what to drink. That's what he needed. Probably not recognizing one single label. Christ—no, Walter, not the seventy-five-year-old stuff!

Greg appeared in the doorway.

"He was in there today, Mr. Daniels. Under the Eagle? Waitress says he acted drunk. Told her he'd been to Lili's Bar, where he used to hang out. She says she stopped in there for a pop after she was through working and he was in there again. Art told her, the bartender, Walter would go out, come back in, go out, come back. Like he didn't know what he was doing."

Robbie looked over, clicking the picture off. "You know where Lili's is?"

"It's right off Campau on Jacob."

"Give me some directions."

Greg said, "Yes sir, but I don't know you want to go there at night."

On the first sheet in the pile of notes and typewritten pages was a list of working titles written in Angela's straight-up-and-down hand.

"Hi, I'm Robbie Daniels"

"What's It Like To Be Rich?"

"I Was Just Saying To My Very Good Friend George Hamilton The Other Day . . ."

"Who Would I Rather Be Than Anyone? . . . Me!"

"Split Images: How Rich-Kid Robbie Daniels Defies Your Viewfinder"

A note below the list of titles said, "Maybe a short dialog exchange would work." And below that, "What would Tom Wolfe call it?"

Bryan got up from his desk. Crossed the squad room toward the wall of mug shots, stopped and turned around, without purpose. He had nowhere to go. He didn't want coffee. He didn't want to turn on the radio. He wanted the telephone to ring and hear Walter's voice, sober. At this moment it was all he wanted because he would not let himself think of anything else. He was standing when Eljay Ayres came in, the inspector of Homicide dressed in a tailored tan three-piece suit, raincoat over his arm, tired eyes looking at Bryan, wondering things.

"Tell me if you're doing something I should know about."

Bryan shrugged, raised his shoulders a little and let them drop.

"You can think it long as you don't do it. You know what I'm saying to you? Ain't worth it."

"How do you know?" Bryan said.

"I don't know much," Ayres said. "Nobody sits down and tells me stories anymore. I have to ask questions, get bits and pieces." He studied Bryan with his tired gaze and began to shake his head. "You don't even have the gun for the job. Little thirty-eight with the bands 'round it so you don't lose it in your pants. What kind ofa gunslinger are you, Bryan?"

Bryan said, "You know how many guns he's got?"

Ayres said, "Has only one I'd be interested in. From what little bit I hear . . . I'm gonna tell you something I would never tell anybody else. Gonna come right out and say you, Mr. Hurd, are the best homicide dick I know or know of. That includes me, giving you maybe a half a step, no more than that. The point being, the best homicide dick I know doesn't fuck up, does he? Doesn't carry the blade to put in the man's hand after, does he? He wins most, he loses a few. But he doesn't ever fuck up. Does he?"

Bryan turned, moved toward his desk. "I've got to write a letter."

"That's cool," Ayres said. "Keep your mind occupied."

Walter parked his sister's Monte Carlo next to a bulldozer that stood in the drive of an abandoned gas station. Every parking place up Jacob and around on Campau was taken. Like somebody was having a party. There were three girls in front of Lili's, standing in the dark smoking, passing around a cigarette. He could smell it now; he was still a cop he could bust them. The hell with them. He had slept about two hours and was still whacked out, half in the bag. The girls moved away, one of them looking at him as he approached the bar, the girl saying, "The Babies bring out the weirdos every time."

What? He put his hand on the door and felt a vibration. The same girl was saying, "Down here, dad."

The fuck was going on?"

They went through a board gate and along a passage with walls that squeezed in close, Walter following sounds in darkness, a girl's laughter, smelling the grass, seeing the glow as the girls took last tokes and went in past a sign that said *Pagan Babies.* Pagan *what?* Art was looking at him through a window in a red door. Art said, "Three bucks."

Walter said, "Wait a minute. I got turned around or something."

Art said, "Three bucks, for the band."

Walter dug in his pocket. He said, "For the *band?* That's the band? I though it must be the fucking wreckers tearing down a building, Art. Hey, Art?" But they were moving him into the wall-to-wall racket of rock sound filling the bar, people behind him now crowding him into people standing inside, the people moving but moving in place, moving up and down, skinny people with painted hair, pink hair, Kraut hair, moving like puppets attached to the beat, skinny girls wired to it together, thighs shining, sliding together with sex on their faces, mouths moving, speaking, but no sound coming out of them, no room for voice sounds in a room filled with electronic sound. Five guys up there by the front with tight suits on and no shirts—no, four guys and a girl playing with them as alike as the guys were alike, moving alike, mechanically, one eating the microphone, saying something about the pope. The pope? *"The Turk did it during her afternoon soap—"* It sounded like the guy singing was saying the girl was pissed off, she missed all her children, yeah, *"She missed 'All My Children'—"* And people around him as he tried to get through them, as he used his shoulders to ram his way, were repeating it, their mouths saying, "She missed 'All My Children'—" But the girl was gonna go straight to hell because she was pissed and the guy up there in the suit and no shirt was saying, *"Don't forget your Sea and Ski—"* And now everybody was mouthing, saying, "Don't forget your Sea and Ski—" Walter raised his face to breathe. He saw Lili, a striped tiger drinking a white drink. He saw a pair of barmaids in shirts that glowed pure white and saw the labels of the fruit-flavored brandy glowing white, girls at the bar moving with their eyes closed and a girl licking the sticky inside of her glass, getting it all, girls squirming in pain to the guys in the suits and no shirts who looked diseased. The sound stopped. It was in the room filling the room and then gone like a plug had been pulled, leaving screams that were moans in comparison. A voice close to him said, "Oh, man, who's got some blow?" Another voice said, "You're busting caps now, man. What do you need with blow?"

Lili's voice said, "Walter? Come on—is that Walter Kouza?"

He stared at her, at her tiger dress.

Lili's voice said, "Walter, you sick? Please don't throw up on my customers, Walter. Go outside."

Art's voice said, "He doesn't know where he is."

Another voice said, "I'll take care of him."

Walter turned to the voice.

To Robbie Daniels smiling at him. "Come on, Walter, let's go outside."

Walter heard his own voice say, "I'm messing up . . ."

Bryan wrote in longhand on a legal pad. He wrote lines and scratched out words and tried other words, trying to explain in the letter why he was writing it. He started again and stopped, picked up the phone and dialed a number. He listened to it ring. He hung up and dialed an out-of-state number.

"Irene? . . . Bryan Hurd. I'm sorry to bother you again. Are you sure Walter's at his sister's? I called a few times, there was no answer . . . Yeah. No, I did see him this afternoon . . . He's fine. Sort of unwinding. Give me the number again, make sure I have it right." He wrote numbers on the yellow pad. "And the address? . . ."

The quiet was good, the sensation of gliding in silence, protected, staring at the gleam of the hood as they passed beneath street lights.

"Is this Belmont?"

"Next one. Hang a left. Go down the second block."

"How do you feel?"

"Shitty. I don't know what happened to me. It was like—you

really want to know what it was like? It was like dying and going to hell.''

''That's interesting,'' Robbie said.

They went in the front door. Walter switched on a lamp, walked through to the kitchen and turned the water on to let it run and get cold. A phone rang.

''That's Irene,'' Walter said. ''She thinks I'm gonna answer it she's crazy.'' Still, he walked back out to the living room to watch it ring.

Robbie, wearing a bulky knit sweater that hung to his hips in soft folds, leaning in the kitchen doorway, straightened. His hands went behind him, beneath the sweater, as his eyes moved over the kitchen. He'd better do it now. Not wait. Bringing out the Colt Python he stepped to the refrigerator, laid the gun on top and stepped back again as the ringing stopped and Walter returned from his vigil. Robbie said, ''You know things don't always go as planned.''

''The first thing I'm gonna do,'' Walter said, ''is quit drinking. The second thing—I don't know, I'm fucking beat. But I was gonna call you.''

''To offer me a deal?''

Walter took time to drink a glass of water. He refilled the glass and sat down at the kitchen table. He said, ''Okay. Two hundred and fifty thousand for the tape I got.''

''You mean tapes,'' Robbie said. ''Two of them.''

''I got one, that's all. I threw the other one away.''

''You sure?''

''I'm telling you I did.''

''Which one do you have?''

''The one you're doing Chichi.''

''Why do you think it's worth a quarter of a million?''

''You're in it too. The headband—fucking Cochise.''

Robbie pulled out the other kitchen chair and sat down. ''I had to pick up after you, Walter. You leave me in a spot and now you're blackmailing me.''

''Bet your ass I am.''

''If in fact you do have the tape.''

''Take my word.''

"Forget it," Robbie said. He rose, pulled his sweater down and started out through the hall to the living room.

Walter said, "Hey, you think I'm kidding?"

Robbie stopped and came half around. "About what?"

"Pay or I mail it to the cops. How's that grab you?"

Robbie came back to the kitchen doorway, hands on his hips, slim, hair mussed. Walter thought of a cheerleader, the first time in what seemed like years.

Robbie said, "Walter, you send it in, I get picked up. What's the first question they ask me?"

"Why you shot him."

"No—who shot the film? I'll give you a hundred grand, flat deal. But only if you prove to me you've got the tape. I mean right now. Otherwise, fuck off."

"I'm sober," Walter said, "you think you can pull anything."

"Come on, Walter, Jesus Christ, I want to go home and go to bed."

Walter got up from the table. He approached Robbie carefully and felt the bulk of the sweater around the middle. "You stay right here, you don't move. Right?"

He went out through the kitchen door, down the steps and across the yard to where his sister had set up her shrine to the Blessed Virgin Mary, a four-foot plaster statue on a pedestal: Mary standing on top of the world, a snake held firmly beneath her foot. Walter looked back at the light showing in the kitchen door before he carefully tilted the statue, bringing it toward him to let his shoulder support the weight, reached into the hollow base and drew out his Browning nine-millimeter that he would throw away right after this deal was completed. He stuck the automatic into his belt, reached under again and drew out the cassette, done up in Saran Wrap.

Robbie had moved a little. Enough to see Walter coming up the back porch steps with a gun in one hand and something wrapped in the other. Enough to place himself next to the refrigerator with his hand resting on top.

Walter stuck the Browning into his belt again so he could unwrap the cassette.

Robbie's hand came off the refrigerator with the Python. He

shot Walter squarely in the chest, three times, giving him one more than he had given the Haitian, and watched Walter stumble around rearranging the table and chairs before he hit the linoleum floor. He felt for a pulse in Walter's throat, something he had not done with the Haitian. It was how you learned.

Twenty-one seventy-two Belmont.

Bryan had to go up the walk almost to the house to read the number next to the aluminum storm door. He rang the bell and waited. The house was dark; the entire street seemed dark, no one up watching late movies. He went around back, along the narrow walk separating Walter's sister's house from the one next door. It was a clear night. He could see a statue standing in the backyard, a robed figure with hands extended: come to me. The back of the house seemed darker than the front.

When the knob turned in his hand he realized the door wasn't shut tight. He pushed gently. The door swung in and stopped, obstructed; but the opening was wide enough for Bryan to slip through, to step inside and feel the bulk of Walter's body against his foot. He turned the kitchen light on.

A Browning automatic and a glass of water were on the table. Walter lay face down, blood on the back of his poplin jacket. Bryan knelt down, tired. He said, "Walter, you dumb shit," raised the jacket and shirt, pulling them up enough to see a ragged tear in pale flesh, blood oozing. He pulled the jacket down, rolled Walter over and opened his shirt. Three entrance wounds, one through and through. Two bullets were still inside Walter. Bryan stood up. He opened the cabinet door with the gouge in it, sifted through broken china to find the third slug and studied it in the palm of his hand. A chunk of misshapen lead. From something bigger than a twenty-two. Bryan turned the light off and sat down at the kitchen table. If police evidence technicians had been watching him up to now they'd have him thrown off the force. And if the Hamtramck Police knew what he was going to do next they might scream or they might thank him, it was a toss-up. But either way, this one was his.

He'd find a shower curtain in the bathroom. Or a blanket.

He'd bring his car around to the alley.

He'd place a call as soon as possible to West Palm and get Gary Hammond out of bed. In fact, before he left the house.

He needed just a little luck. Or kneel by that little statue for a minute. It wouldn't hurt.

20

Robbie couldn't believe how beautifully the video-tape came out. The assassination of Chichi Fuentes. Like he'd directed and choreographed it. The bottles on the bar and the door panes shattering, Chichi staggering out in his golden robe turning red and then, *agggggggh,* falling into the swimming pool. Chichi was a good dier. He even liked—liked?—he loved the unplanned flashes of himself, the bandana and the sun-glasses, firing the grease gun, holding it low and letting it rip with that great gutty sound, muted but very heavy. The whole scene was heavy. Inspirational. It reaffirmed his convictions, made him dead certain he wanted to go on to more significant projects, bag some really bad ones. Maybe not Carlos, but there were some giant assholes out there waiting.

He was learning fast. He'd lucked out with Walter. Walter had been a mistake. Scratch Walter, a genuine pain in the ass. His body probably wouldn't even be discovered until the sister came home from Florida; whenever. The type he needed was not a cop but a seasoned mercenary, a former Green Beret or Recon Marine who'd been to Africa and back and knew the game. A heavyweight. He'd look in the classified section *Soldier of Fortune* and get in touch with a pro looking for action. Some guy practicing his karate moves, opens the letter, the guy wouldn't believe it.

God, it was fun.

Write the real book about it someday.

Robbie watched the tape three times that night after he got home, about ten times or more yesterday and a couple of times this morning. It kept getting better.

Right now he had the footlocker open, going through a seasonal rite: taking out his handguns, oiling and wiping them clean before mounting them in the wall cabinet behind his desk. He liked to keep the handguns handy, show them off. The heavy stuff, the submachine guns, he kept in a half-ton safe that was bolted to the cement floor of the utility room in the Palm Beach house.

There were guns spread all over the desk when the maid knocked on the door, opened it a few inches and said, "Someone here to see you, Mr. Daniels."

He had been half-expecting this so he was ready. The unannounced visitor who would try to catch him off-guard. What surprised him was that Lieutenant Hurd was not alone.

Annie Maguire came in first and Robbie widened his grin as he saw her glance up and around at the sneaky cameras. His hand found the switch under the front of his desk and he flicked it on to activate a record of this meeting, just in case. Robbie's expression changed, became somber. He said to Bryan, "Lieutenant, I can't tell you how sorry I am. If I'd known what Angie was getting into, believe me—"

Bryan cut him off. "You better not say anything. All right?"

"Well, I want to express how I feel—"

"No. Don't say anything."

Robbie said, "You're not inferring, I hope, that anything I say might be used against me."

"I'm not inferring anything," Bryan said. "Can we sit down?"

"Please." Robbie gestured, watched them sink into the soft leather chairs across the desk from him. He remained standing, deciding to feel his way a little deeper into it. "I thought, since I introduced you to Fuentes—remember, at Seminole? . . . Well, I'm sure you've talked to the police in Florida . . ." He paused a moment, not sure what to say next. Hurd was staring at him. Not with an expression that described an emotion, but simply staring. It gave Robbie a strange feeling, the thought that he might have overlooked something. But if it wasn't about Florida . . .

"How're you doing with the Curtis Moore investigation?" Robbie's gaze moved to Annie Maguire. Much better, a definite sign of life in her eyes.

"Well, since you asked," Annie said. "We know you were at the hotel. I mean at the time of the homicide."

"I told him that." Robbie's eyes flicked at Bryan and returned. "I was at the Renaissance Center about ten o'clock. I picked up some Mexicans. I told him all about it and he checked it out."

"You forgot to say you went down to the parking garage," Annie said.

"Are you serious?"

"We've got a witness."

"Where, down in the garage?"

"Right by the valet parking."

"I might've stopped there. I was looking for the Mexicans. But if you're trying to tell me somebody *saw* me down in the garage, that's pure bullshit."

"Where was the pistol, in your car?"

"What pistol?"

"The one you used on Curtis."

"Jesus Christ—"

"The same one you showed us in your office. The High Standard."

Bryan watched him begin to smile, getting back on safe ground.

Robbie said, "You ran a ballistics check on the shells you picked up, didn't you? Compared them to the ones you got out of Curtis Moore? Isn't that the way it's done?"

Annie said, looking at the desk, "Do you have it here?"

Now Robbie looked over his display of handguns. "I don't see it. Oh shit, that was the one I lost in Florida. I was out in a boat, shooting, and dropped it over the side . . . Gee, I'm sorry."

Annie said, "What were you shooting, fish?"

"Yeah, I like to shoot fish." He gave Annie his interested, serious look. "Is this the way you do it, honest to God?"

Annie said, "Well, you asked about Curtis Moore."

"And that's all you have?"

Annie said, "No. As a matter of fact we have a warrant for your arrest . . ."

"You're kidding." Beginning to smile.

". . . on a charge of first-degree murder."

Robbie was smiling sincerely now. It was a con, he was positive. These rinky-dinks were giving him the grim-cop number, Hurd playing stone-face, and he was supposed to, what, break down? Confess? He couldn't believe it.

"You're not serious, are you?"

Annie said, "You have a constitutional right to remain silent. You don't have to answer any questions . . ."

"Wait a minute."

". . . or make any statements. If you do . . ."

"Wait a minute, goddamn it! Hold it!"

There was a silence.

"Now then," Robbie said. "You've got a witness who wasn't actually there. You don't have a murder weapon . . . How in the hell can you associate me, in any way, with Curtis Moore? It's impossible."

Bryan said, "The warrant doesn't mention Curtis." He waited to make sure he had Robbie's full attention. "It's for doing Walter Kouza."

Bryan waited some more. He liked this part. The chair was comfortable, soft but firm. It was Robbie's turn. He watched Robbie pull up the high-backed desk chair, giving himself a little time as he sat down on the edge and tried to look interested in an objective way, at ease, slouching over to rest his arms on the desk full of handguns.

"Let me get this straight," Robbie said, giving himself more time, "Walter Kouza was murdered?"

"The night before last," Bryan said. He had the hook in now.

"Wait a second," Robbie said, but added nothing to it.

Bryan said, "I understand you were with him at Lili's about eleven." Giving him a little more of the hook. In a moment now he'd watch Robbie jump.

"Where," Robbie began, and then said it quickly. "Where was his body found?"

"In front of the art museum," Bryan said.

Robbie jumped. "The *Art* Museum!"

"Lying under that statue. *The Thinker,*" Bryan said.

"You found his body—you're telling me in front of the Art Museum on Woodward Avenue?"

"Why," Bryan said, "did you think it was someplace else?"

"I dropped him off—" Robbie stopped, but knew he had to go on. "It was a house in Hamtramck. That's where I saw him last, in Hamtramck."

"And you're wondering how he got over to Detroit," Bryan said, "with three bullets in his chest from a Colt Python, three-fifty-seven Mag, that match a couple bullets taken out of a Haitian burglar and sent to us courtesy of the Palm Beach Police. Is that what's bothering you?''

Hunched over the desk, his blue cashmere hanging loose, Robbie stared with a numb look, his mouth slack.

Bryan said, ''You want to hear the rest of your rights, or you want to call your lawyer first? . . . Don't know what to think, huh? We've also got a search warrant that says we can pick up evidence. That Colt Python you think so much of and the tape over in the VCR. You got any movies you want to show us?''

Annie said, ''If you do make a statement it can be used against you in a court of law. You have the right to have a lawyer present—''

Robbie said, ''Goddamn it, shut up!'' He came alive and hung there in a knot, losing his good looks, before easing back into the chair. Now he seemed stunned, amazed. He said, ''Walter *Kouza?*''

Bryan said, ''There must be some mistake, huh? Who's Walter Kouza?'' Poking at the nerve center of Robbie's pain. ''He sure wasn't one of your international assholes, was he?'' Bryan said, ''No, Walter was just a local asshole trying to make it big.''

Bryan got up. Annie dug into her bag before she rose and came out with a pair of handcuffs. Bryan took them, jiggled them at Robbie and he got up very slowly.

Robbie said it again, ''Walter Kouza . . .'' Like he would never get over it.

Bryan said, ''Put your hands behind you, we'll ride down to the Wayne County jail. It ain't Seminole, Smiley, but they do serve a lot of macaroni and cheese.''

21

He said to himself, Shit, just write it. It's only a letter. Go ahead.

Under *Dear Editor* he wrote:

Here is the material that Angela Nolan was preparing for your magazine according to the assignment you gave her on rich people. You will notice there are 15 finished pages of the interview typed up that are great and seem to describe exactly the kind of dangerous show-off Robinson Daniels is, or at least was. He is going to have to change his ways very quickly where I hope he is going or else get his ass knocked off. (If you need any information about the Southern Michigan Prison at Jackson, which has the largest inmate population in the nation, let me know.) There are also some very interesting notes you can fix up a little and use to finish the article yourself. (Enclosed also are photos of both Daniels and Angela.) If you are in not too big a hurry, wait and I will let you know how the trial comes out. I'm betting the son of a bitch will get mandatory life. If he doesn't, I'll settle for 99 years.

Bryan was going to end it there and sign it, but he thought of something else and added:

If you have trouble deciding whether or not to run this great article by Angela Nolan, let me know. I'll come to N.Y. and hold you out the window by your heels until you decide.

See if they had a sense of humor.

ABOUT THE AUTHOR

ELMORE LEONARD has written twenty-nine novels, including such best sellers as MAXIMUM BOB, GET SHORTY, GLITZ, FREAKY DEAKY, and KILLSHOT. In 1992 he received the Grand Master Award for lifetime achievement from the Mystery Writers of America. Many of his books have been made into movies. In addition, he has written numerous screenplays. He lives with his wife, Joan, in Birmingham, Michigan.